THE KREMLIN'S CANDIDATE

THE DAZZLING FINALE TO THE RED SPARROW TRILOGY

JASON MATTHEWS

NEW YORK TIMES BESTSELLING
AUTHOR OF *RED SPARROW* AND *PALACE OF TREASON*

Praise for the Red Sparrow Trilogy

REDSPARROW

"A primer in twenty-first-century spying . . . Terrifically good."
—*The New York Times Book Review*

"A smart, intriguing tale rooted in his own experience . . . Fans of the genre's masters including John le Carré and Ian Fleming will happily embrace Matthews's central spy."
—*USA Today*

"You, too, may also conclude that *Red Sparrow* is the best espionage novel you've ever read."
—*The Huffington Post*

"[A] sublime and sophisticated debut . . . *Red Sparrow* isn't just a fast-paced thriller—it's a first-rate novel as noteworthy for its superior style as for its gripping depiction of a secretive world."
—*The Washington Post*

"This debut novel from a thirty-three-year CIA veteran delivers action as pulse-pounding as it is authentic."
—*New York Post*

"Matthews's exceptional first novel will please fans of classic spy fiction. . . . The author's thirty-three-year career in the CIA allows him to showcase all the tradecraft and authenticity that readers in this genre demand. . . . [A] complex, high-stakes plot."
—*Publishers Weekly* (starred review)

"An intense descent into a vortex of carnal passion, career brutality, and smart tradecraft, this thriller evokes the great Cold War era of espionage."
—*Library Journal* (starred review)

"A compelling and propulsive tale of spy versus spy . . . *Red Sparrow* is greater than the sum of its fine parts. Espionage aficionados will love this one."
—*Booklist* (starred review)

"Features enough action to satisfy even the most demanding of adrenaline junkies . . . The author's CIA background and the smart dialogue make this an entertaining tale for spy-novel enthusiasts."

—*Kirkus Reviews*

"Not since the good old days of the Cold War has a classic spy thriller like *Red Sparrow* come along. Jason Matthews is not making it up; he has lived this life and this story, and it shows on every page. High-level espionage, pulse-pounding danger, sex, double agents, and double crosses. What more can any reader want?"

—Nelson DeMille

"[Jason Matthews is] an insider's insider. He knows the secrets. And he is also a masterful storyteller. I loved this book and could not put it down. Neither will you."

—Vince Flynn

"The spy thriller is back in full force thanks to newcomer and CIA insider Jason Matthews. . . . I have not read a more exciting, gripping novel in a long time."

—Doug Stanton, *New York Times* bestselling author of *Horse Soldiers*

"All the tradecraft and cat-and-mouse tension of a classic spy thriller—a terrific read."

—Joseph Kanon, author of *Istanbul Passage*

PALACE OF TREASON

"Matthews's latest is an extraordinarily commanding, acidly relevant, and unrelentingly suspenseful tale of espionage, brutality, and conscience."
—*Booklist* (starred review)

"Matthews's vast experience working in the shadowy world of espionage and spycraft lends an authenticity to his story that few can equal. And it doesn't hurt that he can write. . . . This is another must-read for fans of the spy genre."
—*Kirkus Reviews* (starred review)

"Jason Matthews has an amazing feel for the insider lingo and relentless intrigue of the spy's life. *Palace of Treason* is a harrowing look into the lives of spies. . . . This is stay-up-all-night reading, and we're pummeled by hair-trigger actions on every page."
—*BookPage*

"His real-life experiences in the shadowy world of spying make the story fresh, timely, and nearly authentic. . . . A sophisticated, behind-the-scenes, powerful story . . . Well written, creative."
—*Missourian*

"The world of a spy is unique and claustrophobic, but this bold tale captures its every nuance with expert precision. A tantalizing premise and a heroine who's an alpha female forge a piece of thrilling entertainment that does not disappoint."
—Steve Berry, *New York Times* bestselling author of *The Patriot Threat*

THE KREMLIN'S CANDIDATE

"Jason Matthews has found a formula that is making him one of America's most readable spy novelists. . . . *The Kremlin's Candidate* doesn't disappoint."

—David Ignatius, *The Washington Post Book World*

"Jason Matthews steers his popular Red Sparrow Trilogy to an exciting conclusion. This one's timely, too, exploring how Russian espionage can place agents in positions of power."

—*Entertainment Weekly*

"On every required level, *The Kremlin's Candidate* is superb: a slam-dunk conclusion to a superlative series."

—*Claremont Review of Books*

"A stellar conclusion . . . [*The Kremlin's Candidate*] races to a heart-pounding and unexpected resolution."

—*Publishers Weekly* (starred review)

"Delivers a wallop on all fronts, from adrenaline-charged action to dark political intrigue to gripping emotional stakes. . . . Matthews stuffs his always-hungry characters with onions, garlic, and personalities that make the last of this trilogy both satisfying and bittersweet."

—*Kirkus Reviews* (starred review)

"With nail-biting suspense, scorching eroticism, dark wit, lashing contempt for politicians dismissive of intelligence work, and fury over Russia's disinformation campaigns, this is a riveting and knowing dramatization of today's clandestine geopolitical conflicts."

—*Booklist* (starred review)

"Jason Matthews's finale to the Red Sparrow Trilogy is both timely and timeless; an espionage tale that takes the reader behind and beyond the headlines of Russia's assault on America. If anyone doubts that we are in the midst of Cold War II, *The Kremlin's Candidate* will erase those doubts, page by eye-opening page. Matthews's writing is elegant and self-assured, and we know we are in the capable hands of a man who is writing about what he knows and who he knows. Twenty-first-century spy novels don't get any better than this."

—Nelson DeMille, bestselling author of *The Cuban Affair*

THE RED SPARROW TRILOGY

Red Sparrow

Palace of Treason

The Kremlin's Candidate

THE KREMLIN'S
CANDIDATE

A NOVEL

JASON MATTHEWS

SCRIBNER

NEW YORK LONDON TORONTO SYDNEY NEW DELHI

Scribner
An Imprint of Simon & Schuster, Inc.
1230 Avenue of the Americas
New York, NY 10020

First Scribner trade paperback edition August 2018

SCRIBNER and design are registered trademarks of The Gale Group, Inc., used under license by Simon & Schuster, Inc., the publisher of this work.

For information about special discounts for bulk purchases, please contact Simon & Schuster Special Sales at 1-866-506-1949 or business@simonandschuster.com.

The Simon & Schuster Speakers Bureau can bring authors to your live event. For more information or to book an event, contact the Simon & Schuster Speakers Bureau at 1-866-248-3049 or visit our website at www.simonspeakers.com.

Manufactured in the United States of America

10   9   8   7   6   5   4   3   2

Library of Congress Control Number: 2017299893

ISBN 978-1-5011-4008-2
ISBN 978-1-5011-4009-9 (pbk)
ISBN 978-1-5011-4010-5 (ebook)

To Zsu Zsa,
for pressing all the buttons

The jealous and intolerant eye of the Kremlin can distinguish, in the end, only vassals and enemies, and the neighbors of Russia, if they do not wish to be one, must reconcile themselves to being the other.

No matter how big and powerful, Russia always feels threatened. Even when they are feeling weak, they bluster and bully to hide their vulnerability. In this sense, Putin's policies and beliefs are largely consistent with Russian history and the legacy of the Russian Tzars.

—George Kennan

PROLOGUE

The Metropol

September 2005: Despite the velvet-flocked, gold-leaf splendor of the Metropol Hotel, the enduring fetor of Moscow clung to the drapes and lay thick on the carpet, an incense of fusel oil, boiled cabbage, and ruined pussy.

Twenty-four-year-old Lieutenant Dominika Egorova of *Sluzhba Vneshney Razvedki*, the SVR, the external Russian foreign intelligence service, stood in her underwear (black lace from Wolford in Vienna) and looked down at the naked woman on the bed, snoring on her back, a feral, protruding incisor visible in her open mouth. The American woman—her name was Audrey—had been a biter. Dominika looked in the smoky gilt mirror at the purple half-moon bite mark on her shoulder, the irregular notch from Audrey's snaggletooth clearly visible.

The nineteenth-century bed, formerly from the Pavlovsk Palace in Saint Petersburg, had a soaring rococo canopy framed in falls of musty satin and faded silk ropes. The twisted sheets under Audrey's tall, bony body were darkly wet in a wide circle. Besides the biting, there had been the throaty grunts more characteristically heard from boars in the thickets of the Smolensk hunting preserve. Audrey was what they called a *khryuknut* in Sparrow School: a screamer in bed.

———

Loud, but nothing to faze a *Vorobey*, a Sparrow, a State-trained courtesan sent to the gabled mansion on the Volga River that was the secret State School Four, sent to learn the art of sexpionage—sexual entrapment, carnal blackmail, moral compromise—all with the aim of recruiting susceptible human targets as clandestine intelligence sources, targets who had been maneuvered into an intricate *polovaya zapadnya*, an SVR honey trap.

Dominika looked at the horse bite on her shoulder again. *Suka*, bitch. How she loathed being a Sparrow, how low she had sunk. Two years ago, the world had been hers for the taking. She had been destined for the Bolshoi as a future prima ballerina, until a rival had broken Dominika's foot, resulting in the abrupt end of a nearly twenty-year ballet career and a permanent slight hitch in her gait. The following year had been a nightmare descent into wanton indenture. To keep her ailing, widowed mother in their State-provided apartment, she let her uncle—then Deputy Director of SVR—coerce her to sleep with a man, a repugnant oligarch whom President Putin wanted eliminated.

To keep her quiet after the assassination, Uncle Vanya had magnanimously admitted her into the Andropov Institute, "The Forest," the SVR's foreign spy academy, where Dominika found to her astonishment that she had a natural aptitude for spook work and, consequently she hoped, a new future serving the *Rodina*, her Motherland, as an intelligence officer. Her fluent French and strong English learned at home in a house full of books and music were attributes. She had the skills, the ideas, the imagination, and great expectations for operations in the foreign field.

Ah, what a *prostodushnyy*, a guileless naïf, she had been! The Service, and the Kremlin, and *Novorossiya*, Putin's New Russia, were still the preserve of men, namely, the *siloviki*, the myrmidons around the blue-eyed new tsar, Vladimir Vladimirovich. These weasels purloined the patrimony of Russia, and spread a blanket of corruption so completely over the land that if you were not a billionaire running the energy monopoly Gazprom out of your pocket, then you were a Muscovite who could not afford meat more than three days a week. The *siloviki* were the inheritors of the Gray Cardinals, the sclerotic members of the old Soviet politburo, who had starved Soviet Russians for seventy years with their ineptitude as implacably as this new crowd had been starving modern Russians for the last twenty years with their avarice.

After graduating with top marks, Dominika Egorova had basked in the signal achievement that she was now an *operuolnomochoperuenny*, one of a few women SVR operations officers. But the sweet Dead Sea fruit of success turned to ashes in her mouth when Uncle Vanya sent her packing to State School Four, the Kon Institute in Kazan on the banks of the Volga, otherwise known as Sparrow School, where women were taught the unceasing, inexorable, inescapable indignities of learning how to be one of Putin's Prostitutes. Part of Dominika's soul died in Sparrow School—other women literally died, suicide among the forlorn was not uncommon. The dead parts inside Dominika were replaced by *beshenstvo*, an enduring white fury against the system, and a simmering hatred for the *podkhalimi*, the toadeaters surrounding their taciturn sovereign.

She was determined to succeed. After Sparrow School and back in Moscow, she did her homework and identified a seduction target on her own: a mild French diplomat whose wife was absent and whose adult daughter in Paris worked in a department of the French Ministry of Defense, which oversaw France's nuclear weapons. Dominika knew the man was falling in love with her, and that he would ask his daughter to whisper to Papa any French atom secrets that Dominika wanted to know. It was an easy seduction—and not altogether unpleasant, because he was a lonely, decent man. The difference was that this was a genuine operation. The potential intelligence harvest for the SVR was unparalleled.

But the seduction went too well, and Dominika's potbellied chiefs were envious, so they willfully and with malice ruined the pitch and spooked the Frenchman. He reported his dalliance to his embassy and was sent home. The case was lost and Egorova, the blue-eyed upstart Academy graduate, was put in her place. Solicitous Uncle Vanya commiserated with her and announced he was going to offer her something that was a real operation, something substantial, something even more desirable because it included being posted abroad—in glamorous Finland, he said. *This is more like it*, thought Dominika. *A real operational mission.* But one small assignment first; it would take three hours, said her uncle, smiling: seduce an American in the Metropol Hotel. Do this final honey trap for the Service, and then pack for your assignment in Helsinki. *One last time*, she had thought.

———

US Navy Lieutenant Junior Grade Audrey Rowland had been in Moscow for a week with a group of senior students from the National War College on a junket to observe Russian "bilateral geopolitics," whatever that meant. As was customary with any official visitors to Russia, on receipt of the students' visa applications months before, SVR targeteers began their research, combed through open-source databanks, and asked clandestine sources in the Pentagon for bios and assessments of the dozen War College students who would arrive in Moscow six weeks hence. Running traces was standard procedure: SVR targeteers were like patient wolves on the hillside, watching the horse-drawn *troika* filled with drunken *kulaks*, waiting to see if someone would fall out of the sled insensate into a snowbank and provide fresh meat.

LTJG Rowland's unique profile especially caught their sharp-eyed attention. The targeting study noted that Rowland had graduated with a PhD in advanced particle physics from Caltech, had enlisted in the US Navy, and had breezed through Officer Candidate School, already marked as a fast riser and a sure bet for eventual selection to flag rank. After OCS, Audrey had been assigned to the Electromagnetics Division in NRL, the US Naval Research Laboratory in Washington, DC.

From a purloined classified technical NRL newsletter, the Russians read that in the first three months of her assignment, Audrey Rowland had impressed senior scientists with a monograph on heat diffusion in the MJ64 experimental naval railgun. This tidbit stirred considerable interest among Russian intelligence circles: US railgun technology was a prime collection requirement of the Russian Navy. The threat of an electrically propelled, powderless projectile with a velocity of 2,200 meters per second and unerringly accurate at ranges beyond 150 kilometers, was a concern to Russian naval command. The US Navy had put it another way: a railgun projectile fired from New York City would score a direct hit on a target in Philadelphia in less than thirty-seven seconds.

Because Rowland was a potentially attractive target, an extra effort was made to collect what the spook world called lifestyle-and-personal bio. There was more gleaned from a Russian illegal buried in the administrative staff of the University of California, Irvine, who had access to certain restricted databases in the UC and local law-enforcement systems. Posing as an employment investigator, the illegal also interviewed neighbors, landlords, and one former roommate at Caltech. The results were interesting: Rowland was solitary, remote, with a weakness for margaritas, after two of which she tended to pass out. Beneath what appeared as a shy exterior was a highly competitive nature. There were unflattering stories about obsessive behavior in the classroom and laboratory. Then the jackpot: She'd had an abusive father—himself a navy pilot—there were possible sexual overtones, and a complete absence of men during her university years, culminating in an unspecified date-rape incident about which no official record existed. Vestal virgin, physics androgyne, or a woman who prefers vacations on the Aegean island of Lesbos? If the last, there could be an opening for a bit of lesbionage during her visit to Moscow. Targeteers noted that Rowland would not have been admitted into OCS or the War College, regardless of recent liberalization policies in the US Navy, if her predilections were known. A secret vulnerability.

LTJG Rowland was to tour in Moscow for the week, staying at the Metropol with twelve classmates and a professor/chaperone. Word went up the line—to the SVR's America Department; then to the FSB, *Federal'naya Sluzhba Bezopasnosti Rossiyskoy Federatsii*, the internal security service; then to the GRU, *Glavnoye Razvedyvatel'noye Upravleniye*, the military foreign intelligence service of the General Staff of the Russian Federation. The usual puerile squabbling among these agencies for primacy to target Rowland was stilled when the Kremlin ordained that every organization would have a role: The FSB would control the other students and chaperone; an SVR asset would be used for the honey trap; and the GRU would exploit the take. As for the actual recruitment pitch, a Kremlin specialist known as "Doctor Anton" would be introduced. Big trouble, Doctor Anton.

———

During the students' week in Moscow, FSB watchers noted with interest that LTJG Rowland seemed to enjoy more than a single after-dinner vodka in the Metropol's ornate Chaliapin Bar, invariably saying good night, then sneaking back and drinking long after her fellow classmates retired for the evening. Sergei, a handsome SVR-trained *Voronoy* (a Raven, the male version of a Sparrow), was assigned the task of meeting, charming, and eventually bedding the angular beanpole who wore cardigans buttoned to the neck, opaque panty hose, and sensible flats, in sharp contrast to the hotel's usual sea of cantaloupe busts, see-through tops, and Jimmy Choo glitter pumps. When after two nights of Sergei's musky blandishments it became obvious that Rowland preferred to swim facedown in Veronica Lake rather than be with a man, the targeteers ordered an urgent change. Time was short, and the SVR and GRU were frantic that Rowland not slip through their fingers.

Rowland's *delo formular*, her operational file, was flipped onto Dominika's worn metal desk in SVR headquarters in Yasenevo district in southwest Moscow, by a warty, dismissive section chief. He told her to read it, go home, change into something water soluble, get to the Metropol by 2100 hours, and compromise the American. Dominika's short fuse flared and she told the pudgy deputy to go to the Metropol himself since it was obvious the target preferred pussies (which in Russian came out significantly more profane).

As if he had been listening via a microphone in her cubicle, Uncle Vanya called four minutes later, assuring Dominika this would be the last such assignment—hereafter she would be an ops officer on assignment in Helsinki and the Sparrow seductions would cease. "Take this assignment, please, don't tell me no," Vanya had said, his voice suddenly edgy. "Your mother would tell you the same thing." Translation: follow orders or your mother with her rheumatoid arthritis and spinal stenosis will be out on the sidewalk by the time the real Moscow winter arrives.

Four hours later, with a tab of Sparrow-issue Mogadon, a mild benzo-diazepine relaxant, under her tongue, Dominika sat at the Chaliapin Bar next to an already bleary-eyed Audrey Rowland, who looked sideways at the antique Ottoman necklace Dominika wore around her throat, the hammered silver pendants of which were rattling in the deep vee of her breasts.

"Service at this bar leaves something to be desired," said Audrey, apparently assuming Dominika spoke English. "I thought this hotel was five stars." The tumbler in front of her was empty.

Dominika leaned close and whispered conspiratorially. "Russians sometimes need a little encouragement," she said. "I know this barman; he can be a bit contrary, we say *upryamyy*, like a mule." Audrey laughed and watched as Dominika ordered two iced vodkas that were served instantly and with great deference. Audrey ignored the barman, drank the vodka in one gulp, and appraised Dominika with heavy-lidded eyes. She could not know that the barman and three other patrons in the bar were all from Line KR, counter-surveillance assets looking for opposition coverage as Dominika moved on the tall American woman. The bar was clean; Audrey was alone.

Dominika did not have to work it too hard. A light legend—cover story—that she was a salaried office worker was sufficient, and really couldn't afford drinking at the Metropol but once a month. She told jokes about Russian men, gently steering the conversation, holding on to Audrey's wrist occasionally, establishing physicality, straight out of the Sparrow manual. Dominika purposely showed no curiosity about Audrey's work or her navy career. There was no need to elicit: Audrey showed herself to be utterly self-absorbed and inclined to talk about herself—*a narcissist perhaps, ego will be a button with this one*, thought Dominika, who asked what her hometown of San Diego was really like, eyes wide and interested. Audrey said that she was the only child of a naval aviator father and a quiet mother (biographical facts already in her SVR file), then went on at length about growing up a lithe surfing California beach girl, which Dominika suspected was fiction. Audrey was an *unmik*, a physics geek, and looked it. After the third vodka, Dominika became serious and cocked her head toward the barman.

"Russian men. Beware of them. Not just stubborn, but mostly bastards too," she said. Audrey pried the story out of a seemingly reluctant Dominika in stages. Drying her eyes with a cocktail napkin embossed with the "M" logo of the hotel, she eventually told Audrey of her broken engagement with a fiancé who had been unfaithful by sleeping with a cashier who worked at the GUM department store in Red Square, a total fiction.

"She was a little harlot with hair dyed purple, newly arrived from some rural *oblast*, how do you say, some unimaginable province," said Dominika. "Two years we were engaged, and it was over in a night." Audrey patted Dominika's hand, incensed at the nameless philandering fiancé. The "hook" was always more believable by adding incongruously specific detail like the dyed hair (*No. 87, "The short stories of Pushkin stir the imagination"* was the relevant tagline, and one of scores memorized at Sparrow School to illustrate tradecraft points).

Audrey's eyes searched Dominika's, now expectant and intense. Audrey was moved by the story only slightly less than by the high cheekbones and bee-stung lips of the chestnut-haired beauty sniffling beside her. Agreeing that all men were *svinya* and toasting to eternal sisterhood, Audrey huskily said she wanted to show Dominika her hotel room. Dominika put an elegant finger to her lips and whispered that instead of Audrey's room they could sneak into the opulent Yekaterina Suite on the fourth floor—her cousin was a chambermaid at the hotel with a passkey. Audrey shivered in anticipation and grabbed her cardigan. Her profound knowledge of electromagnetic physics sadly provided no warning of the curved tail of the scorpion poised above her head.

The suite was magnificent, ablaze in gold and green, with an imposing red tombak samovar on an oval Fabergé tea table in the corner of the room. They looked at the furnishings, and at each other. Neither said a word. Dominika knew the nectar trap was about to snap shut. She pretended to stare at the frescoes capering across the Baroque vaulted ceiling when Audrey—now in musth—stepped up to her, put her hands on her breasts, and mashed their mouths together. Dominika kissed her back, then slowly disengaged, smiled, and poured two flutes of champagne from an ice bucket on the settee (she palmed a tab of Mogadon into Audrey's glass to smooth her out), and pushed a silver platter of *pecheniya* toward her, powdered sugar Russian tea cakes stacked high in a snowy pyramid, taking one herself. Audrey did not register the incongruity that Dominika's chambermaid cousin apparently had provided the expensive champagne and delicate cakes along with the passkey.

It was too much watching Dominika nibble the pastry with her even white teeth. Audrey's Dutch oven was at a rolling boil, and with trembling fingers she brushed powdered sugar off the front of Dominika's little black dress, and pulled her across the salon into the bedroom. The next thirty minutes were filmed by four remote-headed, infrared lenses (and slaved COS-D11 mikes) concealed in the ornate acanthus moldings in each corner of the ceiling, operating at 29 megapixels. The feed was being digitally recorded by an SVR technical team in a special utility room down the hotel hallway. Not taking their eyes off the monitors, two sweating technicians bundled and encrypted the images, immediately routing them for real-time review to the Kremlin offices of a few relevant ministers—all former intelligence cronies of the president—a half kilometer away, on the other side of Red Square. Watching the live-action feed was decidedly better than looking at Brazilian bikini girls in *National Geographic.*

Tall, ferret-faced, all hip bones and rib cage, with light brown hair styled in a Prince Valiant cut last seen in the 1928 French silent film *The Passion of Joan of Arc,* mousey Audrey was a Gordian knot of guilty passion, fumbling awkwardness, and anorgasmia, with a tendency to spritz the bed as she vainly chased her elusive release. *Thank God,* thought Dominika, *nothing complicated.* Without much effort, she could avoid active participation and instead assume the role of masseuse and bring this bony scarecrow through the four corporeal stages of arousal—in school they called them Fog, Breeze, Mountain, and Wave—to coax what the instructors called *malenkoye sushchestvo,* the little creature, out of her, which is exactly what happened thirty teetering minutes later, the first shuddering spasm triggered by the unexpected introduction of the ribbed rubber handle of Audrey's hairbrush (*No. 89, "Pray at the back altar of Saint Basil's Cathedral"*).

Moaning and wide-eyed, Audrey came off the mattress like a vampire sitting up in a coffin, wrapped her arms around Dominika's neck, sunk her teeth into her shoulder, and rode her successive, shuddering orgasms like a witch on a broom, out of the hotel, over the Kremlin walls, past President Putin's bedroom window, and around the star on the spire of the Ukraina Hotel, two hundred meters above the Arbatsky bend of the river.

That should give the GRU recruiter enough to work with, thought Dominika, with technical aplomb, as Audrey collapsed on her back, sighing. Dominika draped a towel over Audrey's trembling loins.

The last time, she thought, *and thank God she was leaving this behind. Helsinki was going to be a dream.* She couldn't know she was both right and wrong.

Audrey was stirring out of her benzodiazepine-fueled, four-climax coma, her head surprisingly clear, her thighs sticky and trembling. As per procedure, the Sparrow always slipped out of the room as the recruiter came in, and Dominika shouldered past him, ignoring his courteous nod. Audrey didn't even see her go, and she didn't know that the inveigling Sparrow's role was complete. For Audrey, what's-her-name would be only a fading memory—a Venus with blue eyes holding that hairbrush—albeit immortalized permanently on digital video.

Audrey likewise didn't know that the Kremlin recruiter was the renowned Doctor Anton Gorelikov, the fifty-year-old director of Putin's mysterious *Sekretariat*, a shadowy office in the Kremlin with a single member—Gorelikov himself—that handled delicate, strategic matters of importance, such as the coercive recruitment of a young US Navy officer. Uncle Anton had scored monumental recruitment successes over the years. Speaking in fluent Oxfordian English, Gorelikov had a number of issues to discuss after Audrey finished dressing and came out of the gilt bathroom nervously combing her hair with the still-hot hairbrush. He rarely used threats, preferring instead to rationally discuss the benefits of cooperating with Russian intelligence, and ignoring the "unpleasantness" that had just concluded.

They sat in the salon, Audrey apprehensive but clueless. It was two o'clock in the morning.

"It's a distinct pleasure to meet you, Audrey," said Uncle Anton.

Audrey shifted in her chair and looked at him. Some of her starch was on display. "How do you know my name?" she said. "Who are you?"

Gorelikov smiled the smile that had doomed a thousand blackmailed recruits. Audrey's voice was not calm; he heard the telltale wavering tone.

"Please call me Anton," he said. "I know your name because your bona fides are superb: a brilliant career in weapons research ahead of you, excellent prospects for promotion, influential mentors, and powerful sponsors who will supercharge your navy career."

"How do you know so much about me? What entity do you represent?" said Audrey, still not comprehending what this was.

Uncle Anton ignored her questions. "As for the brief *liaison* this evening with the young girl from the bar, it is wisely left unmentioned—best for all concerned," said Uncle Anton. "I greatly admire the wisdom of the US Navy's Don't Ask, Don't Tell reforms. Sadly, our Russian military is too monolithic for such liberal farsightedness," he sighed.

"What's that got to do with anything?" said Audrey, whose exceptional mind was beginning to connect the dots. A cold wave ran down her back.

"I have an abiding worry," said Uncle Anton. "I fear that if your sapphic indiscretions become public, the old institutional prejudices in your service regrettably would almost certainly reemerge, putting you at risk of early retirement on the beach at half pay. That would be both unjust and unfair." With prescient timing, Gorelikov pointed the remote at the television in the corner of the salon, which began showing precisely which indiscretions he was talking about, namely, images of Audrey's trembling legs in the air with what appeared to be a lemur's tail protruding from between her buttocks. Audrey sat numbly in the armchair, watching expressionless, giving few psychic clues to the wily old wizard, which was interesting—she was placid, emotionless, acquiescent. She accepted a cigarette and drew on it deeply. Gorelikov knew she was considering the consequences. *Good sign.*

Audrey indeed was considering the consequences. She knew what would happen as they had been given security briefings on just these situations. She had chosen to ignore them; they were regulations that would not, *did not*, apply to her. She was going places in the navy, and she didn't have the time. But she knew she was in a jam: The Russians would concoct a charade. The young Russian girl would come forward, tearfully claiming to the authorities that she was coerced into making a salacious sex tape, which was a violation of at least half a dozen Russian morality laws. Such a scandal would destroy Audrey's career, this career she had been preparing for since graduate school, through Officer Candidate School, to the research lab, in order to climb the ladder, to outdo her ungenerous father, to best his own accomplishments in the navy, and to earn the benefits and prestige of flag rank in a service that was the impenetrable preserve of smugly solicitous men. All this would be hers; nothing was more important. Her physicist's mind leapt ahead with comprehension.

"In the simplest terms, you are blackmailing me, an officer in the US Navy." Audrey couldn't keep the tremor out of her voice. Uncle Anton held up his hands in an expression of alarm.

"My dear Audrey," he said. "That is the furthest thing from my mind. The very notion repels me."

"Then perhaps you'll have the courtesy to tell me exactly what it is you *have* on your mind." Gorelikov noted that she already could give orders like an admiral.

"Gladly," he said. "Enough of hypotheticals. I have an exceptional offer. I would like to propose a discreet relationship between you and a sympathetic Russia to work together *for a year* toward peaceful global parity, a relationship that would be beneficial to both countries, and to all nations. A twelve-month collaboration. I ask you to consider: after all, even military research has the avoidance of war as its defining goal, does it not?"

She did not move, but he knew she was listening. Audrey assessed his words. He was, in a sense, right. Audrey's long-suffering mother had lived under the callous weight of her regnant husband for thirty years. She was a kind soul and, well, a love child of the sixties who danced at Woodstock and believed in global peace, in a world devoid of strife, cruelty, and hate. Audrey's analytical mind knew that such things as railguns did not exist in her mother's Elysian world, but she never forgot her placid words, in the quiet months before the tumult when her father came home after sea duty.

"But no one can live on world peace alone, can they?" said Uncle Anton, breaking into her thoughts. A discreet relationship would bring other tangible, less abstract benefits, such as a consultant's fee, including a monthly "stipend," an alias offshore bank account into which *significant* deposits would be made regularly and, most important, *opekunskiy*, tutorials for her prepared by Russian military experts, the North American Institute, and Kremlin staffers on strategic naval doctrine, weapons design, global forecasts, international political priorities, and economic trends. (Never mind that all intelligence services use the fiction of "tutorials" for their assets as elicitation sessions to extract even more information from their agents while giving nothing important away.)

With such a start, Audrey Rowland would become the US Navy's rising star in military research, assuring promotion, management of entire R&D programs, and plum Pentagon billets. These kinds of assignments often led to national politics after a military career—the Senate, the cabinet, even higher. Audrey flicked ash onto the floor. She knew what was happening, yet the rewards were exactly the emoluments she coveted.

Gorelikov analyzed her in layers, like turning a baluster on a wood lathe. She was a social narcissist with an inflated sense of herself, a compensating careerist with a deep need for admiration and yet a lack of empathy for others, like her father. She was in a system that made her by definition a sexual misfit. She had been a brilliant PhD student with an orderly mind, now impressing superiors at NRL. She was not by nature reckless or impulsive, and yet she was picking up women in a Moscow hotel bar, clearly ignoring ironclad security practices stipulated for criteria countries, high-security-threat nations. *Odarennost* and *sobstvennoye*, genius clouded by ego, with the albatross of conflicted sexuality heavy around her neck. Indeed, a potent profile in a recruitment candidate. Based on his assessment of her, he doubted she would refuse his pitch and choose to face the consequences.

Audrey blew a stream of smoke toward the ceiling, winding up her indignation. "Thanks for the offer, Anton, but go fuck yourself," she said flatly, not looking at him. Gorelikov was delighted: it was just the response he'd been waiting for.

PECHENIYA—RUSSIAN TEA CAKES

Mix butter, sugar, baking powder, and vanilla. Incorporate flour, salt, and chopped almonds until dough holds together. Roll one-inch balls, place on ungreased sheet, and bake in a medium oven, but not till brown. Roll still-hot balls in powdered sugar. Let cool, then roll in the sugar again.

1

A Mole in Their Midst

Present day. Colonel Dominika Egorova, Chief of Line KR, the counter-intelligence section in the SVR, sat in a chair in the office of the Athens *rezident*, Pavel Bondarchuk, and bounced her foot, a sign of nettled impatience to those who knew her. Bondarchuk, also an SVR Colonel, was Chief of the *rezidentura* and responsible for the management of all Russian intelligence operations in Greece. He technically outranked Egorova, but she had acquired patrons in the Kremlin during her career, and a professional reputation that was whispered about over the porcelain telegraph at SVR headquarters (gossip only repeated in the headquarters toilets): recruitments, spy swaps, gunfights; this Juno had even blown the top of a supervisor's head off with a lipstick gun on an island in the Seine in Paris on Putin's orders. Who was going to pull rank on this fire-breathing *drakon*? thought Bondarchuk, who was a nervous scarecrow with a big forehead and sunken cheeks.

Not that she looked like a dragon. In her thirties, Egorova was slim and narrow-waisted, with legs still muscular from ballet. Chestnut hair piled on top of her head framed a classic Hellenic face with heavy brows, high cheekbones, and a straight jaw. Her hands were long-fingered and elegant, the nails square-cut and unpolished. She wore no jewelry, only a thin wristwatch on a narrow velvet band. Even under her loose summer dress on this spring day, Egorova's prodigious 80D bust was obvious (the subject of inevitable frequent comment in Yasenevo hallways). But this was nothing compared to her eyes that held his as she watched him look at her chest. Cobalt blue and unblinking, Egorova's eyes seemed to look inside one's head to read thoughts, a decidedly creepy sensation.

What no one knew was that Dominika Egorova could indeed read minds. It was the colors. She was a synesthete, diagnosed at age five, a condition her professor father and violinist mother made her swear never to reveal, ever, to anyone. And no one knew. Her synesthesia let her see words, and music, and human moods as ethereal airborne colors. It was a great advantage when she danced ballet and could pirouette among spirals of red and blue. It was a bigger advantage in the hated Sparrow School when she could see the gassy cloud around a man's head and shoulders and gauge passion, and lust, and love. As she entered the Service as an operations officer, it was a superweapon she used to assess moods, intentions, and deceptions. She had lived with this ability—a blessing and a curse—picking out the reds and purples of constancy and affection, or the yellows and greens of ill will and sloth, or the blues of thoughtfulness and cunning and, only once, the black bat wings of pure evil.

Bondarchuk's yellow halo of craven bureaucratic panic pulsed around his shoulders. "You have no authority to initiate an operation in my area of responsibility," he said, twining his fingers nervously. "To pitch a North Korean is doubly risky. You have no idea how these *giyeny*, these hyenas, will react: diplomatic protest, cyberattack, physical violence; they're capable of anything."

Dominika had no time for this. "The hyena you refer to is Ri Sou-yong, Academician Ri, deputy of the Yongbyon Nuclear Scientific Research Center in North Korea, the institution that is working diligently on designing a nuclear warhead to use against the United States. We need a source inside their program. With Chinese encouragement, the North Koreans are as likely to launch a missile at Moscow as at Washington in the next five years. Or perhaps you disagree?"

Bondarchuk said nothing.

"I sent you the operational summary. Ri has been at the International Atomic Energy Agency, IAEA, in Vienna for a year," said Dominika. "Never a wrong step, unwavering loyalty to Pyongyang, politically reliable. Then he mails a letter. He wants to talk to Moscow. Conscience? Despair? Defection? We shall see. In any case, calm yourself. This is not a coercive pitch; he called us."

"You burned a perfectly good safe house from my list for this unknown target, with no guarantee of success," said Bondarchuk.

"Complain to Moscow, if you wish," snapped Dominika. "I'll deliver your written demarche personally to the Director, explaining you would have met the target openly on the street." Dominika's foot bounced like a sewing machine. The man was an imbecile among imbeciles in the Service.

"We have two days to soften him up. This is a furtive weekend away from his Vienna security detail. He's at a beach house in Voula with a housekeeper-cook," she said.

Bondarchuk sat back in his swivel chair. "The so-called housekeeper, the twenty-five-year-old Romanian student, she wouldn't happen to be on your payroll?"

Dominika shrugged. "One of my best. She's already provided useful insights into his midlife crisis," she said.

Bondarchuk laughed. "I'm sure she's providing other useful insights. You Sparrows are all alike," he said, implicitly including her.

Dominika stood. "Do you think so? Can you tell we are all alike?" she said, all ice. "For instance, is the woman you're seeing every Thursday afternoon a Sparrow from the Center, would you say, Colonel? Or just your Greek mistress? Can you guess? And if you refer to me as a Sparrow ever again, your own midlife crisis will arrive ahead of schedule."

Bondarchuk sat rooted in his chair, his yellow halo quivering as Dominika walked out.

———

When Dominika arrived at the safe house, Academician Ri was out at the weekly street market in Voula, the sun-bleached seaside suburb of Athens on the southern coast, buying produce so his Romanian house sitter, Ioana, could prepare lemon meatballs with celeriac like her mother used to make. Even after he had spent a year experiencing the culinary delights of Vienna, Ri's starved North Korean palate still craved meat, vegetables, and rich sauces, and Ioana had been preparing hearty meals for the two days since he arrived in Athens after slipping out of Vienna before the start of a long weekend.

"We have quite the proper domestic scene here," said Ioana to Dominika, who took off her sunglasses as she entered the little second-floor rented apartment, all whitewashed walls and marble floors with balcony sliders completely open to the balmy sea breeze. "He's a strange duck—separate bedrooms, doesn't want back rubs, and doesn't look at me in my undies. He shops for food, I cook, he washes the dishes, then he watches English-language news all night. Devours it."

Ioana Petrescu was a veteran Sparrow, tall and broad shouldered, a former volleyball player, fluent in English, French, and Romanian, and with level 4 Russian. She had a degree in Slavistics from the University of Bucharest. She disliked most people—officials, SVR officers, and Russians in general—but worshipped Dominika, who was a sister in arms, a former Sparrow who treated her as an equal. With her Dacian goddess face, Ioana could have made a fortune in the West modeling, but her cross-grainedness kept her working as an SVR Sparrow for Dominika, once whispering that she relished the nuances of seduction in a properly managed honey trap. There was a bit of the predator in her, which endeared her to Dominika even more. She was perceptive, educated, irascible, irreverent, and skeptical. Dominika protected Ioana inside the Service, kept the philandering colonels and generals away from her, and valued her canny assessments of targets. The two women were friends—Dominika planned to eventually extract her from the Sparrow cadre and bring her into the Service on a permanent basis as an officer.

"Does he mention why he posted the letter to the Vienna *rezidentura*?" said Dominika. "What does he want? Is he going to defect?"

"I do not wish to defect," said a voice at the door. They hadn't heard him come in. Ri Sou-yong carried a brimming plastic string bag from which protruded a head of celery and the leaves of a leek. He set the bag on the kitchen counter and sat down in a chair opposite the women. He was short and slight, dressed in a simple white shirt, slacks, and sandals. He had jet-black hair, a ruddy moon face with high cheekbones and a light mole on his chin, like Chairman Mao. "May I assume your colleague is the representative from Moscow?" he asked Ioana. "I will not ask for names." He turned to Dominika. "Welcome. Thank you for coming all this way to see me. I have information for you." He went into the back room and came back with a creased button-and-string manila envelope and handed it to Dominika. "Please excuse the condition of the envelope. I had to smuggle it out of my office under my clothing. But I hope the contents make up for its disheveled appearance."

Dominika emptied a sheaf of pages onto the coffee table. The documents were written in Korean script; they may as well have been Paleolithic scratchings on cave walls in Lascaux.

Ri instantly read Dominika's blank stare, and blushed in contrition. "I apologize for the *Chosŏn'gŭl*, the Korean script, but I know that original scientific documents have more intrinsic value than translated or transcribed ones." *This is quite the little perfectionist*, thought Dominika, appraising the deep-blue halo around his head. *A thinker, brilliant, anticipates reactions.*

"Quite so, professor," said Dominika, "but a peddler of spurious information might bring documents whose value cannot be immediately established." It was a discourteous suggestion made to gauge his reaction. In the back of her mind, this still could be a North Korean intelligence trap concocted for some inscrutable reason by the infantile mind of the Outstanding Leader or whatever they called the butter-bean chairman these days. By habit, she and Ioana both subconsciously listened for the crunch of gravel footsteps on the driveway outside. Ri smiled and clapped his hands.

"Quite right, indeed; you are prudent to raise the question," he said.

"And we still have not heard exactly why you requested this meeting or precisely what you are offering, or what specifically you expect in return," said Dominika.

"I will answer your questions, gladly," said the little man, with a little bow. "First, I ask nothing of you in exchange for this information. I have no need for money. I do not want to defect. My family in Pyongyang would be fed alive into a steel rolling furnace one by one if I was to disappear from my post in Vienna.

"Second, I offer you intelligence—state secrets—on recent successes in Yongbyon's nuclear program, specifically efforts to construct a reliable trigger to a nuclear device, one that eventually will be sufficiently miniaturized to be fitted atop an ICBM. I will summarize in English what I have provided in these technical reports for your preliminary report to Moscow. Will that be satisfactory?"

"That would be quite satisfactory," said Dominika. "But the third question remains: Why are you doing this? And why offer the information to Moscow?" Ri looked Dominika directly in the eyes, his blue halo unwavering, his hands still. She did not detect any deception.

"I chose Moscow because Washington has lost its global gravitas in the last decade, it has become an eagle with no talons or beak. CIA has been politicized and contorted, and tends to leak intelligence at the behest of their administration for political gain." He smiled. "Collaborating with an intelligence service that leaks to serve ideologue politicians tends to shorten the life expectancy of its reporting sources. I am willing to run risks, but I am not suicidal."

Ri wiped his palms on his trousers. "You ask why? A person can sit silent only so long. Nuclear weapons in the hands of a man-child who calls himself The Saint of the Sun and the Moon would be disaster for our country, for the Asian region, and for the world. I risk my and my family's lives to see that never happens. There is no hope in our country. Perhaps I can bring some hope for the future."

"I admire your conviction, professor," said Dominika. "Are you prepared to continue reporting from Vienna, from the IAEA? I will not lie to you; the risks will not diminish. But I personally will be responsible for your security."

"Collaborating in Vienna will be significantly more difficult," said Ri. "There is a cadre of security guards who watch our delegation very closely. We are required to live in the same apartment building, two delegates in each flat, so everyone informs on everyone else. Solitary time is very rare."

"These are difficulties that can be surmounted," said Dominika. "We have much experience in these matters."

With the exquisite timing of a trained Sparrow, Ioana stood and walked into the kitchen. "I will start dinner while you discuss business," she said. "I think a bottle of wine tonight, to celebrate?"

———

Academician Ri sat beside Dominika on the couch and summarized what was in the reports he had provided, occasionally turning a page over to sketch a simple diagram to illustrate a point. He spoke like a scientist, logically and in an ordered sequence.

"We could talk for weeks about nuclear-weapon design development, but in a few words, these papers document that our intelligence service has given our nuclear program certain foreign technology that will enable North Korea to build a more powerful nuclear device, and to miniaturize it to fit into the warhead of an intercontinental ballistic missile. If I may, there are three important points:

"One: Our intelligence service, the RGB, the Reconnaissance Bureau of the General Staff Department, is not a global service. They operate regionally, are hopelessly insular, and generally ineffective. They could never have, under any circumstances, acquired the technology on their own.

"Two: The technology involves advanced electromagnetic components, heretofore only seen in the development of a US naval railgun, an experimental weapon that can propel a projectile at great speeds over immense distances.

"Three: Harnessing the electromagnetic power of a reconfigured railgun will enable Yongbyon to develop what is called a gun-type detonator—slamming two subcritical hemispheres of U-235 together—for a uranium fission device in a very short period of time. The technology is relevant because it will also facilitate miniaturization of the trigger to fit inside a missile warhead." Dominika knew this was immensely important.

"Professor, how soon will the trigger be ready for use in its miniaturized form?"

"I estimate six months, unless there are complications," said Ri.

"Does North Korea at this time have a missile with sufficient range to reach Washington, DC, or Moscow?"

"Those are secrets held by the army's Missile Forces of the General Staff. My understanding is that as of today, they do not, but in twelve months, perhaps. That is only a guess."

"How did the RGB acquire the electromagnetic railgun technology?"

Ri shook his head slowly. "That I do not know. We are given plain copies of the research, but we see no original documents or plans. The RGB would never disclose the source of their intelligence. Two things are certain: The stolen technology is authentic—it is accelerating our program, saving us years of research and development."

"And the second?" asked Dominika.

"This science could come from only one place. The Americans have a big problem. They have a mole in their midst."

IOANA'S LEMON MEATBALLS WITH CELERIAC

Mix ground beef, chopped onion, chopped parsley, raw egg, allspice, salt, and pepper, and form into short oblong kebab shapes. Aggressively brown the kebabs, then set aside. Sauté celeriac root cut into matchsticks, crushed whole garlic cloves, turmeric, cumin, cinnamon, crushed fennel seeds, and smoked paprika, stirring on high heat. Return kebabs to pan, add chicken stock, lemon juice, and salt and pepper. Bring to a boil, then simmer until celeriac is tender and sauce is thick. Serve with a dollop of thick yogurt and a sprinkle of parsley.

2

Bread in the Oven

Twelve years ago, when LTJG Audrey Rowland, in the suite of the Metropol Hotel, told Kremlin recruiter Anton Gorelikov to go fuck himself after he had proposed an arrangement by which she would share classified information on US Navy weapons research projects with Russian military intelligence in exchange for cash payments and discreet career assistance, Gorelikov was delighted. In the handbook of intelligence recruitments, this blasphemy was not a refusal. The young woman had not said no and, more important, she had not indignantly declared her intention to report the pitch to American counterintelligence officials, which would have definitively blown the approach. Her thirty-minute dalliance with an SVR Sparrow clearly was a reportable contact that would have had grave consequences for her promising navy career. Gorelikov assessed that she would be motivated by her desire to keep the episode secret. There was something more, he thought. This young woman was ambitious, and she already had shown herself to be a brilliant researcher in a critical program, a gold-plated skill that would guarantee rapid advancement in a male-dominated US Navy, which clearly was important to her. She also carried some as-yet undefined baggage regarding men, which perhaps manifested itself in her sexual behavior, even at her young age. Ambition leavened by ego, seasoned by a forbidden taste for tribadism. A potent recruitment cocktail. He had let her consider overnight—in the espionage lexicon otherwise colloquially known as leaving the bread in the oven.

When Audrey Rowland the next day archly stipulated that she would limit her reporting strictly to the railgun project, Gorelikov graciously agreed to her condition. He knew the hook was set. Most agents start by declaring moral limits to their treason, insisting on close-ended arrangements, usually limited to a single topic, in exchange for keeping their original transgressions secret. What none of them immediately realized was that agreeing to provide *any* secrets to Moscow multiplied the initial infraction a hundredfold, enveloping the agent in the spider's web for as long as the Russians stipulated, or until she lost access, or until her luck ran out and the mole hunters called her in for the inexorable interviews. Gorelikov knew from long experience that the inevitable outcome—the universal fate of all agents—was that Audrey eventually would be blown by careless tradecraft at the hands of a ham-fisted GRU handler or, more likely, by a CIA source inside GRU who would report the existence of a Russian mole in the US Navy. The goal, therefore, had been to compartment the case, and run the asset for as long as possible, extracting as much intelligence as quickly as was secure. Audrey Rowland's survival as a reporting source was not Gorelikov's bureaucratic responsibility, but he told himself he'd rather it be handled by the SVR, a service more adept at handling foreign sources, or better yet, by an anonymous illegal, impossible to trace and trebly compartmented.

Now the lofty Vice Admiral Rowland—encrypted MAGNIT—nevertheless had defied the actuarial odds for agent survival. She had been reporting for twelve years—there had been breaks in contact, unsuccessful turnovers to unacceptable new handlers, and a hiatus after a security scare—but she had been on the books since her recruitment in the Metropol.

VADM Rowland had, as Gorelikov predicted, long ago become accustomed to the act of espionage. She initially rationalized the treason by telling herself that sharing science with Russia would level the technology playing field, engender mutual confidence, and actually lessen the chance of a third world war, a conflict no sane person thought would be survivable for either side. She enjoyed the florid notes of thanks and admiration from astonished Russian scientists praising her technical brilliance, just as she reveled in the yearly meetings with Uncle Anton, who was elegant, well dressed, and urbane, and could discuss art, or music, or philosophy as well as the limits of shipborne phased array radar, or the megawatt generating capacity of the *Zumwalt*-class destroyer.

The relationship between agent and masters matured. As MAGNIT's performance continued unabated, and her reliability ratings remained at the highest level—all services constantly assess their canaries, for the first sign of trouble in a case is an anomalous change in intel production—Gorelikov, at Putin's direction, began parallel handling: GRU officers handled MAGNIT inside the United States, although they were little more than mailmen, collecting drops and passing requirements. Gorelikov, however, began meeting MAGNIT during her annual personal leave, her one break from her otherwise total devotion to the laboratories, Special Access Programs, personnel management, and budget-oversight duties that consumed her. Everyone knew that stork-like Admiral Rowland chose rugged campestral destinations for her solo monthlong holiday travels: hiking in Nepal; photo safaris in Tanzania; camping in Jamaica; or kayaking down the Amazon. To colleagues unaccustomed to seeing rawboned Audrey Rowland in anything but her uniform, vacation photos of her in hiking shorts, boots, cargo pants, or a wet suit usually raised eyebrows and occasioned muttered comparisons to Ichabod Crane.

Meetings with Anton were arranged on the margins of Audrey's exotic vacations, in luxurious rented houses in the nearest large cities to avoid extra travel and incriminating stamps in her passport. The agent's initial, delusional rationalization for spying evolved under the philosophical tutelage of Uncle Anton, who sought to keep Audrey motivated. The notion of "level playing fields" seemed less relevant in the New Cold War of active measures and cyberoperations. Anton instead often raised the inequity of the system for women in the navy, drawing from Audrey's progressively less-guarded comments about a childhood clearly and completely dominated by an overbearing father, a rakish naval aviator who cowed his quiescent wife and as much as told Audrey he would have preferred a son. If her father were alive today, Audrey told Anton, he would have to salute *her*. Anton agreed that women had the same problem in Russia: forced by society, customs, and institutions to let men steal emotional strength away from them. Anton's wry empathy struck a chord in Audrey. What she was doing—passing secrets, meeting furtively, accepting payment from the Kremlin—she was doing for herself, and she was doing it to excel in her career despite the men, despite the system. The growing balance in her Center-managed accounts—she already had five million dollars' worth of the Kremlin's euros, Krugerrands, and uncut diamonds—was further personal validation that this was due her.

Anton recognized that the notion of espionage as an engine of Audrey's emancipation was a potent control factor. Additional control naturally came from her sexual appetites. Despite liberalizations in the US armed forces, Anton continually harped on the necessity of keeping her predilection for female lovers a secret lest she derail her career. The closeted world that Audrey inhabited kept her in an itchy state and made her a better agent: nervy, edgy, and resentful. Her annual vacations abroad were delicious opportunities to spot, pursue, and bed tantalizing lovers. Anton several times had to intercede with local authorities when sessions with Audrey and a local partner became too spirited—Audrey on the boil occasionally became physical. Anton even arranged for forged-alias identity cards to keep her true name out of local police blotters if things got out of control. The sex was a handling problem, but it was worth the bother as a tool to control MAGNIT, for when she was back in Washington behind her desk at ONR, the Office of Naval Research, broad stripes on her sleeves and three stars on her collar, she was by necessity benignly celibate, and had to live the part.

Anton even advised her to eschew battery-operated boyfriends at home because she was assigned a live-in navy steward and cook in the gabled Victorian Quarters B on Admiral's Row at the Washington Naval Yard in SE Washington. He sternly told her that her snow-white image as a laudably asexual professional would be sullied if her staff found any sex toys, and rumors would quickly circulate about the wild-haired, three-star stoker in the attic at midnight with a 220 V massager making the lights flicker and scaring the mice. The same applied when Audrey one year discovered spicy Thai cucumber salad while on a temple tour in northern Thailand, and announced she would have her cook in Washington prepare it often. During their meeting in the swanky Anantara Resort in provincial Chiang Mai, Anton sternly told her to leave the contents of the reefer crisper alone; the household staff would be bound to notice missing cucumbers. Audrey laughed at the image. After so many years, Uncle Anton could talk to her about such things freely.

Between her sustaining foreign meetings with Uncle Anton, MAGNIT met once a month in Washington with GRU handlers who were military intel officers from the Russian Embassy on Wisconsin Avenue. Covered as run-of-the-mill military attachés, GRU spooks rarely ran true clandestine sources, inhabiting instead the margins of classic intelligence of elicitation, open-source collection, and technology transfer. The meetings were held in suburban parks and along nature trails and greenswards in Washington and suburban Maryland and Virginia. These meetings were little more than five-minute brief encounters during which Audrey would pass her intel and send messages to Uncle Anton. Audrey's quantitative mind took to the challenge of finding imaginative meeting sites, ones that she could surveil from a distance to ensure the GRU dolt-of-the-month hadn't dragged FBI surveillance with him. Audrey had discussed the fine points of site casing with Anton—

her tutor in so many things—and had become quite adept. Audrey had lost count of the endless discs, thumb drives, digital cameras, hard drives, and, occasionally, sheaves of physical documents, bound volumes, and print-outs on every aspect of naval-weapons research, antisubmarine warfare, ship design and radar, stealth technology, and encrypted communications she dumped in the laps of her handlers. After twelve years in harness, she couldn't have accurately listed the sum total of the secrets she had passed the Russians. She really didn't care. The three stripes on her uniform coat were reason enough to continue.

A source such as MAGNIT unquestionably was the jewel in the GRU crown, as well as a constant burden on the collective abilities of GRU Head-quarters, commonly known as the Aquarium. From the beginning, Anton Gorelikov had been secretly assigned by Putin to monitor the MAGNIT case, and observe the quality and durability of GRU tradecraft. When MAGNIT received her third star, Gorelikov none-too-gently began prying the case away from the military, eventually to be assigned to an illegals officer in New York who would be anonymous, invisible, and inviolate. At that time, the MAGNIT cryptonym would be changed and the files tightly restricted. Gorelikov also had his eye on SVR Chief of Counterintelligence Colonel Egorova, who he thought eventually could share MAGNIT handling duties abroad, based on her previous experience in street operations and counterintelligence.

President Putin had for years been on a low simmer for his counter-intelligence chief, the former busty ballerina, since the night he had vis-ited Dominika's room in the Constantine Palace at midnight and casually fondled the lace bodice of her nightgown while ordering her to fly to Paris and eradicate her chief, the psychopath Zyuganov, who had got-ten on Putin's bad side. The president had not forgotten how Egorova's nipples had responded to his touch, could not forget the faint scratching of the dockyard rivets swelling beneath the lace, and how her lashes flut-tered in coy arousal. He would own her eventually, it was inevitable. He had intentions of promoting Egorova in the near future, but not yet. And handling MAGNIT could wait: the mole's continued production was criti-cal. Gorelikov assured Putin this was just the beginning: as the US Navy would founder and disintegrate, so would the United States. "*Chto bylo, to proshlo I bylyom poroslo*, what used to be will be gone and overgrown with grass," said Gorelikov to Vladimir.

MAGNIT'S SPICY THAI CUCUMBER SALAD

Peel and deseed cucumber and slice paper-thin, preferably on a mandolin. Put cucumber slices in a colander, sprinkle with salt, and let drain, squeezing out excess water. In a bowl, mix rice vinegar, lime juice, thin slices of garlic, lots of finely diced Thai bird's-eye chilies, *nam pla* (fish sauce), chopped cilantro, a dash of sesame oil, sugar, finely diced scallions, and thinly sliced red onion (soak onions in ice water briefly beforehand). Toss cucumbers in dressing and sprinkle with either dried shrimp powder or finely ground peanuts. Serve immediately.

3

You Are Mine

Dominika uncapped the lipstick tube and wrote *Ti Moy* on Nathaniel Nash's naked chest as she lay on top of him in bed in CIA's safe house: a sun-blasted, white stucco cottage at the end of a dusty road at the top of a rocky cactus hill in Vouliagmeni, fifteen kilometers south of Athens, with a hazy view of the island of Aegina across the dead-calm turquoise Saronic Gulf. White island ferries heading into the Port of Piraeus left intersecting foaming wakes as they passed. Outside the window, hummingbirds flitted around the blossoms on the wisteria vines that grew up the outside walls of the one-room villa. Dominika hitched herself a little higher and kissed him on the lips.

"I hope that wasn't one of your lipstick guns," said Nate. Two years earlier, SVR's Line T (technical) had given Dominika two electrically fired, single-shot weapons disguised as lipstick tubes that she had used in Paris to separate the skullcap from the brainpan of her diminutive and psychotic chief Zyuganov, who at the time was raking her ribs with a stiletto, trying to shiver the tip of the blade between her ribs and into her heart. He had divined that Dominika was working for CIA, and when the exploding dumdum bullets from the lipstick guns aerosolized the poison dwarf's brain into the river Seine, she was safe, again, for the time being, until the next crisis.

———

That had been five years after her first overseas tour in Helsinki. Finland had been a dream. Gingerbread-trim houses, and sizzling venison cutlets, and the excitement and ecstasy of a real operational mission: to find CIA officer Nathaniel Nash of the American Embassy, meet, befriend, and, if necessary, seduce him to elicit the name of a high-ranking Russian the SVR knew, *just knew*, Nash was handling, but could never catch. Nash and Dominika started working on each other—dinners by the light of candlewax-covered wine bottles, walks in leafy city parks, coffees along the breezy harbor promenade, the girls' summer skirts billowing above their hips. Elicitation, bone throwing, verbal snares, and assessment traps. They both knew all the developmental tricks, and banged heads for three months, trying to recruit each other. She noted that his crimson halo—passion, devotion, constancy—never wavered or rippled. He told the truth and she could see his interest deepening by the day.

Then the impossible happened. Nate's easy, honest nature; his mild—but accurate—criticism of the current mess in Russia; the earnest, flirty attention he paid to *her* made her question what she was doing, for whom she was doing it, and why. When her friend in the Russian Embassy disappeared (Dominika was positive she had been assassinated over a minor infraction of security), it pushed her over the edge. On a rainy Helsinki night, she accepted Nate's recruitment pitch to spy for CIA, and she was encrypted DIVA. How better could she do maximum damage to the tsar and his bandits? What more could she do to feed the *otvrashcheniye*, the loathing for them she felt? By spying for CIA, Dominika was helping the *Rodina*, not betraying it.

Bozhe, God, they were a different breed, these CIA men who gathered around to train her, and coach her, and support her like family, beneficence unheard of and impossible in her own SVR. A small group of them had come into her life. Chief of Europe Division, Tom Forsyth, the salt-and-pepper-haired legend in the DO, the Directorate of Operations, and beneficent mentor to Nate Nash. The urbane Forsyth had recruited prime ministers, Emirati princes, and, once, the pampered mistress of a Red Fleet admiral by taking her to an orphanage in Paris to watch children gambol in the playroom (Forsyth knew the admiral had refused to marry her and give her children). Recruitment was all about human needs, vulnerabilities, and motivations. Deeply affected by his solicitude, she started stealing Soviet naval secrets for Forsyth the next day.

Then there was Marty Gable, career-long colleague of Forsyth. He was usually dressed in khaki bush shirt and hiking boots, and slouched on a couch. There wasn't much Gable hadn't seen. He had run assets in Africa, Latin America, Southeast Asia, and the Maghreb. He had recruited a penetration of the PKK terrorist group in Istanbul and rescued the blown agent by shooting a PKK enforcer between the eyes. To him, protecting his agents—namely DIVA—came first. Dominika took to calling him *Bratok*, big brother. He had taken the young Nate under his wing, lovingly kicking Nash's ass to learn the Rules of the Game.

The last of these new friends was Chief of Counterintelligence Simon Benford—podgy, angry, necktie perpetually askew. Most days the hair on one side of his head stuck out in a wing, exact cause unknown. Like Forsyth, Benford was an obelisk in the DO. In the last five years alone, the mercurial genius had led three separate investigations to unmask Russian-run moles inside CIA and the US government. Benford hated bureaucrats, careerists, mooncalves, mutton-heads, most of the special agents in the Federal Bureau of Investigation, the entire Defense Intelligence Agency, and what he called the "homoerotic" Department of State. Due to the extreme sensitivity and restricted-handling protocol within the compartment, Benford became the senior Headquarters officer personally directing the DIVA case.

Under their careful guidance, Dominika emptied the Helsinki *rezidentura* of all its secrets and, when she returned to Moscow, began reporting sensitive blue-stripe intelligence (designating the most sensitive and perishable secrets) from the vaults of Yasenevo, which soon made her CIA's premier Russian source. For more than seven years, Dominika had stolen everything she could, and her CIA men kept her sane and alive, through heart-pounding personal meetings in Moscow alleyways, furtive rendezvous in foreign capitals, and abbreviated burst transmissions from her SRAC (short range agent communications) equipment. She laid open for CIA the Kremlin's clandestine activities around the world.

There was also the situation with her recruiting case officer, Nathaniel Nash. Dark hair spilling across his forehead, his exceptional falcon eyes on the street, the crimson aura around his shoulders, worked cumulatively on Dominika, already dazzled by CIA men and the wild sleigh ride of spying for them. What else happened between Nate and Dominika in Helsinki perhaps was inevitable. Thrown together under the unrelenting pressure of recruitment and espionage, Nate the agent handler and Dominika the clandestine asset fell in love. Their passion was unrelenting, their lovemaking volcanic, furtive, and limited to the rare occasions they were alone together. For Nate, an affair between a case officer and his asset was a career-ending infraction. For Dominika, sleeping with Nate the American would be fatal if discovered by the Center.

Their liaison did not—could not—remain secret from CIA for long. Gable's pheromonal instincts and Benford's warlock prescience soon detected the forbidden affair. Nate was called on the carpet, but Benford chose for the moment not to fire him summarily from the service in the interests of intel production and keeping DIVA motivated. For her part, Dominika unconcernedly acknowledged the situation, accepted the risks, ignored *Bratok* Gable's warnings, and reveled in her love for Nate. Nash had tried to stop the affair several times, but their passion was overwhelming. She refused to give him up, and he could not extinguish his crimson ardor.

═══════

Brushing her heavy breasts across Nate's face, Dominika got out of bed and padded over to the tiled corner of the tiny kitchen that was a makeshift shower, and doused herself with the handheld nozzle, wetting a substantial patch of the marble floor. Nate watched her wash her lithe body, white scars crisscrossing her ribs, ballet calves flexing as she rotated under the water. He got out of bed and joined her in the shower. Nate was muscular and thin with unruly black hair and brown eyes that missed little.

"Can you see what I wrote?" asked Dominika, soaping his chest, tracing his own scars, the brown one across his belly, the angry red furrows on his arms. They were stitched mannequins, the two of them. Nate did not answer, but kissed her, holding her head in his hands, enveloping her in his red cloud.

"*Ti moy*," she said, wrapping her arms around his neck. "You are mine."

"Does Vladimir Putin know?" he said.

They sat on the tiny balcony of the cottage, the sun setting below the mountain behind the house. The rickety table had uneven legs and wobbled. The wicker chairs creaked loosely. They ate a peasant dinner with two oversized spoons, communally from a chipped terra-cotta bowl with painted blue dolphins around the rim. Nate had cooked the green beans slowly all day in olive oil, with onions, garlic, and crushed tomatoes. A separate dish was piled with olives, feta, and crusty country bread. They drank cold Retsina from a bottle floating in a tin washtub with the last of the ice slurry from yesterday. The shadows on the hillside were growing longer as they talked.

"All I'm saying is that it's dangerous for you to continue bouncing around the world personally recruiting North Koreans—or anyone for that matter—considering Putin could make you Director of SVR soon," said Nate. They had spent the entire first day in the safe house discussing Dominika's recruitment of Professor Ri, and the other intelligence Dominika had brought out of Moscow. Especially the most exciting news.

Dominika had told Nate that as a result of President Putin's continued sponsorship, he had hinted that he might soon promote her to the rank of general and, just possibly, give her the Directorship of the SVR, an astounding development that Nate immediately reported to Langley on his THRESHER encrypted satellite phone that was approved for limited use in NATO countries. Gobsmacked by the notion that his star agent might soon be running the SVR, Benford had spilled coffee on his tie, already liberally spotted with crab bisque and mayonnaise.

In one blink, DIVA would have access to all SVR secrets; would automatically claim a seat at the National Security Council; and would become a fledgling member of the *siloviki*, Putin's gaggle of insiders with access to not just secret plots roiling the halls of the Kremlin, but also the *plans and intentions* of the circumspect and coy Vladimir Vladimirovich, whom many foreign observers had analyzed, but few genuinely knew.

"It helps, not hurts. When I acquire intelligence assets, it raises my stock," said Dominika to Nate, sopping up tomato sauce with a crust of bread. "No one in that crowd besides Bortnikov of the FSB, the internal service, recruits foreigners. The president was a KGB officer; he appreciates the accomplishment."

"But there's added risk," said Nate. "If word leaks out, for instance, that CIA knows the North Koreans are using US railgun technology, you're immediately compromised as the obvious source. Moscow's got too many ears in Washington."

Dominika poured two more glasses of wine. "If your people cannot keep secrets, perhaps I should not tell you secrets."

"That's a fine solution," said Nate.

"Well, then tell Benford to *prosmatrivat* the information, how do you say it?"

"Compartment the intelligence," said Nate, who was fluent in Russian. "In Washington that means only a thousand people will read your reports—the air force, navy, Department of Energy, ODNI, DIA, NSC, FBI, and half the committees on Capitol Hill. We have a single leak, you'd be on the Center's short list of suspects in a week."

"And then I suppose you'd get your wish for me to defect," said Dominika, smiling. From the beginning, for seven years, she vowed that she'd never accept exfiltration. She was spying to save her Russia, and nothing else mattered, she would not contemplate fleeing. Nate knew the higher she rose in the SVR, the more exclusive her reporting would become, and the more likely she could be compromised by a leak from Washington. She had to keep a low profile, and CIA had to increasingly obfuscate that she was the source of exceptional reporting.

To the extreme annoyance of Benford, Nate had been preaching for a year that they should exfiltrate Dominika *before* she was compromised. She'd had two close calls, and once had even been interrogated in Lefortovo prison after an operational flap. She'd survived that ordeal and been cleared, but Moscow teemed with counterintelligence bloodhounds, jealous rivals, and political enemies who would relish destroying a competitor, especially the lissome Egorova, the rising star. Nate argued that losing her would be a dereliction of their duty to keep her safe, and it would be debilitating to future CIA recruitments worldwide. Plus, even in safe retirement, she would be an invaluable observer and a useful operational adviser.

Gable and Forsyth disagreed with Nate, but provisionally understood, having themselves extracted blown agents before. But Benford was furious that Nate was rocking the boat and distracting the asset with his mewling arguments. Simon was old school: run your assets and gather the intel until the bitter end, *then* extract them, if possible. If the agent got the chop, it was the hard reality of operations. Benford's operational catechism was codified in an age when an agent could climb over the Berlin Wall, or wait for a rubber raft on a Baltic beach to escape the Iron Curtain. Now moles were caught in cyberstings and by drone surveillance and facial-recognition software. The tenets of espionage were immutable—go forth and steal secrets—but technology was changing the Game.

It didn't help that Nate, despite an unreal gift for denied-area ops and surveillance detection, was the junior officer in the quartet of officers who oversaw the DIVA case, and thus, despite the tradition of civilian informality in CIA that belied its wartime military OSS roots, should have known to speak only when spoken to. They all knew Nate was spoony over Dominika and dreamed of settling down with her behind a white-picket fence. But the DIVA case was too valuable to consider pulling the plug. Gable advised Nate with characteristic candor.

"Listen up, rookie," he said. "*You* recruited her cuz she had access. Now her access may reach all the way to the top. *You* pitched her and put her in harness. Now *you're* her handler, and it's all on you. You use everything in your limited bag of tricks to keep her alive and productive. Everything. Anything. But she's an asset and you run her like a pro, got it? Now go put on your big-boy pants and shut the fuck up."

─────────

Dominika took the dishes in, came back out, and sat on his lap. "I don't want you to worry," she said. "There will be hundreds of people in Moscow who will read the same reports I give you, providing plenty of cover. And I'll be the one investigating any leaks; I will be the Russian Benford!"

Nate shook his head like a dog. "You're saying that I'm sleeping with the Russian Benford? Better get off my lap. The image will stay with me for months, maybe years."

Dominika laughed and ignored him. "I will travel quarterly to Vienna to debrief Academician Ri. My Sparrow Ioana is relocating there to be close to him, to keep him calm, and to rent a place nearby where we can meet. We can discuss the case and you can lecture me, and I will continue to, how do you say it, straighten you out? *Vypravlyat?*"

"You're going to straighten me out?" said Nate, pulling her close. "I'm the handler here. I'm sure you remember."

"In some circumstances I become the handler," said Dominika, lifting his T-shirt over his head. "And yes, I will straighten you out." She deftly pulled the drawstring of his trousers, lifted her skirt, and sat back on his lap, wiggling to seat herself more deeply on him. "Are you straightened out?" she whispered. She rocked back and forth, moaning softly, Nate's face buried in her bosom. Then the dried-out, flimsy wicker chair fell apart, dumping them on the still-warm marble of the warped little balcony. Farther north, the gods on Mount Olympus looking down from above the alluvial pans of Thessaly might have said this was a portent of things to come.

They moved onto the bed, laughing, Nate holding a bruised elbow. Dominika rested her head on his shoulder. It had been a short time together, yet she was full of *bien-être*, a contentment, a tender proximity with Nate that she had not felt during other hurried and dangerous meetings. Perhaps it was the brassy Aegean sun, the salt air, and lying in bed with him, smelling his body and the wisterias and watching the hummingbirds. Nate laughed as Dominika scolded them in Russian, showing the little birds the correct technique for drawing nectar from a stamen; halfway through her demonstration he had stopped laughing and was bucking his hips off the mattress. The bullfrog horn of the night ferry from Rhodes bellowed congratulations from the sea.

Dusk. Surcease. The kerosene lantern attracted a giant emperor moth, silver wings printed with spots as luminous as owls' eyes, and it dive-bombed around the flame, casting shadows as big as bats on the walls. Dominika propped herself on one arm and Nate made her repeat the next contact skeds for Vienna in a month, with preliminary and secondary meeting sites, recognition paroles and countersigns, alternates and safety signals, including brush passes with Ioana, who would be a cutout. This would be an important follow-up debrief to hear more about the Noko nuke program, and see if they could develop any identifiable information on the US source of the technology leak.

"I wish you would let someone else meet the Korean in Vienna," said Nate, worrying the bone one last time. "Surely you can designate another officer, someone who speaks Korean or someone who knows weapons design."

"We talked about this for two days," said Dominika. "Why would I do that? It would be illogical. I told you this will help me politically. I'm more likely to receive the promotion that Putin—"

"—You won't get the promotion if you're in the cellars of Butyrka with a strap around your neck, all because of this *obsession* with revenge and this stupid jihad you're waging against them all. You're poised at the pinnacle. You're too stubborn to realize that you can hurt them a *hundredfold* by just being Director SVR and keeping a low profile."

He felt her stiffen beside him. Dominika got out of bed, wrapped a cotton skirt around her naked body, and started stuffing her few belongings into a shoulder bag.

Nate recognized the flashing eyes and flared nostrils. "Where are you going? We're leaving tomorrow morning," he said.

"Jihad? Obsessed? Stupid?" shouted Dominika. "That is what you think of me, of what I am doing? *Zhópa*, asshole. I'll die for my country before I sit still and watch them rob us blind. Thank you for your *predannost*."

"What are you talking about? I'm devoted to you more than anyone. I want you to survive."

"By giving up and running? *Poshël ty*, piss off! I'm catching the bus to town." She jammed her feet into flats and slung her bag over her shoulder.

Nate got out of bed. "It's pitch-black out there. You'll walk off a ledge in the dark. Let me get a flashlight."

"*Ischézni*, get lost," she yelled and slammed the door and started crunching down the goat path in the dark. Nate threw on pants and flip-flops, grabbed a flashlight, and ran to catch her. She was crying silently as he held her arm and shined the light at their feet. She wouldn't look at him as they stood in the dark under an olive tree waiting for the late 122 bus, which eventually wheezed around the bend in the road and pulled to a stop. As the doors swung open, Nate expected to see Gable driving and Benford sitting disapprovingly in the back row.

"Call when you arrive in Vienna," said Nate as the doors hissed shut in his face. The bus ground out of sight toward Glyfada, where she would take a taxi to her embassy.

She's changed in the last few years. Hotheaded and impossible. Uncontrollable as an agent, and sure to get caught soon. Some clandestine meeting. Some agent handling. Some Romeo. He could hear Gable already. "Congratulations, rookie, you just hit bottom and started digging."

━━━━━━━

Langley. They were gathered in the small, chaotic conference room of Benford's CID, Counterintelligence Division, the gray fabric-covered (and soundproof) walls of which were adorned with a row of framed photographs of previous Chiefs of CID in an unsettling chronological sequence, all the way around the room, like a ghoulish martyrs' wall in a Christian catacomb. Photos from the sixties were sepia-toned, with forgotten Ivy Leaguers in thin ties (JFK years). Kodachrome photos from subsequent decades depicted CID chiefs with hipster sideburns and vapid smiles (Carter); expressions of guilty calculation (Nixon); and the thousand-yard stares of hemispheric liberators (Reagan). The final digital photos were of the modern generation of CID chiefs with expressions of mystified alarm (Clinton, Bush). At the end of the row hung the photograph of the most-recently retired CID director during the modern era, a chuff famous for his implacable conceit. The US flag in the room had with malice been moved partially in front of this photo, so only a single eye of the fomite peered around the fabric, rendering him even creepier in memory than he had been in person. There was no remaining wall space for any additional frames of future ex-chiefs, and rumors of commissioning a ceiling fresco depicting a cherubic, bare-assed Benford with a tiny bow and arrow were, up until now, unsubstantiated.

Like all of Benford's personal spaces, the conference table was messy, cluttered with paper, coffee mugs, and a doughnut box. Rolled-up maps were stacked in a corner, and a projection screen was torn down the center and patched with duct tape. Two shattered flat-screen monitors were discarded in the far corner of the room, along with the shards of a US Navy coffee mug, which almost certainly had been the projectile that had destroyed at least one of the monitors. Benford, Gable, Forsyth, and Nash were at one end. Hearsey, the tall ectomorph tech chief, came in with two notebooks and sat at the far end. Rugged, rangy, and leather tough, Hearsey looked like someone who should be on the prairie mending barbed-wire fence or using a Burdizzo Emasculatome on bull calves, instead of spending a year in a lab concocting a chemical acid fog—sprayed at night by stealth drone—to embrittle North Korean missile gantries, or developing wrist-worn fitness monitors molded out of Semtex that could be detonated in Dubai from a laboratory in Maryland. An engineer by training, Hearsey knew about railguns, plus he didn't take guff from Benford, and Gable liked him, so he was read into everything, including the DIVA case.

He was known in the Agency simply as Hearsey—only the mavens in personnel knew his given name was Gayle, and they never revealed anything. Hearsey looked around Benford's squalid conference room, ran a finger across the crumb-covered table, and contemplated the surrounding detritus.

"I thought the Hindenburg crashed in Lakehurst, New Jersey," said Hearsey, who could get away with being a wiseass. Benford blinked once.

Sitting at the other end of the table taking notes was Benford's new assistant, Lucius Westfall, a WMD analyst transferred from the Directorate of Intelligence to the Directorate of Operations, one of scores of CIA Director-mandated sabbaticals designed to forcefully integrate DI analysts with DO operators, which was in most cases like partnering the pastor's daughters with bargees at a barn dance.

Westfall was blond, thin faced, with wire-rimmed glasses that tended to fog when he spoke publicly or talked to pretty women. It was demanding enough to work for Simon Benford, but Westfall constantly had to decode the aboriginal patois of the Operations Directorate. These ops officers were unintelligible when incessantly talking about bumps, dangles, peddlers, old whores, burn notices, drops, caches, headhunters, scalps, dry cleaning, rabbits, chicken feed, barium enemas, 201s, PRQs, natural reverses, flipping, fluffing, fluttering, and a million other mysteries. As terrifying, Westfall had to weather the depredations of the hulking Marty Gable, who Westfall was convinced had once been a serial killer from Kansas.

"Make sure you take good notes, *Luscious*," said Gable, mispronouncing his name with a fake French accent. Gable's particular style of mentoring a newbie colleague fell somewhere between drill instructor and a chariot driver in the hippodrome. Gable ironically had himself also been dragooned from his rough-and-tumble Africa Division to be Benford's unlikely deputy. CID was a spooky counterintelligence shop typically staffed with brilliant, quirky introverts who worked in the dark with the shades drawn. Outsiders called it the Island of Broken Toys. Benford wanted Gable less as a substantive deputy, and more as someone who could solve unstable, delicate foreign crises wherever they developed, a function Marty demurely characterized as "breaking the dishes." DIVA also idolized Gable—he could talk her down out of the tree when she went into her increasingly more frequent connniptions about commo, risk taking, and security.

Benford gaveled the meeting to order with the solemnity for which he was known in Washington, London, Ottawa, Canberra, Bonn, Paris, Rome, and Tel Aviv, by slamming a file folder on the table, with his trademark invocation.

"Jesus Fucking Christ. If DIVA's intel is right, we have a fucking fuckwad selling fucking secrets on the rail-fucking-gun to North Korea."

Just back from Athens, Nash read off a paper. "DIVA just reported by SRAC this morning. The SVR has encrypted this North Korean Professor Ri Sou-yong PECHKA, which means 'furnace' in Russian," he said.

Gable grunted. "Furnace, huh? A dictionary would take up less space and wouldn't eat all the doughnuts," he said.

Nate slid the box of glazed doughnuts across the conference table. "You're welcome," said Nate. "I bought the doughnuts for everyone, thought it would be okay to eat one."

Gable lifted the lid of the box. "You buy doughnuts and you don't even bring an assortment? No chocolate? No jelly?"

Benford stirred in his chair. "Can we concentrate on what appears to be the transfer of US Navy electromagnetic railgun technology to the North Korean nuclear program?"

Forsyth put down a copy of DIVA's report. "How did the Nokos get this technology?" said Forsyth. "The RGB can't tie their own shoes. All they normally do is shoot coup plotters inside their own country. You're telling me they're running an American source in-country? No way."

"Someone's passing the technology," said Hearsey. "The translated Korean document DIVA provided has verbatim US terminology: 'conduction path,' 'ionized gas,' 'compact pulsed power.' The Nokos aren't coming up with that on their own."

"Got to be Beijing," said Gable. "I bet the MSS popped some California peacenik working in a navy lab who's dedicated to trans-Pacific harmony; or a zit-faced contractor in DOD who wants a Corvette; or a weapons officer on board a frigate who's in love with a Chia Pet from Shanghai who's keeping his personal railgun on pulsed power."

Westfall squirmed in his seat. Benford saw it and pointed at him. "Westfall, you have a view on the issue?" Gable slid the doughnut box down the table, as a collegial encouragement to speak up. Westfall let the lid of the box drop when he saw Gable had eaten the last two doughnuts and the box was empty.

"I don't think Beijing wants Pyongyang to have the bomb," Westfall said. "The Chinese think they still control the Nokos with food shipments and military aid. They like that the West comes begging for help in moderating North Korean behavior. And they ultimately know that once Pyongyang has a *reliable* nuke *and* a delivery system, their pit bull has slipped the leash, and is likely to do anything. Even against them. I looked it up: flight time of a basic Rodong-1 ballistic missile for the eight hundred kilometers from Sohae satellite launch center to Tiananmen Square is about five minutes, not even time for the politburo to kiss one another good-bye. Nope, China doesn't want them to have the bomb." There was silence around the table. *The kid wasn't dumb.*

"A real Ulysses P. Grant," said Gable. "So who do you think's running our railgun mole?"

Westfall looked over at Nate. "DIVA's the only one who can tell us that," he said. "But if she can't find a name pretty darn quick and Pyongyang figures out how to squeeze a uranium device into a warhead, the Seattle Space Needle is gonna be ground zero."

NATE'S AEGEAN GREEN BEANS

Top and tail green beans. Mix minced garlic, parsley, dill, mint, salt, and pepper. Layer thin-sliced onions on the bottom of a Dutch oven, cover with a layer of crushed tomatoes, beans, the herbs, abundant olive oil, another layer of onions, tomatoes, beans, herbs, and olive oil. Finish with a layer of onions and drizzle with more olive oil. Simmer covered until beans are very soft and tender. Season and add lemon juice. Serve warm or at room temperature.

4

Stealing Secrets

Alexander Larson, the sitting Director of CIA, was the first DCIA in thirty years to have come up through the operational ranks. He was a mustang, like the OSS-vintage directors who led the Agency in the fifties and the sixties—before the unrelieved string of successors selected from the military, or from the unctuous halls of Congress, or from the ranks of the Directorate of Intelligence—and tried their hands at directing an organization the arcane mission of which they imperfectly understood and had never experienced firsthand. Some directors were disasters, some of them unmitigated disasters, and a precious few achieved a certain synergy with the notoriously skeptical and ungovernable workforce at Langley before they left. The confirmation of veteran ops officer Alex Larson as DCIA broke the drought.

Alex Larson had gone through training at the Farm in the early seventies with Simon Benford. Larson the smooth extrovert became friends with Benford the irascible misanthrope, the result of an unlikely personal chemistry that had endured thirty years. It was logical that their disparate personalities would push Alex into the overseas clandestine service and the business of recruitment of foreign assets, and that Benford naturally would gravitate to the slough of counterintelligence and counterespionage. Geographical separation over the years did not dull the friendship, which automatically renewed itself whenever their paths crossed. Now Larson was DCIA. He knew his rumpled friend was brilliant, and had the tenacity of a pit bull, albeit with a maloccluded bite. Benford consulted with him often.

The past administration had selected Larson as DCIA in recognition of his moral rectitude, bureaucratic acumen, and top-flight recruitments (which Benford over the years had supported by vetting the assets as they came online). Sixty-five-year-old Larson looked the DCIA part: He was short, a bit stout, wore ginger-colored tortoiseshell eyeglasses, and sported what Benford called an Allen Dulles wannabe mustache. This, along with thinning white hair and white eyebrows so bushy that subordinates had to resist the temptation to run a comb through them, made him look like a college professor. But he was every inch the operator, and the troops respected him.

Larson was not popular with the current White House or with the derivative progressives on the National Security Council, the twentysomething English majors who were advising POTUS on Mideast policy. DCIA Larson moreover had obliquely contradicted his predecessor's statement during the latter's farewell foreign tour. "We don't steal secrets," the outgoing DCIA had said of CIA intelligence collection to an allied liaison audience. "Everything we do is consistent with US law. We uncover, we discover, we reveal, we obtain, we elicit, we solicit."

Asked about his predecessor's statement at a closed session of the Senate Select Committee on Intelligence (SSCI), Larson unsmilingly and without a trace of irony had replied to the senators, "Fair enough. An asset, for instance, *discovers* the existence of a Russian mole in NATO headquarters, the CIA case officer *solicits* the info, the asset then *reveals* it, and thereby CIA *obtains* perishable counterintelligence information." Partisan snitches reported the disloyal comment promptly, but Alexander Larson was not fired. He could not be fired. The reason was COPPERFIN.

During his fourteen years in the operational field, Larson had built the COPPERFIN espionage network, the massive, pervasive penetration of the entire State aerospace design, construction, and testing combine in the Russian Federation. Larson had personally recruited the first two Russian principal agents years earlier, one in India, the other in Brazil, who in turn had themselves recruited subsources in the Sukhoi, Mikoyan, Ilyushin, Tupolev, and Yakovlev design entities, all of which in 2006 had merged into OAK, *Obyedinyonnaya Aviastroitelnaya Korporatsiya*, the United Aircraft Corporation, located in the Krasnoselsky District in the central Moscow *Okrug*. Larson's COPPERFIN agents regularly emptied the top-secret vaults of OAK to report on the advanced capabilities of fourth- and fifth-generation Russian fighters such as the Su-27, the MiG-29, and the new Sukhoi PAK FA. The US Air Force was ecstatic.

The administration's intention to eventually jettison Alex Larson in favor of a DCIA more conformable to the White House's pigeon-hearted foreign policy was stopped cold by howls from the Pentagon after the acquisition through the COPPERFIN network of the technical parameters of APFAR, *Aktivnaya Fazirovannaya Antennaya Reshotka*, the new Russian phased array radar, an inestimable prize. Next came the delivery of an actual Zvezda Kh-35U antiship missile, NATO designation KAYAK, but nicknamed the harpoonski because of its similarities to the US Harpoon missile. The Zvezda was brought across the Lithuanian border by a courier in the COPPERFIN network who bribed border guards to ignore the tail of the missile protruding from the broken-out back window of his UAZ Patriot, which was the only way he could fit the 520 kg, 380 cm missile into his compact SUV.

Immune from dyspeptic antagonists, DCIA Larson, in consultation with Simon Benford, launched his own active-measures campaign against the Putin regime—an offensive long overdue in the eyes of many to repay the Russians in their own coin for seven decades of disinformation, forgeries, and political meddling that was the Kremlin's stock-in-trade. Larson became a vocal critic of Vladimir Putin's Russian Federation, testifying in open committee sessions about congenital Russian use of active measures to influence political outcomes, mostly with mediocre results. He increased intel sharing with allied services, especially in Ukraine and the Baltics, which resulted in several flashy spy arrests of red-faced Russian intel officers. Their identities had been provided by DIVA and Larson had passed along his compliments to her via Benford. (The Director and DIVA had never met; Larson properly left the case in the able hands of Benford and company.)

After a career of working the Russian target, Larson understood the depredatory worldview of Vladimir Putin, and knew that the Kremlin would stop misbehaving only when the costs of Putin's delinquency exceeded the perceived gains. Then came the explosive report: COPPERFIN assets smuggled out documentary proof of massive fraud in the OAK aerospace consortium. OAK had been set up by President Putin as an open joint-stock company combining Russian private and State-owned assets, the lion's share of which disappeared into the pockets of favored cronies. Supported by Benford, Larson pushed the White House and the hand-wringing Department of State to publicize the corruption (citing foreign sources to protect internal assets), to denounce Russia in the United Nations, to levy sanctions on companies selling Russian commercial airliners, and to block any reinstatement of Russia to the G7. Reluctant to antagonize the Kremlin, the White House dithered, but finally acted at the urging of a bumptious Congress that had been briefed by the DCIA. Alex Larson was everywhere in town, pressing official Washington to bestir itself.

Benford huddled with Alex in Larson's office. "Finally. This is an opening to discommode these coarse Slav fuckers," Benford said. "We're collecting comprehensive technical and military intelligence, and the negative international publicity will cow Putin, at least for a while. I only wish we could more accurately predict his reaction. Handling a cornered snake and so on, if you follow the metaphor."

"As I recall, your metaphors used to be markedly more erudite," said Alex, deadpan. "Perhaps DIVA will soon have better access to Putin's plans and intentions if she becomes Director of SVR, assuming, of course, that your handling of her is as inspired as you claim it to be."

Benford did not smile. "You can be sure that even in the absence of your signature flamboyant rococo operational style, the DIVA case is being managed securely."

Larson laughed. "Is the young officer still primary handler? What was his name?"

"Nash, Nathaniel," said Benford. "He is possibly going to assist the Australians in the Hong Kong operation I briefed you on last week. Marty Gable will hold DIVA's hand in the interim."

Larson's nose was too good. "Any trouble?"

Benford shrugged. "The recruiting case officer and DIVA have a relationship that falls slightly outside the usual parameters."

"Meaning what?" asked Alex.

"They are in love and are intimate, whenever circumstances allow," said Benford. "Until now I have stayed my hand from firing Nash. I assess his separation from the service would have a significant effect on DIVA's production."

"How significant?" said Alex.

"As in she would quit. With Nash in Hong Kong for a few weeks and Gable to steady the asset, there are no immediate concerns." The two men thought alike and the matter—and Nash's future—was shelved for now.

Larson opened the file on his desk that contained Benford's script for tomorrow's briefing of POTUS and the NSC Principals Committee on CIA's continued covert-action campaign against the Kremlin. He was silent as he read. "One misses the field," he said, looking up.

Benford opened his file too. "The organization needs you behind this desk. You've had your debauch overseas for thirty years. Now you have to turn this pig's breakfast back into a spy service."

"Run through your notes for me," said Alex.

Benford spoke briefly and succinctly. This brief was a matter of reassuring the jittery US president, and ensuring continued Pentagon support. Jamming a stick into Putin's spokes at this time was critical, given his brazen interference on the world stage. He was emboldened by confusion and anxiety among Western governments. Publicly embarrassing the Kremlin would disrupt multiple Russian active measures in the Baltics, Europe, and in places like Montenegro. Russia's moribund economy would be trebly stung by any publicized malfeasance within OAK, scaring away investors, reducing customers for Russian military material, constraining the military budget, and complicating Kremlin adventurism in Africa, Latin America, and the resource-rich Arctic. Twisting the Russian bear's tail abroad, moreover, would distract the Kremlin and thus protect valuable assets, such as COPPERFIN. The Russians would be driven frantic in the face of withering international disparagement. The DCIA would politely insist that POTUS could not ignore the opportunity and must not remain quiescent.

"We'll see how it works on him," said Alex. "At least the top brass will support me."

"Don't worry, this will stir the hornets' nest," said Benford. He was correct, but he would set in motion events no one could have even remotely predicted.

―――――

The Russian reaction to the first American exposé was to cry provocation (ironic: the inveterate plotters always assumed their own misfortune was, naturally, the result of an outside plot). But the international embarrassment, and the innate Russian paranoia of being laughed at as manure-speckled *kulaks* and relegated to second-world status, drove Vladimir Putin into a rage, in part fueled by fright. This was how leaders were toppled. He summoned Gorelikov to his personal, most-isolated dacha in the town of Solovyevka, 130 kilometers outside Saint Petersburg, on the shore of Lake Komsomolsk. He wanted privacy and to be away from the prying eyes of his *siloviki*. They would smell his panic like the pack hunters they were. He trusted Gorelikov.

"How did word leak of financial arrangements at OAK?" raved Putin, pacing the room, kicking the snarling head of a Siberian tiger rug each time he passed. They were in the dacha's large main room, redolent with wood smoke, decorated in rustic style with leather couches and chairs scattered about and a vintage 1936 7.62-caliber Tula hunting rifle above the roaring fireplace. Outside the panoramic picture windows—uncharacteristically lavish in a typical lakeside dacha—snow covered the shoreline and dusted the pines, but the black water of the lake had not yet frozen.

Gorelikov did not want to excite the president any more than he was now. "It is likely that the corporation's foreign contacts—bankers, salesmen, and government buyers—were the sources of these defamations," he said, quoting the news releases.

Putin looked at Gorelikov like a week-old sturgeon with milky eyes. "No. We have a *gemorróy*, a big problem. Someone inside OAK, someone who knows the books."

Gorelikov had by choice never prospered from the bacchanal of corruption in the Kremlin, and was secretly amused now that the spoils of greed had stung the tsar. "There are thirty thousand employees working at OAK," said Gorelikov. "We'd have to tear the place apart." He took a breath. "Ignore the accusations. They will be forgotten in a week." Putin swore.

Those specific accusations were in fact forgotten the next morning when a message from MAGNIT was relayed from the Center to the dacha's commo room reporting that an intact Zvezda Kh-35U antiship missile had been delivered to the Dahlgren Division, Naval Surface Warfare Center test facility in Virginia for evaluation of guidance, propulsion, and warhead systems.

Putin swore again. "*Bljad*, son of a bitch; so you think this will be forgotten in a week?" he said to Gorelikov. "Not only is Washington defaming us on the world stage, but also CIA appears to have at least one asset inside OAK."

Gorelikov chose his words carefully. "We sell Zvezda missiles to India, Brazil, and Vietnam. The Americans could have acquired an export model from a third-world agent without our top-of-the-line seeker head and telemetry."

Putin gave him another fishy stare. He had trusted Gorelikov since knowing him from law school, recognized his brilliance, and appreciated his analytic mind. He also knew Anton was not corrupt, or susceptible, or power hungry. He would never covet Putin's throne. Most important, Putin recognized Gorelikov's proclivity for and love of *naneseniye uvech'ya*, covert mayhem. Just as a chess player relishes organizing defenses, traps, attacks, and feints to achieve checkmate, Gorelikov reveled in concocting an intricate *intriga* just for the sheer joy of causing havoc. In this he was unmatched:

Bortnikov of FSB, or Patrushev of his Security Council, were accomplished schemers, but no one was like Gorelikov.

"Enough of the rationalizations," said Putin. "I want a solution. Washington and CIA are making fools of us. The loudmouths in the Moscow press and on the street will spread the word and agitate."

Gorelikov shrugged. "Repina especially," he said, referring to one of the most vocal anti-Putin, anticorruption dissidents recently noticed in the West and raising money as a result.

"*Suka*, bitch, forget her. I want *sredstvo*. I want a *remedy*," said Putin, leaving the room, and Gorelikov, to contemplate the snow-laden landscape and the ink-black water.

———

The next evening, Putin lighted two thick candles in eighteenth-century red, gold, and turquoise cloisonné candlesticks on a plank table placed near the dacha's picture windows. The rest of the room was dark—only the light of the burning logs in the vast fireplace cast additional flickering shadows around the room. Two steaming bowls of *kormya*, Russian lamb stew, were in front of them with two heels of black bread for dipping into the gravy. The stewards serving them had withdrawn. Putin and Gorelikov both drank tea from a hissing samovar on a side table. Tonight was no night for vodka. The wind had kicked up after dusk and frozen crystals of snow adrift in the utterly black night scratched invisibly against the glass. With the roaring hearth, the hiss of the samovar, and the storm raging outside, this was the Devil's waiting room. The two men were sitting at either end of the table eating stew and looking at each other, as if waiting for *Shaitan* to join them.

"The Americans are timorous," said Gorelikov. "They avoid conflict in the foreign field; they ignore their allies and coddle those who oppose them."

Putin slurped a spoonful of stew. "And yet we see this attack against the reputation of Russia and the calumny directed at me." His voice shook.

"This is my point," said Gorelikov. "This campaign does not originate from the craven White House. This comes from CIA; it is their brand of active measures directed back at us."

"Why does it come now?"

Gorelikov wiped his mouth, and leaned forward. "It could be for a hundred reasons, all of which we know well. We ourselves concocted a legend to camouflage the intelligence Snowden brought with him. Or we send a dispatched volunteer to discredit a genuine defector. We focus criticism elsewhere to mask the existence of a high-level agent or network."

Putin set his spoon down. "We can discuss American motives all day," he said. "And we can speculate about how many moles we have in place in each other's pantries. But it does not solve the problem." His voice rose. "It is *my* reputation, *my* prestige, and *my* public image." *Which is more important than any spy stealing our secrets*, thought Gorelikov.

Gorelikov commiserated. "The Director of CIA is Alexander Larson," said Gorelikov. "He is a legend among the operational cadre in CIA's Ops Directorate. He is also the first ops-trained DCIA since the midseventies, and is aggressive. Reports from *rezidenturi* indicate CIA is ramping up activity worldwide—CIA officers are pitching our officers in scores of foreign capitals. For every one who reports a hostile pitch, how many do not? We cannot know, but we must assume a small percentage accept recruitment. Egorova in Line KR also regularly reports operational flaps and ambushes, as though a mole in SVR is advising the Americans."

"We have our own triumphs," said Putin, distractedly.

"Of course. I'm only emphasizing that DCIA Alexander Larson is an activist director who is not only accelerating operational tempo against us in the field, but also, in my view, putting together a covert action to stimulate regime change in our country, modeled after their successes in Ukraine and Georgia. He must have leverage to persuade the administration to permit it, perhaps with support from congressional hawks."

Gorelikov spoke calmly. "You know I speak openly to you." Putin nodded. "I say to you with confidence that Larson and his Agency are working to destabilize our country. Why now? Suppression of dissidents may have been the catalyst, Crimea, the alliance with Iran, or ten other factors. But the threat is real, and we will have a crisis unless we act."

Putin poured himself more tea. "You've had a day to think on it. What do you propose?"

"I have considered multiple options. Only one recommends itself."

"Tell me."

A gust of wind-driven snow made the plate-glass window flex in its frame—*Shaitan* knocking to be let in. "That we eliminate the Director of

CIA," said Gorelikov, softly. A log collapsed in the fireplace, spewing sparks into the room where several embers glowed on the pine floor. *Shaitan* was in the dacha now.

Putin stared at Gorelikov, who continued, almost in a whisper. "His death— it must appear accidental—will derail this covert action against the *Rodina*. His agency will be demoralized and in shock, its case officers vulnerable and disillusioned. The US administration will hitch up their skirts in panic, and Congress will blubber until it is time for them to go into their next recess."

Putin had not blinked once. "The hand of Russia will of course remain invisible, even though the world will suspect, no, will marvel, at the utter imperturbability of Vladimir Putin and *Novorossiya*," said Gorelikov, wondering if he was laying it on too thick, but deciding it could never be too thick for V. V. Putin.

"How would you undertake such an action?" said Putin. "The CIA Director is protected at all times."

Gorelikov sipped his tea. "I will examine the pieces to see how they might fit. None of our usual organic compounds; no forensic toxicology is acceptable. An indisputable accidental death will forestall open hostilities between our services."

Putin nodded. "Put all your energies into the plan," he said, curtly. The president of the Russian Federation had just green-lighted the assassination of the Director of the Central Intelligence Agency. "Do you need anything?"

Gorelikov looked at the flames of the candles. "What do you think of including Egorova in the planning? She knows the field, has a cool head, and will not shrink from extreme measures."

Putin shook his head. "Only the two of us. No one else. I insist on that condition. We will refer to the project henceforth as *Kataklizm*."

"Understood," said Gorelikov. The two men fell silent, and Anton knew the president—slayer of tigers, accomplished horseman, skilled jet pilot, and master of judo—appreciated the enormous risk of attempting to assassinate the American DCIA.

"With your approval," said Gorelikov, "I would like to posit an additional refinement for your consideration. Any of our unicellular colleagues in FSB or the armed forces could have arrived at the solution of assassinating the head of CIA in five minutes. This, however, can only be the beginning of a larger plan that is infinitely more consequential and far-reaching."

Putin dunked his black bread into the stew, waiting. Refinements. This is why he liked Gorelikov.

"Since MAGNIT's recruitment I have been monitoring her career," said Gorelikov. "As you know, she was recently promoted to vice admiral and is what one could call the US Navy's senior flag-rank science manager. She has access to technologies, research and development, and the navy labs. Even though she is recognized for her brilliance, she is still generally considered *meshkovatyy*, awkward, pouchy, and three-cornered—without a political network outside her limited naval orbits. Accordingly, when she retires, the technical-reporting-asset MAGNIT disappears. For the last two years I have steered her to balance her scientific career with duties that would burnish her political bona fides; she is ambitious and followed my instruction with her characteristic quantitative precision. She was recently assigned to a position on the Bureau of Navy Personnel advisory board, which wields considerable influence. This year she was also considered for adjutant to Admiral Richards, the Chief of Naval Operations, but was not selected, I suspect due to her lamentable lack of what the Americans call front-office appeal. I fear MAGNIT will never have that quality; she could not acquire it any more than you or I could master her particle physics.

"But there has been more recent progress. She has been selected as a briefer to the Joint Chiefs because of her ability to explain science theory clearly and concisely to unschooled superiors. Part of these briefing duties includes accompanying the chairman to the White House every week. We are collecting some interesting national security intelligence now, which is the transition I wanted MAGNIT to make. You see, I have an endgame in mind, it's—"

Putin put up his hand for silence. The corners of his mouth lifted microscopically, which for him suggested barely suppressed mirth. "What of her preference for *lohmatka*, for women?" he asked.

Gorelikov was not fazed at the interruption; he expected the inevitable question from the president. "Her addiction is aperiodic and controlled," he said. "She indulges her appetites during discreet annual vacations abroad when under my supervision. She occasionally loses control with her partners, which I attribute to her social narcissism and pent-up sexual repression, a result of psychological conflict during childhood with an abusive father."

"Loses control how?" asked the president.

Gorelikov shifted uncomfortably. "Frenzied lovemaking, too-rough use of sex aids, biting, and slapping."

"Have you filmed this behavior for later control?" asked Putin, who was once a spook himself.

Gorelikov shook his head. "Coercion is not a motivating factor with MAGNIT. Apart from her initial—and short-lived—refusal to collaborate during her recruitment, she has grown into a model agent—her narcissism fuels her spying. The only film ever taken of her was during the original *polovaya zapadnya*, the honey trap in the Metropol, nearly twelve years ago."

"Do you have the recording of that encounter?" said Putin.

Gorelikov shrugged. "I have no idea where it is. I suppose somewhere in the archives."

"My loyal counselor, you wouldn't be protecting your protégé Egorova, would you? She was the Sparrow in question."

"Mr. President, you are referring to your next Director of Foreign Intelligence, or have you changed your mind? I will admit I am a supporter of Colonel Egorova. I think she shows enormous promise."

It was enough that he had twanged one of the unflappable Gorelikov's nerves. Putin had already seen all of Egorova's Sparrow-vintage films. She indeed showed enormous promise then, as now. He was itching to get at her. "I agree," said Putin. "Now, tell me about your additional refinement."

The wind outside howled. "It goes without saying that when a sitting DCIA passes away, the administration must select replacement candidates for consideration, one of whom will be put forward as the final nominee for congressional confirmation."

Putin knew what was coming, but stayed silent so Gorelikov could finish spinning his web.

"I have instructed MAGNIT to dangle herself conspicuously in front of the president during briefings in the Oval Office, especially when she is the sole briefer on the occasions the chairman cannot come to the White House for the weekly brief. I have coached her to interject comments that would suggest she is politically aligned with the president, that she agrees with his defense and intelligence policies, and that she looks forward to working on his team, either before or after her retirement."

"You believe these blandishments will work?" said Putin.

"Analysts in the Americas Department posit that the president is driven by ego and ideology, and that now, in the fifth year of his presidency, is increasingly thin-skinned to criticism, and as a result surrounds himself with sycophants. If MAGNIT can establish herself as a sympathetic ally, and the DCIA position is suddenly empty, I predict her name would be one the president at least would consider. The notion of naming a brainy, liberal woman, an admiral from the navy, to undo Alexander Larson's bellicose legacy and unsettling covert action, would appeal to him."

"Too bad we don't have that other president, that *rasputnik*, that satyr, still in the Oval Office," said Putin. "MAGNIT could have solicited the DCIA job on her knees. But this scheme appears extremely tenuous—the chance that MAGNIT would be tapped for the position is remote."

Gorelikov counted on his fingers. "We endeavor to influence outcomes—often with no guarantees—and hope for the desired results. The *utter implausibility* of making MAGNIT the DCIA is the hallmark of the perfect *zagovor*, an exquisite conspiracy without Russian fingerprints. She has no high-profile civilian patrons, no covert sponsors, so there are no invisible strings. MAGNIT, the brilliant but unlovely stork, solidly partisan, able to manage the challenges of technology and the new cyber age, is the perfect candidate. If she is selected, you, Vladimir Vladimirovich, will own the CIA."

More sparks flew from the fireplace as *Shaitan* flew around the massive pine rafters of the dacha, mightily pleased.

———————

Just beside the Situation Room under the West Wing of the White House was a smaller briefing room with a short walnut table and three plush armchairs on each side, POTUS's chair at the far end under the presidential seal. Unlike the spacious, mahogany-paneled SitRoom with seating for twenty—including chairs for backbenchers—and multiple teleconferencing flat screens along the walls, the small briefing room featured only two compact screens on the far wall, above which were six digital clocks: one that displayed the time in Washington; a clock labeled "President," indicating the time wherever the president was located; one for Zulu time; and three additional time-zone displays, today labeled Baghdad, London, and Kabul.

Vice Admiral Audrey Rowland had just concluded a solo briefing to the president, his national security adviser, and the deputy NSC adviser on tests conducted by ONR on cavitation propulsion for littoral combat ships, an in-the-weeds subject usually not of interest to this commander in chief, whose idea of power projection was to enlist the tepid support of prevaricating allies, and to sign treaties with hostile states that had no intention of honoring any diplomatic concordant. POTUS, however, was taken by the smaller, more lightly armed, and relatively inexpensive vessels as good examples of "nonconfrontational naval platforms." One could hear admirals' teeth grinding in the Pentagon all the way from the South Lawn.

The briefing concluded, Admiral Rowland told the president that his notion of a more restrained US military footprint, a more inclusive internationalist US foreign policy that would abandon nineteenth-century practices of nation building, regime change, and gunboat diplomacy (Audrey couldn't remember the other talking points Anton had drilled her on) were critical concepts in an unstable world. His feet characteristically propped up on the table, showing the soles of his shoes to the others—a grave insult to foreigners, but merely boorish in the conference room—POTUS said he was glad to hear her views. Audrey hastened to add that, from her perspective, restraint likewise applied to intelligence collection—whether DIA, navy intel, or CIA.

"We just acquired a Russian antiship missile—I don't know the source—and we'll assess its capabilities and develop countermeasures, against which the Russians will develop counter-countermeasures," said Audrey. "And the process will continue, endlessly, with enormous cost, with so many other domestic priorities facing us." Anton had coached her to invoke inferences that would appeal to the president's well-known social progressivism.

"Mr. President, my retirement window is opening in a year. If I at any time can be of any assistance to you and your team (she nodded at the slack-jawed NSC adviser, then at the slug of a deputy), it would be my singular honor to continue to contribute." Audrey stopped there, not wanting to overdo it. POTUS thanked her, and he and the NSC adviser left the room, but the young deputy stayed behind and stared at Admiral Rowland as she packed up her briefing materials.

"Don't you really know how the CIA got that missile?" he said. He was short, balding, with a round face that perpetually hovered somewhere between mean and deceitful. He had the dark eyes of a hanging judge.

Audrey closed her Kevlar portfolio and secured the zipper pull under the lockable clamp. "No, and it really frosts me," she said, with her carefully chosen prim vocabulary, which would, said Anton, bolster her Vestal image. *Anton constantly considered such details*, thought Audrey. "I know I'm in the science end of things, but I could really add value to the requirements process."

Young Caligula shook his head. "They never told you, a three-star admiral, about COPPERFIN? You have got to be fucking kidding me."

In three minutes he had told MAGNIT about the COPPERFIN network, and about some of the reporting in the compartment.

MAGNIT knew she had to cauterize the leak. "Listen, don't tell me any more. It sounds pretty restricted. I've already forgotten it." The ferret's eyes narrowed, realizing he shouldn't have mentioned anything, but he knew the admiral would be discreet. He'd keep his mouth shut too.

He shrugged, trying not to acknowledge his mistake, and changed the subject. "Sounds like you're looking for a job."

"The navy's been good to me, but I'm ready for a new challenge. I have the science thing down, and cyber's the next big hurdle. Intel would be a good fit."

"Let me talk to the president," he said, puffing up, the White House kingmaker. "It's an interesting idea."

Audrey smoothed her uniform coat and extended her hand. "I'm glad we talked. It's good to feel connected to someone downtown with real pull."

The deputy nodded, as if validating Newton's three laws of motion. "I'll be in touch."

LAMB STEW *KORMA*

Crush cloves, peppercorns, and cardamom seeds into a powder. Sauté chopped onions with spices until golden brown. Stir in cumin, cinnamon, turmeric, chopped coriander, and paprika. Add crushed garlic and grated ginger, and continue cooking until fragrant. Add peeled tomatoes with their juice, simmer, then add boneless lamb chunks and continue cooking. Add water and yogurt, and cover and simmer until lamb is tender. Serve with basmati rice.

5

Welcome to the Club

As Benford began his morning blaspheming about moles in Washington, there was an icy late-afternoon meeting in progress seventy-eight hundred kilometers away, around another conference table in the Kremlin. This room, right off the president's office in the Senate building, was immaculate, carpeted in blue and paneled in rich wood. The polished walnut table had dark mahogany inlays in a star pattern—a five-pointed Soviet star—an antique kept in use for reasons of nostalgia. It was the president's conference room after all, and he liked the discreet reminder of the past glories of the USSR.

The meeting was called and directed by the goateed Anton Gorelikov, elegant in a blue suit from Brioni, a light-blue spread-collar shirt from Turnbull & Asser, and a maroon seven-fold silk necktie from E. Marinella in Naples. His silver hair was combed straight back.

Gorelikov's duty was to advise the president on foreign and domestic affairs, national security, and manipulating world events in favor of the Russian Federation, a modern-day Mikhail Suslov, who had been the Chief Ideologue of the Soviet Communist Party. He had graduated from the Faculty of Law at Saint Petersburg State University in 1975 with Putin, both with law degrees, and both had joined the KGB, Putin in foreign intelligence, Gorelikov in analysis. When Vladimir ascended in politics during the boozy last days of Yeltsin, he tapped his friend from law school to join his political satrapy, and thanks to Anton's poise, acumen, and foresight—as well as a studied avoidance of all Kremlin intrigues—eventually attained chief of the *Sekretariat*. He had never married, was agnostic in matters of sex, trusted nobody, and was an astute and suspicious observer of human reactions. He had the president's confidence (as far as Vladimir Putin conferred his total trust on anybody) chiefly because he never sank to sycophancy. He occasionally reminded the president that surely there were moles in the Kremlin, just as Russia ran agents in Washington.

Anton Gorelikov knew Putin's Russia was atrophying slowly from within, buoyed only by her poorly managed natural resources and the geopolitical misadventures that kept Putin on the world stage. But like a chess master brilliantly defending a losing game until an advantage revealed itself, Gorelikov reveled in the intrigue, in the manipulation of events, and in the wielding of power. His putative allies were Bortnikov of the FSB, Patrushev of the Security Council, and, he hoped, Egorova, the rising star who had already been noticed by the Kremlin. Gorelikov was quietly maneuvering for her elevation to Director of SVR. It would be a tall order for a woman to be appointed Director of SVR, but the resourceful Gorelikov was known as a *volshebnik*, a conjurer, who could turn water to wine. There was no rush.

Aside from acting as Vladimir's Machiavelli, Gorelikov was an aesthete. He collected paintings, bronzes, and antique maps, and was an immaculate clotheshorse. He appraised the incomparable beauty of SVR Colonel Dominika Egorova, who was sitting on one side of the table, a thin file folder in front of her. Her blue eyes were extraordinary, her hands in repose were serene, and that face could launch a thousand ships—if the rotting Russian Red Fleet *had* that many left. Gorelikov knew Egorova's personal and service history, where she lived, how many times she had been posted or traveled abroad (quite a lot for her age and rank), and the more spectacular episodes of her career, including her service as a Sparrow. One thing he did not know was that the beautiful Colonel Egorova was assessing the cerulean halo around his head, the luminous blue halo of the sophisticated thinker.

It was time to begin. Gorelikov knew this meeting would be unpleasant; he disliked churlish behavior, which was in abundance among the oxen of Putin's inner circle of former KGB, gangster, and police colleagues, including the men opposite Egorova at the table.

"Are we all present?" said Gorelikov, his voice smooth as a cello. "May I make introductions?"

Across from Dominika sat Major Valeriy Shlykov of the GRU, the military foreign intelligence service of the General Staff of the Russian Federation. Dressed in a tailored suit with a blue necktie, Shlykov was in his thirties, a blond, broad-faced Great Russian with lazy blue eyes and big lips. The yellow cloud that hung over him like a plague flag signaled conceit, envy, duplicity. Shlykov did not acknowledge or look at Dominika, but dismissively flipped the pages of a folder in front of him. *This one is ambitious and privileged*, thought Dominika. *Why is he here?* The summons to this meeting was vague, but she assumed it was to discuss her North Korean recruitment, Academician Ri. Why would the GRU be present to discuss an SVR case?

In Russia, competition among the services, and inside the branches of the military, and among the ministries was always feverish, and sometimes desperately ruthless. When the KGB split into the SVR and the FSB, it just meant two more muzzles drinking from the same trough. And they all disdained the *krestyaniki*, the peasants in the GRU.

To Shlykov's right sat a squat, chunky man in a too-small suit with a patterned necktie knotted loosely around a drainpipe neck. He was older than Shlykov, in his late fifties, with immense, scarred hands, like a retired wrestler. His hair was gray and thinning, and his gnarly face and crooked nose were creased and weathered. His broad forehead was a shiny mass of scar tissue, as if from a terrible burn. Large brown eyes looked down unwavering at his hands. Gorelikov introduced him as *Starshy praporshchik* Iosip Blokhin, Master Sergeant Blokhin of *Spetsgruppa* "V," or Vega group, or more commonly known as *Vympel*, the Spetsnaz Special Forces unit used by the GRU for assassinations and covert foreign military operations.

Gorelikov's instincts vibrated like a tuning fork: Blokhin was a senior Spetsnaz sergeant in a cheap civilian suit, physically powerful, immensely experienced, outwardly calm and still. Impossible to control, ready to slaughter anything that moved. Blokhin said nothing, hardly moved; there was an air of controlled expectation in those downcast eyes—as if he were waiting for a bell to ring to murder everyone in the room. His burned forehead was striated where the flesh had melted and run like candle wax. With obvious irony, Gorelikov wryly explained that the sergeant had been seconded to work with the major, but to call Blokhin Shlykov's "aide" would be like calling a chain saw a pair of pinking shears.

Gorelikov saw Blokhin raise his eyes to stare at Dominika and watched how his future protégé handled the ferine challenge. She stared unblinkingly at him, hands relaxed, then turned away dismissively to look at Gorelikov to continue. *Satisfactory*, thought Anton. He could not know that Dominika had seen black bat wings of elemental evil unfolded behind the ogre, and stretched wide, like a seabird dries its wings in the sun. Dominika had shuddered slightly, and Blokhin saw it. Only one other human—Zyuganov, her former psychotic supervisor—had black wings like this instead of colors.

Blokhin blinked slowly at Dominika as if wondering how her liver would taste roasted on a stick over a campfire.

"Perhaps Colonel Egorova would give us a précis of her new case," said Gorelikov. His tourmaline cabochon cuff links peeked out of his sleeves.

"Are these gentlemen cleared for the details?" she asked.

Shlykov looked up at her with a sneer. "Yes, Colonel, we're familiar with all aspects of the case with Academician Ri, which is an infernal nuisance and must be terminated immediately."

"Perhaps the major can explain how the GRU is familiar with an SVR case?" said Dominika. Gorelikov smiled inwardly. Egorova outranked this *khvastun*, this swank-pot bully, and she wasn't going to back down.

"We are familiar with every aspect of your so-called case, because it intersects and interferes with a case of much greater importance that the GRU is running," said Shlykov. Dominika smiled.

Gorelikov interposed, like a judge separating two attorneys. "The deconfliction of intelligence operations is always critical," he said. "I am all eagerness to hear about your cases. Both of them."

"Sadly, Egorova is not cleared for it," said Shlykov.

Gorelikov raised a hand. "Now, Major," he said. "I believe the president gave instructions that both efforts should be coordinated. Please brief Colonel Egorova."

Shlykov heard the edge in Gorelikov's voice and complied. "The GRU has been running a sensitive asset for nearly twelve years. The source is encrypted MAGNIT, an American source with broad access to technology and policy." Shlykov sat with his arms across his chest.

"That is quite impressive, Major," said Dominika. "I presume since the GRU is handling the case the asset was a volunteer?" Gorelikov again stifled a smile. Egorova was pulling Shlykov's tail with a backhanded comment, made on purpose. Military dolts in the GRU would be incapable of recruiting such an asset from scratch. *They'd stumbled on a volunteer.*

"I'm not at liberty to describe the source in any more detail," said Shlykov, red-faced.

"And I am still not clear," said Dominika, "how my new source Academician Ri interferes with your source MAGNIT. Can you clarify that?"

"I should have thought it would be obvious, even to an SVR officer," said

Shlykov. "MAGNIT has provided a certain technology that the GRU has shared with the North Koreans to assist their nuclear weapons program."

Dominika smiled. "So let's summarize. MAGNIT has passed railgun technology to the GRU, which in turn has passed it to the North Korean intelligence service, the RGB, which has in turn provided the data to be used in nuclear trigger design at the Yongbyon Scientific Research Center." Shlykov looked back at Dominika without expression.

"Why would the GRU under any circumstances wish to accelerate the development of a North Korean nuclear device?" asked Dominika. *Bravo*, thought Gorelikov, *Egorova arrives at the correct issue in five minutes*.

"That is not an intelligence matter," snapped Shlykov. "That is a policy consideration far outside your purview." Gorelikov from the end of the table looked at Dominika with a blank expression that meant drop it.

"And what does the SVR Director think?" said Dominika. *No answer; the current SVR Director is a nonentity*. "Is it the president's edict that Academician Ri be terminated? I see no conflict between the two cases. MAGNIT is only providing the technology. Professor Ri is a penetration of the North Korean nuclear program. Cannot both cases be run concurrently and in close coordination?" Gorelikov noted how Egorova kept her temper, while Shlykov fumed.

"When an asset of immense potential value is threatened by another asset of lesser value, priorities must be set. There is no question that Egorova's case must be terminated. The SVR must withdraw from the operational field," said Shlykov.

"I believe we can discuss the compatibility of these cases at a later date," said Gorelikov. "But what the major says is true. MAGNIT is of immense importance, now and in the future. But this brings us to another subject, the ultimate reason for this meeting: the secure handling of MAGNIT. The president has ordered the SVR to assist the GRU in establishing an enhanced handling protocol for this asset." Shlykov bristled in his chair.

"The GRU is more than capable of handling its assets securely," he snapped.

"You may wish to express your opposition to the president's wishes in person," said Gorelikov softly, using the time-honored Kremlin threat. Shlykov looked down at his folder, retreating, knowing the conversation was probably being recorded.

"No one has the experience and acumen that the SVR can bring to a foreign operation," said Gorelikov, ticking points off on his fingers. "MAGNIT will be more safely handled in the United States by an illegals officer. SVR administers Line S, the illegals directorate. Colonel Egorova has handled illegals before. Besides," he continued, as if any of it made a difference, "the president expressly wishes that Colonel Egorova be involved in the handling and communications plan for MAGNIT," said Gorelikov.

"I did not agree to this," said Shlykov.

"The president did not solicit your approval," said Gorelikov, impatiently. "MAGNIT has been handled adequately for a decade, with tradecraft commensurate with the asset's position." Gorelikov was devilishly clever not to use the masculine or feminine pronoun. *Be patient; someone will make a slip sooner or later*, Dominika thought.

"But the internal handling protocol must now be strengthened," said Gorelikov. "With the prospect of MAGNIT's improved access, handling can no longer be left to inside GRU officers. A top illegals officer in New York City encrypted SUSAN will handle MAGNIT internally from now on, and Egorova will travel to the United States to meet her and pass dedicated communications equipment." *Well, we at least know SUSAN is a she.* New York: it would be Dominika's first trip to America.

What none of them at the table knew was that for at least ten years MAGNIT was also being met once a year outside the United States by Gorelikov himself. Gorelikov considered MAGNIT *his case* despite Shlykov's pettifogging and now, as MAGNIT's access was going to mushroom, he wanted to jettison clunky GRU handling and institute more secure handling in the United States.

"The SVR will try to usurp the case," said Shlykov, unhappily. "The General Staff will not stand for any attempt to purloin the intelligence."

"You mean steal your credit," said Gorelikov dryly. "Do not worry, the case will remain with the GRU. Colonel Egorova need not even know MAGNIT's true name when she passes the equipment to SUSAN." *Wrong answer, Anton. I need to know where our friend MAGNIT lives and breathes. There will be time.*

"That's most reassuring," said Shlykov. "But I want Blokhin to accompany the colonel to New York to protect our operational equities."

For a million reasons, no way, thought Dominika. *I'll be meeting Nate and Bratok in New York.* "Now I'm afraid I must object," said Dominika. "Two officers cannot make a clandestine meeting in tandem. Though I'm sure Sergeant Blokhin's skills in the field are many, I suspect surveillance detection is not one of them."

Blokhin's strange bass voice surprised everyone. "I'll show you my field skills whenever you like," he said. His vacant look was more alarming than had he been growling. The black wings folded back on each other.

Shlykov and Blokhin pushed back from the table, gathered their folders, and left the conference room. The metronome click of their heels faded, until they turned a corner in the gorgeous hallway.

———

Gorelikov heaved a deep sigh. "Dealing with that *presmykayushchiysya*, that reptile, is always tiresome," said Gorelikov. "His grandfather was a hero in the Great Patriotic War, until Stalin purged—shot—him in 1949. His father was an army marshal in the seventies, and young Valeriy has done well in the GRU. He is ambitious, privileged, and unethical, so watch your back with him."

"And MAGNIT?" asked Dominika casually.

"An immensely productive case with unimaginable promise," said Gorelikov, who was not ready to reveal the agent's identity to Egorova on the eve of her trip to New York. "The asset has risen through the bureaucracy and is now poised on the US national policy stage. If things develop the right way, the source will be handled by the illegals officer in New York and directed from the Kremlin as a Director's case, despite our ill-mannered Shlykov's wishes." *Okay for now. No more questions about the mole; you'll have the name for Benford in a month.*

"And would it be overstepping my bounds to ask why in heaven we are helping the North Korean nuclear program?" said Dominika.

"Because I want to disorient the Chinese, and flatter that little dumpling in Pyongyang," said President Vladimir Putin, entering the conference room from a side door. The usual blue suit, white shirt, aquamarine tie, and darting blue eyes complemented the well-known phlegmatic expression somewhere between a grin and a leer. Putin came around the table with his characteristic rolling sailor's gait, which an obsequious Kremlin biographer had recently described as a KGB-taught fighter's stride, but Dominika suspected was just a short man's waddle. Without speaking, he sat opposite her and rested his hands on the table. His blue aura—intelligence, guile, calculation—was like a *kokoshnik* on his head, the traditional conical Russian headdress, half-tiara, and half-diadem.

"I would like you to meet the illegals officer in New York," he said. Dominika had no doubt he had heard the conversation with Shlykov five minutes before.

The clairvoyant leader, the all-knowing tsar. "Yes, Mr. President."

"I trust you to take the necessary precautions."

"Of course, Mr. President," said Dominika.

"Take Blokhin with you as support," Putin said.

Gorelikov stirred. "Mr. President," he said, "a Spetsnaz trooper is not exactly what the operational situation—"

"Take him along, nonetheless," said Putin. "Keep the major happy until he begins his other project." Gorelikov kept quiet.

"And when you return," said Putin to Dominika, "I want to discuss new initiatives in the SVR with you. The recent favorable results of the *activniye meropriyatiya*, our active measures in the United States tells me we should expand our capabilities in this area."

"I will look forward to it," said Dominika. Putin's face softened as his eyes settled for an instant on the tight buttons of her tailored blouse under her navy suit. *I'll kill Benford if he asks me to do what melon head is thinking right now*, she thought.

Dominika was used to men staring at her figure, and reveled in staring them down. But it was different with the leers of the president. They had a history of sorts. She shuddered as she remembered Putin's late-night visit to her room years ago during the weekend at the palace outside Saint Petersburg. He wore red silk pajamas and walked in without knocking. Sitting upright in bed in her lacy nightgown, she had held the bedclothes up under her chin to cover herself, then remembered she had to captivate the tsar and lowered the sheet. She had dared to put her hand in his lap as he ran his fingers inside the full cups of her babydoll, to demonstrate her willingness, but her practiced (Sparrow) ministrations had, to her alarm, no immediate effect on him. The president had silently departed soon after, but the encounter hung over them, a preordained coupling sometime in the future, whenever the tsar would appear to claim his prize. And she would let him. She had to.

"*Schastlivogo puti*," said the president. "Bon voyage." He got up, nodded at Gorelikov, and exited by a separate side door that was opened by one of a score of werewolf aides who were always lurking. The door clicked shut, and Gorelikov sighed. Directing Putin's one-man *Sekretariat* was a trial.

"I've ordered a light lunch," he said. "Will you join me?"

———

They walked down the corridor to a small executive dining room and sat at a table. A waiter wheeled in a cart with a platter under a silver cover. "*Sel'd pod Shuboy*, herring under vegetable salad," said Gorelikov, serving Dominika a plate. "I hope you like it."

"It's very good," she said, thinking that the average young Russian probably never tasted such a delicacy.

Gorelikov chewed thoughtfully. "Too much mayonnaise," he said, wiping his mouth. "I have much to tell you."

"I will appreciate your guidance," said Dominika.

"First, I must mention that the president applauds your service record. He is following your career with interest." *Unfortunately with an erection,* thought Dominika.

"I predict he will promote you in the next trimester. The Directorship of SVR will follow, in my view."

Gorelikov's blue halo held steady, suggesting that he was telling the truth. "The president also likes Major Shlykov," said Gorelikov. "Perhaps he admires how *naglyy*, how brazen he is."

"Do we terminate Academician Ri in favor of the MAGNIT case?" said Dominika.

Gorelikov shrugged. "I agree that your case has merit, an invaluable look inside the Hermit Kingdom's nuclear program. But I predict the president will tire of pitting the North Koreans against Beijing, and withdraw his support. We can decide later."

"I am still not clear how one case threatens the other," said Dominika. "Both streams of intelligence will be handled in compartments."

Gorelikov observed how much ops sense this beauty had. He toyed with the notion of briefing her on MAGNIT, but decided it was too soon. He admired how she was not shy about pressing her point, even to a superior in the rarified air of the Kremlin. He strongly suspected she would be suitable for what he had in mind. "Shlykov believes the fact that the North Koreans are receiving railgun technology incontrovertibly reveals that an American source exists. If MAGNIT continues to move up, the case will eclipse all others and must be protected."

"Is MAGNIT that good?" said Dominika. *Last question, don't press.*

"The asset has the potential to be the best source in the history of our intelligence efforts against the Main Enemy," said Gorelikov with a chuckle, "if you'll excuse that old Soviet phrase—the Main Enemy—which, incidentally, is enjoying a resurgence in this building. You should keep that in mind."

"I will," said Dominika.

"Good. Now for politics," said Gorelikov. "Beijing is agitating the region with those damn artificial islands in the South China Sea. They're defying Washington; they're annoying the president. Putin wants to distract the Chinese, insert himself between the Beijing politburo and Pyongyang, and shake up the cozy relationship that's been unchallenged since the fifties."

"But forgive me, I can see the merit in active measures to disrupt the relationship, but at the cost of letting them have the bomb?" asked Dominika. Gorelikov laughed.

"I know, I asked the same question," said Gorelikov.

This man is a right-thinking adviser, thought Dominika, *not a lickspittle.* "It just seems like quite a risk," said Dominika. "My experience with the Iranian nuclear program taught me that research and development can stall, then accelerate unpredictably."

Gorelikov smiled at her. "Our work is fraught with risk," he said. "You yourself run risks every day, don't you?"

The familiar douche of icy alarm ran up Dominika's spine, the ageless affliction of the clandestine agent who lives with the dangling dread of discovery every waking moment. *What's that supposed to mean?* An innocent comment? A coy hint that she is somehow suspected? Nate would howl in distress and demand anew that she immediately defect.

"Your experiences with the Iranians were risky, your duel with the lamented Zyuganov was risky, the spy swap in Estonia was exceptionally risky," said Gorelikov. "No, Dominika—may I call you Dominika? And you will call me Anton—you run risks with courage and resolve, which is why the president has his eye on you. And so do I." A spiderweb trap? Or the start of a rare allegiance in a Kremlin where there are no allies?

"I value your support . . . Anton."

"Excellent. So we use Academician Ri for the time being to monitor those cabbage eaters and their infernal nuclear triggers," said Gorelikov. "Meeting him in Vienna will be delicate."

You have no idea, thought Dominika. "I have a support asset assisting me locally," said Dominika.

"The Petrescu woman?" said Gorelikov. "She's quite impressive." *Jesus, this elegant haberdasher knows a lot.*

Gorelikov pushed the platter toward her. "More salad? There's another delicate task the president intends to assign to you. He's convinced the Chinese intelligence service, the MSS, is spying on us, a view I do not necessarily share.

"Since you are SVR Chief of Counterintelligence, President Putin wants you to handle official liaison relations with the Moscow representative of the MSS." *A lot to tell Benford, right away. A SRAC shot to Langley, tomorrow night, at the latest. After dinner with Ioana, just back from Vienna.*

"It appears I will busy," said Dominika.

"Welcome to the *siloviki*," whispered Gorelikov, as he put more salad on her plate.

SEL'D POD SHUBOY—HERRING
UNDER VEGETABLE SALAD

Finely dice boneless herring fillets. Separately grate cooked carrots, potato, peeled apple, and hard-boiled egg whites (reserve yolks). Finely grate cooked beets (drain well) and whip with mayonnaise to make a velvety spread. Layer grated ingredients in a deep oval relish dish, pressing each layer firmly, starting with herring, potatoes, a thin coat of mayonnaise, carrots, apples, and egg whites, then mayonnaise, herring, potatoes, and carrots. Completely cover compressed salad with the beet spread on the top and sides, like frosting a cake. Garnish with finely grated egg yolk and refrigerate. Serve with crusty country bread.

6

Behave Like a Bull

The Uzbekistan Restaurant on Neglinnaya Ulitsa in Moscow's theater district was a Central Asian seraglio lavishly decorated with framed mirrors, chandeliers, and overstuffed banquettes littered with kilim pillows. Dominika pushed through the brushed copper door into the restaurant, registering the aroma of baked lamb laced with cardamom, coriander, and fenugreek. She brushed past the maître d', squeezed between opulent tables in the main room, and took the three steps up to the raised dining level. At the back of this private space, under a purple-and-blue striped canopy, sat Dominika's Sparrow, Ioana Petrescu. She was sipping a glass of white wine and did not wave or otherwise acknowledge seeing Dominika approach. Ioana had lost the tan from her time in Greece, but was elegant in a pair of leather pants, and wore a red silk blouse with a bateau neck. There was the familiar pulsing crimson halo around her head and shoulders, the aura of passion, and lust, and heart, and soul.

"I automatically thought I'd have to buy new lingerie for babysitting your nuclear scientist, but then I remembered he's not interested. So instead I bought a fur coat to keep me warm in Vienna," said Ioana in French, without a word of greeting.

"It's coming out of your pay *vorishka*, you sneak-thief. Did you find the right apartment? It's going to be important to keep him safe. When he comes to you for dinner, or when we have meetings, you have to make sure he arrives clean. Those maniacs watch their people closely. And the IAEA is like a small village: everybody knows everybody else's business." Ioana nodded.

"I found a house on the island, a riverside beach cottage on the other side of a little lake called Kaiserwasser half a mile from the International Center, five minutes' walk from IAEA. He can walk to the house and back in fifteen minutes, if he has to. The houses are summer rentals; they're all empty now. The Danube feeds the lake and surrounding inlets, the neighborhood is very wooded, and the cottage is quiet and cozy. A shame the professor doesn't care for fun."

Dominika laughed. Ioana hated the Sparrow life as much as she had. She was smart and efficient, which is why Dominika drafted her to do the preliminary ops work in Vienna.

"Have you considered that the professor is not interested in fun *with you*? With your backside spreading north and south, he may not be attracted." In truth, Ioana's buttocks were like sculpted marble from years of championship volleyball.

"I have decided I like you less and less each year," Ioana said.

"Forget about your *zadnitsa*, your fanny," said Dominika. "Did you install the recorder in the cottage?"

Ioana nodded. "A long-play wire recorder in the cupboard. Two wireless pickups around the chairs and table. The machine is voice-activated so I don't have to turn it on. Not as good a job as a tech could do, but you can't see a thing." More to tell Benford, but it could wait until the next SRAC shot. She already was up to the character limit for tonight's transmission.

"We'll go back to Vienna after I return from New York. It will be time to talk to him again by then."

"Buy me something expensive in New York," said Ioana.

"You already bought yourself a mink," said Dominika.

Ioana shook her head. "A watch; the one that shows phases of the moon."

"You need a $10,000 Swiss watch so you'll know how long to play the French flute with a recruitment target?"

"From someone who used to *faire une turlutte* before breakfast, that's a bit rich," said Ioana.

"A wristwatch is out," said Dominika. "Maybe a pair of shoes with round heels instead."

"Liking you less and less."

"What are we eating?" said Dominika, looking at the time. She still had two hours.

"There's chicken with mushroom cream, like our *ciulama de pui* in Romania," said Ioana. "Even beastly Uzbeks know our food is best."

"*Slava Bogu*, thank God for Romanian food," said Dominika, ordering two plates, which arrived quickly. Tender pieces of chicken in a rich *sauce suprême* of cream and mushrooms fortified with egg yolks and sour cream, served with Russian mashed potatoes. The women looked at each other after the first bite, approving.

They ate in silence. Ioana was content knowing that Colonel Egorova depended on her and was satisfied with her. This late dinner was proof of that. Dominika trusted her to rent the Vienna safe house. There would be other operations, maybe even the possibility of being made an officer in the Service. Egorova would take care of her.

On the sidewalk outside the restaurant, they kissed on both cheeks and without a word of farewell, Ioana walked north on Neglinnaya Ulitsa. Dominika watched her go, leather pants hissing like a snake, and thought how she would have preferred to be going with Ioana for a nightcap. But there was work to do, and Ioana had nothing to do with it and could know nothing. She would be *porazheny*, amazed if she knew.

———————

Carrying the heavy bag with her signaling equipment over her shoulder, Dominika started walking south on Neglinnaya, feeling the ice water flow into her chest as she went operational. It was a transformation both mental and corporeal, the mark of a street operator, partly learned, partly instinctive. Her pulse quickened and she tamped down the adrenaline rush in her neck and shoulders. Dominika's vision became acute—crystal clear and focused on the middle distance. Her hearing likewise was tuned to the timbre of the street around her—she heard car engines, the hiss of tires on wet cobbles, and the shuffle of footsteps on the sidewalk. It was late; Moscow traffic, while never nonexistent, would be light. She had to determine her status: she had to know she was surveillance-free, she had to get black.

Walk south on Neglinnaya, stair-step west, use the empty high-end walking street Stoleshnikov, luxury stores dark, surveillance would shy away from this funnel, this choke point, so look for the squealing, leapfrogging units hurrying to get ahead, *negative*, turn north on Bolshaya Dmitrova, cross street for a snap look, parked car with sidelights on, *negative*, past Muzykalnyy Teatr, its bas-relief columns illuminated, woman with shopping bag, second hit, but she's hurrying home, *disregard*, and cut through Petrov-skiye Vorota, leafy walking path lined with empty weekend market stalls, *no flanker silhouettes under the trees*, get to the little car parked under the sooty overhang of the Rossiya Theatre, no stakeout units, no finger smudges around the door locks, get in, pause, *smell* the car for the lingering reek of an entry team, *proceed*, check the trapped glove box, *tape still in place*, pull out in traffic, ignore horns, look for trailing units reacting, swerving to keep up, keep windows down, *hear the street, feel the street*, north out of town on Tverskaya, change lanes, watch for reaction, keep speed slow, lull coverage, no turn signal, merge onto the M10, gradually increase speed, traffic sluggish, articulated trucks belching smoke, headlights slotting behind? *Negative*, Sokol District coming up, *pay attention*, take split onto Volokolamskoye Shosse, lighter traffic, *goose it*, watch for reaction, *negative*, nearing timing point, black ribbon of Mosky Canal, check time, Svoboda overpass coming up, reach into the oversized purse on the passenger seat, feel for the button under the fabric, light rail overpass for number six tram coming up, *check mirror*, clear, *now*, two-second, low-power burst, 1.5 watts waking up the SRAC receiver buried six inches under the grassy rail embankment under the catenary lines, yellow light inside the purse winking green, electronic handshake, *message received*, message to Nathaniel, *secrets in the night, moles in our midst, ICBMs and warheads*, now the roar of the tunnel underpass, check mirror, *drifting, steer straight*, don't jackrabbit away, looping ramp to the elevated E105 ring road, traffic faster now, *your six is still clear*, past sleeping towns, Strogino, and past Myakinino, and past Druzhba, the *Rodina* dark, Mother Russia in shadow, her countrymen snug in their homes, believing only what their blue-eyed tsar told them to believe, eating only what the tsar fed them, hoping only for what the tsar let them hope for, fatigue now from gripping the steering wheel for so long, *watch for the exit*, west on Rublevskoye, take it slow, left, right, left, natural reverses in the triangle formed by Rublevskoye, Yartsevskaya, and Molodogvardeyskaya, look for swirling coverage, *negative*, cross Rublevskoye and east on Kastanaevskaya, her building, Number nine, dark windows, half-covered by ivy, bulb burned out over the entrance, dim staircase, she'd have to finger the key into the lock of her apartment door.

She rested her forehead against the steering wheel. Kastanaevskaya at this early-morning hour was completely lined with parked cars, both sides of the street. Cursing, Dominika had to cruise several blocks west before she found an empty spot near an all-night Almi pharmacy, its green neon sign coloring nearby trees and the scrawny grass verge in front, its front door reinforced with bars and opened remotely by the duty clerk. Trash paper swirled in the empty lot. Dominika locked her car door and started walking on the darkened sidewalk toward her building. The neighborhood was deathly silent. She clutched the oversized tote with the stiff bottom that was the concealment for her SRAC unit, antenna wires and transmit button sewn into the leather, standby and receive LED lights concealed as interior compartment snaps.

Once home, she would fit a thin lead into a port inside the bag to download the incoming message from CIA: intelligence requirements, or personal meeting skeds (schedules), or occasionally the rare operational requirement. Since her recruitment five years ago, she had met her CIA handlers overseas—sparingly and cover permitting—to participate in a recruitment, or in a false-flag approach, or in a debriefing, all of them glorious, heady trips to meet her secret CIA colleagues, including Nate, with whom she was still furious, but missed terribly. What message awaited her? Last week's message had mentioned Istanbul, and Dominika anticipated new instructions.

She thought about Nate as she walked. *Bozhe*, God, loving him was against all the rules of tradecraft, but Dominika wouldn't stop, and Nate couldn't stop. She had told them she was committed, that she was not spying *against* Russia but *for* Russia to flush out the Kremlin sewage farm, and send them all back to their filthy little beginnings. So, if she was CIA's irreplaceable agent, valued beyond all measure, and she wanted to love Nate, they should shut up. *Pravil'no?* Right? She dreamed of kissing Nate again, in a taxi or an elevator, or pressed hard against a hotel-room door. His hands on her, and—

Dominika saw movement under the trees in front of the pharmacy, silhouettes coming up off the grass, one, two, three, like demons emerging from the underground. They began moving through the trees, parallel to the sidewalk, heads turned toward her. Dominika's first thought was that somehow the internal security service, the FSB, the spy catchers, had discovered her, knew she was spying for CIA, and had intercepted tonight's burst transmission to the Americans on Volokolamskoye Shosse. Impossible. How? A mole in Washington? A breach of security in Moscow Station? A cracked cipher? However they did it, all the evidence they needed to bury her was sewn into the oversized purse hanging on her shoulder. Could she resist, somehow get away? How many of them would swarm out of the night and overwhelm her? She'd soon find out. Beside her hands and feet, the only weapon in her purse was a key ring. Keeping an eye on the silhouettes, Dominika laced keys between three fingers of her right hand.

Dominika had been trained—and kept up a weekly sparring session—in *Systema Rukopashnogo Boya*, the hand-to-hand combat system used by Spetsnaz, the ferocious Russian Special Forces. *Systema* was an amalgam of classic martial arts, ballistic hand strikes, management of an attacker's momentum, and devastating strikes against the six core body levers. She had killed, with desperate luck, trained assassins in hand-to-hand encounters. But she knew that in combat, one slip, one missed block, or sustaining a crippling strike would be the end.

The three silhouettes stepped into the light, and Dominika breathed a sigh of relief. *Gopniki*. Not an FSB arrest team. A *gopnik* was a male street tough—head shaved, gap-toothed, perpetually slurry eyed and red faced on cans of Jaguar alcoholic energy drink. Invariably dressed in Adidas tracksuits, pointed-toe leather *tapochki*, and *gondonka* flat caps, they infested suburban Moscow street corners, bus stops, and city parks, sleeping, drinking, puking, pissing, and mugging passersby. Their byword was *bychit*, to behave like a bull. They would want her purse, and would bludgeon her to death to get it. She would be just as compromised if these reeking deadheads dragged the purse off her shoulder and found the concealed SRAC burst transmitter as she would if FSB had.

The three were whip-thin and malnourished, but Dominika knew they would be quick and able to absorb punishment. It would be critical to keep them off her. She would trap the lead attacker with a joint hold, and drag him in circles to keep him in front of the other two. She would use the keys to rake their eyes, then sweep their legs with her foot and stomp a high heel into their throats or temples. That was the plan, at least.

"*Suka*, bitch, give me your purse," said Number One, stepping toward her, front right. They were indistinguishable from one another, simply incoming threats. Their yellow halos mingled, and matched the color of their crooked teeth.

"*Blyad*, whore, did you hear?" said Number Two, coming in front left.

Dominika stepped slightly right as Number One reached out to grab her. He smelled sour—urine, beer, tobacco, and pigsty. She covered the top of his right hand with her left hand and bent his wrist down and back. He howled as Dominika pivoted with him to the left, blocking Number Two, then continued pivoting to swing Number One, on his toes with pain, into Number Three in a tangle of legs and arms. She held on to Number One's wrist and turned him again into Number Two, foreheads cracking together. Number Three was coming in fast, his arm raised above his head. Knife. Leaning back, Dominika turned Number One into the line of the downward slash. The blade flensed down the side of Number One's shaved head and cut his ear off at the root. Dominika let the bellowing Number One drop to the ground holding his head, his neck black with spurting blood. She instantly stepped forward with a corkscrew punch, driving the three keys clamped between her right knuckles into the right eye of Number Three, feeling ocular fluid spurt over the back of her hand. She raked the keys out of the eye socket, across his nose, and into his left eye, a glancing blow. Maybe he'd still be able to see out of that eye later. Number Three collapsed shrieking *Suka*, covering his bloody face with trembling hands.

It had taken three seconds, and two of them were on the pavement writhing amid gouts of spattered blood, but Number Two was almost on her, and she knew if he knocked her down, all three would swarm her, maddened by their pain, and slam her skull against the concrete until they saw gray brains in the streetlight. Without thinking, Dominika dipped her shoulder as she grabbed the leather handles of her purse, and swung it in a flat arc into the left temple of Number Two. The four pounds of steel-bodied SRAC components sewn into the bottom of the tote bag hit skull bone with a flat metallic sound. Number Two wobbled, and sat down with a thump, cross-eyed.

Breathing hard, Dominika looked at them on the sidewalk, one face-down and unconscious, the other curled up and whimpering, the third still sitting up, staring but not seeing. These three roaches had come close to ruining everything, to exposing her, to sending her to the basement room in Butyrka Prison with the pine-log wall designed to catch ricochets, and the drains in the sloping, brown-stained cement floor placed to sluice away the fluids of the executed prisoners. Five years of unimaginable risks, of narrow escapes, of precious intelligence—*measured in linear feet*—passed to the Americans, of countless meetings in countless safe houses, only to be nearly unseated by three besotted *gopniki* two blocks from her apartment. This was another charming part of her Russia too, these louts who were as indolent, and cruel, and predatory as Putin's inner circle sitting in the jeweled halls of the Kremlin. They were the same cancer. She risked her life, and tonight they had almost ended it. She could be in a freezing cell awash with sewage, or dead and staring out of a cardboard coffin with a cloth tied under her jaw to keep her mouth closed, *these animals . . .*

In a rage, Dominika stepped up to the dazed punk, set her feet, and swung her stiffened arm under his chin and into his throat—a Spetsnaz killing stroke—fracturing the hyoid bone and rupturing the larynx. He fell backward and began gasping, eyes staring at the top of the trees.

"*Ublyudok*, bastard," said Dominika, watching his legs jerk.

She was still shaking so badly three minutes later that the sticky apartment key skittered over the lock before she could open the door with two hands. She left the lights off except for a small lamp near the front door. Her skirt was spotted with something dark and wet. The SRAC message downloaded to her laptop blinked once, flashed green for two seconds—she read the word "Istanbul"—then it went black, with the words "error 5788" appearing on the screen. *Chyort*, damn it! The *gopnik's* head apparently was harder than the components. Now she would have to trigger a cringingly dangerous personal meeting with an officer from Moscow Station—*Why couldn't Nate come to meet her?*—to exchange the damaged equipment for a new SRAC set.

She left her clothes in a pile on the floor, kicked off her shoes, and looked at herself in the mirror. The skin between her knuckles had been torn by the keys, and her hand throbbed. The little lamp cast a shadow over the curves of her body. Five years was a long time. Her figure was softer now, her rib cage didn't show, and her breasts were fuller. Thank God her stomach was still flat, and her hips had not spread to all points of the compass. The French bikini wax had been a silly impulse, but she was getting used to it. She was satisfied that her legs and ankles were slim.

Looking at herself suddenly deformed into an out-of-body dream; the image in the mirror was someone else. An unbearable melancholy washed over her. She stifled a sob, momentarily overwhelmed by her situation, by tonight's danger, and by her whole existence as a spy. *Look at you*, she thought. *What are you doing? Who are you? A ridiculous fanatic fighting alone in the dark, overwhelming dangers arrayed against you, the odds of surviving slim, your friends far away, separated from the man you love. How long will you last? How did her mentor General Korchnoi—he spied for CIA for fourteen years—summon the will and determination to keep going?* Dominika blinked as tears slid down the cheeks of the revenant in the mirror. It wasn't her; it was someone else crying.

CIULAMA DE PUI—IOANA'S CHICKEN WITH MUSHROOM SUPRÊME SAUCE

Cut chicken into small pieces, boil in salted water with rough-cut carrot and onion until tender. Make a Suprême Sauce by melting butter, then stir in flour, add chicken stock, egg yolk, and sour cream to make a velvety sauce. Sauté thin-sliced mushrooms in butter, add to the sauce, and finish cooking without boiling. Add chicken pieces, chopped parsley, season, and simmer. Serve with Russian mashed potatoes. (Mix mashed potatoes with sour cream, heavy cream, egg yolks, dill, and butter. Spread half of potatoes on greased pan, layer with caramelized onions, cover with remaining potatoes, and top with sour cream. Bake uncovered.)

7

Polestar of Humanity

Two aides escorted her down the brilliantly lighted corridor, while Dominika composed her features for a last-minute meeting with Gorelikov, probably routine, but she always half expected the room would be full of security goons gathered there to arrest her. The life of a spy.

She was on the third floor, residential wing of the Senate building, where Lenin and Stalin both had maintained comfortable apartments and where Stalin's second wife, Nadezhda Alliluyeva, in 1932 committed suicide. *With a revolver probably*, thought Dominika, *after she realized she was married to the messenger of Lucifer on Earth.* An aide knocked on a plain wooden door, waited a beat, and then indicated that she should go in. Anton Gorelikov stood from behind the desk in his Kremlin office, a corner room on the north angle of the three-sided Senate building. The office was spacious, lined with bookcases, and richly carpeted in deep red. An ornate crystal chandelier hung from the center of the ceiling. Gorelikov's desk was littered with papers and folders in assorted colors. *How many other operations are you hatching around the world?* Dominika thought. Today Gorelikov wore a blue shadow plaid suit by Kiton, a light-blue shirt by Mastai Ferretti, and black knit Gitman Bros. tie. He was more elegant than a London banker—no match for the damp tubs of suet on the Kremlin Security Council.

"Ready for your trip?" Gorelikov said, arms outstretched in greeting, like a grandfather welcoming a grandchild back home for spring break. Dominika shook his hand and sat gingerly in a plush leather chair in front of his desk, crossed her legs, and told herself not to bounce her foot.

Gorelikov had read Dominika's New York ops proposal—a document outlining alias identity, clandestine travel, and meeting protocols with the illegal—which she had wired directly to him last night from SVR headquarters in Yasenevo via an embargoed privacy channel. "Excellent plan, Colonel, excellent tradecraft, quite satisfactory." He beamed at her as the blue halo around his head shone and pulsed. Strange. He normally didn't vibrate like this; Gorelikov had some other villainy in mind, she was sure of it. "Sergeant Blokhin is making his own travel arrangements, and he will contact you on arrival. He will lightly countersurveil for you in New York City, but will not, repeat not, accompany you to the meeting with SUSAN the illegal. I made that quite clear to him and Major Shlykov both. If you have any trouble with Blokhin following instructions, abort the meeting rather than risk SUSAN." Dominika nodded, thinking how in the world she could stop Blokhin from doing anything he wanted to do. Her self-defense moves in *Systema* could not match his brute strength.

Dominika had done a little research on Iosip Blokhin. He had served five years in Afghanistan, where in his twenties he led the Spetsnaz Storm 333 assault in 1979 on the Tajbeg Palace to depose Afghan President Hafizullah Amin, killing more than two hundred presidential bodyguards. Unofficial reports documented that he had hung the naked body of the president's mistress from the balustrade of the palace balcony as a message to the people of Kabul: the Soviets were now in town. Blokhin then reportedly swung the president's five-year-old son by the heels against the wall, resolving any questions regarding primogeniture.

But Blokhin was neither a hallucinating veteran nor a psychotic executioner. Dominika was surprised to read that after the war, Blokhin completed noncommissioned officer's command school, trained with fraternal Special Forces units abroad, learned Vietnamese, and wrote a well-received article on small-unit tactics that had been accepted and included in a classified edition of the newsletter of the Centre for Analysis of Strategies and Technologies in Frunze Military Academy. And he showed black bat wings of evil. Savage or savant? She'd have to take care.

Blokhin and Gorelikov, two ends of the spectrum. Dominika looked out the curtained window over the crenellations onto Red Square and the onion domes of St. Basil's cathedral and the just-visible roof of Lenin's mausoleum, hard against the Kremlin wall. The wax mummy of V. I. Lenin under glass in that flowered bier no longer influenced events in *Novorossiya*, Putin's New Russia, but she wondered whether Gorelikov stood at this window and telepathically communed with Lenin and the other visionaries in repose just below in the Kremlin necropolis—Suslov, Dzerzhinsky, Brezhnev, Andropov, and Stalin, the *Vozhd*, the Master of Mayhem. Did they speak to him from the grave? Did they coach him in the tenets of deceit and betrayal? Gorelikov found the folder, and came around his desk to sit beside Dominika in a matching armchair.

They spent the next two hours discussing the mission, which Dominika did not need—she could put together an ops plan in her sleep. No, this was Gorelikov co-opting her, drawing her close, offering his affinity and support, she knew. She remembered what Benford had once told her about Kremlin allegiances: Soviet officials used to say that the beginning of one's ruin was the day one became Stalin's favorite. Gorelikov gazed up in thought at the chandelier above his head as Dominika spoke. Like every chandelier in the Kremlin, it was wired with a tiny 24-bit/48 kHz digital microphone in the bobeche, the fluted glass cup from which the crystal pendants hung, so she was speaking to the president at the same time.

She would fly from Paris to Toronto and travel by rail on the Maple Leaf down the Hudson River Valley. US Immigration controls were not as stringent at train stations as at airports. The next matter of business: communications.

Dominika's primary mission was to pass two special, 256-bit encrypted EKHO phones to SUSAN designed by Line T to synchronize only with each other, and to defy geolocation by frequency hopping simultaneously between cell towers. SUSAN would give one of the phones to MAGNIT during a personal meet, and the secure commo link would be established. With the delivery of the EKHO phones, MAGNIT, henceforth, would communicate only with SUSAN, an untraceable person, an anonymous American citizen, unknown to the FBI or CIA. Even if personal meetings occasionally were necessary, security would be preserved.

During her time in the United States, Dominika would have no way securely to communicate with the Kremlin from an official installation—the *resident* in New York City at the Russian Consulate on East Ninety-First Street was not briefed and would be unaware of Dominika's presence in the city. She would be on her own, a point that displeased Shlykov and moved him to insist that Blokhin stay close. *Not likely*, she thought.

Gorelikov handed Dominika an envelope with a description of a meeting site located on an island off the coast of New York City called Staten. "An island?" asked Dominika. "How do I get there to meet SUSAN?"

Gorelikov flipped through the pages. "There apparently is a ferryboat to this Staten Island from Manhattan. The illegal knows how to operate in the city. I'm sure the site is secure." He handed Dominika a small black-and-white ID photo of SUSAN, and Dominika was surprised to see an attractive blond woman with reading glasses. "This officer has been in the United States since the late nineties, she is a top pro, our best illegal. Her legend is impenetrable," said Gorelikov, reading from the folder. "She has a position of influence—she is an editor at one of the top liberal magazines in Manhattan, widely known and respected in her profession. Her colleagues are totally unsuspecting. They have no idea they have been working beside an SVR officer all these years. It is perfect cover.

"If necessary, you may initiate contact by calling SUSAN's sterile number from your nonattributable cell phone, but only in an emergency. Conversely, if I want to send you a message via SUSAN, she in turn can trigger a meeting by calling you. Here are the numbers, recognition paroles, and meeting schedules. Simple, straightforward." Dominika tried to palm the photo—Benford would sell his firstborn to get his hands on SUSAN—but Gorelikov took it back.

"You'll receive a full trip report," said Dominika. *After I brief Gable and Benford.* With her SRAC transmitter damaged by the *gopnik*'s skull, Dominika would have to wait until she arrived in New York to rendezvous with her handlers and tell them these details.

"I have every confidence in you," said Gorelikov, looking at his watch, an elegant, wafer-thin Audemars Piguet Millenary Quadriennium with an openwork face, the intricate movement visible, like Gorelikov's mind, minutely whirring, oscillating, and pendulating.

═══════

New York, New York. It was a dream. Dominika—in French alias Sybille Clinard—flew from Paris to Toronto, then rode the slow Maple Leaf train down the scenic Hudson Valley, stirring the American gothic ghosts of Sleepy Hollow, and drowsy Dutchmen. Dominika had researched the city and was excited to see it all. On the train, US border agents didn't look twice at her, and she had felt no fear. Pulling her suitcase across the concourse at Penn Station felt like home, but there were more people on the Moscow metro and the stations were grander. This rather grubby underground terminal couldn't compare with the magnificent Kiyevskaya Station on the Arbat line, with its mosaics and chandeliers. There were shops and music here, a man with a hat was dancing for tips, and an old woman stopped and started dancing with him. Americans. Russians were more reserved, more serious, and they dressed up to go out in the city. These New Yorkers were half-naked.

Dominika trudged up the stairs, pushed through the doors, came out onto the street, and stopped, frozen.

The roar of the city enveloped her like a wave, the traffic on Seventh Avenue like a river in flood, the sun blotted out by the buildings—towering, majestic, glass canyons filling the sky in all directions, an impossible concentration of them, and their mass pressed down on her. Dominika craned her neck to look up at them like a *derevenshchina*, a hayseed from the country, not caring. To be sure, Moscow was a city, so too Paris, Rome, London, Athens, but nothing like this. This was someplace without equal, electric and buzzing, a polestar of humanity. Dominika was like a mouse inside a violin, claws gripping tight, stunned by noise and surrounded by vibration. She shook her head. She knew the name and address of her hotel, had memorized the walking route there, and she needed to find a secure telephone to call *Bratok*, but first she wanted to walk, to see everything. This great city was America, this energy, this industry, *this overarching freedom*. This is what she aspired to for Russia. This is why she was spying for CIA and this defined her *nutro*, the impossible-to-explain Russian concept of a person's inner being.

She threaded through pedestrians on the sidewalk, and as if to match the frenzy of these streets, unrelated thoughts came to her *voley-nevoley*, all in a rush. My God, how do you check for opposition coverage on these streets? Was the *shashlik* from these food trucks edible? Did they have *gopniki*, street toughs, in New York? It would be impossible to pick out surveillance in this crush of bobbing heads, faces of every color and every ethnicity, appraising eyes, twitching hands, and shuffling feet. Overhead a fog bank of peoples' colors, indistinguishable, useless, was overwhelming. As Chief of Line KR counterintelligence, she knew how her colleagues in the New York *rezidentura* blithely reported managing operations on these streets—she'd reported it all to Benford for the last five years. But now, seeing it firsthand, she knew the truth. *That's why the Center uses illegals here for the really sensitive cases*, she thought. *Who could find surveillance in this woodwork?*

The Jane Hotel in the West Village was something out of a movie, chosen for her by Gorelikov for its small size and anonymity. An annoyingly voluble bellhop at the front desk had grinned at her (Russians reserve smiling for their friends and family members—to smile with no reason is a sign of a fool) and insisted on telling her that the hotel had been a sailor's boardinghouse at the turn of the century, and that survivors of the *Titanic* in

1912 had recuperated here. Dominika thanked him, then ignored him. The lobby was high Victorian, a riot of colored mosaic pilasters and leafy palms in tarnished copper kettles. The bar/lounge was Bohemian crazy, filled with a thousand candles, velveteen upholstered couches, zebra-print armchairs, a brown-leather hippo, and a toffee-colored stuffed bighorn sheep with a cowbell around its neck, standing high atop the fireplace lintel. It would be fun to seduce Nate in this hideaway.

Walking down the dim wainscoted corridor to her room she felt the shipwrecked spirits of 1912 around her. As she fumbled with her key card, an old woman in a woolen suit and matching pillbox hat came out of a room at the end of the corridor. Under the ridiculous hat her white hair was up in a bun, and she wore half-moon glasses. She shuffled soundlessly toward Dominika on the threadbare carpet, her right hand running along the wooden wall panels for balance. Dominika flattened against the wall to make space for the biddy to pass. Behind the glasses, the old woman's eyes locked onto Dominika's for a second; they were the color of amber. Hunter's eyes, wolf's eyes, raptor's eyes. A strong blue aura around her head. Cunning, calculation, deception. What was the *starukha*, the old crone, looking at? She didn't belong in this trendy hotel either. Dominika suddenly knew: They were watching her. This old woman was a bird dog to report that Dominika had arrived. The MAGNIT case was running on many different levels. The old lady slowly disappeared around a corner.

Dominika's room was train-compartment narrow, with a ship's berth instead of a bed. She imagined making love with Nate in this little room, her foot braced on the far wall for purchase. She left her suitcase and purse on the bed, stuffed the EKHO phones, a small snap wallet with money, and her own mobile phone into a shoulder bag, which she zipped shut. She must not lose the phones to be delivered to SUSAN. The old lady in the hallway was a wake-up call: Dominika had no doubt that They would use her personal phone to track her movements as well as hot-wire it to listen to her conversations. Into the other coat pocket she clipped the fat ballpoint pen with pointed metal tip—a tactical fighting spike—that was her only weapon.

She hit the street, wanting to get away before Blokhin appeared, determined to clear her six so she could call *Bratok*. Never mind the FBI, now she had to worry about Gorelikov's tricks, her own countrymen following her. Did Gorelikov's *vliyaniye*, his influence, extend to the streets of New York?

Who would they be, the people checking up on her? Well, she had survived this long spying for Nate and the others, and wasn't about to be played. As she left the hotel and walked east, she put on the big fashion sunglasses that were designed by the boys in Line T, with beveled mirrors ground into the outer edges of each lens, which permitted a limited view behind her. You didn't rely on such toys—detecting coverage on the street was much more complicated—but it did not hurt to have them.

Dominika walked for three hours, searching for and finding relatively quiet side streets, stripping away repeats, possibles, ghosts, and suspects. If her cell phone was beaconed and her route plotted later, she would be guilty only of executing a thorough and professional surveillance detection run. She used Union Square as a surveillance trap, knowing that any team scurries to cover exits along all sides of a park and inadvertently show themselves. She scanned the outer edges of the park. *Nothing.* She plowed up endless, bustling Fifth Avenue, the Empire State Building coming closer with each block—beckoning, bigger, taller, and somehow more substantial than the *Vystoki*, Stalin's gothic Seven Sisters skyscrapers in Moscow. Nothing showed behind her. Occasional switches to the other side of the street revealed no telltale behavior of handing off the eye. She reversed her direction by taking a taxi south, past the Washington Square Arch, bailing out and walking through the urban campus of New York University to detect pedestrians who stood out among younger casual students. *Nothing.* Dominika popped into The Smile restaurant on Bond Street—she liked the look of the weathered boards on the ceiling and the rich brick walls—and asked to use the phone behind the bar, explaining in an exaggerated French accent to the skeptical barmaid in a dirty apron that she was from France, and that her mobile phone did not receive service in New York. *Besides, I'm calling my CIA handler to discuss foiling a Kremlin attack on the political and security foundations of America, with the express goal of preserving your gravy-stained way of life.*

She left her phone in her coat pocket, and hung the coat on a wall hook away from the bar. *Bratok* answered on the first ring. She told him about her cell phone and the old lady at the hotel, his low chuckle reassuring and comforting. He kept his comments short and cryptic, they'd reviewed meeting procedures a hundred times. "Five o'clock, go to the museum and wait outside. Got it? I'll be looking out for you." The line went dead. Gable had just told Dominika to rendezvous with him at the Monkey Bar, at three o'clock.

The power-lunch restaurant was renowned for the iconic celebrity murals on its walls (hence "the museum"). Gable had also cryptically told her she'd be countersurveilled as she walked to the restaurant on East Fifty-Fourth Street. She wondered whether it would be the old team again, whether she'd see Nate's slim features across the street, whether she'd hear his voice, and whether he'd sit beside her close enough to touch him, feel the heat of his body, smell him . . . *Stop it.*

━━━━━━

Gable was chewing an unlit cigar and driving a wheezing, beat-up sedan with torn plastic seats and an Orthodox cross hanging by a plastic chain from the rearview mirror.

The officers from Benford's CID countersurveilling Dominika gave Gable the all clear, and he had pulled up, thrown open the passenger door, and scooped her off the sidewalk in front of the Monkey Bar. Once rolling, he put fingers to his lips, nodding at the cell phone in her hand. He made two violent right turns, narrowly missed a pedestrian, and careered through crosstown traffic at high speed, shooting the gaps between taxis, trucks, and buses. After one near collision, Dominika reached up, grabbed the swinging cross, and theatrically kissed it. Gable winked at her, delighted. He ran a red light and cut left across oncoming traffic to turn onto Ninth Avenue in the direction of Dominika's hotel. In classic alteration of surveillance detection run (SDR) pace, Gable now drove south slowly in the right lane, letting honking, gesticulating New York drivers pass him. They were black, no tails. After ten blocks, he swerved to the curb in front of a dingy storefront restaurant with "Turkish Cuisine" written in a faux mosaic over the door. He gestured for Dominika to leave her phone under the seat, and follow him into the restaurant.

The place was dark and cozy, with copper trays and ceramic *nazarlik*, blue evil-eye talismans, mounted on the walls. Gable ordered a *çoban* salad, two kebabs, and *kiymali ispanak*, sautéed ground beef, spinach, and rice. "You'll love it," said *Bratok*. "Nash and I used to eat it at a Turkish joint in Helsinki."

"Helsinki," said Dominika, staring. "*Skol'ko let, skol'ko zim*, so many summers, so many winters; it seems like a million years ago." Gable looked at her while chewing a piece of bread.

"Yeah, we've all come a long way, you most of all," said Gable. "Now tell me what's going on." Dominika sat back and talked fast. She told him about Gorelikov's instructions and the meeting with SUSAN. She showed him the EKHO phones—they would not be hot-wired if they were meant for an illegal—thinking he'd want techs to take them apart to inspect, but Gable shook his head. "They could be trapped to reveal tampering, and you're the only one who holds them." Dominika described the meeting site on Staten Island.

"You know how to take the ferry?"

"I studied the entire route. I know how to get there," said Dominika.

"This illegal, what's she look like?" said Gable.

Dominika shrugged. "It was a little black-and-white photo," said Dominika. "Blond, reading glasses, steely blue eyes. Short hair."

Gable rubbed his face. "Christ," he said. "A top illegal in the city and we can't ID her. How many more of them out there, I wonder."

"There is no way of knowing," said Dominika. "Line S, the external illegals department, and Line N, the officers who handle them in-country, are compartmented from the rest of the Service, even from me in KR." The food came to the table and Gable spooned a mound of glistening spinach onto Dominika's plate. She tried a forkful. It was a savory combination of sautéed spinach and curried ground beef with a hint of rice. Delicious. *And Nate used to eat it.* The question popped out before she could stop herself.

"*Bratok*, where is Nate? What is he doing?" said Dominika.

Gable put down his fork. "Benford sent him to take care of another op. In Asia. Right now, that boy is busier than a cat covering crap on a marble floor. He'll be back in a couple of weeks. You steamed at him again?" Gable just asked questions, no matter how sensitive.

Dominika smiled. "In Russia we say *nalomat drov*, to mangle the firewood. You say to mess something up. That's our love affair. Messed up."

Gable patted her hand. "I'm not supposed to say this to you," said Gable, "but you should either cut it off with him once and for all, or defect and concentrate on your lives together. Maybe recruit your replacement before you go. Loving each other and spying at the same time is gonna get someone hurt." Dominika was silent; she knew Gable understood her. "Don't tell anyone I told you that," he said, smiling. Then he got back to business.

"You gotta fly straight with that Spetsnaz guy hanging around. Let him see you nice and relaxed." Dominika nodded. "Make the meeting with that gal on Staten Island alone, but otherwise keep him close. He's going to file a trip report and you want them all to think you were never out of pocket. We'll meet once more after your meet with the illegal. And try to get some ID on her without being too obvious." Gable waved to a young man at a table across the room and Lucius Westfall walked over.

"This droopy bit of wet wool is Westfall," said Gable. "He's backup if you see him on the street, here to help you and me if we need it." Dominika smiled and shook his hand, noting a blue halo quivering with nervousness. She felt sorry for him, especially since she knew what a bear Gable could be.

"Glad to meet you, Westfall," said Dominika. He nodded wordlessly, obviously overcome at meeting the famous DIVA. He'd had no idea she was so beautiful. He turned and left the restaurant after an awkward final bow.

"*Bratok*, you do not torment him too much, do you? He's so young, like you were once." Gable grunted.

"I was born old. But tell me more about the Spetsnaz sergeant."

"This man Blokhin is worse than either Zyuganov or Matorin. He is intelligent, but behind his eyes are, how do you say, hot rocks like when you grill *shashlik*."

"Like hot coals? Well, don't arm wrestle him," said Gable.

"I am forcing myself to go with him to an event at the Hilton on Sixth Avenue in two days. A Russian journalist, Daria Repina, is speaking at a Free Russia fund-raising event. She is a loud critic of everything Putin does. She is without fear, but now that she is in America raising money it will become dangerous for her."

"Is it smart for you to be going to something like that? Why would a Spetsnaz snake eater want to go to hear some dissident?" said Gable.

"Attending with him will be a good appearance—I mean bona fides—for me," said Dominika. "It is a public event. I will stay in the background and leave early. As for Blokhin, I think he is curious. Like a dog sniffing a lamppost. It will be his last night in New York. We both return separately to Moscow the next day."

"And when you get back, you find out the name of MAGNIT, fast as you can, right?"

"Someone will make a slip. I will hear the name eventually," said Dominika.

"That's all well and good, but we gotta wrap MAGNIT up before then, preferably before you're briefed on the case, before you're officially told his name. How's it gonna look if he gets arrested the very weekend you're read in? Plus that prick is selling secrets wholesale. So let's blow him up ASAP."

"There is a problem." Dominika told Gable about the malfunction with her SRAC transmitter after she had brained the street mugger. Gable shook his head.

"We wondered why you hadn't sent anything for a week. I told them you had a boyfriend and wouldn't get out of bed."

"*Nekulturny,*" she said. Crude and rude.

"Dammit. Bad time to lose your commo," said Gable. "I'll cable the station to get you another set. You want them to cache it or do a personal meet?"

"If you have a good station officer who won't bring surveillance with him, a personal meet is faster than me digging up a package in the forest. There are five new brief-encounter sites left in the inventory that are still good."

"You sure? I'd rather break one nail using a shovel than have ten nails pulled out in a prison basement," said Gable. One normally did not remind agents about being captured and tortured, but Gable and Dominika dealt with each other on a different plane.

"*Bratok*, that is because you are delicate and sensitive," said Dominika.

"You fucking got that right," said Gable, as he signaled for the bill.

KIYMALI ISPANAK—TURKISH SAUTÉED SPINACH

Sauté finely chopped onion in olive oil and butter. Add ground beef and cook until browned. Add diced tomatoes, red-pepper paste, tomato sauce, and a handful of rinsed rice. Season and stir to incorporate. Layer coarsely chopped spinach on top, cover and cook on medium heat until spinach is wilted and rice is tender. Serve with a dollop of yogurt and crusty country bread.

8

To Shoe a Flea

Dominika sat on the upper deck of the crowded, lumbering Staten Island Ferry, drolly appraising the collection of people lining the rail—they looked primarily like tourists—talking about, pointing at, and photographing the receding skyline of Manhattan. They would then rush to the starboard rail to snap the Statue of Liberty, then stampede back to gawk at a vintage gaff-rigged schooner tacking up the bay. They honked like a flock of geese. They were dressed in shorts, T-shirts, and brassiere tops, and wore boots, sneakers, shoes, and sandals, a bizarre tribe that rasped at Dominika's Russian sensibilities. She was dressed in a light cotton summer-print dress, with fashionable flats, and carried a beige over-the-shoulder bag. She wore her Line T sunglasses. Despite the raucous passengers, she thought these ferries were a marvel, big orange birthday cakes that never stopped crisscrossing the bay, nothing like the belching, shark-nosed hydrofoils that skimmed across Lake Ladoga from Saint Petersburg.

She literally had been swept down the ferry boarding ramp by the crush of laughing, excited sightseers, past placid bomb-sniffing dogs, and was able to find a quiet seat along the outside rail where she enjoyed the salt breeze and thought about today's meeting with the illegal, SUSAN. She had returned to her hotel room last night and felt the rubber band around her doorknob, a signal confirming a meeting at the site on Staten Island tomorrow afternoon. Dominika wondered if the old lady down the hall had snapped the band in place. She had reviewed the memorized drill, the surveillance detection route she would take: ferryboat, Staten Island train, walking route up to and through the sprawling Moravian Cemetery on Todt Hill, and final approach to the site (which was inside the ornate mausoleum of Gilded Age billionaire Cornelius Vanderbilt, constructed in 1886, and secluded in a private, wooded corner of the park). She had studied the satellite images and memorized the way along the lanes that wound through the forty-five hectares of the graveyard, and knew she could find her way to the site at the appointed time, without coverage. God knew who she had to worry about more on the street during this insane operation—Russians, the illegal, or the FBI.

Gable had been right: Moscow had moved fast. This call-out for the meeting with the illegal came less than forty-eight hours after Dominika had arrived in New York. Dominika could imagine the hurried consultation between Gorelikov and Putin in the Kremlin, their quiet voices briefly discussing options and then the stoic, blue-eyed nod validating whatever tactics Gorelikov suggested to enable the contact. Dominika immediately had gone back out and called Gable from a public phone at a nearby bar, to tell him that "lunch was on tomorrow." Gable told her to stay cool, that everything she did or said would get back to the men who would be evaluating her. They agreed to meet after Dominika returned to Manhattan.

A swarthy young man leaning against the ferry rail in front of Dominika was obviously a local from Staten Island, dressed in a sports jersey, his dark hair slicked back. He noticed Dominika and came to sit beside her on the plastic molded seat. He flirted, charming and irreverent, his face close, pointing out landmarks as the ferry plowed across New York Harbor, including the arching Verrazano-Narrows Bridge—he called it the Guinea Gangplank although it was unclear to Dominika why—connecting the two boroughs of Brooklyn and Staten Island. Dominika could understand about half of what he said, but smiled and looked where he pointed. When she told him she was from France, he winked at her and knowingly said "Nice wines."

The thrumming of the ferryboat engines moderated, then the deck shook as the engines were put full astern to ease the nose of the ferry into the exit ramp at St. George Terminal on Staten Island. *Time to go, time to turn on, time to go to work.* Dominika slung her bag over her shoulder, and nodded vaguely to the young man. Moving quickly, she followed the signs to the adjacent rail platform to board the southbound train. Quick checks to either side did not pick up the loitering passenger, or the too-long look from the young woman on the sidewalk, or the ticket clerk diving for the phone. *No coverage*, she thought, as she stepped into a train car. As the doors closed, Dominika saw with annoyance that the young man had boarded the next car, and was staring at her through the window of the connecting door. She didn't have time for this: a Romeo following her, thinking he might get lucky with a hot tourist from France.

The train rattled and swayed and stopped frequently at suburban stations. A different world was unraveling in front of Dominika's eyes on each side of the tracks. Commercial areas had petrol stations on every corner; there were supermarkets with tomatoes stacked on display in front, and she counted restaurant after restaurant—most of them claiming they made the best pizza in New York. *Was this even New York City?* The train clanked past working-class neighborhoods of tidy two-story houses, shingled, with lean-to greenhouses and tiny fenced yards, some of which had curious aboveground swimming pools hardly big enough to hold a person. On every roof was a gray satellite TV dish, all pointed up in the same direction. The houses were nothing like the luxurious dachas of the *siloviki*; these were not rich people, but these houses looked comfortable. The cars parked along the street were big and relatively new. If this was not wealth, it was at least *prosperity* on a wide scale. In Russia, they would say *blagopoluchiye*, bread buttered on both sides, well-being. Not many people, not even in Moscow, were living lives with such possessions, with such abundant food. Her countrymen struggled to survive, they despaired of improving their lives, they dared not think grand thoughts or speak the truth. They could not *choose*.

Dominika had memorized the strange names of the train stations: Grasmere, Old Town, Dongan Hills, Jefferson Avenue, Grant City. People bustled on and off as the train doors opened and closed—no observable surveillance behavior, nothing amiss. She could see the young man in the next car watching her through the glass. The next station was her waypoint, New Dorp, where she had to get off. She stepped out to the platform and quickly walked in the middle of a crowd of passengers up the steep exit staircase to street level and onto a broad boulevard with light traffic. On the opposite corner stood an Italian bakery owned by someone named Dominick. *Perhaps I will have a bakery someday named Dominika's*, she thought. *Idiot you don't know how to bake.* She went inside, assaulted by the heavy aroma of fresh bread, noting there were no lines at the counter, was no one screaming for service, no churlish salesperson cursing at customers. She bought something called a calzone, which looked like an oversized *chebureki*, a Russian meat pie. This calzone was baked golden brown with a fluted edge, and was served with a small cup of tomato sauce.

Dominika sat at one of a few tables by the window and checked the street. The persistent Romeo was loitering on the opposite sidewalk, smoking. An American *gopnik*, but he didn't look as tough as the Moscow species. *Bozhe*, God, she didn't need this distraction right now. The mixture of sausage, peppers, and onions inside the calzone was delectable and oozed out, and she wiped her mouth with a paper napkin. *Izobiliye*, she thought, abundance. This was an American neighborhood bakery, not a state store, one of hundreds in this borough alone. Enough. Get moving.

Dominika walked up New Dorp Lane, the sidewalks broad and clean, people in storefront offices working. A corner food market, the "Convenient Mart," whatever that meant, had cases of bottled water stacked high on either side of the door. The young man was still following her and she knew she had to shake him before she neared the cemetery. The illegal might be observing her approach and it would be a disaster if she couldn't get rid of him. As she was entering the store in an effort to shake him off, Dominika heard footsteps and the young man called "Hey, Mam'sell!" and she turned to see Romeo take a picture of her with his cell phone at a distance of five feet, then hold it up to admire. Besides her official academy photo, and the ID pics Gable had taken of her in Helsinki, and ops alias passport photos, there was no extant photograph of SVR Colonel Dominika Egorova, especially not on the mobile phone of some *durak*, some idiot, in front of the Convenient Mart, on New Dorp Lane, on Staten Island, forty minutes before a clandestine contact with an illegals officer. She'd be on this boy's Instagram, Facebook, and Twitter accounts in three minutes.

Dominika made an instant calculation. "Since you seem so intent on following me," said Dominika to him, "perhaps you can show me a good bottle of American wine in this store."

The young man stepped up to her, exuding his snail-trail charm. "Show you a bottle of wine, or share it with you?" he cooed.

Dominika let a slight smile move her lips. "It depends how good the wine is," she said.

The young man led her into the little market, down a food aisle where Dominika stopped in amazement to count no fewer than ten different types of breakfast cereals on the shelf, an impossible riot of color. She followed Romeo to the back of the store, and stood in front of a wine cooler with sliding glass doors, while Romeo pointed out the reds, then the whites.

They had everything, anything she wanted. Almaden, Gallo, Carlo Rossi, Blue Nun, Lancers. He said the Franzia box wines were underrated. If she didn't like any of the wines, they had pints behind the counter: gin, vodka, rye. Dominika chose a white and let Romeo pay, then followed him across the avenue to sit on a step that was part of a cement bridge that carried ribbed steam-heat pipes over the commuter train tracks and was screened from the main road. The cement bridge shook when a train passed beneath. Blokhin would have driven the tactical spike through Romeo's eye and into his brain, but Dominika took a sip from the bottle—the wine was sweet and metallic—then handed it back. She turned and hit him on the side of his neck with a hammer fist that started down by her left hip and snapped around with torque provided by her hips. The strike overloaded the nerves in his mastoid process, and his head slumped forward as he pitched unconscious face-first onto the concrete. If he wasn't dead, he would be out for several hours, and Dominika would be long rid of Staten Island. She fished Romeo's phone out of his back pocket and used a broken, pointed chunk of concrete as a Paleolithic tool to pulverize the modern appliance into plastic crumbles, none remotely recognizable as a phone. She scattered the smithereens onto the tracks under the bridge, took a final vile sip from the bottle, and threw that too, to smash on the rail bed among all the detritus piled along the tracks.

"*Zvezdá*, big shot," said Dominika, looking down at Romeo, knowing it would have been easier and more secure to have killed him. She wondered if she would eventually get to that point: the Blokhin/Stalin default solution—kill and erase the obstacle, regardless of circumstances.

Moving quickly, Dominika turned right onto Richmond Road and walked uphill past houses with painted fences and trimmed bushes. Many of the houses had American flags hanging from the porches. The street was quiet, she was black, and there was no trailing coverage, she was sure. She was a Russian intelligence officer loose in America, proceeding to a meeting with a sleeper agent.

The temperature was mild, the sky was clear, the sunlight was bright. The ornamental gate to the Moravian Cemetery was open, flanked by lush orange trumpet vines. As if she had visited this graveyard every weekend, Dominika unerringly took the left-hand path, walked past the placid lake, its surface stirred by the drooping branchlets of willows. She continued along the paved drive flanked on either side by acres of tombstones. Some of the stone markers were extravagant: twenty-foot obelisks or ziggurats topped by ecstatic angels. She passed rows of small ornate mausoleums protruding out of grassy tumuli, family names carved on the lintels. These were nothing like the outlandish headstones of assassinated gangsters, or murdered journalists, or martyred dissidents in Novodevichy Cemetery in Moscow, with startlingly realistic images of the departed carved into the marble. Where would President Putin be laid to rest in Moscow? she wondered. Would the monsters resting in the Kremlin wall scoot over to make room for him? Or would he prefer a twenty-story porphyry obelisk on the Moscow Hills so he could gaze down on the *Rodina* he so energetically defended?

At Dominika's thought of Putin, the warming sun went behind a cloud and she felt a cold shiver. The cemetery was utterly still now, no birds, no traffic noise, as if the spirits knew what was happening. The grass around the gravestones stirred; she heard whispers around her, or was that the breeze? But there was no breeze. *Get a hold of yourself*, she thought as she walked, *keep your head, meet this bitch, and let's complicate Vladimir Putin's life.* Dominika kept left, and followed the footpath into a dark forested section with very little sunlight. It smelled cold here, and she pushed her sunglasses onto the top of her head. Her hand drifted into her purse and around the shaft of the tactical steel pen in the side pocket. She looked left and right into the trees, her Russian imagination conjuring up wolves weaving through the coppice, keeping pace with her.

She rounded a bend in the path and saw the massive wrought-iron lychgate, the entrance to the private cemetery grounds of the Vanderbilt family. The gate was secured with a heavy-duty chain, but Dominika followed the boundary wall ten meters to the right, and was able to hitch up her dress and boost herself over. The path curved left, and the woods opened up to a grassy clearing ringed by a low-curved curb. The white-stone mausoleum at one end dominated the space. It resembled the front of a Romanesque church, with three arched doors, a tall central gable, and two conical cupolas on the roof. The crypt itself extended from the ornate façade into the earthen hill behind.

It was deathly quiet, the sun behind the clouds. Dominika stood still and watched the woods, listened to the air around her. There would have been no way for Gable to set up on this spot without spooking SUSAN. The veteran illegal knew what she was doing picking this site. Dominika checked her watch; it was time. She walked up the five curving steps to the entrance, and pushed on the central steel door with matching ornate handles. Dominika knew the crypt doors normally would be locked and probably chained, but mechanical locks posed no problems, *ever*. The door swung in easily, soundlessly, and a fetid breath of cold stone hit her, a coffin smell, a whiff of endless time. The dim vaulted room was flanked by wall crypts with stone coffins, and a massive tomb with a curved top and adorned with intricate carved decorations—presumably the sarcophagus of the paterfamilias—dominated the center of the chamber.

"*Dobriy den tovarishch*, good afternoon, comrade," said a silky voice in Russian. Dominika willed herself not to jump. Gripping the fighting spike in her purse, she turned slowly toward the voice and saw a dark silhouette in the corner of the crypt, completely in shadow. No halo was visible in this darkness. The only illumination came from the milky bar of light through the cracked central door, keeping most of the room in darkness. "You are precisely on time, but that is to be expected from the famous Colonel Egorova." *Moscow accent, educated, but originally from the south, with a trace of* yakanye, *the broad vowels of the lower Volga*, thought Dominika.

"Good afternoon. I am glad we could meet," said Dominika, holding out her hand. *Will you come closer to shake?* The woman didn't move, and Dominika lowered her hand.

"How much time do you have? I presume we both have to return to Manhattan tonight," said Dominika. She had a mild goal of getting the woman to talk a little, to see what she could learn. *But carefully.* "This Staten Island is a strange place." The silhouette shrugged.

"It is remote, quiet, and parochial. I find it well suited for operations," she said. *Okay, you operate here. Interesting.*

"I would find all of New York operationally challenging," said Dominika.

"One becomes accustomed to the rhythms of the city," said the woman, vaguely. *She isn't going to volunteer anything. She's too smart.*

"I imagine you do," said Dominika, now talking a little shop between professionals. "But in my assignments I have had to contend with active, hostile opposition on the street. As a civilian you, of course, have greater latitude to operate than does a diplomat officer in the *rezidentura*." The silhouette shifted slightly.

"I suppose so. The magazine industry has provided effective cover over the years," said SUSAN. "It fortuitously is dominated by savvy and aggressive women—our timorous male counterparts are less dynamic. Still, there are disadvantages: dealing with writers can be a trial, you have no idea." *This is going nowhere. Back to business.*

"I have the devices—one each for you and MAGNIT—which will provide secure voice communications. If you need to meet personally, you are to coordinate with Line S. I imagine there are ample discreet sites, equidistant from New York and Washington," said Dominika. She slid the zippered pouch with the EKHO phones across the dusty curved lid of Commodore Vanderbilt's sarcophagus, half expecting to hear him complain from inside about being disturbed in his sleep, by Russians no less.

"MAGNIT has less latitude for travel than I," said SUSAN. "And Washington is an easier counterintelligence environment, even within the city." *Okay, you meet in Washington, in the city. Benford will be glad to learn that.*

"Is there anything else I can do for you?" asked Dominika. "Is there anything you or the asset requires?" A long shot—what couldn't MAGNIT obtain in the United States that SVR could? Gold bullion? Blood diamonds? Polonium? *No more questions. Maybe walk out into the sunlight with her? A glimpse of her halo?*

"*Spasibo*, there is nothing I require," said SUSAN, condescension edging into her voice. Then Dominika saw the smear of dust on the sarcophagus lid where she had slid the zippered pouch, and her thoughts raced.

"Then I have a requirement for you," said Dominika sternly, holding her breath, hoping this would work. "I was given a third encrypted mobile phone for contingency use, including for contacting you. I would not like to carry it back to Moscow through airport security. I will pass it to you to dispose of securely the night before I return home. I, of course, could myself throw it into the river, but that kind of haphazard destruction has proven to be disastrous in past cases—equipment has been recovered by the opposition. You must melt the chip, break apart the handset, and disperse the pieces widely so they will not be associated with each other. Passing the phone to you would not require another personal meeting—I will emplace it at a timed drop of your choosing."

"There are a million places in the city where you can dispose of a phone," said SUSAN, pettishly. She'd been on her own for twenty years, met by servile Line N handlers who never questioned her. Dominika put some menace into her voice, the vocal grit all Russians recognize as looming trouble.

"Your long record of service in America—how many years has it been?— undoubtedly has given you encyclopedic knowledge of the city, which is precisely why I am enlisting your assistance. Given that your own contact numbers are on the instrument, it moreover is an *operational requirement* that we do this," said Dominika, flatly. The shadow of the woman stirred, clearly nettled at being told what to do. But all illegals, especially the long-time ones, feared one thing even more than exposure and capture: recall to Moscow, the end of this cushy existence, the end of comfort and abundance, to be cast down again into the pit of Russian sloth, and bureaucracy, and depravation, with a headquarters desk, a dingy apartment, and perhaps a subcompact car, with a medal to wear at ceremonies, the end of foreign assignments, and even of personal foreign travel. Forever. And this blue-eyed chief of CI just made reference to SUSAN's many years in America, and could conceivably make trouble over a stupid regulation. She sullenly gave Dominika the address of a dead drop in Manhattan along with a description. *Okay, a way to identify our silky-voiced friend.*

But now Dominika had to get to Gable to tell him her plan, before her last two days were spent in the protective shadow of Sergeant Blokhin. No more pushing Little Miss SUSAN. She mustn't become suspicious. Conversation tailed off. The meeting was over.

Consistent with established tradecraft procedures, Dominika left the mausoleum first and returned to Manhattan. She never saw the other woman again. Russians don't say that someone is a top pro, they say *podkovat blochu*, that someone can shoe a flea. This woman was like that: even after a fifteen-minute meeting with the illegal, standing three feet away, Dominika couldn't have picked SUSAN out of a crowd if her life depended on it. And she knew eventually it probably would.

DOMINICK'S SAUSAGE, PEPPER,
AND ONION CALZONE

Sauté thinly sliced red and yellow bell peppers, thinly sliced half-moons of onion, and finely minced garlic until soft. Season, add dried oregano and red pepper flakes. Add crumbled Italian sausage and continue cooking until meat is browned. Let mixture cool, then stir in mozzarella, Parmesan, and chopped parsley. On a floured surface, roll out seven-inch rounds of pizza or bread dough. Place a small amount of meat mixture in the center of the dough circles, then fold over and seal the edges with a water-wet finger. Use a fork to press a flute pattern into the dough along the seam, and poke a small steam hole on top. Brush tops with olive oil. Bake in a medium-high oven on a cookie sheet until golden brown. Let rest slightly and serve lukewarm with heated marinara sauce.

9

Cradle Snacking

The bohemian charm of Staten Island left behind, Dominika and Gable were sitting shoulder to shoulder on the banquette in the back of a little bar in Chelsea on Hudson Street called Employees Only. It was late and the bar was half-full. A small plate of Parmesan frico cups filled with tomato salad sat untouched between Gable's beer and Dominika's wine. Dominika had just finished telling Gable about her trip to Staten Island, going into the Vanderbilt mausoleum, and the spooky meeting in the dark with the illegal. Gable shook his head and took a sip of beer.

"You didn't see her face at all?" Gable said.

"Not even the color of her hair," said Dominika. "She stayed in the shadows the whole time. She was very good. I did not push it."

"Jesus wept. And you think she uses Staten Island to meet agents?" asked Gable.

"She said it was well-suited for operations," said Dominika. "But Staten Island goes on forever. How could you cover it?" Gable shrugged.

"Facial-recognition software in cameras at the ferry terminal might pick her up," said Gable.

"If we knew what she looked like, perhaps," said Dominika. "But we do not."

"Yeah, tell me something I don't know," said Gable. "She could drive her ass over one of the bridges too."

"May I tell you an idea about how we could identify her?" said Dominika. "I am thinking we could take a page out of the old KGB handbook." Gable drank some more beer.

"I could order two more drinks if this is going to take long," he said. Dominika smiled and patted his arm.

"*Terpeniye*, patience, *Bratok*, you will like this," she said. "Now listen. Before I leave New York, I ordered SUSAN—yes, ordered her most sternly—to retrieve my encrypted personal mobile phone from a dead-drop site of her choosing in Manhattan, for destruction and secure disposal."

"And she went for that?"

"I used my colonel's voice on her. Russians respond to bullying."

"You sure as hell don't," said Gable.

"That is because you never bully me," said Dominika.

"I'm too scared to," said Gable. "Okay, you dead drop your phone, we set up an ambush, and bag her ass? That's no good; it puts you in hot water."

"I am not thinking of an ambush, which we must avoid for exactly that reason. We just have to pass the physical item in a timed drop at a site of her choosing, someplace that offers her absolute security. No ambushes, no surveillance at the site."

Gable looked sideways at her. "I'm waiting for the punch line," he said.

"We dust the cell phone with *metka*."

"Smegma?" said Gable, being obtuse. "What the hell's that?"

Dominika laughed. She knew the obscure word from Sparrow School. "You are a real *krutóy páren*, a sharp fellow. You know very well what I said. *Metka*, not smegma. Spy dust, like the KGB used in Moscow to track Americans. I'm sure Benford has chemists who could prepare a compound."

"Moscow will still wonder how they lost their sleeper," said Gable.

Dominika shrugged. "They will not connect me with her eventual arrest, not if you catch her months later by using spy dust. Of course, the Kremlin will be annoyed, but the Center will rationalize that twenty years as an illegal in the United States exceeds all expectations of survival," said Dominika. "I know the Russian mind; they will be looking for someone to blame, but if we do this right, Line S will never divine how she was identified, nor will they appreciate the irony that *metka* was used against them, after all these years. SUSAN will naturally follow orders and destroy the phone, leaving no evidence but her invisibly contaminated hands."

"Not bad. I'll run it by Benford." He picked up his phone, pushed a speed dial, and Westfall appeared in the bar two minutes later, gulping as he shook Dominika's hand again, mumbling like an embarrassed butler. Dominika got up and gave Westfall a chaste hug of greeting, with the result that he turned vermillion. Gable repeated a summary of Dominika's plan to him, told him to call Benford on the secure line and get working on it. They had two days to cook up their own batch of *metka*. Lucius bowed that he understood.

Gable shook his head at Westfall's awkwardness. "You gonna click your heels like a Prussian?"

Dominika dug her elbow into Gable's ribs. "Leave him alone," she said. "Lucius, do you understand the plan?" Lucius nodded.

"We do this right, Domi's in the clear, and sugar britches glows in the dark until Christmas," said Gable.

"What is this sugar britches?" said Dominika.

"Skip it, figure of speech."

"I am sure," said Dominika, looking sideways at him. "Westfall, do you know what it means?" Westfall gulped, shook his head, and left, saying he'd call Benford right now. Dominika felt even sorrier for him than before.

"Okay. So the FEEBS check after hours the offices of the leading literary magazines in Manhattan—how many of them can there be—and see whose spaces glow under a black light," said Gable.

Dominika held up a cautionary finger. "There is some need for attention with *metka*. The KGB had difficulty with overcontamination. In a week, SUSAN will shake many hands, distribute memos, and conduct business lunches in restaurants. In several months, everyone in publishing in New York will be covered in the stuff, not to mention half the talent agents in the United States."

"No one's gonna worry about *them*," said Gable, finishing his beer.

———

Iosip Blokhin was walking down Hudson Street in Chelsea, head pointed down, fixated on the sidewalk, bulling forward without apparent regard for other pedestrians, lampposts, or garbage cans. He did not care about the in-congruity of wearing a massive pair of wraparound fisherman's sunglasses at ten o'clock in the evening, and he ignored the occasional stares from amused passersby. He looked like a sightless wrestler without the tapping white cane. The glasses were in fact developed by Line T to detect faint residual traces of nuclear isotopes in order to track a target at undetectable long ranges. Blokhin was tracking Dominika, on the secret express orders of Major Shlykov, and unbeknownst to Anton Gorelikov. Shlykov had instructed Blokhin to begin tailing "Miss SVR tits," after her Staten Island meeting (even Shlykov would not meddle with that) but continuously thereafter until they departed New York. Shlykov wanted Blokhin to ensure that the SVR would not steal the MAGNIT case, and that Dominika was not meeting with officers from the

New York *rezidentura* preparatory to claiming primacy, or engaging in any number of bureaucratic maneuvers to usurp the case. Shlykov stipulated to Blokhin that Egorova was not to know about the surveillance—he would not risk the wrath of Gorelikov—so coverage was to be invisible.

"She's supposed to be good on the street, so let her go if you can't cover her discreetly," Shlykov had told Blokhin. "Do not let her see you."

The Spetsnaz gorilla picked his teeth. "What if I see her doing something interesting?" he said quietly.

Shlykov had looked at the scarred forehead. "Like what?" he said.

"Like meeting someone I don't recognize," said Blokhin.

Shlykov looked him in the eyes. "It could be an officer from the *rezidentura.*"

"Perhaps. But if it's not someone I know, it could be a double deal. Maybe even on Gorelikov's orders."

"What are you saying?" said Shlykov.

Blokhin looked at his hands. "Egorova is not yet Director of SVR, and she is already causing problems. When they give her a star she'll be untouchable."

Shlykov turned away from Blokhin to shuffle some papers. "You already have one problem to eliminate."

"Why leave a second one to fester?" asked Blokhin.

"Only if you are one hundred percent. No traces."

"Chemu byt, tomu ne minovat," said Blokhin, "things that were meant to be will happen, no matter what."

With Shlykov's brevet to operate against Egorova, Blokhin waited for Dominika's departure for Staten Island, entered her hotel room, and using a tool resembling a grommet punch, sunk a pinhead-sized disk of the medical isotope Palladium-103—used for cancer radiation treatment—into the leather heels of the three pairs of shoes in her little closet and returned them exactly as he had found them, after an appraising sniff at each shoe. The tiny Palladium tags in her shoe heels would leave luminous orange dots viewable by special gamma glasses on pavement, flat carpet, marble, or wood, but would be scattered and obscured in leaves, grass, or sand. Palladium-103, moreover, had been chosen as a surveillance tool for its rapid decay rate, which would ensure a target would not inadvertently discover the tracking technique. The orange dots therefore would just support "over-the-horizon" surveillance but had a tendency to dissipate in adverse weather or on less than ideal surfaces. Stronger, more pervasively radioactive isotopes had been ruled out when tests on Gulag prisoners resulted in an unacceptable rate of bone marrow cancers and foot amputations.

Blokhin was trying to follow Egorova in Chelsea from her hotel using "trailing-bread-crumb" surveillance but the brisk temperatures and a light mist were dissipating the tag marks. When he lost the trail for the third time, he crossed the street to see if he could pick up the trail, but after another thirty minutes, he gave up. There were two more days, and perhaps something would develop.

─────────

As Dominika sat in the little bar next to Gable, her face blanched and a shot of ice went up her spine. She saw through the bar's far window Blokhin's thick body walking on the sidewalk. In five seconds he would be past the window directly opposite their banquette table. All he had to do would be to look inside—the interior was brighter than the street outside—and he would see Dominika sitting alone with a man in a city she didn't know, had never visited before and conclude only one thing. *Spion*. Spy. She grabbed Gable's arm in a panic; the banquette trapped her, and she couldn't slip under the table. She pointed with her chin and whispered "Blokhin, outside."

Gable didn't hesitate, and he moved so fast that Dominika felt his arms around her shoulders in a twisting clinch that had his broad back to the window and Dominika totally screened before she felt his lips on hers. "Move," Gable growled into her mouth, and she ran one hand through his crew cut. His arms were like steel around her, and his kiss was dry and firm. He smelled like soap and leather. She opened one eye and looked out the window and saw that Blokhin was gone. "Clear?" whispered Gable.

"Give it ten seconds more," said Dominika, giggling, her cheek against Gable's. He let her go and sat back, looking at her ruefully.

Dominika knew there was not a thought of sex in the kiss. Gable had reacted as quickly as he would have drawn his pistol on a gomer with an AK-47 in a Beirut alleyway—he just used what was available: an enveloping smooch. But Gable for all his gruffness was chaste to her, always had been. Nate had told her once that a young Gable had been married when he joined the Agency a million years ago to a beauty who was on her way to becoming a first-rate concert pianist. But the Life in the Third World claimed more of Gable than his bride was willing to give, and his frequent absences, the constant moving, and having to boil the tap water to kill the *Giardia* parasites was too much. She left Gable the morning that F-sharp above middle C wouldn't play, and she lifted the lid on the baby grand and found a horned puff adder asleep on the felt hammers. Gable resolved to patch things up, but a year later she died in a crash on an icy highway four miles from home. Gable was in Peru facilitating the kinetic retirement of a local drug dealer who had brought a knife to a gunfight when they told him. He never married again, but Nate had whispered that her name was Moira—he never talked about her, except once to Nate. That's what the Life leaves you, Nate had said to Dominika during one of his harangues about defecting.

Gable's face was serious over the near miss with Blokhin. "Is this gonna be trouble?" he asked. "Was he tracking your phone?" Dominika shook her head.

"I did not carry the phone today. I made sure I was black before I met you tonight, absolutely, but yes, I think he was looking for me. He knows where my hotel is, he could have done a long tail from there and was just casting blind along my general route to see if he could pick up my scent. We call it *promyvochnyye ptitsy*, to flush a bird, an old technique. Gorelikov swore Blokhin wasn't in New York to check up on me, but I don't believe it. I will see if he asks about where I was tonight. *Na Volosok ot*, a close call. Imagine being caught in such a big city."

She looked at him, tilting her head. "It is not just shooting bad men; you also kiss very well, just like James Bond. I had no idea. But after tonight I can no longer call you *Bratok*, big brother. It would be inappropriate, after kissing you. I'll have to call you *ledenets* from now on."

"Don't start with me," growled Gable, blushing. "The fuck's that mean?"

"*Ledenets*," said Dominika. "Sugar candy, like your sugar britches." Gable blushed some more, and Dominika laughed, slid over to him, kissed his cheek, and mussed up his crew cut with her fingers. He wouldn't look at her, which she found endearing.

A slovenly waiter sidled up to the table with the bar bill, having watched the old guy and Chesty McThrust necking in the corner. Gable glowered at him. "What're you looking at?" he said. Dominika was red in the face from holding in laughter.

"Nothin,'" said the waiter. "No law against cradle snacking." Dominika clapped a hand over her mouth, eyes streaming.

———————

Benford sat behind the ruin of his desk in the Counterintelligence Division at CIA Headquarters. A three-tray inbox bursting with papers on one side of the desk was missing a foot and tilted dangerously. A dozen three-ring binders were stacked on the other corner of the desk, creating a redoubt from behind which Benford scowled at the two people sitting in his office. Benford was short and slightly paunchy, and this morning his hair looked as if it had been tugged on like a salt-and-pepper beret. His big brown cow's eyes passed over the two officers sitting in front of him and settled on a sepia-toned framed photograph of James Jesus Angleton, the legendary mole hunter whose fanatic belief that the Soviets were running moles inside CIA had paralyzed Langley's Russian operations for a decade. The photograph of Angleton, like a number of other objects in Benford's office, tilted drastically. No amount of straightening would keep the photo frame squared off—every morning it would be slanting again, confirming for Benford his private belief that the spirit of James Jesus resided in his office and knocked the photo askew every night, which suited him just fine.

The two officers sitting in torn bucket chairs with wobbly casters waited. One was Lucius Westfall, the precocious analyst from DI, and Benford's new aide. In the other chair slouched the laconic technical officer Hearsey, whom Benford liked and trusted. "Show me what you have done," said Benford. "Time is of the essence. We need to dust her phone tomorrow night."

Hearsey dug into a zippered pouch, took out half a dozen black-and-white photographs, a large tablet, and what looked like an antique perfume atomizer with a black rubber bulb and an oval glass receptacle. "The photographs are of the various items we used to test adhesion of the compound," said Hearsey. "Results are what we expected. Fibrous material—clothing, floor mats, bedclothes—retain the material better and for a longer period of time. Other surfaces like plastic, glass, or metal are not as good."

"The item DIVA will pass the illegal is a cell phone," said Benford. "It's our only choice." Hearsey nodded.

"Yeah, we figured that," he said. "So we bought a cover she can slip over her phone." He slid a photograph across the desk to Benford. "It's made of stretchy silicone that turns out to be sticky as hell, and actually attracts the compound like a frigging lint roller." He held the tablet up, tapped the corner of the screen twice, and the image of a cell phone in a glass laboratory tray appeared in normal overhead light. "We doused the lights and hit it with ultraviolet." The cell phone in the next image glowed a luminous green. Benford looked up from the tablet.

"Why green?" asked Benford.

"Why not?" said Hearsey. "The Soviets used luminol and nitrophenyl pentadien. They added hydrochloric acid that turned their compound red under UV light. We didn't want to mix the same chems, so we used tetrahydro-beta-carboline, the stuff that makes a scorpion carapace glow green under UV. We have a chemist named Bunny Devore in the lab. She loves scorpions, knows all about them, keeps them as pets." Benford gave Hearsey a look like bent rebar.

"Hearsey," said Benford, "I am puzzled by why you think I would be even remotely interested in the chemistry, or about this woman and her unsavory interest in predatory arachnids. All I care about is whether the compound is undetectable. Our agent's life depends on it." Hearsey held up the antique atomizer.

"Spray a target object about two feet away and let the droplets settle evenly. Don't worry. It's invisible; you can't feel it, you can't taste it, you can't smell it. We dissolved the chemicals in methanol so we're actually spraying a light mist on an object, not like dusting something with fingerprint powder. It fluoresces like crazy under UV light in the ten- to four-hundred-nanometer range, and also shows up on a gas chromatograph."

"Yes, I'm sure it does all this and more," said Benford. "How long does it last?"

"We don't know, simply because we haven't had enough time to test perpetuation," said Hearsey. "It adheres well, and propagation—how it transfers—seems good. If your illegal handles that phone cover, then hits a light switch in her office, touches her keyboard, or drinks coffee from a mug, we can find her." Benford nodded.

"I'll trouble you to courier this personally to New York today with Westfall, connect with Gable, and explain it all to him. I'll ask you to spray the phone and its cover yourself—keep DIVA completely away from it—and ensure she can load the phone in a dead-drop site of the illegal's choosing without contaminating herself." Hearsey nodded and unfolded his lanky frame to stand up and get going.

"Hearsey, I'm appreciative of the work you have done in such a timely manner," said Benford. "You have my thanks. I would have in years past written up an exceptional performance award for you, or a laudatory unit citation for your team, but in the achromatic Agency of today, I am reduced instead to presenting you with a gift certificate to the Starbuck's coffee emporium here in Headquarters so you can enjoy what the gum-chewing young woman behind the counter astoundingly calls a grande café latte, with milk."

Angleton looked down on them slantidicular from the wall.

PARMESAN FRICO APPETIZERS

Mix coarsely grated Parmesan and flour, then season with red pepper flakes and black pepper. Spoon cheese in a medium-hot nonstick pan, flatten gently into a thin disk, and cook until golden on both sides. Drape still-hot frico over an inverted shot glass or teacup and let cool and harden into a Parmesan cup. Fill with a bruschetta mixture of diced tomatoes and shallots, seasoned with sugar, oregano, red wine vinegar, and olive oil.

10

Heaven vs. Hell

The penultimate day in New York. The meeting with SUSAN was concluded, there were no messages from Gorelikov in the Kremlin, and the fund-raising event with Russian dissident Daria Repina was at six o'clock that evening at the Hilton on Sixth Avenue. Dominika made a big show of meeting Blokhin in the morning and walking around Manhattan with him. They had all day. She planned to slip away after the Repina event and meet once more with Gable to spritz her phone with spy dust and emplace it in SUSAN's Manhattan dead drop site, an unknown pocket cemetery on a residential side street. She wouldn't have to accompany Blokhin after six o'clock: they were returning separately the morning after, Dominika through Paris and Bucharest, Blokhin through Berlin.

Blokhin wore a jacket with all three buttons tightly secured, bumpkin-style. He was stiff and formal as they walked, affecting not to look at the wonders of the city: the traffic, the people, and the display windows, as cool as if butter wouldn't melt in his mouth. But Dominika saw him sneaking looks, and she wondered how his Spetsnaz-wired brain was processing the maelstrom of wealth and industry swirling before his impassive face. He walked well-balanced, with his arms at his sides, and his wood-clamp hands hanging loose, free and ready for action. His forehead gleamed in the sunlight. Dominika darted glances at his ruddy profile; he could have been a farmer or an outdoor laborer. Yet the peasant's face reflected God-knows-what horrors. He did not speak to her, and Dominika elected not to make small talk with him. What would they say to each other in any event? Look how tall the buildings are? How much is that in rubles? What did you use to hang the Afghan president's mistress off the palace balcony?

Dominika was taller by a head, but Blokhin's body was thick, no, *dense*, like stone. From behind there was a small bald spot visible through his thinning hair, but he combed his hair to cover as much of it as he could. They were walking on one of the avenues, moving through the crush of pedestrians, when a lanky street person blocked their path, calling Dominika "honey," and asking for a dollar. Dominika had seen this several times before and knew there was no danger but Blokhin, perhaps not understanding—he had told Dominika he spoke no English—in a gliding step put his forearm across the beggar's chest and swept him aside as if walking through a field of ripe wheat. The beggar caught himself, and took a step back toward Blokhin, but the irresistible force of the shove transmitted some jungle warning to avoid confrontation with this cat, and he let them go, shouting obscenities as they walked away.

"You show restraint on the street," barked Dominika to Blokhin in Russian. "We are here in undocumented alias. Back in Moscow you can kill whomever you want. But not here, not when you're with me." Blokhin looked at Dominika as if deciding whether to bite, then looked past her and said *obozhdat*, wait, and pulled open the door to a bookstore, and went in, Dominika on his heels. The store was enormous, with three floors of books on shelves and tables and people reading in overstuffed chairs, the air laced with the aroma of brewed coffee from a café on the second level. Dominika watched Blokhin scan a store directory, squinting like a Visigoth reading a milepost on the road to Rome, until he walked to the fiction section and found Dostoyevsky's *Crime and Punishment*, which he looked at closely, riffling the pages.

"You have no English," said Dominika. "How can you read it?" Blokhin looked at her blankly. "There are editions in the original Russian you could read instead," she said.

"I want to learn English. I will teach myself," he said, as casually as if he had declared "I will learn to bake bread."

Blokhin's black bat wings spread, then folded. He was lying about something, she decided; perhaps he read English. "Why this book?" said Dominika. It was quite amazing, this squat commando gripping the paperback like a pistol, determined to start reading.

"I have been told about this work. It is a great Russian novel." *Told by whom? Sitting around the Spetsnaz squad room honing bayonets, discussing Dostoyevsky?* "It is about permissible murder in pursuit of a higher purpose," said Blokhin with surprising lucidity. *Something you would feel at home with, no doubt,* thought Dominika. She left him gazing at the books, left the bookstore, walked to a shoe store three doors down, and began looking at strappy sandals on display. She meant to conduct a little street test: How would Blokhin react when he looked up from his books to find Dominika gone? Was he here in New York to keep tabs on her?

"Do you like this style?" asked Blokhin, suddenly behind her, making her jump. He was slipping a pair of sunglasses into his jacket pocket, and he took the sandal from her and inspected it, rubbing his dill-pickle fingers over the leather. How had he found her so quickly with hundreds of shops fifty meters from the bookstore? She'd have to double-check her status before meeting Gable tonight. Sergeant Blokhin was someone with secret skills, and not just cutting throats. A copy of his novel was in a small plastic bag.

Blokhin then declared himself hungry and insisted they go into a Korean restaurant for barbecued ribs, which he had consumed in great quantities during past joint-commando exercises in North Korea. Blokhin inhaled the gleaming ribs accompanied by mounds of vermillion kimchi, green onion and cucumber salad, and *ssamjang*, a spicy paste smeared on accompanying lettuce leaves.

Blowing garlic like a contented whale, Blokhin next dived into a sprawling sporting-goods store and spent an hour looking at wire saws, camp hatchets, machetes, and survival knives. His eyes said everything: he expertly appraised each item as a weapon, a killing instrument. "This is an ingenious tool," said Blokhin, running the teeth of a wire saw lightly over his fingertips. "Loop this over a branch, pull it back and forth with these handles, and it cuts wood like a regular *pila*, a saw." *Ingenious indeed*, thought Dominika. *A throat would cut easier than a pine bough.*

"You won't be allowed on the plane with any of this stuff," Dominika told him in Russian. "Cable the *rezidentura* to pouch one back for you, or two: one for Major Shlykov as well. I'm sure his trees need pruning too." Blokhin ignored the comment and put the saw down. Dominika wanted to create just enough enmity between them so that she could feign mounting dislike and impatience, and leave the Repina reception early to rendezvous with Gable.

"It would be wise not to make an enemy of the major," said Blokhin softly, several minutes later, back out on the street.

"Why is that?" said Dominika.

"Because then you would become my enemy," he said, the tips of his black airfoils extending slightly behind his head, like a cobra flaring his neck hood in threat display.

The Grand Ballroom of the Hilton was a colossal space, lighted by chandeliers and triple-gilded lanterns in recessed circular alcoves high on the walls. A crowd of a thousand people filled row upon row of chairs lined up almost to the back of the room. Loggia levels on either side had been reserved for press; television cameras on tripods bristled and television lights bathed the raised stage, framed with a royal purple velour border and leg curtains. A solitary lectern and microphone stood center stage. Blokhin wanted to sit in the front row to listen to Repina's presentation, but Dominika refused, preferring instead an aisle seat halfway back, near the exit doors. Blokhin argued that closer was better until Dominika sat down where she wanted, and refused to budge.

"The seats up close will be in sight of those cameras. You wish to be on the evening news?" Blokhin did not respond but sat down next to her.

The ballroom was abuzz and raucous. Different groups of supporters waved signs printed with FREEDOM FOR RUSSIA, and PUTIN MURDERER, and OUT OF FREE UKRAINE. A number of other placards were printed in Cyrillic. Blokhin nudged Dominika to look at one of these that said HANG PUTIN BY THE NECK. Blokhin's face had taken on a sleepy-eyed languor that, had she known the Spetsnaz sergeant better, would have telegraphed his building rage.

An official came onto the stage, spoke about donating funds to Daria Repina's Free Russia Movement, then began a lengthy introduction, which was briefly interrupted by a knot of young students waving little Russian flags and chanting "Repina, *poshël ty*," which loosely translated meant "Repina, fuck off." Blokhin and Dominika exchanged glances. They knew these pro-Russia agitators were one of the tentacles of the Kremlin's active-measures octopus, a global machine designed to perpetually sow discord, drive wedges, and influence opinion. Tomorrow it might be *dezinformatsiya*, disinformation in a respected US or international paper; the day after, a forged document that would inflame the Arab street against socialist Europe or pit member EU states against one another; and the day after that, political sabotage to fuel a coup in Montenegro to destabilize the Balkans. Active measures were an unceasing staple of the Kremlin's foreign policy, and had been since the Bolsheviks annihilated White Russian exiles hiding in Europe in the 1920s.

A brief scuffle between agitators and supporters broke out, chairs were overturned, and hotel security bustled the pro-Russia hotheads out of the ballroom. As their departing chants died away, the lights dimmed, a spot focused on the podium, and Daria Repina walked onstage to thunderous applause. She was tall and gaunt, with short brown hair in a tight pixie cut that fell in bangs to one side of her face. Her face was severe, lined by the strain of opposing, campaigning against, and exposing the crimes and corruption of the Putin regime for close to a decade. She had begun her jihad against Vladimir Vladimirovich as a little-known journalist, and was muzzled, shoved, and fined by the police for her misdemeanors. The world began noticing when Repina began touring Europe and the United Kingdom, raising awareness during impassioned rallies—the famous speech at Royal Albert Hall in London marked a turning point—and the Free Russia Movement was born. After two months in the United States, serious money started pouring in, and Repina became the face of dissident Russia.

Coy interviewers frequently asked her if she feared for her life. After all, Daria had been preceded by prominent journalists, disloyal government officials, and opposition party luminaries, all of whom were now gone: Nemtsov, Berezovsky, Politkovskaya, Khlebnikov, Litvinenko, Estemirova, Lesin. Shot, poisoned, or fed Polonium-210, they all had been eliminated as threats to the president's sole priority as head of state: to preserve his kleptocracy. Daria would invariably reply that Putin's time was running out, because what he feared most—Russian citizens demonstrating in Red Square—was an inevitability. The eyes of the world were on her now; *she was inviolate.*

Repina started speaking. Her mannish voice was electric, her passion and energy flowed into the ruby-red halo that shone about her head and shoulders, proclaiming passion, courage, and her love for the *Rodina* and for the people of Russia, once serfs, then inmates in a Soviet Union without windows, and now, *impossibly,* serfs again, crying out to the West to understand, to help them be free.

When Repina came out from behind the lectern with the microphone in her hand like a rock star, and railed against the corruption, and the plunder, and the assassinations, and the wars, and the unholy alliances that had to end, the audience came out of their seats and cheered. Dominika kept her face impassive, but inwardly she was amazed to hear a Russian speak the truth, and give voice to her own indignant rage that had pushed her to CIA and a mortally dangerous life as a spy. She, Dominika, was working in the shadows, underground, while Repina was standing on the ramparts, in full sight. Her heart raced; this was an epiphany: she wasn't alone; her countrymen were with her.

Blokhin was still in his seat, chin slightly raised, eyes locked on Repina.

———

"I cannot listen to any more of this *kramola*, this sedition," said Dominika, getting up, faking impatience. "I'm going to my hotel to sleep. I have an early flight." Blokhin didn't move, but kept staring at the tall crusader in the spotlight, who was walking back and forth along the length of the stage, now excoriating the *siloviki*, the remora attached to the belly of the great white shark, feeding off the tendrils of meat dribbling out of the apex predator's jaws. "Don't start any trouble tonight," she hissed, but he ignored her. Dominika paused at the door to watch Repina onstage, thinking she'd like to meet this charismatic woman someday. Perhaps Benford could arrange it. Then she pushed through the door, late for her rendezvous with Gable (she planned to tease him about her being tormented all day by memories of his kiss, to watch him squirm). A last look at Blokhin, whose black wings were unfolded over his head like a raptor about to take flight.

Repina's presentation had concluded, and she was surrounded onstage by press reporters, admirers, and even people asking for autographs. Blokhin was standing quietly at the fringe of the hangers-on, smiling pleasantly and applauding with the rest of the crowd. It took an hour before Repina and her assistant, Magda, a scruffy young Muscovite activist, were free to go to their room on the sixth floor of the hotel (paid for by the City of New York). They were escorted by two officers of the NYPD, Sergeants Moran and Baumann, veterans of the force—Baumann had served on NYPD SWAT for six years before blowing out a knee during an assault and returning to regular duty. Both men had volunteered for this light protective detail because they needed the overtime; this gig qualified as premium double overtime, and there wasn't any heavy lifting, basically just sitting on a hotel couch watching TV, eating chips, and drinking Coke. Going to the rallies was a pain, but no one was going to mess with Repina in New York City. Both sergeants were in civvies—they wore tweed sports coats over white shirts with Glock 19s in belt holsters on their right hips. Blokhin's practiced eye saw the slight bulges of the 9mm pistols through the cops' coats—called "printing" in concealed-carry circles, but not normally a concern to uniformed cops.

Blokhin just caught the elevator with the four of them, apologetically skipping through the closing doors and nodding courteously to them as he moved to the back of the car. Magda was chatting with Baumann, while Repina stared at Blokhin, her Russian nose sensing something familiar about him, his face, his clothes, the pheromones coming off him.

"Na kakom etazhe vy khotite?" asked Repina quickly in Russian, What floor do you want? Blokhin blinked at her, and in slightly accented British English said, "Excuse me, I'm afraid I don't speak Polish." Repina smiled back and asked, "What floor?" Blokhin said, "Five please," having seen that Sergeant Moran, unmindful of one of the basic techniques of tradecraft, had already pushed the sixth-floor button, thus revealing their destination. Repina stared at Blokhin all the way up, and shrugged as he stepped out on the fifth floor with another nod and a muttered "good evening." The two sergeants watched Scarface Blokhin walk down the hall as the doors eased shut.

"Most popular in his class," muttered Moran to Baumann, who nodded. Repina and Magda didn't get the joke.

In the fifth-floor alcove, Blokhin peeked out, scanned the ceiling, and identified the black fish-eye lenses of the security cameras, one at each end of the corridor. They could not see him in the elevator alcove. He slipped a light full-face neoprene balaclava over his head, pushed through the stairwell fire doors, and ran up one flight. Repina's group was just entering a room halfway down the hallway, and Blokhin waited for them to get inside and close the door. He waited another five minutes, subconsciously flexing his shoulders and loosening his wrists. He walked up to the room, took a cleansing breath, and knocked lightly, as hotel staff or a chambermaid would knock. He dragged the hood off his head and kept his head down.

If Iosip Blokhin had been wired to monitors at that moment, his heart rate would have registered 50bpm, blood pressure, 110/70, and ventilation rate, 12 breaths a minute. His galvanic skin response, an indication of stress measured in microsiemens, was at "resting" levels. He recognized the calm clarity that always came before combat, the sudden acuity in vision, and the sharpening of both his sense of smell and hearing. He savored the icy edge of immediate action and the gummy relish of imminent killing. He could hear muffled footfalls on the carpet coming closer. The peephole darkened a second, then came the rasp of the dead bolt moving past the strike plate as the door opened.

Blokhin hit the door with his right shoulder, snapping the security chain and hitting Officer Baumann in the forehead with the edge of the door, and he fell back hitting the wall with his head, trying to get on his feet, but Blokhin closed like a leopard on a baboon, and hit him in the throat with a web-hand strike, compressing his trachea, and sending the cop gasping to the floor, where Blokhin stomped on his Adam's apple, totally crushing his windpipe. Blokhin rolled the strangling cop butt-high to fish out the Glock from his holster; extracted the fifteen-round magazine to check it; then racked the slide as he walked into the sitting room of the minisuite, picking up a bright throw pillow from an armchair and stepping up to Sergeant Moran, who was lying on the couch in his stocking feet watching a baseball game.

"Who was at the door?" said Moran, not looking away from the TV, as Blokhin shot him from a meter away through the pillow four times in the temple, cheek, and jaw, then turned to an openmouthed Magda sitting at the desk and shot her six times through the now-shredded pillow into her gaping mouth, forehead, and throat, knocking her backward in her chair to the floor amid a welter of pillow stuffing and fabric, floating bits of which settled on and stuck to her bloody cheek. Eleven seconds had elapsed since Blokhin knocked on the door.

Daria Repina walked barefoot into the sitting room in a cloud of steam from the bathroom, wrapped in a hotel bathrobe too big for her, toweling her pixie hair. She stopped short, seeing Blokhin in the room, the queer bloke in the elevator, and her natural combativeness took over. She asked him what he was doing in her suite, and to get the hell out, and who the fuck did he think he was? Blokhin faced her, and quietly said, *"Tolko choromu I ne vezot,"* Only the black cat, and no luck. *Mother of God*, thought Repina, only then noticing one of Magda's bare feet sticking up in the air over the upturned chair, and the blood-smeared face of one of the policemen on the sodden couch, and she knew this man was from Moscow sent by Putin, and she ran to the bedroom, turned to slam the bedroom door and get to the phone, but Blokhin threw her on the bed and hit her massively four times with a knife-hand Spetsnaz Cross: a strike to the right side of her neck, crushing the brachial plexus between the collarbone and the first rib, then across backhand to strike the lower left rib cage, staving in the seventh and eighth ribs, which pierced the lower lobe of her left lung, then up across to the left side of the neck, and back down to fracture the right rib cage, puncturing the right lung, each time forcing a grunt out of Repina, now barely conscious. Her body shook as Blokhin sat her up and wrapped his lobster-claw hands on her chin and slowly twisted her head first one way then the other, listening to the green-stick snap as the C2, C3, and C4 cervical vertebrae separated. Repina flopped back on the mattress, staring sightlessly at Putin's henchman. Elapsed time: seventeen seconds.

Blokhin had been instructed to destroy the target with maximum *unizhenive*, maximum humiliation. Moscow wanted Repina to be found in the morning, reduced to a savaged pile of flesh, a demonstration of Russian wrath and a warning to others who dared follow her example. He roughly stripped the bathrobe off her corpse—her skinny body already was a lurid mass of hematomas—and dragged her by one ankle off the bed, her head thumping onto the floor, into the living room, broken neck wobbling, into the middle of the carpet, wrists crossed above her head, and legs kicked out wide, genitals cruelly exposed. He left the other bodies where they were in mute testament to the Kremlin's wrath. Blokhin scratched a *B* on Repina's stomach with the minibar corkscrew (the Cyrillic V for *Vympel* group of Spetsnaz) for investigators to puzzle over. He did not interfere with either of the women; the massacre tableau was enough, and he took a panoramic photo of the room with his cell phone. Total elapsed time: three minutes. *Only the black cat, and no luck.*

As he left the room, sliding his balaclava back over his head, he looked at his handiwork: *Only one thing missing*, he thought. *Colonel Dominika Egorova should be lying on the carpet alongside Repina, staring at the ceiling. D'yavol*, the Devil. He'd tailed her after her return from meeting the illegal, but had lost her too easily—the isotope device was too weak. Shlykov said she was good on the street, and she was, better than anyone he'd encountered before, but she was a spy, after all. He knew she'd eventually make a mistake, and then Blokhin would crush her, like stepping on a snail in the garden.

BLOKHIN'S KOREAN BARBECUED RIBS

Rinse flanken-style ribs in cold water. In a separate bowl, mix soy sauce, brown sugar, rice wine, sesame oil, black pepper, and cayenne. Combine onion, garlic, pears, and ginger, and process to a smooth purée, then add to the soy mixture. Add toasted sesame seeds and a splash of water to thin. Pour marinade over ribs and toss to cover. Chill overnight, then bring to room temperature and discard marinade. Grill or broil until caramelized. Serve on lettuce leaves with *ssamjang* paste, pickled peppers, kimchi, cucumber salad, and steamed rice.

11

Pitch and Roll

Director Alexander Larson owned a Georgian row house on P Street NW in DC, but on the weekends he regularly escaped to his late father-in-law's five-bedroom ranch house near Edgewater, Maryland, on the banks of Pooles Gut, a narrow tidal creek that emptied into the South River below Annapolis, one of the hundreds of tributaries that made up the Chesapeake Bay watershed. Down the sweeping lawn from the house, there was a fixed pier alongside a paved boat-launching ramp. An extended garage behind the house contained two small boats on trailers: one a twenty-five-foot black rigid inflatable boat (RIB) with a center steering console, a Decca radar mounted on an aluminum frame aft, and two 115 hp Mercury outboards, beasts that could push the RIB along at forty knots. The RIB was used by the DCIA's protective detail and had a waterproof locker just forward of the steering console in which were stored two .223-caliber Colt M4A1 carbines.

The second vessel at the back of the garage was Larson's pride and joy: a seventeen-foot Lyman Runabout built in 1961, with a restored lapstrake hull, graceful flared bow, and mahogany spray rails and brightwork. The distinctive angled windshield and the jaunty Lyman pennant on the bow marked the Runabout as a classic, but not as much as the 1955 forest-green, teardrop Johnson Seahorse 25 hp outboard, an antique refurbished to flawless working order, and perfect for running the smooth-riding hull ahead of frequent Chesapeake squalls at twenty knots, or slow trolling for striped bass at nine knots. Two Shimano fishing rods were in beckets along the gunwales with expensive Tekota trolling reels. In a seat locker under the aft banquette were two tackle boxes with lures, jigs, and spoons.

Alex Larson was not a fanatical fisherman, but he enjoyed solitary time out on his boat, and loved preparing striped bass à la Fiorentina, the way he had first tasted it in Rome. His wife did not enjoy going out into the middle of the bay, which could get quite rough and make the round-bottomed Lyman pitch and roll like a floating ninepin, especially in a beam sea at lazy trolling speed. Simon Benford had once reluctantly agreed to go out with

Alex, but the plunging and yawing made him green, and he detested handling live bait, so he vowed the next time to stay ashore and drink Larson's scotch while his friend caught dinner.

At 0600 hours on a crisp fall day, the cloudless eastern sky was going pink as the two agents of DCIA's protective detail backed both trailers into the green water of the creek. They knew Larson would be walking down from the house in fifteen minutes with a thermos of coffee, a flask of bourbon (which they knew he hid from his security guys), and a roast-beef sandwich wrapped in foil made by his housekeeper. The agents today were Bennett and Scott, each with five years' experience on the detail and more than ten years' time in Special Forces. They had examined the undersides of both boats for limpet mines on the keel, checked the lockers on the Lyman, and started the Johnson outboard to let it warm up. Before the Old Man came down from the house, they snapped 30-round magazines into their M4s, charged and snapped the bolts closed, safed the weapons, and put them back into the footlocker. They both additionally carried 17-round, 9mm Glock 17s in Frontier Gunleather CC1 holsters under their sweaters and foul-weather jackets—they knew from experience that once out on the bay, it could get cold and wet in a hurry. They weren't experienced watermen, but they knew the basics.

Once afloat, Bennett and Scott spun the RIB on a dime, and skimmed ahead along the creek to make sure it was clear, the Lyman sedately following, raising hardly a wake in the early light. No one noticed the man in the pickup truck parked on the side of Waterview Drive watching through the trees as the Lyman chugged down Pooles Gut and out onto the South River.

The RIB was infinitely faster than the Lyman, even when the antique was running with the outboard full-out, so Bennett and Scott pushed the throttles flat and bounced ahead to check for traffic downriver as it opened up onto the vast Chesapeake. One of them would always keep the Lyman in sight, and periodically check the radar display set at ten miles range to keep an eye out for the heavies: the tankers and container ships plowing up the channel to Baltimore. They would then pound back to the DCIA, take station astern in a violent turn that sent spray flying in the early sunlight, and throttle back in his wake, smelling the boss's pipe smoke even two hundred feet astern. The process of darting ahead, then racing back was repeated as required, especially if an unknown boat—runabout, cabin cruiser, or tacking day sailer—looked as if it would pass close by.

There was only one rule: the RIB had to keep off at least one hundred yards when the DCIA began fishing. The noise of the burbling Merc outboards would scare off finicky stripers in the Gulf Stream for Christ sake, not to mention around Thomas Point Shoal at the mouth of the river, or Bloody Point Bar, five miles across the bay, off the tip of Kent Island on the Eastern Shore. These two spots were Larson's favorites—productive and not too far from home. He tied on a Slug-Go, a five-inch bone-white plastic worm with a flattened tail that made the lure undulate irresistibly to predatory stripers. He tried the rock ledge around the historic Thomas Point lighthouse: the frivolous hexagonal house on stilts with green shutters and six gables, with the Fresnel light in a pagoda-roofed cupola, like a cherry on a sundae.

No one was home around the ledge; stripers sometimes go deep and suspend, feeding on deep baitfish schools, *not unlike some members of Congress*, Alex thought, retrieving his lure, setting down his rod on the aft deck, and clambering over the front-seat stanchion to sit behind the wheel, a little tricky with the Lyman's tipsiness. He cranked up the Johnson with the electric starter, eased the throttle ahead, and waved to the guys in the RIB who, bored stiff and soporific from the rocking of the waves, actually didn't see the Lyman settle down in the water and swing east to cut across the bay to Kent Island, until the DCIA gave them two shorts and a long on the horn. Embarrassed, they escorted the Lyman across the ship channel, watching for traffic. Larson could estimate where Bloody Point Bar was by taking bearings between the breakwater of the Kent Island Marina and the collapsed seawall off Bloody Point beach. Alex kept his eye on his bearings and about a mile offshore, killed the outboard, stood in the aft deck, balancing easily against the roll, and tried a few casts with a silver spoon. Bennett and Scott in the RIB took station 150 yards upwind of the little Lyman so they'd be drifting down to it instead of away from it.

A typical grimy oyster boat, a Chesapeake deadrise—describing the hard chine or angle of the bottom built for stability—with a plumb bow, forward doghouse, and long open stern, was working closer to the beach, dragging for oysters. The single oysterman was reeling in the sharp-toothed dredge that dislodged the oysters from their beds and scooped them into a steel mesh basket by the bushelfuls. Bennett and Scott didn't know enough to notice that the oysterman was not emptying his dredge, but rather was just casting up and down the beach without result, about half a mile from the Lyman. Alex Larson didn't notice either, because he had already hooked a thirty-inch striper that probably went fifteen pounds, and was intent on bringing in another one. Something else. None of them noticed what an instinctive sailor would have marked in the sky by late morning: the weather.

Heated by the sun, moisture from the Gulf of Mexico was rising over the bay into the atmosphere, where it collided with a stream of cold air, eventually spreading out to create the anvil top of a storm cell. As water built up in the thunderhead, it began to rain, and the temperature variants created wind shears of sixty knots, accompanied by thunder and lightning. Neither Alex Larson nor the agents in the RIB recognized that the thunderhead was building into a classic squall. The rest of the sky was blue, and the surface of the bay was riffled by a mild chop. The oyster boat incongruously kept up its nondredging, marginally closer to the Lyman. Then it happened. From the surface of the bay, the black lowering clouds with slanting rain bands were preceded by a sick gust of hot air, followed by the white froth of torrential rain moving across the water like a visible shock wave. The first sheet of horizontal rain and gale-force wind heeled the Lyman over as a tremendous clap of thunder tore the sky apart and a bolt of lightning lanced into the water beside the boat, the shaft surrounded by green plasma. Larson balanced precariously on the runabout, which was rolling from gunwale to gunwale, as he threw on a rain slicker from the locker. The rain stung his face like needles, and the insane wind got up inside the jacket until he could zip it. He dropped his rod on the deck, and he held on to the side rail, deafened by thunder, wondering if the Lyman would roll all the way over to turn turtle. The wind dropped for a beat, then came roaring back stronger than before, shifting ninety degrees, making the Lyman roll so far over that she shipped a bathtub's worth of slate-gray water. Two more of those and his precious antique would sink from under him. He tried inching toward the forward stanchion to get to the wheel, to start the outboard and get her bow into the wind where she'd settle down and where her nose-up attitude would let the self-bailing bilges get the seawater out of her, but he couldn't let go. The damn hull was still rolling, and Larson's face was slapped by sea spray at each downward roll. He looked with amazement as a rubber glove rose out of the foaming water, then another, to grasp the side rail and pull violently down with the next roll. Larson was tilted so far forward that the gunwale banged his knees and he catapulted into the water. The salt stung his eyes—his glasses had flown off—and he felt his clothes and boots filling with water, and he knew he had to shuck off his boots, get out of his slicker, and kick to the surface. Bennett and Scott would be alongside to haul him into the RIB, bail out the Lyman, and tow her home. Instead he felt the rubber glove grasp him by the collar of his rain gear, turn him upside down, and begin pulling him deeper, where the water was colder, and where the stripers eyed the fluorescent lures dangled by men in cockleshell boats up there in the sunlight. Alex Larson did not think of Vladimir Putin as his breath gave out and he swallowed seawater.

———

Like their protectee, the agents in the RIB saw the squall line too late. They watched from about two hundred yards away as the Lyman was overtaken by a curtain of rain, obscuring it completely. The lightning and thunder were incessant. Scott had already pushed the throttles forward to get the RIB closer to the Lyman to steady her and help their chief. A large wave broke over the snub nose of the unsinkable inflatable, but they still shipped green water that cascaded down the vessel and around the steering console, knocking both of them off their feet. With no one at the wheel, the RIB careened in an insane circle just as the wind shifted ninety degrees and partially lifted the rubber hull, almost flipping it airborne and upside down. Both agents hung on to the straps along the pontoons while the RIB at full power continued to pound into the waves in wild crazy eights. Bennett finally got to the wheel, reduced power, and tried to get his bearings. With the sheeting rain and the spray, visibility was less than twenty feet. With no landmarks, and no shoreline visible, both agents were disoriented and didn't know where the DCIA's boat was. They checked the radar and saw a speck that could have been the Lyman and raced to it in the stinging rain to find instead a crab-pot buoy that had broken loose and was bobbing in the waves. They still had no idea which way the Lyman lay—they might as well have been in midocean and racing around could take them farther away. After ten more minutes, the squall passed, and as the last of the fat drops pattered on the rubber hull of the RIB, the sun came out. Half a mile in the distance, the Lyman's white hull was visible through the water mist that still clung to the surface.

The agents raced up to the Lyman, which was still rolling madly, the fishing rod and reel sliding on the deck. There is nothing as ominous as an empty boat drifting on the water, mute testimony of a soul reclaimed by the sea. As a frantic Bennett radioed the Coast Guard, then called the security-duty office at Headquarters, Scott at full speed started a grid search downwind for any sign of the DCIA, who they knew did not wear a life jacket. They had been out of visual sight of the Lyman for approximately nineteen minutes, and there was no other boat within a mile of them. The foul weather had even driven the oyster boat into harbor. What followed was the usual two days of Coast Guard daylight searches by helicopters and crash boats, concentrating on the lower bay, based on the estimated time of the accident and the prevailing ebb tide. Alex Larson's body was finally found on the third day, facedown on a sandbar off Race Hog Point on Pone Island, about fifty miles south of Kent Island. The FBI investigated the incident with the Coast Guard, and both concluded that the DCIA had drowned as a result of the boating accident.

When official news of the accident was released, President Putin, against the advice of Anton Gorelikov, called the US president to express his sympathy at the loss of a dedicated professional, a committed public servant, and a man of honor. The Slavic mordancy in Putin's comments was lost on POTUS, who already was considering candidates to fill the DCIA position. As Gorelikov had presciently predicted, VADM Rowland was on the president's short list of DCIA nominees. All that toadying to POTUS's vanity had paid off. She was an outsider, a brainy woman, and someone who believed in diplomatic solutions with coalition partners, rather than resorting to armed conflict at the drop of a hat. He looked to Admiral Rowland to continue the reforms within CIA in diversity, promotion quotas, and, frankly, fewer dirty tricks that only antagonized foreign governments.

At Langley, relevant branches in the Operations Directorate tasked Russian and counterterrorist sources to determine whether there were any known plots to harm the Director. Not even DIVA had heard anything in the Kremlin, and she sent her condolences via a Moscow Station officer to Benford, who was inconsolable.

Simon confided to Forsyth that he suspected the Russians had engineered the boating accident, which was nothing less than a political assassination ordered by Putin. Benford summoned Hearsey to ask him about short-range drones that could be fitted with an explosive payload, or aerosolized biological compounds, or even with a single 2.75-inch rocket. Maybe an infiltrated operator could fly a drone close enough to catch Putin outside during a fishing or hunting trip and avenge the DCIA. Hearsey looked at the floor without saying anything until Forsyth told Benford to stop hallucinating and to concentrate on their more immediate problem: vetting the White House's three nominee candidates for DCIA, a triumvirate of progressive Washington insiders, none of whom was well-disposed to the Agency.

"Maybe we should reconsider those drones," said Hearsey, walking out the door.

Three combat swimmers from Spetsnaz *Vympel* Group 3—a unit based in Moscow and normally used by SVR to execute sensitive "wet work" assignments abroad (beatings, kidnappings, and assassinations)—were not returned to their unit after an unspecified special assignment, but rather were reassigned to a naval infantry unit at the Northern Fleet's Bolshaya Lopatka naval base above the Arctic Circle, on the Kola Peninsula, seventy kilometers east of the sliver of Norway's northern border with Russia. The three troopers were given privileges to the officers' commissary on base, and weekend passes to Murmansk once a month. They knew enough never to mention the Chesapeake Bay, especially since a goateed dandy in the Kremlin had warned them of the consequences of indiscretion. They had no desire to be residents of *Upravlenie solovetskogo* and *Karelo-Murmanskikh ITL*, the Directorate of Solovki and Karelia-Murmansk Camps, once Gulags filled by Stalin, but now grim modern district prisons, albeit with the original 1935 plumbing.

STRIPED BASS À LA FIORENTINA

Sauté fish fillets in butter and oil until golden. Set aside. In a saucepan, sauté whole peeled tomatoes, anchovies, chopped garlic, chopped cilantro, capers, a splash of balsamic vinegar, and thinly sliced potatoes until potatoes are soft and sauce is thickened. Serve fish on a bed of sauce.

12

Merit to the Fatherland

The drowning death of DCIA Alex Larson devastated the CIA workforce, and the turnout of silent, numb employees at the service in front of the memorial wall of stars chiseled into the marble, representing CIA officers lost in the line of duty, was so large that the front lobby overflowed and hundreds of attendees had to watch on closed-circuit screens set up in the cafeteria. Simon Benford was convinced that the Kremlin had engineered the DCIA's death, and continued tasking operational desks to canvass assets for any indication of Russian complicity in the matter.

The shocking loss of the DCIA was compounded by another catastrophe: sudden and inexplicable arrests inside the COPPERFIN spy network. A score of recruited design engineers in the OAK aerospace consortium were suddenly arrested by the FSB, and interrogations were being held around the clock in an attempt to identify other network members. Only two assets continued sporadic reporting, and their messages were panicked and barely coherent. COPPERFIN couriers were able to exfiltrate a handful of agents—in one case an entire family—but an equal number were caught and arrested at the border. At last count at least twelve sources did not respond to "sign of life" signals, and were unaccounted for, their status unknown. Benford knew very well that this was the worst case in the running of a large network—the inexorable unraveling, the continuing interrogations, the desperate attempts to escape, the arrests, and, ultimately, the triumphant news releases from the Kremlin.

Benford knew that the COPPERFIN meltdown was the work of MAGNIT. But based on the chaotic counterintelligence performance of the FSB—they were picking apart the network in fits and starts, rather than in a complete roundup—Benford was convinced that the mole did not have direct access to COPPERFIN and had learned about the network incompletely and serendipitously. In the lexicon of spooks, MAGNIT had "vacuumed up" the information: an overheard conversation, whispered gossip, an intemperate aside, the contents of an inbox read upside down. Windfall collection that could not implicate the mole, and left the FSB free to act decisively. No BIGOT list, therefore, could be used to flush the traitor.

"The trouble with running a mole hunt," said Benford to Gable and Forsyth, "is that you cannot announce it, or drag suspects in for CI interviews, or immediately begin combing through one hundred thousand computerized personnel files, or tap the phones and computers of likely candidates without approvals and warrants. And you cannot brief a bunch of FEEBs, whose immediate reaction is to get into a black Crown Vic and interview suspects at home, asking them outright whether they are currently, or have ever, cooperated with a foreign power. They expect immediate compliance—it's a crime to lie to the FBI, after all. The cumulative effect of their blandishments, of course, is to alert the mole, who heads for the hills, resulting in a permanent-resident visa from the Russian Ministry of Foreign Affairs, and an FSB-provided high-rise apartment in Babushinsky District, from the shabby comfort of which the traitor can listen through the clapboard wall every Saturday night to his neighbors fucking."

"Now we have a new problem," said Forsyth. "MAGNIT apparently is getting around some more. He's hearing about secrets like COPPERFIN. He's disappearing into the woodwork."

"He's a fucking flaming cactus," said Gable. "The key is the goddamn railgun. Domi told me MAGNIT has been in harness for ten or twelve years. That's gotta be key; who's been on the railgun project that long?"

Benford swiveled in his chair. "We're running all the combos, but it could be someone who *previously* worked on that project, but no longer. DIVA reported that MAGNIT is moving up to a policy job. That widens the field."

"Okay," said Gable. "But Domi mentioned that fancy-pants guy in the Kremlin wants to handle MAGNIT solely by the New York illegal, and take the case away from GRU goobers. With so much infighting, Domi may eventually find out MAGNIT's true name on a restricted list."

"We can't wait that long," said Benford. "We're hemorrhaging secrets."

"We may not have to. There's a lot of intrigue going on in the Kremlin," said Forsyth. "Not like the years Brezhnev shit his diaper and they held him upright to sign the disarmament treaty. DIVA says Gorelikov runs his own shop, is loyal to Putin, but does things his own way. He's gunning for the GRU. DIVA is ripe for promotion. She's going to get that name." Benford shook his head doubtfully.

"Dangerous territory for our girl with all these plots," said Gable. "We got to keep an eye on her. She's running a little hot these days, temperamental-like. She needs replacement SRAC gear ASAP."

Benford groaned at that. "There is no replacement SRAC. Our inscrutable colleagues from China Operations requested and received the last two available systems, which already are slaved to satellites in geosynchronous orbit to cover the Asian theater. They would not give up either one of them. Their refusal was polite but implacable, which I believe once again proves my contention that operational offices acquire the cultural characteristics of their target countries. Quite inscrutable.

"The SRAC larder is now officially bare. The last time this happened, the Carter White House suggested we use HF radio and Morse code. The Acting Director just ordered that R&D for the next generation of SRAC be put on hold. He wants to divert the tech budget to launch satellites that calibrate global warming. Orders from the NSC."

"Are you fucking shitting me? Leave inside assets without covcom?" said Gable.

Benford ran his fingers through his already anarchic hair. "I am throwing histrionic fits at every leadership meeting, but the bureaucrats are unmoved and singularly focused on the one degree Fahrenheit change in global temperature since Charlemagne. Hearsey is racking his brains on cobbling together some sort of emergency-signaling gear, but as of today we've got nothing on the shelf for her.

"We will have to rely on personal meets for the time being," said Benford, wearing his February face. Every person in the room knew that each time Moscow Station—or any denied-area station—tried a personal meet, the probability of catastrophic flap (and loss of agent) rose to 90 percent. Opposition surveillance had to get it right only once, and your agent was dead. Russia, China, Cuba, North Korea, it didn't matter.

"Personal contact with Domi is coming up in three days," said Gable. "They got a good operator to meet our girl?"

"Case officer named Ricky Walters," said Benford, reading off a cable from Moscow Station. "Looked him up. Good on the street, ice for nerves, likes the ladies, but no zipper trouble in Russia. He looks okay."

Gable grunted. "In her current pissed-off state, she's not gonna be happy without covcom. Hope he doesn't try to get saucy with her," he said. "He'll start his return SDR with a kick in the nuts. She doesn't need another Romeo. Nash is pissing her off enough as it is."

"Tell me that's still not a problem, Nash and DIVA," said Forsyth.

"They're fucking in love," said Gable, holding up his hands. "I know, I know, but if you fire Nash, Domi might flat-out quit on us; she's in that frame of mind lately. So you tell me what's worse, them belly thumping or her quitting."

"We may be able to put some space between those thumping bellies," said Benford. "The Aussies have a clambake brewing in Hong Kong, and they think they might need a Russian speaker. If we send Nash it'll keep him away from her for a while. We can only hope that an extended separation will result in atrophy of one or both of their libidos." No one laughed.

"Christ, is there any good news? What about that illegal in New York?" said Forsyth.

"Everything's done," said Gable. "Hearsey spritzed the phone and we wrapped it so Domi could load the dead drop in some crazy little 1805 Jewish cemetery on West Eleventh Street in the Village. Thirty moss-covered tombstones on a little triangle of land behind a peeling wall. You'd walk by it all day without seeing it. She put the package behind the middle headstone of three against the brick wall; it tilts forward, so she wedged the package down low. We left it alone, lots of apartment windows around. That gal could be watching the drop."

"We'll give it some time, to insulate DIVA, then go up to New York with fifty UV flashlights and bag us an illegal," said Benford.

———

After New York City—even including Staten Island—feeling the energy, and prosperity, and *freedom* of America, Dominika had returned to Moscow, which in comparison she now found sluggish, gray, and sad. Back in her office, she attacked her in-box and read through the backlog of SVR global counterintelligence developments. Overseas *rezidenturi* reported three separate recruitments—in Venezuela, Indonesia, and Spain. The Signals Intelligence Agency, the FAO, had developed access to an encrypted military communications channel in the Baltics. The *rezidentura* in Washington, DC, reported the beginning of discreet developmental contact between an SVR intelligence officer operating under nonofficial business cover and a Congress-woman from California. The legislator was showing herself to be amenable to a lucrative consulting contract on international development policy and multilateral foreign assistance. The Washington *rezident* cautiously predicted that an eventual recruitment would be based on money—the representative had previously been implicated in a House banking scandal involving check kiting—and was judged to be corrupt and venal.

These were important intelligence tidbits, but she could not report them to Langley for lack of functioning SRAC equipment. Last weekend, she had buried the SRAC gear damaged in the fight with the street toughs in a hole in Vorontsovsky Park, ten kilometers outside the ring road southeast of Moscow, on the forested grounds of the abandoned eighteenth-century neo-Renaissance Vorontsov-Dashkov Manor. It would be decades before the excavations for the high-rise developments inexorably spreading out from Moscow would reach this far, and by then the city might well be re-named Putingrad, with homeless zombies roaming the dystopian suburbs. By then she hoped she would be lying on a sun-drenched veranda some-where tropical, sipping rum while Nate painted her toenails Island Pink and, maybe, she dreamed, with a little girl at their feet chattering to her dolls in Russian and English. *Would my children be synesthetes? What would Nate say after all these years of keeping the secret? Would we be happy together? Will it ever happen?*

Dominika instead minutely printed her report in pencil on both sides of two sheets of water-soluble paper—it would dissolve to mush instantly on contact with liquid—and rolled the sheets into a tight tube. She unscrewed the bottom of a clunky Russian Pukat-brand thermos bottle and slid the pa-per into the narrow space between the interior glass vacuum chamber and the plastic outer case. In an emergency, throwing or whacking the thermos against a hard surface would shatter the inner-glass chamber, flooding the space between the outer shell, rendering the paper the consistency of *ovsy-anaya kasha*, Russian oatmeal. If you had to use this prehistoric destruction device (Nate had showed it to her in Finland), you already were probably stopped at the roadblock about to be carted off, but it was effective. The per-sonal meet was in two days, and pray God they're sending someone smart. She fantasized it would be Nate coming out of the shadows to wrap her up and kiss her forever in the fog-shrouded woods.

Then the inevitable courtly call from Gorelikov, welcome back, congratulations on the meet with SUSAN, and the president would see them this afternoon at his Novo-Ogaryovo residence outside Moscow in the Odintsovo District on the Rublyovo-Uspenskoye Highway. The yellow mansion, nestled among pines, with its classical peaked façade and four Corinthian columns, seemed small and modest when compared with the regal apartments of the Kremlin. They were shown into a living room of pale blue with peach-colored satin curtains, sat at a small antique table, and listened to a clock ticking from a corner bookcase across the room. Anton Gorelikov was stylish as usual, in a tailored dark suit and starched tape-stripe shirt. Delicate ceramic cuff links in blue and green showed at his sleeves. The blue halo about his head and shoulders was like a diadem, and glowed in exultation.

They were served tea in elegant *podstakanniki* glasses emblazoned with the double-headed eagle of the new Russian Federation, ironically similar to the bygone imperial eagle of the Romanovs and the tsar. *Plus ça change, plus c'est la même chose*, thought Dominika, *The more things change, the more they stay the same.* A young aide in a light-blue suit stood against the wall near the door, eerily blending into the blue paneling like some color-adaptive rain forest lizard, so that only his face was visible and seemed to be floating in the air. Dominika reflected that disembodied heads floating in the air seemed normal in a Putin residence.

The little gold and ormolu clock chimed eleven, and at that instant the door opened and the president walked in. *How does he do that?* thought Dominika. *Was he outside the door, hand on the knob, waiting for that infernal clock to chime? Or was the clock connected to an unseen power source and made to chime as the president entered?*

Vladimir Putin was, as ever, dressed in a navy suit, white shirt, and trademark aquamarine tie. His blue halo likewise was pulsing with energy. Why shouldn't it be? He had consolidated his hold on Crimea and secured his Black Sea naval base; the rearguard action in Eastern Ukraine kept Kiev off balance; alliances with Damascus and Tehran were paying dividends politically, and he was a major player once again in the Great Game. Oil. Munitions. Uranium (ROSATOM even owned 20 percent of America's mined uranium). And there was more.

Activniye meropriyatiya. Active measures, political subversion, propaganda, media manipulation, forgeries, and assassination. Gorelikov's campaigns in Europe and the United States were shaking the trees of NATO, the EU, and those upstart pricks in the Baltics. That maniac Kadyrov kept Chechnya quiet, and his own presidential domestic approval rating was holding steady at 85 percent. Gorelikov was conceiving new mayhem, and Egorova was a new talent, a steady hand in the field. The president wondered how steady her hand would be in bed. He had checked: no husband or significant other, a former Sparrow, and the resident expert in honey traps. He was sure Egorova would figure into his further plans, especially with his gift today. The president nodded to Gorelikov and Dominika, and sat down. An aide put a square velvet box on the table in front of the president, and read from a sheet of paper.

"*Medal ordenia «Za zaslugi pered Otetchestvom» I Stepeni,*" he bellowed. "Medal for the Order 'for Merit to the Fatherland,' first-class. Awarded to citizens of the Russian Federation for outstanding achievements in various fields of industry, construction, science, education, health, culture, transport, and other areas of work." *Other areas of work*, thought Dominika.

The president opened the velvet box and stood. Dominika and Gorelikov also stood, and Putin presented the box to Gorelikov. Nestled on a bed of blue satin was a starched claret ribbon with a tooled hanging gold medallion with the ubiquitous double eagle. Order for Merit to the Fatherland. Putin stepped up and pinned a small red ribbon bisected by a single yellow stripe to the lapel of Gorelikov's suit. Gorelikov bowed slightly and shook the president's hand. The aide unobtrusively reached over and took the velvet box, softly snapped the lid shut, and left the room. In the nature of commendations for clandestine missions, the award would be stored in the Kremlin—Gorelikov would not be allowed to hang the medal in his office or take it home. All he could do was finger the rosette in his lapel and bask in the knowledge of his accomplishment.

"The planning for the Repina operation was flawless, its execution precise, the results exceedingly satisfactory," said Putin. Gorelikov bowed again, slightly.

"Thank you, Mr. President," he said. Dominika's mind reeled. *The Repina operation? What is this? Was she assaulted? Or simply framed in some false scandal?* Then she knew. *Blokhin. That's why he came to New York. Repina was getting too loud, raising too much money, and attracting too much attention. She's gone.*

This was a crushing shock, to find out a full two days after the act. She had been traveling the entire day after and hadn't seen any news reports—perhaps the New York authorities had held the news of the murder for a day. And it was no mystery that the assassination was not mentioned in the SVR news roundups stacked in her Line KR in-box. What would they say? *We report the unfortunate demise of activist Daria Repina, who passed away from unspecified causes in New York City, once again exposing the unchecked violence in American cities, and the lawlessness inherent in American culture?* The news would break in Moscow soon enough, but Putin's control of the Internet and television would distort the reporting and the Moscow *militsiya* would disperse mourners before serious demonstrations could coalesce, while Putin sanctimoniously called for bogus investigations.

Dominika swayed on her feet, telling herself to stay in control, to remain impassive. She felt faint and pinched her wrist to clear her head. She did not have to obsequiously applaud this kind of murder, but neither could she show revulsion, which would be considered a fatal weakness. Gorelikov was speaking again and Dominika forced herself to concentrate. They had killed Repina.

"I must highlight that Colonel Egorova's performance in support of the MAGNIT operation was brilliant. Without her operational acumen we would not be congratulating ourselves. I commend her highly." Dominika could see only the lanky body of Daria Repina on the stage pacing back and forth, railing internally against this man with a wry smile of satisfaction on his face standing a meter from her.

"I am aware of Colonel Egorova's performance and contribution," said Putin. "Her diligence is constant affirmation of my decision to appoint her Chief of Counterintelligence in SVR. I am confident that she will attain to the Directorship of the Service." He looked slyly at Dominika, judging her reaction to essentially being told that she one day would be Director. She nodded her head in thanks. *You bastard.* Putin was pleased. Gorelikov was pleased. *Benford would be pleased.*

"Thank you, Mr. President," said Dominika, fighting to conceal her rage. "I will try to continue to be worthy of your trust." *Such verbal pap,* thought Dominika, *the Russian version of small dogs lying flat in the presence of an alpha dog. But* zlodey, *you hellkite, you do not know that I am inside your house to bring it down, to rid the* Rodina *of you. What do you think of that? Can you read my thoughts?*

As if he had heard, Putin gave her his trademark watery smile, like slivers of ice in warm beer. "I have designated a dacha on the compound at Cape Idokopas for your exclusive use. The weather on the coast is mild well into October."

Through her fury, she was caught unawares. It was something. Even as Dominika thanked the president anew, she calculated furiously. A *gosdacha*, short for *gosudarstvennaya dacha*, was a State-owned vacation home on a lake or river, or in the cool piney forest, parceled out to functionaries to reward diligence, productivity, or loyalty. This particular dacha, however, was more than a three-room birch-plank cottage with a garden plot outside Nizhny Novgorod. This was one of the luxury hillside concrete villas within Putin's seventy-hectare complex on the Black Sea coast, on wooded Cape Idokopas. The presidential residence there, an Italianate château as big as Buckingham Palace, was said to cost a billion dollars. Being given this sort of dacha on this particular compound signaled patronage on a grand scale.

Dominika knew this was all a sticky spiderweb. Gorelikov's medal was presented to him today with her present for two reasons: Putin was establishing that Gorelikov was senior, and that men gave important medals to other men, a Slavic reminder of her subordinate gender. Everyone knew the president greatly preferred the company of men—the *siloviki* comprised only men, but Egorova was edging toward becoming a potential insider. The second reason was this was a medal for eliminating a dissident, a look inside the furnace. *Kill as I command, and you will be rewarded.* There was still another nuance: though a handsome reward, the villa carried with it the hint of setting up one's mistress in her own residence, connected to the master's manor by a secret garden path. As the *levsha zhena*, the left-hand wife, you are expected to be ready for the tsar, bathed and perfumed, on satin pillows, your ruby fruit wet and swollen, waiting for the discreet scratching on the garden door, day or night.

He expected her to be his left-hand wife. Dominika swallowed the familiar rage in her gut that joined the anguish in her heart for Repina. All the villas and all the ribbons in the world could not lessen what this queer little blond schemer was doing to her Russia as citizens waited for their delinquent pension checks to buy bread. Putin and his inner circle—*Does this include me, am I now a* silovik, wondered Dominika, *as a luxury dacha recipient?*—had starved the country. *And no end in sight*, she thought, *to this corruption, and no end in sight to my life as a spy.* She wondered whether General Korchnoi had felt the same, committed to this mortally dangerous work, strangely fueled by midnight adrenaline, yet trapped with no way out. God, how she needed Nate right now.

This all skittered through her mind in a second. Putin was saying something, and she struggled to focus.

"We now must wait for fortune to smile on MAGNIT," said Putin. "In the meantime, Colonel, I want you to renew the liaison relationship with the Chinese MSS general; what is his name?"

"General Sun," said Dominika.

"He claims his service has a counterintelligence problem, and they want our assistance. I don't trust them at all. See what he has under his fingernails, find out what he wants from us. We don't need any surprises from Beijing. *Men'she znayesh', krepche spish',*" said the president. "The less you know, the more soundly you sleep."

"Yes, Mr. President," said Dominika.

"And now lunch," said Putin. He led the way down a parquet-floored corridor with white walls picked out in gold leaf, and onto a broad sunny terrace ringed by a heavy white balustrade. At the center of the terrace, under a billowing canopy, was a table set for three, with sparkling crystal and elegant plates with blue and gold borders. On each plate was a ramekin, swaddled in a nest of snowy linen. Dominika could smell the heavenly aroma of crabmeat and Imperial sauce. The tops of each ramekin were baked golden brown, and the sauce still bubbled around the edges.

"Crab Imperial," said Gorelikov. "Marvelous. We used to eat this in Odessa as students."

"Try a forkful, and see if this is not better," said Putin. The delicate crabmeat melted in Dominika's mouth. An ice-cold Vernaccia was the perfect wine, and she accepted a second glass. But the image of Daria Repina floated in front of her: the sun went behind a cloud, and the piquant Imperial sauce in her mouth turned to copper.

Dominika would add this news about the murder to her thermos concealment for tomorrow's personal meeting, but she would withhold Blokhin's name. He was hers, and she vowed to kill Sergeant Iosip Blokhin herself someday.

⸻

"Didn't I tell you the president had his eye on you?" said Gorelikov in the official car back to Moscow.

Dominika smiled. "It's quite an honor. I can hardly believe it," said Dominika. "And congratulations on your award." Gorelikov bowed graciously.

"I was a bit surprised to hear about Repina, though," said Dominika. "What actually happened? You could have told me, Anton, seeing as how I was meeting SUSAN." Gorelikov waved her comment away.

"Repina was beginning to embarrass the Russian Federation, the Russian people, and the president," said Gorelikov. "We previously sent emissaries discreetly requesting that she moderate her activities and manifestoes. She chose to ignore those requests."

"So Blokhin was assigned to eliminate her? In America, in *midtown* New York City? What would have happened if there had been a mishap? This is bad operational security. I should have been warned. Really." Gorelikov patted her hand on the center armrest.

"Shlykov guaranteed that there are seldom mishaps when Blokhin is assigned a mission," said Gorelikov. "Besides, I did not want you burdened with the foreknowledge of the impending action. You sound upset that Repina was dealt with," he said. *Tread softly here, but show a little flag*, thought Dominika.

"I have scant sympathy with citizens who would harm our country," lied Dominika. "But I will tell you something, Anton. If I had known of the plan to assassinate Repina, I would have tried to disrupt the plot. Russia is skilled and ingenious in achieving its goals—and no one more so than the president himself—but destroying dissidents sullies the Federation and makes them enduring martyrs. We must abandon the old ways."

Gorelikov looked at her, then turned to stare out the car window. "I happen to agree with you," he whispered, "but the president knows his mind, and has the requisite experience. I have mentioned to him the exact views you have just expressed, and he realizes the cost, and is willing to pay the price. *Kak auknetsya, tak i otkliknetsya*, what you shout into the forest, so shall the echo come back to you."

=====

Gorelikov called Dominika back to the Kremlin the next day, ostensibly to backbench a meeting of the Security Council, but in reality to introduce her to the most powerful men in the realm—a coming-out appearance for the soon-to-be SVR Director. These *siloviki* could be potential allies or, if their interests diverged, lethal adversaries. They all obviously respected Gorelikov, and wondered whether Dominika was more than a rising SVR star, or merely the new pintle-maid of the president. To a man, they dropped their eyes to assess her jutting top hamper, today draped in a black wool knit dress, which accentuated her curves. First there was Nikolai Patrushev, former Director of the FSB, now influential secretary of the Security Council, with thinning hair, a lined narrow face, a slash of a mouth, and the hook nose of a Cossack, all backlighted by a yellow halo of cunning and distrust. He was marginally polite before turning away. Dangerous.

Then Alexander Bortnikov with the surprising cerulean halo, strong and constant, suggesting ratiocination and regard. The FSB Director was sixty-five years old, slight, and shorter than Dominika. He had a high, broad forehead and startling gray-blue eyes that crinkled at the corners whenever he smiled. He had a large mole on his left cheek and a fleshy nose, a hint of the raptor in him. Dominika knew he was an engineer by training, and it was whispered that it was he who had directed the FSB operation in London to spike dissident former KGB officer Litvinenko's afternoon tea with enough lethal Polonium-210 to heat an apartment block in Voronezh for a month. Dominika knew Bortnikov would be wise, sly, cautious, and cunning—he also would be her security service counterpart for internal domestic security if Dominika was handed the Directorship and SVR's foreign intelligence portfolio. She resolved to establish good relations with him.

Finally there was Igor Korobov, an air force lieutenant general and Chief of the GRU, crisply uniformed, with a shaven head, steel-blue eyes, and the green aura of career trepidation from being head of military intelligence in a club of former KGB cohorts. Major Shlykov hovered behind Korobov, doubtless currying favor by kneading his chief's buttocks periodically. Korobov nodded stiffly at Dominika, but Shlykov ignored her. *You tried to torpedo me in New York, you bastard*, she thought. *Worse, you sicced Blokhin on me—*

he would have left me in some alley after eliminating Repina, if he'd had the chance. She measured the inches from his smirking face.

Gorelikov stepped between them before Dominika could put her thumbnail in Shlykov's eye and whispered for her to take a seat against the wall behind him, as Putin gaveled the Council to order. For the next utterly unreal two hours, the Council discussed Operation OBVAL (Landslide), which was conceived, refined, planned, and proposed by Shlykov, who guaranteed success and stunning results. The covert action, whereby Russian weapons and explosives would be smuggled to Kurdish guerilla separatists to be used in terror attacks in Istanbul to destabilize Turkey, was a massive active measure on the extreme end of the scale. Gorelikov and Bortnikov opposed the plan, both pointing out that the military aspect was exceptionally risky and that such a supply-the-rebels-with-guns operation was laughably 1960s Soviet primitive. Bortnikov called it a reckless misadventure—all the more so in Turkey with its vigilant and aggressive police and security services. Lieutenant General Korobov disagreed, saying this insurgency would destabilize the southern flank of NATO, a theme he knew, all of them knew, would gain the president's favor. Which way would it go?

Dominika saw Putin looking at her down the length of the chamber table. What was she going to do if the Pale Moth (one of the president's old KGB nicknames) tried to hoist a leg over her one night in her luxury *dacha*?

Then it happened. Gorelikov leaned back toward her and whispered, "What do you think?"

"Yes, Colonel," said Putin from head of the table. "What do you think of OBVAL?" Twenty faces turned to look at her. *Bozhe moy, mother of God,* she thought.

She looked around the table, then directly at Shlykov, sitting behind his chief. *"Strich porosenk,"* she said. "Like shearing a pig—lots of screaming but very little wool. A fool's errand, and one countered easily by Turkey and the United States." *Especially when I alert Benford.* There were guffaws around the table, and wily Bortnikov of the FSB appraised her anew. Gorelikov was delighted. The GRU contingent sat sullenly. Putin sat with his hands folded, his Stonehenge face impassive.

Dominika realized she was being drawn into her first Kremlin intrigue. Gorelikov intended to usurp the MAGNIT case, and Shlykov had to be brushed aside. Discrediting his paramilitary scheme in Istanbul was a start.

Dominika studied the patrician Anton, saw his blue halo pulse, and read his mind. Why bring her into this? Because as counterintelligence Chief of Line KR, Dominika could credibly criticize Shlykov's tradecraft, operational planning, and judgment if there was a flap. Gorelikov knew Dominika would line up on his side: He knew Shlykov's boorish and dismissive attitude had made him an opponent—oh, this was how quickly sides were drawn up in these jeweled hallways. Allies, competitors, self-interest, personal grudges, career traps, and blood feuds; these were the swirling mosaic politics of the Kremlin.

"Do these chiefs know about the MAGNIT and Academician Ri cases?" Dominika asked Gorelikov when they were alone. She would meet Ri in ten days. Ioana was already in Vienna, preparing the Danube cottage. Dominika reminded Gorelikov that they'd have to prioritize cases, hoping to elicit a name for MAGNIT, but Anton was cautious.

"No one knows about MAGNIT, besides GRU, and we won't disseminate it, not yet, especially not after recent developments. In time, a few members of the Security Council will be briefed, but not all of them."

"What developments?"

"We received a report from SUSAN last night. MAGNIT is being looked at by the US president to become part of his administration. Nothing specific, but it is unprecedented—the *Kandidat Kremlevskogo*, the Kremlin's Candidate in Washington. MAGNIT may be offered something important. We will wait patiently and see what our harvest will be."

"Will you brief me eventually on MAGNIT? Or shouldn't I ask?" *Be direct, confidential, a little piquant; that's what he likes.*

"Of course, once the case stabilizes," said Gorelikov, tickled at her pluck. "The president agrees completely. MAGNIT is a political case now, a Director's case, one he wants handled only by an illegals officer. Not you. Not me. Only SUSAN. Period."

Gorelikov had just given her the lead to the extra pages she would have to prepare for tomorrow's personal meeting with a Moscow Station officer: *MAGNIT, the Kremlin's Candidate.* Dominika mentally drafted the additional intel: Vienna meeting with Ri; her new Black Sea dacha; the Repina assassination; Shlykov's urban terror plot in Istanbul; Gorelikov's prediction that she would be given the Directorship of SVR. She was going to need a bigger thermos bottle.

Dominika was unsettled; this was too much. Putin was like a raging Siberian blizzard boiling across the steppes, headed for the little cabin, a blizzard whose icy fingers would work their way under the eaves, pry up the roof, splinter the bolted door, and collapse the walls to devour the huddled beings inside. *Beregites*, beware Benford, the blizzard is approaching.

PUTIN'S CRAB IMPERIAL

Combine diced red bell pepper, minced parsley, lemon juice, raw egg, mustard powder, paprika, celery salt, bay leaf, black pepper, red pepper flakes, Worcestershire sauce, mayonnaise, and melted butter in a bowl and whisk until smooth. Gently fold in lump crabmeat, spoon into ramekins, and bake in a medium-high oven until bubbly. In a separate bowl, make Imperial sauce by whisking mayonnaise, light cream, lemon juice, and Worcestershire sauce. Top each ramekin with Imperial sauce, butter-moistened bread crumbs, and paprika, and place under broiler until golden brown. Serve with a green salad.

13

Natural Enemies

Ricky Walters hated climbing into the trunk of a car, swaddled in a crinkly silver space blanket, knees bent to fit inside the space, his butt hard against the spare tire. The sweat would start almost immediately, partly nerves, and partly from trapped body heat. Three years ago, a defector told his CIA debriefers that the FSB, in lookout apartments across the street, scanned cars of US diplomats leaving the Moscow Embassy compound from above with infrared scopes to determine if there was a glowing heat source in the trunk, which would indicate a hiding CIA officer (Who else? The knife-and-fork set in the Department of State wouldn't be caught dead playing these cops-and-robbers games) was trying a "trunk escape" to get black to meet a Russian agent and steal national secrets (of which there were as many in Putinstan as there had been in the cave bear days of the Soviet Union). The space blanket trapped the body heat, and through an IR scope the trunk looked cold and empty.

In midafternoon, Walters was driven out of the underground garage in the trunk of the Honda sedan of the junior consular officer (a Station colleague) by that officer's twenty-seven-year-old wife, Helen (who had herself received months of training in surveillance detection). The couple's two-year-old twins were chattering away in rear car seats as Helen watched her mirrors through multiple turns as she headed for Smolensky Passage Mall in the Arbat, a glitzy collection of shops affordable only to the lithe wives of oligarchs and the less lithe, thick-ankled wives of government ministers and heads of industries who found their positions provided gratifying amounts of disposable income skimmed from the official coffers of the State.

A last check for the telltale trailing LADA two blocks back—negative, she was totally clear of ticks this afternoon—and Helen entered the ramp to the underground parking garage, punching in the twins' favorite music disc—Raffi singing about the wheels on the bus going round and round to which the twins resoundingly joined in (the more noise for the FSB-planted microphone in the car the better), and which was also the "ready" signal to Ricky listening from the trunk. Helen rounded the corner of the ramp, totally screened in the gap, ejected the disc ("go" signal) to howls from the twins, popped the trunk, and pulled on the emergency-brake handle to slow the car without showing brake lights. Ricky shed the blanket, rolled over the lip of the trunk, slammed the lid, and darted through a service door up a short staircase, and out into the street. Elapsed time: four seconds. Helen smoothly continued down to park and browse the stores, pushing a two-seat stroller. On the street, Ricky wore a Soviet-style cloth cap, dirty whipcord trousers, a padded light jacket torn at the shoulder, and a pair of scuffed Duolang "acid-resistant safety shoes" imported from China.

As he walked, head down, he wedged silicone spacers between his gums and cheeks, and slipped on clear-lens eyeglasses, making himself look older and heavier. He cleared the ritzy Arbat neighborhood, entered Khamovniki District, and walked slowly along Ostozhenka Ulitsa, a broad commercial street. Halfway down the boulevard, Walters loitered at a bright-red public-phone sidewalk kiosk and checked his watch. The standard four-minute window was just opening, and Walters saw the little dusty navy Skoda hatchback approach and pull over to the curb, a box of tissues on the dash. All clear. Ricky lifted the red phone off the cradle and put it back. Clear here. He scooted to the car and got into the passenger seat, scrunching down just enough to mask his profile, and the car moved off. He felt the plastic cover on the seat, a precaution against spy dust, though his Russkie disguise clothes had been kept in the Station and were unlikely to be contaminated.

This was an agent car pickup, substantially dangerous because a recognizable CIA officer was in the agent's vehicle, the license plates of which were as good as her name being printed in block letters on the side of the car. The reverse procedure—a case-officer car pickup—was generally preferred but there was still risk: now you had a sensitive source in a US diplomatic-plated vehicle. "Pick your poison," Gable once told Nash and Dominika during tradecraft practice. "Doesn't matter who drives and who gets picked up. Just fucking get there black, both of you. That's all there is to it."

Walters looked over at DIVA, who, his chief had told him last night, was the absolute "gold standard," so don't make any mistakes, *not one*, because if he screwed this one through a tradecraft error, he'd be muscling a floor buffer in the Headquarters front lobby, making sure the Great Seal of CIA on the terrazzo marble was nice and shiny for when his replacement reported for duty. No pressure, mind you, and have fun out there.

Walters didn't know what to expect: a mousy librarian or a rotund administrator, but not this Venus driving the car, not the classic Hellenic profile, flower-petal lips, luminous chestnut hair piled on top of her head, concentrating on traffic, electric-blue eyes darting constantly between her mirrors. Her elegant hands held the steering wheel professionally at the ten-and-two position, and she moved through traffic aggressively, shifting smoothly out of the district, east onto the third ring road, weaving through the belching blue traffic, then suddenly off again at Lyusinovskaya Ulitsa south to the 390-hectare Kolomenskoye Park on the river. DIVA parked and they quickly walked through crowds of tourists—no one paid them any attention—past the bone-white Church of the Ascension and the fanciful seventeenth-century wooden palace of Tsar Aleksey, bristling with gables, onion domes, and bell towers. DIVA led Ricky down a steep wooded slope to a small streambed, mossy paths following the water, surrounded by thick woods. It was suddenly dark and cold—and utterly silent. A slight mist hung over the trickle of water, and Walters looked around for three hags stirring a bubbling witches' cauldron. Ricky knew they could spend more than the requisite four minutes in this creepy wooded glen for the meeting. Good screening.

"Pretty spooky down here," said Walters, in English. He had no Russian. "We could probably find a couple of long-term cache sites somewhere along here."

"Golosov Ravine," said DIVA, looking around. "It's very famous to Muscovites. There are sacred stones, holy natural springs, and tales of phantoms appearing out of the fog. Thank you for coming. No problem getting clear?" *This CIA boy looks smart, he's calm, and handles himself well on the street. Not like* Bratok *but solid.*

Walters shook his head, unzipping his backpack, mentally reviewing his meeting agenda. "Thank *you,* Colonel, for all you've done," said Walters. "I'm aware of only a fraction of your service, but enough to know what you contribute." *A charmer, like Nathaniel Nash,* she thought. *Same purple halo too. Passionate.*

"Call me Dominika," she said. "Do you have my replacement equipment?" She saw his face fall. He told her quickly about the SRAC situation, and said that Simon Benford was working to get commo gear to her as soon as possible. In the meantime, Mr. Benford wanted her to have this. He held out a chunky sports watch inside a plastic bag, a precaution against *metka*.

"Are you people serious?" she said, carefully dipping into the bag, extracting then fingering the watch. Walters hurried to explain.

"Without SRAC, we'll have to use personal meets—or dead drops—to pass intel and requirements. You know all the call-out signal sites, right?" Dominika nodded.

"This is different. The watch is a beacon, for emergencies. It's connected to something called the Cospas-SARSAT rescue system, which is a maritime rescue locator with a GPS capability," said Walters. "The beacon frequency is encrypted and hops around. It looks like background noise to nearby receivers. No triangulation."

"Quite lovely, but what is its *purpose*?"

Walters did not know about Dominika's militant opposition regarding exfiltration. "An exfil trigger. If you activate the beacon, and we geolocate the signal in Moscow, we'll check every day at 2100 hours at the downtown pickup site," said Ricky, reading off a small tablet. "You remember it, the twin phones to the right of the Filevsky Park metro station entrance? It's less than a kilometer from your current apartment." Dominika nodded. "If we geolocate your beacon near Petersburg, we use Red Route Two. You know that site. If your beacon transmits from Cape Idokopas, which we have designated as the Black Sea exfil site, you wait on the beach for pickup."

"Exfiltration again? Another submarine?" asked Dominika, her voice suddenly edgy. She had once rescued a blown CIA agent by delivering him to a minisubmersible crewed by Navy SEALs in Neva Bay, near Petersburg.

"No, there's something different," said Walters, sweating despite the dank air in the ravine. He swiped at the tablet. "A manned minisubmarine takes time to deploy, and is slow. We have something new that's always ready, and very fast. You will be taken off the beach in a USV, an unmanned surface vessel." He showed her streaming images of a low-slung, fifty-foot, flush-deck speedboat painted gray overall, with wavy patterns of white and black camouflage. Dominika looked at Walters.

"You are telling me this boat has no one driving? There is no crew?" Ricky swallowed hard. Gable had warned him that DIVA could quickly get in a "horn tossin' mood."

"It is precisely computer controlled, steered by satellite, undetectable on radar, can loiter indefinitely, and is always available," said Walters. "With this platform, maritime exfiltration from Putin's Palace on the Black Sea becomes a viable option."

"I will only be at the cape during the president's four-day reception this fall in November, so it is not a viable site," she said. "Besides, *Gospodin* Benford knows my attitude regarding fleeing and defecting. Didn't he mention it to you?"

"I'm sorry, I don't understand," said Walters, trying to keep this together. *Agent handling. More like playing a snake charmer's pungi flute in front of a swaying cobra.* He hurriedly dug into his backpack for another plastic envelope. "You wait on the shore, night or day, and you wear these infrared sunglasses so you'll see the USV's IR strobe two klicks out to sea. Just stand there and it'll home in to the wristwatch. The thing'll beach itself, glide up to you without a sound, like a horse nuzzling for a sugar cube. You climb up the toeholds on the stern, open the deck hatch and get in; watch your head, it's tight. There's a recliner-like chair, a seat belt, headphones, food and drink, heat control. Close the hatch, and the USV will do the rest." He showed her more images.

"Where is this thing supposed to take me?"

"At fifty knots you'll be twenty miles offshore at the pickup point with a gray hull in twenty-four minutes," said Walters, proudly.

"Where you gentlemen will greet me aboard the navy ship, and we watch at the rail as we sail away and my *Rodina* sinks below the horizon forever," said Dominika, dully. "And I will have effectively deserted my country." *Pissed-off agent.* Walters couldn't remember this precise situation coming up during role-playing exercises at the Farm.

He searched for the right words. "It's an exfil plan, Colonel . . . I mean Dominika. In case of hot pursuit, to get you to safety." She shook her head, finished with arguing, and handed Walters the thermos bottle. Walters wiped the thermos to get rid of DIVA's prints.

"There are six single-spaced, double-sided printed sheets inside the shell. If you smash it to break—"

"—I know the thermos trick." Walters smiled. "What more?"

"Please tell *Gospodin* Benford I will be in Vienna in ten days to meet with my North Korean. I will call to confirm my hotel, but we have used the

König von Ungarn, on Schulerstrasse, behind St. Stephen's previously. Please tell him I believe Professor Ri will accept the introduction of an additional debriefer. We have done it before, with Mr. Nash impersonating a Russian officer, thanks to his Russian language. In this case, it would be easier, as our meetings are conducted in English. CIA can service your own North Korean requirements without risk." Walters nodded.

"If you handle him in English, then any nuke analyst can—"

"—I would prefer the officer be Nathaniel Nash," interrupted Dominika. "We have worked together for years and operate compatibly." Walters thumbed DIVA's request—demand—into his tablet, not knowing the phrase "operate compatibly" would result in knowing glances at Headquarters, for he was unaware of the forbidden relationship. The woman was something.

"I'll pass the word," said Ricky. Dominika's face darkened, and her voice became low and serious.

"Also, please tell him that I can confirm that President Putin approved the assassination of dissident Daria Repina in New York City."

"That created a panic in Washington," said Walters. "It was all over the papers. Who did it?"

"Never mind his name. I know who is responsible, and I will deal with him," said Dominika.

"I'll tell them," said Ricky. *This Amazon is serious. Look at that face.* "I suppose I should say, for the record, that you should not try any dangerous or risky action against the assassin. You're too valuable and—"

"—and a frail woman?" said Dominika. Walters held up his hands in armistice. His tablet, a second-generation TALON device, was recording their conversation, standard procedure for restricted-handling cases. *When they play it back, I should get a medal if I get through this meeting without DIVA punching me in the face.*

"That's not it at all," said Ricky, thinking furiously for the correct word. "I just meant you're too precious to us." *Precious. Fortuitous word.*

DIVA's face softened. "I do not mean to snap at you," she said in apology, then became serious again. "Next item: I have written details of a GRU covert action in Turkey. They propose to supply weapons and explosives to Kurdish separatists in Istanbul. Despite objection from the intelligence services, President Putin last night approved the operation. I have included all the details."

"So much intel. Your reports will go out tonight," said Walters, stowing the thermos in his backpack.

"One last thing. Are you aware of the situation with someone called MAGNIT?" said Dominika. She knew Benford's penchant for compartmentation, and did not want to say too much. Walters nodded.

"Simon Benford briefed me by secure phone when they tapped me to meet you. I know the general facts, as much as any of us knows."

"I've reported all I have heard," said Dominika, "but please emphasize to Benford that MAGNIT is being looked at for an unspecified job in the administration. The Kremlin is very excited. I still do not know MAGNIT's identity."

"This will create a storm in Headquarters," said Ricky.

"It will create more than a storm if MAGNIT begins reading my intelligence reports in his new position, and begins feeding them to Moscow," said Dominika. Ricky for the first time in his young career saw and appreciated the icy danger this woman—all agents—live with every day, and marveled at the courage required to keep operating.

He checked the elapsed-time counter on the tablet. "Fifteen minutes, I should get going," he said, remembering a last item. "Mr. Benford wanted me to ask you for confirmation—when you can—on who was behind the death of our late Director Alex Larson. He's obsessed with finding out."

Dominika looked at her shoes. "Please tell Simon only the president could have given the order. I suspect Anton Gorelikov would be entrusted to design such a plan. I will confirm when I can."

Walters nodded. "You'll be talking to Nash in ten days." Dominika could not shake his hand; she had heard that the FSB had absolutely stopped deploying *metka* when its use against Western diplomats became an embarrassing international story in the heady years of *glastnost*, but CIA continued the prophylactic protocol nonetheless. "You trust Putin wouldn't ever start spritzing our asses again?" Gable had snorted. When they saw each other in Vienna, she would ask Nate about any results from using spy dust on SUSAN.

Her Nate. As mad as she had been at him in Athens, she missed him and yearned to see him.

She smiled at him. "You know your way back? Take care with the thermos. And thank you for the watch and glasses."

Walters shrugged on his backpack. "Stay safe, Dominika," he said. "I'll come out anytime, anyplace, if you need me. I'll be checking the signal sites every day." He turned and disappeared around a bend in the streambed, stirring the ground fog as he moved. *Let one of the seventeenth-century Tartar ghosts living in the mossy Golosov Ravine speed you safely home*, Dominika thought.

———————

Benford raved in his office, prompting Dotty, his secretary of eight years, to shake her head in warning at various CID officers who wished to speak with the Chief this morning. "Best not; perhaps this afternoon" was the whispered refrain.

Dominika's newest tidbit about MAGNIT's being looked at by the president for a big job should have made sorting the possibles easier, but he needed a name. Benford already suspected and feared the worst: the senior vacancy that the Kremlin was steering MAGNIT toward was the one the Russians themselves had created by killing his friend Alex Larson—DCIA. He knew he was looking for a senior figure who, sometime in the last decade, had known enough about the US Navy railgun to have reported technical details to the Russians. The scores of witting navy personnel—officers, enlisted, scientists, and civilian contractors—could now in theory be whittled down, as none of them was likely to be tapped by the president. Or was it someone they had not thought of? Of the dozen high-ranking bureaucrats, only the current secretary of the Department of Energy had occasionally been briefed on the railgun, but he had spent years in other departments on other projects. According to Dominika, MAGNIT had been an *active* reporting source for a decade. An anomaly. Could she have misreported the facts? More ominous, could that slick bastard Anton Gorelikov be parceling variants of the same story to different people—called a barium enema in the Game—as a loyalty test to see which variant later surfaced to finger the traitor?

In London, MI6 called the barium trap a blue-dye test, describing the same mole-catching principle metaphorically as pouring blue dye down a pipe to observe from which downstream outlet the dye would eventually issue. At a counterintelligence liaison conference in London several years earlier, Benford had declared the British terminology idiotic, pointing out that pipes—especially the decrepit plumbing in the United Kingdom and

Europe—became clogged, or they broke underground, and that the metaphor of a barium enema was more to his liking. "That, Simon, is because you are an uphill gardener," said *C*, the Chief of Six, which slang Benford did not understand, and no one told him it meant sodomite. *Thank God for the special relationship*, breathed the Brits in the room.

Gable and Forsyth met Benford in the Executive Dining Room at Langley for lunch, where they tossed around ideas and theories. The elegant room—as narrow as the dining car on a train—on the executive seventh floor of Headquarters, overlooking the tree-lined Potomac River, featured tables placed closely together, so that new arrivals were forced to walk between them, nodding to friends or cutting enemies. Everyone saw everyone else, and with whom they were lunching, and the cabals and cliques and gangs among the seniors at Langley were therefore common knowledge. Benford ordered a plate of pasta with anchovies, parsley, *pangrattato*, and lemon, while Forsyth chose the crab bisque, and Gable, the grilled shrimp.

"This alarms me," said Benford, slurping pasta. "A Russian mole could wind up in the Cabinet room."

Gable stabbed a shrimp. "What I don't get is that Domi says the fucker's been working for a decade," he said. "That means his previous job was of interest to the Ruskies."

"I'm worried it's a trap, a test before Putin gives her the SVR job," said Forsyth. "Christ, we vet *our* directors before putting them forward. So might the Kremlin."

The chief of the Office of Congressional Affairs, Eric Duchin, a galloping careerist, busybody, and gossip, arrived with a posse of his toadeaters, making their way between tables, stopping to greet fellow division chiefs amid great laughter and guffaws. Duchin stopped at Benford's table, surrounded by his grinning acolytes, who were known as "the Duchebags" on the ops floors. Duchin had a Gumby-square head, thick snow-white hair, and a narrow face. Students at the Farm had nicknamed him Q-Tip.

"Simon," he said, nodding.

"Eric," said Benford. Silence. Gable fingered the skewer that his shrimp had been served on.

"I'm calling a meeting on Friday," said Duchin, finally. "SSCI, the Senate Select Committee, wants CIA to provide courtesy briefings to the possible nominees for the Director's job. Just a heads-up to prepare. The committee wants all nominees to be able to discuss current operations during closed hearings, including your Russian antics."

Benford put down his fork, choosing to ignore the word "antics." "Am I given to understand that operational briefings are to be provided to multiple individuals, *only one* of whom will eventually be confirmed as CIA Director? It is customary to provide a limited briefing to the final nominee, and only to the final nominee."

Duchin shrugged. "Your precious secrets will be safe with them," he said. "I'll send you their bio packets. All currently hold SI/TK (Special Intelligence/ Talent Keyhole), top-secret clearances, including Special Access Program tickets. Besides, the Director wants it done this way. Greater transparency." After Alex Larson's drowning, an acting Director had been appointed, whom the obsequious Duchin was already calling "Director."

Benford bristled. "Greater transparency? In an intelligence service?" he snapped. "Duchin, you are incapable of sentient thought. You are my natural enemy. Go away."

Duchin shrugged. "Take it up with the Director," he said. "He's committed to a smooth transition. See you Friday." The three sat silently at the table, thinking of a pair of electric-blue eyes alone in the Kremlin, flitting across the slack, beefy faces around the table, any one of whom would pull the trigger on her without hesitation. These nominees' briefings necessarily would include, at the least, a mention of a CIA-run penetration of the SVR, and at worst, DIVA's true name. Heresy.

"How does this work, the possible nominees for Director all being briefed, and all being interviewed by SSCI?" said Gable. "Whatever happened to POTUS picking his man—one person—and nominating him? What the fuck is this, a beauty pageant?"

"The Acting Director suggested it," said Forsyth. "This way he can push forward different candidates, all of whom will dismantle Alex Larson's policies, placate Congress, and keep the Agency focused on the environment instead of the kiloton yield of the uranium device the Nokos detonated underground two months ago."

Benford shook himself, pushed his plate away, and looked at Forsyth. "What did you say before?"

"The Acting Director wanted it this way."

"No, before that," said Benford.

"That we vet our own directors before putting them forward."

"Exactly," said Benford. "And the Russians had Alex killed, and we're looking for a mole."

"Who's gonna get a big-ass job in the exec branch," said Gable.

"Which vacancy is the Director of this Agency. It's clear now. The Kremlin's candidate is for DCIA," said Benford, pounding the table.

Forsyth looked at Benford over the top of his glasses. "You better be sure before you pull the fire alarm. Not even Putin could pull this off."

"Maybe not," said Benford, "but that Gorelikov mastermind could if what DIVA says about him is true."

Gable stopped picking his teeth. "You saying one of the three nominees for DCIA is the mole? Could they swing that?" he asked.

"Maybe yes, maybe no," said Benford. "But we can't sit by and do nothing."

"We have to brief them all before one's confirmed." Forsyth groaned.

"Too obvious," said Benford. "Let us consider how to pour some blue dye down a pipe."

Gable started picking his teeth again. "If you're talking barium enema, I got a turkey baster in my office."

BENFORD'S LEMON PASTA

Sauté anchovy fillets in olive oil with finely diced leeks until the fillets dissolve and the leeks soften. In a separate pan, toast bread crumbs with a little olive oil, garlic, and dried red chili flakes until the crumbs (*pangrattato*) are golden brown. Cook bucatini, drain, and toss with the anchovy oil and leeks. Sprinkle with chopped parsley, bread crumbs, and a generous squeeze of lemon juice. Serve immediately.

14

Expedient Amorality

DIVA's handwritten report meticulously documented the Security Council debate in the Kremlin regarding the GRU military covert action in Turkey encrypted OBVAL, put forth by Major Shlykov, who argued that Turkey was in chaotic transition: Fundamentalist Islamic political parties were eroding the secular military Atatürk traditions. The country had, since 1984, been struggling with a prolonged, low-intensity armed urban insurrection by the socialist Kurdistan Workers' Party (PKK) in their bid for political rights and self-determination. Current US military aid to the Kurdish Peshmerga in Iraq had discommoded the Turkish government (even though the Iraqi Peshmerga had no political connection to PKK terrorists). Ankara moodily conflated this military support in Iraq with American endorsement of Kurdish desires to secede from the country and to claim a substantial swath of sovereign Turkish territory as their hereditary homeland. Recognizing a developing bilateral schism and subsequent opportunity to drive a wedge between Washington and Ankara—something Putin and his coterie of valets knew how to do best—GRU planners had developed a plan for Turkey.

DIVA's narrative—printed in Russian in space-saving letters so small that translators had to use magnifying glasses to read the text—reported that the aggressive Shlykov had laid out his plan by which Moscow would supply PKK cells in Istanbul with RPG-18 "Mukha" antiarmor rockets, MON-200 antipersonnel mines, and larger PMN-4 pressure-fired blast mines, for use in urban terror attacks in Istanbul, designed to create a crisis in the government, exacerbate tense relations with Washington, and ultimately to destabilize Turkey, the traditional southern bulwark of NATO.

Russian Naval Special Forces would support the operation. The matériel would be delivered in a series of nighttime forays by small boats disguised as fishing vessels to PKK members waiting at a deserted out-of-season picnic grounds on the banks of Riva Creek, four navigable miles inland from the Black Sea coast of Turkey. PKK would then truck the weapons into Istanbul, stage them in a number of warehouses, and distribute them among cells. Despite objections to the covert-action plan from the civilian intelligence services, President Putin had approved the operation. He was willing to undertake this foreign adventure and run the risks—which the GRU assessed as minimal—to weaken NATO, and especially to destabilize the only Muslim member state of the coalition. After that, no one objected any longer. DIVA concluded her report by writing of Shlykov: "This Golden Youth intends to provide enough explosives to PKK to set Istanbul ablaze on both sides of the Bosphorus, from Europe to Asia."

———

DIVA's reporting triggered a hasty meeting in CIA Headquarters in Langley.

Benford recently had designated Gable as DIVA's primary handler.

Benford, Forsyth, Gable. These three veteran officers were as different in temperament and style as imaginable. But they had come together as a team when Nate Nash recruited DIVA in Helsinki, and under their subtle tutelage she had developed into a world-class reporting source. Nash, the fourth and most junior member of the coterie, was absent from this meeting: he had recently been posted as Chief of Operations in CIA's London Station, on the face of it a plum assignment in a solidly advancing career, but really designed to keep him busy and away from DIVA. Forsyth—arguably the best case officer among them—had called Nash "a magician" on the street, working against hostile surveillance in denied areas. Forsyth had been Nate's Chief of Station twice before, and he knew what a good officer he was, despite the sex-with-DIVA problem.

"I seem to remember your unapproved infatuation twenty years ago with a certain safe-house keeper in Rome," Forsyth had once reminded Gable while discussing Nash. "You knew it was against the rules, but you used to run over there bowlegged to see her every week."

"That was different," growled Gable. "We were young, she used to cook carbonara for me, and I was helping her out."

Forsyth looked at him deadpan. "Carbonara? Did she use pancetta, guanciale, or some other pork product?"

"Very funny. If it was such a big fucking deal, why didn't you kick me in the balls?" said Gable, red faced.

"Maybe I knew you could handle it, or maybe I knew you had the discipline to keep her safe," said Forsyth. "Like maybe we give Nash the same slack. I'm not saying he's a choirboy, but Domi's half to blame. Godammit, they're in love with each other, you said so yourself." Gable shook his head, but agreed.

Today, Forsyth had included Lucius Westfall, who, as Benford's new assistant, was cleared for DIVA material, and thus was on the very small BIGOT list for the case, the abbreviated roster of officers who had been read in to her file, and who were cleared for the RH (restricted handling) compartment. Westfall sat quietly in a chair in the corner—he knew his place on the food chain in this room.

"The facility these Russians have for mayhem is awe inspiring," said Forsyth. He looked up from DIVA's reports about Istanbul, and pushed his half-moon glasses to the top of his head.

"They're fuckers," said Gable, "but we take this to Turkish liaison and help them, they're gonna kiss our asses for a decade."

"I agree," said Forsyth. "But not to TNIO, the intel guys. They don't trust us. We take it to the TNP, Turkish National Police; they're serious and accessible."

"And when you say 'help them,'" said Benford, turning to Gable, "you mean exactly what?"

"Interdict the shipments, wrap up the gomers waiting in the swamp for the delivery, let the TNP sweat 'em, and clean out the rest of the cells," said Gable.

Lucius Westfall cleared his throat and scraped his chair. Gable looked over at him. He liked the young guy, but as with Gable's protégé Nate, he would never say so. "If you have something to say, say it," said Gable. "Don't keep us squeezing our legs together."

"I was thinking," said Lucius. "Istanbul's population is over fourteen million. The Kurds in the city number about four million."

"Admirable command of the facts, which I trust will soon be shown to be relevant to this discussion," said Benford, rubbing his face.

"The point is that we'll never be sure of taking out one hundred percent of the PKK cells with a couple of raids and a score of arrests," said Westfall, swallowing. "The city's too big, the Kurdish population is too diffuse. We have to consider this in three parts."

"Tell us," said Benford. He liked linear thinking, which, he frequently raved, was uniformly absent in the US government.

"We have to interdict *all* the Russian matériel without exception," said Lucius. "We can't let even one mine get through. We then have to identify as completely as possible the PKK organization in the city. Finally, we have to neutralize the source of the problem: GRU Major Valeriy Shlykov." The men in the room shifted in their seats.

"You're a regular Alfred Einstein," said Gable. "Keep going." For all his gruffness, Gable knew how to draw young officers out, make them think, stick up for what they believed.

"To stop the whole thing I think we have to beacon the weapons before they get to Turkey," said Westfall. "That way we track them from inland creek, to warehouse, to backyard potting shed, to safe-house cellar, so we get them all."

"Before they get to Turkey?" said Gable. "As in Russia?" The others were quiet, thinking the same thing.

"Out of the question," said Benford. "DIVA's already in jeopardy as it is, reporting this unique intelligence. We fuck up in Istanbul, she's one of twenty Council members in the room—not even a full member yet—who know about the PKK covert action. Trying something with the shipment when it's still in Russia would be doubly suicidal for her."

"Maybe not," said Westfall. "DIVA told us the crates were going to be trucked to Sevastopol and staged in a warehouse, then ferried across the Black Sea to Turkey in small fishing boats when they get the green light from Shlykov. It's a GRU covert action; they'll keep this quiet, and they'll stay away from official Russian naval installations. It'll be a commercial warehouse, an easy target."

"Okay, hotshot, you take the responsibility for invading Russia and starting World War Three?" said Gable. Westfall kept quiet.

Benford got up from the couch and started pacing, looking at Westfall sideways. "How would you propose to break undetected into a warehouse in Russian-controlled Sevastopol and install beacons on a dozen crates?" he said.

"We could use the WOLVERINEs," said Westfall.

Heads around the room came up. "Ain't they all retired?" said Gable.

"They're on reserve status," said Forsyth. "They didn't like to be sidelined. I kept them busy for as long as I could."

"I heard they were pretty effective," said Westfall. "The file is fascinating."

"Cold War throwbacks," said Benford, head cocked to the side, thinking.

"Forget it," said Gable. "They were crazy anticommie Polaks, out of control. Who's going to handle them?"

"We'd need a Russian speaker, strong operator, denied-area expert," said Westfall.

Everybody was thinking of the same name. "And who, pray tell, might that be?" said Benford.

"Nate Nash," said Westfall. No one said anything. Westfall didn't know about Nash's penalty-box status.

"Put that aside for now," said Forsyth. "What do we do with Shlykov?"

"I've been thinking about that," said Westfall, swallowing. "DIVA says Gorelikov wants to sink Shlykov. What if we give him a reason to do it, make it appear that Shlykov himself is responsible for the collapse of the entire covert action in Istanbul?"

"Keep going," said Gable. All three seniors were listening hard now.

"I believe you ops officers call it 'burning' someone," said Westfall. "What if we make it look like Shlykov is double-dipping—taking money from CIA and not reporting it? The Russians are so suspicious, they'll believe it."

"Tall order. It would have to be convincing," said Forsyth, already calculating. "Bank account, spy gear under the mattress, signals."

"It really doesn't have to be one hundred percent convincing," said Westfall. "DIVA and Gorelikov will have enough to ruin him: implicating and convicting innocent people are Russian art forms."

"And the lead investigator gets credit for catching a rat," said Forsyth.

"A blue-eyed Chief of Line KR," said Gable. "It protects her and gives her another CI scalp."

"It's still a risk. Shlykov is supposed to be very good and popular," said Benford, looking around the room. They were thinking of the same name . . . again.

"I'll call London," said Forsyth. "He can be here in two days."

"I want to see him personally," said Benford. "We all should reconvene when he gets here. If we are going to unseat this GRU ruffian, Nash must be brilliant about it." Benford stopped pacing. "Tell Nash specifically from me that Benford says he should endeavor to be brilliant."

"And I'll send the re-activation call out to the WOLVERINEs," said Forsyth. "They'll be pleased."

"Pleased?" snorted Gable. "Who's gonna tell them Stalin died?" Westfall swallowed twice.

═══════════

Nate walked into Benford's office at noon of the second day, having taken the early-morning flight from London. The cable from Chief EUR Forsyth recalling him to Headquarters had mentioned only that he was required for "consultations," which in the patois of cablese could mean he was in trouble for an unknown transgression, or had been chosen as the sacrificial goat for assignment to a liaison billet in FEEB headquarters—a nightmare exile that no ops officer wanted; or there was a spectacular operation that Benford wanted him to handle. Nate the case officer studied Benford's French bulldog face for a clue, but the mole hunter was inscrutable. Benford pointed to a chair beside his littered desk—his whole office looked like Pompeii after Vesuvius—opened a restricted-handling file and read silently. Like any astute operator, Nate read the block-letter title upside down on the RH title page: GCDIVA. *What was this? Were they going to discipline him over the spat he'd had with Dominika in Athens? That was weeks ago.*

Nate knew his stock with Benford, Gable, and Forsyth had taken a hit over the years since Helsinki because of his relationship with DIVA. He also knew very well that he had not been summarily separated from the Service only as an accommodation to keep the agent in harness. As it was, he was hanging by a thread. Nash's mind raced back to the beginning.

The hiatus in contact with Dominika between meetings in Europe always cooled things down, but these officers were not dummies. Benford expected recidivism; Forsyth ruefully understood him; Gable was the worst: he knew both Nate and Dominika as protégés, could read them like the carny who guesses your weight at the country fair. Worse, he could smell coitus from across the room. The tear-filled and disastrous conclusion to the contact in Athens had not helped.

Nate fretted over the futility and unprofessionalism of their love affair— it was *besperspektivnyak*, a hopeless situation, a fruitless exercise. Dominika loved him passionately, and didn't care about the rules. Dominika would tease him for acting like a dour Russian while she soared like a liberated

American love child. The issue of her defection and resettlement was the tinder that always started the arguments.

How do you feel about her now? he thought to himself, thankful that among Benford's other vampiric skills, mind reading *was probably not* numbered. That was fortunate, since Nathaniel Nash at this minute knew, had always known, that he loved the beautiful Russian with the serious scowl that would melt into a dizzying smile from across the street when she saw him approach. He loved the way she breathed his name—*Neyt*, with the broad Russian vowel—when they made love and how her head went back, eyelids fluttering and chin trembling, groaning *Ya zakanchivayu*, I'm finishing (Russians never say "I'm coming" in bed).

The bubble popped when Benford looked up and spoke. "Are you jet-lagging now, Nash?"

"No, Simon, I'm fine. It's an easy flight," said Nate, trying to blot out the image of Dominika's face on the pillow.

"We have something in mind for you, something rather important," said Benford.

"Just don't tell me I should buy a twelve-month meal plan for the cafeteria at the J. Edgar Hoover building." Nate had meant this as a joke, to establish bonhomie, and corporately to suggest—or plead—that he mustn't be sent over to the FBI to work on the joint task force. Joking with Benford was like lion hunting on horseback with a spear: you could in theory do it, but odds were it would not turn out well.

Benford stared at Nate for ten seconds. "Do you know anything about science, Nash?" Benford asked. "I mean apart from the fluid mechanics of nocturnal emissions, of which I am sure you are a longtime student." Nate shrugged, already regretting his joke.

"Since light travels faster than sound, some people appear bright until you hear them speak," said Benford. "Endeavor not to be one of those people. A good place to start is not to speak unless spoken to."

"Okay, Simon," said Nate.

"Now we have a critical operation ahead of us. It's rather complicated as it's in three parts. Alarming as it may be, you would have an axial role in each part." Nate opened his mouth to ask a question, but Benford put up his hand, and shook his head in a "don't spoil it" look of distaste.

"If you would permit me to summarize," said Benford. He sat back in his chair and propped his stocking feet on his desk, starting a minor avalanche of papers that fluttered to the floor.

"DIVA just reported that the Kremlin seeks to destabilize Turkey by supplying antiarmor rockets and pressure mines to separatist PKK insurgents in Istanbul. Part one: We will beacon the weapons crates at their staging point in Sevastopol using an experienced raiding team of reservists that, considering your Russian-language and denied-area experience, you will lead. The operation should take no longer than two days, with time on target approximately two hours."

"Reservists from Desert Storm or Afghanistan?" said Nate.

"No, closer to the years of the Berlin Wall," said Benford.

"I beg your pardon?" said Nate. "Berlin Wall?"

"The Berlin Wall," said Benford. "Perhaps you missed it while watching *Dance Fever* on television."

"*Dance Fever?*" said Nate.

"Never mind. There is no reason for you to have heard of them, the WOLVERINEs. They distinguished themselves during the Cold War in Poland."

"Distinguished themselves how?" said Nate. "Like they blew things up?"

Benford waved his hand in the air. "Let me continue," he said. "Part two: You will liaise with the Turkish National Police as they prepare counterterror raids against PKK, informed by our beacon tracking of the matériel. Those preparations include teltaps on the phones of the SVR Istanbul *rezidentura*, and GRU Major Valeriy Shlykov, who is the on-the-ground Russian intel officer supporting PKK cells, which is why we again need your Russian.

"Part three: Simultaneously, we need to burn Comrade Shlykov. One idea is to make it look like he is a CIA asset, and to suggest he subverted his own covert action. We think this idea has merit, but the plan is unformed; I want you to think about it. A feature of this final act is for DIVA herself to investigate, expose, and defame Shlykov, which will protect her as the source, as well as bestow additional counterespionage credit on her as Chief of Line KR."

"You anticipate personal meetings with her in Istanbul?" said Nate nonchalantly. "We'll be able—"

"Marty Gable is primary handler," said Benford. "You can participate in meetings, but I want you to be smart, to exercise restraint." Nate looked down at his hands.

"*Restraint.* I trust I'm clear?" said Benford.

"Yes, sir," said Nate. "You know I would never jeopardize her security. I mean that." Benford's face moved.

"I for one remember it was you, a young case officer just expelled short-of-tour from Moscow by that damp squib Gondorf, who recruited DIVA. It was a signal achievement. She has developed into a source surpassing Cold War stars like Penkovsky and Polyakov, and even Korchnoi in the modern age." Nate felt hot in the face; Benford never complimented anyone.

"All the more reason to preserve the case and protect her for as long as we can," said Benford.

"And then get her out and resettle her somewhere safe," said Nate.

"Perhaps," said Benford, "if she at some time wants to defect. But she won't. And unless she wants out, this Service runs her as long as we can, to preserve the intel stream until it stops." Nate searched Benford's face.

"You mean until she's caught and executed," said Nate flatly.

"Don't be dramatic," said Benford, sitting up and leaning forward. "We all do everything to protect her."

"But we keep the intel flowing, is what you're saying," said Nate, "above all else, even her life, down to the last report."

"If necessary, yes. To safeguard national security and to preserve the Republic, if you'll forgive the fustian. It is what we do."

"She committed to us. She's risking her life for us," said Nate, getting out of his chair. "I'll huddle with Gable about everything, and get back to you with details." He walked to the door, hand on the doorknob, when Benford spoke.

"Nash, we operate in a hostile fog bank, we deal with ambiguity, and if we must, we apply expedient amorality to accomplish moral goals. Embrace it or tell me what else you want to do with your life."

GABLE'S SAFE-HOUSE CARBONARA

Sauté lardons of guanciale until chewy-crisp. Whisk egg yolks and grated pecorino Romano together to form a hard ball. Cook the pasta one minute less than al dente, then use pasta water to whisk egg-and-cheese ball until creamy. Toss cooked pasta with guanciale-and-egg mixture and serve immediately.

15

The Second Cold War

DIVA's request that Nash participate in the second meeting with her North Korean nuclear recruitment did not please Benford, who wanted Gable to handle it. But Ricky Walters in Moscow reported that Dominika had insisted Nash specifically be there, which was only going to last a couple of hurried hours, the cottage being so close to IAEA Headquarters and the prying eyes of Noko security gorillas. Benford relented, reasoning they would not have time in two hours to squabble over exfiltration, much less be able to engage, in Gable's words, in any "gasp-and-grunt."

Nate flew direct to Copenhagen and took the two-hour flight to Vienna on Austrian Air, then booked a room at the Pension Domizil, half a block down Schulerstrasse from Dominika's hotel. He left a note with his room number for her, and had breakfast in the curtained dining room. She walked in just as he was finishing. She was elegant in a black skirt, leather tunic with a narrow fur collar, and black-leather ankle boots. It had been three weeks since Greece and, as was usually the case between them, sweet absence dulled the acrimony over her determination to keep spying, despite the mounting dangers. She didn't want any breakfast and looked at her Line T encrypted ops phone repeatedly for texts from Ioana, who was waiting at the cottage/safe house in case Professor Ri arrived before his scheduled 1200 meeting. They would have two hours with him, the entirety of an extended lunch break, which the five thousand pampered Euro bureaucrats working in the Vienna International Centre in Donaustadt, north of the river, were accustomed to. The complex of glittering Y-shaped buildings was permanent home to an alphabet soup of UN offices, from which phalanxes of international jacks-in-office churned out hectares of documents, all of which were without doubt critical to the continued survival of the planet: IAEA (atomic energy), UNIDO (industrial development), UNODC (drugs and crime), and UNOOSA (outer-space affairs).

Dominika checked her phone again, then leaned over the table, grabbed Nate's sweater, and pulled him close to kiss him. "Our agent isn't arriving for two hours, and it takes seven minutes to get there on the Number Eight tram," she said, sitting back down. "I would therefore like to go upstairs to your room and bump bones."

Her previous choler from the safe-house spat thankfully eclipsed, Nate relaxed and sat back. "We normally say 'jump your bones' to describe what you're thinking."

"Why?" said Dominika. "I would think 'bumping' describes what I'm thinking more accurately."

Upstairs, Nate barely had time to hang the BITTE NICHT STÖREN sign on the doorknob and close the door. Dominika's leather-faced tunic squeaked as they made love, fully clothed, in an armchair, mouths plastered together and Dominika's hair fallen down around her shoulders, tendrils stuck to her sweaty cheeks. A second round consisted of a frantic shedding of clothes, the yanking of the extravagant Austrian eiderdown off the bed, and the re-invention of what historians first called the missionary position, but without any of the original evangelical restraint.

They sat on separate seats across from each other on the tram, with trembling sewing-machine legs and flushed faces, trying not to look at each other. Dominika's hair had been restored to order, but an errant strand hanging down one side of her face hinted at recent maidenly debauchery. Off the tram, they walked through the garden of the Arcotel, and on the footpath around the reedy Kaiserwasser Lake, and down the last stretch of Laberlweg, a leafy road that ran along a spit of land fronting the upper Danube, a placid branch of the river that rejoined the main river farther downstream. The houses were all cute two-room summer cottages with red or blue ornamental shutters and screened porches. The cottages had grassy front yards that ran down to the shore, each with a pontoon dock for summer canoes and skiffs, now bare and rocking gently in the slow-moving winter water.

It was just 1200 and Professor Ri would appear a few minutes from now. Nate would play a subordinate role during the debriefing, asking CIA intel requirements at appropriate times. Ioana would take a walk during the meeting, standard procedure, but also convenient in that Dominika wouldn't have to explain who Nate was, at least not right away. Dominika had been toying with the idea of recruiting Ioana for CIA—she would adore *Bratok*, she knew—and the notion of a subagent, a confederate, helping her in this work was something she wanted to discuss with Benford. She was sure it would work, especially if Ioana graduated from Sparrow status to operations.

When she opened the cottage door she knew the world had caved in. The little living room was a mass of splintered furniture and fallen bookcases, including an overturned, blood-soaked armchair that had been slashed a dozen times, its stuffing scattered over the floor. The galley kitchen was ankle deep in broken plates and glasses. Nate silently motioned to the door, indicating that they should get the hell out, but Dominika shook her head and whispered "Ioana." Stepping over detritus in the living room, they checked each of the tiny bedrooms. In one, Ioana's clothes were strewn across the bed and a bedside lamp had been thrown in a corner and smashed. Dominika's face was white.

They found Professor Ri facedown in the tub in the bathroom, remnants of the five liters of his blood slick along the tub walls, most of it already down the drain and likely feeding the Danube carp. They went back out into the living room, Dominika's face a grim mask.

"This was Shlykov. He just terminated my North Korean case."

Nate kept looking around, listening for footsteps. "Shlykov did this?" he said.

"No," said Dominika. "This is the work of his Spetsnaz bulldog. A man named Blokhin, who killed Repina in New York."

"Where's your girl?" said Nate. "Wasn't she here waiting for your agent?"

"I don't know," said Dominika. "I'm worried." She snapped her fingers. "The recorder." She went to the sideboard cabinet—it had not been touched—and took out the wire recorder Ioana had installed in anticipation of the debriefing. She plugged it into a wall socket, rewound it, and punched "play." Nothing but the hiss of dead air. "It's voice activated," said Dominika. "She would have put it in standby mode before Ri arrived." The hissing stopped and Dominika froze, staring at the spools. The two concealed wireless mics had picked up muffled conversation.

Blokhin's voice suddenly came through clearly, speaking English (*so the bastard spoke English all this time, concealing it*, thought Dominika). His voice was quiet and silky, then Ioana's voice, angry and indignant, then Blokhin switched to Russian, harsh and brutal, followed by the cacophony of a struggle. Ioana was strong and lithe and it went on for some time, the sound of her ragged breath first faint, then loud as she moved away from or toward the microphones. There was the constant sound of breaking furniture. Dominika looked imploringly at Nate, then back at the recorder, as Ioana cried an abrupt *"nyet!"* followed by a groan, then silence, then moaning, and Blokhin's silky voice again, in English, asking when the Asian gentleman was expected, and would Egorova be coming with him, and Ioana's voice spitting an obscenity. The sound of a slap, then a heartrending scream, quickly muffled, and Ioana woodenly droning that the meeting was postponed, Egorova wasn't even in the city, and another scream, What was he doing to her, was she tied in a chair? and then a faint knocking at the front door and Blokhin's voice moving away, then disappearing altogether until a man's high-pitched wail was faintly heard while Blokhin did in the bathtub whatever he had decided for the North Korean. While he was out of the room, Ioana, breathing heavily, spoke to the concealed microphone in an urgent trembling whisper. Her voice was tinny and hung in the air.

"He is a Russian, sixty years old, sixty-eight centimeters, ninety kilos, fleshy face with scar tissue across his forehead, thick arms, very strong. I cut his cheek with a glass but it did not cost him a step." Ioana started crying briefly, then stopped and sniffed. *"I think he broke my wrist. He has tied my wrists and ankles and he is using the edge of a broken dish between my legs."* Dominika, eyes streaming, looked at Nate in horror. Ioana knew she was going to die, yet she was leaving a message for Dominika. *"He is asking for you, when you will arrive. I have told him you are not coming, but he does not believe me. He intends to kill you too. I'm praying you are not on your way. When it starts again I will scream my head off, maybe you will hear, perhaps he will flee. My broken wrist is bent sideways. Wait. I hear screaming from the bathroom. Your scientist is gone. I'm next, he is coming back. Kill him if you can. Ya tebya lyublyu, I love you, take care* scumpo, *sweetie."* Dominika put her head in her hands and sobbed.

Blokhin's voice came back in range of the mike, again cooing to Ioana about when Dominika was expected, perhaps not before Ioana had softened the professor up with this pretty little thing between her legs, and another nightmare scream that subsided into a sob, and Ioana slurring over and over that Egorova was not coming, then she began screaming, bellows from the pit of her stomach, over and over, and her screaming was suddenly cut short, followed by awful gurgling and gasping—Nate recognized the sound of someone drowning in her own blood from a slashed throat—then a grunt from Blokhin as if he had slung her over his shoulder, then the sound of squeaky screen-door hinges. Several minutes of silence then Blokhin was back inside, followed by three solid minutes of the sounds of him smashing everything in the cottage not already broken, then the front door slamming and nothing else but the hiss of the recorder.

Dominika pointed to the overturned armchair, the seat cushion sodden with blood. Ioana had died there. Nate walked to the screen door facing the yard and the river, and pushed it lightly with a finger. It squeaked like on the tape. Blokhin had carried her outside. She was in the river, floating downstream to Budapest, if she hadn't already fetched up in the crook of a floating log. Nate stopped Dominika, red eyed and teeth bared, from going outside. "Stop," said Nate. "He could be out there. Let me check." The yard was empty, but there were drops of blood on the pontoon dock where Blokhin had walked out to reach deeper water and dumped her in. Nate walked to the end of the dock, holding his breath, half expecting to see her staring up at him from the blue-black water under the pontoon floats. Nothing underwater and nothing farther out in the current.

The Alte Donau tributary flowed steadily to join the main branch of the Danube several hundred meters south, and there was more than an even chance her body would be seen bumping through the pilasters of the A22 overpass or another downstream bridge, unless he had wired something heavy around her feet, in which case she would come up in the spring, bleached and swollen, an unidentifiable Jane Doe to confound Austrian authorities until she ended up in the communal section of Zentralfriedhof Cemetery, another Sparrow who finished up away from her home, unclaimed by the country she served, her fate and grave unknown to her family.

Nate heard Dominika coming up behind him; he caught her and steered her off the tipsy dock, and she looked out at the black winter water, screamed and bent over, and vomited on the grass. He led her back inside, splashed her face with water, pocketed the spool of wire from the recorder, rummaged around Ioana's bedroom and retrieved her Romanian alias passport. They both knew there could be no thought of tipping the police. Professor Ri would be reported missing, but God knows how long it would be before they found him in a rental cottage on the river. Austrian state police forensics were exceedingly thorough. As he closed the front door of the cottage, Nate wiped the doorknob, thinking that between the tub, the furniture, the dishes, and dredging the river bottom under the dock, the owner would have a little spring cleaning to do before the summer rental season began.

They walked back down Laberlweg, the way they had come, Dominika's cheeks wet with tears. As they walked, Nate half watched for Blokhin to emerge out of the Kaiserwasser in an explosion of foam, like a Nile crocodile ambushing a baby gazelle. But Nate was pretty sure Blokhin would already be halfway to Schwechat and the airport. He had knocked off Dominika's agent per instructions, had slaughtered the safe-house keeper as a bonus, but had not waited for Egorova, probably because she had been designated a target of opportunity—take her if you can, but don't loiter on target and don't get arrested. Ioana's screams had hurried him on his way. Their late arrival and the North Korean's early appearance at the cottage probably saved their lives. Nate had no illusions about being able to fend Blokhin off in hand-to-hand combat.

Nate was shocked at the brutality of the Spetsnaz killer. He must be quite the lad. All those guys were hard cases, but this one had a screw loose. It was obvious now that Dominika was a target and in danger. Could her new Kremlin patrons protect her? Inside the palace, sure, but on the street? Opposition party leader Nemtsov had been shot on the busy Bolshoy Moskvoretsky Bridge, in the very shadow of the Kremlin's Vodovzvodnaya Tower. One thing was for sure: Dominika was dead unless CIA could take out this Shlykov asshole and his dancing bear, Blokhin.

Dominika sagged against him, her body trembling and voice shaking. "We were in your room, making love, while she was being tortured, stalling for time, giving herself to save me," she sobbed. "She had the courage to describe the man who was torturing her, even though she knew she was going to die. Oh, *neschastnyy* Ioana, poor ill-fated sister. We should have been there."

"We didn't know, and if we had been there, we'd be in the river too," said Nate. "That guy wasn't going to let anyone walk away."

"I should have been there," said Dominika.

Nate stopped in the middle of the pathway and shook her by the shoulders. "Listen to me. Not your fault. A little less guilt and a lot more thinking about surviving. Will this Shlykov take a whack at you in Moscow?"

Dominika shrugged and shook him off. "In the *Rodina* anything can happen."

"Then fucking him up in Istanbul is critical. Will you be able to finish him if we can complicate his life?"

"If he fails and embarrasses the president, he is lost. But what will you do?"

"You wouldn't believe me if I told you," said Nate. As they walked, he outlined the plan to burn Major Shlykov, and her part in the operation. She stopped crying, her eyes blazed, and she thought of Ioana.

In Washington, the ponderous process of selecting a new DCIA heated up and Langley was told to prepare for briefings for the candidates' use during congressional testimony. Benford contemplated this requirement with unease.

The only policy position of the president that preoccupied Benford was the former's oft-stated distrust of CIA and the president's conviction that it was an anachronistic organization, organically prone to misdeeds and illegal acts and, consequently, overdue for demolition and a thorough reorganization. Happily, said the president, a new DCIA would begin critical reforms. To this end, the White House was putting forward three candidates for DCIA, one of whom would be selected by his staff for Senate confirmation. The unsympathetic SSCI approved the plan and ordered CIA to brief the three candidates equally in preparation for confirmation hearings. Briefing sources and methods to *candidates* before a formal nominee had been selected was heresy, but both the sitting director and the congressional bootlicker Duchin saw to it that division chiefs complied.

Benford sat at the end of the massive oval conference table on the seventh floor of Headquarters, sourly listening to Forsyth finish briefing the three nominees for DCIA on a sensitive EUR Division asset—the representative of the Palestinian Authority to the International Court of Justice in The Hague, which case was producing voluminous intelligence on Iranian support to the PLO and Hezbollah. Forsyth's presentation had been preceded by a briefing from Chief of Latin America Division, the garrulous Johnny Cross—with a pencil mustache and as handsome as a matinee idol—on a case in Caracas, the recruited deputy minister of Petroleum, who had developed into a gold mine of information on the moribund Venezuelan petrochemical industry, including secret payments in the billions from China to keep the spavined government afloat. Next up was Chief of East Asia Division Brenda Neff, blond, busty, and profane, who would tell the nominees about an EA asset, a captain in the Philippine navy who was providing useful assessments and imagery of the fortified atolls in the South China Sea being constructed by Beijing.

Benford wryly noted that his colleagues were briefing on important, but midlevel assets. No division chief was going to totally lift his or her skirt and give up any crown jewels, at least not yet. Duchin knew enough to suspect they were slow rolling, and when the Acting Director heard—as he certainly would from that woodpecker Duchin—the chiefs would be ordered to open the books to the nominees completely. Only a matter of time.

The three nominees sat at the opposite far end of the table, respectively bored, attentive, and mystified. US Senator Celia Feigenbaum was seething: based on her many years on the Senate Appropriations Committee, she was utterly convinced that duplicitous CIA needed to be radically downsized *if not abolished*, commencing with the ceding of various Directorates to the DOD, the NSA, and the FBI. If confirmed as DCIA, she was determined to clean house, and to Benford, this was a calamitous notion, made trebly astounding by the senator's expressed view that the abiding clandestine tenets of the Agency—stealing secrets and exploiting vulnerabilities to suborn human targets—were immoral. "It's not who we *are*, it's not what America *stands for*," purred the senator frequently and piously to any reporter who thrust a microphone in her face. She was a leading contender, in part because her Pecksniffian views mirrored the president's.

The senator had arrived with her senior staff director, Robert Farbissen, and she blithely demanded he receive the same briefings as the nominees, to which Congressional Affairs Chief Duchin immediately agreed, seeing as how Rob also had TS clearances. Benford gritted his teeth; it was an outrageous concession. He knew all about Farbissen: he'd been a fixture in Washington for decades, flitting from staff to staff, wreaking havoc with his revanchist fevers and partisan distemper. Short, and squat, with a lopsided mouth and capped teeth beneath a hedge-apple nose, Farbissen triumphantly sat down at the conference table to listen to the cherished secrets from the vaults of the detested CIA. He turned to notice for the first time that Simon Benford was sitting next to him, made a face of great distaste, got up, and moved three seats away, as if Benford were "patient zero" in a plague ward. *The measure of the man*, thought Benford, *is the distance of three seats at the table.*

More attentive was US Navy Vice Admiral Audrey Rowland. Trim in her service dress dark-blue uniform, she sat with hands folded on the table, the thick gold sleeve stripes of her three-star rank resplendent against the dark walnut conference table. She had been named Distinguished Student after advanced studies at the Industrial College of the Armed Forces at Fort McNair in Washington. During the next twenty years, she'd held increasingly more important positions, most recently as commander of the Office of Naval Research on the shores of the Potomac River in Virginia. At ONR, she energetically supervised nearly three thousand scientists, permanent civilian researchers and contractors, while managing an annual research budget of more than a billion dollars.

Audrey had risen meteorically, passing through flag ranks of rear admiral (bottom half) to rear admiral in two years, and three years later, her third star as vice admiral was awarded. Benford watched her through lowered lashes, noting that she wore more fruit salad on her chest than Bull Halsey, including the Defense Superior Service Medal, the Legion of Merit, the Defense Meritorious Service Medal, the Meritorious Service Medal (three awards), the Navy and Marine Corps Commendation Medal (four awards), and the Navy and Marine Corps Achievement Medal. None was an award for combat or sea duty.

At forty-nine years old, VADM Aubrey Rowland was the modern empowered woman of the twenty-first-century US Navy: brilliant, an able administrator, and decorous. She had never married—the inevitable gossip occasionally floated around, mainly among envious male peers who were still lowly captains commanding destroyer groups out of Yokosuka—but VADM Rowland otherwise was discreetly considered a benign maiden, totally dedicated to the navy and its mission. When the call went out for prospective nominees for DCIA, Rowland's name was immediately proposed by the Chief of Naval Operations, the Secretary of the Navy, and seconded by POTUS.

There was precedent: an admiral had helmed CIA in the midseventies; it was too long ago to remember the lasting damage caused by that dour interloper's so-called Halloween Massacre in 1977 when two hundred operations officers were fired as nonessential, followed by another eight hundred case officers through 1979, uprooting in one stroke an entire generation of experienced street veterans, most with near-native language skills, a priceless commodity. But that was thirty years ago, and today the navy would be tickled to have one of its own again running CIA, none of whose ops officers ever showed much respect to naval intelligence or NCIS, the criminal investigative service. Benford studied the admiral's long mannish face, jutting chin, and salt-and-pepper hair pulled into a braided bun in back, but with a poufy prairie-wife curl in front that, even to Benford's blind fashion eye, was bizarre. Rowland noticed Benford looking at her, nodded across the table, and smiled pleasantly, flashing a protruding left incisor. *Okay, maybe physicist admirals don't have to be lovely looking, especially not the brainy ones*, he thought. As DCIA, she predictably would focus on the science and technology side of the house, but with luck she'd at least support a clandestine service in dire need of resuscitation.

At the far curve of the table, clearly mystified by at least two-thirds of what had been briefed so far, sat the third nominee for DCIA, Ambassador Thomas "Tommy" Vano, who had starred as a B-film actor in the 1980s (*Space Rage, Maniac Brainiac*), and was voted sexiest man alive in 1985, but started fading and got out of Hollywood before he permanently crashed and burned. Using modest earnings from the movies, he began buying strip malls in Florida, together with an entrepreneur brother-in-law, at the start of the nineties real-estate boom. More lucky than prescient, Vano made millions, then formed a company, a consortium of investors buying global commodities, including rare and precious metals. Over the next two decades, he followed his partners' leads and made additional millions, several of which he donated to the right campaign, and in 2008 was named ambassador to Spain. He stayed for four years in a perpetual, if pleasant, state of mild bewilderment, where he first encountered and was transported by the wines of Rioja and *caparrones*, the earthy Riojan stew of white beans and smoky *pimentón* pepper.

Inexplicably retained by the State Department after his return from Madrid, he became Ambassador at Large for Intelligence, which meant he had a shabby office in an interior corridor at Main State, with a two-person staff, and attended countless meetings. The position had been unfilled for eighteen months, primarily because no senior State Department diplomat wanted to wet his shoes in the squishy peat bog of the spy world. But Ambassador Vano found liaison meetings with various intelligence agencies around town tolerably interesting, if not particularly demanding and as the State Department rep he was rarely asked to participate (*the leper at the square dance*, one

NSA wit had muttered). He'd had intel briefs as Chief of Mission in Madrid, and found them thrilling, sort of like movie scripts.

However, one day Tommy Vano interrupted a discussion about strategic metals being purchased and hoarded by Moscow and Beijing, and casually mentioned that his consortium was familiar with the global commodities markets, government ministers, commercial buyers, extraction mines, and stockpiles. All of it. From that day, he had a seat at the table and, despite being more affable than discerning, was accepted as a subject-matter expert.

When the call went out for nominees for DCIA, the milk-and-water outgoing secretary of state (who still believed in the code of conduct which held that gentlemen don't read each other's mail), proposed the Honorable Thomas Vano for DCIA, citing his business acumen, his foreign experience as a diplomatist, and his attributes as a current Ambassador at Large for Intelligence, with deep ties to, and contacts within, the intelligence community. It was Washington-speak to be sure, and patent nonsense, but Vano made the cut for the final three.

He was tall and bird chested, with a buccaneer's wavy black hair, limpid pools for eyes, and a Cary Grant cleft on his chin. Benford noted with interest that the sole visible respondent to Vano's money-Hollywood-sex vibe was EA Division Chief Neff, a known free spirit once referred to by the deputy of the organized crime section in Counternarcotics Division as a habitual receiver of swollen goods. Senator Feigenbaum was too old and mean to care, and Admiral Rowland didn't move her gold stripes an inch, and seemed oblivious.

God preserve us, thought Benford. A harpy from the Hill intent on destroying the Agency; an awkward physics bluestocking from the navy; and a stuffed-toy millionaire who as ambassador in Madrid thought the Basque terror group's acronym ETA stood for estimated time of arrival.

Benford had demurred in today's briefing session, "in the interest of time," to discuss any Russian cases, and was determined to stall for as long as possible. MAGNIT was still out there, Nash had just reported that the GRU was gunning for DIVA, and all hell was going to pop in Istanbul if they didn't do something immediately. Istanbul was going to be a disaster.

The WOLVERINEs. In Sevastopol. *God help us, I hope they're as sharp as Forsyth swears they are. The First Cold War ended thirty years ago. We're fighting the second one now.*

RIOJAN *CAPARRONES* STEW

Fry sliced chorizo and chopped onion and garlic in olive oil until soft. Add *pimentón* (hot Spanish smoked paprika) and red chili flakes and continue frying. Add chopped fresh tomatoes, water, vegetable stock, canned chopped tomatoes, and tomato paste. Bring to a boil, then simmer covered. Add chopped parsley and white beans (cannellini or navy) and continue simmering until thickened, somewhere between the consistency of a soup and a stew. Let stand an hour (or overnight), and reheat to serve piping hot, with a drizzle of olive oil and a poached egg floating on top.

16

The WOLVERINEs

During the salad days of the Cold War, the breathless arrival in bustling Rome Station of first-tour case officer Tom Forsyth, fresh out of training at the Farm, was greeted variously by colleagues. A number of them helpfully showed Tom around Rome and pointed out the best trattorias for Roman *cucina povera*, peasant home cooking, and where to find a bottle of Cesanese del Piglio from Lazio. His branch Chief got him on the invitation list for half a dozen national day celebrations at foreign embassies where he could begin trolling for developmentals on his own. The reports chief sat him down and went over the target lists, so he'd know what to look for.

Senior Rome Station officer Gale Stack was fifty-five years old and close to retirement. Earlier in his career he'd had opportunities at management, but it hadn't worked out due to competing priorities that included three-martini lunches, creative accounting on his ops revolving fund (RF), and chatting up bar hostesses. Stack resented that he'd never been appreciated for what he brought to the mix. He'd been stepped on and stepped over—plenty. The arrival of young Forsyth—they were in adjoining office cubicles—presented an opportunity for Stack to unload a bothersome case encrypted VZWOLVERINE. It was going nowhere, at least not with the amount of effort Stack was willing to put into it. The asset, a young Polish émigré named Witold Zawadzki had volunteered as an embassy walk-in, and Stack had elbowed other officers aside for the case. He thought it would be a gravy train—lots of intel for little work—as well as a nice line item on his RF for charging off lunches and dinners.

VZWOLVERINE was from an aristocratic family in Kraków, one of the *szlachta*, the Polish nobility, dating back to 1360 and King Casimir III the Great. Sent to Rome as a boy to live with an aunt, Witold, now twenty-five and an Italian citizen, hated the Soviets only slightly less than he hated the *zdrajcy*, the traitor Poles who sold out their own country. At their first agent meeting, the firebrand young Pole—nervous, thin, blond hair slicked back—looked intently at his white-maned case officer with the manicured fingernails, whose hand shook as he pulled the martini olive off a toothpick with his large white teeth. Witold leaned forward and told this CIA officer that he was willing to return to Poland, and that his family knew patriotic like-minded Poles in the government, the Party, and the military. Stack burped, signaled for another martini, and told VZWOLVERINE to order anything he wanted off the menu, anything at all.

At a second boozy lunch at the fabulously expensive seafood restaurant La Rossetta in the shadow of the Pantheon, VZWOLVERINE brought a list of influential Polish families who would, with careful encouragement, provide information on Polish Communist Party leadership, Soviet intelligence activity in Poland, and Warsaw Pact military readiness levels. Putting down his lobster claw, Gale Stack took the paper with a butter-slick thumb, put it into his coat pocket, and told Witold he'd "run traces" on the names. Stifling his ready temper, VZWOLVERINE told Stack that he wanted to talk to someone else in his organization. Alarm bell. Bad idea to let another Station officer get his nose under the tent to see how Stack was expensing meals off this case, never mind letting this wannabe freedom fighter complain about his handling officer.

Stack the next day told the branch Chief that VZWOLVERINE was a bitter émigré with no access to intel, and that he was recommending that Station cut the asset with a $1,000 termination bonus (he'd give the young man $500 and keep the rest as pocket money) and stop wasting time. The branch Chief wearily said okay, but something made him change his mind, and he told Stack, instead, to turn over the case to another officer, that maybe changing the chemistry would help. Alarm bell. An experienced Station officer would see the real story and report back. Then Stack remembered that new kid Forsyth in the next cubicle. He wouldn't know the ropes yet; he'd be perfect. How about it? asked Stack. Easy case to cut his teeth on, push the asset to develop access, nice and slow. The branch Chief shrugged and said to go ahead.

That was the start of the WOLVERINE network. After a bibulous turnover meeting, Tom Forsyth and his new agent Witold Zawadzki warily began to feel each other out: Witold saw that his new rookie case officer was honest, energetic, and driven to be successful; Forsyth saw that the impatient young Pole's fierce commitment needed to be controlled. Nothing would be accomplished by running suicide missions. VZWOLVERINE's return forays to Poland started slowly—covered as commercial buying trips for an Italian design company—letting the SB, the *Sluzba Bezpieczenstwa*, the Soviet-controlled Polish intelligence service, get used to seeing the young man with the Italian passport come and go.

After two trips, VZWOLVERINE recruited a childhood friend, now a Polish Army captain, who was encrypted VZWOLVERINE/2. Family friends, VZWOLVERINE/3 and /4, a comely former art student, now special assistant in the party secretariat, and a police sergeant respectively, were acquired in the next six months. Witold's next recruitment was VZWOLVERINE/5, his cousin, who was coincidentally a communicator in the headquarters of the Ministry of Interior, who processed KGB message traffic between Warsaw and Moscow. The intelligence streams started slowly. Reports were collected from those subagents by WOLVERINE/1 (as principal agent) and brought to Forsyth in Rome.

Rome Station management sat up and started taking notice, then Headquarters followed. The reporting from the WOLVERINEs was superb, including photography of classified Warsaw Pact and Soviet Red Army documents never seen before. Counterintelligence analysts looked at the take with a skeptical eye: too-good-to-be-true intelligence always aroused suspicions, but the reports were corroborated and they kept coming. Forsyth had to continually rein in Witold, to tell him to slow down, to balance production against risk. In his continuing effort to protect his WOLVERINEs, Forsyth trained Witold in clandestine photography, impersonal communications, secret writing, and advanced intel reporting, who in turn trained his network members inside Poland.

A month later, Witold presented Forsyth with an *audio tape* of a closed meeting of the frantic Central Committee of the Polish Communist Party arguing about whether to comply with or ignore an order from KGB Director Chebrikov to arrest fractious Wujek miners and Gdánsk shipyard workers in the Solidarity movement. WOLVERINE/3, the statuesque clerical assistant in the secretariat whose name was Agnes Krawcyk and who, alarmingly, was an adrenaline junkie, had stuck a microphone and small wire recorder (assembled by WOLVERINE/5, the electronics whiz named Jerzy) under the president's dais before the meeting. Even as he submitted the reports—subsequently graded a rare O for outstanding—Forsyth freaked. The WOLVERINEs would not last if they kept taking the insane risks of the past months, he yelled at Witold. And the use of two WOLVERINEs in the same operation violated the tenet of keeping WOLVERINE network members compartmented from each other. It was risky enough that Witold knew everyone's name. This had to stop.

Over a holiday dinner of *zrazy zawijane*, succulent roulade of beef with onion, mushrooms, and silky dark gravy, at his aunt's Rome apartment, Witold smiled at Forsyth—how far they had come together—and said that given Forsyth's motherly concern, he would postpone for now his plan to kidnap the KGB *rezident* in Warsaw and deliver him hog-tied to Forsyth in time for Christmas. They toasted with a glass of Chopin *wódka*. In the three years of Forsyth's Rome tour, the WOLVERINE network had produced hundreds of intelligence reports of high interest, and had informed Washington policymakers on the dangerous last throes of Soviet domination of Eastern Europe. Headquarters promoted Forsyth and presented the Medal of Achievement to Witold.

======

When the Soviet Union imploded in 1989 and Poland came back into the light, Forsyth proposed that his five WOLVERINEs be kept together and on the active-duty roster. He envisioned the team traveling as commercial reps for various Polish companies selling machine tools, pumps, and software in denied areas—North Korea, Cuba, Iran, Russia—countries murderously difficult for traditionally covered CIA officers. The statuesque Agnes Krawcyk, moreover, had joined the Faculty of Conservation and Restoration of Works of Art at the Academy of Fine Arts in Krakow where she finally earned her degree as a licensed conservator of antique terra-cotta, plaster, and ceramic artworks. Forsyth envisioned operational foreign travel for Agnes with cover as a restorer of art.

With relative freedom of movement in these countries, said Forsyth, the team could discreetly conduct required operational acts. The WOLVERINEs had been trained over the years and were proficient in street surveillance, surreptitious entry, site casing, recruitment, and intelligence reporting. All of them spoke fluent Polish and Russian, as well as the requisite French, German, and Satellite Proto English. They were self-sufficient, aggressive, natural risk takers, and fiercely loyal to Forsyth, who was like a god to them. Then Headquarters intervened.

There was protracted bureaucratic wrangling over Forsyth's proposal for the WOLVERINEs. The new breed of CIA leadership—mostly politically ambitious former analysts and administrators who for decades had resented the verve and hegemony of the Directorate of Operations and now perversely sought to reform the DO into oblivion—viewed these five fanatic Slavs (or whatever they were) as retro Cold War dinosaurs. Besides, collection in the modern age was shifting to drones, and satellites, and massive electronic listening posts. Classic HUMINT (human intelligence) such as an officer talking to a clandestine source, the one sure way to obtain the *plans and intentions* of the opposition, was atrophying as an overly dangerous and time-consuming method of collection. Most CIA bureaucrats frantic to avoid operational flaps wanted nothing to do with case officers, collectors, operators, cowboys, scalp takers, mustangs, old whores, headhunters, or five fucking Eastern European WOLVERINEs for that matter, who could create only blue ruin and wind them up in front of a congressional oversight committee.

———

When it appeared that Headquarters' ignorance and acedia would prevail, and that the WOLVERINEs would be put out to pasture, a crisis arose in 2001 involving CIA employees in Syria. Three visiting analysts—two women and one man—from the Office of Near Eastern and South Asian Analysis (NESA) had ignored Damascus Station guidance to stay within the embassy compound in central Damascus on Abu Ja'far al Mansur Avenue. They were in Syria to gather "ground truth" on the Syrian civil war, and thought they knew what they were doing. Two of them spoke rudimentary Arabic. They set out on a Tuesday morning, intending to visit the offices of the International Red Cross on Arwada Square, the Italian Hospital on Omar Al-Mukhtar Avenue, and the Souq Al Khoja on Al Thawra Street, a total round-trip of three hours and ten miles.

When they did not return to the embassy at the close of business, the security officer called the metropolitan police who several hours later found the body of one of the women in the eastern suburb of Jobar, on the ground floor of the burned-out Teacher's Tower Building, a blackened ten-story shell amid rubble and rusted tanks with hatches flung open and tracks thrown off the drive wheels. The forty-six-year-old divorced mother of two had been wired in her Maidenform underwear to a rusted bedspring propped upright against a shrapnel-pocked wall, and a plastic cable tie had been cinched around her neck. With a shrug, police said it might have been rogue soldiers from the National Defense Forces, or Sunni-led insurgents, or a Hezbollah unit, who could tell, but they expected the torture tape would be delivered to the embassy in several days.

That night, the security officer received a frantic call from the other two analysts. They had narrowly escaped being taken by running down an alley when their taxi had been blocked by two cars. They had flagged down an elderly man in a dented truck and offered to pay him to drive them to the embassy, but Hezbollah roadblocks and a thunderous explosion a block away had panicked the driver who instead drove the protesting analysts to his house in the village of As Saboura, eight miles west of the city along Route One. The old man and his wife were terrified that local Islamist insurgents would discover the Americans and murder them all—the streets at night were full of roving armed bands of men in *keffiyeh* head scarves. The analysts were trapped, unable to move. They had water and had been fed—the old lady made a batch of *kurrat-barasya*, a fragrant Syrian leek-and-lamb stew, to last the week. They spent the night on the couch, listening to voices in the courtyard. They didn't have much time: some neighbor eventually would notice and talk, or militants might search the houses.

Complicating matters further was that someone in the police had whispered to the local Iranian Qods Force commander that two CIA officers were stranded and hiding somewhere in Damascus. The call went out from Tehran to compliant Syrian security organs, militia, and army units to find and apprehend the perfidious Americans who, significantly, were not accredited to the Syrian government, and therefore had no diplomatic immunity. Despite repeated protests from the acting ambassador, Hezbollah roadblocks were set up around the US Embassy. Station officers tried several times to get clear and drive to the village, but had to abort when they picked up heavy harassing surveillance. They stood down.

At Headquarters, the dire situation in Damascus was the first topic of discussion during the nightly Director's executive-review meeting in the seventh-floor conference room. The caliphs in Langley who normally sat in the high-backed chairs waiting for orders from downtown were gloomy: they had a dead analyst on their hands, and the possibility of losing two more would be no end of trouble. No one had any ideas, nor was anyone going to suggest a solution, and conversation withered. The dyspeptic silence was broken when now Chief EUR Forsyth submitted to the collected leadership that his team of Polish agents could infiltrate Damascus without attracting attention, make contact with the two surviving analysts, and exfiltrate them out of Syria, probably west to Lebanon. There would be no contact with the beleaguered Station. Faces around the table brightened. This was a solution on two levels: either the analysts would be rescued, or the train wreck of a blown op could be blamed on Forsyth and his polka-dancing retinue.

Three WOLVERINEs flew into Damascus International via the intermittent Syrian Air flight from Algiers, posing as representatives of the Polish Business Board looking for business opportunities in new urban-renewal projects, a cover that was marginally plausible given the growing devastation of the suburbs of Damascus. Two other WOLVERINEs, including Forsyth's friend Witold, traveled by jeep from Lebanon and staged in Jdeidat Yabous, a Syrian town forty-five kilometers west of Damascus. It was three kilometers from the Lebanese border, the official border crossing. Witold and his colleague arrived in a white Toyota Land Cruiser with the logo of Heritage for Peace on the door, a familiar organization dedicated to protecting World Heritage sites and antiquities in Syria. No locals paid them any attention.

After a desultory call on the Ministry of Housing and Construction, the WOLVERINEs in Damascus determined they were black and operated flawlessly. They located the house by geolocating the analysts' cell phones in As Saboura with a CANINE unit, a CIA proprietary GPS-satellite tracking system, operated from an innocuous seven-inch tablet, and accurate to five meters. The exhausted analysts were shaken awake at four in the morning by VZWOLVERINE/4, the Polish ex-police sergeant who somehow had entered the little house without a sound. They were bundled into a waiting car and driven north on Highway One where they met Witold's Toyota at dawn. Transferring to Witold's vehicle, the CIA analysts were given khaki field shirts and jeans, floppy hats, desert boots, and Belgian passports. Witold then drove to the border, timing the crossing at noon when truck traffic was heaviest and potbellied customs officers were thinking about lunch. One of the Syrian customs men fingered the alias Belgian passport of one of the terrified analysts, and asked him a question in French, a language he did not speak. The swooning analyst instead threw up the remains of leek-and-lamb stew on the customs man's boots. Witold ruefully explained that his colleague had drunk water from a stream below the last village, and had been sick for the last two hours. Shaking his head at the *ajami*, these non-Arabic barbarians—everyone knew to drink from streams *before* they ran through towns—the customs man waved them through. The analysts were on a Paris-bound flight from Beirut the next morning. The other three WOLVERINEs meanwhile returned to Damascus for another meeting with the flummoxed minister, dropped off the rental SUV, and flew out to Abu Dhabi the next day. No trace, no flap, no fuss, courtesy of the WOLVERINEs. Damascus Station breathed a sigh of relief, the grandees at Langley preened, and Forsyth had his WOLVERINE team intact.

<hr>

The WOLVERINEs remained on active duty for another three years, but with their sponsor and advocate Tom Forsyth assigned abroad and then Headquarters-bound, they were eventually retired, and were paid their sizable annuities that had accrued over the years. There was an awkward awards ceremony in Headquarters during which the five WOLVERINEs were presented with individual Distinguished Service medals, a Meritorious Unit Citation, as well as engraved brass-and-wood mantel clocks with a world-time bezel and CIA logo on the face. The presenter who read the citations—she had been born the year Witold had eluded the guard dogs in the Kampinos Forest outside Warsaw—had a little trouble with the Polish names, but the Deputy Director had memorized *gratulacje*, "congratulations" in Polish, which he kept repeating while shaking hands.

Thanks to their performance in Syria, Forsyth kept the WOLVERINEs on the reserve list, but there was only intermittent work, and they all eventually dispersed to comfortable if spiritless retirements. Three returned to Poland and their families. Agnes, the only woman of the network, was single, earthy, and still a wild child. She settled in Southern California, and found work restoring art at the Getty Museum. Witold, forever serious and driven, and chronically unmarried, chose to live in New York, where he occasionally did freelance security consulting.

So Forsyth's unexpected call for the WOLVERINEs to pack their bags and meet in New York City was the long-hoped-for recall from their blancmange existences. The rendezvous was set at the exclusive Tiro A Segno Club (established 1888) on Mulberry Street in the Village, where Witold—thanks to his Italian citizenship—was a member. It was a special place: The club's façade of three nondescript brownstones was identified only by a brass plaque and a red canopy. The entrance foyer was graced by two antique shotguns hung on the wall. The adjoining bar room, sitting rooms, and card rooms were all wood and leather, and the table in the billiard room was gorgeous in orange felt. The dining room was bathed in subdued lighting from copper-bowl pendants, and the intimate tables sparkled with crystal and white linen. The air of the club was heavy with fragrant savory things going on in the Italian kitchen. Members of Tiro (as it was called) knew one another and nodded politely.

Witold had booked the narrow private room with a table that could seat thirty, and had ordered a simple dinner of buttery imported *mozzarella di bufala* with prosciutto, a sinfully rich lobster risotto, and fresh fruit for dessert. The WOLVERINEs were all there early, greeted by Witold with a glass of prosecco. Their faces lighted up when Forsyth entered the room, and the Poles moved to shake his hand and buss him on both cheeks, a happy Cold War reunion. It had been too long. Faces turned again to the door as Nate Nash walked into the room. Attentive and fit, dark and intense, Nash wore a blazer over a pinstripe shirt with a dark-blue tie. The WOLVERINEs made their individual canny assessments: Witold carefully observed how Forsyth addressed Nash to gauge the young man's status; Ryszard, the former army captain watched how Nash made eye contact when speaking; Piotr, the former police sergeant registered the strength of Nash's handshake; Agnes from afar appraised Nash's shoulders under his blazer.

"You all have been lazing around," said Forsyth. "We have work to do." Piotr the ex-cop huffed.

"You kept us waiting long enough," he said.

"I wasn't sure you hadn't grown fat and slow in retirement," said Forsyth deadpan.

"Piotr is the fattest," said Jerzy, the electronics whiz. "Too much *sernik*, Polish cheesecake."

"Do not worry about me," said Piotr. "You should worry about losing your hair." The rangy Jerzy's hair was thinning on top.

"Thomas, as you can see, discipline is as bad as ever," said Ryszard. "These worthless fellows have not changed."

"Enough," said Witold, always in command. "Thomas, tell us what work you have for us." He was ever the aristocrat, dressed in a light-charcoal double-breasted suit.

"Russia, the Crimea, Sevastopol."

"*Fenomenalny*, marvelous," said Ryszard. "The weather will be warm and sunny."

"How long?" asked Witold. He sipped his prosecco, looking at Nate over the rim of his glass.

"Two days, three; the target is a warehouse," said Forsyth. Faces turned to Nate again.

"But first tell us something of this young man," said Agnes. She was tall and sharp featured, with gray eyes and thick black hair that fell to her shoulders. She had a snow-white streak in her hair, a white forelock that began at the forehead and swept back. She was wearing a black knit sweaterdress that clung to a body that hinted at Mount Rushmore.

"This is Nathaniel Nash," said Forsyth. "I've worked with him for six years. He will be coordinating the operation." The Poles were silent.

"Coordinating, or leading?" asked Piotr.

"Leading. He has significant experience in denied-area operations," said Forsyth.

"May I ask where?" said Witold softly. Forsyth knew this wasn't going to be easy.

"Moscow," said Nate, speaking for the first time. "Helsinki, Rome, Athens." Agnes thought he was attractive, the confident man-boy.

"*Vy govoríte po-rússki?*" asked Ryszard. Do you speak Russian?

"I studied in college and kept it up afterward," said Nate in Russian. The Poles instantly heard in his accent and phrasing that he was fluent, probably better than any of them.

"He's the best officer I've seen on the street, ever," said Forsyth. Nate looked at his shoes. *Yeah, good on the street, my ass in a sling*, he thought. Piotr sipped his drink, and Agnes tilted her head, still looking at him.

"Thomas, forgive me, but I'm thinking *Pani* Nathaniel, Mr. Nate, is too young to be that good," said Piotr. Heads turned. Everybody knew Piotr the cop—he was testing. Forsyth held his breath. *Come on, Nash*, he thought.

"If I agreed with you," said Nate in colloquial Russian, looking Piotr in the eyes, "we'd both be wrong."

There was a moment of silence, then Witold held out a glass to Nate. "Care for some prosecco?" he said.

———

After the mozzarella, they had twenty-five minutes before the risotto would reach the final *mantecatura* stage where cold butter is stirred into the finished rice, so Witold suggested they go down to the basement firing range. The name "Tiro A Segno" in fact means shooting gallery and the incongruous fifty-yard range with three leather-padded firing points was popular with members. Piotr looked at Nate and pointed to the bolt-action rimfire rifles at two of the shooting positions, put on earmuffs, slapped the four-round magazine into the rifle, and worked the bolt to jack a round into the breach. Nate did the same, and both men rested their elbows on the leather padding and looked through the sighting scopes. The paper targets were simple three-ring bull's-eyes hung on tracked clips that could be run the length of the spotlighted range, to vary distances or to be retrieved up close for inspection.

Agnes moved to stand behind Nate and whispered *udachi*, good luck, in Russian. The little rifles popped and each target flapped as the .22 rounds tore ragged holes in the center of the paper—excellent, tight groups on both bull's-eyes. At the fourth shot, both Forsyth and Witold saw Nate's rifle barrel waiver for a second. The rifles were safed and the targets run back to the firing line. Nate's target was perfect; all the rounds had gone through the same expanded hole in the smallest ring. There was a bellow from Piotr. His target had a hole outside the rings, near the edge of the paper—a disastrous "flyer." Nate shook Piotr's hand with a serious expression. Piotr looked over at Forsyth and Witold, who were smirking, red faced. He looked back at Nate, who was still serious, but his eyes were twinkling. Piotr finally got it: Nate had shot across the lanes to place the apparent pulled shot into Piotr's target, an old range-master's prank Gable had once pulled on Nate himself. Piotr held on to Nate's hand, glowering.

"*Beris druzhno, ne budet gruzno,*" said Nate in Russian. If all of us take hold of it together, it won't feel heavy. Piotr clapped Nate on the shoulder.

"Now I will buy you a drink," he said.

ZRAZY ZAWIJANE—POLISH ROULADE OF BEEF

Pound slices of round steak very thin. Put thin-sliced onions and pickle, and a finger of trimmed French bread, on each slice, roll tightly, and secure with toothpicks. Boil dried mushrooms in beef stock. Roll beef rolls in flour and brown in butter with additional onions in a Dutch oven. Cover rolls with stock and bake until beef is tender and braising liquid has reduced to a rich gravy.

17

Phase One

The narrow *S*-shaped Balaklava harbor on the southern coast of the Crimean peninsula was too short to be called a fjord. Protected by craggy headlands topped by the ruins of a Genoese fort built in 1365, the sunbaked little harbor was flanked by empty warehouses and two sleepy restaurants with tables and umbrellas. At the end of the harbor, on the west side, yawned a decrepit concrete adit that was the entrance to the defunct Soviet underground submarine base with a five-hundred-meter channel built under the mountain during the Cold War to shelter Red Fleet submarines from nuclear attack. Clustered on the hills above the east side of the harbor were newer buildings of the town, including the red-tile-roofed Dakkar Resort Hotel with stone balconies overlooking the little jewel harbor. At night, under the riotous Crimean stars, the few city lights glittered on the still water.

Nate and the WOLVERINEs sailed into Balaklava harbor at midnight, on a fifty-two-foot trunk-cabin cruiser with a dark-blue hull and graceful varnished topsides. The leased yacht with two crew from CIA's Maritime Branch had departed from Varna, Bulgaria, and in two days had navigated the three hundred nautical miles, out of sight of land, directly to Balaklava Bay on the placid Crimean coast of pine-covered peaks and rocky islets. The boat backed into an empty slip at the modest Golden Symbol Yacht Club, too late to check in with the authorities. The next morning, uninterested Ukrainian customs officers recorded the Polish alias passports of the passengers on a coast-wide holiday cruise. Instead of staying aboard the yacht, the passengers booked six rooms at the Dakkar Hotel and spent the rest of the day exploring the little town, climbing the hill to the castle ruins, and taking the organized tour of the underground submarine pens, now a museum. By the end of the day, they had satisfied themselves that there was no coverage of them by local police or regional security services. It had been a consideration that Nate—known by Moscow FSB as a CIA officer—technically was in Russian-controlled Crimea, but he was anonymous in the company of the team.

They ate at the crowded Café Argo, dipping crusty bread into vermillion Georgian beet-salad spread, squeezing lemons over *shashlik*, sizzling lamb kebabs sprinkled with wild oregano, chased by ice-cold Lvivski beers. The WOLVERINEs were watchful but at ease. Steady nerves, top pros. Nate tried to tamp down his anticipation, the edginess he always felt before an op. He saw Agnes looking at him from down the table, sensing his mood. Tomorrow they would go active, travel to Sevastopol, and break into the warehouse; DIVA had reported the address from Moscow. Nate and the WOLVERINEs had rehearsed how they would tag the crates with quick-plant beacons, and Nate saw how good they were. So good, in fact, that they expanded the original plan. He had bonded with the Poles during the two days of training—Witold and Ryszard, rigidly proper; brainy Jerzy, well, brainy; and gruff Piotr, a Polish version of Gable. Agnes had kept looking at Nate, categorizing him, sizing him up. Now in Balaklava, she appeared calm and collected; perhaps the only sign of pre-op nerves was her habit of twisting a strand of her thick hair around a finger.

An hour later, Nash stood on the darkened balcony of his hotel room before going to bed, looking at the black harbor and the starlight on the hills across the water. Dominika. He would see her soon, if nothing went wrong in the next two days. He played in his head what he would say to her in Istanbul. Gable would be hovering, watching them, his big sheepdog head turned into the wind, sniffing. Jesus, he wanted to hold Dominika in his arms, put his hands on her back, and pull her tight against him. If he did that, Gable would feed him to the lions.

He knew, just knew, however, that Dominika would fly into a rage if he fended her off; she had done so before. She was of the view that she could be a spy and still be in love with her CIA handler, whom she desired. And she did not sympathize one bit with his conundrum that his superiors disapproved of their doing what they both most wanted to do. She would see to it he was not fired. If they loved each other, that should be enough.

If you love me, then nothing else matters, Dominika had told him. Nate resented being in this situation, resented Benford looking over his shoulder all the time, resented Gable's acuity, resented Dominika's damn Russian incorrigibility. And tomorrow he and this team would break into a warehouse in broad daylight and futz with antipersonnel explosives designed to blow them up. *Chill, what's the matter with you*? he thought. He heard his door latch click and turned to see a sliver of hallway light widen, then go dark again. Someone was in his room. FSB? Had he missed hostile coverage today? Breathe. Heartbeat up. Nate moved quietly off the balcony, reaching for the heavy glass ashtray on the side table. He smelled perfume and his stomach flipped. *No way.* Agnes came out of the shadow into the bar of starlight slanting across the room. She was wearing a baggy sleep shirt and was barefoot.

"The locks on these doors are ridiculously easy," she said.

Nate swallowed. "Agnes, what are you doing? Are you all right?" He knew the answer.

"I always am a little nervous before an operation," she said. "Aren't you?"

"Nervous about what?" asked Nate.

"Well, not nervous, exactly," said Agnes, running her fingers through her hair.

"What exactly?" said Nate.

"More like amorous," she said.

"Amorous?"

"As in horny," she said, stepping toward him. She touched his cheek.

"Agnes," said Nate, "this is not a good idea. We have work tomorrow."

"It will steady our nerves," she said, trailing her hand down his chest.

"My nerves are fine," said Nate. Her perfume was citrusy and made his head swim. She was exotic and primal. He could feel the heat of her hand through his shirt, and he felt dizzy. *Benford, Gable, Domi, regulations, kicked out of CIA, separated from the Service, the citrus-and-musk bloom of this busty tuning fork named Agnes standing a foot away, breathing on him.* His arms involuntarily moved a fraction; he knew that in three seconds he was going to twist his fingers in that mane of hair with the white forelock and crush their mouths together. He could see the rise and fall of her breasts under her shirt; the bottom hem vibrated as her body trembled. Three, two, one. Fuck. Stop. His hands stayed at his sides. Agnes took her hand off his chest, stepped back, and shook her hair.

"I'm thinking about the team, that's all, about us doing this right," said Nate.

"So I shall go?" Agnes said.

Nate took her hot hand in his. He didn't want her to leave mad. The last thing they needed in hostile territory. "You're incredibly beautiful and sexy. But don't you think it's not the right thing?"

"I think it is the right thing," she said flatly. She turned and slipped out the door without a sound. *Jesus, she's furious.*

Nate woke up an hour later, his room pitch-black, the smell of citrus in his nose again. He felt Agnes slip naked under the single sheet, mash her breasts against his chest, and swing a leg over his hip. He registered a soft wetness on his leg. Her skin was feverish, and she breathed into his ear. "I have changed my mind," she said. The white streak in her hair fell across his face.

The bustling port city of Sevastopol simmered under the Crimean sun. Its eight scalloped inlet harbors were bordered by war memorial parks, pebbly public beaches, and elegant whitewashed mansions. Farther inland, high-rise apartment blocks were squeezed between thoroughfares clogged with traffic. In the largest of the harbors, Sevastopol Bay, were the massive concrete piers of the Russian Black Sea Fleet, a dozen bristling gray hulls moored stern-to. Sevastopol was twelve kilometers from little Balaklava, over the mountains. At noon, Nate and the WOLVERINEs took the Number 9 *marshrutka* bus from Balaklava harbor to the five-kilometer exchange outside Sevastopol, and then rode the Number 14 city bus to the Omega Beach stop at the bottom of Kruhla Bay. The route had been charted by Headquarters photoanalysts who had "walked" the entire twelve kilometers via digital satellite imagery. The small buses were crowded and Nate shared a seat with Agnes, who that morning looked as if she had ridden a long distance on horseback, which was not entirely inaccurate. As the others dozed in the hot, swaying bus, Agnes pushed her thigh against Nate's.

"When do I meet your parents?" Agnes said in Russian.

Nate closed his eyes. "Agnes, stop kidding around." He was experiencing remorse on two levels: Sleeping with Agnes—a member of the team that he was leading, with a sensitive job ahead—was reckless. Sleeping with her weeks before he was going to see Dominika was worse. It had been as if he were observing himself from an opposite corner of the room, unable to control events. Fuck, had he weakened maybe as a way of defying his scolding superiors? Maybe to create some space between him and Domi? *Go ahead*, he thought, *rationalize your ass off.* Agnes had been active and insistent, clapping her own hand across her mouth so as not to wake the whole hotel. Wet-lipped, she had held his face in her hands and whispered *jestes taka sliczna*, you are very beautiful in Polish, without Nate's knowing what she had said.

Now she was the debauched older woman, with a morning-after glow, having fun. "I never told you I can bake," she whispered. "What kind of cake do you like?"

"I'm not listening to you," said Nate. Secretly he was amused and interested. This woman, from her early twenties, had risked everything fighting in the shadows for her country. She was second only to Witold in planning sessions, and it was obvious that he respected her. During training, Benford had once glowered at her, and she had glowered back, earning Benford's grudging approval. Nate had seen hurt in her eyes only once, when Piotr had teased her about becoming an old maid. She was different, strong willed, and passionate.

"Oh, yes, I feel marvelous this morning," she said, conversationally. "You're quite a musician, do you know that?" she said. She pushed sweat-damp hair off the back of her neck and fanned herself with a piece of cardboard.

Nate shook his head. "Let's concentrate on today. We're not clear until we're on the boat tonight and outside the twelve-mile limit."

"Don't worry, I'm ready. We are all ready," Agnes said. She put her hand on his arm. "We will succeed, you will see."

Nate did indeed see. From the Omega Beach stop, the team walked separately and casually down busy six-lane Mayachina Street, mingling with afternoon shoppers and citizens heading home. Three carried backpacks over their shoulders, the other three carried well-used zippered shopping totes seen in open-air markets. They maintained the same distances from each other that surveillance would take—in effect becoming their own counter-surveillance. Halfway down the boulevard they peeled off into three pairs: the first crossed a vacant lot; the second walked through leafy courtyards between apartment blocks; the third ghosted down a dusty lane strewn with garbage. Besides hostile surveillance, they looked for *druzhinniki*, the pensioners sitting on stools in front of apartment blocks who were the unofficial neighborhood watch. Nate was in hyperdetection mode, senses alert, scanning, listening, smelling. Nothing. Maybe the citizens were all at the beach. Status: Black. Time check. Go.

They converged from three directions on the four gray-metal warehouses, standing in a row on a weed-choked cement apron. The traffic roar on Mayachina a block away was barely audible. The buildings were streaked with rust and the roofs sagged. Hand signals from the flankers indicated there was no one around. A bird chirped and a cricket zinged from the weeds. Nate squatted and took a breath. Too quiet? A thought of ambush flickered in his mind. Would the GRU leave munitions unguarded like this? He processed sounds and looked into the shadows under the far trees. All clear. Witold knelt beside him.

"What is it?" said Witold. The back of his shirt was wet.

"How does it feel to you?" said Nate.

"I know what you mean," said Witold. "Doing this in daylight is not normal. But we need the light, and the buses stop at nine. The plan is solid."

"Would they leave rockets and mines unattended?" said Nate.

"Do not forget, these are Russians," said Witold. "This is the GRU engaged in an illegal operation; they will be determined to keep it secret, especially from the Ukrainian locals."

"Alarms? Booby traps?" said Nate. DIVA had not reported anything, but she might not have been briefed on such details.

"Jerzy will check the door and look for motion sensors. They have not made the system he cannot defeat," said Witold. "Ryszard will look out for trip wires."

Nate signaled, and Jerzy knelt by the dented, tin side door, and ran his fingers around the edges, feeling for protrusions or gaps in the door that could indicate alarm heads on the other side. He shook his head. Nate nodded at Piotr, who picked the tarnished lock with a snake rake and torsion wrench in fifteen seconds, then eased the door open an inch while Jerzy again ran his fingers along the edges. Negative. Piotr eased the door open, leaned inside, then stuck his head back out and waved them forward. Nate clicked his fingers softly and the last pair came from the other side.

The interior of the warehouse was relatively small. A cracked concrete floor was powdery with fine gray dust. Rusty vertical steel beams set in the floor supported the latticework roof joists. "Watch footprints, handprints," whispered Nate to Witold, pointing to the dusty floor. There were no windows along the walls, but milky light came from two bird-spotted skylights. An angular shape in the center of the warehouse was covered by a dark-green tarp. The crates.

"Don't touch the tarp," whispered Ryszard. "It could be wired to a pull fuze."

Nate nodded. He started to walk around the covered mound, but Ryszard stopped him. "Shine your light along the floor," he said.

Nate pointed his light—a 250 lumen NEBO SLYDE—in front of him. A double line appeared on the floor—an invisible trip wire and its shadow—running to the closest beam where a black box with a copper cone held by a metal arm was strapped. The cone was like a small megaphone and pointed at the tarp-covered pile.

"SM-70 antipersonnel device" whispered Ryszard. "Eighty tiny steel cubes, twenty-five meter kill zone; they used to put them on the frontier fences."

"Can you defuse it?" said Nate.

"Have to leave it intact. They'd notice if we disarmed it," said Ryszard. "We have to work in a live kill zone. Take our time. Don't fixate on the trip wire. They want you to follow the line and miss a pressure plate concealed somewhere else. Booby trapping the booby trap."

They slowly peeled the tarp off the crates. The trip wire from the SM-70 disappeared under the near crate. "Don't lift or move that one," said Ryszard, pointing.

There were a total of fifteen crates of unpainted pine, with hinged tops, stamped metal draw bolts, and folding metal handles at each end. There were no stenciled markings of any kind to indicate the contents. The lids and bottoms of each crate were reinforced by wooden skids, to facilitate stacking. Nate estimated that eight of the crates were about five feet long—they each looked like a coffin for a child—and would contain the RPG-18 Mukha launchers, and the separate propelled grenades. The remaining seven crates were square and deep with rope handles on the ends. Those would be the mines.

Nate and the WOLVERINEs started working silently, their movements coordinated and efficient. Normally a team of six would be too large for this sort of work, but now it meant they could work faster, dividing the tasks. Based on how well they had performed in training, it had been agreed that as well as beaconing the wooden crates, there would be time to render the mines and rockets inert. The black plastic PMN-4 blast mines, each the size of a holiday fruitcake, but only slightly less lethal, were sabotaged by lifting the plunger caps and snipping the points of the firing pins flush to the Belleville spring plungers. The snipped pins would never contact the detonators for each mine's main charge of fifty-five grams of high-velocity RDX. The rocket-propelled grenades, nestled in wooden cradles six to a crate, were fixed by the simple expedient of trickling three drops of superglue into each detent hole to freeze the actuator to the secondary rocket motor that guided the round to its target. Surprised PKK gunners would now aim the launchers, pull the triggers, and gape at projectiles that farted out of the tube for three feet and rolled around on the sidewalk, harmless.

Agnes and Witold meanwhile had emptied the contents of the backpacks and laid them in a row on the floor. They were duplicate wooden skids that would be switched to replace the original cleats. Each new skid had been mortised and was filled with two beacons—one a short-range HAMMER proximity beacon, designed for use in dense urban environments, the other a QUICKHATCH geolocation beacon that reported long-range position via GPS satellite. With QUICKHATCH, you could follow a camel across the Sahara from a laptop in Manhattan. With great care, the original skids were unscrewed and the "hot" replacements were fastened in place with silent push screwdrivers. Agnes was a marvel, collecting discarded wood, counting tools, and ensuring the crates were left exactly as they found them by comparing photos she had taken with her cell phone at every stage of the operation. Once verified, the pics would be deleted.

The afternoon sun was dimming, and Nate looked at his watch. He didn't want to work by flashlight. Witold saw him, smiled, and mouthed "five minutes more." Nate took a cautious walk around outside, still worried by the prospect of a trap not yet sprung, but the zone around the warehouse was clear, nothing moved. He went back inside and Agnes was waiting near the door, out of earshot of the other WOLVERINEs.

"We are almost finished," she said, smiling. "Everything went smoothly."

Nate nodded. "You guys do good work," said Nate. "Forsyth thinks your team is the best, and so do I."

Agnes smoothed her hair. "Do you think we leave tonight or tomorrow?" she asked.

"If we get back at a reasonable hour, there's no reason not to leave tonight, as if we're taking a moonlight cruise," said Nate.

"I just wondered if we'd be in the hotel another night," said Agnes, looking at him with her gray eyes.

"Oh, no," said Nate, shaking his head. "Don't start, Agnes."

"That little boat will be cramped with all of us aboard, no privacy."

Nate tried to imagine Agnes naked in a narrow upper berth with Piotr snoring in the lower rack. "I thought the *start* of an operation made you feel this way," said Nate. "It's over; we're finished."

"Sometimes before a mission, sometimes after," she said, sighing. "Sometimes during."

Nate reached out and took her hand. "What am I going to do with you?" he said.

She squeezed his hand. "Do I have to tell you, or can you guess?"

The WOLVERINEs finished their work, leaving the pile of crates as they found them and draping the tarp exactly as it had been, according to digital photos Agnes had taken of the warehouse interior before they started. They blew smudgy footprints away, and raised a cloud of dust that evenly coated crates, tarp, and floor as before. Nate checked Agnes's photos to verify the scene—she stood close to him, holding the camera, the heat from her body palpable—and they backed out and watched Jerzy relock the door and wipe surfaces clean, not that the Russians would be dusting for prints considering the haphazard way they had cached the munitions.

The swaying bus ride back to Balaklava through the Crimean dusk seemed to take longer. Nate listened for sirens and the sound of motorcycles coming up from behind, and he strained to focus far ahead, at the curves, looking for the striped sawhorses of a roadblock, cars angled across the road. Nothing.

They stayed below to reduce the profile as the cruiser slowly moved away from the pier, down the harbor, past the sea buoy, and into open water. It was night now, the horizon to the west still a little light, the blackness to the east and south impenetrable. The crew signaled Nate when they had gone twelve miles, outside Putin's territorial waters, and Piotr opened a bottle of *Sliwowica*, and they stood close together on the afterdeck and drank under the stars. Agnes contrived to bump shoulders with Nate as Ryszard sang *"Hej Sokoly,"* "Hey Falcons," from the Polish-Soviet war. The cruiser rolled in the gentle sea swell.

Phase one finished, thought Nate, *two and three coming up. Istanbul. Gable. Dominika.*

GEORGIAN BEET SALAD

Put boiled beets, pitted prunes, garlic, walnuts, and sour cream in a food processor and pulse to a grainy paste. Garnish with rough-chopped walnuts and cilantro. Serve with crusty bread.

18

Phase Two

Nate's primary liaison contact in the TNP was a thirty-year-old captain named Hanefi. He was short and dark, with a single caterpillar eyebrow and a thick black mustache, which would twitch sideways whenever he was agitated. He was learning English and tried to use it at every opportunity. The backs of Hanefi's hands were something out of *Phantom of the Opera*—burned during an explosion—and he self-consciously hid the shiny disfigurement by keeping them in his pockets. Nate and Hanefi worked well together, but not before the intense police officer began trusting Nate. Gable had warned him about working with Turks: "No recruitment attempts, no case-officer moves, not even if one of them volunteers. They take their time warming up, but once they're satisfied you're not working them, they're your friends for life. But if they later catch you trying to pick their pockets, they'll never forgive or forget."

Nate spent hours with Hanefi, listening to teltaps of Shlykov on the phone with Moscow and various PKK cell leaders—Russian and fractured English were used—discussing the upcoming weapons delivery. For an officer of his rank, Shlykov's comsec (sense of communications security over the phone) was nonexistent. Each careless call to a separatist would identify five more members, those five, ten more. Each identified location led to the next two, then the next three, all of them in Istanbul's sooty suburbs: Cebeci, Alibeyköy, Güzeltepe; an apartment in a rust-stained high-rise; a daub-and-wattle shed on a muddy lane; or a sagging farmhouse in a garbage-choked gully. There were so many sites that additional police units were brought in from Ankara to assist in surveilling all the locations.

Then the munitions arrived and a TNP helicopter with a HYENA receiver vectored TNP surveillance teams—they were as good as Nate had ever seen anywhere—to warehouses where the explosives would be stored before dispersal. The patient Turks set up on each location, watching, marking suspects. A coordinated assault plan was finalized. The Turks were impressed with Nate's beacons; they were a marvel, said Hanefi.

"How did you do it, Nate Bey?" asked Hanefi late one night in a smoke-choked listening post, referring to the crates. Nate smiled.

"If you asked me whether we did it in Russia, I couldn't tell you," said Nate. Hanefi put back his head and laughed.

"Aferin, sen Osmanli," said Hanefi. He meant, Bravo, you're an Ottoman, a righteous stud.

The night of the multiple raids, Nate checked the QUICKHATCH beacon readouts from a terminal in the consulate. That technology was not releasable to the Turks—they were unaware of the redundant system—but all locations were corroborated 100 percent. Benford called on the secure phone and uncharacteristically praised Nate's performance both in Sevastopol, and in working with the Turks in Istanbul, which he called "satisfactory." Benford confirmed that the tech team for Phase Three would arrive the next day. Part of Nate's plan to frame Shlykov had already been running for a time, a denigration ploy so insidious that a chuckling Gable had said Shlykov was already screwed, only he didn't know it yet. "Good luck, tonight," Benford had said, then terminated the secure link.

———

Nate hung up, remembering that Agnes had also wished him good luck after the WOLVERINEs returned by boat to Varna. He didn't know it, but Agnes had booked a flight a day later than the rest of the team. Nate likewise was waiting for his flight to Istanbul, and was staying one night at the Central Hotel, a tired Romanian Black Sea resort where the lobby, corridors, and rooms smelled of hot elevator oil. Agnes had sneakily taken an adjoining room, and surprised him by pounding on his door while announcing *servitoare*, housekeeping!

Nate was secretly pleased. He was contemplating a dreary evening alone in his threadbare room watching the *Berlin Euro Pop Contest* on television. Agnes had other ideas. Whatever servomotor was ticking inside her, the chaste three-day return cruise apparently had spun it up to red-line levels. They made love everywhere but the bed: on the floor, in an armchair, in the bathtub with a sputtering hydro jet, and standing up on the tiny balcony ghost-lit by the neon hotel sign on the roof. Her heady perfume—she told him it was Chanel Cristalle Eau Verte—mingled with the whiff of Bunker C fuel oil from the harbor around the headland. She had whispered *czuje miete dla ciebie*, I feel mint for you, in colloquial Polish, meaning she had feelings for him. Mint wasn't the only thing she felt.

Hours later, hands shaking, Nate poured Agnes some bottled water, but she was asleep on the bed, on her back, mouth open in a six-orgasm syncope, hair fanned out on the pillow, her witch's streak partly visible. Nate floated a blanket over her and sat on the armchair across the room, looking at her breathing. Sleeping with Agnes the first time had been a midnight impulse fueled by pre-op nerves. Tonight it was a celebration, relief at getting out of Russia in one piece, maybe a bittersweet farewell. Nate rubbed his face and groaned. Maybe he wanted to put impediments between him and Dominika, so he wouldn't—could not—stumble with her again. He resolved to properly act as backup to Gable during meetings in the safe house. He would arrive late, and leave early, making sure Gable was always in the room. He would let Gable explain to DIVA why Nate was acting like a skittish puppy, let *him* deal with the inevitable outburst. Only one problem: Nate loved Dominika. As if Agnes could hear his thoughts, she mumbled fitfully in her sleep, and turned over. *She feels mint for me*, thought Nate, miserably.

The next day they were waiting for their separate flights at the airport. In a white blouse, pink skirt, and sandals, Agnes looked cool and collected.

"Do you think I am too old for you?" she asked Nate, who looked up in alarm.

"After last night, I'll let you know once my chiropractor hammers my spine back into alignment," said Nate.

"I am being serious," said Agnes.

"No, I don't think you're too old for me," he said. "But Agnes, there must be somebody in your life."

"I think there is somebody in your life," she said, ignoring his question.

"What makes you say that?" said Nate. *Scary good radar*, he thought.

"*Zerkalo dushi*," said Agnes in Russian, searching his eyes. *Mirror of the soul*, thought Nate. *Christ.*

"Things are complicated," said Nate, who had no intention of discussing his seriously contorted personal situation.

"You live in London, isn't it?" Agnes said.

"And you live in California."

"Not so far, I think," she said, not looking at him. Nate didn't answer.

"Would a visit to London sometime be a bad idea?" Agnes said, then kissed him good-bye.

———

The Station's outside line rang with an exultant Hanefi on the other end. "Nate Bey, come quickly; there is a police car waiting for you downstairs." He was shouting over the sound of gunfire, a lot of it, including automatic weapons.

"Hanefi, where are you?" yelled Nate. "Are you all right?"

"Godamn hell, shit-bitch," said Hanefi, who was still learning to swear properly in English. "*Çabuk olmak*, come at once."

The drive in the dented police car, blue lights flashing and hee-haw siren wailing, driven by a jug-eared twenty-year-old police corporal who pounded the steering wheel when traffic did not part, was transcendental. Gable's phrase "scared as a sinner in a cyclone" came to mind. Metal ammunition boxes strewn on the rear seat slid back and forth on the curves. They weaved through traffic across the Galata Bridge, and rocketed down the south side of the Golden Horn, past the darkened Greek Orthodox Patriarchate, under the O-1, and into the dingy Eyüp district. The corporal took a steep road up the hill, tires squealing and fenders scraping along the stone guardrail. At one of the switchback curves, the entire sprawl of Istanbul was visible, its city lights bisected by the black slash of the Bosphorus; the end of Europe and the start of Asia. Dominika would be down there, and they'd be together in two days.

The police car locked its brakes and slid to a stop. More police cars were up ahead, stacked behind a big-wheeled Kobra armored car in blue and white TNP colors. The driver shoved two ammo cases into Nate's hands, took two himself, jerked his head, and started running uphill. It was a steep, narrow street with houses on either side, the windowpanes reflecting the two-score flashing blue lights. The echoing cracks of incessant firing became louder. Clustered at the corner of a wall ahead were a group of TNP officers, some in uniform, others in jeans and leather jackets, peeking around the corner of the wall. Hanefi saw Nate and ran to greet him.

"You bring ammunition," he said, clapping Nate on the back. The wall across the street was suddenly riddled by bullets that chipped cement and filled the air with dust. Hanefi pulled Nate closer into the lee of the wall.

"Hanefi, what's going on?"

"Four people, PKK, in top apartment," said Hanefi, loading a magazine for his MP5. Other officers were digging into the ammunition like kids around a bowl of candy. Nate looked past them. The street was covered in spent casings, thousands of them, brass winking in the flashing lights.

"How long have you been shooting?"

"Many hours; we ran out of ammunition." He held his weapon out to Nate. "Here, you try." Nate shook his head. Hanefi barked something in Turkish to another officer, who held out his weapon, a heavier assault rifle. "Try this one." Nate held up his hands in polite refusal.

A bullhorn blared and the shooting slowed, then stopped. Hanefi pulled Nate by the sleeve to peer around the corner. The small apartment building was bathed in spotlights. The top-floor apartment was marked by thousands of bullet holes, the windows were ragged gaps in the walls, and the concrete balcony railing was chipped and broken. It was a miracle that anyone could survive up there. *And this is going on all over Istanbul*, thought Nate.

Hanefi nudged Nate and pointed with his chin. Two shadows—police commandos—were sliding slowly headfirst down the roof tiles. At the edge, they would reach over the gutter and throw fragmentation grenades down into the PKK apartment. Before they were in place, a young woman in a red parka ran onto the balcony with an RPG over her shoulder. Hanefi shouted and tried pulling Nate back. The woman aimed at them and fired the missile, but the back blast from the launching charge rebounded in the small space and blew the woman off the balcony. She cartwheeled four stories into a pile of rubble, followed by the missile that arced harmlessly to the ground. Hanefi looked at Nate in amazement. "Bad luck," said Nate.

The grenades cracked and a thin plume of gray smoke came out of one of the windows. Another boom was followed by a flurry of shots, then silence, then the shrill blast of a whistle. "All over. Let us go up," said Hanefi.

The interior of the little apartment was an eye-stinging charnel house, with a bullet hole in every square inch of the room. Wallpaper hung curled off the walls, the few pieces of furniture had been reduced to kindling, and a prayer rug smoldered in the corner. Bits of upholstery stuffing floated in the air. Two men lay on the floor on their backs, bloody shirts pulled up to their chins. In the back bedroom a young woman lay between the pulverized wall and a shredded box mattress, her fists clenched and mouth puckered, eyes half-open. Black hair showed beneath a head scarf.

Hanefi looked with interest at Nate's face, which had gone somewhat pale. He would not make fun of his new American friend. He patted Nate's shoulder. "It is our job," he said, holding up four fingers. "*Dört*, four terrorists, captured dead," he said using the TNP vernacular.

Shlykov's covert action had been ruined: twenty-four PKK cells had been wrapped up; the morgues were already full. The Russian munitions had been recovered, and the publicity would be devastating when the weapons would be put on display for the TV cameras. *Now let's take Shlykov for a ride*, thought Nate, *and then it's up to Dominika.*

About the time Major Shlykov arrived in town to supervise his covert-action arms shipments, the CIA Base in Istanbul had begun transmitting covert-agent electronic-burst messages into the Russian Consulate. Every day for a week, base officers, stiff wires running beneath their jackets and warm battery packs in spandex holsters under their skirts, walked among the shopping crowds on Istiklal Caddesi and past the consulate gate topped with the double-headed eagle of the Russian Federation. They fired three-second, five-watt burst transmissions into the building. The energy bounced invisibly up the ornate marble staircases, ricocheted through the hallways, and rose like clear smoke up to the attic receivers; the consulate was awash in low-powered signals. They were encrypted gibberish, but the signals themselves were detectable and dutifully recorded by Russian SIGINT (signals intelligence) officers who endlessly monitored frequencies across the spectrum. A report was sent to FAO/RF, the Moscow SIGINT headquarters, immediately. The mysterious daily transmissions continued on a regular basis.

A week later, when phone intercepts flagged that Shlykov was traveling from Istanbul to Ankara to confer with the senior *rezident*, the burst transmissions in Istanbul ceased, and commenced in Ankara. CIA Station officers twice a day drove past the Russian Embassy on Cinnah Caddesi, pushed the recessed buttons, and volleyed the encrypted energy over the embassy fence, through the granite walls, into the elegant Baroque sitting rooms, and out the back of the building to the withered formal gardens behind the embassy. This had not happened before. The astonished Russian SIGINT officers in Ankara also reported their readings to FAO/RF. These reports in turn were sent to the FSB. As a potential counterintelligence matter, neither Shlykov in GRU nor SVR headquarters was privy to the SIGINT reports, nor were they aware that a secret FSB file had been opened on "unidentified encrypted electronic messaging activity in Istanbul." Signals of this sort were sophisticated and clandestine, and clearly suggested that someone in the Russian diplomatic contingent in Turkey was the recipient. The genetic, reflexive Kremlin assumption that there was a traitor in their midst—a cultural paranoia first introduced by the tsars, nurtured by the Bolsheviks, refined by the Soviets, and perfected by Putin—smoldered in Moscow.

Shlykov returned to Istanbul, and the transmissions ceased in Ankara and again followed him. And when he traveled to Moscow, for consultations regarding his covert-action operation, the transmissions stopped altogether, only to start up again on his return to Turkey, when he touched down at Istanbul's Ataturk Airport. The SIGINT log of these encrypted signals grew and the FSB counterintelligence file got fatter. It was not long until signals analysis matched the transmissions with Shlykov's movements.

This delighted Gorelikov, whose refined, gracious exterior concealed an inexhaustible capacity for subterfuge and plotting. When Dominika had quietly brought home news of the murder of her North Korean asset, Gorelikov had listened implacably to Shlykov's dismissive explanation that the North Koreans almost certainly had detected Ri's treachery through some tradecraft error of Egorova's and had eliminated the scientist themselves. And as for the missing Sparrow, either the North Koreans had dealt with her, or she had run off with a ski instructor from the Tyrol. Gorelikov later listened to the recording of Blokhin's voice in the cottage, and had, incongruously, smiled. Additional evidence to hang this GRU apostate, but never a thought for Ioana, Dominika bitterly noted.

Gorelikov took Dominika aside and for a day briefed her on the developments in Istanbul. Shlykov's operation had imploded, the munitions had been captured, the Turks were apoplectic, and Russia would be embarrassed on the international stage. The president no longer numbered Valeriy Shlykov as one of his favorites. They began choreographing a discreet counterintelligence investigation—SVR would have the lead role in the foreign field—meticulously led by a dutiful Colonel Egorova. "It's a shame you have to fly all the way to Istanbul; the findings of the investigation are already drafted," said Gorelikov. "Shlykov is responsible for the OBVAL disaster, for which he must answer, but it is now more serious. He is suspected of espionage. But there it is, appearances matter, and you must play the part." But then came the sly question Benford had warned her about. "What do you think is going on in Istanbul with these transmissions? Did the Americans suspect something? Why did they focus on Shlykov?"

"In Turkey it could be any of a dozen things; that's why this covert action was ill-advised," said Dominika, matter-of-factly. "The Turks certainly have informers inside PKK; perhaps a tradecraft problem with the delivery of weapons; US SIGINT might be listening to chatter." Gorelikov polished his wire-framed eyeglasses.

"Or we could have a mole in the Kremlin," he said, softly. Dominika willed her scalp not to creep.

"Always a possibility, but unlikely," she said. "Everyone in the Council approved the plan."

"Except for you, Bortnikov, and me," said Gorelikov.

"I can hardly credit the Chief of FSB working for the opposition, and I know I am not a mole . . ."

"Which leaves me," said Gorelikov, amused.

"A dangerous counterrevolutionary of the criminal Trotsky gang. Line KR will have to keep an eye on you," said Dominika, and the moment passed. *Is this a ghastly game to tell me he thinks I'm a spy? Take care.* Gorelikov was a serpent, tongue flicking, constantly testing the air. That night, she wrote up the details and dead dropped them to Ricky Walters to pass to Benford. She would have to be very careful.

———

In Istanbul, CIA officers, in addition to sending burst transmissions, had begun marking signals—chalk marks on stone walls, tape on light poles, thumbtacks in trees—along Shlykov's walking route between his temporary Istanbul apartment and the Russian Consulate. Because Shlykov wasn't looking for them, he didn't notice them. Very discreet surveillance of the major, done from the front and in phases, soon determined which cafés and restaurants he favored for solitary lunches and dinners. One of these was in Cicek Pasaji, a covered street arcade with a nineteenth-century Beaux Arts latticework and glass roof. Whenever Shlykov ate there—he habitually ordered *kadinbudu köfte*, ladies' thighs *köfte*, plump lamb and beef meat fingers, fried crispy on the outside and succulent on the inside—one of half a dozen CIA officers sat close by, always facing him, always with a folded newspaper, or a book, or an eyeglass case on the table in plain sight. No contact was ever attempted.

A steady stream of local commercial brochures, advertisements, and flyers were mailed to Shlykov's address announcing Bosphorus tours, condos for sale in Esentepe, bus excursions to Bulgaria. The junk mail was collected and delivered by his toothless concierge. Shlykov thought nothing of the brochures and threw most of them away, but one or two of them were tossed in desk drawers and forgotten. They all had been lightly sprayed with household insecticide, a chemical component of which is phenolphthalein, a telltale of secret writing developer. There were no messages on this junk mail, all of it stiff and glossy with the dried aerosol patina.

Nathaniel Nash sat in a nondescript Fiat Scudo van parked on a narrow side street in Istanbul with three technical officers from Langley. It was dusk and the final call to prayer had finished minutes ago; the steep Beyoğlu neighborhood of grimy apartment buildings and first-floor shops was quiet and dark. There were intermittent rainstorms scudding across the city, and the alleyways, stairways, and gutters were periodically awash in a brown chyme, the composition unchanged since the Byzantine Empire. A cat sat under the eaves of a ground-floor apartment window shaking its paw. The van was parked three doors down from a brick-and-stone apartment building with a fabric canopy over double glass doors in front. They were waiting for the crone who was the concierge in the building to leave her little desk in the entrance foyer and walk down to her basement apartment to start dinner for her husband. Instead, she stuck her head out of the door and poked the underside of the bulging canopy with a mop handle to empty it of accumulated rainwater.

Nate and the three entry techs were waiting to break into the personal apartment of Valeriy Shlykov. The van was filled with the collective fragrances of the tool satchels each of them held in their laps: the bitter stench of electric motor oil; the pungency of wood putty and quick-dry paint; the gritty whiff of graphite powder, the sweetness of talcum. The techs, veterans all, sat silently, looking straight ahead; three good ol' boys, two from the Deep South, who didn't use aftershave because it could linger on doorknobs and drawer pulls, and who didn't smoke because they sometimes had to lie on their stomachs in an attic for seventy-two hours straight.

The books had them down as surreptitious-entry techs, but it was less formal than that: these men had jimmied, shimmied, and picked their way into embassies, boudoirs, code rooms, and missile bunkers around the world. They called themselves "rum dubbers" or steel-bolt hackers; their Harley-Davidson and Jack Daniel's belt buckles had squeezed past laths and joists, under electrified wire, around cable runs, over roof slates covered in snow. Older now, in their fifties and sixties, they traveled less. A new breed—cuticle chewers with laptops—was needed to get past infrared cameras and biometric electronic locks. And the Golden Age of Surreptitious Entry had passed. No modern ops manager in the intelligence community today wanted to authorize a delicate physical-entry operation with career-ending risk written all over it.

But there were exceptions. In Shlykov's case, the object of this clambake was not to emplace microphones or cameras, nor was it to open safes and quick-copy classified materials with a roll-over camera. Rather, the object of this surreptitious entry was to leave things behind.

KADINBUDU KÖFTE— LADIES' THIGHS MEATBALLS

Divide ground lamb and beef into thirds. Sauté two-thirds of the ground lamb and beef with chopped onion until meat is cooked and onions are soft. Mix with remaining one-third raw meat, egg, parsley, salt, and pepper. Knead mixture to incorporate and refrigerate until firm. Form thick finger-sized *köfte*, roll in flour, dip in egg wash, and fry in oil until *köfte* are crispy on the outside. Serve with a tomato salad and garlic-yogurt dressing.

19

Checkmate

Nate and the three technical officers stood in the darkened hallway in front of Shlykov's apartment. The old concierge finally had left her post for the evening and the CIA men had silently walked up four flights of stairs, each stepping in the slipstream of the others' tension. Last in line, Nate saw that even though the staircase was well-washed marble, the good ol' boys by habit walked on the outside of the treads to avoid squeaks; each step likewise was taken supinating on the outside of their cowboy-boot soles, eliminating the sound of footfalls in the stairwell.

This had all been Nate's plan, the ghost transmissions, the signals, the surveillance. For the final act he had blithely suggested an entry to Shlykov's Beyoğlu apartment. But Nate had never before gone in with a veteran surreptitious-entry team; he was nervous as the whole show revolved around this break-in. Thank Christ these old boys were unflappable. The lead tech, a fifty-five-year-old peckerwood from Alabama named Gaylord, knelt in front of Shlykov's door. He had a potbelly and knuckly hands; his white hair was wavy. His teammates had told Nate that he could pick any lock. Gaylord looked at the lock, turned to the others, and whispered "We got a Russian, in an apartment in Turkey, and the door's got a Yale lock." Nate was unsure whether the discovery of a Yale lock in Turkey was in effect good or bad, but concluded it must be good. With bird-like fingers on those beefsteak hands, Gaylord inserted a brass bump key into the keyway, feeling the pins through the tips of his fingers. He seated the key firmly, applied slight pressure on the cylinder, and sharply rapped the bow of the key with the rubber handle of a screwdriver. The pins jumped with the shock transmitted through the bump key, the cylinder rotated, and they were in. No emotion out of any of them; they just straightened and quietly entered the darkened apartment.

Shlykov's apartment smelled neutral, like an intensive-care unit, hot and sanitized. It was neither messy nor neat; he didn't have many possessions. The great repositories of a man's secrets—the bedside table drawers—were empty: no books; no porn; no pics, empty. The second window into a man's life, the fridge: no beer; no veg; no spice; no ice. The box was cold and sour. Most of all, Nate could not identify in the apartment where Shlykov's personal spot was. No armchair with reading lamp; no ass-worn couch in front of the television; no canvas chair on the grimy little balcony. Did this guy hang by his heels from the closet rod until dusk?

Nate checked his watch. They had an hour-long window. Shlykov was propping up a wall at a dip party, watching fellow Russians, not working the crowd. He was too important to bother with dip targets. He had the covert action to propel him to his colonelcy. Three base officers in a loose circle around the Russian, eating, drinking, laughing, and handing off the eye, would punch Nate's number when the major started moving. The techs were moving separately in the apartment, in a smooth, practiced choreography, dividing the rooms into cylindrical search sectors—high, low, middle—looking for the telltale wires of bugs or cameras, though it was unlikely that arrogant Major Shlykov would take such security precautions. No touching, no talking, their eyes moving in the dim light; Nate stood in the middle of the living room and waited.

The Mississippi boy named Lee, baby of the group at age fifty-two, moved to Shlykov's bedroom and in thirty seconds had found a well-worn, hard-sided suitcase under the bed. He weighed it in his hand and nodded. He dipped into the small bag slung over his shoulder, no rummaging around, no sound, and came out with a pair of pincer pliers that looked as though they had first been used in 1415 at Agincourt. Nate kneeled beside him as Lee gently pulled off the aluminum flashing around the upper lid and using a long, thin spatula carefully pried apart the two sandwich layers of molded plastic. He snapped his fingers softly to attract Nate's attention. From his own bag Nate took out the glassine envelope and carefully slid two secret writing carbons—specialized, essential, and incriminating—between the layers of the lid. Lee then squeezed the layers together, applied a dot of adhesive, and fitted the flashing back around the edge of the lid. He crimped the aluminum tight and pointed with his finger. Nate saw that Lee's crimping tool had purposely left tiny teeth marks in the aluminum. Lee slid the suitcase back under the bed.

Nate again checked his watch through sweat-stung eyes and moved back to the living room. Gaylord and the third tech—a jolly Falstaff from upstate New York named Ginsburg—meanwhile had spread a tack cloth on the floor and were feeling with artisans' hands the grain of a large wooden chessboard standing on its edge. Where had they found it? *All Russians love chess*, thought Nate. Was this Shlykov's defining hobby? It was his bad luck, whatever it was. Ginsburg took an instrument of the Inquisition out of his bag, black handle, guide rails, battery pack. The tool itself made only a faint crunching termite sound as he plunged a three-inch-deep mortise into the wood along the end; Gaylord sucked up the sawdust with a silent handheld vacuum as it came off the bit, and cleaned out the hole. They both looked at Nate, who stepped forward and inserted a tiny two-inch square notepad with gummed edges—a onetime pad, called an OTP—into the cavity. This was a block of tiny pages of printed numbers in random sequences used to provide an ever-changing (and therefore unbreakable) key to encrypt messages. Onetime pads had been used forever—in the Great War, inside the Bastille dungeons, and on the Roman roads of Judea.

Gaylord meanwhile had taken the collected sawdust and mixed it in a shallow beaker with an odorless chemical from a squeeze bottle to create a thick batter. Fitting a plastic plug into the cavity to protect the OTP, he smeared the paste over the mortise hole and troweled it even along the edge of the board, like a pastry chef smoothing frosting on a cake. He blew on the spot, tested it with the tips of ridiculously sensitive fingers, and in a few minutes, lightly sanded it smooth. Nate shined the penlight as Gaylord held a color wheel to the chessboard, then painted the area; it disappeared into the exact shade of the wood. "You sure they'll find this?" whispered Nate.

Ginsburg looked him up and down. "If they're looking for it, guaranteed. The cavity'll light up on a fluoroscope like a polyp on your colonoscopy." Nate looked at Ginsburg and nodded thoughtfully; given his age, the grizzled tech perhaps was speaking from recent experience. Whatever Ginsburg intended to say, there was a certain anatomical irony: when the chessboard and suitcase were discovered by Russian counterintelligence officers, Shlykov figuratively would be bent over and would experience the long arm of Kremlin justice.

———

As it turned out, they did, and he was. After a month of burst communications heating up Russian SIGINT antennas in Turkey, followed by the shootouts, the Kremlin had enough. Colonel Egorova traveled unannounced to

Istanbul to observe the situation in the consulate, accompanied by two FSB heavies collegially lent by FSB Chief Bortnikov, who expected Egorova would discredit Shlykov and prove to the president that the Security Council members who opposed the rash OBVAL operation had been correct.

Intermittent rain squalls blown in from the Sea of Marmara were slashing across the runway when Dominika's Aeroflot flight from Moscow arrived at Istanbul's Ataturk Airport. As the plane taxied to the gate, the rain pattering against the smudged windows, she could feel the thready pulse under her jaw; she was about to initiate a *konspiratsia* against a dangerous adversary and, she presumed, his Spetsnaz bullmastiff, though Blokhin had not been seen in the city at all. She was in a foreign country now and the Turks were shrewd and aggressive. This was hostile territory, and she was here to conduct a mock counterintelligence investigation, the result of which had to be the arrest of Valeriy Shlykov for treason. She had a delicate role to play; a too-facile conclusion to her investigation might raise suspicions. She would have to "discover" the evidence against this ambitious officer plausibly and convincingly. *The role-playing starts now*, she thought as the plane jerked to a stop.

As she entered the modern arrivals hall with its soaring vaulted ceiling, the burnt-nut aroma of Turkish coffee in the air enveloped her, and reminded her she was now in the mysterious Orient, among the small dark men who watched all *yabanci*, foreigners, with distrust and uncertainty. She walked past a small take-out cantina, the steam table laden with appetizers—roasted peppers and garlic, flat *köfte* sprinkled with sumac, a tray of *kabak graten*, golden zucchini gratin. Past Customs, two nervous officers from the Russian Consulate rushed up to greet her, bobbing their heads. An SVR colonel was an important visitor. Chin up, Dominika walked with them to the waiting car, saying nothing.

Istanbul was this morning a mass of blocked roads, snarled traffic, and emergency vehicles. The police action of last night had resulted in the capture of lethal munitions of Russian manufacture. Endless television news reported the killing of scores of PKK separatists in as many firefights. The Grand National Assembly met in emergency session. The TNP put the captured land mines and rocket tubes on display. In the Russian Consulate, an apoplectic Valeriy Shlykov cursed. He suspected perfidy and betrayal from some quarter. As Shlykov raved, the junior officers in the *rezidentura* cowered, clueless. This ambitious GRU major had lorded it over everyone, and had not briefed them on the covert action, to ensure compartmentation and security, but really so he could hog the credit.

Gorelikov regrets I have to make this trip, thought Dominika, *but I do not.* Apart from their compromising Shlykov, the Istanbul trip would, of course, be an opportunity to meet her CIA handlers, their first contact since New York. She had been passed the address of an Istanbul *yali*, an elegant three-story wooden Turkish Baroque mansion in Anadolu Kavagi, a resort town on the Asian side of the Bosphorus, designated CIA safe house AMARANTH. The mansion had been rented by a real estate firm in Beverly Hills ostensibly for peripatetic senior Hollywood studio executive Blanche Goldberg, who used the house twice a year to meet mesmeric French film star Yves Berléand, with whom she'd had an on-again, off-again love affair for three years and counting (you never knew with a French lover). Blanche was only vaguely witting that the house was paid for by CIA—she didn't ask the reason—but made her contribution to the love-nest cover-for-status by keeping a bedroom armoire full of expensive Beverly Hills lingerie and toiletries, including a bottle of Swiss Navy Lube in the elegant master bathroom medicine cabinet.

In Moscow, Dominika had been passed descriptions of the CIA moves to discredit Shlykov via thumb drives placed at a timed-drop site in the bushy verge against the ornamental wall of the Zhivonachalnoy Troitsy Temple on Kosygina Ulitsa on the southern border of Vorobyovy Gory (Sparrow Hills Park) on the Luzhniki bend of the Moskva River. Benford himself had included the key information regarding what Dominika should look for in Shlykov's apartment: chemically treated brochures, suitcase lining with crimped flashing, chessboard.

The result was that Dominika was aware of every nuance of the CIA sting, and could direct her investigation unerringly to the evidence, to the astonished admiration of her FSB wingmen. She noted that suspicious Western foreigners were sitting across from Shlykov at lunch (were they signaling him?). The FSB boys followed them and they turned out to be US Consulate employees, presumed CIA. She spotted a thumbtack signal in a tree near Shlykov's apartment that was pushed in too low to affix a poster. A horizontal chalk mark that was noted on a wall outside Shlykov's apartment building on one day had a fresh vertical cross stroke two days later. And the electronic burst messages continued. Things were looking decidedly worse for Major Shlykov.

———————

At no time did Shlykov mentally connect the massive operational flap culminating in running police shootouts at twenty locations in the city with any singular, personal failure in tradecraft, comsec, or planning. He was rarely burdened by introspection. Now this ridiculous Egorova had arrived to conduct a preposterous investigation on some nonsense about transmissions, and the timing ensured she would be here to witness his humiliation. He had been ordered to remain in Istanbul until the postmortem of OBVAL was complete.

The interview with a scowling Shlykov seated at a table in the *rezidentura* secure room developed nicely: Valeriy reacted angrily when asked about the mysterious transmissions, claimed not to know any Americans in town, and dismissed as ridiculous the existence of clandestine signals near his apartment. The FSB officers present looked at one another skeptically. Things got more interesting when Shlykov flatly refused to let the FSB "donkeys" search his apartment. The yellow halo around his head, bleached by rage and pulsing with fright, told Dominika a lot. His fear of career disintegration was eclipsed by his *bol'shoe samomnenie*, his self-importance, and his outrage at being challenged and questioned, especially by a woman. *He'll hang himself with that ego*, Dominika thought. This would be easier than she expected.

"This is an uncomfortable situation for us all," said Dominika equably. "I personally regret the need to interview a fellow colleague from the GRU."

"Then fly back to Moscow and leave me to my work," said Shlykov. "I have critical operational tasks, which you should realize take precedence." He glared at Dominika with the disdain of privileged Soviet Golden Youth.

"Yes, well, the police shootouts in this city with your terrorist protégés seem to suggest that your critical operational tasks have not been totally successful; in fact, they were unrelievedly disastrous," said Dominika. "They almost certainly may yet prove to be damaging to the Russian Federation and embarrassing to the president." In the silence that followed, every Russian in that interview room knew that damaging the country was by far the lesser delinquency.

"I'll attend to the operations," said Shlykov, seething. He decided to add a towering insult. "Why don't you concentrate on what you do best: filming yourself seducing men?"

"I suggest you take a less defiant line," said Dominika. "It is unfortunate." The FSB men heard something in her voice that made them shift in their seats. Shlykov seemed not to register the danger.

"There are anomalies that correspond to your movements," said Dominika. "I trust they will amount to nothing, but I am here to confirm that there are no counterintelligence issues."

"Do you think I'm working for the Americans?" Shlykov shouted. "You're ridiculous, *Po'shyol 'na hui*, fuck off." He stood and loomed over Dominika.

"I advise you to sit down and cooperate," said Dominika, looking up at him. Shlykov bent over her, and stuck his face in hers. The FSB men sat on the edge of their chairs.

"Your reputation precedes you," said Shlykov. "The wonder girl with the big *sis 'ki*, the well-titted-out prostitute trained to suck off—"

Dominika's hand shot out and grabbed Shlykov's jutting bottom lip between forefinger and thumb, and pulled down hard. The major grunted with the pain and went to his knees. Dominika twisted his lip and slammed his head against the edge of the table. Shlykov sat on the floor and held his head. His lip had already swelled and gone purple, and his right eye was closed.

"Consider yourself confined to the *rezidentura*," said Dominika, standing. "You can sleep on the duty-officer cot. A security officer will be with you at all times." She turned to the FSB men.

"Get the keys to Comrade Shlykov's residence, both front door and apartment," she said. "I want to go there now."

At the apartment, the FSB bloodhounds did Dominika's work for her—she didn't have to prompt them at all. In fact, she praised their diligence. They gathered all the papers in Shlykov's desk drawer and found the suitcase under the bed and showed Colonel Egorova the telltale marks on the lid, suggesting some tampering. They hefted the big wooden chessboard they found on the upper shelf in the front closet, shook their heads, and were going to leave it.

Dominika shrugged, pulled out more drawers, and rummaged around the closet. "Strange," she said. "Have you found chess pieces, a chess set?" The FSB men looked around, shook their heads, and suggested they take the chessboard back to the consulate and examine it under the fluoroscope used to screen incoming mail and packages. Dominika looked doubtful.

"Very well," she said. "It's better to check, to be thorough."

"*Bez truda, ne vitashis i ribku iz ruda,*" said one of the FSB men loftily, without effort you won't pull a fish out of a pond.

"I suppose you're right," said Dominika. "Let's see what we find."

―――――――――――

Iosip Blokhin had not appeared anywhere in Istanbul during the disastrous failure of OBVAL. There had been a firefight between TNP shock troops and PKK cell members barricaded in a private house in the historic Rumelihisari neighborhood on the Bosphorus that had been fierce and prolonged, suggesting that the normally unsophisticated PKK terrorists had received tactical advice from a professional. A police picket line in the woods around the house detained a stocky man making his way through the trees as the shooting began tapering off, and he was taken into custody in the police precinct house in Arnavutköy on the basis that he had no identification.

When the burly man in East Bloc English claimed he was a Russian diplomat and demanded to see a consulate official, the police lieutenant called the coordinating captain (it was Hanefi), who in turn called his American friend Nathaniel Nash and offered him the opportunity to speak to the Russian who the Turks strongly suspected was a professional soldier. Hanefi said he could give Nash an hour alone with the Russian before Russian dips arrived to spring him. Nate accepted and quickly called Benford to say this had to be Blokhin who, Dominika was sure, had killed the two women and two cops in New York, her North Korean asset, and her Sparrow in Vienna.

"Go hard on this ape," said Benford. "Pitch him—your cover's blown to these Bolsheviks anyway—and tell him we know what he did. Say we got him on Hilton Hotel security cameras, to protect DIVA. Tell the son of a bitch the next time he shows a hair of his ass outside Russia, we'll extradite him to New York to stand trial for the dissident's murder," said Benford. "Burn him so badly he'll be useless to them from now on."

"It's highly unlikely, but what if he's ready to play ball? How high are you willing to go to get him in harness?" said Nate.

"Three years *substantively* working in place inside, he gets one million dollars. He wants out now, he'll get two hundred fifty thousand dollars after a *meaningful* debriefing in the United States. Money contingent on production—the usual. See if that shakes his tree. Get something solid from him as a sign of good faith before you agree to anything," said Benford.

"Okay, I'll talk to him tonight and let you know," said Nate. "I'm prepping for the meet tomorrow with Domi. I'll get over there early and get things set up for Marty. When's he get in?"

"He's not coming," said Benford, thinly. "I had to send him to Sudan; a wheel came off in Khartoum Station."

"Marty's not coming?" said Nate, his stomach flipping.

"I trust you heard me, unless your ears were affected by the blood rushing to your lower extremities," said Benford.

"Gable is DIVA's primary handler," said Nate.

"And you are her backup officer," said Benford. "You know how this works, Nash. You debrief her, review commo and sites, make sure she is operating safely. Did you receive the requirements cable?"

"It came in this morning," said Nate.

"Then go and do your job," said Benford. "And endeavor not to ruin the asset with your beastly manner. Or do I have to come out there myself?"

"No, I'll handle it," said Nate. "You'll get a wrap-up cable when we're done."

"Good hunting," said Benford, hanging up.

———

Blokhin was in a small gray interrogation room at the police station that was bare except for two metal chairs. Hanefi met Nate outside the door and they took turns looking at him through the peephole.

"*Bir esek oglu*," muttered Hanefi. A son of a donkey. "Nate *bey*, he looks dangerous. *Dikkatli ol*, be careful. Do you want a man in the room?" Nate shook his head. "*Tabanca?*" A pistol?

"No. I want to squeeze him and don't want him to lose face. But if you hear me screaming, come in and shoot him," said Nate.

"I am thinking he is in Istanbul for organizing the cells," said Hanefi. "With no diplomatic papers we put him in Silivri Prison for twenty years, but because Ankara fears trouble with Moscow, he is free after you finish with him. *Iyi sanslar*, Nate *bey*, good luck."

Nate pulled open the door and stepped into the room, which was dimly lighted by a single bare bulb. Blokhin stood in a corner, leaning against the wall, his tree-trunk arms crossed over his chest. There was a bruise under his right eye, probably a corrective love tap from a TNP jailor who didn't like Russians. Nate sat in one of the chairs and slid the other chair a foot toward Blokhin, an invitation to sit, but the sergeant remained standing. Nate knew he was unlikely to find this guy's buttons, but there was nothing to lose. A brief bio on Blokhin had been spun up, but there wasn't much.

"Sergeant Iosip Blokhin," said Nate in fluent Russian. "Congratulations on the *sharada*, the charade of last night. I thought Spetsnaz was better than that." Blokhin stared at him.

"It's hard to imagine you going along with such a half-baked plan, but that's GRU for you—amateurs," said Nate. Blokhin didn't move. *Push another button.*

"Of course you'll be blamed for the unsatisfactory operation," said Nate. "No one in the Kremlin, or the Security Council, or the General Staff will support you. Major Shlykov will cast you aside, like the pack animal he thinks you are. They may even cashier you out of Spetsnaz. What group are you in? *Alpha or Vympel*?" Blokhin uncrossed his arms, pushed off from the wall, and stood behind the metal chair looking down at Nate. He slowly sat down, back straight, hands on his thighs. Nate braced for a lunge.

"You are CIA?" Blokhin asked. His voice was like gravel poured out of a bucket.

"If they kick you out of Spetsnaz, what will you do in Moscow?" said Nate, ignoring the question. "Become a driver on a city tram? Collect tickets at Dynamo Stadium? Do you have a family to feed? Parents?" *Come on big boy, tell me something, anything.*

"You come from Washington?" asked Blokhin, tilting his head as if Nate had blown a dog whistle.

"Washington is close to New York City," said Nate. "Ever been there?

Ever been to the Hilton on Sixth Avenue?" Blokhin's face was impassive but his pupils dilated.

"What do you want?" said Blokhin, sitting back in his chair. *An opening? Work it.*

"We both serve our countries loyally, sometimes endure hardships, but in your system there are no rewards except the pride you take in having served. But that will be gone when you return to the *Rodina*. They will take that away from you in the space of a deep breath." Blokhin said nothing.

"We are not enemies," Nate said, with a straight face. "We are both soldiers, in different uniforms perhaps, but we both understand loyalty. In America we value loyalty and friendship, and repay it. Our soldiers retire with benefits, and live in comfort."

"What do you want?" Blokhin repeated.

"I have a proposal, a way for you to reap the benefits you have earned. Something for you, apart from Russia, and Spetsnaz, and Shlykov." Blokhin waited.

"Talk to us about what is happening in Russia, in the army, in Spetsnaz," said Nate. "Do it for yourself; you deserve the rewards."

"I would dishonor my uniform, my oath," said Blokhin, shaking his head.

"They dishonor you already," said Nate.

"You dishonor me; your proposal is an insult." *He didn't ask how much, he just slammed the door.*

"I want you to know that authorities in New York have fingerprints and DNA found in Daria Repina's hotel room," said Nate. "They will be compared against samples just taken from you by the Turks. There is no doubt there soon will be an Interpol warrant out for your arrest, and Washington will request your extradition to stand trial." Blokhin smiled thinly. He knew Moscow would never agree to that.

"What this means is that you will be obliged to remain in Russia indefinitely, to avoid immediate arrest by a foreign government," Nate continued. "Your days as a clandestine military operator are over. This *neudacha*, this fiasco, in Istanbul will be your last operation, an unfortunate professional legacy for which you will be remembered." A bit dramatic, that. Nate knew Shlykov was already well and properly framed, and Blokhin at most would be criticized and demoted for his part. The added indignity of being pitched by the Americans after being arrested would be intense. Blokhin got up from his chair, returned to the corner, and leaned against the wall.

"I hope our paths cross again," said Blokhin in English.

———

As he walked out of the police station, Nate erased Blokhin from his mind. He was meeting Dominika tomorrow. Nate took a deep breath. *Godamn hell, shit-bitch*, as Hanefi would say. This was going to be tricky. He could attend to the debriefing professionally, no problem. Intel first, followed by ops intel and CI. Establish a sked for future meetings, then review security, sites, and signals. Doing all this in five hours (the last Bosphorus ferry back to town was at 1800 hours) was going to mean they would sit down and work straight through. It would mean Nate must keep his mind on business, even if Dominika put her slim, cool hand on his arm, or if her just-washed hair brushed his cheek, or if she laughed and stuck out her tongue at him. He would ignore that trademark sideways glance that meant she wanted him, invariably accompanied by the barely perceptible lifting of the hem of her skirt, a come-on from her Sparrow past. He could imagine Gable's comment (*"Nash'll be playing twenty toes with her in five minutes"*) and Forsyth would shake his head ruefully, disappointed.

Maybe he'd surprise everyone and instead convince her about coming out with him, defecting, quitting, leaving the danger, and the dread, and the risk, and starting a new life, together. *What if she says, "Yes, let's go, right now, I'm ready"?* Nate thought. Besides meaning the end of his CIA career and the work that defined him, it would also mean the loss of the Agency's best Russian source with irreplaceable access to Putin's Kremlin. And he'd be the cause.

Dark ancillary thoughts emerged: Could either of them live without the sustaining excitement of this work, the knife-edge bustle of the street, the adrenaline high of stealing secrets from an implacable foe? What would their retired life be like? Would they look at the snowy Rockies from the porch of a log cabin? Or eat breakfast on a white balcony overlooking Biscayne Bay? Or throw another log on the fire in a cozy New England farmhouse? A conjugal dream or a constricting nightmare? Could either of them survive retirement? Gable always said that spooks dried up and died when they left the

Game. Most Russian defectors went around the bend away from the *Rodina*; they missed the Motherland, the black earth, and the pine forests. Could he do that to her, to himself? Jesus, maybe he had scared himself straight, maybe she'd see the light too. Maybe they would move to the next chaste and professional level of superasset and sagacious handler, coolly taking care of business against Vladimir Putin and his predatory kleptocracy. Maybe.

And, anyway, what was that fucking Gable doing in Khartoum, now of all times?

TURKISH ZUCCHINI GRATIN

Halve small zucchinis lengthwise, then scoop out pockets, and fill with cubed feta cheese, chopped dill, and parsley. Cover zucchinis with béchamel and bake in medium oven until zucchinis are soft and topping is golden brown.

20

The Great Confluence

It was midnight. From the plane window coming in, Gable saw the bulbous, luminous blue-glass Corinthia Hotel on the river, a fat teardrop rising above the low brown wattle of Khartoum, otherwise punctuated only by a forest of lighted minarets. His plane banked farther and he could make out the *al-Mogran*, the Great Confluence, where the chocolate-brown Blue Nile joined the milky-blue White Nile. Outside the terminal, the brakes of the canary-yellow taxi squealed like a pissed-off baboon. *Probably the red Sudanese dust on the pads*, thought Gable. *The shit gets everywhere.* The drive from the airport to the US Embassy—it was south of town, on the banks of the Blue Nile—took an hour, down riotous four-lane Madani Street cloaked in blue exhaust, with traffic coming in and out from all directions, even at this hour. It was a familiar zoo. Khartoum. Gable was back on his old stomping grounds—the benighted Third World—where you debriefed recruited generals with sweat-shiny faces in gritty Land Rovers parked in stinking alleys, and the cotton-candy sandstorms three hundred feet high would rattle the house, red sand hissing under the door despite the wet towels jammed against the threshold, and where you got used to the sudden tire thump while driving at night, which was either something four-legged and furry, or a local sleeping off a *tshwala* beer bender in the middle of the road. You didn't stop to find out, not at night.

The Third World. Russian diplomats posted to Paris didn't need CIA guys to buy them baguettes, but meet a lonely Russian in barren, alien Khartoum, his family back in Moscow, and give him some *shchavelya sup*, sorrel soup, like his mama used to fix, and put on a DVD, and open a bottle of bourbon, and you could talk to him endlessly about American salaries, or muscle cars, or Las Vegas pussy, or maybe just about *the freedom to choose*, and some dust-stormy night with the shutters rattling, he'd say yes, and you'd have an SVR recruitment in the bag. Some of Gable's best scalps came from the Sandbox.

COS Khartoum Gordon Gondorf was sitting at his desk in the Station on the top floor of the embassy, a two-wing, three-story blockhouse on a five-acre compound, with grenade-proof slit windows and a curved-steel porte cochere. COS Khartoum was short, pig eyed, and preternaturally obtuse. Gable often said Gondorf couldn't pour water out of a boot if the instructions were printed on the sole. Known as "little feet" by the beleaguered officers in his stations, Gondorf seemed to reappear every two years, like a fever blister. He had been the Chief in Moscow where he tried to fuck Nash's career, then went on to ruin Latin America Division, and subsequently became COS Paris where he refused to mobilize resources to look for an escaped CIA traitor loose in the city. This consistent performance had earned him everlasting scorn from Benford, who arranged for Gondorf to be given his current command—this uncomfortable third-tier Station where you had to check to see if a boomslang was coiled under the rim, resting in the cool of the toilet porcelain, before you sat down.

Gondorf's office was dominated by a huge wooden desk, reflecting his belief that the larger it was, the more gravitas it conferred on the person sitting behind it. This theory was vitiated somewhat by the fact that the glass top came up only chest high on the Chief, giving the enduring impression of a red-faced little boy sitting at his father's desk on family day. A dusty A4 rifle was propped in a corner, as if the Chief personally engaged terrorist cells in Khartoum every day before lunch. Of course there was the usual vanity wall, covered with photographs of Gondorf being greeted by members of Congress, foreign dignitaries, and diplomats in tuxedos. A single framed photograph of Gondorf incongruously dressed as a Bedouin with a *jambia*—the curved ceremonial dagger of the Arab world—stuck in his belt, epitomized his catchpenny career. A camel in the background of the photo glared at him as if the half-pint desert nomad owed him money.

Gable was only faintly aware of Gondorf's current dilemma. Benford had not related the details. The story came out in halting sentences, punctuated with "through no fault of mine," or "no one could have anticipated," or "events beyond anyone's control." Months ago, Washington had resolved to covertly deliver shoulder-fired surface-to-air missiles to rebels in Darfur—southern Sudan—to offset massive military aid from Russia and China flowing to the genocidal host government in Khartoum. It was vital that the US aid be kept secret to avoid bilateral friction. At the eleventh hour, a dithering National Security Adviser changed her mind, resulting in canceled plans to deliver the missiles. A pallet load—twelve five-foot dark-green aluminum cases with metal handles—of the missiles were stranded in a secure storeroom in the basement of the embassy.

The cases were smuggled in as construction materials, but getting them out was a different matter. They could not be driven to the airport and flown out on the weekly support flight. If Sudanese Customs officials inspected the pallet, the diplomatic flap would be unsustainable. During a heated embassy principals meeting, the ambassador declared himself unwilling to keep a dozen FIM-92 stinger missiles with high explosive annular blast fragmentation warheads in his chancery indefinitely. The military attaché (called Milatt), marine Colonel Claude Bianchi, respectfully submitted that he had no way to extract the cases until the carrier USS *Nimitz* transited the Red Sea in a week, at which time a Seahawk helicopter could be flown in to extract the missiles; extended-range tanks could be fitted on the bird to make the 450-mile flight. COS Gondorf, eager to curry favor with his Chief of Mission and outshine the Milatt, coyly declared that he had "assets" capable of disposing of the munitions right now. In this he overplayed his hand.

Displaying monumental bad judgment, Gondorf had directed three low-level Sudanese support assets to load the cases onto a stake truck, exit out the back gate of the embassy, drive a hundred yards east across a fallow sunflower field, and dump them into the river.

Gable sat up. "In the fucking Nile?" he said.

"The cases are fifty pounds each," said Gondorf miserably. "They sank right away."

"I don't care if there was a frigging glacier over there," said Gable. "You dumped them *a hundred yards* from the embassy?"

"We did it at night, so no one could see," said Gondorf.

"I don't know what's wrong with you, Gondorf, but I bet it's hard to pronounce," said Gable.

"There's another problem," said Gondorf. He walked to the window, raised the blinds, handed Gable a pair of binoculars, and pointed toward the river. Gable focused on the riverbank, fringed by a thin line of vegetation.

"Holy shit," said Gable. The black mud bank was littered by the missile cases, some on their sides, some sticking straight up, like uprooted coffins in a flooded cemetery.

"Rivers aren't supposed to have tides," said Gondorf.

Centuries of Egyptian pharaohs, nomadic Baggara tribesmen, and Nile basin farmers were familiar with the amaranthine floods. Not Gondorf, however. Between July and October, the Nile would swell from snowmelt in the Ethiopian mountains. In June, the river would subside, leaving dark fertile mud, *kemet* in Arabic, behind. Gondorf had dumped the crates months ago, at high water. Now he had a fifty-foot mud bank with missile crates sticking out of the muck a hundred yards from his office window. Gable looked at the narrow pinched face, the close-set jerboa eyes, and the pinched mouth that was full of "it's not my fault" right behind his teeth.

"There are militia patrols everywhere, boats on the river, scavengers on the riverbanks," said Gondorf.

"How long have those cases been out there?" said Gable. "Why don't you get your gomers to retrieve 'em?"

"I can't. They're out of contact," said Gondorf.

"What're you talking about? You can't contact your assets?"

"I can't find them; they don't respond."

"Jesus wept," said Gable, flipping the binoculars to Gondorf. He walked down the hall to the Milatt's office and introduced himself to Colonel Bianchi, who was tall, dark, ramrod straight, with hair combed straight back and shiny with brilliantine. He was in civvies: a light suit with a blue shirt and plain black tie. He wore a marine corps pin on his lapel. Gable sat down and explained the problem. Bianchi shook his head.

"I've known a lot of you spooks over the years," he said, with Mississippi in his mouth. "But that boy of yours is as sharp as a sack of wet mice."

"Yeah," said Gable, "he's a real asshat. Colonel, those cases have been immersed for three to four months, and now they're covered in mud. Any chance those stingers will be functional?"

"Those cases are water-resistant, but not waterproof," said Bianchi. "If some of the gaskets on those cases held up, you probably got a handful that would light up and fly. But nothing reliable." He shook his head. "But that's not a worry. The militia finds those Stingers there will be more political trouble than we can handle."

"Militia any good?" asked Gable.

"They ride around town, four to a jeep, with AKs, looking for trouble. Not much training, but pretty mean."

"You got anyone who could help me get those cases out tonight?" said Gable. Bianchi shook his head.

"My office is down to two, my deputy is on home leave, and the ambassador wouldn't approve of using the marines. Something happens out there and we lose our embassy watchstanders." He watched Gable's reaction before he spoke again. "We might be in luck. Two SEALs from Team Eight working with AFRICOM are here doing embassy-evacuation surveys. They might be willing to help." He picked up a phone, and in two minutes the SEALs knocked on the door.

They were both in their twenties, lean and quiet. They wore jeans and flip-flops. Senior Chief Petty Officer Gilbert "Gil" Lachs was blond and freckled. He was a breacher, a demolitions expert, who could open a can of peaches with a few grains of RDX without spilling the syrup. Petty Officer First Class Richard "Ricky" Ruvo, was Italian swarthy with Staten Island wise-guy eyes. He was a sniper who could drive a nail into a tree at fifteen hundred yards. They sat slumped in chairs, arms crossed over their stomachs, looking at Gable like sleepy leopards on a tree limb.

"I need some backup. I figure we get a truck with a winch and drag those cases out of the mud," said Gable. He turned to Bianchi. "What we got for weapons?"

"Not much," said Bianchi. "Glocks in 9mm and Remington 870s. We have rifled slugs and buck." Gable nodded.

"Glad to help," said Ruvo. "I'll stand overwatch while you guys get the cases."

"Bullshit," said Lachs. "I outrank you. You get in the mud."

"Gil, you can't hit shit," said Ruvo.

"I always shoot first and call whatever I hit the target," said Gable.

The SEALs nodded. An unspoken code had been transmitted and received: Gable was okay. "You CIA guys still recruiting frogmen?" asked Lachs, whose time in the Teams was running short.

"Yeah, we got a whole division that teaches squids how to use a knife and fork," said Gable. "But it's filling up fast."

Ruvo, Lachs, and Bianchi all laughed.

It was pitch-black when Gable drove the F-350 truck in second gear across the dusty field with lights doused, and put the nose of the truck into the break of the riverbank scrub. There was a dilapidated fisherman's shed made of irregular sheets of corrugated tin at the river's edge. Lachs peeked through a gap in the metal and shook his head. Empty. Ruvo shoved five Sabot shells into the 890, jacked the slide, and clambered up onto the roof of the cab. He did a 360 turn and whispered okay. Gable and Lachs put their pistols into their belt holsters at the smalls of their backs. Silently cursing Gondorf, Gable went knee-deep into the mud, pulling the wire rope off the spool, while Lachs stood beside the winch, holding the remote controller. A tactical flashlight between his teeth, Gable waded to the nearest case, put the snap hook onto one of the metal handles, and waved to Lachs. The truck swayed a little, but the ninety-five-hundred-pound pull of the winch broke the suction and the case slithered up the bank. One down, eleven to go.

An hour later, there were three more cases left, but Lachs had to get in up to his thighs to help Gable dig away mud so they could clip on to a handle. The two of them were on either side of a partially buried case, flashlights in their mouths. Lachs's back was to the black river. Then it happened. A warning shout from Ruvo came seconds before a fourteen-foot Nile crocodile erupted out of the water behind Lachs in an explosion of spray, jaws open. Unable to move in the mud, Lachs could only throw himself across the top of the muddy case. Gable never moved faster in his life. He drew his pistol and pumped all seventeen 9mm rounds into the croc's cotton-white mouth, but it only shook its head and slammed its jaws down on Lachs's buttocks. Perhaps distracted by Gable's light, the croc miraculously did not bite down on flesh, but rather hooked an eye tooth on Lachs's hip holster, tore his cargo pants down to the ankles, shook its head, spit out the gun, and turned to bite again.

Ruvo's shotgun barked from the bank. A two-inch spot between the croc's eyes spouted blood and the croc collapsed in the mud, its tail whipping twice, its walnut-sized brain vaporized. The sounds of the shots echoed over the river and across the fields. A dog began barking. Gable looked at Lachs, who gave a thumbs-up. They both looked at the black water, specifically at two more gray shapes moving toward them. "Fuck this," said Gable, who quickly threaded the snap hook through the handles on the first, then the second, then the third case, and gave Ruvo the sign. The winch groaned, the handles bent, the cases groaned and popped, but all three broke free and slid up the bank. Gable and Lachs pulled each other onto dry land, the grunts of crocs in the river behind them. Lachs was pantless and muddy to his chest.

"First time I ever saw a croc give someone a wedgie," said Ruvo.

"Thanks for getting that fucker off me," said Lachs. "Slug went right by my left ear." Ruvo had snapped the twenty-yard head tap with a shotgun's iron sights, in low light, from the upper bank, a remarkable shot.

"I was gonna wait to see how big a croc's dick was, you bent over like that," said Ruvo. Lachs flipped him the bird.

They finished loading the filthy cases onto the truck when the sound of an approaching jeep came out of the night, its headlight beam bouncing as the jeep jounced over the dried furrows in the field. Militia.

"Heads up, ladies," said Gable out of the side of his mouth. He seated a new magazine into his Glock.

"None of these fuckers goes home," said Ruvo, holding his shotgun slightly behind his leg.

The jeep pulled close, its engine windmilling until it fell silent. The four men in the jeep wore a collection of watch caps, kepis, and berets. The Americans stood in the light of the single working headlamp. The driver stood up in his seat and said *"Kayfa halak?"* His tattered, sweat-stained shirt was unbuttoned. The passenger also stood up in his seat to look at the men over the filthy cracked windshield. No weapons were visible. The driver again yelled *"Kayfa halak?"* to raucous laughter. The passenger pointed at Lachs's bare legs, said something, and spit on the ground, to additional laughter.

"That guy likes your package, Gil," said Ruvo.

"These fuckers are all loopy, chewing *khat* all day," whispered Gable.

The driver reached down beneath the dashboard and tugged on the barrel of an AK-47. "Weapon," barked Ruvo, who brought up the shotgun, shot through the windshield, and blew the driver off the jeep in a cloud of pulverized glass. Gable shot the passenger in 1.5 seconds with a double tap in the chest, and a third round in the head, a triple called The Mozambique. The guy collapsed and slid beneath the dashboard. Even before he hit the floor, Ruvo and Lachs advanced on the vehicle in the bent shuffle of close-quarter combat, each firing three rounds, simultaneously knocking the two in the backseat over the rear of the jeep. The sounds of the shots rocketed into the night air, and more dogs on both sides of the river started barking. Aspirated grunts came from the black river. The dead passenger in the jeep settled sideways. The whole evolution had lasted twelve seconds.

"You CIA guys all this good?" said Lachs. He had last seen The Mozambique used in Panama.

"Yeah, it's the sensitivity training we get," said Gable. "And the pistol instructors from Texas." The SEALs looked sideways at Gable.

"You could do with more time on the range," said Ruvo to Lachs. "You hit that last guy a little high."

"Didn't hear him complain," said Lachs.

"Let's get the fuck out of here," said Gable. "Check these guys for IDs, usually little paper booklets."

"I'll ditch the jeep behind the shed," said Lachs. "You want me to rig a bang on the ignition?"

Gable shook his head. "Odds are some kids will find it first. Let 'em have it."

"What about these guys?" asked Ruvo, looking at the tangle of legs on the ground.

"Wait a minute," said Lachs. "Listen." The sound of multiple vehicles coming across the field and the babbling of excited voices were faint, but getting louder.

"Fuck," said Gable peeking around the tangle of riverine brush. "More militia. I make three jeeps a klick out, coming slowly."

Ruvo racked the shotgun slide. "That makes no more than twelve loopy lovers; we each take out a jeep and we're done." Gable shook his head.

"They heard our shots. They'll come in expecting trouble. Odds are too great something happens and we lose the missiles."

Lachs slapped a muddy missile case on the truck bed. "Let's fucking use three of these puppies to take out the three jeeps."

"We sure they gonna light up?" said Ruvo. "They been immersed for a long time."

Gable looked through the brush again. "They're slowing down running close to the bank; they don't know what they're looking for. You guys take the truck back across the field to the embassy. Bianchi's waiting at the gate and he'll open the storeroom. Get those missiles locked down and safe."

"What the fuck you think you're gonna do?" said Ruvo.

"I'll knock out a couple of headlights, crawl into the brush, and keep 'em pinned down. They won't notice you guys and the truck crossing the field."

"There's twelve of those gomers," said Lachs. "I'll stay and Ruvo can get those cases back."

Gable shook his head. "You both get those cases back to the embassy, one drive, one riding shotgun, don't stop for anything." The SEALs were pros, and didn't argue. Ruvo kept his pistol, but handed Gable the shotgun and a pocketful of shells. Lachs handed over his Browning pistol and two spare magazines. Gable stuck the pistol in his belt and stuffed his pockets with ammo.

"We'll get back with more firepower ASAP," said Lachs. "Just keep their heads down and stay in the damn brush. Don't be a hero."

Gable shook their hands. "Thanks for giving me a hand tonight. You guys made the world secure for another week at least."

Lachs pointed at Ruvo. "I'm still turning this asshole in to the World Wildlife Federation for killing an endangered species of riverine reptile," he said.

"If *this* asshole hadn't got that croc off you, you wouldn't *have* an asshole," said Ruvo. The sounds of the rattletrap jeeps were coming closer, the beams of the headlights waving in the air as the tires bounced over the dried furrows in the field.

"Back around these weeds and don't go until I start popping at these gomers. Then steer for the yellow lamp on the corner of the embassy. Get those cases under lock and key." The SEALs climbed into the truck, backed it up, and sat waiting. Ruvo gave Gable a thumbs-up.

Gable stood behind the little corrugated hut, peeking around the corner at the approaching headlights. They had spread out from a file into a line abreast as the field had widened, yelling across at one another, not paying attention. But they all held their rifles in their hands. *This is gonna be tricky*, thought Gable. The jeeps slowed and stopped eight meters from the hut— about twenty-five feet, a long pistol shot—but these troops all had rusty AK-47s and the rounds would go through the tin walls of the hut like a hot knife through butter. Gable figured he'd shoot from the direction of the hut, then scurry into the brush and let the gomers have fun demolishing the hut while he dug into the weeds, which would give the SEALs time to get to the embassy back gate. Gable saw the militiaman farthest to the right stand and point at the field. He'd spotted the truck's hood sticking out from the brush. In the next second, they would swarm in that direction and engage the truck, just what he couldn't let happen.

Gable stepped from behind the shack into the glare of six headlights, racking the pump so fast the shots sounded simultaneous, and fired three loads of buckshot into the right jeep, whose windshield disintegrated; the two men in the front seat fell out onto the ground, dead. The two in the backseat, one wailing and wounded, bailed out and hid behind their vehicle. Before the dead men had hit the ground, Gable pivoted to put three more rounds into the middle jeep, killing the driver, while the other three jumped out and hid under the jeep. He aimed his last two shots at the far jeep, knocking a rear passenger backward out of his seat. By Gable's count, four were down and maybe one or more wounded. At least seven left and maybe eight. Militiamen were hiding under the respective vehicles, all of them screaming at one another in what sounded to Gable as, "Ahmed, get up and start shooting," and more jabbering that sounded like, "Are you crazy? You get up and start shooting."

Gable jacked four of the dark-green shells into the Remington, his last shells and these were the rifled slugs—tapered solid-lead projectiles as big as marbles, the equivalent of a .50 caliber bullet—and one by one put a slug into the radiator of each jeep, causing a great whooshing explosion of steam, and cascade of water under each vehicle. Those jeeps weren't going anywhere now, and the SEALs were home free.

Out of the corner of his eye, Gable saw movement along the back wall of the shack; the metal flexed as someone slid along it inside the hut. Gable shot the last slug at the bulging metal, knocking a back-wall panel out and blowing the militiaman through a front-wall panel. Shotgun empty, two fifteen-round pistols left with two spare mags, and maybe seven militiamen left with AKs. Shit odds.

More movement in the bulrushes by the river—where were the crocs when you needed them?—and rifle fire started up from the reeds, too close, and Gable dove into the shed—temporary concealment, but certainly not cover—and slow-crawled behind some broken wooden crates that stunk like fish, and hunkered down as a militiaman stuck his head into the hole in the wall and Gable shot him in the head, but two other gomers were coming through the door shooting from the hip and Gable dropped one of them with a snap shot in the face, and felt a punch in his right shoulder, no pain, just numb down to his hand, so he shot the second gomer with his left hand twice in the chest, feeling another round hit his thigh, this one hurt like a son of a bitch hot knitting needle, and rounds started coming through the flimsy metal, each hole creating a glancing shaft of light from the jeep headlights. Gable wiggled into a corner, putting in a fresh mag one-handed by holding the pistol between his knees with the magazine well pointing up—emergency reload—and he released the slide and started firing at the two gomers coming through the door, but felt two more slugs hit him in the chest, and rounds were still coming through the metal, but Gable was feeling numb and it was like he was breathing through a straw, not enough breath, and he saw Nash in Athens Station, and Dominika in a summer dress, and Moira playing piano barefoot, his only regret, how he screwed up his marriage, and how she died before he had a chance to patch it up. He remembered the happy first month, the honeymoon on Cudjoe Key, and he could smell the salt air.

The two surviving militiamen were leaning against the fender of their hissing jeep shakily lighting cigarettes when both their heads exploded and they dropped like string-cut puppets, the cigarettes still in their mouths. Ruvo and Lachs came out of the darkness and looked at the dead soldiers around the shattered jeeps, then looked inside the shack. Five militiamen lay piled in front of Gable, who was sitting up against the wall, eyes closed, his shirtfront black with blood.

Ruvo checked his pulse. "He's gone," he said. "Goddamn it." They were quiet for a second, fellow gladiators mourning one of their own.

"Let's get him back," said Lachs. SEALs never leave their fallen behind.

"We got a little work to do first," said Ruvo.

The next morning, with Colonel Bianchi sitting in a chair in front of his desk, Gondorf reported by secure phone to Benford, who after a stunned silence on hearing that Gable was dead, cursed for five minutes and told him to stay by the phone. He secretly vowed to drum him out of the Service. Gondorf blanched when Bianchi told him about the firefight with the militia patrols, but he did not appear to be concerned any longer about the missiles, now that they were securely returned to the embassy storeroom. And he seemed not to care that a CIA officer was in a plastic bag, lying on a pallet in the embassy cooler. He saw a way to divert blame as he reverted to the gasbag bureaucrat-careerist his colleagues knew him to be.

"Your guys killed twelve militia troops? Are you crazy? There will be serious repercussions when they're found." Gondorf was thinking about official protests, riots at the embassy front gate, a fuming ambassador, diplomatic expulsions.

"More like fourteen. Your guy got eight himself. No one's going to find anything," said Bianchi. "They parked the jeeps down the road behind a warehouse with the keys in them."

"You're all maniacs. When they find the men, all hell will break loose."

"Those guys ain't coming home for supper. Here." Bianchi flipped a pile of militiamen's ID booklets on Gondorf's desk. They were soggy with sweat and blood, one with a bullet hole through the center. Gondorf's mouth curled with disgust as he flipped open one booklet with the point of a pencil.

"Jesus," Gondorf said. "That's one of my support assets who got rid of the missiles in the first place."

"Any more?" said Bianchi. Gondorf opened the other booklets with the pencil. His face fell.

"This one too, and this one, three of them. I don't know the others."

"Pretty efficient agent network you got going there, Mister Chief of Station, recruiting Khartoum militia as clandestine assets," said Bianchi.

"Who your SEALs gunned down last night, like some gangsters."

"Your so-called assets were coming last night to retrieve those missiles, you dickhead," said Bianchi. "Your man Gable got zapped to save your ass, which I'd personally like to kick."

"What about the missiles?" said Gondorf, ignoring the threat. "I want them out of here."

"*You* want them out?" said Bianchi. "I called up a Seahawk-60 from the *Nimitz* in the Red Sea. The Navy'll fly 'em out—Gable too."

Gondorf looked at the Milatt, trying to decide how to strengthen his position, for there was always some bureaucratic dodge, some refuge. His thoughts raced to creating a distracting controversy with DOD as scapegoat. He pointed at Bianchi accusingly.

"Your office is going to have to answer for murdering those men. I'm filing an official crimes report to DOJ."

"Based on what?" said Bianchi, getting out of his chair. The SEALs flew out for Little Creek last night. (All flights departed Khartoum after midnight when the soft, sunbaked tar runways hardened in the cooler night air.) "The Pentagon isn't going to help you, the way you act on the country team, and the ambassador is pissed at your scary good performance. My guess is that whoever that was from Langley screaming over the phone will make you feel like you were swallowed by wolves and shit over a cliff." Bianchi walked to the office door.

"You're forgetting one thing," said Gondorf, sweating. "When they find those men, there's going to be a shitstorm, with you right in the middle of it." Bianchi looked out at the river through the blinds.

"The SEALs took care of it. Like I told you, those militia troopers won't be home for supper," said Bianchi, over his shoulder. "River crocs already had 'em over for dinner last night."

SHCHAVELYA SUP—SORREL SOUP

Sauté greens (traditionally wild sorrel, or substitute dandelion, watercress, or spinach) with chopped onions until wilted and soft. Add chicken stock, bring to a boil, then simmer to finish. Remove from heat, add sugar and lemon juice for balance. Temper egg yolks with broth, stir into soup, and simmer without boiling. Serve hot or cold with sour cream.

21

Smell a Rat

Benford woke Nate up in the middle of the night with the black news about Gable. Nate felt the icy shock run up his back, and he stood gripping the receiver. Gable. Indestructible. A shootout in Khartoum, for nothing. That piece of crap Gondorf. Nate asked about services, the funeral, memorials.

"Never mind that," Benford said. "You get to the safe house tomorrow and do your job."

"How do I tell her?" Nate said. "He was like a brother . . ."

"You do not, under any circumstances, tell her. She cannot fall apart, not now. Keep her focused. She's got to lead us to MAGNIT, we have to wrap up that illegal in New York, and she's got to make sure Shlykov is thrown in prison."

"Pretty long to-do list, Simon; you forgot 'bury Marty Gable.' " Nate braced for the explosion, not really caring. Surprisingly, Benford's voice was muted.

"You know perhaps better than most, what he would have told you right now. He would have told you to do your job, protect your asset, get the intel, and set up the next contact. I would add that you should make him as proud of you as he always was." Nate swallowed hard.

"I'll send the cable when we're finished," said Nate.

———

Istanbul safe house AMARANTH stood behind a massive wooden gate with iron studs topped by medieval spikes. The gravel drive wound slightly downhill toward the water. The ornate villa—*yali* in Turkish—with its sloping red-tile roof stood alone amid pine trees right at the edge of the Bosphorus, its lower foundation continually wetted by the gentle wakes from passing Black Sea freighters. The interior of the *yali* was magnificent, full of elaborate moldings, and painted ceilings, and walls decorated in endless geometric Islamic patterns in gold and turquoise. A broad central salon was graced by a bubbling marble fountain. The salon was flanked by corner sitting rooms that overhung the Bosphorus, cooled by breezes through panoramic gallery windows. The corner rooms were furnished in high Ottoman style, with low sofas and massive copper tray chargers on carved wooden legs. Up the curved staircase of pink marble, on the second floor, four broad bedrooms featured canopy beds in peacock blue. Each bedroom led to a matching bath.

Nate drove to the safe house via a circuitous SDR over the Fatih Sultan Mehmet Bridge into Asia, where he strung together a series of stair-step turns and loops in the hilly neighborhoods of Üsküdar, Ümraniye, Görele, and Zerzavatçi. During one loop in the scrubland, he stopped at a turnoff and used the surrounding gnarly hills as a sound-catching bowl to listen for the purr of fixed- or rotary-wing aircraft, a denied-area trick Gable had taught him. Nothing. These were poor districts, with muddy lanes and rusted satellite dishes, ruined trucks balanced on cinder blocks, and mountains of discarded tires visible behind corrugated metal walls strung with barbed wire. This Asian Istanbul was nothing like the glamourous enclaves of the coast road on the European side.

He was black; no surveillance team—not even those TNP pros—could stay undetected so completely and still know where he was. He had rented the little Hyundai that morning from the lobby of the Mövenpick Hotel in Maslak, so he was not sweating vehicle beacons. He knew DIVA would be as thorough, running a tight route before she got on the ferry. Given the splash she'd made by bagging Shlykov, a too-long absence from the *rezidentura* would be risky. Nate was not sure they'd have even five hours for debriefings. Nate's final SDR leg—memorized by studying maps like an actor memorizes lines—was along Macar Tabya Caddesi, working his mirrors, and catching glimpses of the water between the trees. He drove through the gate, closed it behind him, and coasted down the gravel drive to the house. Its three stories, with ornate roofline, was painted pink with white gingerbread trim, incongruous in the piney woods.

Nate quickly surveyed the opulent interior. Triple doors on the ground-floor salon led outside to the breezy veranda with the Bosphorus glittering in the morning sun. There was a narrow strip of grass between the house and the pier. White wrought-iron lanterns were spaced along the breakwater wall. *Some pasha must have had glittering soirees in this house*, thought Nate. Time check. 0900 hours. She'd be here in three hours. He sat on a low couch in the Ottoman-style living room and reviewed his notes. He had rehearsed what he would say to Dominika, but he didn't know if he could avoid telling her about Gable despite Benford's orders. Would she still be furious at him? Now she was inside the Kremlin, enveloped by the approving embrace of President Vladimir Vladimirovich. She probably would become Director of SVR, and would be generating staggering intelligence for Langley. Her latest reporting had averted an apocalyptic terror campaign in this city.

Nate was sitting in the relative dark of the room, doors open, the long gauzy sheers floating in the wind. He peripherally registered movement on the lawn. It was Dominika, holding a small case in her hand. She had somehow gotten through the gate (or over the wall?) and come around the side of the house. Two hours early. Nate did not move, watching her through the French doors. She faced the water, dropped her bag, shook out her hair in the breeze, and looked at a freighter thrumming down the channel. She lifted one foot, then the other, slipping sandals off her feet. Her dark-blue summer dress billowed in the breeze, right out of *Wuthering Heights*. Nate walked to the open door and leaned against the frame.

"I'm sorry, but the property is not for sale," he said. Dominika did not turn, but continued to look at the water.

"Are you the owner?" said Dominika over her shoulder.

"I represent the owners," said Nate, stepping down to the grass and walking up behind her.

"Are you sure they will not consider selling?" she said. She turned around and brushed wind-blown hair off her face. She took a step toward him. They were inches apart.

"How much are you willing to offer?" said Nate.

"For a view like this, price is no object," said Dominika. She put her arms around his neck and buried her face in his shoulder. Nate lightly held her waist. They stood like that for a long minute, then Dominika stepped back and wiped her wet cheek.

"*Kak ty?*" she whispered, in Russian, how are you?

"*Privet,*" said Nate, Hi. "I missed you." Business now. "How did you get here early? How long do we have today? I've got a lot of questions."

"I took a different ferry, then a bus, then I walked. It was a lovely morning."

"When are you expected back?" said Nate.

"I told them I was conducting a security survey; no one will question me."

"How long?" said Nate, who could feel his scalp.

"Tomorrow night," said Dominika. "I return to Moscow the next morning."
"You can be out of pocket that long? Are you sure?"

Dominika nodded. "And where is *Bratok*?" she said. He rarely missed a meeting with her.

"He's away on a trip," said Nate, without inflection.

They had two days together, alone. Nate looked at her, the high cheekbones, the straight nose, the smooth forehead. There were new faint lines around those blue eyes that flitted over his face, reading the corners of his mouth, looking for clues about them. The bubble popped when Nate said they should go inside and get to work. Dominika smiled, reached for his hand, and walked barefoot with him into the house. His halo had flickered when he mentioned Gable, but she ignored it.

———

Dominika was on the parquet floor, sitting cross-legged on a plush rust-red kilim pillow. Nate was on the couch, which was covered by sheets of yellow legal pages from the last three hours of debriefing. Nate had also recorded the entire session on his TALON note-taking tablet. It was common practice to both record and take notes: the former would be a precise record of Dominika's words and intelligence reports, the latter a more convenient summary from which to draft cables to Headquarters.

A spiral map book of Moscow lay open on the floor. It had been annotated by Dominika to designate possible new dead-drop and SRAC sites, if she ever received replacement SRAC gear. They reviewed exfiltration pickup sites, the ones Moscow case officer Ricky Walters had described. Dominika sniffed that the exfil sites should be saved for those *hysterical* assets who would agree to defect in time of crisis.

"Domi, stop being dramatic," said Nate. "We have to be prepared to get you out if something happens." But he said it halfheartedly. Usually they argued about defection passionately. She noticed it.

After three hours, they both were tired. Dominika had filled in a lot of detail from her abbreviated previous reports dead-dropped in Moscow. No SRAC gear replacement was on the horizon. And there were still no hints regarding MAGNIT.

"There is one more important item," said Dominika. "Please make sure

Benford is aware of this." Nate nodded. "The SVR has established contact with the Chinese intelligence service."

"The MSS?" said Nate. *Russia and China? This could be big,* he thought.

"At the orders of the president," said Dominika. "But something is not right. We do not trust them and they do not trust us."

"Then what is the point of opening relations?" said Nate.

"We are exploring possible areas of mutual interest," said Dominika. "But I think my exalted president wants something bigger. Tell *Gospodin* Benford that it is my guess that Putin will do what he can to worsen relations between China and the United States. It is only my guess, but tell Benford that." An agent's opinion—a source comment—was valuable.

"Domi, this is important. Can you get more details as it develops?" said Nate.

"Of course. The Kremlin—Putin—has already designated Line KR as the lead office to meet with Chinese representatives. He wants me to report directly to him. I have not received specific operational directions, but the MSS are deceitful. *Podozrevat,* I smell a mouse."

"You smell a *rat,*" he said. Dominika shrugged. She had stretched out her slim legs and was touching her toes to work out the kinks. "When you know more, let us know. But go softly, be careful," said Nate.

"Thank you for the tradecraft lesson," she said, nonchalantly, trying not to smile. "I am to meet the Chinese general in Moscow when I return." Nate made more notes, but she knew something was wrong. Nate's halo was faded and waning.

"Is something bothering you?" she asked.

Nate buried his head in his tablet. "What?" he said.

"You are acting strangely." She wondered if she would ever tell him about the colors. She decided to try to distract him. "You should try stretching, to relax, like we did in ballet."

Demurely holding her dress down, she extended each leg out to the side in a perfect split, toes pointed, then leaned forward to touch her chin to the floor. "In yoga, it's called Upavistha Konasana," she said, "in Sparrow School, the Divining Rod. What do you call it in CIA?" Her chin still on the floor, she looked at Nate and blinked once.

Irrepressible Sparrow instincts, thought Nate, looking at the femoral and adductor muscles of her thighs flex. The familiar passion was there: he couldn't feel his tongue and there was a numb spot on the point of his chin. But Gable's face kept intruding. Now his resolve to stay professional, for her sake as well as his, was also for the memory of Gable. She straightened, brought her legs up and hugged her knees, and blinked at him again.

Dominika saw the pulsing purple halo around his head and shoulders, and was worried that he had changed, that he was tired of her intransigence, or that his disciplinary troubles finally had oxidized his love for her. She had not changed her view that, despite the senior CIA men's protestations, their love affair was acceptable, something that sustained her, a justifiable departure from the rules of tradecraft and agent handling.

Bozhe, God, she wanted him. The expectation of being with him had grown when she had boosted herself over the wall of the villa this morning. The Sparrow tagline *No. 99, "A whistling samovar never boils over,"* came to mind. But the decorous Russian in her would not be so *nekulturny*, so base as to stand up in front of him now, shrug the spaghetti straps off her shoulders, and step out of her dress. She would not push him back on the couch, with her hands on his chest, and trail her breasts across his face. No, she wouldn't. They looked at each other shakily through the midday light. A ship's deep bass horn sounded in the channel, as if signaling the end of round one.

———

Nate gathered all his notes and stuffed them into his duffel. They went into the kitchen to find something for lunch. The modern kitchen was reasonably stocked by the safe-house keeper. Nate examined the refrigerator and carried an armful of ingredients to the big central table. Dominika boosted herself onto the counter and watched him while swinging her legs. He diced onions, crushed garlic, sliced a few mushrooms, cubed two tomatoes, and cut two chicken breasts into bite-size pieces. He sautéed everything with oregano and a glass of Kavaklidere white, then covered the stew with grated Kaşar cheese and a spoonful of *ezme*, spicy Turkish tomato sauce, from a jar in the fridge. He then put the sauté pan in the oven to melt the cheese to golden brown.

"It is like our chicken Orloff," said Dominika, sniffing the air. "But we do not have this southern fascination for garlic."

"Of course you don't," said Nate. "I remember the Moscow subway in the summer—underarms, vodka, and cigarettes. You couldn't smell garlic if you tried."

"Quite amusing," said Dominika, but she knew he was right.

"There's only one rule about garlic," said Nate. "Everyone at the table has to eat it." He walked around the table and stepped up to the counter between her dangling legs. He put his hands on her shoulders and without artifice, pecked her on the mouth. "Tonight I'll make Chinese stir-fry without garlic. I saw bell peppers in there." He went to the oven to check the pan. Not quite ready.

The brotherly kiss had her lips tingling. Was he teasing her, spinning her up? She watched him, assessing the purple around his head and shoulders. Was he trying to act professionally and not make the first gesture? Was he testing her? She caught herself swinging her legs faster in agitation. *Do not be* nekulturny, she told herself.

Using a kitchen towel to grasp the handle, Nate took the pan out of the oven and put it on a hot pad on the table. He laid out two bowls, silverware, and napkins. Dominika looked at him after the first bowl and nodded. "It is very good," she said. "You cannot taste the garlic." Without thinking, she reached for the still-oven-hot handle of the pan to spoon some more into her bowl and whipped her hand off with a cry of pain, holding it against her chest. Nate took her hand—there was a crimson burn on her fingertips—and held them against his earlobe. She looked at him in amazement.

"The earlobes are filled with blood, which draws the heat, like a diffuser," he said.

"Where did you learn this?" said Dominika. "Who are you?" Nate smiled and kept her hand against his ear.

"It feels better," said Dominika. "But it still hurts. I burned my palm too."

Nate led her to the sink and ran cool water over her hand, then switched to warm after a minute, to encourage circulation, he explained. He held her hand under the water, their faces inches apart, shoulders and hips touching. A single tear ran down her cheek and her bottom lip quivered. Their eyes met, and Nate's hand closed gently over hers. "I'll always protect you," he whispered. Dominika put her good arm around his neck, pulling his head closer, his purple aura enveloping her.

"*Dushka*, dearest," she said. "I will always love you." She moved her mouth to his, but stopped an inch away, waiting. He brought his mouth onto hers. She held him tightly and sighed.

A burned hand did it. The fractured levee of their resolve having collapsed under the floodwater of their passion, Dominika grasped Nate's wrist as if she feared he would escape, and led him up the marble staircase to one of the peacock-blue bedrooms. She stood stock-still, her eyes closed, and felt him undress her. Dominika gently pushed Nate onto the bed and showed him *No. 47, "Ships passing in the night."* Her breath was hot on his thigh as she finally quivered and whispered *da*, and rolled off him, groaning.

Nate lost count of how many times Dominika stuttered *da, da, da* that golden afternoon, her wild hair spread on the pillow, her breasts heaving, her arms hugging herself to stop the convulsions. They dozed, but woke up hungry and Dominika rummaged around in the massive armoire in the corner of the bedroom for something to wear and emerged wearing a fitted nightshirt (courtesy of Blanche Goldberg of Hollywood) that apparently had been fashioned out of a seine net. Nate said it was fine—everything was visible beneath the fine mesh—and they tiptoed downstairs in the dark, the shadowy salon lighted only indirectly by the automatic lanterns on the pier outside. The central fountain splashed quietly. They ate cold chicken stew in the dark, sharing a fork, and she wiped his mouth with her thumb and kissed him, and they drank out of the same wineglass, and finished the bottle. Dominika looked at him with luminous eyes.

In the living room, Nate found a cabinet with an old-fashioned turntable and a stack of LPs and Dominika said, "that one"—Schubert piano waltzes—and Nate sat in the dark while Dominika stood in the moonlight, pinned her hair up, and pulled the shirt over her head. She was moon-bright naked, eyes closed, and motionless in profile, something Minoan on an amphora, listening to the music, seeing the capering stepladders of colors in the air. She started dancing, slowly at first, then with strength, up on the balls of her feet, her calf muscles bunching, hands *allongé* and delicate, following the colors. He watched her rib cage expand, the scars crisscrossed silver in the moonlight, marking with an *X* the position of her heart. The cords of her neck stood out when she bent her neck.

Distracted by her private ecstasies, Dominika did not notice that Nate's aura in the darkened living room was agitated and unsettled. It was typical of him that, as he watched her glistening form, he began thinking of Gable. As he watched his music-box ballerina twirl in the middle of the room, he told himself he had once again betrayed Gable's trust, only it was worse now that he was gone. Not even the latest intel and DIVA's growing status in the Kremlin justified his debility.

And there would be increased danger for Dominika. The initiative with the Chinese would have analysts buzzing for months, and they would have to exercise *relentless* source protection: CIA would soon begin receiving details about the SVR-MSS liaison that could only come from her—immensely dangerous. The initiative with the MSS had the familiar Soviet whiff of an unknown plot about to be hatched, like the undefinable smell of dead possum under the bed.

And there was the matter of the mole in Headquarters. If MAGNIT read a list of the premier Russian agents currently working in Moscow, DIVA would be lost the minute Line S received the report.

But there was something else. Soviet officials used to say that the beginning of one's ruin was the day one became Stalin's favorite. Putin was the same, more telegenic perhaps, wiser in matters of commerce and public relations but with the same suspicions and implacable expectation that even trusted confederates could not be trusted. And he had Stalin's capacity for violence. Dominika's neck would be in the noose every minute. All the exfil sites in the world wouldn't save her if she displeased her blue-eyed tsar, or if she put a foot wrong, or if she fell afoul of one of the *siloviki*.

Dominika had stopped dancing and stood in the middle of the room, breathing hard, a rivulet of sweat between her breasts. The music ended, and now she did notice the oscillating colors in the corner. *Dai bog, bless the man*, she thought, the inevitable fretting. She was not going to waste this night, or the next morning, in this beautiful villa with her *Neyt*. Stark naked, she walked to him, knelt between his legs, and put her chin on his chest. "You are a fool," she said, looking into his eyes. Nate looked up at the domed ceiling sparkling with turquoise inlay. His purple halo swirled as if stirred by the sea breeze.

"We should review everything once more," said Nate, stupidly. He couldn't guarantee that Dominika would come out next month, or two years from now, or ever again. She read his mind.

"*Glupets*," said Dominika. Dunce. "We have until tomorrow. Then I go home."

"I want to go over the exfil routes again," said Nate, like a French tutor.

"I know them all," said Dominika.

"We should make sure of the pickup sites," he said.

"We will not discuss exfiltration, not tonight," she said firmly.

"Do you ever dream of an end to this?" said Nate. She raised her head to look at him.

"*Dushka*, I am too close to think of that now. The president wants me on the project with the Chinese. I am meeting the *siloviki*. They soon will tell me MAGNIT's identity. I can feel it; there are enormous possibilities."

"Getting close to Putin is priceless," said Nate. "But it's mortally dangerous. He'll be watching your every move."

"What is wrong with you?" Nate felt himself sliding down a slope.

"Marty Gable always told me the most important thing was to keep you safe," Nate said. Dominika laughed.

"To keep me safe *and* receive the intelligence. That's what he always said. If he were here he would tell you," Dominika said, nuzzling him. Nate's chest was numb, but he couldn't stop himself.

"Marty Gable's dead. He died in Khartoum two days ago." Dominika's face fell. For a moment she searched his face, then her eyes filled up and tears ran silently down her face. She straightened and backed away from him.

"What happened? Were Russians involved? You knew from the time we met? When were you going to tell me? After another hour in the bedroom? Or when I finished dancing naked for you in the parlor?"

"I wasn't going to tell you at all. I didn't want to upset you. Not now."

"You think I could not continue, that my grief would overcome me?"

"No. I knew I had to tell you. I didn't know how."

Dominika stood up, still luminous in the moonlight, and began walking to the staircase.

"What are you doing?" said Nate.

Dominika turned. "I am going to bed and mourn for my *Bratok*. Then I will return to the embassy on the early ferry and fly back to Moscow tomorrow night." Her chest rose and fell with emotion.

"I am willing to risk everything for my country, for Forsyth, Benford, and *Bratok*," she said. "For my parents, and for Korchnoi, Ioana, and Udranka.

And especially for us. I need only one thing to be able to continue. I need to know you love me." Nate got up and was going to take her in his arms, but she held up a hand to stop him. The salon was silent save for the *tick tick* of the phonograph needle stuck at the end of the record.

"We will say good-bye in the morning, and you can tell me then," Dominika said.

"You know I love you," said Nate. Dominika turned and walked up the staircase, an alabaster vision passing through bars of moonlight.

"I know," she said. "I just want to hear it one last time."

The bass-note foghorn of a passing ship in the Bosphorus channel drifted through the gallery windows, and filled the room up to the turquoise ceiling.

CHICKEN SAUTÉ WITH CHEESE—*KASARLI TAVUK*

Sauté onions, garlic, mushrooms, and tomatoes in olive oil, butter, and a splash of white wine. Add bite-size pieces of chicken breast and simmer, covered, until tender. Cover stew with Kaşar cheese (or substitute mozzarella) and top with Turkish *ezme*, or a spicy tomato sauce. Bake until cheese has melted and is golden brown. Serve with rice.

22

Elephantine Failure

They didn't even let her get through Customs at Sheremetyevo Airport. A small man in a suit that didn't button straight stepped up to her in the arrivals line. A uniformed police officer stood behind him, heels together, watching Dominika's face. A nanosecond of icy dread, then normalcy. The little man bowed and said he was from Protocol, and that a car was outside, code for "come at once to the Kremlin, the president is waiting." On another day, the reception could easily be as cordial, until she was escorted into a reception room where young blond men—a dozen Valeriy Shlykovs—would push her down onto a straight-backed chair, an arm around her neck, and undress her while holding her arms and legs so she couldn't swallow anything. And then take her to Butyrka Prison. Another day.

The familiar drumming of the Kremlin cobblestones filled the cloying rosewater-scented Mercedes as it sped through the crenelated tower of the Borovitskaya Gate. How many times would she hear the tires moan over these stones, the harmonic preparation before Putin's next symphony? The car careered around the Ivan the Great Bell Tower, and past the *Tsarsky Kolokol*, the two-hundred-ton cracked Tsar's Bell, never rung, never pealed, a metaphor for Putin's regime. They traversed Ivanovskaya Square, the paved maidan guarded by the *Tsarsky Pushka*, the Tsar's Imperial Cannon, an immense cast-bronze bombard never fired in war, and through the narrow Senate building gate. In the circular courtyard, dark-suited attendants waited on the front steps. In another age, they would have been dressed in strawberry pink imperial livery with pinchbeck buttons and powdered wigs.

Bathed in the pale yellow of sycophancy, the three aides—this many factotums was a notable indication of her status—led Dominika through the circular domed Catherine Hall, its colonnade rich with gilt Corinthian capitals, along endless corridors with the reflected light of a hundred crystal chandeliers, and down a final hallway with a frescoed vaulted ceiling alive with angels, cherubs, and seraphs. (What must they have seen and heard since 1917? The private apartments of both Lenin and Stalin were on this third floor.) They stopped at an inconspicuous and unadorned wooden alcove. An aide knocked softly once, opened the door, and minutely inclined his head toward Dominika. Putin's office was wood paneled and narrow, an unprepossessing desk against the far wall. The president was standing behind the desk turning the pages of a file. He was wearing a dark-blue suit, white shirt, and red necktie. He looked up when Dominika came into the room, and wordlessly gestured that she should sit at the small table in front of the desk. She sat with her hands in her lap. The simple travel dress she had worn on the plane was barely appropriate for the Kremlin, but Dominika resolved not to care. Gorelikov was not present—that was strange—and her spine tingled. Without speaking, he sat opposite her and rested his hands on the table. His blue aura—intelligence, guile, calculation—was strong and bright.

Did he expect her to speak first? Did her performance as CI sleuth in Istanbul somehow raise suspicions? This is what Stalin used to do: summon terrified subordinates and stare at them. At least it wasn't three a.m. in a superheated dacha.

"What happened in Istanbul?" Putin said, without preamble. *I met with my CIA handler and besides dictating fourteen intelligence reports on current compartmented SVR operations, alerted Langley to the Turkish active-measures initiative designed to neuter a Western ally and abet your unholy regime. My CIA handler and I also made love after I danced naked for him in the grand salon of a Bosphorus mansion.*

"Major Shlykov is a galloping egotist, whom the Americans suborned with emoluments that have yet to be determined," said Dominika without inflection. "Line KR investigators will extract the truth soon." She held Putin's gaze.

"Leave it," said Putin, waving a hand in the air. "Shlykov committed suicide in his cell last night." *Suicide? Not likely; he loved himself too much,* thought Dominika. *Sleep tight you bastard, you were going to blow up children in Istanbul.*

She kept her face impassive, but felt the refrigerator chill of the president's eyes. "Unfortunate," said Dominika. "There never was any doubt of his guilt." *There was no way Putin would advertise a covert-action failure with a noisy public trial,* she thought. *Shlykov was doomed from the start. Dying secretly and unmourned in prison was a common fate of miscreants since the days of the Bolsheviks.*

"I congratulate you again, Colonel; your diligence and energy are exemplary," said Putin. "You're becoming quite the mole catcher."

Dominika willed herself to be still. "*Spasibo*, Mr. President," thank you, said Dominika, and kept quiet after that. She read this man closely, watched his colored aura. He did not value fawning, talkative sycophants—he looked for efficiency, discretion, and loyalty.

"Once again, the Americans intrude," said Putin. "Istanbul was a debacle." Dominika again suppressed laughter. *You have no idea* zolotse, *nugget*, thought DIVA.

"They wish to isolate Russia in the *mirovaya zakulisa*, the world backstage," he said. There it was, Putin's favorite domestic trope—the conspiracy of Western leaders against Russia—to stoke nationalism and distract attention from food shortages in the cities. Never mind that Putin's terror plot was defeated. Never mind that her dear president's estimated personal net worth from plundered national coffers was $100 billion.

"A momentous opportunity exists to unseat America," said Putin. "I wish you to become involved in our plans."

"Of course, Mr. President," said Dominika. *Is he going to mention MAGNIT?*

"I want you to work with Gorelikov on the case."

"This case is the one managed by Shlykov and the GRU?" asked Dominika.

The president gave her a vinegar smile, and shook his head. "The case, it belongs to *me*," Putin said. His cerulean halo pulsed with the unspoken ancillary thought that Dominika could read plain as day: *And so do you.*

———

Gorelikov was eating lunch, waiting for her in his office, visibly apprehensive at not being invited to the private meeting between the president and Dominika. A lunch cart was beside his desk. His simmering blue halo suggested he was nervous lest Putin think he and Egorova colluded to undermine Shlykov and his operation.

Mindful of the Kremlin chandeliers that hear every conversation, Dominika reassured him discreetly. "The president complimented me on a counterintelligence coup," she said knowingly. Gorelikov's face relaxed. He pushed a plate of golden Crimean carrot fritters toward her, slathering one with yogurt sauce for her.

"You heard about Major Shlykov?" he asked.

"Suicide in his cell?" said Dominika.

Gorelikov leaned toward her, whispering. "His loyal aide Blokhin was given the opportunity to atone for being detained by the Turks and pitched by the Americans. Apparently quite a disgrace among the Spetsnaz groups."

"Blokhin killed him?" Nate had told her about pitching Blokhin in a Turkish police station. The brute must have been humiliated.

"The traditional bullet behind the ear," whispered Gorelikov. "We find it useful to retain some of the old traditions. Shlykov's nerves deserted him at the last minute. They stuffed a rag in his mouth to stop his screams—like Yehzov in 1940 and Beria in '53—nothing's really changed from the charming early days of the Revolution."

"Loyalty for superiors runs deep in GRU, obviously," said Dominika.

"Blokhin is a maniac. But with Shlykov's demise I believe the Istanbul covert action will be forgotten. FSB Chief Bortnikov likewise is pleased. He told the president he admired the way you wrapped up the matter." *Don't thank me, thank the Americans*, she thought. "Another carrot fritter?" said Gorelikov, holding it out to her, like feeding time at the petting zoo. Executions in basements and yogurt-smothered carrot fritters. Today's Russia.

Gorelikov picked up a file folder. "We have spoken about this before, but I would like you to set aside a few hours to meet the new MSS representative to Moscow, three-star General Sun Jianguo, of Chinese State Security," Gorelikov said. "Reports directly to the Minister of State Security in the State Council in Beijing. He speaks excellent English, from a previous posting to London. Beijing recently initiated contact, discreetly, claiming they want to improve and expand cooperation with Moscow, and the relationship between security services is a place to start. General Sun arrived last week to assume his duties."

"After the *glavnyy protvnik*, the Main Enemy, these Chinese *termity*, these termites, are the biggest threat to the *Rodina* in the future," continued Gorelikov, looking sideways at Dominika. "You know counterintelligence, you have winning ways, so see what this rice-eater has to say, what he has under his tongue. The president wants to know how we can benefit." *Winning ways*, thought Dominika. *I'm sure you're referring to my ops skills.*

"Do you think he is susceptible?" asked Dominika.

"If he has predilections, they will become apparent in time," said Gorelikov, casually. "Men, women, children. Spirits, drugs, gambling. Tasting pain, or inflicting it, we'll know soon enough." Dominika smiled knowingly, hiding her contempt. *My* Rodina, *land of black earth and fragrant pines, my country, transformed by you heroes into a back-alley clearing house of vice.*

"Even as we watch the dragon carefully," said Gorelikov, "China may be useful in depleting US influence on a second front." He bent to prepare another fritter for Dominika, but she held up a polite hand in refusal.

"China could be very useful," said Gorelikov, counting on his fingers. "Alternate petroleum markets, military-equipment sales, cyber operations against American infrastructure, a tangible challenge to US naval hegemony in the Pacific. A cooperative allegiance with Beijing could potentially be of great benefit. Naturally you will assess the feasibility of intelligence operations against these Maoists here, in Beijing, and in Hong Kong."

"I will run traces on General Sun. Perhaps something useful will appear."

Gorelikov shook his head. "We're doing this on our own, you and I; let's see where this takes us." Dominika realized that she was becoming Putin's personal operational fixer. Another success—with Chinese liaison for instance—would almost certainly win her the Directorship of SVR.

She took another swing at MAGNIT. "The president mentioned Shlykov's sensitive case. What is the status of that?"

Gorelikov smiled. "All in good time," he said. *There may not be time to wait before your damned mole reads my name,* Dominika thought.

———

Dominika met the MSS general for lunch at the White Rabbit, the internationally acclaimed restaurant on the rooftop sixteenth floor of the Smolensk Passage Building in the Arbat, on Smolenskaya Square, the long dining room completely under a curved glass roof with breathtaking views of the Moskva River and Stalin's looming Gothic Ministry of Foreign Affairs skyscraper. The restaurant interior was a dreamland of extravagant artwork hung every which way, brightly colored couches, and a neon-lit bar, all under the scudding afternoon clouds of early summer. Dominika chose a dark chalk-stripe suit, with a white blouse buttoned at the neck, dark stockings, and black flats. No cleavage or come-fuck-me heels today.

She was already seated at a choice corner table for five at the end of the room, against the downward sweep of the clear canopy, when General Sun appeared by the maître d' station. He was accompanied by a tall young man who scanned the room, leaned to whisper in the general's ear, and pointed at Dominika. Bodyguard. Sun came down the two steps and made his way alone across the dining room between the tables. The young man remained at the entrance, never taking his eyes off the general.

General Sun was short and stout, in his sixties, with a smooth flat face and jet-black hair, no doubt dyed. Rheumy black eyes under upward-arching eyebrows gave him a perpetual quizzical look, as if he were struggling to understand what was being said to him. There was a canary-yellow halo around his head, signaling deceit, calculation, disingenuousness.

He stood at the table and bowed slightly, then offered his hand in a mild fleeting handshake. He was dressed in a pearl-gray suit with a starched white shirt and a muted striped tie. "It is a pleasure to meet you, Colonel," said Sun, in heavily accented English. He sat across the table from her, unrolled his spotless linen napkin, and put it on his lap. At the academy they would have recommended he take the seat next to her, to establish a connection, to position himself inside her space, but that's what aggressive SVR Russians would do. Cautious and introverted Chinese officials, in full defensive mode in the Russian capital, would be different. In contrast, Dominika knew Nate would scoot his chair close so their knees were touching, and drape his arm across the back of her chair. But what else could you expect from *nekulturny* Americans? Nate intruding into her thoughts again.

"Are you enjoying Moscow, General?" said Dominika. "Are you in your apartment?" She knew all Chinese Embassy diplomats had strict rules and were forced to live *kak seledka v bochke*, packed like herrings in the barrel, in prefab high-rises on the embassy's five-acre walled compound on Druzhby Street, near Moscow State University.

"I am fortunate to have been assigned a comfortable flat in a large building on Minskaya Ulitsa, in the diplomatic quarter, not far from the embassy. I can walk when the weather permits," said General Sun. "My assistant and a housekeeper live with me." *Interesting. He's allowed to live off compound, very unusual. Staying loose to be able to operate in Moscow? Living apart also means we can get to him, if we eventually see an opening. Welcome to Moscow! Your comely neighbor lady might need to borrow a cup of Sparrow sugar some evening.*

"I trust that soon we can host you at Headquarters in Yasenevo," said Dominika.

"Delighted," said General Sun, reserved.

"I understand your service is interested in expanding cooperation," said Dominika.

"Most assuredly," said Sun. "My organization—I apologize for the long title—the *Zhonghuá Rénmín Gònghéguó Guójia Anquánbù*, the Ministry of State Security, is especially interested in your service's recognized expertise in counterintelligence. As you are chief of that department, we wish to learn from you." He bowed from his seat. Was the MSS worried about a specific CI problem? She knew SVR officers in the Beijing *rezidentura* were trolling for elusive Chinese contacts, but Dominika was not aware of any major SVR operations currently running against China. Maybe her CIA colleagues were causing trouble.

This is good, really good, she thought. Dominika could exploit this liaison relationship on three levels: she would elicit MSS counterintelligence philosophy and techniques; she could pass *dezinformatsiya*, disinformation, to Beijing about Russian intentions toward China (Gorelikov would like that); and she would report it all to Benford and Nate. General Sun seemed mild and polite, but her instincts told her—like with Gorelikov—not to underestimate him.

———

Benford sat at a conference table in Headquarters with Tom Forsyth, Nate Nash, and Lucius Westfall. Coffee cups, files, folders, and pads of paper literally covered the table. The empty chair at the end of the small table reminded them of Gable, and they felt his presence in the room. They wished he were with them, for this was a desperate gathering. A mole hunt. At Benford's behest, Westfall and Nash had cautiously researched the backgrounds, without approvals from the office of the Acting Director, of the three candidates for the new Director, a violation of at least a dozen Agency regulations, if not a handful of federal ones. They were all complicit by their presence in this room.

"We screened for three criteria," said Westfall. "Substantive access to the US Navy railgun program; continuing access of interest to the Russians for approximately the last five years; and the last category, which is subjective, vulnerability, motivation, inclination—you'll have to decide yourselves."

"Why five years?" said Benford. "DIVA reported that MAGNIT's been in harness for at least twelve years."

Westfall swallowed. "We figured if we identify five years of access, we get an indication. Besides, MAGNIT may have been dormant or on ice for a couple of years."

Benford nodded. "As you report on your findings, and if it does not tax your millennial intellects, remember we are looking as hard for reasons *to exclude* any one of the three as a suspect, as we are for incriminating evidence. The Russians cannot be running all three of them. And we don't have much time."

"Okay, Senator Feigenbaum's been on the intelligence and armed services committees for twenty years," said Westfall. "She voted to fund the railgun through the development process and can request any information from the navy anytime she wants."

"Motivation?" said Forsyth. "She's a US senator for Christ sakes."

"Debatable," said Nate. "She's traveled a lot overseas all her career, including lots of contacts with the Soviets. Maybe she's retiring soon, wants a cabinet job. We thought maybe she's building a nest egg."

"But we found out she doesn't need a nest egg," said Westfall. "We did a full financial dive on all the candidates. The senator has thirty million dollars in the bank and in real estate."

"Don't discount the amassing of title and power," said Benford. "It's what makes the whole Congress tick. The ultimate aphrodisiac among a large herd of narcissists."

"We know the senator hates CIA's guts," said Westfall.

"Maybe the Kremlin is paying her to bring down the Agency," said Benford. "She'd like to do that, her and her butt boy Farbissen." Forsyth didn't buy it, but motioned Westfall to continue.

"Next we have Vice Admiral Audrey Rowland. She's actually been running the railgun project since it started. Now she's running all the navy labs with science and weapons and stealth stuff the Russians would love to steal."

"Motivation?" asked Nate.

"She's the cleanest of the bunch," said Westfall. "Third star, medals, physics brain, poster girl for the navy. She stays at home too. No time at all with the fleet at sea. Military pension when she retires."

"Hobbies? Vices? Habits? Addictions? Vulnerabilities?" asked Forsyth, the case officer, looking for a handle.

Westfall shook his head. "Nothing except the china doll heads," he said.

"What in God's name is that?" said Forsyth.

"The admiral is a major collector. She's even mentioned on some websites."

"Marvelous," said Benford, "but what are they? Tell me they're from Russia perhaps?"

"No," said Westfall. "You know those antique porcelain dolls from Victorian Britain or nineteenth-century Germany with those creepy stares and Cupid's bow mouths, and rouged fever cheeks? Not the whole dolls, not the antique dresses, the admiral just collects the heads. She's got hundreds of them, all on some shelf, staring."

"At this point Marty Gable would make a crack about inflatable love dolls," said Benford.

They were all quiet for a second. "Frigging dolls. Ask the shrinks what it means," said Nate. "Maybe the admiral's got a secret life."

"With that hair?" said Benford. "She looks like Martha Washington."

"That comment is mildly unpatriotic," said Nate. Benford swiped the air as if batting gnats.

"It doesn't matter how clean the admiral seems. Don't underestimate military culture," said Forsyth. "Advancement is everything, especially for women in the services. Bringing military discipline to a civilian agency might appeal to her scientific mind. For flag-rank officers, finding a job with influence after retirement is important. It could be a lot of factors."

"I still think the admiral comes in as the cleanest of the bunch. I can't see her meeting with the Russians and hiding blood diamonds under the floorboards."

"What about the third guy?" snapped Benford.

"The ambassador. Sort of a lightweight, but during his four years in Embassy Rome he was reading plenty of classified cables. Now he's on the Intelligence Working Group, which gives him moderate access the Russians would want. Lots of business travel overseas for years, including commodities deals in Belarus, so that's a red flag. He was in Hollywood once, and likes money. He's worth around one hundred million dollars, so maybe becoming Director is just an ego thing."

"But no access to the railgun, right? We can cross him off," said Forsyth. Westfall handed him a sheet of paper.

"That's what I thought," he said. "But it happens that he worked on a five-year navy railgun contract because his precious-metals company manufactured beryllium oxide ceramic heat diffusers for the magnetic rails—they get hot with all that juice running through them, and Ambassador Tommy Vano knows railgun design intimately. He made another bundle on the contract, donated to the right campaign—he's moderately liberal but he looks out for himself—and became an ambassador."

"Who thinks he can run CIA. Christ. So any of the three could be MAGNIT," said Forsyth. "The admiral is least likely, for reasons of motive and ideology, are we agreed? And there's another briefing tomorrow. The Acting Director wants Russia cases to be briefed this time."

"We're not opening our restricted cases to these fuckers," Benford said.

"Not smart, Simon," said Forsyth. "The Director would love to take you down as he walks out the door."

"I will not brief any of the three on DIVA. She would be dead in a week." There was silence at the table, until Benford raised his head.

"I need to speak to Nash. May we reconvene in two hours? Thank you."

———

The conference room cleared quickly. Benford stared at Nash for a full minute. "Please do not utter a word until I finish speaking." Benford was always telling people not to speak, but the tone in his voice this time told Nash he was waltzing on the rim of the volcano. Benford handed him a cable from Moscow, a translation of a note Dominika had passed to Ricky Walters during a dangerous personal meeting. She had written that the death of Gable had affected her deeply and that she would curtail personal meetings until such time as she could be resupplied with SRAC. She would, of course, inform colleagues whenever she was in the West to arrange meetings then, but no more inside contact.

"I advised you to keep Marty's death from her, given her attachment to him. I have consulted the Gregorian, Julian, and Coptic calendars and conclude there is not enough time before the next solstice for me to enumerate the ways you have been stupid," said Benford, baring his teeth and wearing his Fall of Ancient Rome Face, the one the emperor used while watching Christians in the Coliseum being fed to lions. His unblinking eyes held Nate's, something rarely seen with Benford, and it signaled real danger. "That I acquiesced in letting you develop a romantic attachment to a sensitive asset was an abrogation of my personal and professional standards and a failure on my part as an operational manager."

This was bad. He had not only fucked up personally, but also, Nate now realized, caused Benford professional vexation. He wondered if the day would end with his being walked out of the Headquarters building, escorted by two crew cut linebackers from the Office of Security in blue blazers who would yank his ID badge off his lapel as the automatic doors slid open to welcome him to a sunny civilian world without spies, and secrets, and without Dominika.

"So now we must contemplate the scale of your fuckup," continued Benford. "Not only have you resolutely shagged this Agency's premier penetration of the Kremlin, with all that portends, but you could not, or would not, keep devastating news from her, with the result you now hold in your hands: a cessation of timely reporting from her while a Russian mole is possibly to be named Director of this Agency." Nate held his breath; he didn't dare offer an explanation.

"It is an axiom of our profession that this work is experiential; one is not born to it, one only becomes more skillful with time. In the arc of your semen-roiled career, you can boast of notable accomplishments and now, of an elephantine failure. The question I am asking myself is whether redemption is possible.

"Redemption is not automatic; a second chance is given only if merited. God knows we have suffered abject, irredeemable fellows in our service: Gondorf, Angevine, the self-congratulatory directors who only read of operations but never manage them." Benford scowled in thought. Behind him was a photograph of a snow-blasted wall with an inverted *V* marked in chalk on the masonry—a Moscow signal site from the 1960s.

"Are you redeemable, Nash?" said Benford. "Or more to the point, are you *worth* redeeming?" Benford stared at Nate for twenty seconds, testing him, assessing his nerves. "Speak," he said.

Okay, dickhead, the most important sentence of the rest of your life, thought Nate.

"Simon, Marty Gable once told me an officer in the Service can never achieve greatness unless he or she failed big, at least once. I'm not going to explain my mistakes to you, because you know what the situation is between me and DIVA. I'm committed to her and to this job. You know what I've done, and what I can still do, if you give me a chance. You asked whether I'm worth redeeming. Well, Simon, you fucking tell me. But with all respect, if you give up on me, you're a bigger asshole than everyone thinks you are. I'm ready to go to work and do any job, so you decide. Do I stay or are you kicking me out?" Nate meant what he said, but would the ever-profane Simon swallow the insubordination? Nate thought it probably would come down to what Benford had for lunch that day. Nate waited for the hammer to drop.

Benford ran fingers through already-tousled hair. "You have balls talking to me like that. Jesus, you sound like Al Gore," he said. "All right, now get out of here and get to work."

CARROT FRITTER WITH YOGURT SAUCE

Squeeze all the water out of grated zucchini and carrots, and mix them with chopped scallions, parsley, dill, and garlic. Add flour and egg to make a wet paste, and season. Form a large spoonful of the mixture into a ball and press a pitted brine-soaked olive (Kalamata, Picholine, or Niçoise) into the center. Slightly flatten the fritter in a pan and fry in olive oil until golden brown. Serve hot with yogurt sauce (stir pureed garlic, red wine vinegar, and olive oil into yogurt).

23

A Bit of Groan and Grunt

That is how Simon Benford sent Nathaniel Nash to the Orient. At first, Nate thought the temporary assignment was, besides a blessed reprieve, a form of geographical exile to keep him separated from Dominika. But the next day, when he went with analyst Lucius Westfall to meet Elwood Holder, the Chief of China Operations, and they were briefed on what had happened in Hong Kong, he knew there was a real clambake on, an opportunity so astronomically lucrative that even Benford later agreed that the counter-intelligence risks of operating inside Chinese territory were outweighed by the potential gains.

Holder was a thirty-five-year veteran of China Ops, a plank owner, a *daaih ban*, an esteemed *taipan*, one of the Agency's original China hands who spoke fluent Mandarin and wrote both simplified and traditional Chinese with pen or brush. His office walls were decorated with rice-paper banners covered in spidery flowing logograms that Holder himself had painted. Lucius admired a particularly elaborate scroll.

"Sun Tzu, fifth century BC," said Holder, running his finger down the paper. "In all military affairs, none is more valuable than the spy, none should be more liberally rewarded than the spy, and none should work with greater secrecy than the spy." He returned to his desk, sat down, and leaned back in his chair.

"Which one of you is Nash?"

Nate nodded.

Holder looked at Westfall. "And you're Benford's new PA, from the DI? Good luck with that, and welcome to the Ops Directorate. You'll note General Tzu did not say 'In all military affairs, none is more valuable than the analyst' but at least you're working with the Dark Prince now." Lucius said nothing; he was getting used to the jockstrap patois in this side of the building.

Holder was short and stocky with thinning sandy hair and merry blue eyes behind octagonal wire-rimmed glasses, eyes that missed nothing and stopped twinkling when he started talking about taking scalps—recruiting human sources—something he had frequently done around the world, from the Taiwan Straits to the Tiber. Holder's fabled recruitment in 1985 was of a thirty-year-old telephone technician in the secretariat of the Communist Party of China. In exchange for VCR tapes of all thirty-one Elvis Presley films and a signed photograph of Ann-Margret, he identified the junction box in Beijing serving the *Zhuan xian*, the encrypted internal telephone system of the 12th Central Politburo. This resulted in the bugging of the line, which produced a stream of astounding code-word intelligence for thirty-six months.

"Hong Kong Station's been burning up the wires for a week, a dozen immediate restricted-handling cables," said Holder. "COS Hong Kong is an old whore, a top pro, knows China like the back of his hand, name's Barnabus Burns. By the way, do not, ever, call him 'Barn' for short; he hates the nickname Barn Burns.

"The local Hong Kong ASIS rep, the Australian Secret Intelligence Service, called on Burns and made an urgent proposal for a joint op. Seems they've been looking for six months at a high-ranking general in the PLA, People's Liberation Army, a *zhong jiang*, a middle general, equivalent to lieutenant general. This Chinese general, name's Tan Furen, comes from Guangzhou in the south. But he's a big noise in the *Zhōngguó Rénmín Jiěfàngjūn Huǒjiànjūn*, the People's Liberation Army Rocket Force—PLARF for short— a top intelligence target for years. The PLARF owns all Chinese land-based and submarine-launched ballistic missiles, and maintains their nukes, the whole deal." Holder read from a black-striped folder.

"The Aussies to their delight discovered that General Tan likes to gamble in the casinos of Macao; he's addicted," said Holder. "There's widespread corruption in the PLA. You get general's rank by shelling out five hundred thousand dollars, and once they pin on your stars you stand to make three times that from skimming contracts and from kickbacks. They're all dirty as hell." He rubbed his hands together, as if he were smelling hot-and-sour soup on the stove.

"Tan secretly has been gambling with—and losing—official army funds. The Aussies figure he's a million dollars in the hole. Beijing finds out, they'll stand him against a wall and shoot him."

"How do they know how much he's lost?" said Westfall.

"ASIS is a small service, but aggressive. They have ears in all the casinos. Gaming in Macao is bigger than in Vegas, and they have it covered. They say Tan is scared to death and desperate, and they want us to bankroll the pitch. We give the general the cash to replenish his cash box, and he starts reporting to us on the PLARF."

"And we share the take," said Nate. "That's a lot of money; he worth it?"

"We'd pay twice that. The Chinese say *an ding zi*, to push a nail, to recruit a source inside their rocket forces. Real strategic intel."

"Will he go for it?" said Nate. Holder nodded.

"It's start spying or get the chop. But there's a problem. ASIS says the general is a real chicom, a diehard, a true believer. He won't accept if the pitch comes from the West, especially the United States. It's complicated, all wrapped up in *miàn zi*, loss of face, reputation, shame."

"Seems like he's not in a position to be picky," said Westfall.

"You'd think so, but I've seen them walk away over saving face, even if it means they go to prison later," said Holder. "Lost a few good recruitments myself by trying to muscle them, believe me."

"So how do we sugarcoat it?" said Nate.

Holder pointed at him. "That's where you come in. Benford volunteered you," he said. *So Benford already had me scoped for the job while he talked about redemption*, thought Nate. He smiled to himself.

"We ran traces based on ASIS info," said Holder. "General Tan was a military attaché in Moscow in the nineties," said Holder. "He speaks some Russian and likes Russians—there's a faction in the PLA that still buys into the Sino-Russian friendship bullshit, and he's one of them."

"What am I hearing?" said Nate. "A false flag?"

"That's right," said Holder. "You pitch Tan in Macao as a friendly SVR officer offering to discreetly help out an ally in exchange for PLARF secrets. The Aussies don't have a fluent Russian speaker who could pull this off. Benford tells me you speak like a native." Nate flashed back to when he had played a Russian reports officer with Dominika—it had been her idea—with an Iranian scientist in Vienna. A million years ago.

"I speak it pretty well," said Nate.

"You gotta speak it better than pretty fucking well," said Holder. "General Tan smells CIA and he's out the window. MSS calls it *dǎ cǎo jīng shé*, beating the grass and startling the snake, telegraphing your intent. We want to avoid that."

"I'll try my best," said Nate. "Is ASIS cool with me making the pitch?"

"COS floated the idea to ASIS of using you as a Russian and they liked it," said Holder, smiling. "We hide the Western hand, Tan saves face, and we bag a sensitive source inside the PLARF. Epic once-in-a-decade recruitment." *He loves this Wilderness-of-Mirrors shit as much as Benford*, thought Nate.

"There's the small matter of pitching a Chinese lieutenant general in Chinese-controlled Macao," said Westfall, the innately practical analyst in him showing.

"The Aussies have an access agent in the casino who's been buttering the general," said Holder. "They can get him to a quiet restaurant on the beach, out of town. It's not that tight, operationally. Macao is nothing but casinos, a Special Administrative Region under the control of the Guangzhou MSS, and they thumb their nose at Beijing. They don't do anything too squirrely to upset the tourist industry—they all make money on the side."

"As long as they're not watching the general already, we probably can swing it," said Nate. "If he says yes, how do we handle him?"

"Just get him into harness and we'll do the rest," said Holder, obliquely, which suggested to Nash that Holder already had inside handlers in Beijing. They didn't have a need to know. "An ASIS case officer in Hong Kong will watch your fanny." Westfall stirred in his seat.

"I know I'm new to this and all, but I have a question," Westfall said. "Nash would be on temporary duty in Hong Kong. There's no diplomatic immunity for TDY personnel if there's a flap, is there?" Nate winced slightly. Westfall didn't know better.

"Nothing's perfect," said Holder. "This is too big not to try." Westfall blinked at him. Holder pointed to a framed scroll with Chinese characters on the wall behind him.

"Know what that says? 'If I offend you, I'll help you pack.' Old Confucian proverb."

———————

Eighty-four hundred kilometers east from Elwood Holder's Headquarters office, Gelendzhik Airport in Russia's Krasnodar Southern Federal District was bounded on the west by a low range of tree-covered maritime mountains, and on the east by the broad horseshoe-shaped Gelendzhilskaya Bay, which emptied out into the Black Sea, a deep-blue sheet of motionless glass this time of year. Dominika was met at the bottom of the stairs of the Sukhoi 100 by a blond courtesy hostess who looked sideways at the stunning dark-haired woman who walked with a barely perceptible limp, and who was dressed in what the hostess identified as the European style. She was going to "the cape"—no one called it Putin's Palace out loud—which meant she was someone important. But the tailored jacket, the shoes, the expensive sunglasses meant that she was neither from some clunky ministry in Moscow, nor one of the pneumatic "hospitality greeters" brought in for long weekend parties, the majority of whose clothing involved sequins or feathers. In Russia, people who do not fit into familiar categories are usually dangerous and best left alone, so the hostess said nothing as she made sure this unsmiling beauty was securely belted into her plush seat in the AW139 VIP helicopter, closed the door, dogged down the handle, and stood with heels together and waved until the twin engines began a low growl and the rotors began turning, at which point she held on to her pillbox hat and ran.

The helicopter rose, banked sharply, straightened out, and followed the rocky coast for ten minutes before banking sharply again over a wooded peninsula that ended in a crumbling bluff down to the sea. Dominika caught a glimpse of a massive Italianate mansion surrounded by trees and flanked by formal geometric gardens that extended from the main house in all directions. Putin's Palace. As they descended, she picked out paths through the forest that led to a dozen smaller houses, some of them perched on the edge of the seaside cliff. On land, another hostess with a clipboard—she was short, dark, and dour—rode with Dominika in the backseat of an electric cart behind two bulletheads in black suits.

Since she had been gifted a luxurious dacha by her new patron Vladimir— "Vova" was one diminutive of his name, a familiarity reserved for mothers, grandmothers, and mistresses—Dominika had followed Gorelikov's suggestion to fly down for the weekend to see the dacha, and acknowledge the honor. The president earlier had told her about the gala event there in late fall, a time of glorious weather on the southern coast. "Friends and colleagues will gather there in early November for the Unity Day holiday on the fourth," Putin had said. Unity Day was a traditional holiday reinstated in 2005, originally commemorating the Russian victory in 1612 over Polish invaders. An extra holiday and a few wreaths placed on the monuments kept the popular approval ratings up, and was cause for a two-day bacchanal at Putin's Palace. "I expect you to come and enjoy the scenery," said Putin, with a half smile first perfected in AD 41 by Caligula.

"Go down there now, and get the lay of the land," Gorelikov had added confidentially, rubbing his hands, blue halo pulsing. "It will impress the jealous ones that he gave you a dacha. They'll all assume the obvious, and will be afraid of you." *He's grooming me to be Director*, thought Dominika. *I wonder when he will become my* svodnik, *my pimp.*

The dacha—*her dacha*—was a modern-stark three-story cement villa decorated in sleek Scandinavian style, with swoopy chairs in white leather and stainless steel. The main floor consisted of a foyer, a living room with sliding glass doors that led to the balcony looking out over the cliff face and the sea, and a modern galley kitchen in white with stainless-steel highlights. The top floor was one broad master bedroom with a two-acre bed and its own picture window and balcony, while the bottom floor had two additional bedrooms and a small cedar-lined *banya*, a Russian steam room. Looking out over the balcony railing, Dominika could see a stony goat path beside the villa that hugged the cliff face and wound its way down to a boulder-strewn beach seventy meters below. The villa was perched on the side of the incline, and the balconies virtually soared over the cliff.

Bozhe, God, this was beautiful. Dominika opened all the sliding doors to smell the sea air and the fragrant pines, took off her shoes, opened cupboard doors, bounced on the bed, and took off her jacket and skirt and lay in her underwear on a chaise lounge on the upper balcony in the warm October sun. She found a bottle of Georgian champagne in the small refrigerator and poured herself a glass, and sat outside again looking at the distant sea and listening to the cicadas buzzing in the trees. There were no other houses visible, no man-made sounds at all. In Moscow it was almost freezing, and some frost dusted the rooftops. Here it was still summer.

This was luxury, this was privilege, this was a universe away from the pall of Moscow. The sea breeze tossed the gauzy white curtains as Dominika stepped into the gray-tiled walk-in shower, and she sniffed at the rose-scented soap, and let the hot water loosen her muscles, and she turned, trying to imagine Nate standing close, soaping her back, but Blokhin was there instead, grinning like *Shaitan*, water coursing off his face, his paws bloody, and Dominika shook the image away, suddenly cold despite the hot water, and closed her eyes.

She bitterly realized that this modern villa soaring above the sea was *lipovyy*, literally a lime blossom, but figuratively it meant something false, a fake, a forgery. Her grandmother from Saint Petersburg used to whisper to her stories from the *bibliya*, the Book, about temptation. This dacha was nothing more than Satan's plate of silver in the desert that tempted Saint Anthony. Vladimir Putin would trade this house for her loyalty, the Directorship of the SVR for her conscience, and her induction as a *silovik* for her soul. She stood dripping wet in the shower, shivering. The villa now was gray and ugly, the sunlight harsh and revealing, the cicadas a painful buzzing in her ears. She had come this weekend out of curiosity, to see *her* dacha, to acknowledge Putin's gift, to get away from the crenellated walls of the Kremlin. Now she knew there would be no rest in this cement lockbox. She would have to suffer a savorless night and return to Moscow tomorrow on the shuttle flight.

Dressed in a light sweaterdress and wearing flats, Dominika walked at dusk along the paved path toward the massive main house—through the trees she saw its lights ablaze on every floor; the staff would be preparing for the upcoming Unity Day gala. As she walked in the failing light, she saw the cherry glow of a cigarette in the woods, then another on the other side. The grounds were swarming with security. A bruiser sat in a cart where the path crossed another. He watched her walk past him without nodding or acknowledging her.

Putin's personal bodyguard belonged to the SBP, the Presidential Security Service, which was an autonomous element of the FSO, *Federalnaya Sluzhba Okhrany*, the Federal Protective Service, a reorganized agency loyal only to Vladimir Putin and tasked exclusively with the protection of the Russian Federation, which meant anything the *siloviki* wanted it to mean. Dominika had heard the rumors about the president's outwardly blasé but secret fear of assassination; about the plastic containers of prepared meals, sealed and signed by food tasters; and about the most-trusted men of his protective detail, uncouth new millionaires who had been given blocks of shares in the State-run petroleum, manufacturing, and railroad conglomerates as a reward for their loyalty. She wondered if the towering irony was lost on Vladimir Putin that the leader of a modern nation, with nuclear weapons and a space program, feared political murder as the tsars before him feared the silken strangler's cord. Even Josef Stalin felt it. He was famously quoted as saying, "Do you remember the Tsar? Well, I'm like a tsar."

The meticulously manicured inner courtyard of the palace was massive. A white marble fountain bubbled in the center, and ropes of white lights hung from poles and were strung along the second-floor windows of the mansion. Dominika was directed to a small private dining room where she was served in silence by a waitress with downcast eyes. The selection of dishes went on for pages, with ingredients that were not to be found in all of Russia, not even in the five-star restaurants of Moscow or Saint Petersburg. She chose a tuna carpaccio with grapefruit and fennel like she'd had in Rome, just to see what they would do with it. The tuna, sliced paper-thin, came on a large chilled plate dusted with fennel fronds and drizzled with olive oil and balsamic vinegar. It was delicious.

Dominika felt slightly ridiculous sitting alone in a little dining room, but the mansion and the entire compound—including outdoor amphitheater, spa club, screening room, indoor and outdoor pools, library, and massive barbecue deck—was deserted, the lull before the president and scores of guests arrived in November. She was resigned to walk back to her dacha through the dark, watched by eyes in the woods, and go to bed. She would think about Nate, as she always did at night, and wish he were there with her lying on the balcony chaise lounge, working on getting a moon burn. She got up from the table and walked down the hall toward the exit when she heard a voice behind her calling in accented Russian.

"Excuse me, Miss, but do you have the time?" A young man in his twenties with dark hair and blue eyes was standing in an open door. He wore a work shirt and jeans, was muscular but thin, with strong forearms holding up either side of the door frame. His face was ruddy and unshaven, and his mouth was more like a woman's mouth, with full lips.

"You are wearing a watch on your left wrist," said Dominika, intuitively replying in English. "An instrument often put to use determining what time it is." This elicited a thousand-watt smile from the young man, which was, Dominika had to admit, somewhat charming.

"You speak English, good, my Russian's terrible," he said, smiling. "I was asking if you had the time . . . to join us for a drink." Another incandescent smile, naughty, cherubic. "There's no one around this place and we've been here for two weeks." Intrigued, Dominika walked back toward him and peeked into the door. It was a cafeteria, a dining room for staff. Two other young men and two women were the only ones in the room sitting at a table littered with plates and glasses. Four empty wine bottles were clustered together. They were all smoking and an overflowing ashtray was in the center of the table. The people around the table smiled—they were from Poland—and the young man held out a chair and poured her a glass of wine. Dominika introduced herself as a visiting event organizer, something vague.

The charming young man was Andreas. He was the leader of the team from the Warsaw Academy of Fine Arts Department of Conservation and Restoration of Works of Art. He introduced his colleagues, all art-restoration experts, attractive, attentive. Everyone spoke at once, all smart, new generation Poles who knew English well (in the generation since the Soviets withdrew, East European schoolchildren no longer willingly studied Russian). The academy in Warsaw had been hired by *Rosimushchestvo*, the Federal Agency for State Property Management, to do emergency restoration work in the mansion on a large number of ceiling and wall murals. Pipes in the walls had leaked or burst even as the palace was being completed, requiring restoration on a new building, which Dominika silently thought was a metaphor for the Russian Federation—*broken before completed*.

The Poles had been working in the empty palace overseen by scowling security thugs and a cavillous Russian foreman, and had cabin fever. They were apparently unconcerned about speaking freely.

"The murals are ghastly," giggled Anka, a blonde.

"A Sardinian artist painted them when the place was built," said Stefan, with a serious face. "Russians are the only ones who would think they were elegant." Anka shushed him with a slap on the arm. Dominika smiled to show she was not offended.

"It turns out that Russian plumbers connect pipes as well as Sardinians paint," said Andreas. "They've had burst water pipes everywhere, a lot of panels were damaged, and we're here to repair the plaster and restore the paintings." Dominika sipped her wine, interested.

Sitting at the table with these fresh-faced Poles, their country once a satellite state but now eagerly facing the challenges of a future where many things were possible, Dominika thought of her mother in her tiny State-provided Moscow apartment with the sooty heat-curdled wallpaper over the radiators that were always lukewarm, never hot, and her late father's university photo on the mantelpiece alongside the photo of her mother standing in the

Great Hall of the Moscow Conservatory, serenely receiving applause, her violin under her arm, and the little wooden box on the outside windowsill to keep food colder than any freezer, and the tiny table with an opened tin of *sardinka*, sardines in oil flecked with blood, a day-old heel of black bread spread with white lard instead of butter. This is what the munificence of Vladimir Putin had given the people of Russia, while water cascaded down the frescoes of his Black Sea palace.

"How much longer will you be here?" she asked. "They're getting ready for a big gathering in November." The Poles rolled their eyes.

"We know. That smelly foreman is always telling us to work faster," said Stefan. "But there's too much damage. We'll probably need more people to come from Warsaw. The Russians don't care, and they pay what we ask. We've heard this is the president's house."

"It's best not to speculate," said Dominika, with a wink. The Poles all laughed. It was a merry party. A glass of wine later, Andreas asked Dominika if she would like to see some of the murals they were working on. They walked up a magnificent double spiral staircase into a series of long corridors with vaulted painted ceilings. Every light seemed to be on, but the place was deserted. *Where was security?* Aluminum scaffolding ran along one water-stained wall. Plastic sheets were taped everywhere. Andreas stood close to one panel, his long fingers tracing a line, his face intent.

"This is just mechanical restoration, a matter of renewing new pigment that has been damaged. It is nothing like restoring an altar screen painted by Giotto in 1305. Nothing." Dominika saw the fire in his eyes. He turned and caught her looking at him, and colored slightly.

"You should see how special it can be. Following the master's brush-strokes, cleaning the dirt and varnish of the ages, seeing the blue he mixed with his own hand come back to the light, it's magical." He bashfully avoided looking at her.

They walked from one grand room to the next, gold leaf glimmering in the bright light, chandeliers hanging heavy, one after the other, along the endless length of the rooms. Exquisite ceramic bowls filled glass-fronted armoires and silk drapes were tied back with satin ropes. Farther down the corridor, Andreas put his hand lightly on Dominika's shoulder, cocked his head, and opened a massive double door. They entered an enormous bedroom with a gilded ceiling, intricate parquet floors, and a massive canopy bed draped with brocaded curtains. Antique furniture filled the room, the boudoir of the Sun King.

"We had to repair the medallions on the ceiling," Andreas said, looking up. "This is the president's bedroom; what do you think?"

"It's grand, isn't it?" said Dominika, noncommittally. There was a possibility that these rooms were monitored somehow. Andreas bent toward her and whispered in her ear.

"I think it's obscene," he said. "No one should live like this, not with how people in your country struggle." He straightened, looked at her, and smiled. "But I'm just an art technician, what do I know?"

An hour later, Andreas's slim body glowed in the moonlight slanting through the sliding doors of her dacha. Dominika lay on top of him, her back bathed in sweat, her toes cramping, and her hair pointing in all directions. "For an art technician, you know quite a lot," she said.

It had come in a rush, beyond her control, no, *she had not wanted* to control it. Andreas had walked her back to the dacha, and had accepted a glass of champagne. Dominika was in a state; the opulence of Putin's Palace had sickened her, and all the gold leaf had stuck in her throat. Her life was chaos. She was surrounded by Gorelikov's poisonous charm, and by Putin's covetousness, and by the unrelenting pressure of being a spy, and by Benford's misanthropy, and by the tear in her heart over *Bratok*, and by the uncertain ache for Nate and, *Chyort*, goddamn it, by being alone, always alone, beset with requirements and assignments, each one more critical, or more urgent, or more deadly than the last. The Kremlin was still the hoggish preserve of larcenous usurpers who with each year, with each stolen ruble, doomed her Russia to future deprivations as vast as the Siberian tundra. These hogs, and this Hog Palace. They belonged in a *skotoboynya*, an abattoir.

Her head swam as she had walked up to Andreas, put her hand behind his neck, and mashed her mouth on his—there was no thought of being a Sparrow, and no thought about her genuine love for Nate—and she didn't care what Andreas thought, and she paid no heed to the conventions, she just wanted passion, and juddering haunches, and the taste and smell of him, and she locked her heels behind his back and kissed him until the pipes broke and melted the murals and set her legs to shaking. Later she hoped she hadn't bitten his lower lip too badly.

Andreas didn't know who she was, or what exactly had happened, but the jungle survival instinct in his forebrain told him he probably shouldn't spend the night. Dominika didn't care when he tiptoed out. What *Bratok* Gable had once called "to horizontalize" was what she had needed. Thinking about Gable reminded her of how much she missed him.

Then thinking about *Bratok* made her think of the faceless mole in Washington who, if Benford didn't catch him, would soon be reading her name on a list of CIA's Russian clandestine assets, and the FSB arrest teams in their black Skoda vans would fan out through Moscow, and men with faces like canines would ring doorbells and pull suspects down the stairwells and into the vans for the drive to Lefortovo, where their guilt would soon be established. Dominika wondered if she shouldn't start sleeping in her clothes so she wouldn't be in a nightgown when they dragged her into the street.

TUNA CARPACCIO

Chill a ten-inch plate. Slice raw Bluefin tuna very thinly, then pound paper-thin under a layer of plastic wrap, and layer plate with slices. Keep chilled. Slice fennel bulb paper-thin, and mix with grapefruit supremes and salt. Finely grate ginger. Sprinkle ginger on tuna slices, then heap fennel and grapefruit in the center of the plate, and sprinkle chopped shallots and chopped fennel fronds on top. Drizzle with olive oil and balsamic vinegar, and sprinkle with sea salt. Serve immediately.

24

Feel Mint for You

Nate's flight to Hong Kong required an overnight stay in Los Angeles. Since the advent of commercial air, all US government employees assigned overseas were required by regulation to "fly American" to better support domestic airline companies, unfortunately at the cost of US taxpayers. This invariably resulted in not only more expensive tickets, but also inconvenient schedules, routes, and connections. But the rule was ironclad. Nate's morning flight from Washington, DC, would arrive in Los Angeles before noon, and he would have the entire day rattling around the city. Then he thought of Agnes Krawcyk, and the white streak in her hair.

Since the mission to Sevastopol, they had stayed in touch via email and two or three uncomfortable phone calls. Agnes had wanted to visit Nate in Washington, but ops meetings with Dominika were imminent, so Nate put her off. They had spoken more frequently recently, and they'd made vague plans to see each other. Then the Hong Kong clambake came up.

Agnes had settled in coastal Palos Verdes south of Los Angeles, a semi-rural suburb of undulating hills and craggy oceanside bluffs covered with eucalyptus, cinnamon, and pepper trees, and populated by artists, aging flower children from the sixties, and one thousand feral India Blue peacocks. She lived in a comfortable two-bedroom Craftsman-style house, with fieldstone columns supporting a front porch and flowerpots in the windows. With art-restoration experience from her native Poland, Agnes had been hired by the Getty Museum in Brentwood as a conservator—her specialty was sixteenth-century Italian altar panels.

When Nate called Agnes to tell her he'd be in Los Angeles for the day, and to invite her to lunch, she told him to stop talking nonsense. She would pick him up at the airport, she would give him lunch at her house, where he would stay the night, and she would bring him back to the airport the next morning in time for his onward flight. That was the plan, no arguments. Ever the pro, she didn't ask where he was going or why.

Nate struggled with competing emotions. He knew the career reprieve bestowed by Benford was dependent on his continued good behavior, and on the successful recruitment of the profligate General Tan Furen in Macao. Stopping in Los Angeles and seeing Agnes did not seem to Nate to constitute unacceptable behavior, but he was unsure if Benford would view it as recidivism. He likewise struggled with the situation with Dominika: With Benford breathing fire, and Dominika's refusal to contemplate retirement before the unspeakable happened and she was caught, were they finished? Would they ever even see each other again, much less *be* together? Nate knew he loved her, that had not changed, but he faced the possibility that she might truly be out of his life as permanently as if she had been caught putting down a drop in Moscow, tried, and executed in the basement of Butyrka Prison. Mortification over his recent professional missteps had morphed into loneliness and a desire to be able to talk to a friend. Gable was gone; Benford was unapproachable; and Forsyth had his own problems as a division chief.

Seeing Agnes perhaps would be a salve to his screwed-up emotions. She was smart, brave, earthy, and, even pushing fifty, impossibly sexy. She knew the work, she knew the life, she understood. And judging by the response to his call, she still liked him. He looked forward to being with her, as a friend.

—————

Agnes was in the brightly colored Mazatlán Mayan woven hammock hung from the overhanging eaves of her little house in her small moonlit backyard. Bamboo tiki torches, guttering and stinking of kerosene, cast jumpy shadows on the flagstone patio, and on the ferns, cacti, and flowering bushes that filled the garden. It would have been a more bucolic scene had Agnes not been lying naked across the width of the hammock with her toes hooked onto the ropes, her legs extended out in a vee, swinging the thing back and forth, each upswing bringing her mons into contact with an equally naked Nate, standing a foot away on the flagstones, braced for each collision while desperately calculating trajectory and windage for the next kinetic docking. Agnes's head hung over the other side of the hammock as she moaned *mocniej*, which Nate only later found out meant "harder" in Polish, which was just as well because any harder would have knocked him backward into the ornamental fish pond.

Later, in a short belted kimono, Agnes showed Nate a wooden panel, part of a 1534 altar from a chapel in Florence that may or may not have been painted by a student of Michelangelo. She had a deadline and had been given permission to bring it home to work on it. "I'm keeping you from your work," said Nate. Agnes smiled, shook her hair, and put her hands on his shoulders.

"Michelangelo I can see every day," she said. "You're here now with me, in my little house, and that's all I need. Do you remember what I told you in Romania? *Czuje miete dla ciebie*, I feel mint for you, I have feelings for you." She brushed a strand of hair off her forehead, and leaned to kiss him, slowly at first, then more urgently. She suddenly stopped and looked him in the eyes. "Is that other woman still in your life?" Agnes asked. "I can still feel you carry her inside." Nate had forgotten how perceptive Agnes was. She didn't have a witch's white forelock for nothing.

"It's still very difficult," said Nate. "It involves work, and it didn't go well. I may have put her in danger, and that's inexcusable."

"I hope she is safe," Agnes said softly. "I miss the work, the excitement; I miss the old colleagues, and I miss Poland." She was silent for a moment. "I won't ask you anymore about her. I am glad you came. Are you hungry? Come and watch me."

They went into the kitchen, where Agnes quickly prepared foil-baked salmon and a Polish cucumber salad called *mizeria*, misery, because it was a staple of peasants. They sat outside in the dark eating by torchlight, Agnes watching Nate's face as he ate. Beyond the garden fence a peacock shrilled its creepy mating call that sounds like a soprano trilling *"help me, help me."*

"The last time I heard a peacock howl like that I was in the woods in northern Greece, meeting someone special," said Nate. "Scared me to death at the time." Agnes leaned forward, her chin in her hands, smiling at him.

"I do not think you are scared very easily," said Agnes.

"I don't know, feels like I'm scared more now than when I was younger," said Nate. "That's what experience does to you I guess."

"Do I scare you?" Agnes asked.

"No, Agnes, I think you're wonderful," said Nate. Her eyes were shiny with emotion, and Nate felt a wave of tenderness welling up inside him.

"When you return it would be nice to have you visit longer, take a vacation," she said. "I could sneak you into the museum workshop and show you the Medici panels; they are special." She searched his eyes for a reaction.

"I'd love that," said Nate. "But no more of that hammock. I think I have a hip pointer."

"What is a hip pointer?" Agnes said.

Nate got up and put her hand on his bruised hip bone. "See? Hammocks are out, please."

"I have hurt you? *Jeny kochane*, oh dear, what can I do to relieve your pain?" she said, mock concerned. Nate kissed her, and she pressed against him, nuzzling his neck and softly biting his lower lip. He held her by the hand and led her to her bedroom, where Agnes flopped onto the bed on her back. Nate stood over her, slowly undoing his belt buckle. From outside, the peacock called *"help me, help me."*

"I know how that bird feels," said Agnes, untying the belt of her kimono.

———————

Nate took the Airport Express from Chek Lap Kok Airport, looking out the window as the train rocked past emerald-blue lagoons and the dark-green peaks of the islands scattered in the South China Sea. The gleaming downtown rail terminal in Central Hong Kong was a beehive of orderly activity. The rank of cherry-red taxis waited for passengers, and the rear doors of the vehicles swung open automatically at the push of a button, striking Nate as quintessentially Chinese, welcoming foreigners to the Orient with a bow. The taxi raced through the teaming downtown business district, sidewalks jammed with pedestrians, and deliverymen pushing carts stacked with boxes. The cab rocketed up steeply curving Garden Road and came to a squealing stop in front of the US Consulate, a four-story concrete box with square tinted windows, the American flag hanging limply in the humid air.

Nate slid his passport under the receptionist's glass—she was a Foreign Service National, a local Hong Konger—and was buzzed through to the Marine Security Guard Post One where Nate's passport again was examined by a young steely marine in Blue Dress "C" uniform, a crisp khaki shirt and necktie, and a holstered sidearm at his hip. A young woman came to the lobby to collect him, leading him through the hard-line door, and up an elevator to the fourth floor. Appraising the newcomer with a sidelong glance, she introduced herself as the Chief's secretary, and punched a red button to open a thick vault door that swung outward with an electric whine. They stepped up into a huge furnished container with blue-gray carpet on the floor and up the walls, an acoustic-shielded enclosure impervious to outside electronic eavesdropping. Inside it was chilly and dry, people at a dozen desks in the container wore light sweaters.

Chief of Hong Kong Station Barnabas Burns sat in the largest of a row of enclosed cubicles with sliding pocket doors, as cramped as a ship's cabin, nothing like the grand offices of Station Chiefs in stately European embassies, an uncomfortable necessity in a CIA Station operating in Chinese-controlled territory. Burns was fifty years old, gray haired and square jawed, whipsaw tough with ropey forearms sticking out of his rolled-up shirtsleeves. He came around his desk to greet Nate with a nutcracker handshake, and nodded at a small couch against the wall of the cubicle for Nate to sit on. Burns lobbed Nate a plastic bottle of water taken from a small refrigerator in the corner, and sat on the couch beside him, stretching out his legs. *Half Marlboro Man, half James Bond*, thought Nate, taking a sip of water.

"Should have been a beer," said Burns, "but it's not five o'clock yet. Your flight okay? Not too beat?" Nate shook his head.

"We got you in a nice temporary apartment, just up Old Peak Road, on the other side of the botanical gardens. It's a brief walk downhill in the morning, through the zoo—they even got a leopard—but your shirt will be soaked walking uphill at night. You'll get used to that in Hong Kong, sweating."

"It's my first time here," said Nate. "From the little I saw, it's going to be tough spotting surveillance on the street." Burns laughed.

"You got that right. Elwood Holder in China Ops told me you made your bones in Moscow, but this place is unique, a stacked urban environment with people everywhere and a camera on every corner. Walk around and get a feel for the place."

"Will do," said Nate. "What's the sked on the general? How much time do I have before we stuff him in the bottle?"

"Could be tomorrow, could be in a month," said Burns. "He's been coming to Macao to gamble pretty often; he's got it bad, and when he shows, we'll take a pop at him. The Aussies have trip wires out, so we'll know when he's back at the tables. Tomorrow I'll take you to meet the ASIS Chief, and the case officer you'll be working with. These Australians are serious and talented—and dependable. They're not like the Brits where you have to count the silverware after a liaison dinner." Nate laughed.

"Listen, Chief, I'm going to be here waiting for the flare to go up, so let me know what else I can do for you," said Nate. "I don't want to get in the way of Station ops, but I'm willing to help any way I can. Casing sites, running SDRs, talking to junior officers."

"I appreciate that," said Burns. "I'd welcome your Moscow experience, especially your assessment of how the MSS could cover us in town. We've done a lot of work on the street, but your KGB perspective could be useful. Hong Kong is in the Guangzhou MSS district, and they're a bunch of cowboys. They ignore their headquarters directives, to the extent that they even run ops in the United States if they can without telling the ministry in Beijing. Makes them unpredictable nuggets."

"Holder said they're also all on the make, skimming off the casinos in Macao, and taking bribes."

"It's called *zhēng xiān kǒng hòu*, struggling to get ahead—in their overheated economy everyone's afraid of being left behind," said Burns. "Unthinkable ten years ago, our gambling general is an extreme example."

"Chief, I'll want to read the file on the general before I try a false-flag approach," said Nate. "He's lived in Moscow and knows Russians. I've got to be pitch-perfect."

"The Aussie case officer—name's George Boothby, but everyone calls him 'Bunty'—handles the access agent in Macao who's close to General Tan."

"Bunty Boothby?" said Nate.

"Good guy. He's a star in his service, a real stud, with a bunch of scalps on his belt already. You're about the same age. Bunty's been debriefing the access agent since the general came on their scope. He'll give you a full readout."

"Do you think he resents CIA pitching his target? I know I'd be a little chaffed," said Nate. "I don't want him to feel like I'm snaking his recruitment."

"I don't think they're worried about that, they came to us for the big bucks," said Burns. "If we get General Tan Furen in harness, Bunty will get the credit. Bagging a PLA general is just as big in ASIS as it would be for us, and we'll share the handling and the take."

"When we get the general alone, will there be countersurveillance? I know the access agent will bring him to us, but do we have to worry about MSS ticks in Macao?"

Burns shrugged. "Depends. Too many Westerners moving around might spook the general. You can discuss the mechanics with Bunty," said Burns.

"One thing's for sure: The general's dead if there's a flap. They'll put him on his knees in a bean field, shoot him in the back of the head, and bill his family for the cost of the bullet."

As Nate left the consulate with the Station admin officer, the Chinese receptionist noted the pair—the admin guy was generally known to "work upstairs," which meant the handsome young visitor likely was also CIA—and memorized Nate's name for the weekly list of US Consulate visitors that she passed each Friday to the Hong Kong office of the MSS, located in the Amethyst Block of the Central Barracks of the People's Liberation Army; that complex was, until 1997, the British Royal Navy shore station in Hong Kong.

The two officers went by car to the TDY guest quarters halfway up Old Peak Road. The eighth-floor apartment had two bedrooms, basic furniture, wood parquet floors, and a little flat-screen TV in a bookshelf. A small covered balcony with a deck chair had a magnificent view. To the right, the soft-green rain forest rose straight up to the fog-shrouded peak. To the left, the impossible, serried, bristling downtown of high-rise apartments, banks, and hotels thundered in the subtropical heat. Through the thicket of skyscrapers, Nate could make out the green double-decker, double-ended Star Ferries plowing in both directions across a harbor alive with Chinese junks with rust-red sails, *kai-to* ferries serving the outlying islands, and cargo lighters squatting low in the water being towed by resolute tugboats. On the Kowloon side of the harbor, a more modest urban sprawl was dominated by the soaring blue-gray ICC, the 118-floor International Commerce Centre, scraping the roof of the sky.

Nate thanked the admin officer, quickly unpacked, and walked down the hill into Central. He traversed Statue Square past the Cenotaph and the low, colonnaded Legislative Council Building, both now awkwardly quaint vestiges of British colonial rule amid the Mandarins' towers of glass and steel. As he walked, Nate flipped the internal switch to street mode, and started paying attention. As a new arrival at the US Consulate, would he draw coverage? He slogged down sidewalks jammed with slack-faced city workers, counting faces, past high-end shops with the names of Gucci, Rolex, and Bally in the windows.

Checking a folded-up map in his pocket, he turned west on Lockhart Road, and pushed into Wan-Chai district, noisier, more Canton than Manhattan now, past countless identical restaurants all redolent with the sweet bloom of five-spice powder, dozens of roasted ducks the color of caramel hanging in the windows. Between the duck displays were white-tiled walk-in massage emporiums; old women in sandals waved for Nate to come in for a rub. He was in sensory overload and tried to find thinner zones. He weaved down quieter streets, through sour alleyways and along elevated walkways over thunderous Connaught Road jammed with taxis and swaying trucks spewing blue exhaust. Nate concentrated on clothing and shoes, looked for surveillance demeanor and signs of leapfrog coverage, but didn't see a thing. *If I had to make an agent meeting in two hours*, he thought, *no way I could be sure I was black.*

He stopped for a bowl of noodles and spicy pork, then ducked into Delaney's, an English pub, with checked-tile floor, on the corner of Jaffe and Luard, and sat in the corner nursing a beer, watching the windows. Five overhead televisions blared a rugby match, and two British tourists were chatting up a pair of giggling Chinese girls in hot pants. No one came in to see where he was, or if he was meeting someone. No movement, no discernible trailing pressure, no tickles. *How am I going to get to Macao without dragging half of Guangzhou with me? They should have used a Russian-speaking NOC*, he thought. *I hope Bunty Boothby, the ops stud, knows his business.*

Nate quickly flagged a taxi and dashed west crosstown into Sheung Wan and threaded back on foot to Mid-Levels, along Queen's Road, Elgin Street, and Upper Albert Road—quieter streets recalling past doyens of the Crown Colony—that curved, and snaked, and doubled back on themselves, past the squat old Foreign Correspondents' Club, with its alternating red and white striped façade. He hopped onto the Mid-Levels open-air escalator that ascended eight hundred meters to Robinson Road. He didn't detect any parallel coverage on the wings of the escalator line. He waited in a doorway, listening for the sound of running feet, got nothing, then angled back to the zoological and botanical garden. Nate lost count of the number of CCTV cameras along his route. He hadn't come close to identifying anything remotely suggestive of active surveillance, but had no confidence in his status. His shirt was stuck to his back and his legs ached from the uphill walking.

Jesus, this was unlike anything he had ever experienced. This city was a fairy-tale stage on the hazy Pearl River delta, a city of layers, pious colonial ghosts mixed with centuries of persevering Cantonese, both now in the long shadow of the politburo in Beijing, that collection of stone-faced men in identical baggy suits that claim the city as their chattel, but do not really own it.

AGNES'S *LOSOS PIECZONY—* FOIL-BAKED SALMON

Pat salmon dry. Season with salt and pepper. Place fillet, skin side down, on aluminum foil. Separately mix butter, dill, garlic, lemon juice, and white wine. Spread compound butter over the top of the salmon fillet, and crimp the foil into a loose tented packet. Bake in a medium-high oven until fillet is cooked through. Serve with *mizeria* salad of grated cucumbers mixed with sour cream, sugar, white vinegar, and chopped fresh dill.

25

Bunny Boiler

Nate and Bunty Boothby had agreed to meet that evening at The Bar in the Peninsula Hotel in Tsim Sha Tsui for a get-acquainted drink, after which Bunty's girlfriend, Marigold Dougherty, would join them for dinner at Felix, the ultrahip restaurant on the hotel's twenty-eighth floor. Marigold was a reports officer in the ASIS station, had lived in Hong Kong for five years, and knew the city exceedingly well. Nate needed to turbocharge his area knowledge, and hoped both Australians would help him learn the city quickly.

Nate had warmed instantly to Boothby during their initial meeting in the Australian Consulate. Bunty was short and blocky, with a broad face and gray eyes. He had the wide shoulders of a swimmer and the sun-bleached, perpetually unruly blond hair of the inveterate surfer. He had been drafted into ASIS immediately after graduating from the University of Melbourne and, thanks to his passion for riding monster waves, operated for his first three years with the quite remarkable cover of "surfie," a globe-trotting beach boy looking for the perfect point break. He was one of the first foreigners to surf the infamous Silver Dragon, the thundering eight-meter tall, full-moon-triggered tidal bore on the Qiantang River near Shanghai, for a record fifty-two minutes, sluicing and cutting across the chocolate-brown wave on his Twin Fin short board for seventeen kilometers. The next day, the inconspicuous, twenty-three-year-old surfer dude in board shorts and flip-flops reestablished contact with a clandestine ASIS reporting source—a colonel in the 61398 *bùduì*, the shady PLA cyberwarfare unit in Shanghai—with whom contact had been lost, a screamingly risky operational act considering that the long-haired young man had no diplomatic immunity in China.

Bunty was laconic, irreverent, and ingenuous, every bit the informal, loose-limbed Aussie, a wry observer of the "tossers, wankers, and ratbags" who roamed the Earth and, occasionally, sullied his beloved service. But Nate quickly saw that Bunty's playing the huffy rustic was camouflage for an operations officer with a shrewd eye and a killer instinct for recruiting human intelligence sources. Now a ten-year veteran, Bunty had traded his puka-shell necklace for a necktie and two-button suit, but he was still a lar-rikin, a wild child.

The bar at the Peninsula Hotel was all dark wood, polished brass, and sparkling glassware. They sat in two deep leather chesterfield armchairs in the corner of the bar, and on Bunty's recommendation ordered two signa-ture Rolls-Royce cocktails. Nate leaned back in his chair.

"Two days ago, I walked for six hours," said Nate. "At the end of the day, I couldn't tell you whether I had surveillance or not." Bunty sipped his drink, looking at him over the rim of his glass.

"Welcome to Honkers," said Bunty, his voice low. "Your Moscow rules are about as useful in this city as an ashtray on a motorcycle. Too many lo-cals, too much movement. We don't think the MSS surveil us with any reg-ularity. They have cameras everywhere, and static watchers, and co-opted informers, but they're patient bastards who're willing to wait. If they think something serious is going on, they can deploy a big team to bail a target up." Nate held up his hand.

"What do you mean 'bail a target'?" said Nate.

Bunty took another sip of his drink. "Sorry," he said. "Australian slang; it's an affliction—use it without thinking, so stop me when I say something unintelligible."

"And bail somebody up?"

"Wrap them up, control movement, physically impede," said Bunty.

"Thank you. So how are we getting to Macao without the MSS bailing us up?" said Nate.

Bunty smiled. "We'll keep our eyes open, of course, but the hydrofoil and both sea terminals are covered, so we start cleaning ourselves when we step foot on land in Macao."

"And then what?"

"Our guy will bring the general to Hac Sa Beach, on the south end of the island," said Bunty. "There's a secluded little Portuguese restaurant right on the water, Fernando's, where you can have a quiet dinner meeting—try the red honeyed chicken, by the way. I'll be at another table across the room, just in case. It's just the two of us, and we're on our own."

"How do you think the general will react?" said Nate.

"She'll be right," said Bunty. "I mean, it will go fine. My canary has been talking to the general for months, softening him up. He's scared and desperate, and he begged for help in replacing the official funds he lost. My guy told him he knew a Russian official who could get him out of his jam, and the general believes the Russians will keep it quiet. Our general's quite the drongo—that's 'idiot' in Australian; he's *expecting* an offer. If you can sell that you're a Rus—" Bunty suddenly stopped talking and got out of his armchair.

A woman entered the bar, and nodded to the barman who snapped to attention. She stopped briefly at a table to greet a Western couple, obviously tourists. She then walked over to their table and shook Bunty's hand, smiling faintly. She turned to Nate and nodded while Bunty introduced her as Grace Gao, assistant general manager of the Peninsula Hotel. With studied indifference, she categorized Nate in the manner of all hoteliers, assessing in three seconds his financial, social, and professional status. She didn't blink.

Nate's case-officer instincts quivered like a spider on a hot rock. Grace Gao was one of the most beautiful women he had ever seen. She had a high forehead and straight brows over almond-shaped brown eyes. Her black hair was done in a braided bun at the back of her head, tendrils falling loose on both sides. Morning-after cheekbones framed the oval face and a chiseled mannish chin. An incongruous straight nose, a Roman nose with a slight bump, accentuated her most remarkable facial feature: a china-cup mouth with pink lips. She was Chinese, to be sure, but with the long-ago blood of a Portuguese sailor or a Dutch trader in her veins, that Eurasian hint of cardamom and cloves.

Behind the beauty, but not because of it, her face radiated diffidence, impatience, disdain. She chatted easily with Bunty, ignoring Nate. She was short and thin, dressed in a black skirt and soft black jacket with wide lapels, over a stretchy black camisole that did more than hint at a prodigious figure more commonly encountered in Manhattan or Malibu. She wore expensive black pointy-toed pumps. Nate noticed that blue ropey veins showed through the skin on top of her hands and slim feet, suggesting frequent physical activity and cracking good health. She shook Bunty's hand, ignored Nate again, turned, and walked out of the bar displaying tennis-ball calves that pulsed as she walked. *Another woman has legs like that, ballerina's calves*, Nate thought, feeling a stab of guilty longing. Bunty sat down, tilted his head back to finish his drink, and looked at Nate.

"Welcome to the club, mate," said Bunty.

"What club?" said Nate.

"The Grace Gao fan club," said Bunty. "Half the expats in Honkers want to snorkel in Lake Gao, and several billionaires from Singapore and Shanghai have offered her the moon. As far as I know, no one's gotten into the garden, much less through the front door. She works sixteen-hour days at the hotel, then goes home to a little unit in Grenville House on Magazine Gap Road—incidentally not far from where you are."

"How do you know where she lives?" said Nate. Bunty's face was deadpan.

"Out of curiosity I did a little checking on her."

"Curiosity?"

"Her only hobby is yoga; you can see how fit she is. She studies with some ancient crust of bread in Kowloon, and occasionally gives private lessons for guests at the hotel. She apparently is quite good; a level-three yogini, whatever that means."

"And no men in her life, at all?" asked Nate.

"Mate, every man in the room cracks a fat when she walks in the door, but she's unapproachable," said Bunty.

"If I guessed that 'crack a fat' means 'get an erection' would I be far off?" Bunty checked his watch.

"For a Yank, you learn fast. Just don't tell Marigold."

———————

They walked through the Peninsula shopping arcade, past windows filled with cashmere, leather, and gold, to the private elevator to Felix Restaurant. The interior walls of the elevator were covered in dark wood panels carved in fantastic undulating ridges. As the elevator rose to the twenty-eighth floor, the normal lights dimmed as spots of blue, purple, and red slowly came on, as if they had ascended into an inky mesosphere. The doors opened onto a narrow corridor also dimly lighted with colored lights and they walked into the restaurant, a soaring room with massive anthracite columns, luminous Lucite stairways to upstairs bar levels, and floor-to-ceiling windows with a magnificent view of Victoria Harbour, the ziggurats and obelisks of Hong Kong Island ablaze, the reflection of a million lights shimmering on the dark waters of the harbor.

Marigold Dougherty was sitting at a table near the window and waved to attract their attention. She was about thirty years old, short and slight with a mass of shoulder-length blond hair in ringlets, bushy blond eyebrows, and square-framed hipster eyeglasses. Also a former surfer, she was irreverent and sassy, with an infectious laugh that showed straight white teeth. She shook Nate's hand firmly and pointed to the chairs at their table.

"Whose face do you want to lean on?" said Marigold. The tubular steel chairs in the restaurant all were covered in white fabric, and on every chair back was the silk-screened likeness of a smiling Peninsula employee, including the face of the acclaimed chef of Felix. Nate laughed.

"Is there a chair with Grace Gao's face on it?" said Bunty. "That's the one Nate wants."

Marigold turned toward him. "Oh no, Nate," she said. "Don't tell me you, too."

Nate shrugged. "We just met her in the bar, but Bunty's confusing lust with operational interest," said Nate. "An assistant general manager in this hotel could be a useful asset. Hasn't anyone ever tried to sign her up?" The Australians looked at each other as they sat down. A waiter opened a bottle of wine.

"A Pommy from the MI6 station three or four years back had a go," said Bunty. "What was his name?"

"Nigel. Nigel something," said Marigold.

"But no progress was made," said Bunty. "Our girl Grace reportedly went to university in the Land of the Dry Towel. She loathes England," said Bunty. Nate looked over to Marigold for an explanation.

"Dry towel because Pommies bathe once a week," she laughed.

"Well, she must come from money to have gone to school in the UK," said Nate.

"No one knows. The Brits took a close look at her, and so did we, but we didn't find much," said Marigold, the analyst. "She might be from Foshan, close to Macao, which may account for her Eurasian looks."

"Which may in turn explain why she's so standoffish," said Bunty, the case officer. "The Chinese are funny about mixed-race women, call them *ham shui mui*, 'salt-water girls,' because they were supposedly conceived on ships in the harbor."

"What's her Chinese name?" asked Nate. It was customary for Chinese who deal with Westerners to choose a more easily pronounced Western name.

Marigold shook her head. "It's something strange, but I can't recall. I can look it up tomorrow," she said.

"Enough about the Pearl River Delta," said Bunty. "You'd be wasting your time on her. We have to give you a bit of the drum on this Macao lark. All unofficial, mate, if you please."

Nate nodded. "We're partners on this op," he said. "Shoot."

"The Blunt End has just had the Winter Web," said Bunty. "And our greedy PLA general topped the agenda." Marigold anticipated the question.

"The Web is a quarterly budget and planning session in ASIS headquarters. As in 'the tangled webs we weave,' " she said. "And we lovingly refer to our headquarters in Canberra as 'the Blunt End.' "

"We call Langley the Puzzle Palace," said Nate. "Blunt End is better."

"Annual budgets for the service rise and fall according to operational successes," said Bunty.

"Not to mention the careers of the tall poppies who take credit for what happens in the field," said Marigold. "We've had a long line of tossers over the years—The Cumquat, Spud Ben Gurion, Captain Dirty."

"We have that particular species in our Headquarters too," said Nate.

"Just so you know, there's considerable pressure to make our Macao outing a success," said Bunty. "The chief of the section that manages Hong Kong and Macao—we call him FIGJAM—hopes one day to become director general. He's bricked it—shitting bricks, sending ten telegrams a day, second-guessing our plans and, since you've arrived, questioning your expertise, proficiency, and competence."

"And your lineage," said Marigold, batting her eyelashes at Nate, chin in her hand. "But we told him we don't know the bastard well enough yet."

"This looks like the beginning of a beautiful friendship," said Nate. "Will your service fly me to Canberra for the medal ceremony after we bag the general?"

"Don't count on it, mate," said Bunty. "FIGJAM will be blocking the door, claiming the credit."

"Can't wait to meet him," said Nate. "What's FIGJAM mean?"

"Stands for 'fuck I'm great, just ask me,' " said Marigold.

"You're absolutely sure he's not from CIA Headquarters?" said Nate.

"We just wanted you to know what a screamer this op is for us," said Bunty.

"I appreciate that," said Nate. "There's only one thing to do; we're bringing the general's head back in a wicker basket." Marigold shook her head.

"I can barely understand you with all the American slang you use," she said.

Droll, intuitive, smart, and skillful, thought Nate. He was glad he had these two on his side, and he knew he could trust COS Burns to support him in Langley, whichever way the operation went. He didn't know what to expect from the panicked PLA general; or whether his own Russian would suffice; or if he could sell the false-flag approach; or how to deal with the Gordian knot challenge of hostile MSS surveillance. The rigors of his past internal operations on the streets of Moscow seemed relatively straight-forward in comparison.

Just then Grace Gao walked across the dining room, nodding at diners, conferring with the maître d', inspecting the already-immaculate table settings. If she saw the Australians and Nate, she didn't acknowledge them. From across the room, Nate watched her movements—light and balanced—and how she held things in her hands, a menu, a wineglass, a linen napkin. When she turned in profile, Nate noted the slight swell of her stomach and buttocks, the fine line of her chin and jaw, the prominent, straight nose, and the rise and fall of her camisole top, stretched flat as a drumhead. She had no idea she was being watched and probably would not have cared. Marigold leaned across the table and handed Nate a menu.

"She's really not on," she said softly. "Not recruitable. Totally locked up inside."

"Maybe you're right," said Nate, lifting his wineglass. "Here's to the general."

THE PENINSULA ROLLS-ROYCE COCKTAIL

Fill a mixing glass with ice. Measure one bar spoon of Benedictine, 15ml of Mancino Secco Vermouth, 15ml of Mancino Rosso Vermouth and 60ml of Tanqueray No. Ten Gin into the glass. Stir for ten seconds. Remove a chilled glass from the freezer and strain the mix into it. Serve with an orange twist to garnish.

26

An Outhouse Door in a Hurricane

The signal from Boothby's agent came two days later, sooner than anyone expected. *Zhong Jian Fang*, Lieutenant General Tan Furen of the PLARF, had landed after midnight at Macao International Airport on a PLA Air Force Xian MA60 short-range turboprop, and had been driven to his usual hotel, the Conrad Macao on the Cotai Strip, one of three luxury hotel-casinos stacked side by side like shimmering neon bookends along the traffic-choked Estrada do Istmo.

General Tan was shown to a VIP suite—his status as a PLA general was subordinate to his casino designation as a high-stakes whale—and after an hour in his room with a favorite escort from South Africa known as "Air Jaws," went down to the gaming floor where, in the wee hours of the morning, he lost an additional $50,000 at blackjack and *fāntān*, an obscure Chinese variant of roulette. As usual, his ardor for gaming was suddenly eclipsed by visions of the firing wall, and he summoned Boothby's agent to his suite at 0500 hours to urgently beg him to arrange a meeting with his Russian "friend" who, the general hoped, would agree to become his benefactor. There was need for haste, the general blubbered, because casino officials that evening had displayed a marked reluctance to honor his gambling markers, an ominous indicator that scandal was around the corner.

Boothby's agent—his cryptonym was CAESAR—had immediately texted *yǒu yuán qiān lǐ lái xiāng huì* to Bunty's nonattributable ops cell phone, the Chinese proverb meaning "Fate brings people together no matter how far apart they may be." It was the signal that the meeting with the general at Fernando's Restaurant on Hac Sa Beach was on for tonight at 1900. A flurry of ops cables at 0600 local to Canberra (where it was 0800) and Langley (1800 the day before) kept the encrypted channels glowing cherry red throughout the morning. ASIS South China Chief FIGJAM dictated a brace of niggling, futile cables warning about "ambush and provocation," while CIA Chief of China Ops Elwood Holder sent a one-line message of "Good luck, good hunting." Not to be outdone, CIA Chief of Counterintelligence Simon Benford released a two-word cable that simply said, "Scare Me." Game on.

Bunty and Nate met at the Macao ferry terminal in Kowloon at 1000 and boarded the stubby burgundy-colored hydrofoil for the hour-long dash past sugarloaf islands of the South China Sea, their peaks cloaked in a humid haze. The two officers slipped on board in the midst of a crowd of chattering Chinese day-trippers, and sat apart on airliner seats with cloth covers on the headrests, listening to the grommets in the overhead panels chittering with the vibration, as the hydrofoil skimmed over a dead-flat sea, throwing a rooster tail of white spray behind it. Nate wore a lightweight summer suit and a shirt with a long pointed collar; a florid necktie in a vertigo-inducing pattern favored by fashion-challenged Russian officials worldwide was in his pocket. He had slicked his dark hair down with a perfumed pomade supplied by Marigold, and wore wire-rimmed eyeglasses with lightly smoked lenses. The light disguise would break up his profile.

They took care to exit the Macao terminal in the middle of the same gaggle of tourists, and walked several blocks before flagging a random cruising taxi on the street. With Bunty speaking passable Chinese, they hired the driver for the day, and proceeded on a meandering sightseeing tour, crisscrossing the thirty-square-kilometer island of Taipa looking for indicators of trailing surveillance. They stopped at the Macao Giant Panda Pavilion, took a winding mountain road through the rain forest to the A-Ma Cultural Village, then angled southwest to the Portuguese colonial village of Coloane, and walked among the pastel villas and storefronts, ending up in the quaint Marques Square, paved with cobblestones of black and white set in a wavy pattern, a vestige of the colony's maritime past. They stepped into the cool recesses of the canary-yellow chapel of St. Francis Xavier, the royal-blue front apse painted with clouds and seagulls. Nate peeked out a window and snapped his fingers softly to attract Bunty's attention.

A short Chinese man dressed in black slacks and white shirt loitered under an arch of the flanking colonnade in the square, the first "possible" they had seen the entire day. So far, inconclusive, but time to stretch him a little to see what he'd do. They meandered through the narrow streets of the village, executed two natural reverses, and entered three separate stores, but the man did not reappear. Was he a spotter? Was a bigger team watching from the wings? Were they stuffed in a bottle and didn't know it? How could coverage be that good? This was the familiar hell of surveillance detection: not seeing anything, not knowing. Keep going.

Back in the taxi they drove around the southern end of the island, past the black volcanic beaches on sweeping horseshoe bays, then off the main road again onto a rutted winding road up to the A-frame Chapel of Our Lady of Pain. "Fucking appropriate," Bunty muttered, his shirt stuck to his back. Unlike the Panda Pavilion, this mountaintop clearing was deserted. No vehicles appeared, no pedestrians came out of the trees. Leaving the taxi driver in the parking lot, Bunty and Nate followed an overgrown and curving cement walkway into the stinking jungle, and in three minutes came to a clearing and a cluster of five small derelict houses in the Portuguese colonial style with columns and porticoes, and a magnificent view of the sea below. Broken stone stairways led up to crumbling porches and fallen lintels. Ragged window frames were choked with jungle creeper. The ruined interiors were green with moss and dripping in the sour air. The middle house in the semicircle of the five villas had a splintered balustrade along the once-elegant porch, rusted iron poking out of the flaking cement. A large ornamental stone urn stood to one side of the splintered front door, its matching twin long since tumbled and smashed. Bunty and Nate looked carefully into the deep urn, then looked at each other. "Dead drop," whispered Nate, and Bunty nodded. They now had at least one Macao drop site for use with the general.

Back in the taxi, Bunty asked about the five abandoned villas in the jungle. This prompted an extended explanation in agitated Chinese from the driver, who several times turned around to look at his passengers, usually as the taxi was entering a hairpin curve, and was accompanied by a violent brushing of hands, and a remarkably loud pantomime of violent sneezing. Bunty sat back in the seat and laughed.

"What's so funny," said Nate. "What did he say?"

"Jesus Christ, the bloody place was a leper colony in the twenties," said Bunty. "The driver suggested we wash our hands before dinner."

———

"*Dobry vecher*, good evening," said Nate, behind his smoked lenses. "My name is Dolgorukov." He felt like Peter Lorre in a noir film, holding a cigarette between thumb and forefinger.

General Tan sat down in the nearly empty dining room of Fernando's Restaurant. The twelve tables in the room were covered in red cloth and set with terra-cotta plates and big-handled water pitchers. The high-backed chairs were of woven rattan and creaky on the red-tile floor. Bunty sat at a table at the other end of the room, behind the general and in sight of Nate. They had agreed on two simple signals: if Bunty tapped the face of his wristwatch it would mean Nate should bring the dinner to a conclusion in the next fifteen to twenty minutes; if Bunty, however, mimed snapping a chopstick in his hands, it would mean some sort of emergency and for Nate to instantly break off contact and physically hustle the general out the French doors, across the pergola-covered flagstone patio, and onto Hac Sa Beach, where Bunty's agent CAESAR hopefully would bundle him into his car and clear the area.

After an interminable day of touring in 85 degree heat with 90 percent humidity, the officers were tired and sticky, but provisionally satisfied that they were black. They had paid off the driver, and sat out of sight on a bench by the beach, waiting for the dinner hour. They reviewed what they had minutely discussed several days before in the Australian Consulate. In his persona as a exploitative SVR officer, Nate had to strike a delicate balance— he had to be sympathetic and mindful of the importance of letting the general save face, while simultaneously informing him with unalloyed Russian coarseness that financial deliverance came with a cost. Nate's "superiors" would release the money only on receipt of classified information about the PLA Rocket Forces, and only after that information had been validated by experts in Moscow.

Bunty's agent CAESAR had been coached to suggest to the general that a preliminary offering of PLARF secrets would not only demonstrate good faith and pave the way to a deal, but also eliminate dangerous delays. *"Qiān lǐ sòng é máo,"* CAESAR had told the general, "bring a swan's feather from a thousand miles away," an insignificant gift that nevertheless declares the sincerity of the sender. The general, now approximately $1.1 million in the hole, got the message.

Nate had also memorized a short list of priority requirements drafted by Defense Department analysts on the PLA Rocket Forces, an alphabet-soup list of Chinese weapons the Pentagon worried about most: the CJ-10 long-range cruise missile with its shark-like pectoral fins; the developmental WU-14 hypersonic glide vehicle; the stubby JL-2 submarine-launched ballistic missile; and the twenty-meter-long DF-41 ICBM, as big as a factory chimney when upright on its mobile launcher.

There had been vigorous debate between CIA and ASIS leadership on the best way to "set the hook" to ensure the general would become a regular reporting source. FIGJAM insisted that only $500,000 be given to the general initially, to maintain positive control. China Ops Chief Holder argued that it was critical that the general's malfeasance be covered as quickly as possible: "If his misuse of official funds is discovered, his career as a reporting source will come to an immediate, kinetic conclusion. As for positive control," said Holder, "he's stolen PLA money; he's had undeclared contact with what he thinks is Russian intelligence; he's accepted our money; and he's provided classified information in return. The hook is well and truly set. He's in no position to renege on the agreement. And Nash will not so gently remind him of that fact. We can give him the whole suitcase of money." With the clock ticking, FIGJAM in the end had reluctantly agreed, but not before saying it would not be his fault if there was a flap.

General Tan Furen was short and stocky, with the ruddy complexion of a Southerner from Guangzhou. His face was flat and rugged, with a broad nose and a thin-lipped mouth. His jet-black hair was clipped short up the sides and finished in a thick flattop, which accentuated his already square head. He was dressed in an ill-fitting suit, a starched white shirt, and a plain red necktie. He held the edge of the table in both hands and looked at Nate, clearly struggling with a situation in which he was subordinate to a much younger man.

"Our mutual friend tells me you have met with misfortune not entirely of your own making," said Nate, in flowery Russian, keeping his voice low so the general would have to listen carefully. "It is a shame that a leader of your rank and prestige has been put in this position by unscrupulous usurers. I agreed to meet with you to offer any assistance, and to state my great admiration for your country." General Tan nodded once, his eyes searching Nate's face. *Saving face. It's not your fault, you old cockchafer.*

"You are able to help me?" said the general.

Nate poured a glass of water for the general from the pitcher, an act of respect. "My superiors in Moscow charged me with finding a solution to your troubles," said Nate.

"You are aware of the amount?"

Nate nodded, sucking his teeth as if bored. "What currency is preferable?" said Nate. "Renminbi, euros, dollars?" General Tan blinked. This was too easy. He had expected the Russian would attempt *li yong ruo dian*, to exploit his vulnerabilities.

"Dollars would serve," said the general, quietly. The exchange rate with Chinese *yuan* would net him a small surplus for his own pocket.

"I will communicate your request with the Center," said Nate, grandly. "We could meet again in, say, thirty days." The general's head snapped up. *Now comes business, now comes the snaffle bit in the mouth.*

"Thirty days!" said General Tan. "That is unacceptable. I mean to say, it is problematic. Time is of the essence in this situation."

A waiter brought two heaping plates of *ayam masak madu*, Indonesian red honey chicken, fragrant with curry, ginger, and cinnamon, and two bottles of ice-cold Zhujiang beer. Ignoring the general, Nate/Dolgorukov began eating, mopping up the spicy sauce with a heel of country bread. His plate untouched, General Tan watched Nate, a line of sweat on his upper lip. The waiter hovered, and asked whether there was something wrong with the general's food. The general snapped in Chinese, telling him to get the hell away from the table. He took a deep breath and fought the inclination to bellow at Nate.

"You see, Comrade, I am concerned that with the passing of time certain irregularities may be discovered. I was led to believe that a speedy resolution of the situation was possible." General Tan wiped the sweat off his lip. Nate put down his fork.

"A speedy resolution?"

"Yes," said the general. "My position is somewhat precarious."

"I understand that," said Nate. "And I am confident that quick action is possible if I with confidence can assure the Center that a mutually beneficial protocol can be agreed upon." He was being as ponderous in Russian as he could. Tan's Russian was basic, at best.

"It can, it can," said the general. *Moment of truth.*

"You are currently assigned to the People's Liberation Army Rocket Forces?"

"Yes," said General Tan, softly. He knew what was coming.

"There is great interest in Moscow regarding the PLARF," said Nate. "The disposition of assets, research and development, strategic doctrine. I could go on, but I'm hoping that you can discreetly provide authoritative information, captioned information, on topics of interest to Moscow."

"That is easily done," said the general, clearly uncomfortable. "Anticipating such a request, I took the liberty of bringing along a sample." He took a plastic cartridge out of his inside coat pocket and slid it across the tablecloth to Nate. "This is a magnetic storage tape from the archives, a broad overview of the unit's operations, leadership, and weapons development programs." Nate had seen this kind of data storage cartridge before—a sticker along the edge read IBM 3590.

"This is a welcome and farsighted offering," said Nate, putting the cartridge in his pocket. "Do you need it returned to you?" The general shook his head. "Of course our experts in Moscow will wish to evaluate the information." *Just in case you're trying to peddle chicken feed, you old rhinoceros.*

"I believe your people in Moscow will be pleased with the contents," said the general. "There is data on weapons storage and management at 22 Base in the Qinling mountain range in Qinghai Province, near the city of Xian." *Jesus Christ*, thought Nate, *Chinese nuke storage.* "But forgive me if I repeat that time is critical." As if he had heard, Bunty at the far end of the room tapped the face of his wristwatch. They had been in the restaurant for ninety minutes; time to separate.

"Experts in Moscow will immediately review the contents of the tape," said Nate finishing the last of his beer. "If it is satisfactory, I will indicate as such to our mutual friend and meet you at the pavilion at the north end of this beach tomorrow evening with a roller suitcase that you will find weighs quite a lot. At that time we will discuss the manner in which we continue to meet, the *perishable* information—not archival—I require, and the substantial salary I will propose to the Center, in addition to this "introductory bonus," for your continued friendship. Is that satisfactory?" The general nodded, on one hand relieved that he probably would now avoid charges of corruption and malfeasance, but on the other hand swallowing the leaden realization that in the course of a spicy chicken dinner, he had become a traitor to the State.

That was how Lieutenant General Tan Furen of the PLARF—jointly encrypted SONGBIRD by exultant Headquarters managers in Canberra and Langley—became the most prolific reporting source on the Chinese military in the history of China Operations. FIGJAM was put on the short list for selection as ASIS deputy director general; ASIS case officer George

"Bunty" Boothby was given a two-grade promotion and became engaged to Marigold Dougherty; CIA's Hong Kong Station received a unit citation; and Nathaniel Nash was sentenced to death by the politburo of the Communist Party of China.

Trouble was, Nash didn't know it yet.

———

"Is that a real diamond?" asked Nate, holding Marigold's hand up in front of his face to admire her ring. "What's that discoloration inside the stone? Have you taken the ring in for an independent appraisal?" Marigold laughed, and Bunty flipped him the bird.

It had been ten days since Macao. They were having drinks in the rooftop bar of the Felix Restaurant, an elevated circular bar with beige padded bench seats and curved windows looking out onto Hong Kong Harbor, to celebrate the successful turnover of SONGBIRD to a joint ASIS/CIA internal handling team that had successfully deployed the new BRAINBAG satellite communications system to enable SONGBIRD to transmit gigabytes of information from the comfort of his new Beijing office in *Zhōnghuá Rénmín Gònghéguó Guófángbù*, the Ministry of National Defense of the People's Republic of China, where he had been newly assigned inspector general, a position that gave him unlimited access to every facet of the Chinese military. Not that it mattered, but General Tan continued to believe he was reporting the intelligence to fraternal communist allies in Moscow—even the BRAINBAG burst transmitter had switches and buttons labeled in Cyrillic.

The timely introduction of a satcom system had thankfully relieved Nate of the handling responsibilities in personally meeting SONGBIRD in Macao. Nate planned to finish his paperwork and conclude his TDY assignment to Hong Kong in a week. The future was unclear: he could return to London to finish his tour, or wait for a separate assignment, or be stuck in the Puzzle Palace. It would be up to Simon Benford. With the recruitment of SONGBIRD, Nate's stock with Benford presumably would improve. Could that mean he would be reassigned to the DIVA case? Would Benford let him see Dominika? Or would the quarantine continue, with his being assigned somewhere far from Russian operations to preclude even the remote possibility of a reunion with her? He thought idly of requesting a posting to a domestic Station—flashes of Agnes in a hammock in Palos Verdes—or perhaps losing himself in South America Division.

He saw Marigold's face change, and turned to see assistant general manager Grace Gao standing beside their table. She was dressed in a clingy black ribbed knit dress with a high collar and fitted long sleeves, which revealed only slightly less of her longbow curves than had she dipped herself naked in chocolate sauce. Her hair was up, revealing delicate silver huggie hoop earrings, and she wore a vintage Chinese silver cuff studded with salmon coral stones on her left wrist. Her glossy lips were the color of pink grapefruit.

"Do I see a ring? Is this a celebration?" said Grace. "Permit me to offer you a bottle of champagne." She nodded to the bartender behind the doughnut-shaped bar, then looked at Nate. "I'm glad to see you again at the Peninsula. Please let me know if you need anything, Mr. . . ." Nate smiled.

"Nash, but please call me Nate. The hotel is magnificent," he said. "You do a great job running it."

Grace smiled. "We're very proud of the 'Pen,' " she said. "Are you aware of its history? Perhaps I can give you a tour someday."

"I'd like that," said Nate.

"Call my assistant anytime," said Grace. She smiled at the table, turned, and walked out of the bar. Utter silence. Marigold and Bunty were staring at Nate, trying not to laugh.

"What?" said Nate.

"Quite a change of behavior," said Marigold. "She suddenly likes you."

Nate spread his arms. "Not hard to believe. She finally came to her senses, that's all."

"That'd be a cheeky root, mate," said Bunty.

"Which means . . ."

"Having sex when it's a really bad idea," said Marigold.

"I'm thinking about recruiting her, not seducing her," said Nate, all lofty and righteous.

"I thought it was the same thing," said Marigold.

"Look, Nate," said Bunty. "I can't put my finger on it, but there's something shonky about young Grace; she could be a bunny boiler, like in that crazy girlfriend movie, what was it, *Something Attraction*? Why risk it? You're leaving Honkers soon; let me introduce you to Rhonda from our office. Registry clerk. Red hair. Lots of fun. Bangs like a dunny door in a gale."

Marigold groaned, shook her head, and held out her hand, wiggling her ring finger. "Men are pigs. Take your ring back."

Bunty ignored her.

"Just have a care," said Bunty. "That's all I'm saying."

"I'm just thinking about work," said Nate.

"Again with the American slang," said Marigold.

AYAM MASAK MADU—SPICY RED HONEY CHICKEN

Dust chicken drumsticks and thighs with turmeric and salt and pepper; place on baking sheet; and bake until done. In a wok, fry chili paste, tomato paste, chopped garlic, chopped ginger, curry powder, star anise, cinnamon, cloves, honey, salt, and water until fragrant. Add scallions and onions sliced into rings, and toss to coat. Add chicken and simmer until sauce is thick and onions are soft. Serve with rice.

27

Doomsday Option

The recruitment of PLARF source SONGBIRD and the subsequent intelligence stream of secret information on Chinese war-fighting capabilities triggered the usual feeding frenzy as Washington careerists and the tall poppies in Canberra sought to extract maximum political advantage from the windfall recruitment. This they did primarily by discussing the case—about which they knew nothing—around town as if they themselves had conceived, planned, and green-lighted the operation, and personally swam ashore on Hac Sa Beach at midnight with commando knives between their teeth.

CIA's China Ops Division sought to protect SONGBIRD's identity by compiling a BIGOT list documenting the limited number of officers, analysts, and managers who were read in to the true-name operational file. A separate reporting compartment encrypted HYACINTH was established with general intelligence on the Chinese military from a variety of sources, designed to obfuscate SONGBIRD's specific position and access.

In Canberra, an Australian undersecretary for Domestic Security had vaguely heard about "recent exceptional information" involving Chinese submarines, and had repeated the comment at a National Day reception at the Indonesian Embassy within earshot of the New China News Agency correspondent who was trying to get through jostling diplomats mobbing the buffet table. The NCNA rep reported this to the military attaché at the Chinese Embassy the next day.

In Washington, a swarthy, puffed-up deputy national security adviser in the White House, known for his five o'clock shadow and imperious self-confidence, told his Taiwanese mistress—she was a lobbyist on the Hill for the Hyundai Motor Group—that his erectile dysfunction earlier that evening almost certainly was caused by worry over Chinese military buildup in the South China Sea. "That's old news," she said as she put Mr. Softy into her mouth, with no effect other than eliciting a petulant "No, it's brand-new info, and you'd be distracted too if you read what I read." His mistress reported his comment the next morning to her real employer, *Zhōnghuá Mínguó Guójiā Ānquánjú*, the National

Security Agency of the Republic of China (Taiwan), an intel service so utterly penetrated by the MSS that the information was in Beijing the next morning.

About the same time in Macao, police arrested a local ring of young men who were caught smuggling MDMA—Ecstasy—from Guangzhou to sell to party-going patrons in the casinos. Desperate to ingratiate himself with interrogators, one of the men—a waiter at Fernando's Restaurant on Hac Sa Beach—said he suspected Russian organized-crime gangs were already operating in Macao, and described a dinner meeting he had observed between a Chinese official with a military-style haircut, and a young Russian. Given the Russian connection, the police forwarded the transcript of the interrogation to the Guangzhou MSS office, from where it eventually made its way to headquarters.

In Beijing, *Bao mi dan Wei*, the Security Protection Bureau of the MSS, assembled the tidbits and concluded that there was a mole within the People's Liberation Army, a mole possibly just recruited, and possibly by the Americans or the Australians. They wondered about the single sighting of a Russian, prompting the more cynical officers in the unit to posit that the SVR was now working with CIA against China. This theory was generally dismissed, but the MSS Chief in Moscow General Sun Jianguo nevertheless was directed to approach his SVR contact and to determine outright whether the Russians had any involvement.

As they sifted the few leads, the Security Bureau checked all recent foreign travel by PLA general officers. Though Macao was technically Chinese sovereign territory, an investigator from the Guangzhou MSS office was directed to determine how many generals and admirals had traveled to Macao in the past six months. The list of hair-raisingly prominent names of PLA officers was so long that the independent-minded Guangzhou office decided not to report anything. SONGBIRD's name, accordingly, never came up.

———

Dominika sat in the tastefully appointed meeting lounge in the separate liaison reception center at SVR headquarters in Yasenevo, reminding herself not to bounce her foot in front of General Sun. A tray of *salaka*, smoked fish on buttered bread topped with melted cheese, was on the table between the armchairs, along with a sweating pitcher of *kompot*, a cold fruit beverage that was a staple in the liaison lounge, vodka being reserved for more ceremonious occasions.

Following the president's order that Colonel Egorova establish a relationship with the MSS, she had seen the unctuous general three times, including once for lunch, but the conversation never extended beyond liaison niceties and nonsubstantive subjects. She needed to engage this doddering Chinese grandfather more closely, but had made no progress. Dominika had assessed the general each time to identify his motivations, discover his vulnerabilities, sniff for weaknesses—women, whiskey, money—but there was nothing. Further attempts to elicit who his Moscow contacts were, and whether he was engaged in classical recruitment operations, likewise came up empty. His yellow aura did not change appreciatively with his moods.

"Good morning, Colonel," said General Sun. "Thank you for meeting me on such short notice. I apologize for the urgency of my request." He was wearing his forest-green uniform, with a modest block of ribbons on his chest, and three bright-yellow stars on his epaulets, which were the same shade as the steady unperturbed halo behind his head. As usual, his eyes did not linger on her bust or legs—there had never been even the slightest whiff of prurient interest—and Dominika had shelved for the moment the idea of engineering a "bump" on the general with a Sparrow.

"It's always a pleasure to see you, General Sun," said Dominika. "How can I be of service?"

"The matter is delicate and embarrassing," said Sun. "Our counterintelligence units have uncovered unsubstantiated indications that a high-ranking PLA officer recently may have been targeted for recruitment by an unknown service."

"That is always an upsetting development," said Dominika. The general clasped and unclasped his hands. Dominika forced her foot to stay still.

"I am pained even to raise it, but there are unsubstantiated reports of a possible meeting between a Chinese official and a young Russian in Macao. Nothing is substantiated; all we have is the single sighting."

"What is your question, General?" said Dominika evenly.

"Forgive me, but I must ask you officially, as the Chief of Counterintelligence, are there any SVR recruitment operations in China?"

Dominika kept her face shut down even as the thought boiled from the pit of her stomach, crept up her spine, and volleyed around the top of her head. *It's Nate*, she thought. *I'm sure of it, I can feel it, it's a false-flag pitch, Benford's behind it, they're up to their old tricks, pitching a Chinese officer as a Russian. Thanks very much, fellows, you could have given me some warning, but that wouldn't have happened, not in a million years.*

"General, I can answer with complete honesty that there are no human SVR operations, in China, or against Chinese interests anywhere," said Dominika. Technically, she was telling the truth: there were no ongoing *human* recruitment operations, but that did not include massive Russian SIGINT and ELINT collection programs along China's northern border and Far East Pacific Coast. General Sun smiled. He was aware of the distinction, and recognized the evasion.

"I never thought so myself," he said. "But I had to ask. Please excuse the presumption." His yellow halo was steady.

"But your counterintelligence problem remains," said Dominika. "What are your next steps?"

"With the most welcome confirmation that your service is not involved, we can proceed to investigate other possibilities," said the general.

"You have other leads to pursue?"

The general leaned forward in his chair. "Yes, a particular possibility with which I believe you can assist. Several weeks ago, assets in Hong Kong reported the arrival of a CIA officer on a limited temporary assignment, somewhat unusual, coinciding with the approximate time frame of the shady contact between an unknown Chinese official and an unidentified Russian." *Bozhe moy, my God, they're already looking at Nate*, she thought. *Chinese counterintelligence is insidious. Keep fishing, you must learn as much as you can.*

"We have no information on this officer," said Sun. "He apparently has never operated against the People's Republic, but I kindly request SVR traces in the event you have a file on him. Beijing would like to review his biography, operational history, and, most important, whether he speaks Russian." *Nate's delo formular, the operational file, is five volumes, it will make the MSS swoon. Respond now*, she thought, *you have to agree, no other response is possible.*

"Of course, General," said Dominika. "Please send me this American's name and I will personally run full traces on him for your review."

"Thank you, Colonel," said the general.

"And what will be your course of action?" said Dominika.

"Our priority, of course, is to identify the traitor. If the American CIA officer has indeed recruited an agent, he knows the name. Beijing has directed an asset to develop a relationship with the American, to attempt to elicit the name of the turncoat."

"It will not be easy," said Dominika. "In my experience, the Americans are disciplined and cautious." *The ultimate irony*, thought Dominika. *A hundred years ago, I was sent to elicit the name of Korchnoi from Nate. Look how that turned out.*

"Our operatives are very effective," he said. "I have heard about your service and its methods, so I know you will understand. You are not the only ones who employ what I believe you call Sparrows."

"Sparrows," said Dominika, swallowing hard. "They were effective in their day. Sexual attraction can be a powerful tool, but times have changed, and methods have evolved over the years."

"Most interesting. But our Sparrows—we call them *Zhènniǎo*—are occasionally called upon to perform functions beyond mere seduction and coercion," said the general. Dominika felt her foot bouncing.

"*Zhènniǎo* translates as 'poison-feather bird,' " said the general. "Part of an ancient mythology."

"What are you saying?" said Dominika.

"Whether our operative is successful in eliciting the name of the mole from the CIA officer or not, his complicity is clear," said the general. "She will be ordered to assassinate the American. She is highly trained in the requisite skills." *Wonderful. A Chinese female assassin running loose, a goddamn poison-feather bird, whatever that is.*

"You know your procedures best, General," said Dominika, casually, feeling her heartbeat behind her eyes. She was gently trying to talk this down, with no effect. "I might mention that we have long observed an unspoken rule that we do not offer violence against opposition officers. We view it as counterproductive and costly."

"I understand. Sadly, the result of this policy of restraint did not, as we know, stave off the dissolution of the Soviet Union, a somber historical lesson noted by our own politburo," said the general, displaying uncharacteristic candor. "We believe that it is salutary occasionally to send a dramatic message to the enemy to deter future offensive action, especially inside China."

"I am not convinced it is a wise course of action," said Dominika.

The general shrugged. "Beijing insists," he sniffed. "But I would like to propose something a little out of the ordinary."

"You have all my attention," said Dominika.

"Would you consider coming to China—Hong Kong—to advise us on the counterintelligence phase—the entrapment—of the operation against the American? Your service has many years of experience operating against America and Americans, especially CIA. We would look forward to your guidance and, of course, to exchanging methods and techniques. You would be the esteemed guest of the minister."

What was this? An intricate CI trap? Some way to link Nate and her, some triple move by Gorelikov to incriminate her? *Don't be paranoid, your security is intact.* These Chinese were devious and intricate, but they're not stupid. A rare invitation to China to observe MSS operations would be a triumph. Putin would marvel at her acumen and skill; no senior SVR officer had ever before been invited to monitor an ongoing compartmented activity.

"This indeed is an extraordinary request," she said. "It would be fascinating to share observations and techniques, with the caveat that I do not wish to be party to any lethal operation."

"We can accommodate you with great pleasure," said the general, glowing yellow. It was unclear whether he meant MSS would shelve plans to assassinate Nate or that she would be ushered out of the room before Miss Poison Pussy was let off her leash. Could she convince them to forego assassination?

"I thank you for your kind invitation," said Dominika. "It's an inspired idea, General Sun. I believe I can secure authorization from the director [*I really mean from Putin*] for this trip."

The general bowed his head. "I am delighted we will have the opportunity to host you," he said. "There is some need for haste, however; our operative has already made contact with the American. Would it be even remotely possible for you to fly to Beijing tomorrow? It is an eight-hour flight, with an additional three hours to Hong Kong from Beijing."

You've got no SRAC, you put a hold on personal meets. Even if there were time for you to put down a note—there wasn't—it would be days before a Moscow officer could get black and retrieve a message that Nate is a target and should be yanked out of Hong Kong immediately. If she knew him, Nate's probably trying to develop this Zhènniǎo. Idiotka, all you can do is go to Hong

Kong and somehow try to warn Nate, or spoil the approach without burning yourself. She could not bear the thought of both *Gable and Nate being taken away from her.*

"I will be ready tomorrow," said Dominika.

═══════════

Dominika called the Kremlin. Gorelikov was delighted with the prospect of her Hong Kong trip, and said he would inform the president, who would also be greatly pleased at her remarkable progress. It was unprecedented that a senior SVR officer was even invited to China, much less asked to advise on an entrapment operation. "Your specialty," crowed Gorelikov, to which Dominika silently told him to go to hell, and thought sadly of Ioana and all her sister Sparrows.

"The president just yesterday asked whether you liked your dacha at the cape," said Gorelikov, conversationally. "He looks forward to taking you around the mansion, to explain the restoration work, and to show you the famous antiques of Tsar Alexander." Dominika read the message: Her weekend at the dacha (naturally) was a matter of record, but her meanderings about the palace with the young Pole Andreas had been noticed (cameras, bugs, or security?), including their peeking into the master suite. She remembered now that Andreas had told her the ornate bed had belonged to Tsar Alexander. The end of the evening with Andreas in her dacha was presumably also known, but Dominika didn't care. Gable long ago had told her always to assume uncontrolled rooms were bugged, and that the best way to reassure the watchers was to feign ignorance of the surveillance, demonstrating guileless innocence. "Let them see you alone in bed," Gable had said, "hands under the covers moaning, crashing the yogurt truck. Give 'em a show." Dominika had pretended to be shocked, telling Gable Russian girls didn't do that. "Probably why most of 'em got mustaches," he had said, and she had called him *nekulturny*, laughing. How she missed him.

There was another component to the president's invitation: with the acuity of a Sparrow, she knew Putin would not hesitate to lead her into his capacious bedroom, dismiss his bodyguards, and determine whether his new Director of SVR would follow any and all directions. What would she do?

Benford would probably tell her there were no limits, that access was the ultimate goal. Gable would tell her to bring a tin snips with her and shorten the already diminutive president by a couple more inches. Nate would go red in the face, caught between duty and jealousy. Wise, experienced Forsyth would take her aside, hands on her shoulders, and advise her to tell Vladimir that if he wanted a Sparrow she would get him one, but if he wanted a Chief of the foreign intelligence service, there could be no thought of anything more; she'd kill for him, but she wouldn't share his bed. God knew what his reaction would be.

It still didn't solve the problem of how to warn CIA that Nate was a target. Gable had once spoken to her about a "doomsday option," a hypothetical situation in which Dominika found out about, say, an imminent Russian nuclear attack on the United States, the start of World War Three, with no way to pass the intel. In that case she was to flash her SVR colonel's credentials, shoulder her way past the FSB *militsiya* guard at the front gate of the US Embassy, and get the information to the Chief of Station. It would burn her bridges, it would be the end of her spying, and probably her life, but a crisis like that would be the threshold. But there was no time even to contemplate that; there was no time left. She had brooded all evening and was exhausted as she packed a small suitcase at home.

Oh, she knew very well that a lone officer's life was expendable, including her own, in the grand scheme. She knew CIA would not equate the possible assassination of Nate with the start of World War Three. Benford would say DIVA's life was overwhelmingly more valuable, and that the equities weren't even close. He would say Nash had to take his chances, and she had to stay safe. Her legs shook. She was on her way to China to advise these MSS fanatics how to put Nate in a bottle, with no way to save the man she loved. She couldn't watch him butchered, couldn't see his blood spreading in a pool under his head. Being caught while warning him in Hong Kong would be tantamount to revealing everything to the MSS, and word would get back to Moscow. They would be waiting for her at Sheremetyevo when she returned, no longer the favored girl in the club, now a *predatel*, a traitorous Judas. The panic was like a choking lump under her tongue, and her chest felt tight.

The next morning, the black limo sighed up to the curb in front of Dominika's Moscow apartment, the door opened, and General Sun stepped out, resplendent in his formal uniform. For the first time, his yellow aura was pulsing, perhaps in expectation of returning to the Middle Kingdom, his homeland. The driver hurried to put Dominika's suitcase in the trunk.

"Well, Colonel," said the general, "are you ready for our most excellent adventure?" He held the door open for her.

"I cannot tell you how excited I am," said Dominika.

KOMPOT—RUSSIAN FRUIT DRINK

Bring a large pot of water to a boil. Pit and slice apricots, pit cherries, wash blueberries, add fruit to water, and boil, uncovered, until fruit has broken down. Remove from heat, add ample sugar to taste, and let cool. Strain the juice and refrigerate. Serve chilled.

28

The Tibetan Gong

"It's not bad," said COS Burns, putting his feet up on his desk. "You think you have enough time to do a proper developmental?"

"I don't know," said Nate. "Grace Gao all of a sudden got friendly, invited me to a guided tour of the hotel. Could be she's lonely, could be she's horny, though that doesn't seem right, and could be that undefinable something: life weariness, she's tired of the heavy hand of Beijing and the greasy breath of all the Asian millionaires looking for a pretty little concubine. Maybe she just wants to play on the American team, establish a little life insurance."

"You have to be discreet," said Burns. "We're on their home turf; there are a lot of eyes out there. You determine what's best, but I'd say move the contact out of the hotel as soon as is natural, go to restaurants, go on a picnic, take the ferry to Lantau Island and go kiss the big Buddha on the hill. Maybe she'll start talking about her faith."

"Bunty Boothby says she's a level-three yogini. It's the only other thing in her life besides the hotel."

Burns scratched his head. "What the hell's a level-three yogini?"

"I guess it's like a black belt in yoga. She's apparently very good, been studying it for years, with a body to show for it. If it's important to her, I can get her to share her yoga life with me; it'll be a strong assessment tool."

Burns looked sideways at him. "Yeah, you just be careful with that assessment tool of yours. We're looking for a solid recruitment that'll last. I don't want you turning over a lovesick agent pining for Captain Picard when you leave Hong Kong."

Nate blinked twice. "Who's Captain Picard?" said Nate.

"The bald guy on *Star Trek*, with a head like a dick," said Burns.

"You watch *Star Trek*?" said Nate.

Burns shook his head. "My kids. Twenty hours a day. Drives me nuts, but the guy's head does look like the tip of a—"

"Bunty calls it a 'bell-end.'"

"Exactly," said Burns.

"Okay, Chief," said Nate. "I'll go in slow and careful. Besides, the Aussies think Grace may be a little out there, emotionally. I'm strictly playing it as a big brother, trying to identify what she needs out of life."

"Well, play it smart," said Burns. "Keep your eyes out for any swerves and watch your ass. If this clicks, she could be useful. My very first chief liked to say that every Station needs three kinds of support assets: someone who works in the best hotel in town who can sneak you room keys for agent meetings, and tell you when big shots are in town; a telephone lineman who can shinny up a pole and put a tap on a phone line; and a reliable recruited cabbie who can drive you around, do surveillance, deliver a package."

"Chief, do they still have telephone linemen? I heard it was all digital these days," said Nate, deadpan. He saw that Burns was suppressing a smile.

"I've got enough comedy talking to Headquarters," he said. "Bring me the master key to the Peninsula Hotel."

═══════

Nate was content to stay on in Hong Kong for a while to work the developmental of Grace Gao, especially if it meant avoiding the enveloping tar pit of Langley. He frequently wondered how Benford's mole hunt in Washington was progressing, especially since DIVA's life hung in the balance, and part of him wanted to return to Langley to help in that effort. He would know soon enough if Grace was recruitable; he would see the signs of that metaphysical harmony between two people who think alike, have the same needs, and trust each other. The classic recruitment is when the case officer knows *ahead of time* that the agent's answer will be "What took you so long?" when the officer delivers the pitch. The case officer looks for the sweet spot when two people are in sync, when a look between them is all that's required to communicate volumes.

Grace was a stunning woman, but Nate knew he had to focus on her mind and her needs, to become a friend and confidant, and to explore her eventual willingness to talk to American intelligence in a clandestine relationship about her hotel and its VIP guests. In an accelerated developmental he had to press without pressuring—Gable once explained it as "taking your time, in a hurry." Benford had agreed to this extension of his TDY assignment, but it wouldn't last forever, and the recall order would come the instant forward progress on the case stalled.

Grace met him at the front door of the hotel under the steel porte cochere emblazoned with THE PENINSULA in gold letters. A nervous knot of stewards in white coats and doormen in green livery stood at a respectful distance, wondering what the boss lady was doing outside standing beside one of two snarling stone imperial guardian lions on either side of the front doors. The juxtaposition of Ms. Gao and the mythic statues was upsetting to the staff. Nate's taxi pulled up the circular drive lined with half a dozen forest-green Rolls-Royce Phantom limousines of the hotel's luxury car fleet. Grace stepped forward to shake Nate's hand, and he almost tripped over the curbstone looking at her, a vision out of Shanghai in 1920. She was dressed in a fitted black *qípáo* cheongsam that came to just above the knee, with a mandarin collar, capped sleeves, and scarlet Chinese knot buttons up the front. Only the traditional side slit was missing. Nate decided the dress had been sprayed on that morning because there was no way anyone could actually physically wriggle into it. She wore black pumps over sheer black nylons.

"Welcome back to the Peninsula, Nathaniel," said Grace. *Nathaniel?* The thought flitted through his mind that she somehow had researched his name. He'd told her his name was Nate. The assistant general manager of a five-star hotel had to be resourceful. She followed his gaze as he looked at the line of gleaming motorcars.

"We're very proud of our fleet of Rolls," she said. "We have fourteen of them. Come over here, I want to show you something." She walked to the first limousine in line, triggering a rush by no fewer than three doormen to pull open the rear door of the limousine for her. Grace bent down and pushed a button recessed in the end of the door above the locking mechanism, and the handle of a silk umbrella popped out. She pulled it all the way out and flourished it. "I'd open it to show you the Peninsula name, but that would be bad luck." She replaced the umbrella in the limousine door.

"Don't tell me you're superstitious," said Nate. Grace just smiled, turned, and walked into the entrance lobby patting one of the guardian lion statues on the head as she passed, looking over her shoulder at him. *Maybe superstitious, but certainly playful.* Nate followed the dress and the sheer stockings into the hotel lobby.

For the next hour Grace led Nate on a fascinating tour of the venerable hotel, from the gleaming stainless-steel kitchens and rooftop heliport, to the infinity pool on the eighth floor. In the hushed wood-paneled VIP lounge on the top floor, Grace opened a photographic book documenting the Peninsula's history. They stood shoulder to shoulder as Grace flipped the pages, pointing out interesting facts. Nate stole quick glances at her, watching as her eyes flitted across the photos, her eyelashes fluttering, and her mouth pursed in concentration. She was wearing a hint of something lilac or lavender, and he could feel the heat from her arm through his jacket sleeve. She wore her hair in a bun with two black lacquered chopsticks stuck through it. She stopped turning pages and caught him looking at her hair. Nate smiled at her.

"Your hair is very pretty that way," he said. "Not many American women wear it like that." *A compliment. Mention the United States. Here's a man who's observant.* She fingered the chopsticks self-consciously.

"I don't know why I wear it like this, they keep falling out," she said. Neither of them said anything, and Nate kept quiet. *How do you handle silence, what do you say?*

"Would you like to see the health club and spa?" said Grace. "It's on the seventh floor." *Smooth recovery. Isn't easily flustered, under control.*

The health club had the usual array of expensive machines arranged along floor-to-ceiling windows with a soaring view of the harbor. The spa, sauna, and massage rooms were all magnificently appointed. As they walked around, Nate ruefully complained that it never seemed that he had enough time to exercise. *Time to raise yoga.*

"What do you do to stay fit?" he asked.

"I practice yoga," said Grace.

"Been doing it long?" *Guileless question, on purpose, talk to me.*

"Since I was a little girl," she said, vaguely. *Reluctance? She's not convinced I'm interested, so sell it.*

Nate had been reading up on yoga styles the night before. "I had a friend who did what I think she called Ashtanga yoga, is that right? And what's that hot yoga called? Where they heat the room?" Grace looked at him through her lashes, assessing his sincerity. *Ask for information, educate me.*

"Yes, Ashtanga, Vinyasa, Bikram; these are modern styles, and very popular," said Grace.

"What style do you practice?" asked Nate.

"An older style, something based on an ancient book," she said, looking at the floor. *A sticking point. Gently now.*

"What's it called?" said Nate. Grace's eyes searched his, her China-doll face hesitant for a moment, then clearing with the decision to share.

"A book of Hindu verses called the *Rigveda* was written in 1500 BC. My yoga is based on that book. It is called Kundalini yoga. It is now a popular style."

"I've never heard of it," said Nate. "What does it look like, do you stand on your head?" *Come on, set me straight.*

"It is a very strong style," she said, smiling thinly. "I do not want to bore you."

Nate shook his head. "I'm not bored," he said. "Tell me."

"It's the use of poses, chanting, and special breathing, all three to release the energy in our bodies," Grace said. "When our energy is blocked, we cannot grow. When we release it through the discipline of yoga, there is health, and stability, and peace. I know this sounds very mystical and silly, but it has helped me." Nate nodded to a wood-floored exercise area surrounded by full-length mirrors.

"Show me something I could learn without tearing my shoulder out of its socket," said Nate. Grace looked at him skeptically. Nate slipped out of his shoes, and held out his arms, the earnest foreigner who wanted to learn about her world.

"All right. This is *Adhu Mukha Svanasana*, it's relatively easy. I'll show you, then you try it." She shucked off her heels, walked onto the wood, planted her feet, then bent forward and put her hands on the floor, walking them ahead of her until she was in a pike position, her hips in the air, her head lowered between her shoulders. Nate saw her triceps flexing, her stomach contracted into a wasp waist and her thigh muscles rippled. A soft hissing note came from her mouth as she exhaled for what seemed like ten seconds. Her fitted dress inched up her thighs, revealing the lacy tops of her stockings and, in the mirror behind her, a glimpse of the black lace vee of her panties. *Whoa. Interesting. Is she oblivious, or is she flirting? No way she's promiscuous.*

Grace straightened up, and motioned for Nate to try it. He put his hands on the floor and copied the pose as she had done it. Grace noted with satisfaction that Nate's form was very good, and that he was strong. She was pleased that he had done it well.

This first contact had gone well. Grace was friendly and modest, and she'd responded to Nate playing the informal, friendly American. She wasn't so tight-assed shy that she didn't demonstrate a yoga pose in a short skirt. *Now comes the second meeting*, thought Nate, a critical contact in any developmental, when the target decides whether the relationship continues. Embroidered stocking tops and pink-grapefruit lips aside, Nate hoped it would.

———

Three days later Nate invited Grace to dinner. She knew Hong Kong and suggested they go to the China Club, a chic restaurant done in colonial Shanghai style with red walls and Chinese screens, an ornate carpeted staircase to the dining room, and funky framed daguerreotypes of Marx, Lenin, Stalin, and Mao on the walls, a tongue-in-cheek retro pantheon of the crew who plunged the world into flames. The club was on the top three floors of the old Bank of China Building—the first postwar skyscraper in then-British Hong Kong with a 1950s vintage lobby of polished marble columns and terrazzo floors—on Des Voeux Road in Central. Grace suggested Nate try the Ma Po eggplant in garlic sauce, a specialty. Fragrant, spicy, glistening; it was delicious, Nate told her.

Grace had two glasses of wine at dinner, and coyly told him her Chinese name was *Zhen*, which means precious and rare. She wore a simple black dress, a double strand of pearls, and tiny pearl earrings. Her perfume was exotic and smoky; Nate had never smelled anything like it, and it lingered in his nose and mouth. She giggled when Nate threw her a bone, joking about growing up in a family of rapacious Southern lawyers, priming the pump to get her to start talking about herself. Her history came out haltingly. She was an orphan whose liberal-minded parents—one a professor, the other an artist—were imprisoned during the Anti-Spiritual Pollution Campaign in 1983, the year she was born. She was remanded to a reluctant government-assigned foster family who received a stipend for taking the baby girl. She never saw her real parents again. She endured an unhappy adolescence, spent a lonely four years in a British university, and returned to a cynical, smog-choked China of new millionaires and a censored Internet—an emergent superpower paradoxically caught in its imperial past. With an uncertain future, Grace went to hotel school, then moved to Hong Kong and prospered, eventually becoming assistant general manager at the Peninsula.

"How is it you went to university in Britain?" asked Nate. Grace lowered her eyes and sipped her wine.

"I received a scholarship," she said, vaguely. *Huh. Not usual*, Nate thought, *unless you have a patron who pays. Or unless the State pays for you. There's a slightly false note here. Circle around and ask her later.*

"And the yoga?" asked Nate. Grace leaned forward, no longer defensive.

Searching for comfort and company in a rootless childhood, twelve-year-old Zhen spent hours in the back room of the neighborhood *Zhōngyī* shop that sold traditional Chinese medicines. The nut-brown old woman who swept the floor was a Bengali Indian, improbably stranded in China after a shipwreck, who whispered to the young girl, became her *Jiàomǔ*, her godmother, and sang the ancient Sanskrit Vedic mantra, the *Gayrati*, to her. The old crone was a yogini, a guru of the ancient practice, and began teaching Grace poses on the rough coir mats in the fragrant back room lined with amber jars of preserved coiled snakes, yellow flasks of bear bile, and gray dried *lingzhī* mushrooms, stacked on shelves like cordwood. Besides its physical benefits, Grace, in time, discovered the abiding spirituality of yoga. It gave her serenity and made her melancholy adolescence bearable. She never stopped studying yoga, not even when she moved to Hong Kong.

"So here I am," she said, tipping back her wine, accepting a third glass. She brushed a strand of hair off her face, softly bit her lower lip, and blinked at Nate. "No family, fourteen-hour days, nothing but my yoga to keep me whole." She took another sip of wine. "I don't know what the future holds."

Holy crap, thought Nate, *this is a psychological smorgasbord.* He processed her story in parts: lingering resentment of the system; absence of communist ideology; strong work ethic and meticulous attention to detail; feeling isolated and disenfranchised and contemplating an uncertain future; and committed to and dependent on the spiritual aspects of yoga. This was an astounding collection of exploitable motivations right out of the textbook—*almost too good to be true.* A few more contacts, a sympathetic ear and a friendly smile, and he could subtly determine Grace's willingness to help him, her need to belong to a cause, her desire to give meaning to her life, to work toward a more liberal China. The case officer in him noted that she did not ask questions of him, which was a little strange.

They walked after dinner in Central, on empty sidewalks past buildings too tall to see the tops shrouded in fog. Grace linked her arm in Nate's—that mystery perfume washed over him—and he steadied her a little. They flagged a taxi, which careered up Garden Road onto Magazine Gap Road to the front door of Grenville House, fifteen stories of luxury apartments perched on the side of the jungly hill looking over the tops of the high-rises on the next level below, slices of the harbor visible between the forest of buildings. Grace said the Peninsula Hotel paid her astronomical rent; otherwise, she would be living in a moldy flat in Kowloon. Propriety in mind, Nate chastely bussed her good night on the cheek and was going to leave, but she spilled her purse on the lobby floor digging for her keys, and giggled that she shouldn't have had that third glass of wine. Nate chivalrously rode up in the elevator with her, and got her key in the door. She tilted her head, and said he should come in to see how she lived, because, after all, he seemed interested in her. "You *are* interested in me, *aren't you*, Nathaniel?" she drawled. *Okay, take this slow*, he thought.

Grace kicked off her shoes and led him into a large living room with picture windows and a herringbone parquet floor, without a stick of furniture or anything on the white walls—Nate cracked wise that he loved what she did with the room. The air was redolent with that same fragrance. Three large wicker baskets were lined up against the wall. At the end of the room an immense gong (from Tibet, Grace said solemnly) hung from a varnished standing frame, with a large white pillow on the floor in front of the dimpled seven-foot bronze disk. On either side of the gong were black lacquer console tables with matching Chinese cloisonné candlesticks, a deep copper bowl, and a squat black-granite carving that Grace called a *shivalinga*, an idol to the Hindu deity Shiva, the patron god of yoga. *This is nothing less than an altar in a yoga church*, thought Nate.

Nate picked up the gong hammer, but Grace said, "No, not that way, I'll show you," and lightly ran the felt head of the hammer around the edge of the dimpled disk that started a low moan as the palpable vibrations started, then were overlaid with a higher whine as the harmonics mingled. She dropped the hammer, and shook herself, and Nate figured the wine had caught up to her, but she straightened and walked close to him, and he braced for either a kiss or projectile puking, but in a small voice she asked whether he wanted to see Kundalini energy, her style of yoga, the coiled snake at the base of the spine. It was a little creepy. Nate remembered Bunty thinking maybe she was a bunny boiler, but she was tipsily offering to show him the wellspring of her soul after two dates, and he said yes, of course; the snake at the base of the spine, sure. Then things got weird.

Grace took two steps back, unzipped her cocktail dress, and stepped out of it, the straps of the straining black-lace balconette bra loose on her shoulders, and her boy shorts smooth between her legs. She sat on the cushion in front of the gong, folded her legs in the classic yoga *Padmasana*, and placed her hands on her knees. "First comes *Kapal Bhati*, skull shining breath," she whispered. She began slow, controlled breathing, with deep inhalations and explosive exhalations. After a dozen breaths, she nodded to Nate, okay, make the gong sing like she showed him, and the low Tibetan rumble started, and Nate could feel the buzz in his own spine, but he had to concentrate on a smooth circular motion with the hammer as the second sympathetic higher note started, and he looked at Grace who was sitting rocking her torso in a circular movement, chin up and eyes closed, gaining speed, and she began an indecipherable chant at the same musical note as the gong. Four minutes, five, six, shoulders in a circle forward and back, hands braced and eyes closed, and the sweat started pouring off her face and ran in rivulets between her glistening breasts, and down her stomach to soak the waistband of her panties. Nate's arm was getting tired, but he was afraid that if he stopped with the gong she would breathe fire at him, and levitate off the balcony into the night sky. At about the ten-minute mark of unabated violent torso swinging, Grace leaned back, arched her spine off the wood, the back of her skull planted on the floor. Her sweat-transparent bra strained high, and she clasped her hands together in a *Ksepana Mudra* above her heart. She bent back even farther, her rib cage expanding like a bellows, her prayerful hands pressed between her breasts, and she started trembling, tsunami spasms rolling up her heaving belly, the long muscles of her legs pulsing, her feet twitching, and her quivering chin pointing at the ceiling. She suddenly tensed, her eyes rolled white, and her mouth opened as she expelled a huge breath and lay still, hands now slack on her chest.

Nate figured the telephone he'd use to call the ambulance was probably in the kitchen, but first he leaned over Grace who was now lying flat on the floor, eyes closed, legs unfolded and outstretched. Her rib cage was still expanding with her breathing. "Are you okay?" he asked, putting his hand on her shoulder. Her eyes slowly opened and focused on him. She smiled, put a hand behind his neck, and pulled his mouth down onto hers for a hint of a kiss, a single caress of her lips. Her sweet fragrance enveloped him, and his head swam. "What is that perfume?" he said. She pulled his mouth down on hers again.

"*Ylang-ylang*," she whispered in his ear, pronouncing it *ee-lang, ee-lang*. "It is very old."

"Are you all right?" said Nate. "What happened to you?" Grace rolled to her feet, unhurriedly unclasped her sopping bra without covering herself, and walked to one of the wicker baskets, pulled out a linen kimono, and slipped it on.

"What was that?" said Nate. Grace ran her fingers through her hair, then knotted the belt of the kimono, looking him in the eye without blinking, not at all embarrassed.

"Awakening Kundalini," she said. "It's when I lose myself."

"Awakening what?" said Nate.

"Have you heard of the seven chakras in the body? Life-force centers? No? I will explain it another time. It is too late tonight."

Another whisper of a kiss at the door, and Nate walked home along Bowen Road, mentally drafting tomorrow's cable for COS Burns's release on what appeared to be a notable start in the developmental to recruit Grace Gao, aka Zhen Gao. Nate's case-officer antennas were vibrating a little, assessing factors: This was going faster than normal, maybe artificially faster? This Kundalini energy thing was unexpected; could it be exploited? She had sobered up fast enough. She was an enigma, but irresistible: erotic without being salacious; alluring without being wanton; at once sophisticated and naive. If he could swing it, he had a feeling this could be an exceptional recruitment. The foreign scholarship in the United Kingdom was still an unexplained anomaly, as was her apparent uninterest in his personal history. These were false notes, but he'd resolve them.

The MSS counterintelligence team in the apartment next door listened to the audiotape of the dinner at the China Club, and reviewed the video of *Zhènniǎo*, the poison-feather bird's performance in the honey-trap apartment on the other side of the bare wall—with the choreography of the gong and *Matsyasana*, the provocative bowstring fish pose, and the chaste kiss—and were satisfied with the evening and with future prospects for entrapping the American CIA officer and eliciting the name of his agent. His assassination was a foregone conclusion. The team leader politely congratulated their esteemed guest from Moscow, the beautiful blue-eyed Russian SVR officer who sat in an armchair in front of the monitors, bouncing her foot. Her guidance on how best to concoct Grace Gao's fictitious personal legend to inveigle the American was sibylline—almost as if she knew how he thought.

MA PO EGGPLANT IN GARLIC SAUCE

Mix ground pork with rice wine vinegar, chili sauce, cornstarch, and soy sauce. Refrigerate. Cut Asian eggplants in half lengthwise, brush with peanut oil, season with salt, and broil cut side down on baking sheet until charred and tender. Whisk chicken stock with sake, sugar, sesame oil, bean paste, and soy sauce. Stir-fry minced scallions, garlic, and ginger until fragrant, add pork and brown, then add chicken stock mixture and bring to a boil. Simmer until sauce thickens. Place eggplants cut side up on a platter and spoon over with pork. Garnish with sliced scallions. Serve with steamed rice.

29

Your Chakra Is Showing

Dominika had arrived in Hong Kong several days earlier after a day of ceremonial courtesy calls in MSS Headquarters at the Ministry of State Security. General Sun stayed in Beijing for consultations, so Dominika was turned over to an English-speaking captain of the Guangzhou MSS office, named Yuán Chonghuan. He had chosen the inexplicable Western business name of "Rainy," *yu tien* in Mandarin, which was phonetically close to Yuán and lyrical, or so he thought. Rainy Chonghuan was exceedingly short and thin, with all the built-in malignancies of the physical runt. He had the toxic temper of a low-level officer who one minute relishes mistreating subordinates, and shamelessly toadies to superiors the next. He had caramel-colored teeth and stubby fingers with nails bitten to the quick. The halo around his head and shoulders was caramel-colored too, the color you get when the yellow of conniving treachery mixes with the browns of sloth and envy. Dominika knew she had to be careful around him.

Colonel Dominika Egorova of the SVR was an alien being to Rainy—the leggy, busty Slav with the high cheekbones might as well have been from another planet. His English, learned at MSS Officer's school, was just fluent enough to discuss strategy with her in the operation to trap the American. Rainy Chonghuan had, however, immediately seen that this Russian was held in high esteem by General Sun and MSS leadership, which meant he would butter her remorselessly. He moreover saw that she had long experience working American targets. Her suggested amendments to the entrapment-phase plan, including tweaking *Zhènniǎo*'s personal history to appeal to the Yankee's operational instincts, were impressive. Anything that would ensure success and bring him credit and promotion was welcome. Rainy provided a translated copy of *Zhènniǎo*'s service docket for Colonel Egorova's review, and suggested the two women meet to discuss nuances of the nectar bait. To his surprise, the Russian demurred, explaining that Sparrows in the Russian Service operated most effectively with fewer distractions. Rainy hurriedly agreed, complimenting the colonel on her foresight and wisdom.

Zhen Gao's personnel file was fascinating to Dominika. The autobiography she had recited to Nate was mostly fiction, with some nuggets of truth. She had not lost her parents, she was not adopted, and she never went to hotel school. She was never taught yoga by a wizened yogini when she was twelve, she learned it only later, as a way to stay in shape and help her seduce targets.

Zhen Gao was the daughter of a minor State-school teacher from Anxin, in Hebei Province, on the reed-choked shores of Lake Baiyangdian. Already a stunning beauty at age sixteen, Zhen caught the eye of a provincial administrator who appraised the woman's body under the schoolgirl's smock. He used his influence to install the young girl as a housekeeper in a State-controlled villa, took her virginity, and occasionally shared her with other municipal jacks-in-the-office to curry favor. When Zhen was eighteen, the administrator was caught taking bribes and was tried, convicted, and executed for corruption. With no patron, and an undeserved reputation as a "pleasure girl," she was sent to Tianjin, a teeming city of fifteen million on the northeastern coast two hours south of Beijing, and enrolled in State School 2112, a training academy run by the MSS that, the file obliquely explained, trained young women in "intelligence techniques," which included seduction, elicitation, recruitment, and blackmail. Graduates were known as *Yèyīng*, Nightingales.

Based on academics, performance, and an assessment of ideological aptitude, a handful of Nightingales were chosen for continued study at Institute 48 in Beijing, a classified facility in the northeastern Shangjialou District where students were trained in the use of firearms, exotic weapons, and poisons. At age twenty, Zhen was sponsored by a storefront Sino-Anglo friendship society controlled by MSS for study in the United Kingdom, both to master English and to be exposed to Western ways. Four years later, she graduated as a full-fledged seductress-assassin of the State, known as a *Zhènniǎo*, the poison-feather bird. Because of her excellent English and British manner, Zhen was quietly placed in a cover position as assistant general manager at the Peninsula Hotel in Hong Kong, available for assignments as required.

Bozhe, thought Dominika, reading the file, *a young girl defiled by a swine, passed around the pigsty, then forced into the Chinese version of Sparrow School*. Her pulse raced as she read Zhen's life history—it was like her own.

But Russian Sparrows don't kill people, Dominika told herself, *but you have, haven't you?*

Throughout the second volume of the file, Zhen now was referred to as *Zhènniǎo*. Dominika asked Rainy what a poison-feather bird was, and he haltingly described the mythological bird, with coal-black plumage, that fed exclusively on serpents, and whose feathers as a result were highly poisonous. One could stir a glass of wine with a single such feather to make it mortally toxic, he said. *Only in China*, thought Dominika.

The file documented fourteen assassinations credited to *Zhènniǎo*—the most recent being a drug-dealing Burmese police chief who had been poisoned with a distillate of the monkshood bloom. There had been no witnesses and no blowback connection to Beijing. Dominika turned to a pharmacological annex in the file that listed monkshood as a poisonous plant that produces aconitine, a lethal tetrodotoxin readily absorbed through the skin. Even slight contact with the delicate, purple bell-shaped flower would, between two and eight hours later, induce cardiac arrhythmia, ventricular tachycardia, ventricular fibrillation leading to respiratory paralysis or cardiac arrest. *Zhènniǎo* had applied the poison on the skin of the police chief blended with *ylang-ylang*, a fragrant essential oil used in aromatherapy.

———

As she watched Zhen's Kundalini demonstration on the surveillance monitor—the entire apartment was covered by cameras and microphones in the fixtures, woodwork, and ceilings—Dominika's heart stopped when she heard Zhen tell Nate her perfume was called *ylang-ylang*. That's how they would do him. Zhen would dab him with fragrant oil spiked with the monkshood toxin during some yoga tryst, which would kill him by the next morning.

Would Nate sense the danger? Why would he? He was an operations officer on the hunt, intent on recruiting a beautiful Chinese girl. Benford and CIA had no idea of the threat; they couldn't warn him. Dominika herself was in a screamingly perilous position. She couldn't call CIA; she was in China. She couldn't throw a package over the wall of the US Consulate as it was surrounded by MSS lookouts. She was constantly accompanied by MSS escorts, and the diminutive Rainy Chonghuan was always at her side.

They had put her in a luxurious guest apartment one floor up, directly above this one, which Dominika had no doubt, was also humming with multiple digital microphones and lenses, making it exceedingly risky to try to leave the building and somehow make street contact on the fly with Nate who, she also assumed, was under MSS surveillance.

If she acted to save Nate and made a mistake, the Chinese would report it to the Kremlin, and she would be lost. Dominika had tried to send Nate subtle warnings. She had advised the MSS that Zhen must not seem overly inquisitive, and ask no personal questions, the mark of an intelligence officer. She recommended that Zhen downplay her UK university years by simply saying they were paid for by a "scholarship." Dominika told her hosts it was "safer to be vague," but in reality these were inconsistent notes that she hoped would be the silent dog whistle in Nate's head to get him to start smelling a trap. She also strongly advised that Zhen should mention Fernando's Restaurant in Macao to shock the American into blurting something actionable, really knowing it would be a premature and aggressive note, sure to alarm Nate. She feared these would be too subtle, too diffuse warnings. Would Nate pick up on them? She couldn't try any more subtle sabotage, for the Chinese were too smart. Dominika didn't know how else to confound MSS plans to kill Nate.

Grace had invited Nate back to her apartment for a home-cooked meal, in repayment for the dinner at the China Club. She opened the door, smiled, and pulled him by the hand into the apartment. She wore a beige shirtdress that came to midthigh, with floppy sleeves rolled up past the elbows. She briefly pressed up against him—he could feel the softness of her breasts under the shirt—and kissed him lightly. She padded barefoot through the living room—the air was thick with *ylang-ylang*—around the corner, and into a small but modern kitchen done all in white tile and stainless steel. On the counter were a number of ingredients, and a small black-handled Chinese cleaver.

"I'm making a Burmese tomato salad," said Grace. "The word for salad in Burmese is *'lethoke.'* It means mix by hand."

"Were you ever in Burma?" said Nate. "What's it called now?"

"Myanmar," said Grace. "Only as a tourist. But a Burmese woman there taught me how to make the salad. Her name was Kyi Saw." Grace chopped the ingredients skillfully, whisked lemongrass vinegar, canola oil, and fish sauce, then fried sliced onions and garlic in a small pot of oil. Nate watched how she moved effortlessly around the kitchen, her hands quick and deft. She assembled the salad in a large wooden bowl, lightly tossed it with her hands until everything was incorporated, and handed Nate a fork. He tried a thin slice of tomato. The taste was salty, sweet, and pungent, with a slight crunch of crushed peanuts.

"This is really delicious," he said. "I've never had anything like this before."

Grace leaned on the counter and looked sideways at him. "I think they serve a version of the salad at a restaurant in Macao," she said. "It's a little restaurant on the beach called Fernando's. We should go there sometime, and I'll show you." Nate kept his face neutral. *Don't like the sound of that at all*, he thought. *Coincidence? Maybe, maybe not.*

"Sounds like fun," said Nate. They brought plates of salad out to the balcony and ate while looking at the harbor and the scudding clouds in the night sky blushing pink from the city lights. "I find it inconceivable that this vibrant city was actually returned to China, and is now under the thumb of Beijing," said Nate. "Do you think the spirit of Hong Kong can survive?"

"The people here are trying, resisting and demanding their rights. But I do not know if they will succeed," said Grace.

"I know the rest of the world hopes they will succeed," said Nate.

"So do I," said Grace.

"It would be a worthy effort, to help Hong Kong stay free," said Nate. "Something with meaning." He stopped and came off the gas, putting it in neutral, not wanting to overdo the theme. They could come back to it; at the right moment, Nate could tell her specifically how she could help. Work for CIA.

"I could see that," said Grace. "Right now I devote myself to the hotel, nothing else. And yoga is my only escape."

"I have to be honest with you," said Nate. "When you showed me that Kundalini Awakening, I was a little startled, scared even. I didn't know what had happened to you."

Grace laughed. "Do you want to learn a little more? I can tell you about the chakras, the energy points in your body. They're very important; they control everything," said Grace. *Okay, stud, keep this under control.*

Nate so far had kept things platonic, despite the black bra and the arched back, and the cursory kisses. He could imagine Benford's reaction if it became known that he had recruited Grace Gao by bedding her; it would be an affirmation of Benford's lingering belief that Nate should no longer be employed by CIA. He had not dwelled on it in some time, but now Nate contemplated what a nightmare it would be if he got kicked out of the Agency, and returned home to Richmond, Virginia, where his family all along had brayed that Nate wouldn't make it as a spook, never mind that his downfall took ten years and not two, as they had predicted. *So how do you handle this Chinese beauty who wants to show you her chakras?*

They sat on the floor facing each other, cross-legged, knees nearly touching. Grace took the wide copper bowl off one of the altar tables, put it on the floor beside them, and struck the rim lightly with a small wooden dowel. The bowl gave off a clear, smooth note like the chime of a grandfather clock. "Singing bowl," said Grace, "to clear your mind." She ran the dowel around the lip of the bowl, which began a pulsing hum that grew into a second bullfrog tone overlaying the first. She stopped stroking the bowl, and the tones slowly faded. She shifted herself slightly forward so their knees touched.

"There are seven chakras in your body, and they all represent different emotions," said Grace. She took a small bottle out of her dress pocket, unscrewed the cap, and tilted it forward to wet the tip of her finger. The dizzying fragrance of *ylang-ylang* enveloped them, and Grace dragged her fingertip along the sides of Nate's neck, on the undersides of his wrists, and on his ankles. "The oil will help you relax," she said.

She touched the top of his head. "This is the seventh chakra, the violet chakra, the crown, which brings bliss." She leaned forward and kissed his forehead.

"This is the sixth chakra, the indigo chakra, the brow, which controls intuition." She kissed his eyelids.

"The fifth, blue, the throat for healing." She moved lower and nuzzled his throat with her lips. *Jesus, she's heading south, is there a Captain Picard chakra?*

"The fourth, green, the heart for love." Grace unbuttoned his shirt and kissed his chest.

"The third, yellow, the solar plexus for purpose." Her lips grazed his stomach.

"The second, orange, the spleen for desire." She ran her fingers around his navel.

Grace moved her hand between Nate's legs and underneath his body, pressing up through his khakis on the fleshy pad of his perineal muscle. "The first, the root chakra, red, controlling passion," she said. She kept her fingers there, and looked into his eyes.

At a time like this, with Grace's *ylang-ylang*-infused fingers pinpointing his first chakra, Nate unaccountably and psychotically flashed to Kramer, his case officer–colleague in Vienna, who once told him that the perineum was commonly called the "taint" because "t'aint your balls, and t'aint your butt." Nate wondered what that nugget was doing now. He shook himself as Grace removed her hand.

"And when you awaken Kundalini," said Nate, trying not to squirm, "these chakras do what, exactly?"

"The energy expands from the root chakra, like an uncoiled snake, up the spine to the head, like an electrical current. It brings a profound consciousness."

"I can feel mine expanding as we speak," said Nate. Grace scooted forward to sit on Nate's folded legs, and wrapped her legs around his back. She put her arms around his neck and looked into his eyes. They were inches apart, from noses to crotches, and Nate could feel her body heat, like sitting too close to a woodstove.

"This is called *Yab Yum*, sitting like this," she said. "The union of wisdom and compassion." She took his hand, pressed it on her heart, and held it there. "Can you feel my heart? Let me feel yours." They sat motionless, eyes closed, hands on each other's hearts, foreheads lightly touching. "Now we cannot move for a thousand years until we achieve Samadhi," she said.

"Samadhi—whatever that means—is going to happen sooner than that," said Nate. "I'm just warning you."

"Stop talking," she said. "Samadhi is a state of mind. Concentrate." Nate felt her breath deepen, and her heartbeat slowed, and he could hear it in his head, and he could feel his own heartbeat exactly matching hers. Her legs were wrapped tightly around him, her heels hooked softly into his back. Nate suddenly felt a lightness in his pelvis, his legs, his spine, and his arms.

A loud rushing noise filled his head, as if he were in an underground grotto above a thundering waterfall. The lightness moved into his head, behind his eyes, and under his tongue.

"Do you feel it?" whispered Grace. Nate nodded. "Samadhi is wonderful," she said. "It can carry you, carry you over mountains, and across the oceans. What is over the ocean for you, Nate? What is in your heart?"

"A woman far away," he said, his eyes still closed, marveling at the feeling in his brain, and at his answer, which just popped out of his mouth before he could think. Grace shifted closer to him, her arms around his neck.

"Breathe with me," she said, inhaling deeply. She put her mouth on his and started inhaling and exhaling into his mouth, surrounding him in hot velvet and electricity. Her breath controlled his breath. She rocked slightly and leaned forward, so their expanding stomachs touched. Grace whispered into his lips.

"Who else is in your heart?" she said. Nate thought of Agnes in Palos Verdes, and Hannah killed, and white-haired General Korchnoi murdered, and Gable gone, and Benford, Forsyth, and Burns who were his colleagues and family, and the bucket-headed image of PLA General Tan, that profligate beetle whom Nate had just recruited, and he almost said his name out loud. *Shit, what is this?*

Nate, struggling, blinked three times, very quickly, and she knew she had lost him, at least for now. She moved back slowly, sliding off him.

———

Dominika sat in the armchair, legs crossed, squeezing her thighs together, sweating. She had forced herself to sit still as she watched the monitor and imagined the feel of Nate's body pressed against Grace in *Yab Yum*, and her lips tingled imagining those kisses. Thank God she didn't have to hide an *orgasm*, sitting a meter from the appalling Rainy Chonghuan, who was watching the screen with his mouth open. She had panicked when Grace had dabbed Nate's neck with fragrant oil, but she realized this was not the assassination night.

That last kiss. She was astounded by Grace's apparent skill in dragging Nate into a meditative state, something she knew she could never do. Strangely she was not mad at him—seeing him after all these months on a high-resolution screen was a shock, and she felt a million kilometers away. She knew he had not planned for this to happen, that he was working on the Chinese woman, and it was she who had initiated the contact. To be sure, Dominika would break a vase over his head when (if) she saw him next, but she realized she still loved him; he had said he loved a "woman far away," which she knew meant her. She was the first person he thought about from his *Yab Yum*– addled subconscious. Oh, how this espionage got in the way of their lives.

But right now jealousy, pique, longing, and horniness were superfluous. Dominika didn't know if Nate could resist the mind-warping blandishments of this gorgeous Chinese girl, but she knew that whether or not the MSS pried the name of Nate's agent out of him, they would very soon reach the point where they would give Zhen the order to eliminate him. He was a beetle in a matchbox and they were going to step on him.

Rainy Chonghuan watched the screen as Grace said good night to Nate at the front door to the apartment. He ordered the technicians to shut down the surveillance monitors and microphones, and turned to Colonel Egorova.

"You can see *Zhènniǎo* is extensively trained and meticulously prepared," he said. "She uses the mystical aspects of this yoga to manipulate her targets, to employ *tao qu de zuo fa*, elicitation methods. If she succeeds, it will happen next time. If at the conclusion of the next contact the American does not reveal the name of the mole, the order to eliminate him will be given."

"You know your operation best," said Dominika, casually, wondering if there was a wet spot on the back of her skirt. "But eliminating the American now seems premature. Your girl is making good progress. You could potentially learn additional secrets from this officer about CIA operations in China."

Rainy shrugged. "Beijing insists," he said. "She will invite him for another dinner in two days, and we shall see what happens. *Zhènniǎo* will stay in this apartment from tonight, in case the American becomes lonely and amorous, and decides to visit unannounced."

"And how will you eliminate the target?" said Dominika.

Rainy Chonghuan showed a muddy riverbank smile. "*Zhènniǎo* is an expert with firearms, edged weapons, the rope, and a variety of classical weapons. She is also expert in hand-to-hand combat. Her knowledge of poisons and toxins is encyclopedic," said Rainy. "The requirement, as in most cases such as this, is to mask the hand of the Service. She will choose the appropriate method."

"It doesn't sound like she will have any trouble," answered Dominika, suddenly overwhelmed. The lingering terror waiting for her back in Moscow if she were exposed by the mole in Washington came back to her suddenly. Both she and Nate were teetering on the knife-edge of ruin.

KYI SAW'S BURMESE TOMATO SALAD

Slice medium tomatoes into crescents, cut cherry tomatoes in half, and slice sweet onion into crescents and place in a bowl; add toasted sesame seeds, crushed peanuts, dried shrimp powder, diced chilies, and chopped coriander. Deep-fry garlic and additional onions until crispy and add to bowl. Whisk lemongrass vinegar (or substitute rice wine vinegar), canola oil, fish sauce, lime juice and palm sugar, and pour over salad. Mix gently with hands and garnish with reserved fried garlic and onions and a chiffonade of cilantro. Goes well with a rare steak.

30

Emptiness

Zhen disliked staying in the honey-trap apartment. Her personal flat was in a smaller building in Mid-Levels, where she was surrounded by her books, yoga materials, and comfortable furniture. Staying in this nearly empty apartment was an inconvenience. It, moreover, meant the assassination phase was near, and although she had no compunction about eliminating a target, she was always depressed at the conclusion of an operation. She enjoyed the hunt: engineering first contact, coyly developing the relationship, the heady thrill of seduction, and the dizzying anticipation of the final act, up to the moment she eased a steel needle between the cervical vertebrae of the neck, or looped a silk rope around a throat, or watched a victim's eyes grow in alarm as the chest-constricting effects of a poison were first felt. But afterward there was an emptiness, a depression, a melancholy. An emptiness that yoga helped relieve.

Zhen always told herself that she worked as a poison-feather bird to feed her stomach, but she practiced yoga to feed her soul. Practice gave perspective, energy, and the strength to accept what she could not change. But there were some things she could indeed change. Her unhappy childhood and subsequent exploitation as a teenaged concubine, and the humiliating scurvy years in Nightingale School and at the Institute in Beijing learning to kill increased her resolve never to let anyone mistreat her again. The first time had been in London, at university, where she had been singled out as a shy exotic by a group of male students, the majority of whom were simply bullies, but one of them had wanted more. Zhen did not bring any of the usual weapons from the institute with her to the United Kingdom, except for two *gongfu shàn*, pleated kung-fu fighting fans, one black, one red, wide and delicate with expanding wings of edged metal affixed to the fan folds. These were medieval martial-arts weapons and Zhen could make them flutter like birds wings, snapping them open and closed with a report like a gunshot.

There was a complicated social protocol as well in the use of fans, ancient Chinese conventions essentially lost on most Britons, but Zhen had studied them because they would be most relevant when she returned to the Orient as a seductress. Drawing a closed fan along the cheek meant "I want you." Touching the edge of the extended fan lightly with the fingers meant "I want to talk to you." To tap the lips with a closed fan meant "kiss me." None of these applied to the rangy British Romeo named Rowdy White who pushed his way into Zhen's dormitory room one night, and stood amused as she held two puny folded fans in front of her, ready to defend herself. Rowdy's cumulative experience with fans was limited to the big ostrich-feather variants used by the dancers in the strip clubs off High Street. When Rowdy reached to grab Zhen by the arm the black fan opened with a pop, deflecting his hand. Chuckling to himself, Rowdy again reached for her and the red fan snapped open, blocked his other arm, then folded in the blink of an eye, and snapped down across his wrist. That hurt. He snarled, stepped forward, arms extended, and both fans snapped open with a clatter like pigeons taking flight in a park, and the leading edge of one fan was raked across his face an inch above his eyebrows, slicing his forehead and blinding him as blood streamed into his eyes and down his cheeks. It was *Zhènniǎo*'s first blood, and she was mildly surprised how easy it had been.

———

She wasn't hungry but she made a small pot of *shēngcài* soup, simple lettuce soup, and let it cool on the stove. She opened the balcony door for the night breeze, and sat naked on the big pillow on the floor in the darkened empty living room inhaling great draughts of air, distending first her stomach, then her diaphragm, then her lungs, and expelling her breath in reverse order, pulling her navel in and up, and locking her root chakra. She quietly repeated the Adi Mantra: *ong namo guru dev namo*, bowing to the teacher within, and continued breathing. She got to her feet and leaned forward into a deep lunge, her body glistening, breasts straining, muscular arms above her head, then flowed into a series of poses, her breath steady and hissing on the exhale. But something was wrong. Her concentration was off tonight.

She liked the young American, and had to admit to herself that he was decent and charming. His comments about freedom and Hong Kong were obviously recruitment talking points, but she agreed with them. She wondered what he'd be like in bed—she did not sleep with men after Nightingale

School—but she didn't much care whether he lived or died. She was alone in the world, not aligned with anyone, not with Beijing, not with the MSS, not with the hotel to which she devoted all her energies. She knew Nate was CIA, and that he wanted to recruit her. She had used her professional wiles to encourage him, flirted with him, and kissed him, all to maneuver him into the kill zone. Her recruitment was an impossibility, of course—she would never ally herself with the Americans—and besides, the MSS was observing everything. Zhen had been told that she had to elicit, or trick, or fuck the name of a mole out of him but if after two nights she was not successful, she was to assassinate him. It would happen tomorrow night.

She would take a vial of monkshood distillate mixed with fragrant *ylang-ylang* oil and using great care—a drop on her own skin could be fatal—apply the poison on Nate's skin (she had established the practice of dabbing him with the oil over the last two nights), this time with a bamboo stick applicator. The aconitine would slowly flood his system and kill him hours later, long after he returned home. Zhen got to her feet, folded forward with her palms flat on the floor, and exhaled. She straightened, and walked to the bedroom to take a shower before bed, snapping lights off as she walked through the apartment. She lighted a sandalwood taper and took her shower by candlelight.

The woody fragrance of sandalwood was a nice change from the *ylang-ylang* oil, which hung heavy everywhere without dissipating, like the copper stench of stale blood in a charnel house.

———

Nearly midnight. It was a good thing that Benford and Nate were not going to hear what Dominika planned. There were no other options. They were going to kill Nate tomorrow night, and she didn't even have to think too hard about it. She was going to kill *Zhènniǎo*, the poison-feather bird, or try to, anyway. Dominika stood in the darkened living room of her MSS guest flat wondering if she would survive the next half hour. She wore black pajama pants and a black T-shirt over a sports bra that flattened her chest and hugged her ribs. She didn't want to be flopping around if she actually had to engage Zhen hand to hand. She wondered if the Russian Spetsnaz-derived *Systema* fighting technique she had learned over the years would even come close to what she imagined a Chinese assassin's martial-arts skill would be. She still had to try. Otherwise Nate was dead.

Dominika had no intention of standing toe-to-toe with Zhen. She likely had weapons hidden all over the apartment, not to mention bullets, arrows, darts, and daggers, all dipped in lethal compounds. Having seen her move via surveillance monitor, Dominika also knew that Zhen was strong, lithe, and flexible, and no doubt would be able to absorb a lot of punishment in a stand-up fight. Dominika, therefore, had to ambush her and instantly incapacitate her. It would be the only way she could win.

And all this had to be done in an MSS-controlled building filled with surveillance cameras, and dozens of security guards, who would respond instantly to the tumult of an all-out catfight. If Dominika could not take the Chinese girl out quickly and silently, the responding security guards additionally could power the surveillance equipment in the apartment back on, documenting for Gorelikov and Putin Dominika's efforts to save Nate. They would draw the same instant conclusion: Dominika was working for the Americans. She'd be arrested in Hong Kong, flown to Beijing for interrogation, bundled onto the interminable flight to Moscow, and then driven in a closed van directly from the tarmac to the gates of Butyrka Prison, where more than interrogation would be waiting for her. That is if *Zhènniǎo* didn't kill her first.

She knew she couldn't simply walk out of her apartment door tonight—it certainly was connected to an alarm—go down one floor, and gaily knock on Zhen's door—also probably alarmed—to invite herself in for a late nightcap. She had scoped out her balcony, and that of Zhen's apartment directly below. She thought she could climb over her balcony railing, lower herself as far as possible, and take a swinging drop down onto Zhen's balcony. If she mistimed her swing, or if her hands slipped, nothing more would matter. They were nine stories up. Dominika had searched her apartment for any possible weapons. The kitchen was not stocked; there were no chef's knives. She had found a small toolbox in the utility closet from which she took a box cutter with retractable blade and a medium-weight claw hammer. Both these potential weapons were close range and inefficient, but that's all she had. She retracted the blade, tucked the box cutter into her bra, and stuck the handle of the hammer into her waistband. Time to go poison-bird hunting. She remembered to unlock her apartment door from the inside so she could get back in after she settled with Zhen.

The Grenville House building was totally dark. Dominika was relieved to find that by hanging by her fingers she could actually touch the lower balcony railing with her toes, and was able to drop quietly onto the dark balcony of Zhen's apartment. The balcony door was open and she tiptoed in, passing into a wall of *ylang-ylang* fragrance. The sound of shower water came from the bedroom, and Dominika reached for the hammer as she moved forward in the dark. No hammer. She had not heard it slip out of her pajama bottoms or hit the driveway nine stories down.

Dominika peeked into the bathroom. Flickering candlelight was barely enough to see through the fogged glass partition of the big walk-in shower. Zhen stood with her back to Dominika beneath the rectangular rain showerhead luxuriating under the soft deluge, arms above her head, muscles in her buttocks bunching as she moved, wet hair slick on her skull. Dominika tried to remember the locations of the major veins and arteries in the human body, knowing the box-cutter blade was only an inch long. *Get on with it*, she told herself, *before you start moaning like a cow.*

A wave of rage boiled in Dominika's gut for what she was about to do, for what They were forcing her to do. She measured the distance through the opening of the glass, and felt for the box cutter, thinking *Slash, don't stab, slash at throat, eyes, neck.* Just before she stepped forward, her eye caught a kimono hanging on a wall peg and she left the box cutter alone, reached over, and drew the silk belt free, then quickly twisted two loops into a constricting slip knot, stepped into the shower, and slipped the loop over Zhen's head, pulling the knot tight. Moving faster than humanly possible, Zhen turned to face her and tried to bow her head to slip the loop, but Dominika stepped outside the glass, drew the belt over the top edge, and pulled the belt down with all her might, adding her body weight, yanking Zhen's cheek sideways against the inside of the glass with a clunk and, with another pull, off her feet. The glass kept Zhen's hands and feet away from her.

Zhen's toes drummed against the shower wall; her breasts, brown nipples, and pubic delta flattened against the wet glass, her fingers scrabbling at the material around her throat, but the soaked silk had tightened into an impossible knot, the loop pulling her head ear-high, and she shook like a fish side to side, and tried to push off the glass with her feet, her thighs flexing.

Rasping grunts came out of her open mouth, but the noise of the shower covered the sound. After three minutes of violent thrashing, as the oxygen in her brain was used up, her kicking slowed, and her hands fell away from her throat, and she quivered for another three minutes, head canted sideways, spittle drizzling out of the corner of her mouth. Rivulets of water ran down the glass as Zhen stared through it dead eyed and openmouthed at Dominika, who had sat down on the bathroom floor with a thump, feet braced, holding the belt, her arms screaming, staring back at the wet corpse.

Five minutes, ten, an hour later—Dominika couldn't tell—she made her cramping hands let go, and Zhen slid down the partition, her pancaked breasts squeaking on the wet glass, normally a bawdy and erotic sound during shower sex, but now it was ugly and final. Zhen flopped on her back, chin up, legs splayed, the shower water filling her mouth and dribbling down either cheek. Dominika turned off the water. The *tock-tock* sound of the dripping drain beneath the body was her only requiem.

Frantically drying her feet and legs, Dominika moved fast through the living room—no more chakras to palpitate with vibrating gongs here—opened the front door, ignoring the possibility of a silent alarm, and left it ajar, got into the stairwell, and pulled the handle of the fire-alarm box she had marked the day before. Now she wanted noise and confusion. The peculiar Hong Kong fire alarm was a *woop-woop* siren that brought tenants out into the hallway as Dominika ran up one flight to her apartment door, pushed it open, and quickly put on a robe, then stood in the corridor, looking uncertain and frightened. Rainy Chonghuan came running down the corridor in a hoisin-stained sleeveless undershirt and boxer shorts, and he protectively bustled her down nine floors in a stairwell crowded with yelling residents, crying children, and a squawking cockatoo in a bamboo cage.

Dominika was booked into a luxury hotel suite in Kowloon that night, her clothes, toiletries, and belongings packed up and delivered to her the next morning. A shaken and embarrassed Rainy told her that fire investigators responding to the alarm had found Zhen Gao murdered in the operational apartment, strangled in the shower. The MSS were convinced that a CIA action team had killed her—likely they had rappelled from the roof—and that the American Nash had probably assisted. There were other theories as they cast wildly for explanations.

"No single person could have caught *Zhènniǎo* off guard, and bested her in combat," said Rainy. "There's no other explanation."

"It could not have been a random crime? Rape? Robbery?" asked Dominika.

Rainy shook his head. "Impossible. She could have thrown a petty thief over the balcony railing with one arm."

"An unfortunate and frustrating conclusion to this operation," said Dominika. "What will you do now?"

Rainy wanted to regain some face in light of this debacle. "The *gweilo*, the foreign devil Nash, is in Hong Kong temporarily, without diplomatic immunity. Beijing has instructed me to direct the Hong Kong Police to arrest Nash on suspicion of murder. He will be remanded to Stanley Prison until his trial and sentencing, then sent to a *Laogai*, a work camp, in western China where he will learn to dig coal in the mines. That is if something worse does not happen to him while he is in custody."

This was a whole new danger. If Nate was arrested and jailed, the MSS wouldn't have to assassinate him. They would stage a dramatic show trial, with international coverage. He would die in a prison camp on the windswept steppes of western China. He had to get out of Hong Kong immediately. But would the Station learn about Grace's death and the arrest warrant in time? Or would Nate blithely appear at her apartment tonight with a bouquet of flowers? *Bozhe*, God, he could walk right into their arms.

Dominika fought her panic: Would she have to barge into the US Consulate to deliver a warning? She daydreamed about it. The end of her career as a spy and the start of a life together with Nate. It was a warm daydream. He would be astonished to see her in Hong Kong, halfway around the globe. She imagined their first kiss in the lobby of the consulate, not caring who saw them. *Snap out of it.*

But the MSS made up her mind for her. A female escort stayed in the hotel room with her for the evening, and the next morning Dominika was driven to the airport by a dyspeptic Rainy Chonghuan and put on a direct Air China flight to Moscow, with no further courtesy calls in Beijing proposed or offered. It wasn't exactly a snub: The Chinese were agitated and bewildered. The MSS, General Sun, and the Minister of State Security, moreover, were mortified over their operational failure, witnessed firsthand and up close by a Russian intelligence officer. The loss of face was too great for her to be received as a guest at the ministry. *What would they think if they learned that their exalted guest from a fraternal service was the one who had throttled their highly trained executioner?* ˙

Now it was a race against time. Would the Americans learn about the warrant before Nate was rounded up by the Hong Kong Police? She wouldn't know until tomorrow. The flight would take ten hours. She'd read the SVR Asia reports in the morning. Nate was on his own.

———

As it turned out, Dominika needn't have worried. A cooperative young lieutenant in the Hong Kong Police who received an envelope every month for "confidential chats" with Bunty Boothby passed the news about the murder and the arrest warrant. The ASIS officer requested an urgent meeting with Nate and COS Burns. They all were seriously shaken to learn that gorgeous Grace Gao was an MSS bird dog. Nate was utterly gobsmacked when Bunty's agent added that Grace had been part of an MSS operation to suborn Nate and elicit the name of their new PLA recruitment. A close call. But who had killed her? COS Burns paced in the five feet of his cubicle office.

"Right now, it doesn't matter who whacked her. We'll find out sooner or later," he said. He pointed at Nate. "You just avoided the Little Bighorn."

Nate put his head in his hands. "*The university, and the restaurant,* I should have seen it," he said almost to himself. "I was too focused on signing her up."

"You did nothing wrong," said Burns. "By the book. I read and released all your cables and contact reports."

"These things happen, mate," said Bunty solicitously, one leg hooked over the arm of the couch in Burns's office. "Tell me at least she gave you a gobby."

———

Nate couldn't leave Hong Kong or Macao by air, for both airports were being watched closely. There were no cruise ships in harbor. Bunty floated the idea that Nate could, just possibly, take a train from Hong Kong Hung Hom Station to Guangzhou's East Station, and catch a flight to Seoul or Tokyo from there. He thought the MSS would never expect such a bold maneuver. That option would require Nate to wait for an unspecified amount of time for an alias passport from Langley, which was problematic. He couldn't hide indefinitely in the consulate—too many locals.

Finally, the risk of Nate actually traveling *into* China *to get out* of China convinced COS Burns that the option was not viable. CIA Headquarters, meanwhile, was flooding Hong Kong Station with interrogatory cables about the developmental case against Grace, her murder, the continued security of the new asset SONGBIRD, and proposals for smuggling Nate out of Hong Kong. Benford personally spoke to Nate on the secure phone and seemed calm and mild.

"Your performance with SONGBIRD and with this woman was exemplary," said Benford. "Keep me apprised of your exfil plans, and get back here as quickly as possible." He hung up before Nate could reply, but from Benford this was a love letter. That was something, at least.

A day later, COS had a plan. They borrowed a uniform from the curious but cooperative assistant military attaché, a commander in the US Navy. The tech officer in the Station matched the color of Nate's hair in a modified "lip brow" mustache, and gave him slightly longer sideburns and heavy tortoise-shell eyeglasses to round out his face. The next evening, humid and overcast, Commander Nash boarded a bus from the motor pool with twenty consulate employees, the majority of whom were from the Station. The bus drove down Connaught Road, through the tunnel under the harbor, and pulled up to the municipal pier on Canton Road in Kowloon for a public ship visit on the USS *Blue Ridge*, a six-hundred-foot amphibious command ship and the flagship of the US Navy's 7th Fleet, making her biannual amicable port call.

As they arrived, Bunty Boothby and Marigold Dougherty were hectoring Hong Kong Police on duty at the foot of the gangplank to be let aboard without invitations. Marigold was in a long dress and heels, yelling at Bunty for forgetting the invitations at home, calling him a nong and breaking into tears. The busload of consulate employees arrived, and the overwhelmed police privates hurriedly did a head count and let everyone on board. They didn't blink at Nate in all the confusion. Bunty toasted Nate in the wardroom, thanked him for being a mate, and noted that Beijing would be "mad as a cut snake" when they eventually realized that Nathaniel Nash was out of China. At the end of the evening, a young petty officer switched places with Nate and got off the ship while Nate stayed aboard, out of sight.

The *Blue Ridge* departed Hong Kong the next morning and returned to fleet headquarters in Yokosuka, Japan, in three days, a transit of fifteen hundred nautical miles, during which time Nate stayed in his cabin, ate alone in the officers' mess, and watched half a dozen movies. He brooded about Grace; he wondered about Dominika and the mole hunt, the briefing for the DCIA candidates, and his standing with Benford and Forsyth, and waited in uneasy anticipation of what they had in mind for him next. Overseas assignment? Secondment to FBI? A tiny cubicle in the basement of Headquarters?

He didn't know why, but he had a feeling—he just knew—that he would see Dominika very soon.

ZHÈNNIǍO'S SHĒNGCÀI—LETTUCE SOUP

Sauté diced white onions and minced garlic in butter in a soup pot, stirring until softened. Add chopped coriander, salt, and pepper. Add peeled, cubed potatoes, whole lettuce leaves (do not trim the ribs), and water to cover. Bring to a boil, then cover and simmer until potatoes are soft. Purée liquid to a velvety texture, whisk in butter, and season to taste. Serve hot or at room temperature.

31

League of Nations

"You're as bad as Angleton," said Acting Director Farrell to Benford, who was standing in front of the spotless desk in the DCIA's office on the seventh floor of Headquarters. Unsullied by cables, memos, or ops plans, the Director's workspace contrasted wildly with Benford's desk three floors down in CID, which more closely resembled downtown Tokyo after Godzilla walked through. "You counterintelligence fanatics waste time chasing shadows that don't exist." Angleton had been the zealous messianic CI chief in the seventies who saw Soviet disinformation and provocation under every rock. Benford shifted his feet slightly.

Farrell was a lank-haired economics analyst from the Directorate of Intelligence who was, in the eyes of the jaundiced workforce in Langley, an unlikely pick to run the Agency, even temporarily. He had dishwater eyes, a waxen complexion, a reedy cartoon voice, and an abiding, singular interest in promoting himself. Farrell had first been noticed by POTUS as a fellow internationalist with a healthy dislike of CIA cowboys. Farrell had further endeared himself to the White House after publicly declaring he would credit the assessments of Headquarters-based analysts regarding the political situation in any given country, rather than rely on the estimations of the Chief of Station on the ground, an apostasy increasingly in vogue after the drowning of DCIA Alex Larson. As Farrell's comment became common knowledge, operations officers in the foreign field continued their work, silently toasting the Acting Director at recruitment dinners worldwide.

"This mole is hardly a shadow," said Benford, controlling the impulse to tell this ponderous bureaucrat he was a preening cockatoo. "His existence has been corroborated by a sensitive asset in Moscow." The Director snorted.

"It's always the same," Farrell said. "Sensitive asset says something, and we go off on a wild-goose chase. It's absurd. What asset reported this?" The Director had the right to ask about any source, including true name, but Benford protected his restricted-handling cases jealously, usually referring to them only by cryptonyms.

"DIVA, our top source in Russia, her intelligence has been impeccable, she's stolen secrets from inside the Kremlin itself."

Farrell made a face. "I prefer to avoid that hackneyed phrase, 'steal secrets.' Stealing implies extralegal and morally reprehensible methods."

"It's the definition of espionage, since Judas kissed Jesus," said Benford. "What do you call it?"

Farrell looked up, nettled at his tone. The two men glared at each other. "We don't steal secrets," he said.

Benford kept a straight face. "I've heard that homily before, somewhere. It's as imbecilic now as it was then."

Farrell swiveled in his chair, turning his back on Benford. "I didn't call you up here to listen to your old-line retrogressive cant. I called you because I understand you are not fully briefing the three nominees for the Directorship. You are to brief them all unreservedly, with no evasion, including the reporting from this star asset of yours. Do you understand? Full briefings."

"The asset is in a precarious position. The intelligence can be sourced directly to her," said Benford, already knowing what he was going to do.

"Stop this pedantry," snapped Farrell. "The nominees all have top-secret clearances. Brief them. Everything. Am I clear?"

―――

"You're going to get your ass fired, Simon," said Forsyth. They were sitting in Benford's office. Lucius Westfall was squeezed on the couch, trying to keep a teetering stack of files from falling on him and onto the floor.

"We suspect that one of the candidates for the next Director of the Central Intelligence Agency is a mole run by Moscow Center. The Kremlin's candidate. If MAGNIT is selected as DCIA, the Agency will cease to exist, and the United States will be blind to overseas threats. It will be worse than Philby, worse than Ames or Hanssen."

"We'd have to exfil and resettle hundreds of assets," said Forsyth. "Not just the Russians, but sources in China, North Korea, and Cuba."

"The cereal aisle at the supermarket in Alexandria is going to look like the League of Nations, with all the ex-agents grocery shopping," said Westfall, who once babysat for a Chinese defector, and knew how impossible most defectors could be.

"Those will be the ones we agree to settle. There will be a lot of low-level Joes left behind, who'll be tossed in jail, or retired without pension," said Forsyth.

"You're both forgetting the ones who won't leave and will try to gut it out," said Benford. "The ones they'll feed to the lions." They were all thinking about Dominika.

"So you're willing to risk your career to defy the Director?"

"In trade for DIVA? What would you do?" They all knew the answer to the question, including the greenhorn on the couch, who already felt fiercely protective of the blue-eyed Russian.

"Time for a barium enema," said Benford. "Lucius, I'll need your help." Westfall's eyes widened. He frantically wondered whether this could possibly be a medieval secret rite of initiation in the Operations Directorate or, as plausibly, an unsavory personal practice of Benford's in which he, as factotum, was somehow expected to assist. He was sure it had not been listed as one of his professional duties.

Westfall was immeasurably relieved, though alarmed at the scope of the sedition, when Forsyth and Benford explained what "barium enema" meant—a counterintelligence test—and what they wanted. Just then, Benford's secretary walked in with lunch, a cardboard box with Styrofoam cups of egg-drop soup from the cafeteria, which had become popular with the recruitment of SONGBIRD. She handed around cups as the room grew silent except for the sound of Benford slurping.

———

They were fortunate that for the next round of briefings, each nominee had scheduling conflicts, so individual sessions had to be scheduled at different times. Benford obsequiously briefed Senator Feigenbaum and her scowling altar boy Farbissen on a sensitive operation to recruit a Russian code clerk in Buenos Aires, based not on any demonstrated vulnerability or regulatory transgression, but simply because the young bachelor was observed to be lonely. Farbissen snorted in derision and the senator muttered "fishing expedition" under her breath, neither of them acknowledging the immense value of recruiting a code clerk.

In reality, Benford had concocted the entire operation. If Feigenbaum/Farbissen were the moles, the Center would quickly recall the blameless code clerk to Moscow—something the cooperative Argentine service immediately could ascertain—to get him out of the crosshairs of perfidious CIA. Benford wasted an hour playacting, trying to convince these two congressional bivalves that the operation had merit. By then, time was up, and Benford had avoided briefing his most sensitive cases—for today. It was a dodge that would work only once.

The next day, Forsyth briefed VADM Rowland. Benford had suggested that Forsyth turn on a little of his salt-and-pepper charm to see if the dour three-striper would react to him. Forsyth later grumpily reported that mildly flirting with the admiral was like throwing cotton balls at riveted steel plate.

"Christ," said Forsyth. "I wore my dark suit with the Italian pocket square, threw her the case-officer smile, turned on the charm, and complimented her on her inspired management of ONR. I let her catch me looking at her legs, and told her a story about my fiancée who was lost at sea during a typhoon. Nothing. No reaction. I've had North Koreans at diplomatic receptions react more than she did. I went home that night and cried into my pillow."

"Age is the great leveler. It catches up with us all," intoned Benford, commiserating. "Though it may have been the pocket square."

Forsyth had briefed the admiral on a troubling case in Panama City involving a recruited but obstreperous senator in the Panamanian Parliament who had befriended an unidentified (and imaginary) Russian diplomat who was "talking out of school." The senator had refused to identify the Russian until the Station agreed to raise his salary. Benford knew that even the *possibility* of an unknown Russian dip getting cozy with an access agent from CIA would result in a hasty Russian approach to the venal senator in an attempt to identify the wayward diplomat. (The senator, in fact, was a longtime and loyal asset who would report any inveigling contact or surveillance on him.)

"The admiral listened politely but was clearly not interested," said Forsyth.

"Probably thinking about magnetic impedance and joules," said Benford. "She continues to be the least likely of the three, in my view." He turned to Westfall. "You will brief Ambassador Vano tomorrow. He seems less concerned with rank, and is equable in nature, so he presumably will not object to a briefing from a junior snail. Play it with youthful enthusiasm and make it appear you're exceeding your brief. Observe his reaction. He is a successful businessman with access, who is vain and inexperienced in intelligence matters. Play on that."

For a junior analyst who was new to the Operations Directorate, Lucius played his role with a fine hand as the overserious analyst with facts and figures who liked to hear himself talk. He told the ambassador about a (fictitious) Russian naval captain in the Northern Fleet stationed in Murmansk who intended to defect and smuggle himself and his family into Finland in the back of one of the hundreds of 18-wheelers passing through the *Vaalimaan Rajanylityspaikka*, the southernmost Finnish border crossing on the E18. Westfall bragged that the Russian captain commanded a fleet ballistic submarine, would potentially bring kilos of top-secret naval documents out with him, and would attempt the crossing in two months. This would be irresistible bait for the Russians, who would tear apart every truck exiting the Federation, causing holy chaos at the border, which would be easily observed. Benford was enthused now that he had spread his trail of bread crumbs at the feet of each candidate.

"I anticipate FSB and SVR will collaborate, and that DIVA will be involved in the investigations," Benford said. "We, therefore, will have positive intelligence on which variant was reported to Moscow."

"If we ever get her reliable commo," grumbled Forsyth. "We cannot keep meeting her on the street."

"Hearsey tells me a new piece of communications gear has been tested and will soon be ready for deployment. He is coming to demonstrate it this afternoon. You should all be here to assess its suitability for DIVA, especially Nash, when he returns from the Orient."

———

Nash returned the next day, was sarcastically congratulated by Benford on having resisted using his phallus in the Hong Kong operations, and was briefed on the mole hunt. Hearsey came to Benford's office and nodded to the officers in the room. *Definitely channeling Gary Cooper*, thought Nate, noticing his tall man's habit of instinctively ducking slightly under the door frame. Hearsey wore a soft sports jacket over a pinstripe shirt with khaki trousers, and was carrying a silver ZERO Halliburton attaché case. Behind him, dragging a large black plastic Pelican footlocker, was another tech introduced as Frank Mendelsohn, who was short, slight, dark, shy, and twitchy, about whom Benford whispered, "the guy you don't want assembling the bomb in the basement."

Hearsey nodded to Nate. The ops officers had worked with Hearsey before; he'd broken into a German factory with Gable to sabotage centrifuge parts destined for Iran, and he had trained Nate's friend Hannah Archer before she was assigned to Moscow. Hearsey was what they called an operational tech, a trained engineer who knew you couldn't sneak a listening device into an office if it came in twelve pieces and weighed six hundred pounds. He understood operations, and his technical solutions reflected that understanding, a rare bird.

As he did typically, Benford had bypassed the orotund Director of OTS and confidentially asked Hearsey to consider solutions to DIVA's communication problem now that she was to be Director of SVR. He asked the rangy tech to think out of the box, and come up with an answer. It was a little risky for Hearsey to accept and work on a bootleg project for Benford without his own chief's knowledge, but he couldn't abide his boss, a nontechnical outsider whom he called a seagull manager. "Swoops in, starts screaming, shits on everything, then flies away," Hearsey had told Benford.

Hearsey sat on the couch, his knees coming even with his stomach. "I assume it's okay to talk details in front of everyone," he said. Benford nodded. "I had the beginning of an idea, so I asked NGA, that's the National Geospatial-Intelligence Agency—the people who fly the satellites—to image SVR headquarters in Yasenevo. They did an ELINT shot, which reads electronic emissions, then the next pass was a MASINT shot, which measures energy. I was looking for two things: that the main buildings radiate electric energy to the outside; and that there is only one main transformer—step-down transformers block energy—in a separate power plant."

"How'd you do?" said Forsyth.

"Two out of two," said Hearsey. "The buildings radiate, so there must be miles of wiring inside the walls, and the transformers are in a dedicated power plant on the other side of the compound."

"My pulse is racing, but what exactly are you telling us?" said Benford.

Hearsey smiled. "You're going to like this, Simon. The Russians hardened their headquarters on the inside against external eavesdropping, but didn't think about energy leaking through the wires *outside* to the surrounding pine forest. The bottom line is that the two main buildings of SVR headquarters in Moscow are in essence a big honking antenna," he said. "Even the shapes of the two buildings—a fifteen-floor tower connected to a five-floor wing shaped like a Y—act like a Yagi directional antenna."

"I will not ask what a Yogi antenna is. But how does that help us?" said Benford.

"That's *Yagi*, and it's just what we need." Hearsey turned to Mendelsohn, who opened the locker and took out a sleek desk lamp composed of a large ebony base, a stainless-steel, L-shaped arm, and a broad black shade. Hearsey smiled and put the lamp on the arm of the couch.

"Stick this lamp on your agent's desk and plug it into the wall. That's it. She can dictate, record, or type messages to Simon through this lamp, using the building's electrical wires as a carrier, even with people present in the agent's office," said Hearsey. "Another feature: align documents along the base under the shade and you can photograph them, even while signing them, right in front of a secretary looking over your shoulder. And the lamp will tell her when an incoming message from Simon is waiting for her."

"How's it do that?" said Nate.

"An air vortex ring," said Hearsey.

"What does that mean?" said Forsyth.

"It'll blow in her ear," said Hearsey.

"That can't be a bad thing," said Westfall.

Hearsey left after two hours, having demonstrated the functions of the desk lamp concealment for DIVA's covert communications equipment. Hearsey told them the system was encrypted BOLERO, which crypt Simon found fatuous. Nevertheless, he was pleased. Hearsey had outdone himself, supported by the engineering brilliance of Frank Mendelsohn, whose nickname in the office, inexplicably, was Money Shot. The BOLERO transmitter/receiver was interactive, multifunctional, and protected from tampering by retinal-scan permissive-action link. Messages or images that Dominika loaded into the device would be stored until it detected the authentication code from the BATTLEFAT telemetry satellite in geosynchronous orbit above the Arctic Circle. In 3.5 seconds, Dominika's stored messages would flood through the building's electrical grid to the satellite, and simultaneous incoming messages would be read by the BOLERO lamp at the other end of the wall plug in DIVA's office.

"Will these transmissions be detectable inside the building?" Nate asked. "Is it safe?"

"SVR comsec experts solved that problem for us," said Hearsey. "They shielded the building against external eavesdropping, so our communications don't emanate inside. We got lucky."

"I have a question," said Westfall, ever the analyst. "I understand that transmissions to satellites are vulnerable to radio intercept or direction finding."

"You mean triangulation," said Hearsey. "Not with this system. The power is low, like with your SRAC equipment, but, more important, transmissions are diffused. It's the difference between tracing back a beam in the night sky to find the searchlight, and stuffing fog into a gunny sack." Benford grunted approvingly at that, a metaphor he could understand.

Frank Mendelsohn then had explained principles of haptic (tactile) communication, organic user interface, and flexible display with bend interactions until Benford began going purple in the face. The not-insignificant consideration of getting the desk lamp into SVR headquarters without arousing suspicion appeared to be a problem until Nate said Dominika could carry it in herself as she moved into the Director's office and chose new furnishings. The lamp would be cached to her by Moscow Station. Risky but doable. And once the lamp was on her desk, she needn't step foot on the street to meet a case officer—personal meets would be reserved for when DIVA traveled outside Russia. Benford said they should deploy BOLERO as soon as possible.

DIVA would once more be online, and Benford could begin reading other gentlemen's mail again, with the exception of the messages to and from MAGNIT. And that was the problem.

CIA'S EGG-DROP SOUP

Heat chicken stock and use a little to mix with cornstarch into a slurry. In the remaining stock add ginger, soy sauce, diced scallions, thin-sliced mushrooms, white pepper, and bring to a boil. Add cornstarch slurry, stir well, and simmer. Beat eggs vigorously in a separate bowl and slowly pour them into the soup while stirring the stock, so that the eggs cook and spread out in ribbons. An optional ingredient is kernel (or creamed) corn. Garnish with additional chopped scallions and serve immediately.

32

Snaggletooth

Dominika's return from China—rumors of her secret commission to Beijing had the *siloviki* (except Gorelikov and FSB Chief Bortnikov) frantic with envy and trepidation—coincided with the announcement of her promotion to one-star general and to the post of Director of the SVR. Chubby, jowly faces clustered around her after the Security Council meeting to congratulate her, enveloping her in an impossibly cloying miasma of competing colognes underlaid with the earthy fear-sweat of officials who had millions squirreled away in overseas accounts. It, therefore, was important to establish good relations with this *shlyukha*, this former trollop, who now had the organizational means and authorities to investigate foreign bank accounts whenever Vladimir Vladimirovich ordered it. Beefsteak hands with manicured nails and pinky rings pumped her hand and yellow halos quivered above their yellow smiles, interspersed by the rare blue crowns of the few pragmatic thinkers on the Council, the occasional gazelles who roamed among the muddy-flanked buffaloes. The thinkers had a low survival rate in the jungles of the Kremlin.

The official promotion ceremony took place the following week in the gilded Andreyevsky Hall in the Grand Kremlin Palace, in front of the forty-foot curved gold filigreed doors, above which the black double-headed eagle of the Russian Federation stood guard, wings outspread, the orb and scepter in its talons. The relics represented God's dominion over the Earth, and the monarch's benevolent and just rule over his people. Dominika contemplated the towering irony of benevolence and justice in modern Russia as the president approached her to pin the Order for Merit to the Fatherland, First Class, on the lapel of her forest-green tunic, the military uniform the service chiefs wore to ceremonial events to reflect their flag ranks. Dominika hated the baggy cut of the double-breasted jacket, the stiff epaulets, and the straight-line green skirt, more suitable for a librarian or a wedding magistrate's clerk. The clunky black service shoes, she couldn't even look at.

"*Pozdravlyayu*, General," said Putin, looking into her eyes. Felicitations. His fingers lingered while pinning the medal on her lapel, solicitously smooth-

ing the hanging claret ribbon, brushing with knowing fingers the start of
the swell of her left breast. Dominika idly wondered if there was an ornate
general's belt buckle to be awarded next, that would present additional opportunity for the president to smooth the folds of her uniform skirt.

"Thank you, Mr. President, I will continue to serve the *Rodina* with all
my energies," said Dominika, standing at what she imagined was a sem-
blance of attention. Putin's azure halo pulsed once, and he gave her an olive
oil smile that unambiguously transmitted, no, serve *me* with all your energies, stuff the *Rodina*, as he shook her hand and stepped sideways to the
other medal recipient, a twenty-seven-year-old champion rhythmic gymnast,
who was retiring from the sport and had been named as a district organizer
for *Yedinaya Rossiya*, the United Russia Party—the government's party that
controlled 75 percent of Parliamentary seats. Dominika wondered how she
had qualified for that position. The president turned back to Dominika after
laboriously pinning a sports medal on the blushing gymnast.

"I look forward to hosting you at the reception at the cape in several days,"
said Putin, leering. Dominika wondered if her dacha was wired for sound
and video, and if the president had a key to the front door. *Stupid questions.*

"I will be there, Mr. President. Thank you for the invitation. And I must
thank you again for use of the dacha. It's quite beautiful."

Putin nodded. "The view of the sea from that particular dacha is second
only to the view from the master apartment in the main house," he said as
if he were selling shares in a Ponzi scheme.

Dominika smiled. "I have no doubt of that," she said, noncommittally. She
was not going to stick out her chest, wet her lips, and tell him she couldn't
wait to compare the two views. How to keep a suspicious, covetous, and randy
despot's hands off you for two or three days without incurring his wrath, or
worse, embarrassing him regarding performance issues? There were bawdy
rumors on the streets of Moscow that Dimitri Medvedev, Putin's diminutive prime minister, a protégé who had switched leadership positions with
Putin as a way to satisfy term limits laws, was better endowed and, well,
more *feral* than his supposedly ubervirile patron. Medvedev's nickname
from those years was Nano President, but the mere thought that Putin was
not the rampant alpha wolf among the whole pack could not be remotely
contemplated. "Until then," said the president before moving off. She felt
footsteps coming up behind her.

"Congratulations, Director," said a smiling, jubilant Gorelikov with a flourish. "You've earned this honor, and we will accomplish great things in the coming months." *Great things, to be sure*, thought Dominika. *Disrupting democracies, suborning innocents, enabling cloven-footed surrogates, maybe start the next world war.* But Anton was reveling in the possibilities now that his ingénue, his creation, had landed the big job. "With the announcement of your new position, I took the liberty of transferring your belongings to your new penthouse on Kutuzovsky Prospekt. You'll find it elegant and quite comfortable." *How kind and thoughtful.* The courteous favor was an opportunity for Gorelikov's team to rummage through her belongings. Bozhe, *thank God I buried my broken SRAC equipment before I left.* "The penthouse belonged to Andropov before he became First Secretary," beamed Anton. *Charming. I hope they've taken out the hospital bed and oxygen tanks since then.* "Your daily schedule will naturally be taken up with more representational duties, starting tomorrow evening with a formal diplomatic reception in the Georgievsky Hall here in the Grand Kremlin Palace. Besides the embassies, there will be various delegations." Dominika's irrational first thought was that she had no dress for a formal reception. Gorelikov was a warlock, reading her mind.

"Dominika, I also took the quite outrageous liberty of putting a selection of evening dresses in your closet," said Anton like a valet, "but I must apologize in advance for my utter lack of style. I hope at least one of them will suit." The elegant Gorelikov, dressed today in an exquisite gray flannel suit of British cut, a white spread-collar shirt, and a black knit tie, would have chosen, Dominika had no doubt, elegant, expensive frocks in her exact size. *Welcome to the club*, thought Dominika. *Now they're dressing you like a doll.*

"I'm sure they will be quite lovely, thank you," said Dominika, her mind drifting. She knew Benford would hear about her long-anticipated promotion within a day: TASS and Pravda would carry the announcement, doubtless highlighting the fact that General Dominika Egorova was one of the highest-ranked women in the government. *Modern Russia making great strides*, thought Dominika, *despite the unavoidable fact that the entire country was nothing more than a big petrol station with nuclear weapons and heaps of murdered dissidents.*

The crowd made no move to disperse—no one arrived at a State function after the president and likewise no one departed before him—so Dominika continued speaking with Gorelikov, and they were soon joined by a mild and complimentary Alexander Bortnikov of the FSB, in a gorgeous powder-blue uniform with gold braid at lapels and cuffs. Bortnikov was a lieutenant general with three stars, after all. He shook hands with Dominika as he congratulated her, and his politely firm grip was dry and warm, his steady blue halo—matched by the equally steady aura above Gorelikov's head and shoulders—hinted at reserve and good sense. Perhaps she could eventually count these two as true allies in this Kremlin maze. Then she remembered that this beneficent and reasonable grandfather had planned and authorized Litvinenko's assassination in London. *No one, but no one, was an ally.*

Sidelong glances from the milling *siloviki* were ill disguised; nervous noses already had sniffed the air and tentatively identified a newly formed triumvirate—Gorelikov and the Directors of SVR and FSB, a potent cabal favored by the president himself. But Dominika remembered Benford's warning when the subject of her becoming head of SVR first was raised: "You'll be close to the top, but even as you become indispensable to Vladimir, so will you be considered a threat to his suzerainty." Nate had to translate that word, but she knew he was right. From now on, her official life would be plagued with hidden tests, sly traps, and constant assessments of her loyalty. She grimly told herself that gutting the Kremlin for Benford, Nate, and Forsyth would be trebly satisfying from now on, as long as she survived.

The familiar heartache welled up in her breast. Where was Nate now? Would they let them see each other? She would have to pick a plausible foreign trip, her first as Director, to be able to meet with her CIA friends, and from now on she would have to contend with hovering aides and ever-present security personnel.

Dominika would be busy in the next weeks, and she would have to alter her mode of operating. She'd have to concoct a reason to go out alone without an escort, to put down a signal for a personal meet with Ricky Walters, and make arrangements for a foreign trip in the near future. That would take a few weeks to arrange. Dominika had a lot to pass to her handlers, and she desperately needed reliable, secure commo. She still hadn't decided whether to tell Benford and Nate that she had saved Nate's life in Hong Kong. But for now, she had to get ready for a party.

The Georgievsky Hall in the Grand Kremlin Palace was an endless series of massive and ornately decorated coffered ceilings supported by spiraled-fluted marble columns at each pier, with intricate capitals and plinths, an ivory and gold arcade of dazzling opulence illuminated by colossal chandeliers hanging in a line from each dome, three, four, five, six of them, with galaxies of lights reflecting off the polished parquet floor inlaid with colored pieces of precious wood, set in patterns as complex as a Tabriz carpet from Persia. The room was filled to capacity with the boisterous Moscow foreign diplomatic corps, jostling and carrying flutes of champagne above their heads as they pressed through the throng. The oligarchs milled quietly in a corner, each wondering whether, when, and under what pretext their pre-Putin fortunes would be appropriated. The *siloviki* kept loose station around the president as he halfheartedly worked the crowd, dispensing an infrequent wry grin, or very rarely, a lopsided smile, which clearly he managed at a grave cost.

High-ranking Russian military officers from the army, navy, and air force stayed segregated in their herds, respectively green, navy, or light blue, like grazing herds of African antelope, the kudus apart from the sables, separate from the impalas. Dominika had known Gorelikov would stuff her closet with fabulous frocks. Two from Paris (a Vuitton and a Dior) and one from Milan (a Rinaldi), but she had worn the more demure Dior, a silk champagne-pink beaded floral-print gown with hourglass bodice, ruched waist, and low-cut plunge. Gorelikov steered her around the crowd, making introductions. She already knew the buffaloes on the Security Council and the secretary of the Council, dour Nikolai Patrushev, who stayed with her for a few minutes chatting, while looking down the front of her dress. Nikolai drifted off when Bortnikov eased up and kept Dominika amused for fifteen minutes whispering in her ear to point out the known and suspect foreign-intelligence officers from the respective embassies.

"That's the German BND representative?" asked Dominika. "He looks like a *godovalyy bychok*, a breeder hog. He cannot be active on the street." Bortnikov pointed to a thin man with white hair talking to a group of diplomats. "The American Chief of Station Reynolds, capable, cunning, and tricky," said Bortnikov. "His officers are active on the street, but we have not detected their activities . . . yet." *Keep up the good work*, Dominika telegraphed to the American.

Suddenly Gorelikov excused himself and made his way through the crowd, weaving his way around obstructions halfway down the length of the one-hundred-meter room. Russian naval uniforms had gathered at a doorway to greet another arriving group of a dozen foreign naval officers—Bortnikov whispered they were Americans, a US Navy delegation—and there seemed to be as much gold braid and as many chests full of ribbons on the Americans as on the Russians.

"What are they doing here?" asked Dominika.

Bortnikov shrugged. "Some fool discussions proposing joint naval cooperation against Somali and Malay pirates," he said. "Patrushev has decided we do not have the time or the resources for such adventures, but we invited them anyway for appearances and to collect assessment data on these admirals. Some day we may face them in battle," Bortnikov said, chuckling. Dominika watched as Gorelikov, Patrushev, and the Russian admirals stiffly greeted the American contingent, which was accompanied by the US ambassador and a phalanx of aides, including, to Dominika's alarm, the youthful Ricky Walters, her case officer in Moscow for personal meets. *Bogu moy*, my God, if he saw Dominika would he have the wits to keep expressionless? She resolved not to go near the Americans for the entire evening, slightly incongruous behavior for the new Director of SVR, who would be expected to get right in the faces of US Navy visitors. The thought tickled an ancillary fact she could not retrieve.

Dominika kept quartering the room, "cutting the pie," like they taught her a hundred years ago at the Academy, circling in the opposite direction, to stay away from the Americans, but to also keep them in sight. Could she dare scribble a note and try to slip it into Walters's pocket? To say what? What if Gorelikov saw her? *No. A thousand times no.*

Gorelikov was certainly spending a lot of gratuitous time with the US Navy contingent, handing around flutes of champagne, raising his glass to toast the ranking officer of the group, the Chief of Naval Operations, but then he turned and toasted another admiral who Dominika saw was a mannish woman. Dominika eased through the crowd to get a closer look, and something stirred in her, the female admiral was familiar, somehow. She had smiled at a Gorelikov witticism, revealing uneven teeth. What was it? Gorelikov was recommending canapes from the tray of a passing waiter that featured an assortment of *salaka*, toasted brioche with herring and melted cheese. A snaggletooth. Twelve years ago. The Metropol Hotel. The GRU honey trap. The skinny naval student. The biter with the tooth. Her shoulder. She had never asked—or cared—about the result of the snap trap. It was possible, probable, that the blackmail did not take, for the historical success rate on honey traps was only 25 percent. If it did take, the Kremlin had been running a US admiral for more than a decade.

Then Dominika stopped, frozen like an idiot mannequin in the middle of the hall, jostled by partygoers under the blazing chandeliers, and felt her spine grow cold. The selection of the DCIA—Benford had written to her with the names of the candidates. This one here tonight had to be the naval admiral, Rowland. Her visit to Moscow on this delegation could mean nothing, but it could also mean much. The pieces tumbled in her head like a collapsed mosaic ceiling. Shlykov. Naval railgun. She knew who this was, and she knew why Gorelikov was toadying to her. Now all she had to do was get word back to Benford to find out whether MAGNIT liked herring on toast. With no commo she was mute and Benford was blind.

Gorelikov was sitting on a red velvet couch at the end of the empty hall with his feet up on a brocade chair, his tie loosened, and a flute of flat champagne on the floor beside him. Dominika sat at the other end of the couch. A few remaining waiters scurried about, collecting the last of the crockery from the twelve groaning buffet tables that had been spaced along the length of the hall. An army of cleaners would follow to polish the magnificent floor and to dust the interstices of the chandeliers.

"US naval officers are exceedingly adept in unfamiliar social situations such as tonight's reception," said Gorelikov, rubbing his eyes. "They receive schooling in diplomatic conversation and comportment, and handle themselves with confidence. Our senior officers are *krestyane*, peasants and plowmen, by comparison, hesitant to say anything for fear of revealing the color of the hulls of our ships. It's positively Soviet, the way they act."

Dominika wanted to work on him a little. "Back then they were all terrified of Stalin," she said. "He purged the entire officer corps in the thirties."

"Yes, but now? The president supports the armed forces."

"Old habits fade slowly," said Dominika, noncommittedly. "But who was the female admiral you were speaking to? She was the only woman in the bunch." Gorelikov's halo wavered, and Dominika listened for the deception. "I don't recall her name. She apparently is a science genius," said Gorelikov, dismissively. "She is retiring soon, and doubtless will be offered seats on boards of defense contractors as a consultant. These admirals can manage little else in retirement." *Interesting. You don't know her name or where she works, but it has not escaped your notice that she is retiring soon.* Dominika forced herself to yawn, as her mind churned.

IF *this admiral was the girl Dominika seduced twelve years ago at the Metropol, and* IF *Gorelikov had been successful in pitching her as MAGNIT, and* IF *New York–based illegal SUSAN was now undetectably meeting her, and* IF *she were selected and confirmed as CIA Director, the first thing Gorelikov and Bortnikov would ask from her would be the list of active recruited CIA sources inside Russia. DIVA/Egorova would be at the top of the list. A lot of ifs, but Dominika knew there was grave danger.*

Why wasn't Gorelikov telling her the admiral was MAGNIT? Professional covetousness? Orders from the president? Was she somehow suspected? No. They had specifically selected her to meet SUSAN on Staten Island. Were they waiting for her promotion and a further demonstration of loyalty? Perhaps.

Dominika continued to stay away from the US delegation. God knows what trouble would ensue if the admiral recognized her. After a day of liaison meetings with an uncooperative Russian Naval Command, the Americans would stop in London for two days, after which the admiral would return to Washington for more preliminary briefings, and to await the selection of the final candidate. Then congressional confirmation hearings. In no more than ten days Gorelikov would know who would be running CIA. Dominika frantically calculated if she'd have enough time to trigger a crash-dive meeting with case officer Walters to pass an urgent warning to Nate and Benford. Gorelikov, the prescient warlock, seemed to read her mind.

"Will you be flying down to the reception at the cape tomorrow with me? I've reserved the Falcon 7 before Bortnikov or Patrushev could claim it. We all have to fly separately; it's a regulation." *This is a mild test*, thought Dominika. *Do I fly down with him, or show a little independence and go a few days later, try to make a meet with the Station in the meantime? No. You'll never get rid of your new bodyguards, and you'll never get through to the Station. Act naturally. You stick to Anton for now.*

"I'd be disappointed if you hadn't invited me," said Dominika. "How many guests are expected?"

"Total over the four days, not more than two hundred," said Gorelikov. "But you have your dacha and your privacy. The rest of us stay in the main house on the presidential wing, elegant, but nothing like your own sea view. You don't get lonely by yourself?" Dominika knew Anton was not flirting.

"No, I do not become lonely," said Dominika.

Gorelikov smiled. "I'm sure you will not be," he said. *You mean when Randy Vlad comes scratching,* thought Dominika.

When Admiral Rowland was first invited to accompany the delegation to Moscow by the Chief of Naval Operations, she almost panicked and declined. For MAGNIT the mole to visit Moscow and rub elbows with the intelligence officers who were running her was sheer folly. A little more thought on the matter convinced Audrey that this trip would burnish her credentials for selection as DCIA, and that smooth Anton Gorelikov would ensure that no compromising contacts would be attempted. It would be enough for the Russians to see her across the ballroom, and to marvel at her cool nerve and audacity. She accepted the invitation to travel to Russia, sent a short message to SUSAN to inform the Center that she would be arriving, and packed her best uniforms.

After arriving in Moscow, Audrey stayed close to her colleagues, because she was still nervous about her security. After diplomatic pleasantries with Gorelikov and other officials at the Kremlin reception, Audrey assumed that would be the only contact with her handler, and the danger was past. She could finish her time in Russia, fly to London, then return to Washington to find out if she had been selected by POTUS as DCIA. It would be the most audacious penetration of an opposition service in the history of espionage.

She should have known better. The Russians could not resist the temptation to enter her Moscow hotel suite through the door of an adjoining room on the last night of her stay in the capital. The room was dark, and Audrey sat up in bed when the silhouette of Anton glided across the room, backlighted by city lights from the window. Without saying a word, he pulled up a chair and sat next to her bed, leaned close to her, and patted her hand.

"We are very glad to see you," Anton said. "It has been too long. Are you well? Is contact with the woman in New York satisfactory?"

Audrey was astounded that Anton would take the risk of coming to her room. "Yes, yes. Everything is satisfactory," said Audrey. "It's insane coming here like this."

Anton patted her hand again. "There is no way I could not have spent a few seconds with our most productive friend. We are very excited and expect the best of news regarding the selection process. As we speak, we are working on an enhanced communications plan for you if you are named Director."

"Communications better be enhanced," whispered Audrey. "You must not take any shortcuts. You sit here in Moscow reading the intelligence I send you while I run all the risks. And no more Washington meetings with those clods from GRU—I only want to meet with SUSAN from now on." *Too many risks*, she thought. *What if someone from the American delegation knocked on my door right now?*

Gorelikov smiled. "We give you full operational discretion to accept or reject any plan or equipment. If you become Director, even meeting SUSAN will become problematic. We, therefore, are developing a computer-based messaging system that uses an extensive network of international servers, which I believe you know as the cloud. It is utterly undetectable and unbreakable. I'm sure you will approve."

He paused for a moment. "We were wondering about another aspect if you are selected to the position. I do not mean to pry, but with a twenty-four-hour security detail, we must consider how we can manage your social activities discreetly." Anton knew the day of reckoning had arrived. He was preoccupied with the security ramifications of MAGNIT's particular sexual proclivities.

Audrey's face hardened. She smoothed the sheet over her legs and stared at Gorelikov's silhouette in the dark room. "I presume you are referring to my love life. Are you are telling me the days of our secret vacations abroad will end?" she said.

"Yes," said Anton. "I suppose I am. I cannot imagine any other way forward."

"That would be, in a word, unacceptable," hissed Audrey in the dark. "I expect you to arrange a suitable alternative."

The three-star admiral giving orders, thought Gorelikov. *We've come a long way from the meek physicist with a daddy complex.*

Anton leaned toward her solicitously. "Audrey, the security measures required of us if you become Director will multiply tenfold, and with them will come significant personal sacrifice. When your tenure at Langley ends, your personal, permanent vacation begins. You'll have the money to do whatever you want."

"Marvelous. And in the meantime? You'll want me there for as long as possible, right? Some DCIAs have served five years. What do you propose I do all that time?"

"You could tend to your doll collection," said Anton, using his hammer-and-sickle voice. "Those charming little china faces. They will all look on you from the shelves in your living room with approval of your profession-alism and discipline."

Audrey's head came up. "You've been in my quarters? Tell me you're bugging my fucking house."

Prozreniye. Epiphany. It came in every agent's career, the realization of exactly what the relationship amounted to, who was vassal and who was master. It was Audrey's turn, tonight, in a pitch-black hotel room. "Whether your quarters are bugged or not is immaterial," said Gorelikov without emo-tion. "You are one of the most prolific clandestine intelligence sources in the service of the Russian Federation. You are on the threshold of being Russia's best American spy ever. What you want and what you do not want is unim-portant. I *require* you to dedicate yourself without reservation and to remem-ber the mission. If that means you must live for three years without putting your fingers in a Buenos Aires prostitute, then that is what you shall do."

"You can't talk to me that way," said Audrey, her voice shaking.

"Of course I can, my dear," said Gorelikov, pushing back his chair silently. "You belong to me." He left through the connecting door, his steps muffled by the sour threadbare carpet.

———

Dominika's new Moscow apartment was in the massive city block–long build-ing on Kutuzovsky Prospekt with two outlandish neoclassical towers. The address—number twenty-six—had been the residence of Premiers Brezhnev and Andropov, and party ideologue Suslov. Building security bristled with cameras, controlled elevators, manned checkpoints, and twenty-four-hour valet and food service. Her black Mercedes was always ready for her in the underground garage. *Could I tell my driver to follow a surveillance detection route?* The penthouse had been beautifully remodeled in beige and brown, with luxurious bathrooms and a gleaming kitchen that Nate would love to cook in. Dominika looked at the outside private-line telephone on the sideboard. A suicidal overseas call to CIA's SENTINEL number to blurt out her epiphany about MAGNIT would be recorded (at both ends), and she would be finished, but at least Benford would know. Likewise, crashing the gate of the American Embassy to spill the tale to COS Reynolds would forever burn her bridges. She'd become a permanent exile inside the embassy, living in one of the temporary apartments, a historical oddity like Hungarian Cardinal Mindszenty who took asylum in the US Embassy in communist Budapest for fifteen years. Dominika would grow old, the faded beauty giving Russian lessons to young American wives, unable herself to even walk outside in the chancery compound for fear of snipers. A fine end. She wouldn't do that. Without time to make a personal meet, and with no SRAC, she had no way to communicate the intel that would save her life.

As she packed for the reception at the cape, she fingered the sports watch Nate had given her, the satellite beacon that would transmit an emergency signal requesting exfiltration. The beginning of a plan started percolating in her mind. *Nate's always trying to get me to defect. Okay, lover boy, come rescue me.*

KREMLIN *SALAKA*

Toast triangles of bread and spread thickly with butter. Lay a boned fillet of smoked herring on the bread, and cover with a soft melting cheese like Russian *bryndza*. Place briefly under broiler until cheese is melted. Serve with *ogrutsky*, dill pickles.

33

Exfiltration

When DIVA's exfiltration signal was relayed by the SARSAT maritime rescue receivers to Simon Benford's desk in Langley he yelled at Dotty through the door to summon Forsyth, Nash, Westfall, and Gable instantly. She knew he had included Gable as a reflex, and didn't have the heart to correct him; she saw how deeply he had felt Gable's death in Khartoum. Benford also bellowed that he wanted Phineas "Finn" Nikula, the extravagant and boisterous Chief of maritime branch—the section in the larger Paramilitary Staff (PMS) that controlled all CIA maritime assets. Along with other ships, Finn Nikula controlled the Agency's experimental fleet of Unmanned Surface Vessels, and Benford knew he'd need Finn's cooperation to release one of his precious USVs, stage it on a gray hull in the Black Sea, and program it to retrieve DIVA at Cape Idokopas, even though Benford didn't believe for a minute that DIVA wanted exfiltration. Her transmission was meant to signal something else, he was sure of it. He just didn't know what.

Westfall was the first to arrive, then Forsyth, then Nash breathlessly barged through the door, instinctively knowing this crash dive could only mean Dominika was in trouble. Nikula arrived fifteen minutes later, having come from the other side of the Headquarters building where the PMS front office was tucked away as far as possible from the dyspeptic Director and easily scandalized analysts, who were *positively allergic* to the very notion of paramilitary operations. Nikula was broad shouldered and muscular, and his tweed sport coat strained around the biceps and across the back. He was known to confront people in meetings by neighing like a donkey, implying they were jackasses. He had a wide, rugged face, an ice-blue stare, no eyebrows, and a completely shaven head, which Benford said would certainly make a phrenologist back out of the room in alarm. Gable had once told Finn to his face that he was half a bubble off plumb, and they were firm friends after that. Finn had volunteered to bring Gable's casket home from Khartoum, but Benford sent Nash instead, certain Finn would bludgeon Gondorf with a toner cartridge from an office copier and throw him in the Nile. Benford wanted Gondorf back alive so he could fire him.

"The transmission was received at 1100 GMT, which means 1400 on the Black Sea coast," said Benford.

"She's at Putin's compound for the four-day reception," said Nate. "We've got maps of that stretch of coast, and imagery. I can show you where her dacha is and the beach below the house."

"She's got a dacha?" said Finn, rubbing his head. "Whose Mexican corn did she eat the long way?"

Nate's face colored. "Spare us the knuckle-dragger jokes," he growled. "They're bullshit."

"You think so?" said Finn.

"Let's finish operational discussions before the two of you go out back and begin a fight," said Benford.

"Which I'd win," said Finn, grinning.

"Both of you, shut up," said Forsyth. "What do we all think? Does DIVA want out? After refusing to consider defecting over and over?"

"She decided to come out," said Nate. "She changed her mind."

"Doesn't seem consistent," said Forsyth.

"I agree," said Benford. "The transmission is a signal for something else."

"Do we even send Finn's USV to the beach?" said Forsyth. Nate squirmed in his seat.

"We have to," said Nate. "She sent the exfil signal. She'll be on that beach in three days."

"You guys make up your minds," said Finn. "I don't want to send a four-million-dollar USV hull into Russian territorial waters if nobody's gonna be on that beach."

Nate rounded on him. "She'll be there," he said. Westfall characteristically cleared his throat.

"An observation, if I may," he said.

"Where's he from?" Finn muttered to Nate, looking at Westfall's fogged-up glasses. Lucius ignored him.

"We know DIVA was recently promoted to flag rank and that President Putin has named her Director of SVR," said Westfall. "She is aware of our intense interest in the identity of the mole the Russians call MAGNIT. We know only that MAGNIT is a senior official who possibly is in line for a significantly more senior post. Simon, through a process of elimination, has narrowed the suspects to the three candidates being considered as the nominee for DCIA, based on their respective connections to the navy's railgun project and their ancillary access to information of interest to Moscow Center."

"Ancillary? Simon, I thought only you talked like that," said Finn. "You following the candidates around? Reading their mail?"

"We have done background on them, which is all we can do without potentially alerting the mole. Go on," Benford said, turning to Westfall.

"I believe it's logical to assume DIVA's access has dramatically improved overnight, including knowing some of the unwritten plans and intentions of President Putin. She doubtless has participated in informal conversations during Security Council meetings, and shared confidential asides with her patron, Gorelikov."

"We're waiting for the headline," said Benford, but Westfall would not be hurried.

"DIVA has been without SRAC going on three months," said Lucius. "We have not seen her since Vienna. She's at Putin's compound on the cape with no way to meet a case officer face-to-face in Moscow. I believe it is logical to assume that one, she has discovered the identity of MAGNIT, and two, she has activated the exfil beacon—an inconsistent act given her resolute refusal to defect—to let us know. It was the only option left to her." The room was quiet.

"So what do we do about it?" said Forsyth.

"You think she wants the USV as a floating dead drop, to send us a message? You know, put a note inside the USV cabin and send it back empty?" said Finn. He was developing smaller USVs—no bigger than a six-foot torpedo—for precisely that use.

"We still cannot discount that, along with all the factors Lucius listed, she's in jeopardy, and wants out," said Nate. "That's the exfil plan we briefed her on. We've got to stay on script."

Forsyth shook his head. "That's all speculative," he said. "The gala at Cape Idokopas lasts four days. When DIVA gets back to Moscow we can have the case officer ready to meet her the first night back."

"It'll be too late by then," said Nate. Westfall cleared his throat again. Finn Nikula made him nervous, like Gable used to.

"Based on my research, as Director DIVA now has a two- or four-man security detail, a driver, and at least two household staff. How's she going to get out alone at night?" said Westfall. "We need to get her Hearsey's desk lamp ASAP."

"How about direct her to start an affair with some Russkie movie star," said Finn. "Her bodyguards'll stay in the lobby while your girl buries the pump handle where it won't rust, and she can leave her reports hidden in his apartment, and we go in when he's not home and retrieve her intel. Simple."

Forsyth waited for Nate to explode. "Jeopardize the source by getting her involved with an unwitting stranger and have her leave incriminating intel inside a Moscow apartment?" said Nate. "It's moronic."

Finn shrugged. "Better than what you got now," he said, turning to Benford. "I'm not so sure I can deploy a USV if you ladies aren't sure there will be anyone on the beach."

Nate leaned forward. "What if I can guarantee there'll be someone to take aboard?"

"Tell me your thoughts, Nash," said Benford, "so we can brief the medics on the nature of your derangement when we call them to escort you to the infirmary."

"Listen, Simon, Lucius is right. Domi knows who MAGNIT is. She may or may not want to defect, but we've got to contact her. I can sneak into that compound, get her alone, and see what's up."

"How do you propose to penetrate the private preserve of the President of the Russian Federation during an exclusive levee?"

"Domi told me there's a bunch of young Polish art restorers working in the mansion; they're always coming and going. We can whip up ID for me as a Polish art student. My Russian will get me through. I can be in and out in two days."

Benford shook his head. "Implausible, rash, unconvincing, out of the question," Benford said. "They'll wrap you up at the front gate."

"Not if I arrive with other genuine art experts and native Poles."

"Tell me," said Benford.

Nate turned to Forsyth. "Tom, Agnes Krawcyk lives in LA. One of your old WOLVERINEs. She's an art restorer, a real Pole, and she's bored out of her skull. The two of us will look plausible as hell. She's still on reserve status and she can handle herself. We fly in as art experts, maybe in a larger group of students from Warsaw, meet Domi, talk for ten minutes, then hide on the beach till your speedboat picks us up."

Nate looked at Finn. "Can two people fit in your USV?" asked Nate. Finn nodded. "What if DIVA wants out too?" said Forsyth.

Everyone looked at Finn. "Three people will slow her down," he said, "and it'll be a little cramped. Two of you will essentially have to lie on top of each other in a moderate chop for forty-five minutes. It'll mean some bouncing."

Benford stifled a wan smile. "That will not pose any problem for Casanova, here," he said.

"So let's give it a try, Simon, for Christ sake," said Nate. "Look, if the wrong candidate—namely MAGNIT—gets nominated and confirmed in less than a week, Dominika Egorova is the first name that gets sent back to Moscow. Putin and company will be so scandalized and embarrassed that she'll just disappear, no show trial, no spy swap. She'll be headfirst in a wet hole with no marker. I'll bring back the name, and we keep her alive." Benford looked at Forsyth who minutely nodded his head. Benford turned to Finn.

"Can you have one of your infernal machines on the beach below Cape Idokopas in three days?"

Finn nodded. "Then, Nash, I suggest you prepare to crash President Putin's party." He seemed amused at how dangerous that would be.

MEXICAN CORN

Combine mayonnaise, sour cream or *crema*, *cotija* cheese, chili powder, garlic, and cilantro in a large bowl. Stir until blended. Grill shucked ears of corn until cooked through and charred on all sides. Sprinkle hot corn with cheese mixture. Sprinkle with extra cheese and chili powder. Serve hot with lime wedges.

34

House of Cards

As Nash made crash-dive preparations for the mission to infiltrate Putin's Cape Idokopas compound, Benford sat alone with Forsyth. Simon was in a foul mood, introspective, troubled, and heartsick. Losing Gable and Alex Larson had affected him in ways he could not have predicted, and the specter of dispatching Nash into Russia with such slapdash cover troubled him. With DIVA in imminent danger, the outlook was even bleaker. He told Forsyth that he thought Nash might not make it even close to DIVA: She would be in the company of ministers, service chiefs, VIP guests, and the president himself, plus ample security. How could Nash or the Polish woman get near her?

"Maybe Agnes can follow her into the ladies room," said Forsyth, half joking.

"Perhaps, but I anticipate operational ruin compounded by the possible loss of a star asset and two officers," Benford said.

"Nash is one of the best," said Forsyth helpfully. "He'll get through. The son of a bitch has one advantage: he loves her."

Benford snorted. "I assume it did not escape your notice that he seemed to have kept in contact with your former WOLVERINE, what's her name? Agnes, yes, well I suppose there's no reason why this infernal case cannot continue as a ménage à trois."

It did not help Benford's state of mind when he received word that he had this afternoon to brief the three candidates a final time before one was selected as the formal nominee by POTUS and appeared before Congress to be confirmed. The process would be faster than usual, because the president was eager to install his hand-chosen replacement at Langley to begin rolling back what he considered the hyperactive operational focus of CIA under the late Alexander Larson. Acting Director Farrell had it right: CIA should be an information-gathering organization, eschewing dirty tricks, and assassinations, and whatever other skullduggery they always seemed to be hatching. Farrell, in fact, had been promised the Deputy Director slot—everyone in Washington knew he was an obsequious toad prone to vapors, but as deputy, he would be an effective ideologue who would advocate for what he described as a more human face of espionage. "Like Mikhail Suslov in short pants," said Forsyth, referring to Brezhnev's hard-line politburo chief in the seventies.

As usual, scheduling conflicts resulted in the need for three separate briefings, an infernal nuisance. Forsyth and Westfall would backbench the sessions, to provide moral support. Briefing Senator Feigenbaum and her mealy-worm butler Farbissen would be a matter of gritting teeth and weathering the senator's scorn and her doughy aide's ready accusations of being lied to. Briefing Admiral Rowland would be a matter of getting through a polite if impenetrable indifference to intelligence matters: if it wasn't naval science, she didn't seem interested. Ambassador Vano had seemed appreciative of prior briefings while clearly understanding no more than half of what was being said to him.

Benford spent the morning locked in his office. Even Forsyth couldn't get in to see him. At the first of the afternoon briefings, Forsyth watched with alarm as Benford walked into the room. He was chalk-white and moved slightly bent over, as if in physical pain. A heart attack? Forsyth made to rise, but Benford waved him off. He slowly shuffled the papers in his folder. Before he began briefing the senator he turned to Forsyth and Westfall, leaned close, and whispered. His lips quivered.

"I ask that both of you make no comment or otherwise display even a mote of surprise or approbation when I brief the candidates. None. Can you do that?"

"What are you going to do?" hissed Forsyth. "What's the matter with you?"

"I intend to sell my soul."

"What does that mean?" said Westfall. "You can't bullshit these candidates."

"That's not what he means," said Forsyth, in a whisper, divining the truth in a flash. "He's going to save Dominika."

"Senator, I have a new development to brief you on, one that I'm sure you and Mr. Farbissen will find fascinating," said Benford. They both looked bored.

"Another intelligence failure?" said Farbissen. "What's that make it, a major fuckup a year, on average?"

"One a year would be a *good* year," said Senator Feigenbaum. Benford smiled.

"Nothing like that," he said briskly. "It's what we call a crash dive. Something quite urgent."

"Yeah, everything you guys do is urgent," said Farbissen.

"I'm sure you'll be interested to know an important asset of ours in Moscow has discovered the identity of a highly placed mole in the US government, but unfortunately cannot transmit the mole's identity due to technical difficulties. We've sent a case officer to Russia to exfiltrate the asset—code-named HAMMER—to report the mole's name so we can arrest the traitor." Benford heard Forsyth's chair squeak, but didn't dare look at him.

"How do you intend to get your man into Russia to meet this HAMMER?" asked the senator, calmly, no alarm on her face. "And how do you propose to spirit him out of the country?" Her decades on intel committees made her familiar with the Game, even though she despised and derogated the Agency with vigor.

"HAMMER will be among the guests at a large reception at President Putin's Black Sea estate," said Benford. "Gaining access will be relatively easy for our case officer, certainly easier than doing this in Moscow. Exfiltration will be accomplished by a JAVELIN aircraft, a powered stealth glider. The numerous valleys and plains in the area are more than adequate for STOL aircraft to get in and out." The short-takeoff-and-landing aircraft was all hogwash, but it sounded good.

"And where is this Russian mole?" said Farbissen, somewhat agitated, whether from fear or congenital disdain was not apparent.

"We do not know," said Benford. "All we know is that he has been active for some time."

"I thought you were supposed to be some kind of legendary mole hunter," said the senator.

"Maybe he's lost his touch," said Farbissen, looking at Benford. "Maybe it's time to turn in your badge."

From the back, Forsyth saw Benford's hands shaking. God, what a gamble. What a choice. Deliberately setting up Nate as the ultimate bait. Not even the conspiratorial Russians would consider something so extreme to be a counterintelligence trap. Sacrificing a case officer—for instance by abandoning him behind the Iron Curtain—to save a blown agent had happened before during the Cold War, but an officer had *never purposely been set up* to protect a source. They both saw it; Benford's face showed he was trading his soul to sell out Nate. Forsyth knew this was a mortal decision for Simon, one made without the possibility of redemption or exculpation. We all of us are expendable, Benford had once told Nash. Today, that included Benford's devoir and conscience.

The same briefing was given two more times with the other candidates, each with different code names, the classic barium-enema trap. VADM Rowland was told the CIA asset Nate would contact and rescue was encrypted CHALICE. She was calm and collected at the news, bored as usual. Ambassador Vano was told the agent was encrypted CHRYSANTHEMUM, but his blank stare prompted Benford to mercifully tell him the asset was also known as FLOWER. *If he is the mole*, thought Benford, looking at that handsome profile powered by room-temperature IQ, *the Russians must be better than we thought.*

For the three CIA officers, the afternoon was an interminable bad dream, a sightless stumble through a hazy swamp, each of Benford's compounded lies rendered more bitter by betraying Nate. Admiral Rowland once perked up at mention of the JAVELIN stealth glider, and asked technical questions about the airframe, the answers to which Benford promised to supply. He silently wondered whether Westfall could research gliders and invent a variant they could call JAVELIN. By then he hoped it wouldn't matter.

As Benford briefed at the front of the room, Westfall leaned over to Forsyth, his own face ashen and eyes wide. "Why not tell Nash ahead of time?" he whispered. "Give him advance warning."

Forsyth shook his head. He knew how Benford thought. "The surprise has to be genuine," said Forsyth. "The Russians will be looking for false notes. Besides, Simon knows Nash would have gone in anyway, witting or not. He'll figure it out in the first ten seconds and sell the deception."

"And what happens to Nate?" whispered Westfall. He resented this fall-on-your-sword macho bullshit with these ops maniacs. To deliberately do this to Nate was beyond comprehension to Lucius.

"They'll arrest him, interrogate him, and throw him in prison. Knock him around a little, nothing bad. I know Simon will persuade Department of Justice to offer MAGNIT and SUSAN in a swap for him. The Russians like to get their people back. Saves face. Nash'll be home for Christmas."

"Seems like we shouldn't have to resort to kamikaze missions," said Westfall, staring at the floor.

Forsyth gripped his arm. "Whichever of these esteemed candidates is MAGNIT—my money's on that bottom-feeder Farbissen—one thing's for sure: they will not fail to report this operation to Yasenevo, to save their own ass."

"What about the Polish woman, Agnes?" said Westfall. "The Russians will really work her over."

Forsyth shook his head. "You noticed Benford didn't mention her during his briefings? The Russians won't be expecting another ringer. Nash and Agnes will be arriving with a gaggle of new art students from Warsaw, part of the restoration crew rotation. The Russians will sniff at the students and Agnes, but with Nate in the bag they'll have only one concern: who among the two hundred guests is the US-run mole. The cryptonym the interrogators use will tell us who MAGNIT is. HAMMER, CHALICE, or FLOWER."

"And how do we find out which?" said Westfall. "How do we know this'll work? Benford's previous bait stories never got a rise out of the Russians."

Forsyth shrugged. "Not every trap catches a bear," he said. "The mole doesn't report it, no one in Moscow believes it, they decide to wait before acting. Could be anything."

"And getting the name back?"

"DIVA puts a note in the USV," said Forsyth. *Shit house of cards*, thought Westfall. *Selling Nate out for a name.*

"Nate's back by Christmas?" said Westfall, doubtful.

"Safe and sound," said Forsyth. "And DIVA will start reporting the inside scoop on the SVR and the Kremlin right from her director's desk."

"Unless a wheel comes off," said Westfall. Forsyth noticed the young analyst was using more operational slang. And he was also correct: *unless a wheel comes off.*

———

In Moscow, Gorelikov was busy trying to improve MAGNIT's chances: He had set in motion two minutely subtle *activniye meropriyatiya*, active measures, using two agents from the stable of innumerable assets used by the Kremlin for Putin's political-influence campaigns around the world. These were favored tactics during the Cold War to spread the communist cant. Now they were designed to sow discord among those who sought to weaken Putin's kleptocracy. Active measures were most effective when the disinformation was woven into a macramé of truth, which effectively obfuscated the deception. The toolbox was diverse: influence elections, disparage opposition leaders, disrupt inimical allegiances, support friendly despots, circulate disinformation, leak forgeries, and, in extreme cases, use people like Iosip Blokhin to eliminate the most tenacious enemies of the State. The attempted assassination of a Polish-born Pope in 1981 who was encouraging the Solidarity movement in the Gdansk shipyards was an extreme example of an active measure.

A tame journalist named Günter Kallenberger—on Gorelikov's payroll for decades—from the German investigative magazine *Der Spiegel* asked for an interview with Senator Feigenbaum's staff chief, Rob Farbissen. Aware of Kremlin assessment data on the fatuous staffer, Kallenberger asked Farbissen if the senator became DCIA, wouldn't Farbissen surely become executive director, or perhaps deputy director for administration? If that was the case, what changes or reforms within CIA could allied intelligence agencies expect in the coming years? It was a classic journalist's open-ended question, in Russian a *lovushka*, a deadfall, a snare, designed to give Farbissen enough rope to hang himself (and his patron). The voluble Farbissen did not disappoint. He railed to Kallenberger that CIA had evolved from a postwar collection of has-been Nazi hunters to a futile and undisciplined anachronistic agency prone to intelligence failures, and unable to collect on relevant intelligence gaps. Instead, CIA spent its time and resources trying to suborn Russian code clerks in South America in what he called sex traps. The firestorm that erupted in Congress and Europe, and in the indignant editorials in RIA Novosti and TASS went on for a week, at the end of which Senator Feigenbaum withdrew her name from consideration for DCIA. Farbissen left the senator's staff and became a lobbyist on the hill for the ACA, the American Coal Association.

Concurrent with Farbissen's scandalous interview, an article in the *Business Standard* financial newspaper in New Delhi reported a new mineral-supply contract signed with Belarus president Alexander Lukashenko and

IPL, Indian Potash Limited. The article described the chaotic practices of Belarus's state-owned fertilizer group Belaruskali, which in 2013 caused global prices to collapse, as they had in 2008 and 2009. A sidebar—drafted by Gorelikov and obligingly run by a *Business Standard* editor on Kremlin retainer—mentioned that American businessman and former US ambassador to Spain, the Honorable Thomas Vano, had been a member of an international commodities consortium that had benefitted from insider tips from the Belarus government to invest in and then short volatile mineral futures. The sidebar piece finished by estimating that the insider trading had netted Ambassador Vano's group $1.5 billion in 2013 alone, profits realized while he was a US government employee, a serious ethics violation. The facts were fudged: no insider tips were given (who in Minsk would confirm that?) and the figure of $1.5 billion was a fabrication, but uncheckable, giving the further impression of currency sheltering and tax evasion. Though Vano blithely did not withdraw his name as a candidate for DCIA, the ambassador's nomination was quickly characterized as "implausible" by the *Wall Street Journal*, and *vozmutitelnyy*, scandalous, by Channel One Russia in Moscow.

In two deft moves, Gorelikov had eliminated the other candidates as realistic contenders. He knew that this theoretically helped the mole hunters at Langley—they'd now be free to concentrate on vetting Admiral Rowland—but he was not worried. The admiral had no detectable flaws in her cover, and the final decision to confirm was imminent. For all CIA knew, one of the failed candidates could be the mole; the Kremlin would swallow its disappointment, and would direct their asset to an equally sensitive position elsewhere in Washington.

In Headquarters, Benford likewise recognized that the obvious hatchet jobs on Feigenbaum and Vano put the spotlight on Admiral Rowland, *but that was exactly the problem.* In the world of counterintelligence, especially with the Russians, nothing was ever as it seemed. Feigenbaum's and Vano's apparent disqualification might actually be an insidious red herring to divert attention—like fake defector Yurchenko sent to protect Ames. The goal would be that while Benford wasted time looking under Rowland's bed, the real mole would be free to burrow somewhere else: the NSC; the Pentagon; the West Wing. One hope remained. The Center didn't know about Benford's final trap.

Admiral Rowland did not have an adventure vacation scheduled for at least six months. Next spring, it was going to be Argentina: she planned to hike in Patagonia, because she had discreetly done research on a nonattributable Homeland Security library computer downtown—it was already brimming with downloaded porn—and had read about Crocodilo Club in Barrio Norte in Buenos Aires that catered to girls. She wasn't sure what that meant exactly, but it sounded interesting. She'd meet Anton in BA and have fun.

Then she read about Argentine wine. And the food. There was an Argentine food truck in downtown DC that served delicious *choripanes*, mini grilled-chorizo sandwiches with onions and *chimichurri* sauce. If the little girls in Buenos Aires were as tasty as the street food, she would enjoy herself. But the heady prospect of meeting an exotic Latina lover was overlaid by the shock of this afternoon's CIA briefing.

This was trouble, bad trouble, and she needed to talk to Uncle Anton. Not to the Center. Not to the Kremlin. Not to Moscow. She needed Anton. If that unkempt troll Benford at CIA was telling the truth, in a couple of days a CIA case officer would be talking to someone named CHALICE who, somehow, knew that Audrey Rowland, vice admiral, US Navy, was spying for the Russians, and had been spying for more than a decade. She had to tell Anton, which meant she had to call SUSAN to pass the message. That evening, she dug her clunky Line T encrypted phone out of the hinged concealment compartment in the arm of a couch in her bedroom—a crappy piece of furniture delivered by the GRU years ago. Big as a brick, it was a location-spoofing FIPS140-2 encrypted secure phone whose software obfuscated phone position by canceling the device's connection to the nearest cell towers while permitting the call to go through using more-distant towers. A call, therefore, from Audrey in Washington to SUSAN in New York caromed first to Las Vegas, then bounced through Traverse City, Michigan, to SUSAN's New York City phone, which would use similar circuitous routing through Cheyenne, Wyoming, to Tarpon Springs, Florida, and back to Audrey in DC.

SUSAN did not answer her special phone in three separate tries—there was no capability for leaving messages, too insecure—so Audrey had to stew all night and finally connect with an irascible SUSAN the next morning. What the hell was she doing? This was an emergency. Using her admiral's voice, Audrey ordered her hot-shit handler to send a flash message to Anton about the imminent infiltration of a CIA officer at Putin's reception to connect with a spy code-named CHALICE, got that? CHALICE, and he's going to fly the mole out on a stealth glider, no he didn't say from where, but this CHALICE bastard knows my name, and once they tell Langley, I'm finished. Do you understand? And I want to meet you in Washington soonest: I've got new information on cavitation propulsion tests, never mind what it is, and more tidbits CIA has been briefing on, about recruitments of Russians, that's right, recruitments, and one more thing, I want to be ready to bug out if the CIA guy gets CHALICE out of Russia, yeah, well fuck authorization, because if they arrest me I'm going to tell them about a magazine staffer in New York working for Vladimir Vladimirovich, then you'll be swimming the Rio Grande yourself to get to Mexico. You have all that? Do it now, I don't care what time it is there, the CIA guy may already be eating hors d'oeuvres at the buffet table with CHALICE. And call me back about our meet down here. *Good-bye*.

Audrey Rowland's orderly mind was not panicking, yet, but like any astute scientist she was watching the gauges carefully to determine the degree of danger and to identify the propitious moment to contemplate flight. This was not the first time there had been a security scare in her twelve-year career as a spy. She'd had long discussions with Anton about tradecraft, spying, and the mental discipline required of a mole collecting, storing, and passing sensitive secrets from within a large organization. The intricate discipline appealed to her quantitative brain. The US Navy had many layers of security designed to protect secrets, but no navy counterintelligence system could conceive of, much less make allowances for, a three-star admiral and director of ONR operating as a clandestine source for the Kremlin. NCIS, the Naval Criminal Investigative Service, was ill equipped to detect the tradecraft nuances of a Russian-run mole. But it was the little gray rumpled men like that annoying Simon Benford at CIA who were the real danger. Audrey thought it ironic that the famous little mole hunter himself had delivered the warning that would keep Audrey out of trouble. If she was selected for DCIA, the irony would continue.

She thought back to her recruitment at the Metropol in Moscow, and wondered what had become of the stunning Russian girl who had wet her chin between her thighs so long ago. Certainly *she* was not a three-star admiral now. That sexy evening had started the whole thing: Audrey began spying as a way to boost her career, specifically to show the son of a bitch she called daddy that she could match, no surpass, his own career in the navy. As the stripes on her sleeve multiplied, Audrey was confirmed in her belief that she had made the right decision regarding the Russians, despite the initial circumstances. Now she was in danger. Her orderly mind contemplated the odds, and she felt no fear, confident in her own intellect and in Anton's skill.

Audrey was ready to leave the navy, and if she became DCIA it would mean two or three or four more years of bureaucratic torpor, spectacular gains for Moscow, the collapse of CIA, and continued annuity payments from the Kremlin, after which Audrey Rowland would disappear, and retire to a beach somewhere with hot and cold running *chocito* in sarongs and braided hair. *She wouldn't have to be alone anymore.*

But first she had to survive this imminent threat to her liberty, and trust that SUSAN was at this moment speaking to Anton, who in turn was alerting security at Putin's compound, and that both the CIA officer and his confounded mole would be arrested and eliminated so her secret would remain safe forever.

ARGENTINE *CHORIPANES*

Split and toast small rolls on a griddle until brown. Cut chorizo in half, then in half lengthwise, and grill until caramelized and charred on both sides. Grill sliced white onions until caramelized and finish with a splash of balsamic vinegar. Put chorizo and onions on toasted rolls and slather with *chimichurri* sauce. (Process shredded carrots, parsley, vinegar, red pepper flakes, garlic, olive oil, salt, and pepper in a blender into a thick sauce.)

35

Gall, Not Cheek

SUSAN's tardy relay of MAGNIT's urgent warning about the CIA officer who would attempt to penetrate the president's swanky party to contact the mole known as CHALICE was received in the Center, but was further delayed by the laborious special handling required of all incoming messages from illegals. It finally was forwarded from Yasenevo to the communications unit at Cape Idokopas, where it was read by Gorelikov with a mixture of alarm and triumph. He made a hurried inquiry with the security office: they still had time; the new art-restoration shift from Poland was arriving the next morning. He immediately convened an emergency executive meeting in the secure room of the commo shack with General Egorova of the SVR, Bortnikov of the FSB, and Patrushev of the Security Council.

"The *szloba*, the gall of these Americans, attempting this at the president's compound," said Bortnikov behind his blue halo. "I could understand it in Moscow, business as usual, but this is too much."

Patrushev had no time for games. His own yellow halo of deceit and cruelty shimmered in the small gray room. He pointed his Cossack's nose at Gorelikov. "*Gall*, not cheek. What is so complicated?" he said. "When the American arrives with the Polish contingent, it will be a simple matter to arrest him immediately. Let our colleagues here"—he nodded to Dominika and Bortnikov—"arrange a vigorous interrogation, determine the identity of this CHALICE, and settle the matter. The American and his mole can share a cell in the Black Dolphin, in Orenburg."

Gorelikov had his courtier's face on, so as not to offend. "I agree with you wholeheartedly, but if you would please indulge me for a moment." He shot his French shirtsleeves absentmindedly, revealing magnificent cuff links of brushed silver and red coral. "I propose, for your consideration, a discreet alternative to immediate arrest and interrogation, as logical and proper a course of action as it might be. I posit that if we instead let the American roam freely during the three days of the president's reception, under constant and strict surveillance, he is likely to attempt contact and unknowingly lead us directly to the individual we seek, the mole CHALICE."

Bortnikov, whose FSB surveillance teams were prodigious, liked the idea. More credit for him and his agency if he could bag both the case officer and the mole. Dominika kept her face impassive, but internally she knew this diabolical ambush tactic could blow her out of the water in forty-eight hours. And she knew something else. It would be Nate Nash who would be coming from Washington; she knew him, and she was certain of it. As good as he was on the street, Nate could be kept under strict control by static surveillance following his every move around the presidential compound through long lenses that would be impossible to spot. If he made a beeline toward her, convinced that he was black, the game would be over.

Something didn't make sense. How had MAGNIT learned of Nate's mission? And where had the cryptonym CHALICE sprung from? She guessed the answer, but could not believe it. She had been doing this long enough, and knew Benford well enough, to come to the unspeakable conclusion that this was what the Americans called a barium enema, designed to flush out MAGNIT by using Nate as *primanka*, an expendable lure, dangling bait. A desperate gambit, sacrificing him.

How ironic it would be if Nate unwittingly was the engine of her compromise? Just about as ironic as what Dominika knew she had to do now. *Gently*, she thought, *stay objective and kill this idea without offending Gorelikov or alerting the other two wet-muzzled wolves at the table.*

She sat up straight, folded her elegant hands on the table in front of her, and looked them all in the eyes. "It is an inspired plan," she said. "But as you all realize, the enemy of tradecraft is unnecessary complication. If something can go wrong on the street, it invariably will. You all know this. I do not wish to give the impression of negativity, but the list of potential pitfalls is significant."

Dominika took a breath. "CIA case officers trained in denied-area operations are resourceful. This man coming tomorrow could elude our coverage and foil our plans. He could use disguises. He could distract our surveillance units while an unknown second confederate accomplishes their mission. He could have some infernal technical device—we all know how the Americans rely on their little black boxes—that could allow him to make contact with CHALICE under our noses, without ever approaching him. And worst of all, the CIA officer could detect coverage, abort his mission, and escape in the stealth aircraft MAGNIT reported was part of the plan, leaving us looking like fools, and worse off than before. Admittedly, gentlemen, these are all remote possibilities, but they are possibilities. Can we afford to risk coming up empty-handed?"

That is why I'm trying to persuade you tarakany *you cockroaches, to arrest the man I love with all my heart, and allow me to be present when you beat him, and watch him thrown in prison to rot until he dies or is broken and ruined, because there's nothing else I can do.*

To the annoyance of Gorelikov and Bortnikov, Patrushev nodded. "I agree with Egorova," he said. "Immediate arrest and interrogation. That is the only way to mitigate the risk. Are we all agreed? Or should we consult with the president?" No one wanted that—not in Putin's current frame of mind—so it was agreed: the CIA officer would be arrested immediately. Dominika breathed a sigh of relief as her heart went cold and died.

———

Nate and Agnes flew on LOT, the Polish airline, from Warsaw to Bucharest, and then to Odessa. Three hungover apprentice art-restoration students from Warsaw were on the same flight. Bored officials at Customs and Immigration stamped Nate's alias Polish passport without looking at it. Another hour flight on a Ukraine International Embraer 170 had them standing at the front portico of Gelendzhik Airport, waiting for the van that ferried staff and workers to Cape Idokopas. The soft subtropical breeze stirred Agnes's skirt, and they smelled the salt air from the sea. Nate wore wire-rimmed glasses, jeans, and a T-shirt with "Warszawa" in letters across his chest, and they both carried small duffels. A surly Russian driver appeared in a wheezing UAZ minivan, and took them all careering down the M4 to Svetly, where they turned off the highway and got onto a meandering two-lane blacktop that wound its way downhill through pine-forested valleys scarred by limestone cliffs, steeply down toward the water past paltry villages at lonely crossroads—Divnomorskoye, Dzhankhot, Praskoveevka—and finally through the compound gate with a *militsiya* car on the side of the road, and more slowly now, past guardhouses and military jeeps parked in the trees, to stop at the front steps of a large dormitory-type building amid the pines. In the distance, the roof of the massive main palace loomed above the treetops. Agnes was calm and collected, Nate marveled; she was cooler than he was.

They lined up in front of a table to register, surrender their passports, and received security badges on lanyards for access to the compound and the work sites inside the mansion. A militiaman told a Polish student to put out his cigarette, and the young man pretended not to understand, blowing smoke in his general direction. The militiaman stepped toward the student to knock the cigarette and some teeth out of his mouth, but the subaltern barked at him in Russian to step back and "take his position." Nate's scalp moved as he saw other militiamen standing attentively, edging in, and looking specifically at him. Nate made an instant calculation about knocking a guard over and dashing for a door or window. But where would he go? There were hundreds of protective militia and Special Forces troops, plus two hundred SBP (Presidential Security Service) agents on the seventy-four-hectare compound. And God knew where Dominika was. He couldn't sprint for her dacha and hide under her bed.

The Russians' efficiency was chilling. How had his cover been undermined so quickly? Did this mean there was another mole inside Langley who knew about his mission? That could only mean Forsyth, Westfall, or that cue-ball maniac from maritime branch. Impossible. There was nothing that the Russians could have picked up from his alias documents, nothing about his Polish Art Academy cover story. Was it possible he was recognized from his first tour in Moscow? Some misstep at Customs in Odessa? No, not even the FSB were that good. Whatever the reason, he understood what was going to happen.

He leaned close to Agnes and whispered. "Something's wrong, I think I'm blown. Stay away from me and stick with the students."

Agnes didn't budge, didn't blink; she was every inch the top pro. "I'll get clear and get you out if there's any trouble," she said. She looked at him with blazing eyes.

Nate snarled at her out of the side of his mouth while stepping away from her. "You'll do no such thing. We rehearsed this. You lie low and work with the restoration team for two weeks, then fly home. Stay away from DIVA and her dacha, and stay off the beach. She knows enough to send MAGNIT's name out in the boat. Understand?"

Agnes nodded. "I'll follow your orders, but there's one more thing," she said. "I love you." Nate looked at her for a long beat, trying to say it with his eyes. That white forelock, Jesus. He turned away.

The subaltern stood up, the signal. It was time. As the surprised students looked on sullenly, two militiamen stepped behind Nate and grabbed him tightly above the elbows, spun him around, and walked him through a door at the end of the dormitory lobby. He didn't resist, husbanding his strength. Agnes didn't look at him, and the last thing he saw as he was pushed through the door was that no one had seized her. *Thank Christ.* Nate was led down a manicured gravel path through a dense stand of pines, their fresh scent competing with the salt air. Nate thought he could see glimpses of water through gaps in the trees, but the militiamen yanked him straight whenever he looked to the side. At the end of the path, quite alone, deep in the forest, stood an ornate Russian log cottage with decorative fringe tracing the steep gables, a pair of casement windows with rustic diagonal muntins and a polished wooden door with wrought-iron hinge straps and a grated speakeasy. *Fucking Hansel and Gretel.* The guards opened the door and pushed him into a deep armchair upholstered in dark-green fabric. Nate looked around the spartan living room with a single couch and two end tables. A framed picture of Lenin hung on the wall in front of Nate, the unsmiling portrait of him while in exile, around age fifty, with the piercing stare, the goatee, the straight mouth without a trace of mirth or mercy.

The bare logs on the walls and along the pitched ceiling were light-colored and polished, their gleam lighting up the room in the afternoon light. This was a secluded guesthouse, or perhaps the personal quarters of some caretaker. The two militiamen stood on either side of the armchair and pushed him back down into the chair when he tried to get up, apologetically saying *toileta.* He wanted to look around the cabin for escape points, and to test the degree of free movement allowed him, but for now, no dice. Nate knew this was going to be hard or easy, a sophisticated interrogation or a basic police-level interview. He expected the latter, for starters. A lot was going to depend on his attitude, the mood and skill of the interrogators, what exactly they wanted to know, and the urgency of their inquiries. He planned on sassing them, pissing them off, and holding out for as long as possible.

Early in training, Nate had attended classes in interrogation—resisting it, not inflicting it. The instructor, an Argentine operator—with a perpetually flicking eyelid and improbably named Ramón Lustbader (named by his mother after silent-screen star Ramón Novarro) with an attitude worse than Gable's—had told the class that the bottom line was that everyone eventually gave it up; it was just a matter of how long you put up with the pain or drugs. Classically, the goal was to hold out forty-eight hours, an artificial period ostensibly long enough for a blown asset or a compromised network of assets to exfiltrate, but that was largely outdated film noir, Cold War theatrics.

In actuality, Ramón said, it was the pain of physical punishment—and the ancillary techniques of sleep deprivation, starvation, and extremes of hot or cold—that broke prisoners. The mysterious and feared psychotropic drugs such as ethanol, sodium thiopental, amobarbital, and scopolamine that reportedly could compel prisoners to talk, and that could, after prolonged use, plunge the human brain to the cognitive level of one of the lesser apes, in reality did not compel subjects to begin blurting the truth. Rather, these drugs unlocked memories, reduced inhibitions, and heightened suggestive responses that could, in the hands of a skilled interrogator, prompt the blurting of desired information. Common sleeping gas at the dentist, nitrous oxide, had the same effect.

Lustbader's eyelid pulsed as he lectured the class. "If you focus on a thought or person, or on an external object, really obsessively focus, the mind can effectively counteract the effects of the interrogation drugs that coincidentally quickly spike in effectiveness, then dissipate dramatically. Coming out of it feels like rising to the surface after a deep dive. The euphoria at that stage, the rush back to the light, is the danger period where the ebullient subject is most likely to be susceptible to elicitation." He looked at the trainees who were dreaming of future glories in the field, or thinking about lunch. "Unless they want to turn you into a gibbon monkey—though I suspect some of you in this class are already halfway there—they cannot top you off with more drugs for another twelve hours, without risking harm."

None of the students ever dreamed they would in the course of their careers have to recall Ramón's words.

——————

When SUSAN sent the encrypted flash message detailing MAGNIT's verbal report about a CIA case officer infiltrating the compound to contact an American-handled mole, code-named CHALICE—a mole who somehow knew the closely held identity of Admiral Audrey Rowland—Gorelikov was amazed. The tenacity of the Americans to recruit sources deep inside the corridors of the Federation never seemed to abate. Unmasking this CHALICE was not going to be easy. As much as Gorelikov had run MAGNIT meticulously as his own asset recently, there were an infinite number of potential leaks and points of entry into the case: a dozen GRU handlers from the early years, twice as many supervisors, records clerks, the Security Council staff, and technical experts evaluating MAGNIT's voluminous reporting. But none of these people was on the VIP guest list for the Cape Idokopas weekend gala. The two hundred guests were service chiefs, ministers, and the slobbering *siloviki* around the president. But who knew about MAGNIT? Bortnikov of FSB, that idiot from the GRU, the president. But that is not how secrets are lost: mistresses hear things, people get drunk and brag at a party, the president himself might comment on MAGNIT to an old friend from the Petersburg years, and the bird is out of the cage, impossible to trace back to the source.

There was one thing: Egorova did not know MAGNIT's name, which provisionally exonerated her and meant that Gorelikov could depend on her to assist in the counterintelligence investigation, but there was no time to fiddle with suspects and interviews. CHALICE had to be identified and wrapped up within the next five days. Word from the Washington *rezidentura* was that the derogatory stories had been loudly trumpeted by a US press corps with a taste for political calamity: Senator Feigenbaum and Ambassador Vano were out of the running for DCIA, and VADM Rowland would begin congressional confirmation hearings immediately.

Gorelikov contemplated the audacity of the Americans to send an operations officer into Russia, *to the president's compound*, to brazenly meet an agent to scoop up MAGNIT's true name. The bastard case officer being held in the Gorki cottage in the woods was the key: the identity of CHALICE had to be ripped from his throat. Gorelikov had quickly assembled three experts in interrogation methods: a doctor from Moscow State University who specialized in psychotropic drugs; a psychologist from the Serbsky State Scientific Center for Social and Forensic Psychiatry; and a behavioral scientist from Section 12 of Line S in SVR, the illegals directorate. Meanwhile, the honored party guests were arriving by limousine, shuttle bus, or personal helicopter, each according to their place on the food chain. And one of them was CHALICE. Gorelikov frantically summoned Egorova, and briefed her on the situation, and together they hurried through the woods to the cottage. Egorova was smart and capable. Gorelikov saw the color drain from her face as she instantly realized the imminent danger to MAGNIT.

———

Dominika's heart was pounding in her chest as she walked down the path to the cottage with Gorelikov. She knew the American who had been captured *had* to be Nate. Just had to be. *You pushed the exfil signal to get a reaction, and you got one,* she thought. But trying to break into the compound? She knew Nate was brash, but what was Benford thinking? Now she had to supervise the interrogations, her own exposure and ruin one croaking confession away. Anton was frantic to protect MAGNIT, who Dominika was now 100 percent certain was Admiral Rowland. No more hunches. Dominika had read the daily summaries circulated from the Americas Department: Rowland was being confirmed *this week* as next Director of CIA and would surely read Dominika's name as a CIA asset *the week after.* With Nate in custody, Dominika had one option left: she'd have to send Rowland's name back to Benford in that crazy drone speedboat—if they'd send it—that would be on the beach tomorrow night. She had no idea if the information would get to Langley in time.

Her heart fell when she saw him, but if he noticed her in the now-crowded, overheated cottage, he gave no indication. Three experts, five guards (three militiamen and two SBP), Dominika, Gorelikov, and a stenographer were all squeezed into the room. Bortnikov was expected momentarily; this technically was an internal security matter that belonged to FSB.

Nate was in an armchair, wearing wire-rimmed glasses and a ridiculous T-shirt, being talked to by one of the pros from Moscow. The doctor from the Serbsky Institute—his yellow halo hinted at duplicity—was leaning close, a paternal hand on Nate's knee, talking to him in English in a soft voice, which Dominika could barely hear. She made out phrases "futile effort," "early release," and "return home." Dominika sat in a straight-backed chair slightly behind the armchair, out of Nate's line of sight. Anton paced the length of the little living room, looking impatiently at Nate and the doctor, until Dominika grabbed him softly by the arm and made him sit down. The elegant and phlegmatic Gorelikov was a nervous wreck. Hearing Nate's voice for the first time was a knife blade in Dominika's heart.

"Doc, you're either going to have to give me a happy ending, or take your hand off my knee." The doctor sat back and smiled. He was the chief psychologist from the Serbsky Institute, the clinic where dissidents are evaluated and remanded to psychiatric wards instead of Siberian gulags.

"I appreciate your sense of humor," said the doctor, who had snow-white hair and one eye higher in its socket than the other, which made him look like a Dover sole. "But you're in serious trouble, Mister . . . ; forgive me, I don't know your name."

Nate smiled. "I didn't offer it," he said, holding out his hand. "Nathan. Nathan Hale." The stenographer scribbled furiously, but none of the Russians knew who that was. After traces were run, they'd all get a lesson in the American Revolution. Gorelikov stood up and signaled his impatience. The fish-eyed doctor leaned forward again.

"A pleasure to make your acquaintance, Mr. Hale," he said. "But I must now ask you to answer my questions. Your plan has been foiled. Absolutely nothing can come of it. Your cooperation will be viewed favorably by the relevant authorities, including at the highest levels. We can avoid any unpleasantness, and you will be returned home without delay."

"What highest levels?" said Nate. "And what sort of unpleasantness? Just so I can inform *my own* authorities, at the highest levels, of course." Dominika closed her eyes. Nate's smart mouth would be his undoing—and hers.

"Whom were you sent here to meet?" said the doctor brusquely. "We know a great deal. In a matter of hours we will know your true name and a summary of your career. I sincerely hope it was more illustrious than this debacle." Dominika knew the technique: belittle the subject, impress him with Russian omniscience, take away hope, and then give a little back. Hard-soft, push-pull.

"If you know so much," said Nate, "then you know I'm here to work on the art-restoration project and take a look at the compound."

"What did you expect to do on the compound?" asked the doctor.

Nate shrugged. "The usual. Take latitude, longitude, GPS coordinates. So we can bomb it later."

The doctor slapped Nate's face, losing his cool. "Who is CHALICE?" he yelled. "We know all about your ill-fated plan."

"I never heard the crypt CHALICE in my life," said Nate, his cheek red. He knew instantly that he was at the end of a barium enema concocted by

Benford and that the answer was already here: CHALICE. But now it had to get back to Langley. Maybe he could break out of his room at night and make it to the beach. The doctor nodded to one of the guards, who back-handed Nate on the side of the face. Dominika was about to get out of her chair when the doctor from Moscow State University interceded. His halo was blue. Dangerous.

"It would be counterproductive to strike the subject if I am to use certain compounds. As I'm sure my esteemed colleague knows, punches and slaps will raise his levels of adrenaline and endorphins," he said softly, as if he were berating his counterpart from the insane asylum, who knew only about restraints and shock therapy.

"We're wasting time," Anton said. "What are your compounds? Do they work?"

"Let's see, shall we?" the doctor said to Nate. Dominika held her breath.

The doctor took out three separate syringes, and laid them on the side table. Presumably each syringe contained a different chemical cocktail.

"Just so you don't have Polonium-210 in that little black bag of yours," said Nate. A guard clamped his hands on Nate's right arm, but he shook it off, grabbed the guard's lapel, twisted it, and pulled him forward to sprawl on the floor with a clatter. Two more guards clamped down on Nate's wrist. The doctor lanced one of the needles into the vein on Nate's arm, then stepped back to look at his face. He lifted one of Nate's eyelids and looked at his pupils.

"Now I want you to relax," said the doctor. "The experience will be quite pleasant." Nate felt a hot rush travel up his arm, up his cheeks, then up the back of his skull. He experienced an intense wave of vertigo. The walls of the cottage spun in front of his eyes, and he had a sensation of falling a great distance out of the sky. He held on to the arms of the chair and rode the sensation, while quietly taking deep breaths to oxygenate his lungs. The doctor's voice came to him from a great distance away, as if he were talking through a speaking trumpet.

"Psychotropic drugs are chemical substances that change brain function, and result in alterations in perception, mood, or consciousness," said the doctor. "There is a wide range of compounds; the effectiveness of each depends on the personality of the subject. A period of testing is required to determine which specific drug will be most effective on an individual subject. I have chosen one that normally is quite effective." Anton looked as though he was ready to plunge the needle into the doctor's own neck.

"Perhaps you have not observed that this interrogation must be conducted with extreme urgency," said Gorelikov. "We don't have time for your damn chemical analyses, and we don't have time for this other idiot's moronic attempts to establish the subject's trust, and we don't have time for the luxury of Line S's leisurely records searches. I need a name, the name of one of the two hundred guests now arriving for the president's reception. One name. I need it before the sun goes down tonight. Can any of you *duraki*, mutton heads, accomplish that?" The doctor who had injected Nate stood stiffly with nervous indignation.

"I appreciate the urgency of the situation, you can be sure, comrade. I, therefore, have selected a robust compound of 3-Quinuclidinyl benzilate and amobarbital mixed with a stabilizing derivative of Valium. You will observe the effect on the subject quite soon."

He pulled up a chair, and sat close to Nate, whose head was now lolling, his chin on his chest. The doctor looked nervously at a fuming Gorelikov, leaned close, and started speaking softly.

"Now Mr. Hale, we are going on a pleasant trip, you and me. It will be quite enjoyable. Are you ready? By the way, who is CHALICE?"

———

Nate's furtive deep breathing was just keeping the effects of the drugs from totally swallowing up his head, WHO IS CHALICE? and the room was still spinning but his grip on the armchair helped, as did digging his fingernails into his palm so he could concentrate on the pain, which became his tenuous hold on to the lip of the cliff, to the real world, *keep breathing*, he was on the edge of the abyss, WHAT IS CHALICE'S NAME? between consciousness and the dreamy state where he might start talking a blue streak, *keep breathing dammit*, think about Benford, *keep your wits about you, Nash*, and he thought about Forsyth, *you're stronger than they are*, and he thought about Gable, *rookie, don't give those fuckers one thing, I'm proud of you*, and he thought about them all, Korchnoi, and Hannah, and Udranka, and Ioana, everybody but Dominika, she doesn't exist, WHO IS CHALICE? and he thought about Agnes two days ago in the hotel room in Warsaw, *keep breathing*, how her hands felt on his cheeks, feel the sensation, remember the sensation, don't let go, and the room spinning and the doctor's voice intruded into his thoughts, friendly, soothing, insistent, WHO IS CHALICE? *don't let go, stay in this room*, his face was hot, and he could feel the sweat running down his cheeks. He looked up, the spinning got worse with his eyes open, but there was the photograph of Lenin looking down at him with those doll black eyes and the goatee unevenly trimmed, and the tight-lipped mouth waiting for Nate to start talking, but I won't talk unless you do, you bastard, and Nate concentrated on those eyes, he locked on them, nothing else, nothing else, and waited for them to blink or move and the more he stared at Lenin's face the stronger he became and he kept staring at the bridge of Lenin's nose, taking in the whole photo, come down off that wall you bastard, come down and take over the interrogation, because the drugs weren't going to work, Nate knew that now his head was clearer, and he kept breathing and the room slowed, and he kept looking at the photograph, and Lenin's eyes blazed with hatred, and Gable's voice told Lenin, *you can go ahead and blink first, you goat fucker, because you're not getting shit from us, and shove your proletarian revolution up your ass*, and Nate kept staring at Lenin's face, expecting the photograph to combust into the fire of Hades and to hear the roar of rage as his will was denied, and suddenly Nate was through the tunnel and his head cleared with an enormous rush, his eyesight crystal clear, noticing the grain of the logs on the wall, a fly on a windowpane, the frayed collar of the doctor, everything was humming and then Gable's words came to him. *"Listen up, rookie, just when things look darkest, they go black."* And Nate took a deep breath, and looked at the doctor. It had been twenty minutes, or three hours, Nate had no clue.

The doctor looked at Nate and knew he had lost him, the drugs were already dissipating in his system—they typically spiked in the first half hour, then faded quickly. The doctor followed Nate's gaze and saw the picture of Lenin and instantly understood that Nate had used the photograph to focus his attention and resist the soporific effects of the drugs. Smart young man, obviously trained. He would have to wait at least twelve hours before another injection might be effective, otherwise an overload of drugs might put the subject too deep and unable to respond from that desired state of drifty half awareness. This American seemed less susceptible; perhaps it was his apparent lack of fear. The doctor looked at Gorelikov and shook his head, as he nervously started packing up his little black bag. Anton turned away in disgust, and Dominika let out a long silent breath.

Alexander Bortnikov of the FSB came through the door to the cottage and looked around. Gorelikov gave him a shrug of impotent rage. Bortnikov walked in front of Nate's chair and stood looking down at him silently. "So nothing seems to have made an impression on our young American friend, eh? You can go," he said, indicating the doctors. "One guard only. If the American moves, damage him considerably." He pointed at the stenographer. "You. Out." He picked up the receiver of the gray telephone on a side table. "*Serzhánt* Riazanov to the Gorki cottage, instantly," said Bortnikov, hanging up. "We will see if we can keep your attention a little more closely," said Bortnikov, his blue halo pulsing.

———

They waited for thirty minutes. Dominika stayed seated behind Nate so their eyes wouldn't meet. Sergeant Riazanov had to dip his head when coming through the door. He must have been over two meters tall, a giant. The first thing Dominika noticed were his hands, which were huge, with bony knuckles and long fat fingers. He had the face of an ogre—*acromegaly* was the medical name of the affliction commonly known as gigantism—with a protruding forehead, jutting lower jaw, pronounced cheekbones, widely spaced camel's teeth, and a massive fleshy nose. Dominika had no doubt that the skulls of Sergeant Riazanov's early relatives had been found in Pleistocene caves in Spain and France. He wore no uniform, but was in mechanic's overalls, zippered in front, short in the sleeves and cuffs, and a pair of enormous combat boots. No insignia, no mark of rank. That he had been summoned by Bortnikov suggested to Dominika that Riazanov was a member of some FSB unit kept in reserve for extraordinary duties, like right now, in this little quaint cottage.

General Bortnikov pointed at Nate with his chin and the ogre stepped up to the armchair, lifted Nate by the armpits, shook him like a rag doll, and threw him back into the armchair. Nate looked up at him in amazement.

"You must've been the tallest kid in your class," said Nate. "You ever get checked for a tumor on your pituitary gland?" Bortnikov, unimpressed, nodded again at Sergeant Riazanov. The sergeant took Nate's left hand in one of his grizzly-bear paws and started bending Nate's little finger back toward his wrist. Nate thrashed wildly, but could not escape the vise grip of the sergeant as the little finger kept bending back, and back, until there was an audible snap and Nate groaned and fell into the armchair holding his broken finger. As the sergeant towered over the doubled-over figure of Nate, General Bortnikov moved slightly closer. Dominika felt faint sitting there. *Those sweet hands*, she thought.

"Do you recall the name of CHALICE now?" he said. "We would like to know his identity rather quickly." Nate held his wounded hand, his little finger dark blue. From behind, Dominika saw Nate's crimson halo steady and bright, fueled by courage and, she knew, his love for her. But how long could he last?

"I'm telling you assholes, I don't know anyone named CHALICE," said Nate. Bortnikov's face flushed with anger.

"Break his left arm," he said to Riazanov. The giant grabbed Nate's left arm, twisted the wrist, held it out away from Nate's body, and swung a massive fist down against Nate's forearm with more force than an iron pipe. The snap of Nate's ulna made Dominika jump. Nate screamed and held his shattered arm while bent double in the chair.

"Now, the name of CHALICE," said Bortnikov. "Let's be reasonable. All we require is a name. Sometimes it is easier to write it rather than to actually say it out loud." He took out a pen and a notebook and put them on the arm of Nate's chair with an encouraging smile." You see we've left your right arm and hand alone for the time being so you can write the name," said Bortnikov.

"The hospitality and honor for which Russia is widely known," said Nate, gasping and still bent over. He didn't reach for the pen.

"Let the sergeant help you," said Bortnikov. The giant took the pen and placed it between Nate's index and ring fingers and squeezed, lighting up the ulnar nerve in the hand as the pen ground against the bones. Nate's head went back in agony.

"CHALICE?" said Bortnikov. Suddenly Dominika knew she had to do something, anything. She was the Director of SVR. She got up from her chair, put a reassuring hand on Gorelikov's shoulder, and strode forward.

"Let's stop this display," said Dominika, with vehemence. "I wonder if the three of us could talk outside for a second," she said, indicating Bortnikov and Gorelikov. The senior officers were taken aback, especially at the tone of her voice, and they filed outside onto the little decorative porch of the cottage, leaving Nate with Sergeant Neanderthal. She followed her colleagues out, slammed the front door behind her, and stared at the two startled men.

"What the fuck are we doing?" hissed Dominika. She amped up her indignation. "This is not 1937 with Stalin running amok." She paced up and down the little porch while Gorelikov and Bortnikov followed her with their eyes. Dominika knew both of them were capable of pulling rank on her, and probably would, but she had to get them to stop breaking things on Nate.

"We don't have the luxury of time," said Gorelikov. "If this CHALICE reports the name of MAGNIT, we lose the best asset in the history of Russian espionage." *And probably both your heads*, Dominika thought.

"I know that, Anton," said Dominika. "But what do you intend to do with this American? Break every bone in his body? No SVR officer would be safe in the United States or abroad thereafter. And which one of you would care to explain to the president that an American intelligence officer was willfully killed during interrogation?"

"What would you propose we do about discovering the identity of CHALICE?" said Bortnikov.

"Think about it, gentlemen." Dominika laughed. "We have found moles before. The guest list is manageable. Two hundred suspects is nothing," she said, mock hearty and confident. "We'll be able to cross off a hundred fifty names right away, you both know it, and I know it. The morons who run the Joint-Stock Companies, Russian Railways, or RUSAL state aluminum could never know such secrets. The remaining fifty can be interviewed, or put under surveillance, or electronically monitored. The FSB can handle that easily. Better yet, we can order all the prime suspects to attend a weeklong closed conference—something political like Governance in *Novorossiya*—in Nizhny Novgorod, so there will be no possibility of CHALICE communicating with anyone. By then it will be too late and MAGNIT himself will be able to tell us CHALICE's identity. The mole is removed, MAGNIT is in place, and we initiate the systematic destabilization of CIA and the US government." Dominika made a conscious effort to use the masculine pronoun when referring to MAGNIT.

"And the American?" asked Gorelikov.

Dominika shrugged. "He's a discarded chess piece. For the time being, send him to Moscow and hold him incognito. Not in a prison, but in a remote district—or even a provisional capital, under supervision, house arrest. We keep him for future use: a show trial if we need it; a diplomatic concession; a spy swap. He's not going to get near CHALICE, and the problem will be solved in a week's time." Bortnikov looked at Dominika from under bushy eyebrows.

"General, what you say makes sense. Your facility with operations is apparent. But there is still a risk that we do not find the mole in time. Are you willing to accept responsibility if we lose MAGNIT?"

"I do not even know MAGNIT's true name," said Dominika. "This will work and we will succeed without covering the walls of this ghastly little cottage with blood. Sergeant Riazanov will have to kill and eat a bear tonight instead."

Gorelikov was impressed with his protégé. What she said was astute; it was a clever solution, specifically since he secretly had not approved of the physical aspects of the interrogation. He thought them barbaric. He looked over at Dominika.

"You're sure it's not that you're taken with the handsome American?" said Gorelikov. *Joke or hint?* Anton had always circled around Dominika's loyalty, poking and prodding. It was creepy and ominous, the mentor always testing the protégé.

"You have a point, Anton. Not counting Sergeant Riazanov, he's the handsomest man in that room," said Dominika. Both men laughed, their blue haloes positively shimmering.

DOVER SOLE

Place flour seasoned with salt, pepper, and dill in a shallow dish. Pat boned sole fillets dry, season both sides with salt and pepper, and dredge fish on both sides in the flour. Heat oil in a large skillet, add butter and swirl to combine. When foam subsides, add fillets and cook until golden brown on both sides. For the sauce: Heat drippings from skillet, add butter, and cook until slightly brown, remove from heat and add dry white wine, chopped parsley, lemon juice, and capers. Spoon sauce over fillets and serve immediately.

36

Hussar Condoms

It was 2230, and Dominika walked through her dacha, turning off the lights. She had taken off her party dress and was wearing a satin sleep shirt with snaps down the front. The doors to her upstairs bedroom balcony were open and the gauzy curtains heaved back and forth with the land breeze. Dominika knew she would not be able to sleep, not with Nate handcuffed to an aircraft seat flying back to Moscow, his broken arm and finger haphazardly set in a cast and splint. At least she had stopped the interrogation—for now. It had been a relief that Gorelikov and Bortnikov both had ultimately endorsed her plan of stashing Nate in Moscow and holding him in reserve as a hostage. Once commo with Benford was reestablished, she would inform Langley about Nate's whereabouts, and diplomatic negotiations could commence to retrieve him and return him home.

That unmanned boat was due on the beach below her dacha at midnight tonight, according to the exfiltration plan. Dominika would meet the silent craft, open the hatch, and emplace a thumb drive with a detailed report of the events of the past three weeks, but primarily with the presumed identity of MAGNIT. The mole was US Navy Admiral Rowland; Dominika had approximately five days before the admiral was confirmed as CIA Director. Would Dominika's intel get back to Benford, from the 6th Fleet frigate on patrol in the Black Sea through US NAVEUR in Naples, through the maze of the Pentagon, and onto Benford's desk in that short period of time? She would, of course, address the thumb drive to the immediate attention of Simon Benford, CIA, but the ponderous US Navy bureaucracy was an unknown. Would they react accordingly?

Her mind seethed, trying to calculate all the imponderables of the situation, her concern for Nate, her lack of commo. The opening day of Putin's reception had been lavish, with two more days to go, and with enough food and drink to feed half of Moscow for a year. The bovine wives of the *siloviki*, dressed in outrageous satin and velvet frocks in teal, peach, or tangerine, the height of Soviet haute couture, vainly competed with the lithe trophy wives of the oligarchs in their bodycon minidresses and tanned cantilevered bosoms. The heavyweights could not compare in the sex department, but they held their own at the buffet tables. Gorelikov, Bortnikov, and Dominika had watched the exuberant guests from the sidelines as they milled about, whispering to each other, privately assessing the likelihood that one of them could be the mole. A score of one meant unlikely, a two meant a possible, and a three meant a short-list finalist. Dominika went along with the Star Chamber game with mock enthusiasm and grim determination. Some of the threes were going to have their lives rudely disrupted next week back in Moscow.

Dominika padded downstairs to the dacha's stainless-steel kitchen, took a bottle of champagne out of the refrigerator, and started peeling the foil and wire to pop the cork. A slant of silver moonlight was the only light in the room, and cut diagonally across the marble countertop. The sea breeze picked up a little and the house stirred.

"Do you need help with that cork?" said a female voice. Dominika jumped a foot. A sturdy woman appeared out of the shadows of the kitchen and walked toward the kitchen island. She was dressed in a white T-shirt and black leggings, which did nothing to conceal a prodigious bust and athletic legs. She was Slavic and classically attractive; Dominika thought she might be close to fifty years old, with a dramatic white forelock that started in front and was swept back with the rest of a thick lion's mane of hair. She had a crimson halo of passion—like Nate's—strong and bright.

"Who are you?" said Dominika. "How did you get into this house?" The woman smiled and approached closer, but without any menace.

"As elegant as this villa is," said the woman, "the locks installed are of inferior quality, especially those on the sliding doors. But I suppose you don't have to worry about security here on the compound."

"You are right about that," said Dominika. "In fact, I can summon a security patrol to this house in about ninety seconds."

"I have no doubt of that," said the woman. "Forgive my bad manners, but are you General Egorova?"

"As much as I've enjoyed your unannounced visit," said Dominika, "I believe it's time for me to call security. Who are you?" The woman seemed unfazed. She approached closer and began whispering. She obviously knew about the limitations of audio emplacements in a large room with tall ceilings and cement walls. But this conversation was too dangerous in what Dominika assumed was a bugged space.

"I know you are Egorova, and you are exactly as Nathaniel described you." This situation was too bizarre, insane, implausible. Was this a trap or trick conjured up by Bortnikov? Did he think *she* was a three on the suspect list?

"I'm afraid I know no Nathaniel, and I believe I've asked for your name for the last time." She opened a drawer of the kitchen cabinet and took out a small PSM pistol, favored by senior security service officers and politburo members. She racked the slide back.

"You have every cause to be cautious, but before you shoot me, I'd appreciate a glass of champagne," said the woman. Dominika intuitively knew what this must be: this Polish beauty was from Langley. She poured a glass of champagne for the woman, while holding the pistol in the other hand. Dominika waggled the muzzle, indicating they should walk upstairs. Once in the softly lighted bedroom, Dominika led the woman outside onto the balcony. She held the PSM down by her side and sipped champagne. The sea breeze hissed through the pines and the Black Sea moon hung over the horizon.

"Who are you?" Dominika asked.

"I arrived with Nathaniel posing as an art restoration supervisor," whispered Agnes. "My name is Agnes Krawcyk. Nathaniel was arrested within five minutes of our arrival. I could tell he was surprised. Someone must have given him up."

Dominika sipped at her champagne. "How long have you known this Nathaniel?" she asked, still cautious.

"Only several years," said Agnes. "But I worked during the Cold War in Poland for Tom Forsyth."

"Describe this Forsyth," said Dominika.

"Salt-and-pepper hair, six feet tall, and slender; he wears his reading glasses on the top of his head. Very experienced, amazing operational mind. He brought Nathaniel to Helsinki from Moscow and saved his career. Satisfied?" Her halo was steady, assured. Dominika put the pistol on the ledge of the balcony. This was Nate's wingman, and Benford's clever addition: sacrifice Nate, clear the field, and hope for success. Crazy, but it worked; this woman was here, wasn't she?

"I'm sure your instructions were never to come to this dacha," Dominika said.

"I don't care about the rules anymore," said Agnes. "I want to save Nathaniel. Where is he? Do you know? Is he all right?"

More than professional focus, thought Dominika. *There's a personal dimension here too.* "They were halfway to killing him this afternoon. They broke a finger and his left arm. He resisted a preliminary course of psychotropic drugs. As the Director of SVR, I argued that he should be kept incognito in Moscow, in good condition, to use as a future bargaining chip as developments require. He's already on a plane to the capital."

Agnes put down her glass. "You sent him to Moscow? I can't get to him there. There's no way he can escape."

"I saved his life by sending him to Moscow. What were you going to do, shoot your way into the guardroom, grab Nathaniel, and run for the beach? There are five hundred troops in these woods."

"He might be in one of your prisons for five years," whispered Agnes.

"I'll worry about Nate later," said Dominika. "Right now, you and I need to accomplish one thing. I believe Nate's superiors in Langley arranged a canary trap to determine the identity of a high-placed mole in the United States named MAGNIT. Did Nate tell you any of this? No, he probably didn't know himself. During Nate's interrogation they kept asking about an informant with a code name of CHALICE. I believe that is part of a blue-dye test, a telltale incriminating variant, because I've never heard it before. Do you understand what that is? Do you know the word CHALICE? Forsyth and Benford need to know that variant immediately. The word CHALICE will flag the identity of MAGNIT. Do you understand?" Agnes nodded.

"Tonight you're getting on that drone speedboat, whatever they call it, and you're going to bring back that code name, and deliver a thumb drive with the details. Demand to speak personally to Simon Benford the minute you get on board the navy ship. Directly to Benford at CIA. No one else. Do you understand?" Agnes nodded her head again.

"How can you protect Nate in a Moscow prison?" asked Agnes.

"There's only one thing that's important now," said Dominika, ignoring Agnes's mule-headedness. "CHALICE. Bring that name back to Benford. I'll watch over Nate in Moscow."

———————

The dacha's doorbell rang, a strange cacophony of tubular bells that sounded more like wind chimes. Putting a finger to her lips, Dominika signaled that Agnes should hide in the spacious bedroom closet next to the vast bed. Agnes slipped in and soundlessly pulled the louvered doors closed. Dominika ran downstairs, put Agnes's champagne glass in the cabinet under the sink, and left hers on the counter with half a bottle of champagne. Tugging at the hem of her nightshirt, and fluffing her hair, she walked across the living room to the glassed-in front door.

President Putin was standing under the front entrance lantern, the glow casting shadows under his eyes, nose, and chin, transforming him into a blue-haloed gargoyle, an otherworldly creature on a late-night pop over to visit his new Director of Foreign Intelligence, who was barefoot and dressed in a satin sleep shirt that barely covered her sex, and whose wild hair was tied with a blue ribbon. The satin shirt did nothing to hide the swell of her breasts, or the imprint of her nipples, or the rhythmic flutter of her heartbeat. The president's retinue of bodyguards was clustered on the paved path below, in three or four electric golf carts, watching. In an acid flash, Dominika knew the head of state of the Russian Federation would in ten minutes be between her legs, that this was the inescapable moment—no more creepy frottage during furtive midnight visits—the moment that CIA asset DIVA would be required to sacrifice herself to her chosen role as spy, seductress, and implacable foe of the monster in the Kremlin. She thought of Gable as she felt herself shutting down, closing the internal doors of her emotions, marshaling strength to overcome revulsion. She was moving into full Sparrow mode. She wondered if Gable was looking down from Heaven's cocktail lounge.

"*Dobriy vecher*, Mr. President, good evening," said Dominika. "This is a pleasant surprise. Do you have time for a glass of champagne? I was having one myself." Putin waved his security men away into the darkness after one of them asked if he should check the dacha beforehand. As she poured a glass of bubbly, she noticed the extra wet ring made on the countertop by Agnes's glass, but she smeared it away with her hand, and they clinked glasses and sipped.

"To the quick discovery of the traitor among us," said Putin, and Dominika rolled the champagne around her tongue, savoring the secret.

"The American knows who it is. We will grind it out of him like a peppercorn under our thumb. Bortnikov and Gorelikov briefed me this afternoon on the CIA officer," said Putin. "They described the *bumbling* preliminary interrogation this morning about why he came here and what he knows. They also told me about your proposed solution to the problem, which I found astute and well-timed. Are you enjoying the party?" A typical Putin conversational swerve that, Dominika was convinced, was designed to demonstrate the president's rapidity of mind.

"I told them both we cannot be eliminating our opponents as if we were barbarians," said Putin. *Króme Shútok. Are you kidding?* marveled Dominika. She silently thought of the names of the two-hundred-plus journalists, dissidents, and political activists eliminated since the year 2000 under this president's beneficent reign, not to mention half the civilian population of Grozhny, in Chechnya.

"Thank you for your confidence in me, Mr. President," said Dominika. "I am sure we can discover the American mole from a pared-down list of fifty names. In fact, I was going to suggest that you review the final list—your perspective on individuals will be invaluable." Putin smiled and nodded; he could purge other enemies in the process.

"In five days we will know that name, and all the others," said Dominika, soothingly. Putin had endorsed her plan not to damage Nate, and to keep him in reserve as a bargaining chip. Now he was talking about crushing peppercorns. A faint sound came from upstairs and Dominika was terrified that Agnes thought the coast was clear and was coming back downstairs. Vladimir had heard the noise and was looking up the stairs. *Would the tsar care for a threesome?*

"The breeze from the balcony moves the drapes in the bedroom. Come, I'll show you." Dominika put her glass down, took the president's hand—it was callused because he picked at it—and led him upstairs, making as much racket as possible.

"The view from the balcony is exceptional," said Dominika. "I must thank you again for the use of the dacha." Putin stuck his head out of the sliding doors, glanced at the sea and the moonlight shining on the surface riffled by the land breeze that started after sunset. He came back into the bedroom. He didn't care about moonlight. His blue halo pulsed in time with his heartbeat.

"A handsome view, but not as beautiful as you." Dominika imagined Agnes falling out of the closet, hands over her mouth. *Quiet* sestra, *sister, our tsar is a love poet, don't ruin the moment.*

"Mr. President. Are you always this poetical?" She walked up to him, put her hands on his shoulders, and pressed against him, flattening her breasts on his chest. Their mouths were inches apart. *A thumbnail into his eye. A wristlock to lead him onto the balcony, a mighty heave over the wall, and Russia will be done with you.* Instead, Dominika brushed her lips against his and peeled his T-shirt over his head. The musk deer scent of him came back to her—part gaggy cumin and cinnamon cologne, part day-old armpit and crotch. If it had been Nate, she would have run her chin and lips over every inch of him to inhale his sweetness, but not now. She stepped back and pulled open the top three snaps of her shirt, which hung open, revealing a hint of cleavage (*No. 95, "Keep the banya door slightly open to create more steam"*).

Putin put his hands inside her shirt and ran his fingers around her nipples. "I think in these circumstances we can dispense with 'Mr. President,' " he said. Perhaps to illustrate, he trailed his fingers down Dominika's flat stomach, then lower, running his fingers along her pubis, then pushed up and in. The trained Sparrow stifled a flinch—men were always stuffing their fingers everywhere prematurely, as if they were looking for the light switch—and instead closed her eyes and whispered "Oh, Volodya," the affectionate diminutive of Vladimir. "I do not know what to call you," she whispered, "lest someone overhears our intimacy." *What I'm asking you, you, svinya, is whether you've bugged this whore's cottage.*

Putin laughed. "Not tonight. Don't worry, no one's listening." *Not tonight, how charming. Audio emplacements switched off for tonight.*

Every time he got close to her, he was struck by how beautiful she was. Her blue eyes were mesmerizing, and it was as if she could read minds, a psychic skill he himself believed he possessed. Her lush body triggered his organic covetousness: he wanted to own her, to dominate her, to wrap his fingers in her chestnut hair and drag her across the room, simply to validate the power he had over her. He knew very well she was independent and intelligent, and that her operational accomplishments far exceeded his own tepid overseas KGB career in the eighties in communist East Germany. But that did not matter. His control over others—including trusted friends among the *siloviki*—was based in fear, or money, or family, or simply by bestowing access. With Egorova, it would be different. Putin this evening intended to dominate her with carnality. As a former Sparrow, she would get the message.

Putin shucked off his tracksuit pants as Dominika shrugged off the satin shirt, and flicked off the overhead chandelier, leaving only the soft glow of a small bedside lamp bathing her soft curves in pink light. If Putin saw the silver stiletto scars on her rib cage, he did not mention them; after all, they represented the sacrifices his vassals necessarily made to preserve the *Rodina*, or more precisely, his *Rodina*. Putin whipped the coverlet off the bed and onto the floor like a matador performing the extravagant pinwheel *rebolera* pass of the cape.

Putin then wordlessly placed a red foil pack of Hussar brand condoms on the nightstand for reasons not entirely clear, since he made no move to put one on. These were produced exclusively in Russia after a government decree banned imported American Durex prophylactics, alleging the US product promoted the spread of HIV, a transparent bit of *dezinformatsiya* in retaliation for US sanctions. Hussar condoms were known in Moscow as Russian-roulette rubbers because of their unreliability—never mind their overwhelming odor of petroleum. This shortage of reliable prophylactics had resulted in the appearance of numerous black-market products on the street, including the infamous silver packages of condoms printed with a caricature of the president above the English logo, "I've Got Something to Putin You." Samizdat, *protest materials, had greatly changed since the days of Solzhenitsyn and Sakharov*, thought Dominika. *What does he expect me to do with this?* she wondered. She slid the president's condom package into the nightstand drawer.

He gently pushed Egorova onto the bed on her back, and knee-walked on the mattress closer. He grabbed her ankles and spread them to either side, like haggling drumsticks apart on a roast goose. He saw her face was swollen with desire, her breasts heavy, her nipples distended. No one could fake those responses, not even a Sparrow. He mashed his hands on her breasts, then planted them on either side of her head, and loomed over her, looking at her face. Putin had bedded plenty of women since his divorce from Lyudmila Putina after thirty years of marriage—the gymnast Kabaeva, the skater Butyrskaya, the boxer Ragosina. All of them blond, all of them champion superathletes, but this Egorova was different, somehow more continental, less a Slav broodmare. She was also his new SVR Director, a cool operator who started as a Sparrow, had exposed the traitor Korchnoi, and had killed opponents in the field. She kept her counsel, knew operations, appeared discreet and loyal, and Gorelikov approved of her. Other lovers would appreciate the blue eyes, or the smile, or the charitable spirit, or even the exuberant libidinousness, but Vladimir valued other attributes. He wedged his knees between her legs.

Putin liked to plunge straight in, right away, feeling the pinch of the dry spots, looking for the sharp intake of breath, the wince at the initial plunging penetration. He liked when they gasped like that. Then when the woman had finally wetly flowered open, he favored a measured metronome pace—no jackrabbit sprints for him, not with his judo-damaged disc—pounding his pubic bone hard against the woman's sex to elicit huffing grunts of pleasure at each wet slap. He liked that too, their animal huffs of pleasure. He was in control. Egorova's breasts oscillated with each shock, her head was back, mouth slightly open, breathing through her nose. Vladimir felt he was really giving her a workout—her eyes were clenched closed.

Keep your eyes closed so you won't have to look at his blond moon-pie face or his doughy eunuch's chest she thought; *there* must *be at least one albino—a cousin or nephew—in his family, the genes are there.* At least there was no slobbering into her mouth. In bed with Nate, groaning into each other's mouth while she came was ecstasy, but thank God she didn't have to "Suck on Putin's Tongue," which should be the title of a song by the dissident Russian girl band Pussy Riot. And she knew Russian men of his generation did not do the other, put their mouths down there, and he had been too impatient to ask her to put him in her mouth. Thank God for Russian priggishness.

Putin had put his legs over her spread thighs, pinning her like some animal on the veldt, showing his teeth. *And Nate is on a plane to Moscow, by my own hand, and Agnes is in the closet looking at me through the louvers, fucking this man, watching his* khuy *splitting me apart, and I know she loves Nate too. Will she understand what is happening?*

The wrecking-ball stroke of the tsar of all the Russians never changed, just a steady rhythm devoid of all the heady variations of positions, or pillow talk, without the ecstasies of edging or beads, or what she had seen in Hong Kong with those crazy chakras. The president's blue eyes never left her face, looking for the slightest trace of feigned reaction, which, she was sure, would equate in his mind as *deception*, and the equivalent of disloyalty. Fake an orgasm with Vlad, baby, and you're off his favorites' list. Not even Benford would have calculated that bit of tradecraft.

At Sparrow School they intensely studied (and filmed hundreds of women experiencing) sexual climax, including the physical rhythmic contractions, the psychosomatic euphoria, and the chemical release of endorphins during the refractory period. Sparrows faking orgasm, therefore, were trained to avoid the novice's display of histrionic screaming, head thrashing, hair tossing, and the clawing of the partner's back. A pro Sparrow instead knew the orgasmic subtleties of a change in respiration, a stiffening of the limbs, the brief, racking shudder(s) through the body, followed by the frantic levitating off the bed if the man touched overly sensitive plumbing sooner than five minutes after. Dominika put on her Sparrow mask of pleasure-pain, as if waiting for salvation, for ecstasy, at the hands of her blue tsar. Then the impossible happened.

It started as a little buzz in her stomach—the whisper hints of a real orgasm, not faked—that radiated to her crotch, then grew, and hovered like an antique vase on the edge of the mantelpiece after an earthquake, waiting for the next trembler that would set it wobbling over the edge to the floor below. *This cannot be happening*, she thought. Not with *this* lizard cleaning her chimney. The sensation grew; her orgasm was *going* to happen if she let it, and it would be a big one, it had been too long without Nate, a time of prolonged stress, and she had built up a lot of, well, kilowatts, that were ready to arc and burn someone's eyebrows off. She no longer used her grandmother's long-handled hairbrush, for she assumed her official residences—here and in Moscow—were filled with audio and video. *Bogu moy*, my God, the vase on the mantelpiece started chittering, vibrating closer to the edge.

This cannot happen. This will not happen, she thought. Even as she began the Sparrow School routine for Putin's benefit (*No. 44, "A single snowflake will start the avalanche"*), Dominika shut down her real climax, chased it away by thinking about *Bratok*, banished it back to her spleen, or her liver, or wherever it resided. It was easy enough to do, considering the *dibbuk*, the ogre who was hunched over her, nose-whistling as he plowed in and out.

Putin was himself laboring; it was catching up to him too: the image of this unattainable Venus, head back, throat offered to him, eyes white in their sockets, was having its effect, not to mention the quite remarkable sensation of her pubococcygeus muscle *actually milking* his organ with the result that he felt the telltale gathering in his groin, the insidious thickening of his member, and finally the leaden palsy that sweeps over the limbs at the moment of *spuskat*, of ejaculation. He said nothing, blinked once—his expression did not change—and disengaged the moment he was done, wiping his face, sliding off the bed, and collecting his tracksuit pants off the floor. The tsar was not one for kissy endearments, or stroking of hair, or tender embraces in the soft après-sex twilight. It was sufficient that he had deposited on his bedewed Director of Foreign Intelligence, an SVR general, the imperial spoor that marked one of the boundaries of his predatory range.

She was outwardly languid, but breathing hard and sweaty between the breasts. Dominika's thoughts raced madly in the postcoital asylum that was her brain. She had to get rid of the president. Agnes in the closet probably had to pee. Would the freshening land breeze prevent Benford's USV—due in fifty minutes—from landing on the beach below? Ugh, her thighs were sticky. As a trained Sparrow, Dominika knew that a healthy man ejaculates approximately 5 milliliters (a teaspoon) of semen, which contains approximately one hundred million sperm. That meant one hundred million melon-headed Putin spermatozoa with whippy tails were all on the move inside her, intent on annexing her cervix like the Crimean peninsula. (Thank God for the Agency-issued IUD, a copper coil PARAGARD device developed [purely by coincidence] by Lockheed in 1962 during the design phase of the SR-71 Blackbird supersonic reconnaissance aircraft.) The president was saying something, and Dominika stilled the cascade of her disjointed thoughts.

"I would like you to have this," said Putin, sliding a long velvet box onto the end table. "Wear it tomorrow at the concert." Tomorrow's entertainment was to be a live performance by a hugely famous American music artist, also well-known as a vocal and committed progressive activist who, despite the absence of demonstrable human rights in Russia, found he could accept $5 million from the Ministry of Culture of the Russian Federation to appear at Cape Idokopas to entertain the *siloviki*. Dominika opened the case. Nestled inside was a priceless strand of multicolored South Sea and Tahitian pearls, each one 114 millimeters, as big as marbles, sea green, gold, ivory, and mocha, a sublime strand.

"Mr. President, these pearls are magnificent. I couldn't possibly . . ."

Putin put up his hand to quiet her, took the strand from the box, and fastened it around her neck, where a separate pearl nestled heavily in the hollow of her neck. Personal gifts exchanged between governmental colleagues—Dominika's *pizda* in exchange for the pearls—did not pose the slightest conflict of interest in this tsar's Russia. "I would like you to accept them," he said.

Dominika fingered the pearls. "Thank you, Mr. President," she said. "And thank you for a wonderful evening." His blue halo glowed.

CIA star asset DIVA saw Vladimir Vladimirovich to the door. She did not kiss him good night, with all the shining raccoon eyes of the security detail fixed on her in her silk kimono from the darkness. They shook hands instead, the feel of the president's calluses scratching her palm.

―――――

The electric whine of the golf carts speeding uphill faded. It was dead quiet inside, but the pines outside stirred noisily in the breeze. No audio bugs working tonight in the dacha, right? Dominika retrieved Agnes from the closet and they walked downstairs in silence. Dominika opened another bottle of champagne and poured two glasses, leaning on the marble island with her elbows, her head in her hands, exhausted. Forty minutes to the arrival of the USV.

Agnes ran her fingers through her white forelock. "Half a cup of white vinegar with a teaspoon of baking powder," she said, also leaning on the marble top. They were like two cowpokes at a bar.

"What?" said Dominika, looking at her glass.

Agnes shook her head. "Not to drink; it's a homemade douche solution.

I assume you'd rather not carry the president around with you all night." Dominika laughed. She liked this Polish Cold Warrior. Thank God she could carry Dominika's message to Benford personally. And thank God Dominika would be able to get her out of Russia in one piece. But she didn't have vinegar and there was no time.

"How often does this happen?" asked Agnes.

"This is the first time," said Dominika, trying not to sound defensive. She noted Agnes's nonjudgmental expression. "But I expect his attention will grow more acute now that I am a member of his inner circle."

"It's important not to blame yourself. No self-recrimination, not ever."

"I don't dwell on anything but doing what I have to," said Dominika.

Agnes nodded. "In Poland, it was the same for me. I slept with half the politburo for their secrets, and with three Soviet colonels on the military advisory staff in Warsaw."

"I trust you sleep well at night? No nightmares?" said Dominika, impressed.

Agnes averted her eyes. "And what does Nathaniel think about this?"

Dominika stiffened. Here it was. "What Nate and I have together is apart from all this. What we have together is *despite* all this," said Dominika, with an edge in her voice. Agnes looked down at the floor.

"Tell me," said Dominika, standing straight to look at Agnes squarely. "What is it exactly that *you* and Nate have together, if I may ask?"

"You can rest easy, General Egorova," said Agnes softly. "We worked together, and I love the boy, but his heart belongs to you. You have nothing to fear from me." The two women knew the unspoken parts, which needed no further discussion.

Agnes looked at her watch. "When does that damn boat arrive?"

"Exactly at midnight about thirty minutes from now," said Dominika. "You must carry back the thumb drive that explains the whole situation, MAGNIT's identity, and Nate's status. It's absolutely critical that you talk to Benford or Forsyth. Even if you have to call them from a phone booth in Varna, just tell them CHALICE."

"Do you have something that is waterproof that I can carry the thumb drive in?" asked Agnes "I don't want to risk getting seawater on it." Dominika ran upstairs, dug out the thumb drive, and stuffed it into the now unwrapped

Hussar condom from the bedside table drawer and tied a tight knot in the rubber. Back downstairs, she flipped it to Agnes.

"Are you serious?" she said, holding the rubber between thumb and forefinger.

"Don't worry," said Dominika. "One owner, never been driven, low mileage."

"Okay, now it's waterproof. But if I don't get the message to Benford in time, you are in grave danger, isn't that so?" asked Agnes.

Dominika nodded. "If you consider that the execution chamber in Butyrka Prison constitutes grave danger, then you are correct."

"So if something befalls you, something catastrophic, and Nate eventually is released, it leaves the field open for me, wouldn't you say?"

"Absolutely," said Dominika, staring at her. "He would be all yours." This was one cat hissing at another, establishing the relationship. Agnes's crimson halo was steady and bright. She would not betray the cause any more than Dominika would, and they both knew it. Agnes looked again at her watch.

"All right," she said. "Let's get down to the beach."

———————

Dominika left Agnes downstairs briefly while she dressed in tights, black stretch top, and rubber-soled shoes to walk on beach rocks. She stood stock-still when she heard voices downstairs. The man's voice was unmistakably that of Gorelikov. The words were indistinguishable but the tone was pure Anton: courtly, polite, and modulated. Agnes's voice was also calm, but Dominika couldn't make out her words either. *Bogu moy*, my God, what possible cover story could explain Agnes's presence in the personal dacha of the Director of SVR? Old school chums? A shared interest in the decorative arts? Saving water by taking showers together? Dominika set her jaw, and walked downstairs, to confront disaster.

"Anton, what are you doing here at this hour?" asked Dominika. "You just missed the president. He left a few minutes ago after a glass of champagne." Dominika nodded at Agnes as if to say her presence was totally natural. Gorelikov looked from Dominika to Agnes then back to Dominika. *Go ahead, assume we're* pizdolizi, *girlfriends.*

"I have just had the pleasure of meeting this young lady," said Gorelikov. "She tells me she is one of the restoration experts from Warsaw who arrived this morning. In the same group as the American." *This was trouble, undiluted, unmitigated danger.* Dominika felt the ember of rage alight in her gut.

"You recall my proposal to let the American roam the compound freely so he would lead us to the mole?" said Anton. "That idea was vetoed, chiefly on your insistent recommendation, for very logical, very good reasons." Gorelikov walked to the island and poured himself a glass of champagne. "I resolved to conduct my own modest experiment and follow this young woman who seemed to know the American. A coincidence? The other Poles stayed in the dormitory drinking complimentary vodka. Except Ms. Krawcyk, who walked for some time through the compound on a most circuitous route. And she ends up here at midnight, after the president's visit, and now we're all drinking champagne out of a crystal *chalice.*" That word. They stood looking at each other. The pistol was in the kitchen drawer, a step away. It was unlikely that Anton was armed. Not his style. Dominika knew this was the end, unless she was prepared to react violently to eliminate the threat. Whatever scaly beast lived inside her, it crouched at the entrance to the cave, talons gripping the dirt, ready to spring.

It was Gorelikov who broke the silence, looking at Dominika. His voice was calm, his face pacific. "I suppose it is the nature of espionage that the more monstrous the betrayal, the more effective the operation. You enjoyed the confidence of your peers, the Kremlin, and the president. What is more, I trusted you. Imagine the irony. You are Director of the SVR, reporting to the Americans, even as we influence events to place MAGNIT as DCIA." He put down his glass and smoothed his hair. "Where does that leave us? What shall we do to resolve—"

Both women moved simultaneously, instinctively. Agnes lunged forward and hit Gorelikov extremely hard with a hammer fist on the side of the neck beneath the ear, overloading the vagus nerve, disrupting heartrate and blood-pressure signals to the brain, and causing him to wobble and go down on one knee. Without thinking, Dominika circled behind him, and with nothing else at hand, unclasped the president's South Sea pearls and wound the strand around Anton's neck in the counterclockwise Sicilian garrotter's loop, which puts the hands behind the target pushing crosswise—exerting a more powerful constriction than pulling the hands wide apart—a technique taught during Spetsnaz *Systema* training. Gorelikov started struggling, fell back to the floor, reaching behind his head, scrabbling for Dominika's eyes, until Agnes flung herself at him, held his wrists, then lay across Gorelikov's legs so he couldn't kick. He was thin and light and Agnes controlled him easily. Through his increasingly constricted throat he repeatedly rasped, "Don't!"

Dominika expected the necklace strand to break, scattering the priceless pearls across the terrazzo, but whatever had been used to string them together must have been unbreakable, wire or monofilament rather than the traditional silk thread, and her vision tunneled as she went a little crazy, leaned back, put her knee behind his neck, and kept applying torque. At least the big pearls were easy to grasp, and the frail Gorelikov was not exceptionally strong. As she strangled him, she heard herself whispering to Anton that Russia was not the Kremlin's private preserve, that the *Rodina* belonged to the Russians, not the jackals who fed on the carcass, which struck her as sounding like an early manifesto of Lenin's, but she was out of her mind with panicked bloodlust. She didn't know if he heard her over his air-starved grunts. As she whispered to him, Agnes looked at her openmouthed.

Agnes held Anton's wrists and rode out the last paroxysm of his thrashing legs, and he was still, but they didn't move for another five minutes, tense. They knew he was gone when his trousers showed wet and a pool of urine spread on the floor under him. Agnes was soaked too, but didn't say a word as she got to her feet, with wild hair. They both looked at Gorelikov, both panting like murderous ancient queens, Clytemnestra and Electra contemplating crimson bathwater. Dominika saw that Agnes's halo was bleached and faded. Anton's corpse was wet from waist to knee, his eyes were open, his neck was bruised purple, and his halo was gone. Interesting. Dominika wondered if she eventually would feel remorse—Gorelikov had, after all, befriended and supported her in the Kremlin—for she felt none now. The elegant *boulevardier* would have had her executed without hesitation.

Dominika fastened the still-warm pearls back around her neck; they were heavy and slick against her skin. They'd never feel the same again, and she'd always have to contend with Anton's ghost when she wore them. "Are you ready to take a cruise with Monsieur CHALICE?" she asked Agnes. "He's decided to defect."

―――――――――

"You're going to put me in that canoe with Putin's closest adviser, and strap me in with him to bounce around for thirty minutes?" said Agnes.

"With the president's closest *dead* adviser," said Dominika. "His disappearance will prove he was the mole, a devastating scandal for the Kremlin and for the president personally."

"Gorelikov becomes CHALICE? The most-trusted man in Putin's Russia turns out to be the mole who defects? They'll never believe it," said Agnes.

"*Posle dozhdika v chetverg*, we'll see after the rain on Thursday; we have no idea what will happen. It's the only evidence they'll have, and you'll be gone too, the second CIA operative we all missed when we obsessed over Nate," said Dominika. "Final confirmation of Gorelikov as the mole will come when Benford arrests MAGNIT." She ran upstairs to whip the used sheet off the bed and raced back down to the living room to swaddle Gorelikov in the sheet, a burial shroud smelling of Putin's cologne.

"How are we going to carry him down that steep path to the beach?" said Agnes.

"We each grab one end and drag him down," said Dominika, gathering one end of the sheet and lifting.

"This is insane."

"Insane? Now is the time for *vera*, for faith, and unshakable resolve, which I suspect you know very well."

Agnes nodded. "*Wiernosc* in Polish."

Dominika nodded. "Take his wristwatch off. It's one of those fancy Swiss models, worth thousands. Keep it, it's yours, compliments of the Kremlin. Consider it reimbursement for this crazy mission. They never should have sent you. It was an insane risk."

"Nate came to rescue you and I came to help Nate," said Agnes. "So I suppose all of us have lost."

"We have not lost," said Dominika. "But now it's time to end this. This is defeat for Them. They sleep in their beds just up the hill, in the main house, while we will be swallowing seawater for Gable, for a white-haired general and two young Sparrows who gave their lives." She looked at her watch. "We've got twenty minutes before the boat is due, and Anton takes his last Black Sea pleasure cruise. Grab the sheet and help me lift him."

MOUSSELINE SAUCE

Make the sabayon by gently whisking cold water slowly into egg yolks, until triple in volume. Whisk sabayon, slowly adding warm clarified butter until sauce is smooth and glossy. Incorporate lemon juice, salt, and cayenne and continue stirring. Gently fold in whipped cream that has been whisked into firm peaks. Serve immediately.

37

Black Sea Cruise

They dropped Gorelikov's shrouded body twice as they stumbled down the shale goat path to the beach, once just catching him before he rolled off the pathway onto the rocks thirty meters below. The night land breeze came off the face of the cliff and created a small chop on the water, which broke among the many rocks protruding from the sandy bottom. Could an unmanned vessel be preprogrammed to weave between these outcrops, to run aground gently on this small patch of wet packed sand, and to weave its way out again? Dominika and Agnes took turns wearing the infrared glasses that would pick up the invisible beacon from the bow strobe on the USV, and Dominika wore the beacon wristwatch. They thought they could hear some of the sounds of the late-night party high above them, beyond the face of the cliff. As they waited silently, listening for the clump of sentries' boots, the land breeze increased, and the waves turned from small chuckling wavelets to noisier three-foot breakers that hit some of the protruding rocks and gurgled over them, occasionally throwing a little spume into the air. Choppy, but not impossible. Dominika periodically looked back at the shrouded form of Gorelikov lying on the sand beyond the reach of the waves—she fully expected him to sit up and start talking—and wondered first, how the boat could get close enough to them in the surf, and second, how they could possibly load his limp body onto the deck of the USV that had a significant freeboard.

At precisely midnight by Dominika's watch, she saw an intermittent flashing blue light on the horizon. As the minutes went by the light grew brighter and the indistinct shape of a low-slung speedboat with what looked like zebra stripes along its sides and a small white bow wave in its teeth became visible. The shape of the vessel materialized, disappeared, and reappeared as it approached, sliding into the troughs of the waves, and then climbing back out. As it entered the rock field, the boat slowed and, as if driven by a coxswain, slowly made its way around or between the rocks until the rounded bow slid to a stop on the sand right at their feet. The boarding footholds were at the stern of the USV, but the surf was banging the hull back there. Dominika could hear the propulsion jets of the vessel trying to hold the hull straight and to counteract the effects of the waves. Making her way to the aft accommodation ladder, Agnes was soused to the neck by a breaker, then knocked off the second foothold back into the water, completely drenching her, the second time tonight she was soaked. Finally she was able to scramble up the three footholds and balance herself on the deck of the USV. Dominika reached up and gave her the bag that contained the condom-wrapped thumb drive, the infrared glasses, the beacon watch, and Gorelikov's expensive Swiss wristwatch.

The double coffin-lid hatch automatically opened and Agnes looked inside, then back to Dominika, who was in thigh-high water, and gave a thumbs-up. Dominika stayed away from the stern of the boat being pounded regularly by the surf, causing loud slapping booms that would sooner or later attract sentries. Now came the hard part. Dominika went over to the wrapped body of Gorelikov, sat him up, put her shoulder into his stomach, and with a grunt, picked him up like a sack of flour. She waded back into the water and tried to boost him high enough so Agnes could reach down, grab a sheet corner, and haul him aboard. It was impossible with the sloshing water and the bucking hull, but Dominika boosted him by his legs and, miraculously, Agnes was able to grab the top edge of the sheet and pull with all her might. The corpse slid up over the gunwale and onto the deck of the vessel. Dominika walked back on the beach and waited; watching as Agnes slid, rolled, and finally dumped Gorelikov's corpse down the hatchway. Once below, she would have to pick him up and put him on one of the reclining seats, strap him in, then strap herself in, and flip the switches that would close the hatch and initiate the programmed course back to the waiting US Navy frigate twenty miles offshore. Before Agnes disappeared down the hatch she looked at Dominika in the moonlight and waved. The thought occurred to Dominika that Nathaniel Nash was very lucky that such a woman loved him, that they both loved him.

The tone of the jet nozzles grew louder as the USV backed off the beach, the surf still smacking the transom as it moved away. Then a grinding bump as the stern collided with a flat rock protruding above the surface and the vessel stopped dead. From the foam around the stern, Dominika could see that the USV was trying to go forward and backward to free itself from the invisible obstruction, but it kept bumping into the outcrop and could proceed no farther. Cursing, Dominika waded in up to her chest, was swallowed by a breaker, and then managed to swim to the hung-up hull and push the bucking stern with all her might. She finally got a lift from a wave, and heard the transom grind against the rock and float free. Another wave slapped her under, but the jets pulsed in reverse and the zebra-striped boat silently backed out of the rock field into open water. Another wave hit Dominika and she swallowed some seawater and retched, but recovered enough to see the USV spin in her own length, settle by the stern, and pick up speed, headed out to sea. She paused briefly to squat in the shallows. Seawater should do the same job as vinegar and baking powder. There was some satisfaction in consigning the president's DNA to the Black Sea. Dominika struggled to the beach, her clothes streaming with water (she'd win the wet T-shirt contest at the party tonight), and looked back seaward. The stealth vessel had already disappeared from sight. *Good luck, Agnes Krawcyk. Don't fail me.*

Shivering, Dominika staggered up the goat path to her dacha, shucked off her clothes, collected the champagne glasses, and mopped up Gorelikov's mess from the marble. She then stood under a hot shower for twenty minutes, too tired to mind the inevitable nightmare image of Grace Gao hanging by her neck from the glass shower door.

———

It was noon before anyone noticed that Gorelikov was missing. Bortnikov ordered a massive search of the compound, and had spotter planes and fast motor-patrol boats from Sevastopol comb the coast in case Gorelikov somehow had fallen off the cliff into the sea. After an informal roll call it was additionally noticed that Agnes Krawcyk, one of the art-restoration workers, was also unaccounted for. Bortnikov and Dominika met in the compound's security-control building's conference room, to discuss how they would brief the president on these disturbing developments. There was no record at Gelendzhik Airport of either individual boarding a plane and all compound vehicles were accounted for—they had simply disappeared into thin air. Bortnikov remembered that MAGNIT had reported part of an exfiltration plan involving a powered stealth glider that could land in the Balaklava Valley undetected, but there was no way Gorelikov or the woman could have exited the compound unnoticed and walked the ten kilometers at night, on country roads, to reach an exfiltration pickup point. Frustrated and furious, Bortnikov ordered a second complete search of every structure in the compound, including the presidential wing and the president's own private apartments. Nikolai Patrushev deigned to attend the last meeting with Bortnikov and Dominika at the end of the day. Despite the cataclysmic possibilities, Patrushev's conniving yellow halo was steady and unperturbed. *He's already chosen a scapegoat*, thought Dominika. *He'll assume none of the blame.*

"The Polish woman is of no importance," said Patrushev. "She could have been taken by one of the soldiers into the woods, raped, and killed, then thrown into a ravine. It would take months to find her body."

Bortnikov goggled at him. "Are you mad? Why do you assume that?"

Patrushev ignored him. "Anton Gorelikov is a different matter. If he has defected, it is a potential disaster. Your services should have been more vigilant."

Bortnikov looked across the table at him. "You are levying blame on Egorova and me? Are you serious? You are head of the Security Council with an oversight charter over all matters of State security. You share the responsibility." Bortnikov was almost yelling, but Patrushev was blasé and unaffected.

"The FSB exists to catch spies in the *Rodina*. The SVR is supposed to run foreign assets who can give early warning of such breaches," said Patrushev. "It is my observation you both fell short in these duties, and in consequence failed the president." There it was, the cringing, blame-shifting, famous among the Kremlin *siloviki*, with no one taking responsibility, and everyone distraught and disapproving when the president was ill served by others. Dominika calculated that perhaps this criticism would push her and Bortnikov closer—at least until the next palace crisis. Bortnikov still goggled at Patrushev, and his blue halo flickered in agitation.

Dominika understood what Nikolai was doing, distancing himself from any responsibility. But she was now Director of SVR. It was time to assert herself, to establish a voice among these men who, along with the president, would be her competitors, allies, and rivals in the years to come. "With respect, I think no one deserves any blame, and it is unseemly that Nikolai pretends otherwise," said Dominika. "One thing is certain. We will know clearly whether Anton Gorelikov is a CIA mole, and we will know the truth very soon."

Patrushev and Bortnikov stared at her. "The proof will be apparent within four or five days," said Dominika. "If in the next week important SVR assets in the United States are compromised, then it must be the inescapable conclusion that Gorelikov is CHALICE. This is conjecture, but if it happens, it is incontrovertible proof." *That should nail down the notion of Anton's guilt.*

"How do we brief this to the president?" said Bortnikov. Patrushev offered no guidance.

Dominika leaned forward. "Given that Anton was one of the president's closest advisers, I think care should be taken, great care, not to insinuate that the president himself was incautious, or overly trusting, or blind to the obvious signs, if any, that Anton was going down the wrong path." The two magpies on the other side of the table nodded their heads.

"If it suits you, gentlemen," said Dominika, fingering a striking strand of pearls around her neck, "I can brief the president on this difficult situation. We are lucky that we have the American case officer in Moscow to use as a bargaining chip. We can use the American to exchange for our assets, and additionally demand the extradition to Russia of Gorelikov."

"Since it was your idea," said Patrushev, relieved, "it would certainly be appropriate for you to brief the president. Don't you agree?" he said to Bortnikov.

"Absolutely," he said. "The president likes and trusts you."

Dominika nodded. "That would be satisfactory," she said. "Then all we have to do is wait. I intend to return to Moscow tonight to monitor the situation from Yasenevo." *And I want to see Nate.*

Audrey Rowland walked in the twilight on the raised boardwalk over the bog on the northern end of Theodore Roosevelt Island in the Potomac River between Rosslyn and the John F. Kennedy Center in the heart of Washington, DC. The island was part of the National Park System, and would close in ninety minutes. Pedestrian traffic was light. An old coot had been fishing off the causeway bridge that connected the island to the parking lot on the George Washington Memorial Parkway, and two blue-hairs with cameras had passed Audrey fifteen minutes ago, chattering like parrots and idiotically looking for birds to photograph. After that, she was alone. As she walked soundlessly on the planks of the boardwalk in the failing light, lumpy things—turtles and frogs—occasionally splashed in the brackish, reedy water, but otherwise the forested island was eerily calm.

The boardwalk curved east, and the lights of Georgetown and downtown DC were coming on, visible through the dense foliage. Audrey stopped and sat on the secluded bench designated as the meeting site, looked at her watch, sat back, and listened. The creeks and pops of the deciduous forest were muffled by the drone of the evening traffic on the nearby Key and Roosevelt Bridges. Otherwise nothing. Audrey had been making clandestine meetings for a long time, and was accustomed to the jittery stomach and damp palms that came before making contact with her GRU handler or, more recently, with SUSAN, the illegals officer from New York. Meeting with this creepy bitch was a lot safer than meeting someone from the Russian Embassy, but Audrey didn't like her. There was something superior about her attitude; she didn't acknowledge Audrey's rank or importance. Audrey already had resolved to tell Uncle Anton that she wanted a different commo system, and she was sure the Russians would comply, especially since she was two days away from Senate confirmation as the new Director of the CIA.

The confirmation hearings on Capitol Hill had been a joke: legislators read rambling prepared statements and asked extraneous questions off lists handed to them by spotty staffers just out of college. Audrey played the professional navy vice admiral, and the scientist preeminent in technology, weapons, and communications, advances in which would mean less spending and reasonable budgets for the navy while continuing to ensure national security. The addlepated senators, Democrats and Republicans alike, liked the fact that Admiral Rowland was an outsider, a sexless woman, obviously apolitical, and would steer CIA in the right direction, away from profligate spending and away from nefarious covert actions and similar extralegal behaviors.

Audrey's scalp moved when she heard a *thump-thump* coming toward her out of the darkness on the boardwalk. In the fading light, the indistinct shape of a hunched-over human form gradually became clear, and Audrey thought of the irony of being accosted by an estuarine swamp creature while meeting her Russian handler in downtown Washington, DC. More likely it would be a paunchy Schedule C contractor, out at twilight looking for a young tug-mutton. She relaxed when a fogey in a floppy hat and flannel shirt approached. The old man was using a walker, and the thump of the padded legs of his appliance echoed hollowly off the planks. Audrey nodded pleasantly as he passed, but just got a harrumph in return from the miserable bastard, who was clearly hurrying to get off the island before it closed. After the man had disappeared around the bend there was no one else around, no sounds. All she had to do was wait for SUSAN to ghost up to her out of the dusk. Audrey patted her jacket pocket to make sure the thumb drive and two discs with the latest Office of Naval Research secrets were secure. She'd pass the drive and discs, verbally brief SUSAN on her confirmation, and listen to the Center's ideas about communications options when she became DCIA and had a full-time security detail.

What Audrey Rowland did not realize was that the senior citizen fishing off the causeway, and the two biddies looking for birds, and the irascible crusty-pants hobbling behind a walker were all part of Simon Benford's ORION surveillance team, a collection of retired CIA officers who were so adept, and patient, and effective, that they outperformed the crack FBI surveillance team known as the "Gs" who followed trained foreign intelligence officers for a living. The ORIONs' skill was to anticipate where a target would go, get there *ahead* of the rabbit, and undetectably witness a clandestine act without the intelligence officer (and his American agent) ever having an inkling that they were covered. Benford once famously said that the difference between ORION surveillance and the FEEBS was the difference between a cat watching a bird, and a dog chasing a car. The ORIONs had been leapfrogging ahead of Admiral Rowland all day, totally unseen, anticipating her route-of-march—the overall vector of her travel—and logging her general direction, and when, near the end of the day, Theodore Roosevelt Island became a possibility, four of the dozen ORIONs covering Audrey had flooded the zone and were in place before she even pulled into the parking lot. The geriatric team—the two bird-watchers were grandmothers—reported that target demeanor indicated an imminent meeting. That was good enough for Simon. Benford had alerted the FBI arrest team to deploy accordingly, as the ORIONs had no arrest authority and could not detain a suspect by flashing their AARP cards.

Days before, the rendezvous had been made twenty-one nautical miles off the Black Sea coast of Russia. The USV had performed flawlessly, making contact with DDG-78, the USS *Porter*, an *Arleigh Burke*–class destroyer of the 6th Fleet, a little after 0100 in calm seas. The USV was hoisted aboard the helo deck by a specially fitted stern hoist, and rolled on a dolly out of sight into the aft helo hangar by bridge crane. Sailors who opened the USV hatch had been surprised to see a busty middle-age woman in a wet T-shirt emerge, holding a waterproof pouch. They had been further surprised to see the shrouded figure of an elegant gentleman in a suit sleeping in the second reclining chair who, on closer inspection, was determined to be dead. The executive officer on the *Porter* cleared the hangar of crewmembers at the behest of a short rumpled man wearing a navy peacoat who was accompanied by a taller civilian with salt-and-pepper hair, and a nervous young man with fogged-over spectacles.

Agnes had shaken hands with Benford and Westfall, hugged Forsyth, repeated "chalice, chalice, chalice," until they told her to stop, they got it, and handed them the pouch with the thumb drive. They had all sat in the empty wardroom, sipping coffee, reading the thumb-drive report on a laptop. A plate of toast slices smothered in a white sauce with chipped beef, the navy staple known as "S.O.S.," was put in front of her by a grinning steward. Agnes took a cautious sniff, tried a forkful, then had devoured the whole plate. She had not eaten in twelve hours. As she ate, she told them the rest about Dominika and Gorelikov. Forsyth reached over and squeezed her hand. Westfall had hurried away to send flash cables to Langley.

"Alex Larson is in small measure avenged," said Benford, grimly. "MAGNIT will be arrested, and Gorelikov becomes CHALICE. Line KR in SVR, *kontravietka*, counterintelligence, will be doing damage assessment for years." He patted Agnes's hand and congratulated her. "DIVA will be able to tie up Russian intelligence—internal and external—for a decade, especially since she has consummated her relationship with Putin, and there is no longer a competitor for the president's confidence. I wish Alex could see it all."

Agnes had whipped her white forelock back, and looked at him with a murderous look Forsyth remembered from the old days. "How nice for DIVA," she spat. "You are content to let your asset get on her back whenever that pig wants? And what of your officer languishing in a Russian prison?

What is so fortuitous? Your brilliant trap worked but what will you do to repay Nash for your betrayal?" Benford glowered at her, red in the face.

Forsyth had pulled her out of the wardroom and out onto the afterdeck where they stood against the aft rail as dawn broke, watching the ship's yeasty wake trail behind, straight as a pencil. Both of them wore too-large peacoats against the morning chill.

"If you think he's not going through hell over this, you'd be wrong," said Forsyth. "But catching the mole is Simon's first priority, his only priority. He would have used any of us to identify MAGNIT, including himself."

Forsyth put his arm around Agnes's shoulder. He had guessed at the love triangle since Sevastopol. "He's counting on Dominika keeping Nash in one piece and eventually getting him out of Russia, maybe arranging a trade. It'll take some time—the navy and the courts won't let a traitor of Rowland's magnitude avoid prison time."

Still furious at the soulless practicality of these CIA men, Agnes shook Forsyth's arm off. "So Nathaniel rots in Russia?" She didn't care if her affection for Nate showed.

Forsyth shrugged. "If the FEEBS can also identify MAGNIT's handler—a real Russian illegal—a spy swap might be arranged quickly." Forsyth knew this was a long shot. Benford had ranted to Hearsey that nothing had come from dusting DIVA's throwaway ops phone with *metka*, spy dust, as a way to tag SUSAN. Multiple trips to New York City with FBI technicians to fluoresce the offices of fringe, left-progressive literary magazines in New York—*New Politics*, the *American Prospect, Salon*, the *New School Quarterly*, and *Harper's*—had not resulted in a single hit of spy dust. There was some initial excitement when the desktop of an editor had fluoresced slightly under the black light, prompting an FBI special agent to say he knew the place was full of comsymps, but there was no other evidence of *metka* anywhere else in the office. Hearsey later determined that trace amounts of recreational drugs including cocaine, methamphetamine, and psilocybin mushroom crumbs on the desktop had registered a false positive. Benford subsequently concluded that SUSAN either had used a cutout to retrieve the phone from the little cemetery in the Village, or had somehow not physically touched the phone before throwing it into the East River. Smart gal, that SUSAN.

Audrey felt rather than saw SUSAN sit down next to her on the bench in the gloom. Goddamn illegals, sneaking up like that.

"Any problems getting here?" she asked. Audrey shook her head as she handed over the thumb drive and the two discs in a ziplock bag.

"These will be self-explanatory," said Audrey. "I expect confirmation as DCIA in two days or less. We will have to discuss communications on a priority basis."

"The Center is aware of the requirement," said SUSAN brusquely.

"Well the Center had better get moving. In less than a week's time I'm going to have a twenty-four-hour security detail, and . . ."

The dark woods on both sides of the boardwalk erupted into a wall of blinding light. A megaphone voice ordered the two women to stay put, this was the FBI. Blinded by the lights, Audrey heard the sound of SUSAN launching herself out of the bench, and jumping off the boardwalk into the putrid swamp, followed by frantic splashing. Voices were yelling, more splashes were heard, quite a lot of additional splashing, and Audrey, who had not reacted at all because of the blinding effect of the lights (and a physics geek's natural inability to launch into rapid physical movement), felt hands on her arms and the snick of handcuffs on her wrists. She saw that SUSAN had left the thumb drive and discs on the bench, which the FBI was now gathering and putting into a plastic evidence bag. It seemed as if there were hundreds of people milling about in blue Windbreakers with "FBI" stenciled across the back. There was never a moment that a hand wasn't gripping her arm.

It would have been impossible to describe the numb shock that Audrey felt as she was walked back down the boardwalk to the parking lot, already a carnival ground of flashing red-and-blue lights. Part of the shock, of course, was the surprise of the ambush, and the realization that approximately fifty special agents of the FBI had been hiding knee-deep in swamp water for hours before the meeting. How had they known? Audrey's precise, quantitative mind also reeled against the reality that her twelve years of clever, calculated espionage had been detected, and it was irksome not to know how. Those dumpy little men looking for moles were more dangerous than they appeared. The final sour gout of desperate reality hit Audrey when she was put in the back of an FBI sedan reeking of Aqua Velva, her hands still cuffed behind her back, and the car door was slammed shut. She knew this was the beginning of an interminable period of evidence, interrogations, trials, and publicity ending in prison, as well as the catastrophic end of her navy life of privilege and status. She felt no remorse beyond the fact that they would court-martial her and take away her stripes. A female special agent sat in back with her, and Audrey stole an appraising glance at the youthful profile and the stockinged legs. The special agent caught Audrey looking at her, and stared her down. This was the end of that part of her life too, Audrey realized miserably, not ever having seen movies such as *Caged Heat*, or *Kittens Behind Bars*.

Her life was over, her world was upside-down, and she would certainly grow old and die in prison, but as the car started moving onto the parkway, Audrey strangely thought about what her hateful father would have said at this moment. Screw him. She was a three-star admiral, and he never was.

US NAVY CREAMED CHIPPED BEEF

Melt butter in a saucepan, blend in flour, salt, and pepper. Stir in milk and cook over medium heat until boiling and sauce thickens. Tear dried beef and add shreds to sauce. Serve over toast.

38

The Presidential Wood Saw

"You're telling me that there was no conceivable contingency that would have suggested the positioning of a patrol craft or an inflatable dinghy on the river, given that the ambush was taking place *on a fucking island*?" raved Benford to FBI Counterintelligence Chief Charles Montgomery. Benford had just been told that the woman who was meeting Admiral Rowland had plunged into the swamp, had actually outrun a score of special agents in their twenties through thigh-deep swamp water, had gotten to the shoreline, and had escaped across the black Potomac in what the winded SAs thought was a kayak. This was confirmed when a rental kayak was found abandoned on a low-tide mud bank near the Washington Harbour condominium complex in Georgetown the next morning. SUSAN was gone, presumably already back in New York City, editing precious and self-important articles in a literary magazine, and presumably still operationally active for SVR Line S, supporting other sources, talent-spotting prospective assets for recruitment, and probably servicing dead drops and caches from Seattle to Key West. Benford uttered a foul oath as he contemplated how many more MAGNITs could be operating with impunity in the United States.

Benford had told Forsyth they would wait six months, to see whether DIVA could swipe SUSAN's file (illegals' true names are strictly compartmented in Line S—even the Director of SVR does not have ready access to the roster—and a close record of senior people who request their identities is kept). Now that Dominika was Director of SVR, double and treble precautions had to be taken to protect her. In the meantime, the two CIA men began contemplating a double-agent dangle to give DIVA reason to assign SUSAN a new case. Setting up and arresting a Russian operative—any operative—was on everyone's mind so CIA could arrange the swap to free Nash as soon as possible. There was some urgency; prisoners normally did not flourish in Russian prisons.

The arrest of Audrey Rowland was, of course, a counterintelligence triumph for Benford, but it was not trumpeted in the press out of concern for Nash's well-being, only that the admiral had been relieved for cause, with a vague mention of malfeasance. Not only did it eliminate an active Russian mole within the US Navy, but also DIVA and the list of CIA's other Russian assets were again secure. However, CIA was still without a Director: there were no nominees to replace the late Alex Larson as DCIA. Until new candidates could be identified and put forward, an interim Director had been named. This happened to be the preening Frederick Farrell.

———————

Two good pieces of news greeted them the next morning: A Moscow Station case officer had successfully delivered DIVA's communications desk lamp without a problem (a Russian support asset passed the package to DIVA as she retrieved her coat from the cloak room of a fancy restaurant by actually giving it to one of her bodyguards to carry to the office) and Counterintelligence Division had already received a test covcom message from DIVA, indicating that the equipment was in place and working perfectly. A second message (from the Pentagon) informed CIA that the body of an unidentified Russian citizen had been buried at sea; his weighted canvas body bag had slid into the Black Sea from under an American flag, while being saluted by an honor guard of US sailors. Benford forwarded the snippet to DIVA in Moscow, with grim satisfaction.

The initial tranche of intel reports from DIVA's covcom lamp were astounding in their unique perspective and extreme sensitivity. Security Council minutes, weekly meetings with Bortnikov of the FSB concerning counterintelligence cases against foreign embassies, President Putin's executive-committee meetings, the agendas of which indicated he was already worried about an increasingly dissatisfied working-class, and the upcoming Russian elections, Defense Council minutes regarding solid-fuel missile technology shared with Iran and North Korea; the latest statistics from the Central Bank of the Russian Federation noting endemic economic dysfunction, warning of imminent financial stagnation; and Kremlin reaction to enhanced cooperation among North Asian allies with Washington against Chinese expansionism in the Pacific, and against chronic North Korean misbehavior. Plus, of course, DIVA's usual fare—a weekly executive summary of SVR operational activity worldwide. "A hundred case officers working for ten years couldn't collect this kind of intel," crowed Benford. He ordered four separate reporting compartments established, so that the bulk of DIVA's intel would appear to have originated from multiple sources.

———————

In Moscow things were less jolly. Putin had convened a small meeting in his private conference room with Bortnikov, Patrushev, and Dominika after more specific stories about the arrest of a US Navy admiral for espionage broke in the US press. Dominika expected to be the main focus of President Putin's ire, given that it was she who had argued for a looser counterintelligence net to identify CHALICE, with the unhappy result that the presumed real mole (Gorelikov) had escaped and defected. Now with the arrest of MAGNIT, the opportunity to destroy CIA was lost. But Putin raved at the three of them equally, his blue halo luminous with emotion. During most meetings, he rarely raised his voice when berating the incompetents who ran his State industries, or who mismanaged sectors of his economy, or who siphoned off billions from companies at the cost of efficiency and productivity. But he was yelling tonight.

This evening the president told Patrushev, *"Negó kak ot kozlá moloká,"* that he was as useless as tits on a bull. He told a scandalized Bortnikov, *"Mne nasrát', chto ty dúmaesh,"* that he didn't give a fuck what he thought, and turning to Dominika, said her work was *"porót chush,"* literally dog shit. He glared at them as they sat silently around the mahogany conference table with the inlaid Soviet star, telling themselves these blasphemies could not compare with the disciplinary actions that would have been meted out in the thirties by the black *Vozhd*, the Master, Iosif Vissarionovich Dzhugashvili, Comrade Stalin.

Sitting at the table with her hands folded in front of her, Dominika took it as a positive note that she was receiving the president's scorn in equal measure with the other two. This suggested that Putin considered her a full and equal member of the Big Three on the Council. If so, this would be an important indicator to pass along to Benford regarding her elevated status. Perhaps Putin calculated that, with Gorelikov defected to the West and presumably advising CIA in all things, he needed Egorova's cosmopolitan outlook to counter continued American depredations. No one on either side of the old Iron Curtain ever forgot that British traitor Kim Philby, apart from his epic betrayal of MI6, had for the subsequent twenty-five years after his defection to Moscow in 1963 frequently briefed KGB audiences to explain the national idiosyncrasies and cultural vulnerabilities of Britons and the British Secret Service. The really good defectors keep talking for decades, and the men all assumed Gorelikov would do the same.

Putin noticed Dominika wore the pearl necklace he had given her—she wondered if Gorelikov's DNA still lingered between the pearls—his previously thunderous expression cleared slightly, and he half smiled at her, which did not escape Bortnikov's or Patrushev's notice. Not good, especially if word got around that Director SVR was wearing the *chemise cagoule* for the president. In Sparrow School that meant they were intimate, referring to the medieval woman's long nightgown with the demure single embroidered hole for copulation, the Middle Age precursor to crotchless lingerie. That would not do.

———

The night before, after their return from Cape Idokopas, the president had called on Dominika at her new apartment on Kutuzovsky Prospekt, coming up via the underground garage elevator. He ostensibly wanted to discuss counterintelligence, but obviously the president was looking for a return bout with her. Putin was on the boil that evening—it was the day of MAGNIT's arrest, and four days after Gorelikov's disappearance—but his worries did not minutely affect his carpenter-like performance in bed: the presidential wood saw was again wielded steadily but without inspiration, leaving Dominika to daydream about Nate, and to wonder if she could risk visiting him in jail. He was in Butyrka Prison, but in the wing for political prisoners where inmates were treated more mildly. It did not at all mean he was out of danger; dissident attorney Sergei Magnitsky died in the same cell block in Butyrka after being beaten, then denied medical care. Dominika stilled the impulse to raise the matter of a Nash spy swap while still in bed with Putin, chiefly because the president was not susceptible to postcoital euphoria.

After sex, the evening wasn't over, for the president uncharacteristically lingered to chat, so Dominika padded around her spacious new kitchen in a black V-neck, knee-length cotton slip with one spaghetti strap carelessly hanging off the shoulder and her hair tied with a ribbon. She didn't wear a black satin thong underneath, in case Volodya fancied kitchen-counter sex (*No. 81, "Béchamel thickens only with stirring"*) before he left.

Sitting on a modern bar stool in Dominika's deluxe kitchen of stone and wood, Vladimir Putin was content. The headlines about Audrey Rowland's arrest did not overly concern him, as grievous a loss as it was. Lurid news like this was good for Russia's image, was good for *his* image as *muzhestvennyy*, the virile leader who ran spies around the world. The world would know that the secret services of Russia were omniscient apex predators that could penetrate the governments of his enemies, discover their secrets, and exert his will over them. Of course, spies could suffer reverses, but Putin enjoyed seeing foreigners—governments, or companies, or individuals—moderate their behaviors in fear of his wrath. His active measures were creating lasting discord in the West, at minimal cost, and if he wanted to unseat an American politician, he had only to release an embarrassing, unencrypted email through WikiLeaks run by that languid dupe hiding in that exiguous Latin embassy in London. Partisan political hysteria now gripping American society would do the rest.

And he was having his bullish way with Egorova, a delectable bonus. He looked at Dominika's legs as she reached for an upper cabinet and saw how the ballet dancer's calf muscles flexed when she was on tiptoe. He did not at all mind the whispered gossip in the Kremlin already swirling in the hallways that the two of them were bedmates. No one would dare utter such gossip aloud, and it simply validated that the SVR belonged to him, just as the FSB belonged to him, just as the *siloviki* belonged to him.

To go with the Georgian champagne she had opened, Dominika assembled a quick Mediterranean appetizer with ingredients available only at the special government commissary on the ground floor of her building: marinated artichoke hearts with capers and olives on bruschetta under the broiler, a *contorno* she first tasted in Rome while meeting with Nate. They were newly in love then, and had fed each other with their fingers, giggling and drinking Asti. It occurred to her that her thoughts always returned to her *Neyt. Take care lest the tsar sees it in your face.*

She bent to take the tray out of the oven, feeling his eyes on her haunches. Time for her pitch. She was better at this than he was, but she had to be careful. She reverted to more formal address. "Mr. President, given the events of the last four days, I have a suggestion I would like you to consider," said Dominika. Putin sipped a glass of champagne she had poured for him.

"I recommend that the American be moved from Butyrka to a special safe house, where he could be kept under close supervision, and where low-level interrogation by a team of minders could continue without interruption."

Putin looked sideways at her. "Why would we spare the American the discomfort of prison?" he asked.

"CIA was not above mounting a rescue operation at the Black Sea compound. I would hate for them to try the same thing in Moscow. It would not be impossible. Prison guards are paid little, and many are corrupt."

Putin looked at Dominika's figure under the sheer black slip, faint blue veins traversing her cleavage. The savory artichoke hearts sizzling out of the oven smelled delectable. "We can discuss the matter at the meeting tomorrow morning. I want to talk to the three of you. At eight o'clock. To discuss all the security variables," he said.

There was a reason he had lingered in her apartment, sipping champagne and watching the swell of her buttocks as she moved around the kitchen. Putin knew facts the others did not know, and he intended to make tomorrow's meeting unpleasant, because things needed shaking up, perhaps including some purges and firings. He'd done it before to his Council, and it was time again. The shaking up—in General Egorova's case at least—could start tonight. He reached and grabbed her hair, pulling her close to him, looking at her eyes. Dominika kept her unblinking gaze steady, and let him wrap his fingers in her hair, imagining delivering a single ballistic slap—a *Systema* strike—against his jaw. Was he going to push her head into his lap? He held her wrists behind her back with one hand and pulled her closer, so their lips touched. He popped an appetizer into his mouth and smiled.

Dominika felt the rage well up inside her gut, yet she resisted the elemental urge to push away from this *neznatnyy*, this jack-in-the-office commoner with imperial airs. If he wanted her mouth in his lap, she'd use her teeth and spit his severed manhood into his face as he chewed hors d'oeuvres. *Wait. This is five minutes of humiliation. In the end you'll bring him down.*

———

But the next morning in the conference room with a furious Putin, the situation changed. Dominika's love talk—she had cooed *kroshka*, baby, poppet, sugar, to him last night—was a distant memory, her sore crotch forgotten. He was once again the blue-eyed caliph, playing it heavy and serious.

"MAGNIT is blown, a valuable asset prepared over a dozen years compromised," yelled Putin. "And none of you had the wit to manage the case to prevent her arrest." He slammed his hand hard on the table theatrically.

Patrushev of the oily yellow halo sat back in his chair. Dominika waited for the inevitable prevarication. Nikolai looked back and forth between the president and his colleagues. "Mr. President, Anton Gorelikov's treason and defection could not have been foretold. MAGNIT was his case, and he did not share operational details. He had not even briefed Egorova yet. Once Anton revealed all to his CIA paymasters, no operation of ours could remain secure. We must complete a full damage assessment regarding the extent of his knowledge. He was aware of a great deal." Dominika's scalp twitched; Patrushev obliquely was criticizing Putin himself for trusting Anton so much.

Putin stared at the three of them. "My brilliant *tsaredvoreti*, my loyal courtiers," he said, thick with irony. "Gorelikov did not defect. He was kidnapped," he said, matter-of-factly.

The conference room was quiet, as the three of them stayed still, wondering if Putin's penchant for reading minds and foreseeing the future was just now psychotically manifesting itself. Dominika held her breath and wondered how he knew. *Did that mean he also suspected her?* Finally, Bortnikov spoke. "Kidnapped by whom? Mr. President, with all due respect, it's an outlandish theory."

"Kidnapped, taken hostage, assassinated, it makes no difference," said Putin, angrily. "We have been the target of a massively diabolical operation by CIA, a deception unparalleled since the height of the Cold War." The tsar was schooling his professionals.

Bortnikov's FSB was responsible for internal security. How did the president know this? This was FSB turf, his territory. His halo pulsed in agitation. "What deception?" he said.

Putin snorted in derision at his useful fools. "CIA removed Gorelikov—shot, poisoned, threw him to the sharks, it does not matter—so we would conclude the inevitable."

"This is an impossibility," said Bortnikov. "You know how operations are conceived and implemented. You know the Main Enemy. How can you possibly believe—"

Putin held up his hand. "CIA removed Gorelikov to make us believe he is CHALICE, and that he defected. MAGNIT's arrest came immediately afterward, a well-timed coincidence, no? But I am telling you this categorically: Gorelikov cannot be the mole. CHALICE is still among us."

Without knowing why, Patrushev was nodding in agreement like a felt-headed dipping-bird toy sold in kiosks in Gorky Park. "On what do you base this theory?" asked Bortnikov, struggling to retain a modicum of deference. Dominika could see he was furious with Patrushev, a natural *podkhalim*, a real lickspittle.

"A single fact," said Putin. "Gorelikov conceived of, planned, and managed the *Kataklizm* operation to eliminate Alex Larson."

Silence. All of them looked at Putin in shock. They knew everything that went on in the Russian Federation, but none of them had heard of this before. *Eliminate Larson? My God.* Dominika knew she had just heard the most explosive secret intelligence of the decade: Kremlin complicity in the allegedly accidental death of the American DCIA.

"Gorelikov planned the death of Larson?" she whispered. "Do the Americans know? There will be *bedstviye*, calamity over this." *When I tell them.*

Putin did not care; he smirked at their discomfort, and his halo shone. Was he not the tsar? Did he not rule *Novorossiya*? "No asset under the control of CIA would undertake the assassination of its own Director without warning Langley and disrupting the plot," he said. "Other services might martyr their own, but never the Americans. The Chinese perhaps, the North Koreans certainly, and Stalin without a second thought. But not the Yankees."

"So the real CHALICE is active?" said Patrushev, not dwelling on the enormity of *Kataklizm* or statal murder. He seemed eager to please the president, eager to agree.

Putin nodded. "It is clever. We all assume Gorelikov is CHALICE; therefore, the real CHALICE is safe. You all know the Game. We've run such deceptions ourselves. Alex Larson's death proves Gorelikov could not be an American asset. His success in *Kataklizm* exonerates him."

"And CHALICE?" muttered Patrushev.

Putin's face changed from smirking narrator to phlegmatic prosecutor. "The three of you must ask each other that question," said Putin, staring at them.

"Mr. President, what are you saying?" said Bortnikov, sitting stock-still.

That he suspects one of us, thought Dominika. *It's a wonder he didn't pass out pistols loaded with blanks to see who would shoot whom. All right, what would* Bratok *do? What would he tell you? If you don't keep calm, if you don't share the outrage, they'll suspect you.* Like a sleepwalker heading toward the edge of a cliff, Dominika heard herself speak. "The American officer Nash is the key. He certainly knows important details, doubtless even the true identity of CHALICE. It is time for enhanced interrogation to begin." *Idiotka, you better pray you haven't signed his death sentence.*

Putin nodded with satisfaction. "Let it be so, and no more talk of comfortable safe houses or spy swaps," he said, pointing his finger at Dominika. "You are in charge, but I want all three of you there. In the room. I want that name the American hides behind his teeth. I don't care how you get it. But get it. The medical team is already at Butyrka, waiting. Go now."

They all knew they had to out-Herod Herod to prove their innocence. With Putin, demonstrable innocence didn't matter; he just wanted to blame someone.

———

That month, Lucius Westfall officially joined the Directorate of Operations, and soon would be going through operational training at the Farm, as Nate, and Gable, and Forsyth, and all of them had done before him. After the Farm, Westfall was scheduled to begin Russian-language training in preparation for his first tour in Moscow. The irony did not escape either Benford or Forsyth as they looked on benevolently.

As a renewed, rather frantic search for replacement candidates for CIA Director roiled the political waters of Washington, DC, Acting Director Farrell summoned Benford to his office.

"I am told by Senator Feigenbaum's former staff director Rob Farbissen that you obviously and deliberately misled the DCIA candidates during their preparatory briefings, and that you withheld asset information from them," said the Director. "Duchin from Congressional Affairs corroborates Farbissen's accusations. You were expressly ordered to brief the candidates completely and fully, without reservation." He straightened the blotter on his otherwise spotless desk.

"We were conducting a counterintelligence investigation," said Benford, with infinite weariness. "I was convinced, after an exhaustive investigation, that one of the three candidates for the job was working for Moscow. It turned out I was right. We were forty-eight hours from having a Russian mole as Director of the Agency. It was the reason Alex Larson was assassinated."

Farrell scoffed. "You can't leave Larson alone. You're preposterous. That is speculation, but it does not excuse you from your dereliction," said Farrell. "Or from your insubordination. Benford, you've been an irascible, uncontrolled rogue your entire career. Why is that, do you think?"

Benford shrugged. "I don't know," he said. "I suppose, unlike you, I never got accustomed to the taste of cock."

Farrell sat up, red faced, and slammed his fist on the desk. "That will do," he yelled. "You're fired, effective immediately, separated from the Service. Go to that rat hole you call an office, and collect your personal items, and two officers from Security will escort you out of the building. You can surrender your badge to them, and good riddance."

Benford left the Director's office without another word, but by the time the two blue blazers escorted him through the turnstile at the north entrance, two hundred employees were lined up along the length of the atrium, applauding. Benford scowled at the crowd and waved once, then turned and unclipped his badge from his torn jacket pocket, handed it to one of the security men, and went through the automatic doors, which hissed closed behind him. From that instant forward, Simon Benford could have entered CIA Headquarters no more easily than could Vladimir Putin.

DOMINIKA'S ARTICHOKE APPETIZER

In a large bowl, toss marinated artichoke hearts, pitted Kalamata olives, capers, quartered tomatoes, and crushed garlic with white wine, olive oil, salt, and pepper. Spread out and roast on a baking sheet until tomatoes are tender. Drizzle with olive oil, sprinkle with salt, and top with torn basil leaves. Serve on toasted bruschetta.

39

Interview Room Three

Butyrka Prison. Nate was escorted downstairs from his cell by two guards who were careful not to jostle his left arm in a short cast or his little finger swaddled in a splint, which was good because his whole left side ached. Nate was surprised when they did not enter a standard ground-floor interrogation room with the usual table, steel chairs, and photographs of Marx and Lenin, and the ubiquitous bowl of roses, which of course concealed the microphones. Instead they descended to the clammy third basement with the flaking pale-green walls and the chipped steel doors that gave no clue what or who languished behind them. Nate thought he must be the first CIA officer to be marched down this windowless corridor. It was utterly silent as the guards stopped him in front of a door marked OPROS 3, interview room three.

Some interview room. The room was large and looked like a surgical theater with white tiles on the floor and up the walls above chest height. It smelled of disinfectant and was lighted a dazzling white. Several wheeled tables were aligned against the far wall and massive circular stainless-steel pole lights, also on casters, were gathered in a corner. Against the opposite wall there was a strange solitary chair that looked as though it was made of painted aluminum, with a high back and headrest, flat protruding arms, and rolling casters on the legs. The white paint on the chair was chipped and discolored, especially along the front legs, the arms, and the high back. Standing alone in a corner of the room, the chair looked like a discarded eighteenth-century baby's high chair wheeled aside and forgotten. As he was marched in, Nate saw a makeshift gallery of five wooden chairs set up behind him. Interrogations normally did not have audiences, but perhaps these were for interrogator-trainees learning the finer points of their trade. It was typical Russian beastliness that observers were placed inside the room, to hear, see, and smell the proceedings firsthand, rather than behind one-way glass.

The guards pushed Nate into a wooden straight-backed chair and stood behind him, their hands resting lightly on each of his shoulders. Nash saw the prison guards carried OTs-27 Berdysh 9mm automatic pistols in holsters on their belts. He leaned forward to peek around the guards at the rest of the room, but was yanked back to sit up straight. There were glass-fronted medicine cabinets filled with vials, and surgical instruments neatly laid out on sterile cloths. There was also a stainless-steel table in the center of the room with drainage pipes at either end leading down to drains in the floor, clearly a mortician's table for performing autopsies. Nate did not like the look of the undulating tile floor gently sloping toward half a dozen drains around the room. He also didn't like the look of a truck battery on a dolly with a jumble of cables wrapped around the handles, barely visible, leaning against the side of the cabinet. The equipment was incongruous in the gleaming surgical theater; it belonged in a grimy motor-pool garage meant for jumping stalled trucks, not in this room. Nate's spirit fluttered a little as he imagined what the battery was for. Ignore the damn thing.

Despite his arm and his finger, Nate was in relatively good shape. He had figured out that Benford had probably run a canary trap and had told the three DCIA candidates variants of the same story. With luck, Dominika had passed the word to Langley, hopefully in time to prevent a catastrophe. Nate accepted that this was Benford's radical, all-out tactic to expose the mole, and he understood he was being used as a "lizard's tail," an expendable operative who is jettisoned and sacrificed to protect larger equities. He had not seen Dominika since the interrogation in the little cottage on Putin's compound, and he was worried that the mole had somehow compromised her. He was also worried about Agnes, and hoped she was safely out of Russia. No. If everyone was blown, he reasoned, it wasn't likely they'd be putting him through the wringer. He still had agents to protect. If he listened closely, Nate expected he could passively glean an idea from the interrogators' questions about the status of the mole hunt and of Dominika's security situation.

Avoiding looking at the battery, Nate tried to prepare himself mentally and physically for the coming cycle of interrogation. They probably would try drugs again, but with luck and discipline, Nate thought he could resist. If Dominika had any influence in managing the interrogation, he knew she would contrive to keep the physical punishment at a minimum, and to limit the sessions for as long as possible as Langley worked on arranging a swap.

She must not go too far on his behalf and throw suspicion on herself, however. That was critical.

Whatever the Russians had in mind, he had no doubt he would survive. He was a prisoner in Putin's Moscow, but this was the modern age and intelligence officers from opposition services were not harmed, according to a strict protocol. Putin may have eliminated hundreds of dissident Russians, but not ops officers of rival services.

Nate knew he had a long stretch ahead before the State Department would get off their pinstriped fannies to commence talks to arrange for his release. He could be in the slammer for a year, five years, ten years, but CIA would never give up trying to get him back. On his return to Langley, there would be medals, a promotion, choice of assignments, but in reality his career would be over. He would be considered too burned coverwise and too burned out psychologically. By then, he daydreamed, Dominika might be finished at SVR and would be ready to retire and disappear into idyllic resettlement with Nate. It was a hell of a long way around to finally start a new life together, but it would be worth the wait. For the present, Nate intended to give his interrogators as much guff as he could muster. He knew by now the Russians probably had identified him as Nathaniel Nash, the last handler of General Korchnoi, one of the best assets the CIA had run in Moscow for fourteen years. They would also know that Nash was a fluent Russian speaker, which would further infuriate them.

All thoughts about civilized outcomes in the basement of Butyrka Prison evaporated when Sergeant Iosip Blokhin walked into interview room three. He was dressed in a camouflage utility uniform and wore polished combat boots. A green nylon web belt was cinched tightly around his waist with a metal snap buckle with the Spetsnaz seal of parachute and dagger. His uniform was starched and crisp, but nowhere was there any badge of rank. His thin hair was slicked back over his bullet head, his scarred forehead dully shone in the bright lights of the room, and his ham-hock hands hung at his sides.

He approached Nate's chair and leaned close so that their faces were inches apart. Blokhin inexplicably smelled of kerosene—sharp and crisp, not altogether unpleasant. "It is *sudba* meeting again, American. How do you say it in English?" said Blokhin, in his gravely croak.

"Fate," said Nash in English. "Been back to Turkey since we last spoke?"

"Not just fate, Yankee," said Blokhin. "*Sudba* also means 'doom.'"

Nate looked him in the face. "Yours or mine? Or Major Shlykov's?"

Blokhin signaled to the guards standing behind Nate's chair to pick him up and put him into the antique, chipped high chair and wheel it into the center of the room, under a big surgical light. The guards cinched Nate's wrists to the flat arms of that chair and his ankles to the fronts of the legs with clear plastic cable ties, which Blokhin strained tight. Nate's felt slippers were yanked off his feet. A sweat-stained leather strap was passed around his chest and buckled in back. It was tight, but Nate could breathe okay. It dawned on him that this might be worse than he'd anticipated: these restraints suggested they were going to try extreme techniques that would make him fall out of this chair if he weren't tied in. Perhaps he'd be the first CIA officer in the history of the Cold War to actually be tortured in the Butyrka basement. Maybe they'd give him a Trailblazer Award when he got home.

He tested the ties and rocked in his chair, sending it slowly rolling across the uneven floor, just as the door opened and four people walked in, three men and a woman, all senior bigwigs judging by the way the guards snapped to attention. Nate craned his head to see. The woman was Dominika, dressed in a dark suit and dark stockings, a prison-visitor's badge was around her neck, and it swung as she walked, her heels clicking unevenly against the white floor tiles because of her slight limp. It was like a dream seeing her now, here, like this. Her hair was up as always, and their eyes met for an instant. It would have been the most natural thing for her to walk up to his chair, kiss him on the lips, order his bonds cut, and walk him out of this basement and through the front gates while holding his hand. She'd give him some *khren*, some grief, like "*Dushka*, you cannot manage even this without my help?" He smelled a faint whiff of her Calèche perfume in the room over the stench of carbolic disinfectant. He heard the scrapes of chairs behind them as Blokhin pulled Nate's chair back into the middle of the room, so he couldn't see the visitors—Nate had also immediately recognized Bortnikov and Patrushev, former and current Directors of FSB. Dominika completed the trifecta as Director of SVR. These officials were here to observe his interrogation? Unheard of. Maybe the Kremlin was panicking, or maybe Benford had bagged MAGNIT, and they didn't know how and were desperate to identify the American mole. Nate told himself he had to be extra careful—

the mole was sitting in this very room, the one with the pretty legs. He had to protect her at all costs.

Nate couldn't know it was more serious than that. After being berated by Putin and informed that Gorelikov was not the mole, the three Service Chiefs had been escorted to their official cars and had separately driven to Butyrka to observe the interrogation of the American case officer. They instinctively stayed apart to avoid contamination, and they did not speak to one another. Dominika's head was in a fog; she did not remember the drive to the prison through Moscow streets, did not remember the tea served in the protocol room by the prison director, did not remember the clacking footsteps echoing down endless corridors and littered stairwells. Her head cleared when she entered the white-tiled room and saw Nate in the chair, his purple halo shining brightly. Her stomach flipped when she saw Blokhin and his black wings, waiting to begin. This was another Putin touch, using Blokhin: he hated Nate for what had happened to Shlykov and, most of all, for the towering insult of pitching him in the Turkish jailhouse. He would put greater energies into Nash's interrogation. The haloes of her colleagues were bleached out with fear. This exercise was like some throwback to the Great Purges of the thirties: all were suspected and accused; one trusted adviser would be destroyed and the others exonerated.

Blokhin had put on a full-length leather slaughterhouse apron and tied it tightly around his waist. He pulled on heavy black rubber gloves, then wheeled the battery from the corner of the room and uncoiled the cables. A red star was embossed on the side of the battery. The cable ends were clamped to the battery terminals. The opposite ends terminated in dull copper alligator jaws that were wrapped in red felt, which Blokhin dipped into a bucket of water, soaking the felt wraps thoroughly. He touched the felts together, but no Hollywood sparks dramatically arced and snapped. Instead, the felts started smoking from the current, quenched by Blokhin's dipping them into the bucket again. There was a sour, metallic, burned toast smell in the room. Nate heard a chair scrape behind him and willed Dominika to stay still. How long could he last? How long would Domi stay in her seat? *Come on, baby, hang tough.*

Blokhin casually leaned against the arm of Nate's chair. "I require one thing from you, *Amerikanskiy*," he said softly. "The name of your agent in Moscow."

Nate smiled at him. "The name's a secret *malys*, you small prick; that's why we use the word 'agent.' "

Blokhin's eyes narrowed, and his face flushed. He touched a felt pad to each side of Nate's left ankle and looked as Nate's back arched and his left leg involuntarily shot out straight. The electric shock was excruciating, half hammer blows and half pulsing muscle spasm that engulfed his whole leg. *Shit, this could go on for days.* Blokhin removed the felts, and the sudden cessation of pain and spasm was a heavenly relief. But anticipating the next one was enough to drive one mad, which was the point of using shock—the prisoner's dreading the next jolt.

Blokhin dipped the felts in the water again. "The name of the mole? We have all day and all night, until the battery goes dead or you lose your mind, whichever will come first."

Nate remembered how good Blokhin's English was. Nate shook his head to clear it. "You're an ass-picking gorilla, *mandjuk*, dickhead."

With a snarl, Blokhin pressed the felts on the insides of Nate's thighs, an inch from his scrotum. Nate's torso curled forward in a rigid bow against the chest strap, and his lower body started shaking spasmodically, the current running through his skeletal muscle fibers triggering synchronous contraction. The pain between his legs was all-encompassing, radiating through his penis, which immediately stood straight up, followed by a loss of bladder control. Blokhin removed the felts and stood back, avoiding the trickle of urine under Nate's chair. The American raised his head, straightened, and looked at Blokhin through wet hair, which had fallen over his eyes.

"I require the name, Yankee," said Blokhin.

Nate shook his head. He couldn't take much more of the felts. And he was terrified that Dominika would soon react to save him. Only one hope: piss Blokhin off so much that the Spetsnaz sergeant would either kill him or so seriously damage Nate that the interrogation would cease, at least tempo rarily, thus distancing Dominika from a catastrophic reaction. The button would be Blokhin's honor. *Give it a try, hurry. Save her.* His crotch burned and his thighs twitched uncontrollably. During the last spasm it felt as if he had pulled a muscle in his back.

"This is why we pitched you in Istanbul," said Nate hoarsely in Russian, to give the insult more edge. "You are no man of honor, certainly not worthy of belonging to the Spetsnaz brotherhood. *Ty zhenshchina*, you are a woman." *If he ever got out of this, Domi would be sure to give him grief over that.*

Blokhin's eyes goggled at the insult, and he cast aside the battery cables, kicked over the battery cart, spilling the water bucket, walked over to a cupboard, and drew out a meter-length of rebar. His eyes were unblinking, like a lizard's eyes, and his scarred forehead was a livid purple.

For what we are about to receive, thought Nate, looking at Blokhin's face.

Blokhin hit him with the length of the steel bar across his left shin, causing a comminuted fracture of the tibia, shattering the bone into several pieces inside the leg and tearing the interosseous membrane that stabilizes the tibia and fibula, essentially rendering Nate's left leg below the knee the approximate consistency of cooked pasta. Nate roared in pain, but it was a throaty roar of defiance, not the keening wail of a terrified prisoner. Nate looked at Blokhin as he roared, as if he would tear his throat out with his teeth, but the blocky trooper was unfazed—he handled the ribbed length of the rebar in both hands, lovingly, like Benny Goodman held his clarinet.

Blokhin appraised Nate's left leg, which was already swollen and purple and bent unnaturally to one side. Nate could feel the grooves in the arm of the chair as he dug his nails into the soft aluminum; other men and women had clawed against the pain as he was doing now. For all Blokhin's many talents for mayhem, sophisticated interrogation was not his specialty. "I require the name of the Russian traitor working for the Americans," he said.

Nate lifted his sagging head, and a bead of sweat dropped off his nose. Pain radiated up his leg to his gut. "You're supposed to ask the first question *before* you hit the prisoner, *zhopa*, asshole," he whispered.

Faster than Nate could tense up, Blokhin brought the rebar down on Nate's captive left hand, rebreaking his little finger, shattering three of five metacarpophalangeal joints where the digits meet the palm, and pulverizing the small bones of the intercarpal articulation of the wrist. Nate's ruined hand swelled immediately, and his knuckles became dimples. The pain was overwhelming, sharp, electric, radiating up his arm to his armpit and across his chest, the associated nerves reacting to the crushing blows of the steel bar. Roaring like an animal made him hyperventilate and helped the pain. The cable tie on his left wrist was now cutting into his flesh as his hand turned purple.

Nate growled as Blokhin leaned close, coyly resting the tip of the rebar on Nate's undamaged right forearm, a hint of more to come. "The name of your asset in Moscow?" asked Blokhin.

"Someone close to the top," stuttered Nate, "but I cannot recall the name, so fuck you." Through his pain, Nate heard the three senior officials behind him stir in their seats. *That was it*; Putin suspected everyone, even his closest advisers, and he was treating them just as Stalin had habitually denigrated *his* lieutenants. That's why they were present—to observe and sweat a little, for Putin's amusement. But where was the august Gorelikov? Was he above suspicion? "Wait," slurred Nate, as Blokhin tightened his grip on the rebar. "There is one name I know. Conspirators meet at Blokhina's house, your mother's house, after the sailors leave."

More stirring sounds behind him. The American would pay for his smart mouth.

Blokhin walked behind Nate's chair and looked at the three senior officials with a sneer. Bortnikov was fidgeting, whether from witnessing the beating or from anxiety was unclear. Patrushev's face was ashen: the PhD and former engineer had no stomach for this. Egorova's handsome face was a disinterested mask, her crossed legs were still. She looked bored. She was the only proven killer in the room, and since their New York trip, Blokhin had wanted to overpower her, then hog-tie her, then break her bones. He would see if he could get her to vomit over Nash's beating.

Openly opposing Egorova was not feasible now, especially if the rumors of her relationship with the president were true. Oh yes, Blokhin had been briefed on many things. Besides the two guards, a young Kremlin aide with cat's eyes was standing against the wall, observing the Security Council members intently. He would doubtless report back to the president. And there were three smoked glass globes in the ceiling concealing cameras. Blokhin scanned their faces again, turned, and without any windup hit Nate from behind on the point of his right elbow, snapping the constraining cable tie, splitting open the olecranon, the tip of the elbow, like a burst roasted chestnut, and subsequently dislodging the synovial joint between the head of the radius and the radial notch of the ulna. Nate's arm hung limply off the armrest, his elbow joint in pieces and severely dislocated. He would have been unable to lift his arm even if it had flopped into a flame. Nate howled in pain but stopped himself, trembling, and managed a croaking laugh, which enraged Blokhin, who swung the bar in a flat arc at Nate's left shoulder not covered by the chair back, fracturing the acromion and shattering the coracoid process of the clavicle. The shock made Nate pass out with a spectral groan, and his head and chest flopped forward until restrained by the leather strap around his chest.

Dominika and Patrushev got out of their chairs at the same time, but Patrushev strode to the door, slamming it behind him as he left. Weak stomach? Or guilty panic? Dominika instead walked around Nate to face him and raise his lolling head with a finger under his chin. She kept her face neutral—Blokhin was watching her like a mastiff—but her heart beat wildly as she felt Nate's sweaty face and saw his eyebrows, cracked lips, and his closed eyelids, the eyelids she used to kiss to wake him up. *No emotion, show nothing, my God, she couldn't sit motionless and watch him be ground to a paste by this Spetsnaz maniac, she couldn't, she'd confess to save him, he'd be sent back and Forsyth could patch him up, it didn't matter what happened to her, but no! that's what this was, a trap, Nate would tell her so, Benford the same thing, Gable would bellow it from Valhalla, stay whole, we're all spies, spooks, ferrets, survival is worth any price, defeating Putin's monstrous snake pit is worth anything, even if you have to watch Nate die, forgive me,* dushka, ya lyublyu tebya vsem serdtsem, *I love you with all my heart.*

She let Nate's head drop like a rejected melon at the market and turned to the young Kremlin toad. "Go immediately to the Kremlin and tell the president that this interrogation is an abomination, and that this subhuman piece of Spetsnaz shit will kill the American officer before he utters a word." She stamped her foot. "Go! Go now, immediately!" She pointed at one of the armed guards. "You, go with him to see he gets out of the prison without trouble. Did you hear me?" The guard and the Kremlin toad jumped as if scalded and ran out the door.

Dominika turned to Blokhin. "You animal! This American has important information, the identity of a mole operating inside our government, passing our most sensitive secrets, and you are breaking arms and legs with a steel bar. You are an imbecile."

Nate started moving his head and groaning, and Dominika went to a sink at the far end of the room to wet a cloth to wipe his face, and she turned to see Blokhin standing in front of Nate with a swagger, and Nate was saying something through parched lips and swollen tongue, and Blokhin stiffened, then straightened, and raised the steel bar above his head, and Dominika saw Bortnikov leap out of his chair and scream No, but Blokhin brought the rebar down on the right side of Nate's neck with an overhand chop, breaking his right clavicle in a compound fracture—the visible broken tip of the bone punctured the skin—and collapsing the vagus nerve inside the brachial plexus, causing global brain ischemia, a catastrophic interruption of blood to the brain, which resulted in Nate passing out again and slumping forward in his chair, and Bortnikov and the guard both grabbed Blokhin's arms as he raised the bar to strike Nate again, and Dominika walked behind the guard, pulled the Berdysh automatic pistol from the holster, racked the slide, and pointed it at Blokhin, whose eyes went wide. His exceptional reflexes turned his head almost out of the line of fire, but Dominika was too close, and she shot him twice in his shiny, scarred forehead, splattering both the prison guard and the horrified Director of FSB with gray brain matter. Blokhin collapsed face forward onto the floor. His head bounced twice on the tiles, his blood flowing out of his head neatly in two different directions into the two nearest drains, as his legs twitched involuntarily, because the frog's brain was dead but his legs didn't know it, and Dominika watched as Bortnikov and the guard reeled unsteadily out the door, wiping the gore from their eyes, and Dominika wiped Nate's bloodied face and, mindful of the cameras in the ceiling, limited herself to attending to the prisoner, and the cold cloth revived him and he opened one eye, then the other, but the pupils were two different sizes, and a small trickle of blood was coming out of his right nostril, and all Dominika could do was wipe his face and say to him, "American, are you all right?" and Nate's irises wobbled erratically in little circles. "You're safe now," he whispered to her. She heard the edge in her voice as she screamed "Medic!" down the corridor, telling herself to control her panic, and the blood kept coming out of his nostril even though Dominika kept wiping it, and his breath was labored and Dominika loosened the chest strap so he could breathe, but by the sound of his breaths, she guessed he was aspirating blood, and all she could do was wipe his cheek and say, "Medical attention is coming," but somehow knowing it wouldn't make a difference, and Nate's uneven eyes locked on hers and there was a faint smile that passed over his lips and his halo grew brilliant and radiated, and she felt the minute caress of one shattered finger touching her hand, a light touch, brushing the top of her hand, just for an instant, unseen by the cameras, more intimate than a kiss, and he took two more deep breaths and went still, and his purple halo dissolved, and Dominika fought her tears, then heard footsteps pounding down the corridor even as Blokhin's legs on the pinkish tiles wouldn't stop twitching.

=====

Dominika felt the nearly undetectable puff of air from the air-vortex nozzle on her desk lamp sitting on the corner of the desk in the Director's office of SVR headquarters in the pine forest of Yasenevo. It indicated that a message from Benford had just come in. She positioned the flexible display, engaged the system by moving her eye in line with the integral optical reader that biometrically authenticated the pattern of her iris, and began projecting the short message on the flat base of the lamp in a directional hologram. The scrolling letters were invisible to anyone not positioned exactly in line with the lamp, and could be turned off with a casual wave of her hand. Though previously skeptical of the contraption, Dominika now marveled at the efficiency of the covcom device. Just this morning she had undetectably used the digital lens in the lamp to photograph and transmit to Washington a top-secret read-and-return bulletin from the Security Council as the Kremlin courier respectfully waited three feet from her desk for her signature. There was even a self-destruct feature that would fuse the components in case of emergency. The SVR headquarters building, as Hearsey predicted, was proving to be an efficient, massive antenna.

The multiparagraph message was not from Benford, but rather from Forsyth. Strange.

1. FYI, MAGNIT sentenced life imprisonment at Supermax Prison in Florence, Colorado.
2. Request advise current status Nash, including when feasible diplomatic initiative to bring home. Pls advise possibility of swap.
3. Be advised Counterintelligence Chief Simon Benford retired. Forward his deep thanks and regards.

Nate and Gable gone, Benford retired. She had never known any other CIA officers since her recruitment in Helsinki, they were her family, and their comforting presence mitigated the stark solitude of her life as a spy. Now she felt alone, even though she was at the pinnacle. She started drafting a reply, husbanding characters as she typed on the flexible display while her throat closed tight in despair.

```
1. Contact with president two nights per week. He sharing
   opinions of siloviki—Patrushev now in disfavor. He dis-
   cussing Russia clandestine alliances with Iran, North
   Korea. Will advise.
2. Regret inform officer Nash died as a result of injuries
   sustained during unauthorized interrogation.
```

```
DIVA.
```

```
END END END
```

With burning eyes and trembling lip, Dominika pushed "send," and the message was transmitted. She remembered what Agnes had said: "Nate came to rescue you and I came to help Nate. So I suppose all of us lost." Everyone indeed had lost, but Dominika was running the SVR, and she moved inside the Kremlin, and astride President Putin, ironically back to her hated Sparrow roots in a hopelessly febrile world without her *Neyt*. She sighed and shuddered.

Then DIVA got back to work in her large office with the panoramic view of the pine forest and the endless horizon of her beloved *Rodina*.

ACKNOWLEDGMENTS

With each completed book, I find the list of people whom I must thank grows exponentially.

My thanks first to my agent, Sloan Harris, who is responsible for guiding my second career as a novelist (which occasionally has proven more delirious than my first career) and who continues to advise, encourage, and inspire me as a colleague and friend. I add my thanks to the team at ICM, including Esther Newberg, Josie Freedman in Los Angeles, Heather Karpas, Heather Bushong (in case President Putin sues), and Alexa Brahme, for their aeonian support.

I gratefully acknowledge my editor, the supranatural Colin Harrison, without whose discerning novelist's eye and literary acumen this book would not exist, period. Many thanks, too, to the entire Simon & Schuster family, including Carolyn Reidy, Susan Moldow, Nan Graham, Roz Lippel, Brian Belfiglio, Jaya Miceli, Jen Bergstrom, Irene Lipsky, Colin Shields, and Gary Urda. Special thanks to Sarah Goldberg for her unremitting support, Katie Rizzo, and Valerie Pulver for infallible copyediting. At S&S Audio, thanks to Chris Lynch, Elisa Shokoff, Tom Spain, Sarah Lieberman, Tara Thomas, Elliot Rambach, and Jeremy Bobb, who narrated all of the Red Sparrow Trilogy audiobooks.

I thank colleagues in CIA's Publication Review Board for their consistent and timely support in reviewing the manuscript. Any errors in fact or language are the author's, and any similarities to characters in the novel with real people are wholly coincidental. This is a work of fiction.

My appreciation, too, to all my fellow officers in the Directorate of Operations—especially to the CT class of November 1976, for a lifetime of memories and frequent expressions of support. Among these, I must mention the late Stephen Holder, who provided a primer of authentic and obscure operational terms used by the Chinese Intelligence Service, and the late Jack Platt, who taught us, blaspheming, about double corners and trailing surveillance. Former partners and close friends from an allied service, Alasdair and DT, variously advised the author, including passing along several exceptional family recipes, normally more closely held than politburo minutes.

As usual, friends and family contributed endlessly. Yogini Alison introduced me to the sublime essence of yoga; Steve and Michael revealed the mysteries of New York and Staten Island, the latter occasionally more sublime than yoga. Kelly demonstrated the ancient and silent code gestures of the Chinese folded fan. My brother William and sister-in-law Sharon read the manuscript and made helpful suggestions. Brother William also continued in his role as the author's science adviser. How a university professor of economics knows about electromagnetic railguns is a puzzle. I suspect he has one in his apartment. Daughters Alex and Sophie continued in the Sisyphean task of explaining modern music, current fashion, and popular English usage to the author.

Finally, I thank my wife, Suzanne, for being the better half of a tandem couple in CIA for three decades, for raising two independent and accomplished young women as daughters, for her hours of help with the manuscript, and for her aplomb in good times and bad.

Jason Matthews is a retired officer of CIA's Operations Directorate. Over a thirty-three-year career he served in multiple overseas locations and engaged in the clandestine collection of national security intelligence, specializing in denied-area operations. Matthews conducted recruitment operations against Soviet–East European, East Asian, Middle Eastern, and Caribbean targets. As Chief in various CIA Stations, he collaborated with foreign partners in counterproliferation and counterterrorism operations. He is the author of *Red Sparrow* (which was adapted into a major motion picture starring Jennifer Lawrence and produced by 20th Century Fox) and *Palace of Treason*. He lives in Southern California.